Dance Portrait of Garrick.
Folger Shakespeare Library

THE PLAYS
OF DAVID GARRICK

A COMPLETE COLLECTION OF THE SOCIAL SATIRES,
FRENCH ADAPTATIONS, PANTOMIMES,
CHRISTMAS AND MUSICAL PLAYS,
PRELUDES, INTERLUDES, AND BURLESQUES,
to which are added
the Alterations and Adaptations of the Plays of Shakespeare and
Other Dramatists from the Sixteenth to the Eighteenth Centuries

VOLUME 1
Garrick's Own Plays, 1740-1766

EDITED WITH COMMENTARY AND NOTES BY
HARRY WILLIAM PEDICORD AND
FREDRICK LOUIS BERGMANN

SOUTHERN ILLINOIS UNIVERSITY PRESS
CARBONDALE AND EDWARDSVILLE

COPYRIGHT © 1980 BY SOUTHERN ILLINOIS UNIVERSITY PRESS
ALL RIGHTS RESERVED

PRINTED IN THE UNITED STATES OF AMERICA
DESIGNED BY GEORGE LENOX

LIBRARY OF CONGRESS CATALOGUING IN PUBLICATION DATA

Garrick, David, 1717–1779
    The plays of David Garrick.

    Bibliography: p.
    Includes indexes.
    CONTENTS: v. 1. Garrick's own plays, 1740–1766.—
v. 2. Garrick' own plays, 1767–1775.
    I. Pedicord, Harry William. II. Bergmann,
Fredrick Louis, 1916–   III. Title.
PR3465 1980   822'.6   79–28443
    ISBN 0-8093-0862-2 (v. 1)

To
ARTHUR HAWLEY SCOUTEN
and
GEORGE WINCHESTER STONE, JR.
these volumes are
respectfully dedicated

"Go on—prepare my bounty for my friends,
And see that mirth with all her crew attends."
        Prologue to A CHRISTMAS TALE.

Contents

Contents

Illustrations

Preface

WHEN DAVID GARRICK returned to London from his second visit to the Continent (1763–65) in the spring of 1765, he found himself engaged in a struggle for his health, for his rights as manager of the Drury Lane Theatre, and for his reputation as an actor and champion of the works of William Shakespeare. He was also no little disturbed by the fact that John Beard and Mrs. Rich, joint patentees of the rival theatre, Covent Garden, had established in his absence and without consulting him a theatrical fund for the relief of sick, indigent, and aged actors. He was, he thought, weary of management, cautious about resuming his career as England's foremost actor, and increasingly fond of the easier life of a gentleman in his country house at Hampton. Despite his poor health, a command performance brought him back to the stage as Benedict in Shakespeare's *Much Ado About Nothing* on 14 November 1765. When he discovered his reception to be quite extraordinary, Garrick determined to continue functioning as actor-manager, thus taking his career into perhaps its greatest years.

It is significant, we think, that the first collection of Garrick's plays was published soon after this period of indecision. Under the general title *The Dramatic Works of David Garrick*, sixteen plays and alterations of plays were published by an unknown printer in three duodecimo volumes. Volume 1 contained *The Lying Valet, Miss in Her Teens, Lethe, The Guardian, The Male-Coquette,* and *Lilliput*. Volume 2 included some of his alterations and adaptations—*Romeo and Juliet, Cymbeline, Catharine and Petruchio, Florizel and Perdita,* and *Every Man in His Humour*. Volume 3 consisted of *The Gamesters, Isabella, The Enchanter, The Farmer's Return from London,* and *The Clandestine Marriage*.

Five years later, R. Bald, T. Blaw, and J. Kurt brought out *The Dramatic Works of David Garrick* in two volumes, duodecimo, 1774. This edition contained the same sixteen plays as the 1768 publication, leading to the surmise that Bald, Blaw, and Kurt had a hand in the first collection, since the order in which the plays appear corresponds exactly to that of the 1768 edition. And from the care with which these plays were again presented during Garrick's lifetime, we may assume that copy had been approved by Garrick himself.

In 1798 a final collection appeared, published by A. Miller in three volumes duodecimo. This new edition contained not only the previously collected plays but added eight more: *The Fairies, A Peep Behind the Curtain, Bon Ton, The Irish Widow, May-Day*, and *The Theatrical Candidates*, and two plays erroneously attributed to Garrick—the anonymous *Arthur and Emmeline* and James Townley's *High Life Below Stairs*. Except for the occasional appearance of *The Lying Valet* in other collections, Garrick's remaining works were not collected.

Contemporary editing of Garrick plays began in 1925, when Louise Brown Osborn edited *Three Farces by David Garrick* with introductions for Yale University Press. These were *The Lying Valet, A Peep Behind the Curtain*, and *Bon Ton*. Osborn commented that "there have been no editions of Garrick's works. None of the farces here given has been reprinted since the appearance of *The Lying Valet* in *The British Drama*, Philadelphia, 1850." But the very next year brought publication of *Three Plays by David Garrick* (New York, 1926), with which Elizabeth Stein began her lifetime of Garrick studies. Her industry gave us three hitherto unpublished manuscripts among the holdings of the Boston Public Library and the Kemble-Devonshire Collection in the Henry E. Huntington Library: *Harlequin's Invasion* (1759), *The Jubilee* (1769) and *The Meeting of the Company* (1774).

Seven years later, in 1934, George Winchester Stone, Jr., delighted theatre historians with the discovery of "Garrick's long lost alteration of *Hamlet*" (*PMLA*, 49, 1934, pp. 890–921), which he described in detail but of which he printed only Act V of the Garrick preparation copy in the Folger Shakespeare Library. In 1938 Miss Stein published her comprehensive study, *David Garrick, Dramatist*, adding to the Garrick canon and describing in detail each of the plays then attributed to his authorship, but not including his alterations and adaptations of Shakespeare and the other English dramatists. In 1939 George H. Nettleton and Arthur E. Case included *The Lying Valet* in their edition of *British Dramatists from Dryden to Sheridan*.

Garrick studies then shifted from his plays to his biography, his verse, and his correspondence. A rash of biographies appeared between 1948 and 1958. These were of varying quality and included Margaret Barton's *Garrick* (1948); Anna Bird Stewart's *Enter David Garrick*, a book for young readers done with sound scholarship (1951); and Carola Oman, Lady Lenanton's *David Garrick* (1958). To these we may now add Philip Highfill's extensive biography of Garrick which appears in volume 6 of *A Biographical Dictionary of Actors, etc., 1660–1800* and the new biography by George M. Kahrl and George Winchester Stone, Jr. In 1955 Mary E. Knapp published her invaluable *Checklist of Verse by David Garrick* (revised 1974) with its citing of prologues, epilogues, and occasional verse. *The Letters of David Garrick*, an exhaustive work which, however, failed to include letters to Garrick, was published by David M. Little and George M. Kahrl in 1963. Meanwhile, the appearance of *The London Stage*, especially Part 3 by Arthur H. Scouten and Part 4 by George Winchester Stone, Jr., 1960, provided substantiations of the canon, cast lists, contemporary criticism, playhouse conditions, and the actual number of performances for each of Garrick's efforts.

The result of this continuing interest in Garrick has created a climate in which it is finally possible to identify the works of his authorship. The present edition, therefore, represents the first attempt since 1798 to publish a complete edition of Garrick's plays. Believing that no modern edition would be valid without the inclusion of his alterations and adaptations of Shakespeare and other English dramatists, we have cautiously collected them. They are published here for the first time.

In this edition we have printed Garrick's own plays in chronological order in two volumes: 1. *Lethe* (1740) to *Neck or Nothing* (1766); 2. *Cymon* (1767) to *The Theatrical Candidates* (1775). Another two volumes will include the twelve Shakespearean adaptations: *Macbeth* (1744) to *The Tempest* (1773). The final two volumes will include the fifteen non-Shakespearean adaptations: *The Provok'd Wife* (1747) to *The Alchymist* (1777). The plays are presented *seriatim*, with textual notes, references, commentary, and explanatory notes for each play. An index to the commentary concludes each volume. A roster of Drury Lane actors appears at the end of each second volume. Printing the plays in chronological order will enable the historian to evaluate Garrick's progress as an adapter-champion of Shakespeare and as an alterer of other English dramas.

All plays have been based on collation of the editions published during Garrick's lifetime. The first edition is the copy-text in all instances, and the textual notes record substantive departures. Variants of spelling, punctuation, and capitalization are noted only when relevant. Character names contracted in the original texts have been silently expanded in speech prefixes, and stage directions have been regularized. Any added stage directions not found in the copy-texts have been enclosed in brackets. Additional material discovered to be important to the plays has been added from the original manuscripts and enclosed in brackets.

Spelling has been modernized as conservatively as possible to preserve the linguistic quality of the original texts. Punctuation is also modernized from the pointing of the copy-texts, but every effort has been taken to preserve the features of the orignal while making it intelligible to the modern reader. Explanatory notes are chiefly concerned with glossing obsolete words and phrases.

Several printing problems which have surfaced should be explained briefly. Garrick's *Lethe* underwent continuous changes from 1740 through 1772. Granted, most of the changes involve the evolution of the same characters; *viz.*, the Beau into a Fine Gentleman, Mr. Tatoo into a horse-grenadier named Mr. Carbine, Miss Lucy into Mrs. Riot into a Fine Lady. But the most important addition is the Bowman-Lord Chalkstone episode, which did not occur until 1757, the fifth edition of the text to be published. To avoid reproducing two texts, we have printed the text of the first edition (1749) and added the Lord Chalkstone episode following the basic text.

The complete text of *The Institution of the Garter* (1771) has never before been published. When Garrick caused this work to be printed, it was done as *The Songs, Choruses, and Serious Dialogue of the Masque Called The Institution of the Garter; or, Arthur's Round Table Restored*. The manuscript of this production exists in the Larpent Collection in the Huntington Library, and we have restored the comic scenes to the copy-text with the permission of the Huntington Library. These scenes appear in brackets. It is now possible to view this production as a whole and understand its fascination for a playgoing public of Garrick's time.

Mention has already been made of the three plays Miss Stein discovered and published: *Harlequin's Invasion*, *The Jubilee*, and *The Meeting of the Company*. *Harlequin's Invasion* has been edited again from the manuscript in the Barton-Ticknor Collection with permission of the Boston Public Library, and the other two plays have been edited again from manuscripts in the Kemble-Devonshire Collection with the permission of the Huntington Library.

Problems in publishing the adaptations of Shakespeare will be discussed in a preface to that part, especially *Romeo and Juliet* and the "long lost" *Hamlet*. However, it should be noted here that in preparing the texts of Shakespeare and other of the older dramatists we have accepted the conventions of eighteenth-century printing, foregoing the usual form and line-numbering of these plays. With Garrick adding material and cutting hundreds of lines, it makes little sense to try to adjust these altered texts to conventional printing of such works.

George Winchester Stone, Jr., has estimated the number of plays in which Garrick might claim some hand. In a paper read at the Clark Library Seminar, 25 January 1975, "David Garrick and the Eighteenth-Century Stage: Notes toward a New Biography," Stone states that Garrick "was a playwright of remarkable ability who wrote, or adapted, or had a major hand in sixty-eight pieces, each of which was popular on the stage of his time." Our edition includes only forty-nine. While the hand of Garrick can most certainly be discerned in many other plays of the period, we have added only four plays to the Garrick canon: *The Institution of the Garter* to the list of his own plays, and his adaptations of Shakespeare's *The Tempest* in operatic form, Vanbrugh's *The Provok'd Wife*, and John Fletcher's *Rule a Wife and Have a Wife*, despite Garrick's own public disclaimer of this last offering. None of the other plays referred to by Stone appears to warrant inclusion in this edition, not because Garrick did not rework portions of them for Drury Lane, but because evidence is at present lacking as to how much or how far Garrick himself altered a given piece for production.

In addition to the forty-nine plays presented in this edition there is evidence from letters and prompt copies that Garrick did some work on the following plays. From Shakespeare: *Richard III, King John, Othello, 1 Henry IV, 2 Henry IV, Henry V, Much Ado About Nothing, Coriolanus, The Two Gentlemen of Verona*, and *Timon of Athens*. From others: *The West Indian* (Richard Cumberland), *The Orphan of China* (Arthur Murphy), *The Way to Keep Him* (Arthur Murphy), *The Royal Suppliants* (John Delap), *False Delicacy* (Hugh Kelly), *Zingis* (Alexander Dow), *The Earl of Warwick* (Thomas Francklin), *The Note of Hand* (Richard Cumberland), *Braganza* (Robert Jephson), and *The Widow'd Wife* (William Kenrick). Perhaps with somewhat less justification one may add, on the basis of the above sources and the Hopkins Diaries, some or all of the following: *The Jealous Wife* (George Colman the Elder), *Miss Lucy in Town* (Henry Fielding), *The Elopement* (unpublished pantomime), *Pigmy Revels* (James Messink), *Almida* (Mrs. Celisia?), *Harlequin's Jacket* (anon.), *Love Makes a Man*[1] (Colley Cibber), and *The Sultan*[2] (Isaac Bickerstaff).

---

1. *Love Makes a Man; or, The Fop's Fortune* was published in Washington, D.C., in 1825 by Davis and Force with the notation, "Altered, arranged, and adapted to the English Stage by D. Garrick, Esq. Copied by permission from the Prompt Book of the Philadelphia and Baltimore theatres." There is a copy in the New York Public Library.

2. See Peter A. Tasch, "Garrick's Revisions of Bickerstaff's *The Sultan*," PQ, 50 (1971), 144–49. This play was produced in 1775 and printed in 1780. Tasch bases his argument on the differences between Bickerstaff's Larpent version and the French original of Favart and on letters exchanged between Garrick and Mrs. Abington, who was to star in the play. The latter had asked Garrick to give the play "but a touch of that Promethean heat with which you have for so many years past animated the clay of every successful modern Playwright" (14 June 1774). Garrick apparently eliminated some business, cut out a song and a political allusion, and toned down some language thought to be coarse. Likewise, the word *blackamoor* (describing Osmyn) is marked out on the Larpent copy, pretty obviously because Charles Dibdin was no longer at Drury Lane to do blackface roles.

Again and again authors acknowledge the help of Garrick in completing a play: Cumberland, for example, tells us that Garrick helped him work over *The West Indian*, the actor-manager giving it more pace and flourish in the first act. How many more such acts of assistance—beyond those suggested above—went unrecorded is a matter of pure conjecture.

A final word must be given to recognition of the pioneer work of Elizabeth Stein and George Winchester Stone, Jr. We are indebted to both scholars. Miss Stein brought enthusiasm and insight to even the most inconsequential of Garrick's plays. The same should be said for the work of Stone in his studies of Garrick and Shakespeare. In our introductions we have aimed at adding significant stage history, contemporary criticism, and such additional material as we hope will make these plays come alive for the modern reader.

OVER THE YEARS WE HAVE BEEN INDEBTED TO the assistance and courtesy of the staffs of many libraries, notably the Folger Shakespeare Library, the Harvard Theatre Collection, the Henry Huntington Library, the Lincoln Center Library of the Performing Arts, the Library of Congress, the New York Public Library, the Morgan Library, the Lilly Library of Indiana University, the Boston Public Library, the University of Edinburgh Library, and the Library of Brown University. We cannot adequately express our indebtedness to Louis B. Wright, O. B. Hardison, Jr., and the late Dorothy Mason of the Folger Shakespeare Library; to the British Library and Mr. Ian Willison; to Mr. George Nash, Curator of the Enthoven Collection of the Victoria and Albert Museum; and to Anthony W. Shipps, Librarian for English of the Indiana University Libraries.

The funding of our project has included substantial grants from the American Council of Learned Societies, the American Society for Theatre Research, the Folger Shakespeare Library, the American Philosophical Society, the Ford Foundation, and the research funds of DePauw University and Thiel College. Without this assistance the project would remain far from complete.

From among a host of friends and colleagues who deserve our special gratitude we may, for reasons of space, single out only a few: Louis B. Wright; Mary E. Knapp; Jack Reading and Sybil Rosenfeld of the Society for Theatre Research; Philip H. Highfill, Jr., Kalman A. Burnim, and Edward A. Langhans, authors of the invaluable biographical dictionary of the London stage personnel of our period; Commander E. S. Satterthwaite, R. N., Secretary of the Garrick Club, and H. P. R. Hoare of C. Hoare & Company, Bankers, for special assistance with *The Clandestine Marriage*; Hermann J. Real of the Wetfalische Wilhelms-Universitat of Munster, Germany; Dr. and Mrs. James T.

Schleifer; Michael Marshall, Howard Archer, and Stephen and Margaret Reese Jones of London for invaluable practical assistance; Josephine Bergmann of Arlington, Va.; Robert H. Farber, Sarah Jane Williams, Edwin L. Minar, Robert Grocock, Marian Maloney, and Barbara Grimes of DePauw University; the late Vernon Sternberg, Director of the Southern Illinois University Press, whose enthusiasm for David Garrick led to his support and patient guidance of our work, and most particularly Arthur Hawley Scouten and George Winchester Stone, Jr., without whose aid we would have been unable to complete this task. And finally, we can never adequately express our debt to our wives, both for assistance and for extreme patience through the long years in which we have labored.

HARRY WILLIAM PEDICORD
FREDRICK LOUIS BERGMANN

Acknowledgments

THE EDITORS and the publishers gratefully acknowledge the permissions granted by the following libraries, museums, and publishers: The Folger Shakespeare Library, Washington, D.C., the Lilly Library of Indiana University, the University of Pennsylvania Libraries, and the University of Illinois Library at Urbana-Champaign, for permission to reproduce the title pages of first editions of Garrick's plays; the Folger and the Harvard Theatre Collection, and the Theatre Collection of the Victoria and Albert Museum, London, for permission to reproduce the illustrations in these volumes; The Huntington Library, San Marino, California, for permission to edit the Prologue to and the text of *The Jubilee*, the text of *The Institution of the Garter* and *The Meeting of the Company* (and the introductory letter to the play), for permission to quote from The Huntington's copy of *Lethe*, and for permission to reprint The Huntington's copy of the Prologue to *The Tempest: An Opera*; the Boston Public Library, Boston, Massachusetts, for permission to edit *Harlequin's Invasion*; Mr. J. Edward Eberle and the Edward-Dean Museum of Decorative Arts, Cherry Valley, California, for permission to photograph and reproduce a portrait supposed to be one of David Garrick; Doubleday for permission to quote from the Preface to Maurice Evans's *G.I. Production of Hamlet by William Shakespeare*, copyright 1946 by Maurice Evans and reprinted by permission of Doubleday and Company, Inc.; the Modern Language Association of America for permission to quote from "Garrick's Long Lost Alteration of *Hamlet*" by George Winchester Stone, Jr. (*PMLA*, 49 [1934], 890–921), copyright 1934 by the Modern Language Association of America and reprinted by permission of the Association.

Introduction

RELATING A QUARREL which he had had with James Lacy, his partner in the management of Drury Lane, Garrick complained to his brother George in 1768 that in "the last Year, my playing alone brought to ye house between 5 & 6 thousand pounds– . . . you know what sums I have given to ye house in altering *Romeo—Every Man*, &c, &c, &c, without fee or reward,–nay have had ye most ungrateful return for it."[1]

Garrick was justified in uttering the complaint: it was his acting, his management of the company, his handling of recalcitrant actors and actresses, his choice of plays, his long hours of rehearsing the company, his own dramatic pieces, and his alteration of the older plays that made Drury Lane the profitable venture that it was. Moreover, by that year Garrick had produced fourteen of the twenty-two original plays presented in this edition, eleven of the twelve adaptations of Shakespeare, and thirteen of the fifteen nonShakespearean adaptations, or thirty-eight of his forty-nine dramatic pieces. But Garrick did even more than these things. Because of his wide and carefully cultivated acquaintance among the "right" people, he lent a great deal of social prestige to the London professional stage. And he spent incalculable hours discussing plays and corresponding about them with authors and would-be authors. Isaac Bickerstaff, for example, before his disgrace, supplied Drury Lane with a great deal of material for the boards; but the demands on Garrick's time in planning with him original productions and adaptations, and in supplying criticisms and suggestions for improvement, were great. Playwrights frequently acknowledged their indebtedness to Garrick. George Colman wrote in the advertisement to *The Jealous Wife* (1761): "It would be unjust, indeed, to omit mentioning my Obligations to Mr. *Garrick*. To his Inspection the Comedy was submitted in its first rude state; and to my Care and Attention to follow his Advice in many Particulars, relating both to the Fable and Characters, I know that I am

---

1.   *Letters*, II, 618.

much indebted for the Reception which this Piece has met with from the Publick."

Edward Moore acknowledged indebtedness to Garrick for some of the most applauded passages in *The Gamester*.[2] Original plays and alterations, both solicited and unsolicited, poured in to Garrick, and his correspondence testifies to his conscientiousness in dealing with them. One post would bring a petulant letter from Arthur Murphy, who had asked for and received criticism of *The Orphan of China* and was made unhappy thereby.[3] Mrs. Dorothy Celesia would send her translation of Voltaire's *Tancred* from Genoa in order to "submit it entirely to your decision,"[4] and J. Sharp would complain of his assigned task of altering *The Maid's Tragedy*: "I would wish indeed you would set me a better task for my Leisure, for, after all, *king-killing plays* are not the thing."[5] Or Sir Joshua Reynolds would ask Garrick to read and consider *Zaphira*, a play by his nephew, the Rev. Joseph Palmer, and Garrick would dutifully send a long critique, act by act.[6] An almost interminable commentary on Mrs. Griffith's various dramatic pieces runs through the Garrick correspondence; often her incessant requests for aid must have been harassing to the busy actor-manager-playwright. To Richard Cumberland, especially when he was writing *The West Indian*, Garrick gave a great share of his off-stage time, happily, in this instance, to an appreciative writer. Wrote Cumberland: "I have twice the pleasure in following your corrections that I had in composing the piece; and if your patience does not give out, mine never will. I entirely adopt your observation on the first scene, and have already executed it in a manner that I hope embraces your ideas. . . . I have heightened the character of O'Flaherty very much in the new scenes, and tied him closer to the plot, as you advised."[7]

But at another time Dr. Thomas Francklin submitted a tragedy with the request that Garrick "carefully revise it," and yet was put out of humor by the criticism which he received, replying haughtily that he would submit "the whole to some approved judges" for a trustworthy opinion.[8] Garrick must answer Francis Gentleman's charge that *The Institution of the Garter* was stolen from him,[9] tell Mme. Riccoboni that she is on the right track in her scheme to translate an English comedy

---

2.   Davies, I, 167.
3.   Boaden, I, 96.
4.   Ibid., p. 354.
5.   Ibid., p. 333.
6.   Ibid., p. 646. Garrick's comments are recorded in a note preserved in the Forster Collection. See *Letters*, III, 955.
7.   Boaden, I, 387.
8.   Ibid., pp. 630, 632.
9.   Ibid., pp. 438–39.

into French,[10] urge his friend John Hoadly to invoke his tragic muse in an alteration of *The London Merchant*,[11] tell Cumberland, who had the audacity to submit an alteration of *Timon* after it had been rejected by Colman at the other house, "I really believe that the Lovers of Shakespeare would condemn Us for not giving them Timon as it Stands in the Original."[12] On another occasion he must be courageous enough to refuse the great Lord Bute's request that Garrick produce Home's *Douglas* after the author had revised it,[13] tell Mrs. Griffith "with the greatest uneasiness" that the three acts she has submitted will not do,[14] compose an epilogue for Mrs. Pritchard's farewell performance ("I wish that I could write, as well as You have Acted"),[15] tell Alexander Dow how to make an actable play of *Zingis*,[16] read Mrs. Charlotte Lennox's *The Sister* with the object of altering and emending it,[17] wade through an unsolicited dramatic piece based on *Don Quixote* which His Majesty's Quartermaster General had composed (again with the object of adding "a few of your masterly touches"),[18] only to open yet another packet from Mrs. Griffiths, this time her translation of *Père de Famille*.[19]

In addition to his perusal and criticism of manuscript plays Garrick was busy with the works being presented in these volumes. The bulk of the present edition indicates the enormity of his tasks of writing and altering plays. His jubilee at Stratford was a time-consuming and costly enterprise, although it was rewarding in publicity value and in the increased popular interest in "the God of his Idolatry" which it aroused; and the consequent *Jubilee* which he presented on the Drury Lane stage was a profitable venture. He wrote, in addition, nearly a hundred prologues—in one he styles himself a prologue-smith. Although Samuel Foote, as may be expected, deplored them and Francis Gentleman wished he had not written two-thirds of the total, Dr. Johnson delivered himself of the opinion that "Dryden has written prologues superior to any that David Garrick has written; but David Garrick has written more good prologues than Dryden has done. It is wonderful that he has been able to write such a variety of them."[20] His poetical activity was such that there was rumor Garrick would be offered the laureateship, and Warburton, learning of Garrick's stand on the matter, wrote on 21

10. *Letters*, II, 626–27.
11. Ibid., I, 84.
12. Ibid., II, 592.
13. Ibid., I, 244–47.
14. Ibid., II, 576.
15. Ibid., p. 498.
16. Ibid., p. 628. See also Boaden, I, 306, 315.
17. Boaden, I, 319.
18. Ibid., I, 385.
19. Ibid., I, 445–46.
20. Boswell, *Life of Johnson*, 27 March 1775, II, 325.

December 1757: "You have given me fresh occasion to commend and esteem you. I have been told you have carefully avoided the occasions of having the Poet Laureate's place offered you. I will tell you my mind frankly: I think it below you, as some others, who have declined it, think it below them."[21]

In the midst of this busy career of acting, producing, playwriting, and counseling—and, to be sure, socializing—Garrick found time to search the older drama for likely revivals. Many of these he assigned to other writers for alteration; others, including most of the Shakespeare plays, he himself prepared for the Drury Lane stage. These works, made "without fee or reward," were independent contributions of Garrick to the drama of his day. All of them, along with his original works, should be read in the light of his total career as actor, producer, director, manager, playwright, critic, and social lion. In this light, and in comparison with the production of the other playwrights of the day— mostly single-art men—the result, presented in these volumes, is a formidable collection of writings for the theatre.

It is interesting to speculate as to what David Garrick might have accomplished as a serious playwright had not his attention been so generously given to a heavy acting and directing schedule and the ever-present burden of management. His contributions to the drama of his day give him third place in importance behind the work of Sheridan and Goldsmith, but his total output, good and otherwise, far surpasses his two superiors in the craft. We tend to dismiss his plays because we do not really know them and because they represent only what appears to be a minor facet of his genius when compared to his acting and managerial careers. But the fact remains that David Garrick's place in the drama of his century is paramount because he was a solid link between his own age and that of the greater personages of the past—from the Restoration comic playwrights on back to the genius of Molière, Jonson, and Shakespeare.

Garrick as a dramatist was his own worst enemy. As a canny manager he gave his audiences what delighted them, pantomime and musical spectaculars. But these were only occasional productions, usually during the Christmas holidays when the town demanded such. And even in these productions he was careful to provide musical scores of merit done by leading contemporary composers.[22] His more serious efforts at playwriting, however, were offered with a view to improving public taste.

21.   Boaden, I, 81.
22.   Garrick used musicians such as Michael Arne (*A Fairy Tale*, *Cymon*); William Boyce (*The Tempest*, *Harlequin's Invasion*, *Winter's Tale*, *Romeo and Juliet*); Charles Burney (*Alfred*, *Midsummer Night's Dream*); and Dibdin (*Institution of the Garter*, *The Jubilee*, *A Christmas Tale*).

But time after time he affected only a passing interest in his plays, choosing the convention of the advertisement to printed plays to slight his work. In 1757 he introduced *The Male-Coquette* with the statement: "The following scenes were written with no other view than to serve Mr. Woodward last year at his benefit." He remarked of *The Farmer's Return from London*, 1762, that "the following Interlude was prepared for the stage, merely with a view of assisting Mrs. Pritchard at her benefit; and the desire of serving so good an actress is a better excuse for its defects than the few days in which it was written and represented."

A Christmas Tale was presented to the reading public with the hope "that the success attending this attempt, so well supported by the Scenery, Music, and Performers, will excite superior talents to productions of the same kind, more worthy of . . . approbation." In 1775 he warned his readers, "if there should be any, that it was merely intended to introduce the *Little Gipsy* to the public." And he concluded the advertisement by remarking that "the piece was produced at an early part of the season, when better writers are not willing to come forth, [which is] the best apology the author can make for its defects." Even concerning one of his finest plays, *Bon Ton*, produced in the same year, he commented: "This little Drama, which had been thrown aside for many years, was brought out last season, with some alterations, for the benefit of MR. KING. . . . The Author is sincerely apprehensive that the excellence of the performances upon the stage, will greatly lessen its credit with the readers in the closet." Two of these pieces, *A Christmas Tale* and *May-Day*, deserve apology, but the others rank among the finest of Garrick's efforts. Cautious as he was with his public, surely Garrick's humility (assumed as it most likely was) damaged his reputation as a serious playwright.

It is generally agreed that of the twenty-two original plays in the Garrick canon, the following five are unworthy of any but house hacks: *A Christmas Tale, May-Day, The Enchanter, Linco's Travels,* and *Cymon. Linco's Travels* is an interlude; *May-Day* is a miniature comic opera; and the remaining three are Christmas pieces designed for those in search of spectacle. Yet all of them had a brisk following and brought success at the box office.

Garrick's claim to serious consideration as a playwright rests upon seventeen lively theatre pieces from 1740 through 1775. Except for his first three plays, all his work appears to derive from the demands of his management, obligations to favorite performers, and the collaboration with George Colman the Elder on *The Clandestine Marriage*. Only three of his original plays were mainpieces; the rest were afterpieces and interludes. And since these genres have disappeared from the stage, we tend to neglect them and their historic importance.

The demand for the afterpiece as an integral part of the bill each night can be dated as far back as the 1703–4 season in London theatres. Thus by Garrick's time it was not only a necessary feature but also on most evenings the mainstay of the entire program. Percy Fitzgerald described the situation as it existed during the Half-Price Riots of 1763: "The performance . . . began very early, and was so arranged as to be, as it were, in two divisions, each of which might suit a different class of spectators. The farce in those days was not the sketchy imperfect thing it is now [1882], but a feature of the night, and worth the reduced rather than half price that was paid for it."[23] And Friedrich Wilhelm von Schutz said of the English playhouses of 1791: "A unique feature . . . was the afterpiece, in which the greatest variety of entertainment was offered, and for which the seats, hitherto comparatively empty, were invariably filled to capacity."[24] Thus it is not surprising to find the bulk of Garrick's own plays afterpieces, most of them successful.

As a manager Garrick had to fill the latter part of each evening, and the demand for variety far outstripped the material available. Thus management dictated the form and increasing artistry Garrick demonstrates in the genre. Mainpieces were expected to come from the standard repertoire, new alterations of older plays, and usually serious plays from leading contemporary playwrights. Garrick turned to the afterpiece almost through necessity and produced more successful ones than any of his contemporaries. A glance at the following tabulation will demonstrate how he managed the task from season to season. In 1747, it will be remembered, Garrick became manager of Drury Lane.

1740–41	*Lethe*, afterpiece (15 April 1741), Drury Lane
1741–42	*The Lying Valet*, afterpiece (30 November 1741) Goodman's Fields
1743–44	*Macbeth*, adaptation (7 January 1744), Drury Lane
1746–47	*Miss in Her Teens*, afterpiece (17 January 1747), Covent Garden
1747–48	*The Alchymist*, adaptation (21 October 1747)
	The Provok'd Wife, adaptation (10 November 1747)
1748–49	*Romeo and Juliet*, adaptation (29 November 1748)
1749–50	*The Rehearsal*, adaptation (20 December 1749)
	The Roman Father, alteration (24 February 1750)
1750–51	*Alfred*, A Masque, adaptation (23 February 1751)
1751–52	*Every Man in His Humour*, adaptation (29 November 1751)
1753–54	*Zara*, adaptation (25 March 1754)

23. *A New History*, II, 186–87.
24. Quoted in Kelly, *German Visitors*, pp. 148–49.

1754–55 *The Chances*, adaptation (7 November 1754)
        The Fairies, adaptation (3 February 1755)
1755–56 *Catharine and Petruchio*, adaptation (21 January 1756)
        Florizel and Perdita, adaptation (21 January 1756)
        The Tempest, an Opera (11 February 1756)
        Rule a Wife and Have a Wife, adaptation (25 March 1756)
1756–57 *King Lear*, adaptation (28 October 1756)
        Lilliput, afterpiece (3 December 1756)
        The Male-Coquette, afterpiece (24 March 1757)
1757–58 *Isabella*, adaptation (2 December 1757)
        The Gamesters, adaptation (22 December 1757)
1758–59 *Antony and Cleopatra*, adaptation (3 January 1759)
        The Guardian, afterpiece (3 February 1759)
1759–60 *Harlequin's Invasion*, pantomime (31 December 1759)
1760–61 *The Enchanter*, Christmas musical (13 December 1760)
1761–62 *Cymbeline*, adaptation (28 November 1761)
        The Farmer's Return from London, interlude (20 March 1762)
1763–64 *A Midsummer Night's Dream*, adaptation (23 November 1763)
1765–66 *Mahomet*, adaptation (25 November 1765)
        The Clandestine Marriage, mainpiece (20 February 1766)
1766–67 *The Country Girl*, adaptation (25 October 1766)
        Neck or Nothing, afterpiece (18 November 1766)
        Cymon, mainpiece (2 January 1767)
        Linco's Travels, interlude (6 April 1767)
1767–68 *A Peep Behind the Curtain*, afterpiece (23 October 1767)
1769–70 *The Jubilee*, afterpiece (14 October 1769)
1770–71 *King Arthur*, a masque, adaptation (13 December 1770)
1771–72 *The Institution of the Garter*, a masque (28 October 1771)
1772–73 *The Irish Widow*, afterpiece (23 October 1772)
        Hamlet, adaptation (18 December 1772)
        The Tempest, adaptation (12 May 1773)
1773–74 *Albumazar*, adaptation (19 October 1773)
        A Christmas Tale, spectacle (27 December 1773)
1774–75 *The Meeting of the Company*, prelude (17 September 1774)
        Bon Ton, afterpiece (18 March 1775)
1775–76 *The Theatrical Candidates*, musical prelude (23 September 1775)
        May-Day; or, The Little Gipsy, miniature comic opera (28 October 1775)

Garrick's forte was social satire, and he steered a good-tempered course between the ferocity of Fielding and the lampoons of Samuel Foote. A man of reason, and moral for his time, he sincerely despised the callous effrontery of the presumptuous in his society. It is from his first play, *Lethe*, in 1740 that we can trace his role as calm spectator of the foibles of men; and this position he maintained throughout his life. Elsewhere we have indicated the evolution of the Mrs. Riots into Fine Ladies, the Beau into the Fine Gentleman and ultimately into the Fribble. These characters later become the Mrs. Heidelbergs, the Daffodils, the Flashes, the Lord Chalkstone, *et al.* His own role as Aesop the spectator becomes the Tukelys, Bateses, and Trotleys at the end of his career.

Garrick made no secret of his preference for the "old comedy" and its Restoration practitioners despite the wave of sentimentality he had to avoid as manager and still try to please his audiences. As in his Aesop, Garrick would always be amused at the follies of his fellow men, but this Aesop approached the social vices of his time with great seriousness. In other words, Garrick worked hard for his own living and his standards as a gentleman; he expected no less from the rest of his contemporaries. He has no affection for the pretences of fine ladies and fine gentlemen, for gamblers, bullies, effeminate philanderers, or for the Britisher returned from Continental travels a slave to *outré* fashions. As early as 1747, in *Miss in Her Teens*, he was waging war against tavern bullies masquerading as army officers, and in 1757 he waged public war against the Daffodils in *The Male-Coquette*. In a group of afterpieces—*Lethe*, *Lilliput*, *The Male-Coquette*, *The Irish Widow*, and *Bon Ton*—Garrick displays his idea of what he constantly referred to as the true *vis comica*. He stressed moral values not to preach but to provoke derision through laughter. Ben Jonson appears to have been Garrick's great teacher, even if he has had to remain this side of idolatry. Ten of Garrick's plays prove the point.

When Henry Woodward joined forces with Spranger Barry in Dublin (1756), Garrick was left to provide his own Christmas shows and other spectaculars. The result was some of his poorest playwriting, which had to be bolstered by increasing scenic splendor and musical accompaniment to provide excitement for the holiday public. But these spectaculars were rather dull for the most part. They prove only what little real interest the author had, even though the manager aimed for popular success. *Harlequin's Invasion*, Garrick's sole pantomime, was based upon the old one he had known in his apprentice days at Goodman's Fields, *Harlequin Student; or, The Fall of Pantomime*. His devotion to serious drama and Shakespeare appears here in the defeat of Harlequin and an apotheosis of the Bard. The other five spectacular entertainments exhibit the manager at pains to satisfy the public, to rely upon his own growing interest in new deployments of stagecraft, and to introduce young singers such as Master Leoni and Harriet Abrams to the public. In all these pieces one can perceive two intentions: to try as honestly as possible to provide holiday entertainment, asking critics and public to relax and enjoy trifles; and to surmount the inability of a dedicated author sincerely to believe in what was written for such occasions.

In his preludes, interludes, and burlesque plays Garrick established his ideal for his theatre. When he produced his first play in 1747, Dr. Johnson's famous prologue outlined the course Garrick hoped to take in management. The new manager loved Shakespeare and the older dramatists. As late as 1775, having relented somewhat as to pantomime, having banned visitors behind stage, and having fought a good fight for legitimate theatre, he was still insisting that pantomime should hold up the trains of tragedy and comedy, that spectacle was all right for the holidays and special occasions, and that the actors had a right to decorum in their working habitat.

While we must always regard Garrick's plays from the point of view of his position as a manager, the lot of them show his particular genius for theatrical material which continued the historical tradition. If Sheridan and Goldsmith were more polished writers, David Garrick at his best equals them as a playwright, and his total writings combine with his excellence as actor-manager to make him the greatest theatre personage of his century.

The Garrick Canon

[Dates indicate the season each play
or adaptation was first presented.]

GARRICK'S ALTERATIONS OF OTHERS

Chronology

1685		David Garric arrives in London from Bordeaux.
1687		Peter Garrick, son of David Garric, born in France, arrives in England.
1707		Peter Garrick married to Arabella Clough of Litchfield.
1717		David Garrick born in the Angel Inn, Hereford, 19 February.
1718	France and England declare war against Spain.	
1720	Failure of South Sea Company and Law's Mississippi Company in Paris.	
1722	Jacobite Plot.	
1724	The Drapier's Letters and Wood's Halfpence.	
1725	Treaty of Hanover.	Brother George Garrick born 22 August.

1727
| | Accession of George II. | David attends Litchfield Grammar School. |

1728
| | | David sent to Lisbon, Portugal, to enter Uncle's wine business. After a brief stay returns to England. |

1729
| | Resolutions against the reporting of Parliamentary debates. | David re-enters Litchfield Grammar School. |

1730
| | Walpole and Townshend quarrel, Townshend resigns. | |

1731
| | Full Walpole administration. | |

1735
| | Porteous Riots in Edinburgh. | David enrolled under Samuel Johnson at Edial Hall. |

1736
| | | Father returns from Army and David drops out of Edial. Johnson's academy a failure. |

1737
| | Censorship established with the passing of the Theatrical Licensing Act. | Garrick and Samuel Johnson set out for London on 2 March. Garrick enrolled as student at Lincoln's Inn on 9 March. |

1738
| | Jenkins's Ear. | |

1739
| | England declares war against Spain. | |

1740
| | | Garrick's first play, *Lethe; or, Esop in the Shades*, produced at Drury Lane, 1 April. |

1741
| | | Charles Macklin's revolutionary performance as Shylock, Drury Lane, 14 February. Garrick plays summer engage- |

ment at Ipswich under name of Lydall–Capt. Duretête in Farquhar's *The Inconstant*, 21 July.

Garrick's debut as Richard III at Goodman's Fields, 19 October.

Appears in seven other roles during the season.

The Lying Valet produced at Goodman's Fields, 30 November.

Garrick retires from wine trade in London.

1742

Resignation of Walpole.

Garrick plays three performances at Drury Lane: Bayes, 26 May; Lear, 28 May; Richard III, 31 May.

Plays summer season at Smock Alley Theatre, Dublin.

Returns to London as a member of the Drury Lane company, opening with Chamont in Otway's *The Orphan* and playing twelve other roles before end of season.

1743

Defeat of French at Dettingen.

Actors' strike against manager Fleetwood at Drury Lane.

Garrick plays second season at Smock Alley, Dublin.

1745

Plays Dublin, 9 December to 3 May 1746.

1746

Mlle. Violetti arrives from Continent in February to dance at Haymarket Theatre.

Garrick and James Quin compete in performance of Rowe's *The Fair Penitent at* Covent Garden, 14 November.

1747

> *Miss in Her Teens* produced at Covent Garden, 17 January. James Lacy and David Garrick become joint-patentees of Drury Lane, 9 April. New managers alter and refurbish Drury Lane Theatre.

1748

Peace of Aix-la-Chapelle.

1749

> Garrick and Violetti married, 22 June, and reside at 27 Southampton Street, Covent Garden.
> The "Battle of the Romeos."

1751

Death of Frederick, Prince of Wales.

> Garricks set out for trip to the Continent, 19 May.

1753

Founding of the British Museum.

1754

Death of Pelham, who is succeeded by Newcastle as Prime Minister.

> Garrick leases villa at Hampton.

1755

Publication of Johnson's *Dictionary*.

> The Chinese Festival Riots at Drury Lane, 8–18 November. Garrick buys Hampton villa.

1756

Seven Years' War begins.

1760

Accession of George III.

1762

War against Spain.

> Drury Lane Theatre altered and enlarged.
> Half-Price Riots at Drury Lane and Covent Garden.

1763

John Wilkes and *The North Briton*.

> Garricks tour the Continent 1763–65.

1764		
		Garrick stricken with typhoid fever in Munich.
1765		
	The Stamp Act.	Publication of *The Sick Monkey* precedes Garrick's return from abroad. Returns to stage by command as Benedict in *Much Ado About Nothing*, 14 November.
1766		
	Repeal of the Stamp Act.	
1768		
		The Dramatic Works of David Garrick published in three volumes.
1769		
	The letters of "Junius."	Garrick becomes Steward of Shakespeare Jubilee at Stratford-upon-Avon, 6–9 September. Stages *The Jubilee* at Drury Lane on 14 October.
1772		
		Garrick buys house in Adam Brothers' Adelphi Terrace; moves in on 28 February. Isaac Bickerstaff flees to France in disgrace, and Garrick is attacked by William Kenrick's publication of *Love in the Suds*. Garrick goes to court and Kenrick publishes apology on 26 November.
1773		
	The Boston Tea-Party.	
1774		
	Death of Oliver Goldsmith.	*The Dramatic Works of David Garrick* published in two volumes by R. Bald, T. Blaw and J. Kurt.

1775

War of American Indepen-
dence.

Drury Lane altered and deco-
rated by the Adam Brothers.

1776

Garrick's sale of Drury Lane
patent announced in the press
on 7 March—to Richard Brins-
ley Sheridan, Thomas Linley
and Dr. James Ford.
Garrick's farewell performances upon retirement, 1
April to 10 June.
Final performance as Don
Felix in Mrs. Centlivre's *The
Wonder*, 10 June.

1777

Burgoyne surrenders at Sara-
toga.

Garrick reads *Lethe* before the
Royal Family at Windsor Castle in February.

1778

Alliance of France and Spain
with the United States.

1779

Garrick dies at Adelphi Ter-
race home on 20 January.
Burial in Poets Corner, Westminster Abbey on 1 February.
Roubillac statue of Shakespeare and large collection of
old plays willed to the British
Museum.
George Garrick dies on 3 February.

Lethe;
or, Esop in the Shades
A Dramatic Satire
1740

LETHE.

A
DRAMATIC SATIRE.

By *DAVID GARRICK.*

As it is Performed at the

THEATRE-ROYAL in DRURY-LANE,

By His MAJESTY's Servants.

LONDON:

Printed for and Sold by PAUL VAILLANT,
facing *Southampton-Street* in the *Strand.*
M DCC XLIX.

Dramatis Personae

Aesop	Mr. *Bridges.*
Mercury	Mr. *Beard.*
Charon	Mr. *Winstone.*
Poet ⎫	
Frenchman ⎬	Mr. *Garrick.*
Drunken Man ⎭	
A Fine Gentleman	Mr. *Woodward.*
Mr. Tatoo	Mr. *King.*
Old Man	Mr. *Taswell.*
Tailor	Mr. *Yates.*
Mrs. Riot	Mrs. *Clive.*
Mrs. Tatoo	Mrs. *Green.*

Lethe; or Esop in the Shades

SCENE, *a grove.*

With a view of the River Lethe.
Charon *and* Aesop *discovered.*

CHARON. Prithee, Philosopher, what grand affair is transacting upon earth? There is something of importance going forward, I am sure; for Mercury flew over the Styx this morning without paying me the usual compliments.

AESOP. I'll tell thee, Charon. This is the anniversary of the Rape of Proserpine, on which day, for the future, Pluto has permitted her to demand from him something for the benefit of mankind.

CHARON. I understand you. His Majesty's passions, by a long possession of the lady, are abated. And so, like a mere mortal, he must now flatter her vanity and sacrifice his power to atone for deficiencies. But what has our royal mistress proposed in behalf of her favorite mortals?

AESOP. As mankind, you know, are ever complaining of their cares and dissatisfied with their conditions, the generous Proserpine has begged of Pluto that they may have free access to the waters of Lethe as a sovereign remedy for their complaints. Notice has been already given above and proclamation made. Mercury is to conduct them to the Styx, you are to ferry 'em over to Elysium, and I am placed here to distribute the waters.

CHARON. A very pretty employment I shall have of it, truly. If her Majesty has often these whims, I must petition the court either to

---

0.2. With] omit with *O*4.
0.3. Charon . . . discovered] Enter Charon and Aesop *O*4.
 8. passions] passion *W*1.
 9. are abated] is abated *W*1.

build a bridge over the river or let me resign my employment. Do their Majesties know the difference of weight between souls and bodies? However, I'll obey their commands to the best of my power; I'll row my crazy boat over and meet 'em. But many of them will be relieved from their cares before they reach Lethe.

AESOP.   How so, Charon?

CHARON.   Why, I shall leave half of 'em in the Styx. And any water is a specific against care, provided it be taken in quantity.

Enter Mercury.

30   MERCURY.   Away to your boat, Charon; there are some mortals arrived, and the females among 'em will be very clamorous if you make 'em wait.

CHARON.   I'll make what haste I can, rather than give those fair creatures a topic for conversation.

Noise within: "Boat! Boat! Boat!"

Coming, coming. Zounds, you are in a plaguy hurry, sure; No wonder these mortal folks have so many complaints, when there's no patience among 'em. If they were dead now, and to be settled here forever, they'd be damned before they'd make such a rout to come

40   over. But care, I suppose, is thirsty, and 'till they have drenched themselves with Lethe there will be no quiet among 'em. Therefore I'll e'en to work. And so, Friend Aesop and Brother Mercury, goodbye to ye.

Exit Charon.

AESOP.   Now to my office of Judge and Examiner, in which, to the best of my knowledge, I will act with impartiality; for I will immediately relieve real objects and only divert myself with pretenders.

MERCURY.   Act as your wisdom directs and conformable to your earthly character, and we shall have few murmurers.

AESOP.   I still retain my former sentiments, never to refuse advice or

50   charity to those that want either. Flattery and rudeness should be equally avoided; folly and vice should never be spared; and though by acting thus you may offend many, yet you will please the better few. And the approbation of one virtuous mind is more valuable than all the noisy applause and uncertain favors of the great and guilty.

MERCURY.   Incomparable Aesop, both men and gods admire thee! We must now prepare to receive these mortals; and lest the solemnity of the place should strike 'em with too much dread, I'll raise music shall dispel their fears and embolden them to approach.

SONG.

I.

Ye mortals whom fancies and troubles perplex,
Whom folly misguides and infirmities vex;
Whose lives hardly know what it is to be blest,
Who rise without joy and lie down without rest;
  Obey the glad summons, to Lethe repair,
  Drink deep of the stream and forget all your care.

II.

Old maids shall forget what they wish for in vain,
And young ones the rover they cannot regain;
The rake shall forget how last night he was cloyed,
And Chloe again be with passion enjoyed;
  Obey then the summons, to Lethe repair,
  And drink an oblivion to trouble and care.

III.

The wife at one draught may forget all her wants,
Or drench her fond fool to forget her gallants;
The troubled in mind shall go cheerful away,
And yesterday's wretch be quite happy today;
  Obey then the summons, to Lethe repair,
  Drink deep of the stream and forget all your care.

AESOP. Mercury, Charon has brought over one mortal already. Conduct him hither.

Exit Mercury.

Now for a large catalogue of complaints, without the acknowledgment of one single vice! Here he comes. If one may guess at his cares by his appearance, he really wants the assistance of Lethe.

Enter Poet.

POET. Sir, your humble servant—your humble servant. Your name is Aesop. I know your person intimately, though I never saw you before; and am well acquainted with you, though I never had the honor of your conversation.

AESOP. You are a dealer in paradoxes, Friend.

POET. I am a dealer in all parts of speech and in all the figures of rhetoric. I am a poet, Sir; and to be a poet and not acquainted with

---

74. cheerful] chearful *W*1.
83. your . . . servant] omitted *W*1.
83–189. Poet role entirely omitted *O*4.

90   the great Aesop is a greater paradox than —. I honor you extremely, Sir. You certainly, of all the writers of antiquity, had the greatest, the sublimest genius, the —

AESOP. Hold, Friend, I hate flattery.

POET. My own taste exactly. I assure you, Sir, no man loves flattery less
than myself.

AESOP. So it appears, Sir, by your being so ready to give it away.

POET. You have hit, Mr. Aesop, you have hit it. I have given it away
indeed. I did not receive one farthing from my last dedication, and
yet, would you believe it, I absolutely gave all the virtues in heaven
100   to one of the lowest reptiles upon earth.

AESOP. 'Tis hard indeed to do dirty work for nothing.

POET. Ay, Sir, to do dirty work and still be dirty oneself is the Stone
of Sysiphus and the Thirst of Tantalus. You Greek writers, indeed,
carried your point by truth and simplicity. They won't do nowadays. Our patrons must be tickled into generosity. You gained the
greatest favors by showing your own merits; we can only gain the
smallest by publishing those of other people. You flourish by truth;
we starve by fiction. *Tempora mutantur!*

AESOP. Indeed, Friend, if we may guess by your present plight, you
110   have prostituted your talents to very little purpose.

POET. To very little, upon my word. But they shall find that I can
open another vein. Satire is the fashion, and satire they shall have.
Let 'em look to it. I can be sharp as well as sweet; I can scourge as
well as tickle; I can bite as —

AESOP. You can do anything, no doubt. But to the business of this visit,
for I expect a great deal of company. What are your troubles,
Sir?

POET. Why, Mr. Aesop, I am troubled with an odd kind of a disorder.
I have a sort of a whistling, a singing, a whizzing as it were in my
120   head, which I cannot get rid of.

AESOP. Our waters give no relief to bodily disorders. They only affect
the memory.

POET. From whence all my disorder proceeds. I'll tell you my case,
Sir. You must know I wrote a play some time ago, presented a
dedication of it to a certain young nobleman. He approved and
accepted of it, but before I could taste his bounty, my piece
was unfortunately damned. I lost my benefit; nor could I have
recourse to my patron, for I was told that his lordship played
the best catcall the first night and was the merriest person in the
130   whole audience.

AESOP. Pray, what do you call damning a play?

POET. You cannot possibly be ignorant what it is to be damned, Mr.
Aesop.

AESOP. Indeed I am, Sir. We had no such thing among the Greeks.

POET. No, Sir. No wonder then that you Greeks were such fine writers. It is impossible to be described or truly felt but by the author himself. If you could but get a leave of absence from this world for a few hours, you might perhaps have an opportunity of seeing it yourself. There is a sort of new piece comes upon our stage this very night, and I am pretty sure it will meet with its deserts; at least it shall not want my helping hand, rather than you should be disappointed of satisfying your curiosity.

AESOP. You are very obliging, Sir. But to your own misfortunes, if you please.

POET. Envy, malice and party destroyed me. You must know, Sir, I was a great damner myself, before I was damned. So the frolics of my youth were returned to me with double interest, from my brother authors. But, to say the truth, my performance was terribly handled before it appeared in public.

AESOP. How so, pray?

POET. Why, Sir, some squeamish friends of mine pruned it of all the bawdy and immorality, the actors did not speak a line of the sense or sentiment, and the manager (who writes himself) struck out all the wit and humor in order to lower my performance to a level with his own.

AESOP. Now, Sir, I am acquainted with your case, what have you to propose?

POET. Notwithstanding the success of my first play, I am strongly persuaded that my next may defy the severity of the critics, the sneer of wits, and the malice of authors.

AESOP. What, have you been hardy enough to attempt another?

POET. I must eat, Sir; I must live. But when I sit down to write and am glowing with the heat of my imagination, then this damned whistling or whizzing in my head that I told you of so disorders me that I grow giddy. In short, Sir, I am haunted, as it were, with the ghost of my deceased play, and its dying groans are forever in my ears. Now, Sir, if you will give me but a draught of Lethe to forget this unfortunate performance, it will be of more real service to me than all the waters of Helicon.

AESOP. I doubt, Friend, you cannot possibly write better by merely forgetting that you have written before; besides, if, when you drink to the forgetfulness of your own works, you should unluckily for-

---

160. sneer] snear *D*2.

163. sit] set *W*1.

get those of other people too, your next piece will certainly be the worse for it.

POET.   You are certainly in the right. What then would you advise me to?

AESOP.   Suppose you could prevail upon the audience to drink the water? Their forgetting your former work might be of no small advantage to your future productions.

180

POET.   Ah, Sir, if I could but do that. But I am afraid Lethe will never go down with the audience.

AESOP.   Well, since you are bent upon it, I shall indulge you. If you please to walk in that grove (which will afford you many subjects for your poetical contemplation) till I have examined the rest, I will dismiss you in your turn.

POET.   And I in return, Sir, will let the world know, in a preface to my next piece, that your politeness is equal to your sagacity, and that you are as much the fine gentleman as the philosopher.

Exit Poet.

190   AESOP.   On, your servant, Sir.—In the name of misery and mortality what have we here?

Enter an Old Man *supported by a* Servant.

OLD MAN.   Oh, la! Oh, bless me, I shall never recover the fatigue. Ha! what are you, Friend? Are you the famous Aesop? And are you so kind, so very good, to give people the waters of forgetfulness for nothing?

AESOP.   I am that person, Sir. But you seem to have no need of my waters, for you must have already outlived your memory.

OLD MAN.   My memory is indeed impaired. It is not so good as it was, but still it is better than I wish it, at least in regard to one circum-

200   stance. There is one thing which sits very heavy at my heart and which I would willingly forget.

AESOP.   What is it, pray?

OLD MAN.   Oh, la! Oh! I am horribly fatigued. I am an old man, Sir, turned of ninety. We are all mortal, you know, so I would fain forget, if you please, that I am to die.

AESOP.   My good friend, you have mistaken the virtue of the waters. They can cause you to forget only what is past. But if this was in their power, you would surely be your own enemy in desiring to forget what ought to be the only comfort of one so poor and

210   wretched as you seem. What? I suppose now you have left some dear, loving wife behind, that you can't bear to think of parting with.

OLD MAN.   No, no, no. I have buried my wife and forgot her long ago.

AESOP. What? You have children, then, whom you are unwilling to leave behind you?

OLD MAN. No, no. I have no children at present. Hugh! I don't know what I may have.

AESOP. Is there any relation or friend, the loss of whom —

OLD MAN. No, no. I have outlived all my relations. And as for friends—
220 I have none to lose.

AESOP. What can be the reason, then, that in all this apparent misery you are so afraid of death, which would be your only cure?

OLD MAN. Oh, Lord! I have one friend, a true friend indeed, the only friend in whom a wise man places any confidence. I have — Get a little farther off, John. (*Servant retires*.) I have, to say the truth, a little money. It is that, indeed, which causes all my uneasiness.

AESOP. Thou never spok'st a truer word in thy life, old Gentleman. (*Aside*.) But I can cure you of your uneasiness immediately.

OLD MAN. Shall I forget then that I am to die and leave my money be-
230 hind me?

AESOP. No, but you shall forget that you have it, which will do al-together as well. One large draught of Lethe to the forgetfulness of your money will restore you to perfect ease of mind. And as for your bodily pains, no waters can relieve them.

OLD MAN. What does he say, John, eh? I am hard of hearing.

JOHN. He advises your Worship to drink to forget your money.

OLD MAN. What, what! Will his drink get me money, does he say?

AESOP. No, Sir. The waters are of a wholesome nature, for they'll teach you to forget your money.

240 OLD MAN. Will they so? Come, come, John, we are got to the wrong place. The poor old fool here does not know what he says. Let us go back again, John. I'll drink none of your waters, not I. Forget my money? Come along, John.

                                                                    Exeunt.

AESOP. Was there ever such a wretch? If these are the cares of mortals, the waters of oblivion cannot cure them.

Re-enter Old Man *and Servant.*

OLD MAN. Lookee, Sir, I am come a great way and am loth to refuse favors that cost nothing. So I don't care if I drink a little of your waters. Let me see—ay, I'll drink to forget how I *got* my money. And my servant there, he shall drink a little to forget that I have
250 any money at all. And, d'ye hear, John—take a hearty draught. If my money must be forgot, why e'en let *him* forget it.

---

238. wholesome] *O*2, *D*1, *O*5, *O*6, *O*7, *O*8; wholsomer *O*3, *D*2, *O*9, *O*4; whole-somer] *W*1, *O*10, *W*2.

AESOP.   Well, Friend, it shall be as you would have it. You'll find a seat in that grove yonder where you may rest yourself till the waters are distributed.

OLD MAN.   I hope it won't be long, Sir, for thieves are busy now, and I have an iron chest in the other world that I should be sorry anyone peeped into but myself. So pray be quick, Sir.

Exeunt.

AESOP.   Patience, patience, old Gentleman. But here comes something tripping this way that seems to be neither man nor woman, and 260   yet an odd mixture of both.

Enter a Fine Gentleman.

FINE GENTLEMAN.   Harkee, old Friend, do you stand drawer here?

AESOP.   Drawer, young fop! Do you know where you are and who you talk to?

FINE GENTLEMAN.   Not I, demme! But 'tis a rule with me, wherever I am or whoever I am with, to be always easy and familiar.

AESOP.   Then let me advise you, young Gentleman, to drink the waters and forget that ease and familiarity.

FINE GENTLEMAN.   Why so, Daddy? Would you not have me well bred?

AESOP.   Yes. But you may not always meet with people so polite as 270   yourself or so passive as I am. And if what you call breeding should be construed impertinence, you may have a return of familiarity may make you repent your education as long as you live.

FINE GENTLEMAN.   Well said, old Drybeard. Egad, you have a smattering of an odd kind of a sort of a humor. But come, come, prithee give me a glass of your waters and keep your advice to yourself.

AESOP.   I must first be informed, Sir, for what purpose you drink 'em.

FINE GENTLEMAN.   You must know, Philosopher, I want to forget two qualities, my modesty and my good nature.

AESOP.   Your modesty and good nature?

280   FINE GENTLEMAN.   Yes, Sir. I have such a consummate modesty, that when a fine woman (which is often the case) yields to my addresses, egad, I run away from her. And I am so very good-natured that when a man affronts me, egad, I run away too.

AESOP.   As for your modesty, Sir, I am afraid you are come to the wrong waters. And if you will take a large cup to the forgetfulness of your fears, your goodnature, I believe, will trouble you no more.

FINE GENTLEMAN.   And this is your advice, my Dear, eh?

AESOP.   My advice, Sir would go a great deal farther. I should advise you to drink to the forgetfulness of everything you know.

290   FINE GENTLEMAN.   The devil you would! Then I should have travelled to a fine purpose truly. You don't imagine, perhaps, that I have

been three years abroad and have made the tour of Europe?

AESOP. Yes, Sir, I guessed you had travelled by your dress and conversation. But, pray, (with submission) what valuable improvements have you made in these travels?

FINE GENTLEMAN. Sir, I learnt drinking in Germany, music and painting in Italy, dancing, gaming, and some other amusements at Paris, and in Holland—faith, nothing at all. I brought over with me the best collection of Venetian ballads, two eunuchs, a French dancer, and a monkey, with toothpicks, pictures and burlettas. In short, I have skimmed the cream of every nation, and have the consolation to declare I never was in any country in my life but I had taste enough thoroughly to despise my own.

AESOP. Your country is greatly obliged to you. But if you are settled in it now, how can your taste and delicacy endure it?

FINE GENTLEMAN. Faith, my existence is merely supported by amusements. I dress, visit, study taste and write sonnets. By birth, travel, education, and natural abilities, I am entitled to lead the fashion. I am principal connoisseur at all auctions, chief arbiter at assemblies, professed critic at the theatres, and a fine gentleman everywhere.

AESOP. Critic, Sir; pray what's that?

FINE GENTLEMAN. The delight of the ingenious, the terror of poets, the scourge of players, and the aversion of the vulgar.

AESOP. Pray, Sir (for I fancy your life must be somewhat particular) how do you pass your time? The day, for instance?

FINE GENTLEMAN. I lie in bed all day, Sir.

AESOP. How do you spend your evenings, then?

FINE GENTLEMAN. I dress in the evening and go generally behind the scenes of both playhouses; not, you may imagine, to be diverted with the play but to intrigue and show myself. I stand upon the stage, talk loud and stare about, which confounds the actors and disturbs the audience. Upon which the galleries, who hate the appearance of one of us, begin to hiss and cry "Off, off!" while I undaunted stamp my foot so, loll with my shoulder thus, take snuff with my right hand and smile scornfully, thus. This exasperates the savages, and they attack us with vollies of sucked oranges and half-eaten pippins —

AESOP. And you retire.

FINE GENTLEMAN. Without doubt, if I am sober; for orange will stain silk and an apple may disfigure a feature.

AESOP. I am afraid, Sir, for all this, that you are obliged to your own imagination for more than three fourths of your importance.

FINE GENTLEMAN (aside). Damn the old prig! I'll bully him.—Lookee,

---

327. pippins] pippens] *O5, W1.*

old Philosopher, I find you have passed your time so long in gloom and ignorance below here that our notions above stairs are too refined for you. So as we are not likely to agree, I shall cut matters very short with you. Bottle me off the waters I want, or you shall be convinced that I have courage in the drawing of a cork. Dispatch me instantly, or I shall make bold to throw you into the river and help myself. What say you to that now, eh?

340

AESOP. Very civil and concise! I have no great inclination to put your manhood to the trial; so if you will be pleased to walk in the grove there 'till I have examined some I see coming, we'll compromise the affair between us.

FINE GENTLEMAN. Yours as you behave. Au revoir!

Exit Beau.

Enter Mr. and Mrs. Tatoo.

MRS. TATOO. Why don't you come along, Mr. Tatoo? What the deuce are you afraid of?

AESOP. Don't be angry, young lady; the gentleman is your husband, I suppose.

350

MRS. TATOO. How do you know that, eh? What, you an't all conjurers in this world, are you?

AESOP. Your behavior to him is a sufficient proof of his condition, without the gift of conjuration.

MRS. TATOO. Why, I was as free with him before marriage as I am now. I never was coy or prudish in my life.

AESOP. I believe you, Madam. Pray, how long have you been married? You seem to be very young, Lady.

MRS. TATOO. I am old enough for a husband, and have been married long enough to be tired of one.

360

AESOP. How long, pray?

MRS. TATOO. Why, above three months. I married Mr. Tatoo without my guardian's consent.

AESOP. If you married him with your own consent, I think you might continue your affections a little longer.

MRS. TATOO. What signifies what you think, if I don't think so? We are quite tired of one another and are come to drink some of your Le—Lethaly—Leithily, I think they call it, to forget one another and be unmarried again.

345.2. Enter . . . Tatoo] *O5* inserts entirely new scene of Bowman "With the additional Character of Lord Chalkstone." For this new scene from 5th Edition 1757 see following pages. *O5* lines 1–200. Bowman-Chalkstone scene omitted *D2*.

367. Le . . . leithily] Lethily *O4, O5, O9, W1*.

AESOP. The waters can't divorce you, Madam; and you may easily
370   forget him without the assistance of Lethe.

MRS. TATOO. Ay? How so?

AESOP. By remembering continually he is your husband. There are
several ladies have no other receipt. But what does the gentleman
say to this?

MRS. TATOO. What signifies what he says? I an't so young and foolish
as that comes to, to be directed by my husband or to care what
either he says or you say.

MR. TATOO. Sir, I was a drummer in a marching regiment when I ran
away with that young lady. I immediately bought out of the corps,
380   and thought myself made forever, little imagining that a poor, vain
fellow was purchasing fortune at the expense of his happiness.

AESOP. 'Tis even so, Friend; fortune and felicity are as often at variance
as man and wife.

MR. TATOO. I found it so, Sir. This high life, as I thought it, did not agree
with me. I have not laughed, and scarcely slept since my advancement; and unless your wisdom can alter her notions, I must e'en
quit the blessings of a fine lady and her portion, and for content
have recourse to eight-pence a day and my drum again.

AESOP. Pray, who has advised you to a separation?

390 MRS. TATOO. Several young ladies of my acquaintance, who tell me
they are not angry at me for marrying him, but being fond of him
now that I have married him; and they say I should be as complete a fine lady as any of 'em if I would but procure a separate
divorcement.

AESOP. Pray, Madam, will you let me know what you call a fine lady?

MRS. TATOO. Why, a fine lady and a fine gentleman are two of the finest
things upon earth.

AESOP. I have just now had the honor of knowing what a fine gentleman is, so pray confine yourself to the lady.

400 MRS. TATOO. A fine lady before marriage lives with her papa and mama,
who breed her up till she learns to despise 'em and resolves to do
nothing they bid her. This makes her such a prodigious favorite
that she wants for nothing.

AESOP. So, Lady.

MRS. TATOO. When once she is her own mistress, then comes the
pleasure.

AESOP. Pray let us hear.

MRS. TATOO. She lies in bed all morning, rattles about all day, and sits
up all night. She goes everywhere and sees everything, knows
410   everybody and loves nobody, ridicules her friends, coquettes with

---

375. and foolish] and so foolish *O5, D2, W1.*

her lovers, sets 'em together by the ears, tells fibs, makes mischief, buys china, cheats at cards, keeps a pug-dog, and hates the parsons. She laughs much, talks aloud, never blushes, says what she will, does what she will, goes where she will, marries whom she pleases, hates her husband in a month, breaks his heart in four, becomes a widow, slips from her gallants, and begins the world again. There's a life for you! What do you think of a fine lady now?

AESOP. As I expected, you are very young, Lady. And if you are not very careful, your natural propensity to noise and affectation will
420   run you headlong into folly, extravagance, and repentance.

MRS. TATOO. What would you have me do?

AESOP. Drink a large quantity of Lethe to the loss of your acquaintance. And do you, Sir, drink another to forget this false step of your wife; for whilst you remember her folly you can never thoroughly regard her. And whilst you keep good company, Lady, as you call it, and follow their example, you can never have a just regard for your husband. So both drink and be happy.

MRS. TATOO. Well, give it me whilst I am in humor, or I shall certainly change my mind again.

430 AESOP. Be patient till the rest of the company drink, and divert yourself in the meantime with walking in the grove.

MRS. TATOO. Well, come along, Husband, and keep me in humor, or I shall beat you such an alarm as you never beat in all your life.

Exit Mr. *and* Mrs. Tatoo.

Enter Frenchman, *singing.*

FRENCHMAN. Monsieur, votre serviteur. Pourquoi ne repondez vous pas? Je dis que je suis votre serviteur.

AESOP. I don't understand you, Sir.

FRENCHMAN. Ah, le barbare! Il ne parle pas François. Vat, Sir, you no speak de French tongue?

AESOP. No, really, Sir, I am not so polite.

440 FRENCHMAN. En verité, Monsieur Esope, you have not much politesse, if one may be judge by your figure and appearance.

AESOP. Nor you much wisdom, if one may judge of your head by the ornaments about it.

FRENCHMAN. Qu'est cela donc? Vat you mean to front a man, Sir?

AESOP. No, Sir, 'tis to you I am speaking.

FRENCHMAN. Vel, Sir, I not a man! Vat is you take me for? Vat I beast? Vat I horse? Parbleu!

---

433. alarm] O_2, D_1, O_4, O_6, O_7, O_{10}, W_1; alarum O_3, O_5, O_8, O_9, D_2, W_2.
446. you take me] O_2, D_1, O_3, O_6, O_7, O_9, W_2; mistake O_4, O_5, O_8, O_{10}, D_2, W_1.

AESOP. If you insist upon it, Sir, I would advise you to lay aside your wings and tail, for they undoubtedly eclipse your manhood.

450 FRENCHMAN. Upon my vard, Sir, if you treat a gentilhomme of my rank and qualité comme ça, depen upon it, I shall be a littel en cavalier vit you.

AESOP. Pray, Sir, of what rank and quality are you?

FRENCHMAN. Sir, I am a marquis Francois, j'entens les Beaux Arts, Sir, I have been an avanturie all over the varld, and am à present en Angleterre, in Ingland, vere I am more honoré and caress den ever I was in my own countrie, or inteed any vere else.

AESOP. And pray, Sir, what is your business in England?

FRENCHMAN. I am arrivé dere, Sir, pour polir la nation. De Inglis, Sir,
460 have too much a lead in deir head and too much a tought in deir head. So, Sir, if I can lighten bote, I shall make dem tout à fait Francois and quite anoder ting.

AESOP. And pray, Sir, in what particular accomplishments does your merit consist?

FRENCHMAN. Sir, I speak de French, j'ai bonne addresse, I dance un Minuet, I sing des littel chansons, and I have—une tolerable as-surance. En fin, Sir, my merit consist in one vard. I am foreignere, and entre nous, vile de Englis be so great a fool to love de foreignere better dan demselves, de foreignere vould still be more great a fool
470 did dey not leave deir own counterie vere dey have noting at all, and come to Inglande vere dey vant for noting at all, perdie. Cela n'est il pas vrai, Monsieur Aesope?

AESOP. Well, Sir, what is your business with me?

FRENCHMAN. Attendez un peu, you shall hear, Sir. I am in love vith the grande fortune of one Englis lady; and de lady, she be in love with my qualité and bagatelles. Now, Sir, me vant twenty or tirty douzaines of your vaters, for fear I be oblige to leave Inglande be-fore I have fini dis grande affaire.

AESOP. Twenty or thirty dozen? For what?

480 FRENCHMAN. For my crediteurs, to make 'em forget the vay to my logement and no trouble for me for the future.

AESOP. What! Have you so many creditors?

FRENCHMAN. So many? Begar, I have 'em dans tous les quartiers de la ville, in all parts of the town, fait —

AESOP. Wonderful and surprising!

---

451. littel] litel O4, O5, O8, O9.
455. avanturie] advanturier O4, O8, O9, W1.
460. lead in deir head] "lead in deir heels" O3, O4, O5, O8, D2.
462. anoder] another D2.
471. perdie] pardie O4, O9.
474. vith] vit O5, D2, O9.

FRENCHMAN. Vonderful? Vat is vonderful—dat I should borrow money?

AESOP. No, Sir, that anybody should lend it you.

FRENCHMAN. En verité vous vous trompez; you do mistake it, mon ami.
490 If fortune give me no money, nature give me des talens. J'ai des talens, Monsieur Aesope, vich are de same ting. Par example: de Englishman have de money, I have de flatterie and bonne addresse; and a little of dat from a French tongue is very good credit and securité for tousand pound. Eh! Bien donc, sal I have this twenty or tirty douzaines of your vater? Ouy ou non?

AESOP. 'Tis impossible, Sir.

FRENCHMAN. Impossible! Pourquoi donc? Vy not?

AESOP. Because if every fine gentleman who owes money should make the same demand, we should have no water left for our other
500 customers.

FRENCHMAN. Que voulez vous que je fasse donc? Vat must I do den, Sir?

AESOP. Marry the lady as soon as you can, pay your debts with part of her portion, drink the water to forget your extravagance, retire with her to your own country, and be a better economist for the future.

FRENCHMAN. Go to my own contré! Je vous demande pardon, I had much rather stay vere I am. I cannot go dere, upon my vard.

AESOP. Why not, my Friend?

510 FRENCHMAN. Entre nous, I had much rather pass for one French marguis in Inglande, keep bonne compagnie, manger des delicatesses, and do noting at all, than keep a shop en Provence, couper and frisser les cheveux, and live upon soupe and sallade the rest of my life.

AESOP. I cannot blame you for your choice, and if other people are so blind not to distinguish the barber from the fine gentleman, their folly must be their punishment. Therefore, go to the rest of the company, and you shall take the benefit of the water with them.

FRENCHMAN. Monsieur Aesope, sans flatterie ou compliments, I am
520 your very humble serviteur—Jean Frisseron en Provence, ou le Marquis de Poulville en Angleterre.

Exit Frenchman.

AESOP. Shield and defend me! Another fine lady!

Enter Mrs. Riot.

MRS. RIOT. A monster, a filthy brute! Your watermen are as unpolite upon the Styx as upon the Thames. Stow a lady of fashion with

---

491. vich] vech O4, O5, O9.
517. Therefore . . . company] omitted O4, O8, O9, W1.

tradesmen's wives and mechanics! Ah, what's this, Serbeerus or Plutus? (*Seeing Aesop.*) Am I to be frighted with all the monsters of this internal world?

AESOP.   What is the matter, Lady?

MRS. RIOT.   Everything is the matter, my spirits are uncomposed, and
530   every circumstance about me in a perfect dilemma.

AESOP.   What has disordered you thus?

MRS. RIOT.   Your filthy boatman, Scarroon, there.

AESOP.   Charon, Lady, you mean.

MRS. RIOT.   And who are you, you ugly creature you? If I see any more of you, I shall die with temerity.

AESOP.   The wise think me handsome, Madam.

MRS. RIOT.   I hate the wise. But who are you?

AESOP.   I am Aesop, Madam, honored this day by Proserpine with the distribution of the waters of Lethe. Command me.

540 MRS. RIOT.   Show me to the Pump Room then, Fellow. Where's the company? I shall die in solitude.

AESOP.   What company?

MRS. RIOT.   The best company, people of fashion! The *Beau Monde*! Show me to none of your gloomy souls who wander about in your groves and streams. Show me to glittering balls, enchanting masquerades, ravishing operas, and all the polite enjoyments of Elysian.

AESOP.   This is a language unknown to me, Lady. No such fine doings here, and very little good company (as you call it) in Elysium.

MRS. RIOT.   What, no operas, eh? No Elysian then! (*Sings fantastically
550   in Italian.*) '*Sfortunato Monticelli*! Banished Elysian as well as the Haymarket! Your taste here, I suppose, rises no higher than your *Shakespears* and your *Johnsons*. Oh, you *Goats* and *Vandils*! In the name of barbarity take 'em to yourselves; we are tired of 'em upon earth. One goes indeed to a playhouse sometimes, because one does not know how else one can kill one's time. Everybody goes, because, because—all the world's there. But for my part, call Scarroon and let him take me back again. I'll stay no longer here. Stupid immortals!

AESOP.   You are a happy woman that have neither cares nor follies to
560   disturb you.

MRS. RIOT.   Cares? Ha, ha, ha! Nay, now I must laugh in your ugly face, my Dear. What cares, does your Wisdom think, can enter into the circle of a fine lady's enjoyments?

AESOP.   By the account I have just heard of a fine lady's life, her very pleasures are both follies and cares. So drink the water and forget them, Madam.

---

541.   shall] omitted *O3, O4, O5, D2, O8, O9, W1*.

MRS. RIOT. Oh, gad! That was so like my husband now. Forget my follies? Forget the fashion, forget my being, the very *quincettence* and *emptity* of a fine lady? The fellow would make me as great a brute as my husband.

AESOP. You have an husband then, Madam?

MRS. RIOT. Yes, I think so—an husband and no husband. Come, fetch me some of your water. If I must forget something, I had as good forget him, for he's grown insufferable o'late.

AESOP. I thought, Madam, you had nothing to complain of.

MRS. RIOT. One's husband, you know, is almost next to nothing.

AESOP. How has he offended you?

MRS. RIOT. The man talks of nothing but his money and my extravagance. Won't remove out of the filthy city, though he knows I die for the other end of town; nor leave off his nasty merchandising, though I've labored to convince him he loses money by it. The man was once tolerable enough and let me have money when I wanted it; but now he's never out of a tavern, and is grown so valiant that, do you know, he has presumed to contradict me and refuse me money upon every occasion.

AESOP. And all this without any provocation on your side?

MRS. RIOT. Laud, how should I provoke him? I seldom see him, very seldom speak to the creature unless I want money; besides, he's out all day —

AESOP. And you all night, Madam. Is it not so?

MRS. RIOT. I keep the best company, Sir, and daylight is no agreeable sight to a polite assembly. The sun is very well and comfortable, to be sure, for the lower part of the creation; but to ladies who have a true taste of pleasure, wax candles or no candles are preferable to all the sunbeams in the universe.

AESOP. Preposterous fancy!

MRS. RIOT. And so, most delicate, sweet Sir, you don't approve my scheme. Ha, ha, ha! Oh, you ugly devil you! Have you the vanity to imagine people of fashion will mind what you say, or that to learn politeness and breeding it is necessary to take a lesson of morality out of Aesop's Fables? Ha, ha, ha!

AESOP. It is necessary to get a little reflection somewhere. When these spirits leave you and your senses are surfeited, what must be the consequence?

MRS. RIOT. Oh, I have the best receipt in the world for the vapors, and, lest the poison of your precepts should taint my vivacity, I must beg leave to take it now by way of anecdote.

AESOP. Oh, by all means. (*Aside.*) Ignorance and vanity!

MRS. RIOT. (*drawing out a card*).
Lady Rantan's Compliments to Mrs. Riot.

SONG.

I.

610
The card invites, in crowds we fly
To join the jovial rout full cry;
    What joy from cares and plagues all day,
    To hie to the midnight hark-away.

II.

Nor want, nor pain, nor grief, nor care,
Nor dronish husbands enter there;
    The brisk, the bold, the young and gay,
    All hie to the midnight hark-away.

III.

Uncounted strikes the morning clock,
And drowsy watchmen idly knock;
620
    Till daylight peeps, we sport and play,
    And roar to the jolly hark-away.

IV.

When tired with sport to bed we creep,
And kill the tedious day with sleep;
    Tomorrow's welcome call obey,
    And again to the midnight hark-away.

MRS. RIOT. There's a life for you, you old fright! So trouble your head
no more about your betters. I am so perfectly satisfied with myself
that I will not alter an atom of me, for all you can say. So you may
bottle up your philosophical waters for your own use, or for the
630
fools that want 'em. Gad's my life! There's Billy Butterfly in the
grove. I must go to him. We shall so railly your Wisdom between
us. Ha, ha, ha!
    The brisk, the bold, the young, the gay,
    All hie to the midnight hark-away.

Exit singing.

AESOP. Unhappy woman! Nothing can retrieve her. When the head
has once a wrong bias, 'tis ever obstinate in proportion to its weakness. But here comes one who seems to have no occasion for Lethe
to make him more happy than he is.

Enter Drunken Man *and* Tailor.

DRUNKEN MAN. Come along, Neighbor Snip. Come along Tailor; don't
640
be afraid of hell before you die, you sniv'ling dog you.

---

631. railly] rally *O4, O8, D2, O9*.
639–764. Drunken Man and Tailor scene omitted *O4*.

TAILOR. For heaven's sake, Mr. Riot, don't be so boisterous with me, lest we should offend the powers below.

AESOP. What in the name of ridicule have we here? So, Sir, what are you?

DRUNKEN MAN. Drunk—very drunk, at your service.

AESOP. That's a piece of information I did not want.

DRUNKEN MAN. And yet it's all the information I can give you.

AESOP. Pray, Sir, what brought you hither?

DRUNKEN MAN. Curiosity and a hackney coach.

650 AESOP. I mean, Sir, have you any occasion for my waters?

DRUNKEN MAN. Yes, great occasion, if you'll do me the favor to qualify them with some good arrack and orange juice.

AESOP. Sir!

DRUNKEN MAN. Sir! Don't stare so, old Gentleman. Let us have a little conversation with you.

AESOP. I would know if you have anything oppresses your mind and makes you unhappy?

DRUNKEN MAN. You are certainly a very great fool, old Gentleman. Did you ever know a man drunk and unhappy at the same time?

660 AESOP. Never otherwise. For a man who has lost his senses —

DRUNKEN MAN. Has lost the most troublesome companions in the world, next to wives and bum-bailiffs.

AESOP. But, pray, what is your business with me?

DRUNKEN MAN. Only to demonstrate to you that you are an ass.

AESOP. Your humble servant.

DRUNKEN MAN. And to show you that, whilst I can get such liquor as I have been drinking all night, I shall never come for your water specifics against care and tribulation. However, old Gentleman, if you'll do one thing for me, I shan't think my time and conversation
670 thrown away upon you.

AESOP. Anything in my power.

DRUNKEN MAN. Why, then, here's a small matter for you, and, do you hear me? Get me one of the best whores in your territories.

AESOP. What do you mean?

DRUNKEN MAN. To refresh myself in the Shades here after my journey. Suppose now you introduce me to Proserpine. Who knows how far my figure and address may tempt her? And if her majesty is over nice, show me but her maids of honor and I'll warrant you they'll snap at a bit of fresh mortality.

680 AESOP. Monstrous!

DRUNKEN MAN. Well, well, if it is monstrous, I say no more. If her majesty and retinue are so very virtuous, I say no more. But I'll tell you what, old Friend. If you'll lend me your wife for half an hour, when you make a visit above you shall have mine as long as you please. And if upon trial you should like mine better than your own, you shall carry her away to the devil with you and ten thousand thanks into the bargain.

AESOP. This is not to be borne. Either be silent, or you'll regret this drunken insolence.

690 DRUNKEN MAN. What a cross old fool it is. I presume, Sir, from the information of your hump and your wisdom, that your name is— is—what the devil is it?

AESOP. Aesop, at your service.

DRUNKEN MAN. The same, the same. I knew you well enough, you old sensible pimp you. Many a time has my flesh felt birch upon your account. Prithee, what possessed thee to write such foolish old stories of a Cock and a Bull, and I don't know what, to plague poor innocent lads with? It was damned cruel in you, let me tell you that.

AESOP. I am now convinced, Sir, I have written 'em to very little
700 purpose.

DRUNKEN MAN. To very little, I assure you. But never mind it, Damn it, you are a fine old Grecian for all that. (*Claps him on the back.*) Come here, Snip. Is he not a fine old Grecian? And though he is not the handsomest or best-dressed man in the world, he has ten times more sense than either you or I have.

TAILOR. Pray, Neighbor, introduce me.

DRUNKEN MAN. I'll do it. Mr. Aesop, this sneaking gentleman is my tailor, and an honest man he was while he loved his bottle; but since he turned Methodist and took to preaching, he has cabbaged one
710 yard in six from all his customers. Now you know him, hear what he has to say, while I go and pick up in the wood here. Upon my soul, you are a fine old Grecian!

Exit Drunken Man.

AESOP. (*to* Tailor). Come, Friend, don't be dejected. What is your business?

TAILOR. I am troubled in mind.

AESOP. Is your case particular, Friend?

TAILOR. No indeed; I believe it is pretty general in our parish.

AESOP. What is it? Speak out, Friend.

TAILOR. It runs continually in my head that I am —
720 AESOP. What?

TAILOR. A cuckold.

AESOP. Have a care, Friend. Jealousy is a rank weed, and chiefly takes root in a barren soil.

TAILOR. I am sure my head is full of nothing else.

___

688. borne] bore *D2*.

AESOP. But how came you to a knowledge of your misfortune? Has not your wife as much wit as you?

TAILOR. A great deal more, Sir, and that is one reason for believing myself dishonored.

AESOP. Though your reason has some weight in it, yet it does not
730   amount to a conviction.

TAILOR. I have more to say for myself, if your Worship will but hear me.

AESOP. I shall attend to you.

TAILOR. My wife has such a very high blood in her that she is lately turned Papist and is always railing at me and the Government. The priest and she are continually laying their heads together, and I am afraid he has persuaded her that it will save her precious soul, if she cuckolds a heretic tailor.

AESOP. Oh, don't think so hardly of 'em.

740 TAILOR. Lord, Sir, you don't know what tricks are going forward above. Religion, indeed, is the outside stuff, but wickedness is the lining.

AESOP. Why, you are in a passion, Friend. If you would but exert yourself thus at a proper time, you might keep the fox from your poultry.

TAILOR. Lord, Sir, my wife has as much passion again as I have. And whenever she's up, I curb my temper, sit down, and say nothing.

AESOP. What remedy have you to propose for this misfortune?

TAILOR. I propose to dip my head in the river to wash away my fancies. And, if you'll let me take a few bottles to my wife, if the water is
750   of a cooling nature, I may perhaps be easy that way. But I shall do as your Worship pleases.

AESOP. I am afraid this method won't answer, Friend. Suppose, therefore, you drink to forget your suspicions, for they are nothing more, and let your wife drink to forget your uneasiness. A mutual confidence will succeed, and, consequently, mutual happiness.

TAILOR. I have such a spirit, I can never bear to be dishonored in my bed.

AESOP. The water will cool your spirit, and if it can but lower your wife's, the business is done. Go for a moment to your companion,
760   and you shall drink presently. But do nothing rashly.

TAILOR. I can't help it. Rashness is my fault, Sir, but age and more experience, I hope, will cure me. Your servant, Sir (*Aside.*) Indeed he is a fine old Grecian.

Exit Tailor.

AESOP. Poor fellow, I pity him.

Enter Mercury.

MERCURY. What can be the meaning, Aesop, that there are no more mortals coming over? I perceive there is a great bustle on the other side of the Styx, and Charon has brought his boat over without passengers.

AESOP.   Here he is to answer for himself.

Enter Charon, *laughing.*

770   CHARON.   Oh! oh! oh!

MERCURY.   What diverts you so, Charon?

CHARON.   Why there's the devil to do among the mortals yonder. They are all together by the ears.

AESOP.   What's the matter?

CHARON.   There are some ladies who have been disputing so long and so loud about taking place and precedency that they have set their relations a tilting at one another, to support their vanity. The standers-by are some of them so frighted, and some of them so diverted at the quarrel, that they have not time to think of their
780   misfortunes. So I e'en left them to settle their prerogatives by themselves and be friends at their leisure.

MERCURY.   What's to be done, Aesop?

AESOP.   Discharge these we have and finish the business of the day.

Enter Drunken Man *and* Mrs. Riot.

DRUNKEN MAN.   I never went to pick up a whore in my life, but the first woman I laid hold of was my dear, virtuous wife, and here she is.

AESOP.   Is that lady your wife?

DRUNKEN MAN.   Yes, Sir; and yours, if you please to accept of her.

AESOP.   Though she has formerly given too much into fashionable fol-
790   lies, she now repents and will be more prudent for the future.

DRUNKEN MAN.   Look ye, Mr. Aesop, all your preaching and morality signifies nothing at all. But since your wisdom seems bent upon our reformation, I'll tell you the only way, old Boy, to bring it about. Let me have enough of your water to settle my head and throw Madam into the river.

AESOP.   'Tis in vain to reason with such beings. Therefor, Mercury, summon the mortals from the grove, and we'll dismiss 'em to earth as happy as Lethe can make 'em.

SONG.

By Mercury.

I.

Come, mortals, come, come follow me,
800   Come follow, follow, follow me,

To mirth and joy and jollity;
Hark, hark, the call. Come, come and drink,
And leave your cares by Lethe's brink.

CHORUS.
Away then come, come, come away,
And life shall hence be holiday;
Nor jealous fears, nor strife, nor pain,
Shall vex the jovial heart again.

II.

To Lethe's brink then follow all,
Then follow, follow, follow all,
810   'Tis pleasure courts, obey the call;
And mirth and jollity and joy,
Shall every future hour employ.

CHORUS.
Away then come, come, come away,
And life shall hence be holiday;
Nor jealous fears, nor strife, nor pain,
Shall vex the jovial heart again.

During the song, the characters enter from the grove.

AESOP. Now, mortals, attend! I have perceived from your examina-
tions, that you have mistaken the effect of your distempers for the
cause. You would willingly be relieved from many things which
820   interfere with your passions and affections, while your vices, from
which all your cares and misfortunes arise, are totally forgotten
and neglected. Then follow me and drink to the forgetfulness of
vice.
'Tis vice alone disturbs the human breast;
Care dies with guilt; be virtuous and be blest.

Finis

Lethe

with the Additional Character of Lord Chalkstone

Enter Mr. Bowman, (*hastily*).

BOWMAN. Is your name Aesop?

AESOP. It is, Sir—your commands with me?

BOWMAN. My Lord Chalkstone, to whom I have the honor to be a friend and companion, has sent me before to know if you are at leisure to receive his Lordship.

AESOP. I am placed here on purpose to receive every mortal that attends our summons —

BOWMAN. My Lord is not of the common race of mortals, I assure you; and you must look upon this visit as a particular honor, for he is so much afflicted with the gout and rheumatism, that we had much ado to get him across the river.

AESOP. His Lordship has certainly some pressing occasion for the waters, that he endures such inconveniences to get at them.

BOWMAN. No occasion at all—His legs indeed fail him a little, but his heart is as sound as ever, nothing can hurt his spirits; ill or well, his Lordship is always the best company, and the merriest in his family.

AESOP. I have very little time for mirth and good company; but I'll lessen the fatigue of his journey, and meet him half way. (*Going.*)

BOWMAN. His Lordship is here already. There's a spirit! Mr. Aesop— there's a great man! See how superior he is to his infirmities; such a soul ought to have a better body.

Enter Mercury *with Lord* Chalkstone.

LORD CHALKSTONE. Not so fast, Monsieur Mercury—you are a little too nimble for me. Well, Bowman, have you found the Philosopher?

BOWMAN. This is he, my Lord, and ready to receive your commands.

LORD CHALKSTONE. Ha! ha! ha! There he is, profecto!—*toujours le Meme!* (*Looking at him through a glass.*) I should have known him at a mile's distance—a most noble personage indeed!—and truly

L E T H E.

A

DRAMATIC SATIRE:

WITH THE

Additional Character of Lord CHALKSTONE.

As it is Performed at the

Theatre-Royal in Drury-Lane.

The FIFTH EDITION.

By D A V I D G A R R I C K.

L O N D O N:

Printed for and Sold by PAUL VAILLANT, facing
Southampton-street, in the *Strand*.

M DCC LVII.

Greek from top to toe—Most venerable Aesop, I am in this world
and the other, above and below, yours most sincerely.

30 AESOP. I am yours, my Lord, as sincerely, and I wish it was in my
power to relieve your misfortune.

LORD CHALKSTONE. Misfortune! what misfortune?—I am neither a porter
nor a chairman, Mr. Aesop—my legs can bear my body to my
friends and my bottle; I want no more with them; the Gout is
welcome to the rest—eh Bowman?

BOWMAN. Your Lordship is in fine spirits!

AESOP. Does not your Lordship go through a great deal of pain?

LORD CHALKSTONE. Pain? ay, and pleasure too, eh Bowman?—When I'm
in pain, I curse and swear it away again, and the moment it is gone,
40 I lose no time; I drink the same wines, eat the same dishes, keep the
same hours, the same company; and, notwithstanding the gravity
of my wise doctors, I would not abstain from French wines and
French cookery, to save the souls and bodies of the whole College
of Physicians.

AESOP (to Bowman). My Lord has fine spirits indeed!

LORD CHALKSTONE. You don't imagine, Philosopher, that I have hobbled
here with a bundle of complaints at my back. My legs, indeed, are
something the worse for the wear, but your waters, I suppose, can't
change or make 'em better; for if they could, you certainly would
50 have try'd the virtues of 'em upon your own—eh Bowman? Ha,
ha, ha!

BOWMAN. Bravo! My Lord, bravo!

AESOP. My imperfections are from head to foot, as well as your
Lordship's.

LORD CHALKSTONE. I beg your pardon there, Sir; though my body's
impaired—my head is as good as it ever was; and as proof of this,
I'll lay you a hundred guineas —

AESOP. Does your Lordship propose a wager as a proof of the goodness
of your head?

60 LORD CHALKSTONE. And why not—Wagers are now-a-days the only
proofs and arguments that are made use of by people of fashion:
All disputes about politics, operas, trade, gaming, horse-racing, or
religion, are determined now, by six to four, and two to one; and
persons of quality are by this method most agreeably released from
the hardship of thinking or reasoning upon any subject.

AESOP. Very convenient, truly.

LORD CHALKSTONE. Convenient! aye, and moral too—This invention of
betting, unknown to you Greeks, among many other virtues, prevents bloodshed, and preserves family affections —

70 AESOP. Prevents bloodshed!

LORD CHALKSTONE. I'll tell you how. When gentlemen quarreled here-

Garrick as Lord Chalkstone in *Lethe*.
Harvard Theatre Collection

tofore, what did they do? They drew their swords—I have been run through the body myself, but no matter for that—What do they do now? They draw their purses—before the lie can be given, a wager is laid, and so, instead of resenting, we pocket our affronts.

AESOP. Most casuistically argued, indeed, my Lord;—how can it preserve family affections?

LORD CHALKSTONE. I'll tell you that too—An old woman, you'll allow, Mr. Aesop, at all times to be but a bad thing—what say you, Bowman?

BOWMAN. A very bad thing indeed, my Lord.

LORD CHALKSTONE. Ergo, an old woman with a good constitution, and a damned large jointure upon your estate, is the Devil—my Mother was the very thing—and yet from the moment I pitted her, I never once wished her dead, but was really uneasy when she tumbled down stairs, and did not speak a single word for a whole fortnight.

AESOP. Affectionate indeed!—but what does your Lordship mean by pitted her?

LORD CHALKSTONE. 'Tis a term of ours upon these occasions—I backed her life against two old countesses, an aunt of Sir Harry Rattle's that was troubled with an asthma, my fat landlady at Salt-Hill, and the Mad-Woman at Tunbridge, at five hundred each per annum: She outlived 'em all but the last, by which means I hedged off a damned jointure, made her life an advantage to me, and so continued my filial affections to her last moments.

AESOP. I am fully satisfied—and in return your Lordship may command me.

LORD CHALKSTONE. None of your waters for me; damn 'em all; I never drink any but at Bath—I came merely for a little conversation with you, and to see your Elysium Fields here—(*Looking about thro' his glass.*) which, by the bye, Mr. Aesop, are laid out most detestably—No taste, no Fancy in the whole world!—Your river here— what d'ye call —

AESOP. Styx.

LORD CHALKSTONE. Ay, Styx—why 'tis as strait as Fleet-ditch—You should have given it a Serpentine Sweep, and slope the banks of it.— The place, indeed, has very fine capabilities; but you should clear the wood to the left, and clump the trees upon the right: In short, the whole wants variety, extent, contrast, and inequality—(*Going towards the orchestra, stops suddenly, and looks into the Pit.*) Upon my word, here's a very fine Hubbab! and a most curious collection of evergreens and flow'ring shrubs —

AESOP. We let Nature take her course; our chief entertainment is contemplation, which I supose is not allowed to interrupt your Lordship's pleasures.

LORD CHALKSTONE.   I beg your pardon there—No man has ever studied or drank harder than I have—except my chaplain; and I'll match my library and cellar against any nobleman's in Christendom—shan't I, Bowman, eh?

120   BOWMAN.   That you may indeed, my Lord; and I'll go your Lordship's halves, ha, ha, ha.

AESOP.   If your Lordship would apply more to the first, and drink our waters to forget the last —

LORD CHALKSTONE.   What, relinquish my bottle! What the devil shall I do to kill time then?

AESOP.   Has your Lordship no wife or children to entertain you?

LORD CHALKSTONE.   Children! not I, faith. My wife has, for aught I know—I have not see her these seven years —

AESOP.   You surprise me!

130   LORD CHALKSTONE.   'Tis the way of the world, for all that—I married for a fortune; she for a title. When we both had got what we wanted, the sooner we parted the better—We did so; and are now waiting for the happy moment, that will give to one of us the liberty of playing the same farce over again—eh, Bowman?

BOWMAN.   Good, good; you have puzzled the Philosopher.

AESOP.   The Greeks esteemed matrimonial happiness their *Summum Bonum.*

LORD CHALKSTONE.   More fools they! 'tis not the only thing they were mistaken in—My brother Dick, indeed, married for love; and he

140   and his wife have been fattening these five and twenty years upon their *Summum Bonum*, as you call it. They have had a dozen and half of children, and may have half a dozen more, if an apoplexy don't step in and interrupt their *Summum Bonum*—eh, Bowman? ha, ha, ha!

BOWMAN.   Your Lordship never said a better thing in your life.

LORD CHALKSTONE.   'Tis luck for the nation, to be sure, that there are people who breed, and are fond of one another—One man of eloquent notions is sufficient in a family; for which reason I have bred up Dick's eldest son myself; and a fine gentleman he is—is not he,

150   Bowman?

BOWMAN.   A very fine gentleman, indeed, my Lord.

LORD CHALKSTONE.   And as for the rest of the litter, they may fondle an fatten upon *Summum Bonum*, as their loving parents have done before 'em.

BOWMAN.   Look there, my Lord—I'll be hanged if that is not your Lordship's nephew in the Grove.

AESOP.   I dare swear it is. He has been here just now, and has entertained me with *his* elegant notions.

LORD CHALKSTONE.   Let us go to him; I'll lay you six to four that he has

160 been gallanting with some of the beauties of antiquity—Helen or Cleopatra, I warrant you;—egad, let Lucretia take care of herself; she'll catch a Tarquin, I can tell her that—He is his uncle's own nephew, ha, ha, ha!—Egad, I find myself in spirits, I'll go and coquet a little myself with them.—Bowman, lend me your arm; and you, William, hold me up a little—(William *treads upon his toes*.) Ho— Damn the fellow, he always treads upon my toes—Eugh—I shan't be able to gallant it this half hour—Well, dear Philosopher, dispose of your water to those that want it. There is no one action of my life, or qualification of my mind and body, that is a burden to me. And

170 there is nothing in your world, or in ours, I have to wish for, unless that you could rid me of my wife, and furnish me with a better pairs of legs—eh, Bowman,—Come along, come along.

BOWMAN. Game to the last! my Lord.

Exeunt Lord Chalkstone *and* Bowman.

AESOP. How flattering is folly! His Lordship here, supported only by vanity, vivacity, and his friend Mr. Bowman, can fancy himself the wisest, and is the happiest of mortals.

Enter Mr. *and* Mrs. Tatoo.

Epilogue

[From the surreptitious edition printed by J. Cooke, London 1745]

Spoke by Miss Lucy *and Mr.* Thomas.

THOMAS.	Farewell, my cares; farewell, domestic strife;
	How blest the husband when reformed the wife!
LUCY.	I'm not reformed —
THOMAS.	Not reformed, my Dear!
LUCY.	No. —
THOMAS.	No!
LUCY.	No! no! no! can't you hear?
THOMAS.	Then all my hopes are gone.
LUCY.	With all my heart.

10 You may go too—I'm ready, Sir, to part.

THOMAS. Did not you promise, Lucy, to reform?

LUCY. You promised too— and how did you perform?
You well may drop your lip and change your saucy tone.
Go, get you hence, you worthless drone!

THOMAS. Pray follow, Lucy, do.

LUCY. I'll follow strait,
My pleasures—not you —
When thou are gone, I'll ne'er on man rely;
Next time, by golls, I'll taste before I buy.

[*Exit* Thomas.]

20 Contented now, the husband is retired;
Like other wives, I'll stay and be admired.
And now I'll chuse a lover to my goust,
Irish and French I've tried, but they'll not do.
I must have British fare, and one of you.
First, I'll beg leave to view the upper places —
Ha, ha! They grin so, one can't distinguish faces!
I'll pass the footmen; they're not worth my care;

I married one—and lazy rogues they are!
Next, to the boxes let my eyes descend;
30 I surely, there, shall find some one my friend —
O lack! how fine they are! but we shall ne'er agree;
They like themselves so well—they'll ne'er like me.
Besides, of all things, I abhor a beaux;
For, when tried, 'tis doubtful whether man or no.
Next, let me view my last resort—the pit;
Here's choice enough: the merchant, soldier, cit,
The surly critic, and the thread-bare wit.
As for the rakes, they are too common grown,
For men who strive at all are good at none.
40 Nor will the wit or surly critic serve me;
For one would beat me and the other starve me;
The merchant now and soldier's left behind;
To both I feel my heart inclined.
Which shall I chuse? Each has a noble soul.
Which shall I have? I'll have 'em both, by goll.
No doubt you'll all approve my patriot passion;
My heart is fixed for trade and navigation.
I hope you'll not refuse your gen'rous voice;
Applaud me, Britons, and approve my choice.

The Lying Valet
1741

THE

LYING VALET;

In Two ACTS.

As it is performed G R A T I S,

At The

Theatre in Goodman's-Fields.

By D. GARRICK.

L O N D O N:
Printed for and Sold by Paul Vaillant,
facing *Southampton-Street* in the *Strand*; and
J. Roberts, in *Warwick-Lane.* 1742.

(Price One Shilling.)

Dramatis Personae

[Charles] Gayless	[BLAKES]
[Timothy] Sharp	[GARRICK]
Justice Guttle	[PAGET]
Beau Trippit	[PETERSON]
Dick	[YATES]
[Servants]	
Melissa	[MRS. YATES]
Kitty Pry	[MISS HIPPISLEY]
Mrs. Gadabout	[MRS. BAMBRIDGE]
Mrs. Trippit	[MRS. STEELE]
[Prissy, Priscilla, Mrs. Gadabout's *daughter*]	[MRS. DUNSTALL]
[Patty, *a niece of Mrs.* Gadabout's]	[MRS. VALLOIS]

10

[Cast names are taken from *The London Stage*, Part 3, II, p. 946.]

1–2.] *O2* reverses the order of the first two names.
   4. Trippit] name is frequently spelled "Trippet" in the texts.

The Lying Valet

SCENE I. Gayless' *lodgings.*

Enter Gayless *and* Sharp.

SHARP. How, Sir! shall you be married tomorrow? Eh, I'm afraid you joke with your poor humble servant.

GAYLESS. I tell thee, Sharp, last night Melissa consented, and fixed tomorrow for the happy day.

SHARP. 'Twas well she did, Sir, or it might have been a dreadful one for us in our present condition: all your money spent; your movables sold; your honor almost ruined, and your humble servant almost starved; we could not possibly have stood it two days longer. But if this young lady will marry you and relieve us, o' my conscience, I'll turn friend to the sex, rail no more at matrimony, but curse the whores and think of a wife myself.

GAYLESS. And yet, Sharp, when I think how I have imposed upon her, I am almost resolved to throw myself at her feet, tell her the real situation of my affairs, ask her pardon, and implore her pity.

SHARP. After marriage, with all my heart, Sir. But don't let your conscience and honor so far get the better of your poverty and good sense as to rely on so great uncertainties as a fine lady's mercy and good nature.

GAYLESS. I know her generous temper and am almost persuaded to rely upon it. What, because I am poor, shall I abandon my honor?

SHARP. Yes, you must, Sir, or abandon me. So, pray, discharge one of us; for eat I must, and speedily too. And you know very well that that honor of yours will neither introduce you to a great man's table, nor get me credit for a single beefsteak.

GAYLESS. What can I do?

---

8. starved] sterved *W2.*

THE LYING VALET;

A FARCE, IN TWO ACTS.—BY D. GARRICK.

Act II. Scene 1.

CHARACTERS.

GAYLESS	BEAU TRIPPET	MRS. GADABOUT
SHARP	DRUNKEN COOK	MRS. TRIPPET
JUSTICE GUTTLE	MELISSA	KITTY PRY

ACT I.

SCENE I.—*Gayless's Lodgings.*

Enter GAYLESS *and* SHARP.

Sharp. How, sir, shall you be married to-morrow? Eh, I'm afraid you joke with your poor humble servant.

Gay. I tell thee, Sharp, last night Melissa consented, and fixed to-morrow for the happy day.

Sharp. 'Tis well she did, sir, or it might have been a dreadful one for us in our present condition: all your money spent, your moveables sold, your honour almost ruined, and your humble servant almost starved; we could not possibly have stood it two days longer. · But if this young lady will marry you, and relieve us, on my conscience, I'll turn friend to the sex, rail no more at matrimony, but curse all old bachelors and think of a wife myself.

Gay. And yet, Sharp, when I think how I have imposed upon her, I am almost resolved to throw myself at her feet, tell her the real situation of my affairs, ask her pardon, and implore her pity.

Sharp. After marriage, with all my heart, sir; but don't let your conscience and honour so far get the better of your poverty and good sense, as to rely on so great an uncertainty as a fine lady's mercy and good-nature.

Gay. I know her generous temper, and am almost persuaded to rely upon it. What! because I am poor, shall I abandon my honour?

Sharp. Yes, you must sir, or abandon me: so, pray discharge one of us; for eat I must, and speedily too; and you know very well, that honour of your's will neither introduce you to a great man's table, nor get me credit for a single beef-steak.

Gay. What can I do?

Sharp. Nothing, while honour sticks in your throat. Do gulp, master, and down with it.

Gay. Pr'ythee leave me to my thoughts.

Sharp. Leave you! No, not in such bad company, I'll assure you. Why, you must certainly be a very great philosopher, sir, to moralize and declaim so charmingly as you do, about honour and conscience, when your doors are beset with bailiffs, and not one single guinea in your pocket to bribe the villains.

Gay. Don't be witty, and give your advice, sirrah.

Sharp. Do you be wise, and take it, sir. But, to be serious, you certainly have spent your fortune, and out-lived your credit, as your pockets and my belly can testify. Your father has disowned you; all your friends forsook you, except myself, who am starving with you. Now, sir, if you marry this young lady, who as yet, thank heaven! knows nothing of your misfortunes, and by that means procure a better fortune than that you squandered away, make a good husband, and turn economist, you still may be happy—may still be Sir William's heir, and the lady, too, no loser by the bargain. There's reason and argument, sir.

Gay. 'Twas with that prospect I first made love to her; and though my fortune has been ill spent, I have at least purchased discretion with it.

Sharp. Pray, then, convince me of that, sir, and make no more objections to the marriage. You see I am reduced to my waistcoat already; and when necessity has undressed me from top to toe, she must begin with you, and then we shall be forced to keep house and die by inches. Look you, sir, if you won't resolve to take my advice, while you have one coat to your back, I must e'en take to my heels while I have strength to run, and something to cover me; so, sir, wishing you much comfort and con-

SHARP.   Nothing while honor sticks in your throat. Do gulp, Master, and down with it.

GAYLESS.   Prithee leave me to my thoughts.

SHARP.   Leave you! No, not in such bad company, I'll assure you. Why, you must certainly be a very great philosopher, Sir, to moralize and declaim so charmingly as you do about honor and conscience, when your doors are beset with bailiffs, and not one single guinea in your pocket to bribe the villains.

GAYLESS.   Don't be witty and give your advice, Sirrah!

SHARP.   Do you be wise and take it, Sir. But to be serious, you certainly have spent your fortune and outlived your credit, as your pockets and my belly can testify. Your father has disowned you; all your friends forsook you, except myself, who am starving with you. Now, Sir, if you marry this young lady, who as yet, thank heaven, knows nothing of your misfortunes, and by that means procure a better fortune than that you squandered away, make a good husband and turn economist, you still may be happy, may still be Sir William's heir, and the lady too no loser by the bargain. There's reason and argument, Sir.

GAYLESS.   'Twas with that prospect I first made love to her; and though my fortune has been ill spent, I have at least purchased discretion with it.

SHARP.   Pray then convince me of that, Sir, and make no more objections to the marriage. You see I am reduced to my waistcoat already; and when necessity has undressed me from top to toe, she must begin with you; and then we shall be forced to keep house and die by inches. Look you, Sir, if you won't resolve to take my advice while you have one coat to your back, I must e'en take to my heels while I have strength to run and something to cover me. So, Sir, wishing you much comfort and consolation with your bare conscience, I am your most obedient and half-starved friend and servant. (*Going.*)

GAYLESS.   Hold, Sharp! You won't leave me?

SHARP.   I must eat, Sir; by my honor and appetite, I must!

GAYLESS.   Well then, I am resolved to favor the cheat, and as I shall quite change my former course of life, happy may be the consequences. At least of this I am sure—

SHARP.   That you can't be worse than you are at present. (*A knocking without.*)

GAYLESS   Who's there?

SHARP.   Some of your former good friends who favored you with money at fifty per cent and helped you to spend it; and are now become daily mementoes to you of the folly of trusting rogues, following whores, and laughing at my advice.

GAYLESS.   Cease your impertinence! To the door! If they are duns, tell
70   'em my marriage is now certainly fixed, and persuade 'em still to forbear a few days longer, and keep my circumstances a secret for their sakes as well as my own.

SHARP.   Oh, never fear it, Sir. They still have so much friendship for you not to desire your ruin to their own disadvantage.

GAYLESS.   And, do you hear, Sharp, if it should be anybody from Melissa, say I am not at home, lest the bad appearance we make here should make 'em suspect something to our disadvantage.

SHARP.   I'll obey you, Sir. But I am afraid they will easily discover the consumptive situation of our affairs by my chopfallen counte-
80   nance.

Exit Sharp.

GAYLESS.   These very rascals who are now continually dunning and persecuting me were the very persons who led me to my ruin, partook of my prosperity, and professed the greatest friendship.

SHARP (*without*).   Upon my word, Mrs. Kitty, my master's not at home.

KITTY (*without*).   Look'ee, Sharp, I must and will see him!

GAYLESS.   Ha, what do I hear? Melissa's maid! What has brought her here? My poverty has made her my enemy too. She is certainly come with no good intent—no friendship there, without fees—
90   she's coming upstairs. What must I do?—I'll get into this closet and listen.

Exit Gayless.

Enter Sharp *and* Kitty.

KITTY.   I must know where he is, and will know too, Mr. Impertinence!

SHARP (*aside*).   Not of me you won't.—He's not within, I tell you, Mrs. Kitty. I don't know myself. Do you think I can conjure?

KITTY.   But I know you will lie abominably; therefore don't trifle with me. I come from my mistress, Melissa; you know, I suppose, what's to be done tomorrow morning?

SHARP.   Ay, and tomorrow night too, girl!

KITTY (*aside*).   Not if I can help it.—But come, where is your master,
100   for see him I must.

SHARP.   Pray, Mrs. Kitty, what's your opinion of this match between my master and your mistress?

KITTY. Why, I have no opinion of it at all. And yet, most of our wants will be relieved by it too; for instance now, your master will get a fortune; that's what I'm afraid he wants; my mistress will get a husband, that's what she has wanted for some time; you will have the pleasure of my conversation, and I an opportunity of breaking your head for your impertinence.

SHARP. Madam, I'm your most humble servant! But I'll tell you what, Mrs. Kitty; I am positively against the match; for, was I a man of my master's fortune —

110

KITTY. You'd marry if you could and mend it. Ha, ha, ha! Pray, Sharp, where does your master's estate lie?

GAYLESS (*aside*). Oh, the devil! what a question was there!

SHARP. Lie, lie! why it lies—faith, I can't name any particular place, it lies in so many. His effects are divided, some here, some there; his steward hardly knows himself.

KITTY. Scattered, scattered, I suppose. But hark'ee, Sharp, what's become of your furniture? You seem to be a little bare here at present.

120

GAYLESS (*aside*). What, has she found out that too?

SHARP. Why, you must know, as soon as the wedding was fixed, my master ordered me to remove his goods into a friend's house, to make room for a ball which he designs to give here the day after the marriage.

KITTY. The luckiest thing in the world! for my mistress designs to have a ball and entertainment here tonight before the marriage; and that's my business with your master.

SHARP (*aside*). The devil it is!

130

KITTY. She'll not have it public; she designs to invite only eight or ten couple of friends.

SHARP. No more?

KITTY. No more; and she ordered me to desire your master not to make a great entertainment.

SHARP. Oh, never fear.

KITTY. Ten or a dozen little nice things, with some fruit, I believe, will be enough in all conscience.

SHARP (*aside*). Oh, curse your conscience!

KITTY. And what do you think I have done of my own head?

140

SHARP. What?

KITTY. I have invited all my Lord Stately's servants to come and see

---

105. I'm afraid] *O1, O2, O3, O4, O5, O6, O7, W1, O8, W2*; I am *D1, D2, D3, D4, D5*.

123. his goods] omit his *W1*.

124. day] pay *O6*.

you and have a dance in the kitchen. Won't your master be surprised!

SHARP. Much so indeed.

KITTY. Well, be quick and find out your master, and make what
haste you can with your preparations. You have no time to lose.—
Prithee, Sharp, what's the matter with you? I have not seen you
for some time, and you seem to look a little thin.

SHARP (*aside*). Oh, my unfortunate face!—I'm in pure good health,
150   thank you, Mrs. Kitty; and I'll assure you, I have a very good
stomach, never better in all my life, and I am as full of vigor,
hussy! (*Offers to kiss her.*)

KITTY. What, with that face! well, bye, bye. (*Going.*) Oh, Sharp,
what ill-looking fellows are those were standing about your door
when I came in? They want your master too, I suppose.

SHARP. Hum! yes, they are waiting for him.—They are some of his
tenants out of the country that want to pay him some money.

KITTY. Tenants? What, do you let his tenants stand in the street?

SHARP. They choose it; as they seldom come to town, they are willing
160   to see as much of it as they can, when they [d]o. They are raw,
ignorant, honest people.

KITTY. Well, I must run home. Farewell! But, do you hear? Get something substantial for us in the kitchen—a ham, a turkey, or what
you will. We'll be very merry. And be sure remove the tables and
chairs away there too, that we may have room to dance. I can't
bear to be confined in my French dances; tal, lal, lal. (*Dancing.*)
Well, adieu! Without any compliment, I shall die if I don't see
you soon.

                                                        Exit Kitty.

SHARP. And without any compliment, I pray heaven you may!

                        Enter Gayless.
            They look for some time sorrowful at each other.

170   GAYLESS. O Sharp!

SHARP. O master!

GAYLESS. We are certainly undone!

SHARP. That's no news to me.

GAYLESS. Eight or ten couple of dancers—ten or a dozen little nice
dishes, with some fruit—my Lord Stately's servants, ham and
turkey!

---

160.   [d] o] do *O2, O3, O4, O5, O6, O7, W1, O8, W2; D1, D2, D3, D4, D5*.
164.   sure remove] *D1, D2, D3, O1, O2, O3, O4, O5, D4, D5, O7*; sure to remove
          O6, O8, W1, W2.

SHARP.   Say no more, the very sound creates an appetite; and I am
sure of late I have had no occasion for whetters and provocatives.

GAYLESS.   Cursed misfortune! what can we do?

180 SHARP.   Hang ourselves; I see no other remedy, except you have a receipt to give a ball and a supper without meat or music.

GAYLESS.   Melissa has certainly heard of my bad circumstances, and
has invented this scheme to distress me and break off the match.

SHARP.   I don't believe it, Sir; begging your pardon.

GAYLESS.   No? Why did her maid then make so strict an inquiry into
my fortune and affairs?

SHARP.   For two very substantial reasons: the first, to satisfy a curiosity, natural to her as a woman; the second, to have the pleasure of
my conversation, very natural to her as a woman of taste and un-
190 derstanding.

GAYLESS.   Prithee be more serious. Is not our all at stake?

SHARP.   Yes, Sir. And yet that all of ours is of so little consequence,
that a man with a very small share of philosophy may part from
it without much pain or uneasiness. However, Sir, I'll convince
you in half an hour that Mrs. Melissa knows nothing of your circumstances; and I'll tell you what too, Sir, she shan't be here tonight, and yet you shall marry her tomorrow morning.

GAYLESS.   How, how, dear Sharp?

SHARP.   'Tis here, here, Sir! warm, warm, and delays will cool it.
200 Therefore I'll away to her, and do you be as merry as love and
poverty will permit you.
        Would you succeed, a faithful friend depute,
        Whose head can plan, and front can execute.
I am the man, and I hope you neither dispute my friendship or
qualification.

GAYLESS.   Indeed I don't. Prithee be gone.

SHARP.   I fly.

                                                      Exeunt.

SCENE [II]. Melissa's *lodgings.*

Enter Melissa *and* Kitty.

MELISSA.   You surprise me, Kitty! the master not at home? the man
in confusion? no furniture in the house and ill-looking fellows
about the doors! 'Tis all a riddle.

KITTY.   But very easy to be explained.

183.   off] *of D*1.

MELISSA.   Prithee explain it then, nor keep me longer in suspense.

KITTY.   The affair is this, Madam: Mr. Gayless is over head and ears in debt; you are over head and ears in love; you'll marry him tomorrow. The next day your whole fortune goes to his creditors, and you and your children are to live comfortably upon the remainder.

MELISSA.   I cannot think him base.

KITTY.   But I know they are all base. You are very young and very ignorant of the sex; I am young too, but have more experience; you never was in love before; I have been in love with an hundred and tried 'em all and know 'em to be a parcel of barbarous, perjured, deluding, bewitching devils.

MELISSA.   The low wretches you have had to do with may answer the character you give 'em; but Mr. Gayless —

KITTY.   Is a man, Madam.

MELISSA.   I hope so, Kitty, or I would have nothing to do with him.

KITTY.   With all my heart—I have given you my sentiments upon the occasion, and shall leave you to your own inclinations.

MELISSA.   Oh, Madam, I am much obliged to you for your great condescension, ha, ha, ha! However, I have so great a regard for your opinion, that had I certain proofs of his villainy —

KITTY.   Of his poverty you may have a hundred; I am sure I have had none to the contrary.

MELISSA *(aside)*.   Oh, there the shoe pinches.

KITTY.   Nay, so far from giving me the usual perquisites of my place, he has not so much as kept me in temper with little endearing civilities; and one might reasonably expect when a man is deficient in one way, that he should make it up in another.

Knocking without.

MELISSA.   So who's at the door.

Exit Kitty.

I must be cautious how I hearken too much to this girl; her bad opinion of Mr. Gayless seems to arise from his disregard of her.

Enter Sharp *and* Kitty.

So, Sharp; have you found your master? Will things be ready for the ball and entertainment?

SHARP.   To your wishes, Madam. I have just now bespoke the music and supper, and wait now for your ladyship's farther commands.

MELISSA.   My compliments to your master, and let him know I and my company will be with him by six. We design to drink tea and play at cards before we dance.

KITTY. (*aside*). So shall I and my company, Mr. Sharp.

SHARP. Mighty well, Madam!

MELISSA. Prithee, Sharp, what makes you come without your coat? 'Tis too cool to go so airy, sure.

KITTY. Mr. Sharp, Madam, is of a very hot constitution, ha, ha, ha!

SHARP. If it had been ever so cool, I have had enough to warm me since I came from home, I'm sure. But no matter for that. (*Sighing.*)

50 MELISSA. What d'ye mean?

SHARP. Pray don't ask me, Madam; I beseech you don't. Let us change the subject.

KITTY (*aside*). Insist upon knowing it, Madam. My curiosity must be satisfied or I shall burst.

MELISSA. I do insist upon knowing—on pain of my displeasure, tell me!

SHARP. If my master should know—I must not tell you, Madam, indeed.

MELISSA. I promise you, upon my honor, he never shall.

SHARP (*indicating* Kitty). But can your ladyship insure secrecy from
60 that quarter?

KITTY. Yes, Mr. Jackanapes, for anything you can say.

MELISSA. I'll engage for her.

SHARP. Why then, in short, Madam—I cannot tell you.

MELISSA. Don't trifle with me.

SHARP. Then since you will have it, Madam—I lost my coat in defense of your reputation.

MELISSA. In defense of my reputation!

SHARP. I will assure you, Madam, I've suffered very much in defense of it; which is more than I would have done for my own.

70 MELISSA. Prithee explain.

SHARP. In short, Madam, you was seen, about a month ago, to make a visit to my master alone.

MELISSA. Alone? My servant was with me.

SHARP. What, Mrs. Kitty? So much the worse; for she was looked upon as my property; and I was brought in guilty as well as you and my master.

KITTY. What, your property, Jackanapes!

MELISSA. What is all this?

SHARP. Why, Madam, as I came out but now to make preparations

---

55. upon] up *D*1.
58. he never] I never *W*1, *W*2.
79. preparations] preparation *W*1.

80   for you and your company tonight, Mrs. Pryabout, the attorney's
wife at next door, calls to me. "Hark'ee, fellow!" says she, "Do
you and your modest master know that my husband shall indict
your house at the next parish meeting for a nuisance?"

MELISSA.   A nuisance!

SHARP.   I said so. "A nuisance! I believe none in the neighborhood live
with more decency and regularity than I and my master," as is
really the case. "Decency and regularity!" cries she, with a sneer.
"Why, Sirrah, does not my window look into your master's bed
chamber? And did not he bring in a certain lady, such a day?"

90   —describing you, Madam. "And did I not see —

MELISSA.   See! oh scandalous! what?

SHARP.   Modesty requires my silence.

MELISSA.   Did not you contradict her?

SHARP.   Contradict her! why, I told her I was sure she lied. "For
zounds!" said I,—for I could not help swearing,—"I am so well
convinced of the lady's and my master's prudence, that, I am sure,
had they a mind to amuse themselves they would certainly have
drawn the windowcurtains."

MELISSA.   What, did you say nothing else? Did you not convince her

100   of her error and impertinence?

SHARP.   She swore to such things, that I could do nothing but swear
and call names: upon which out bolts her husband upon me, with
a fine taper crab in his hand and fell upon me with such violence,
that, being half delirious, I made a full confession.

MELISSA.   A full confession? What did you confess?

SHARP.   That my master loves fornication; that you had no aversion to
it; that Mrs. Kitty was a bawd, and your humble servant a pimp.

KITTY.   A bawd! a bawd! do I look like a bawd, Madam?

SHARP.   And so, Madam, in the scufflle my coat was torn to pieces as

110   well as your reputation.

MELISSA.   And so you joined to make me infamous!

SHARP.   For heaven's sake, Madam, what could I do? His proofs fell
so thick upon me, as witness my head, (*Showing his head plas-
tered.*) that I would have given up all the maidenheads in the kingdom, rather than have my brains beat to a jelly.

MELISSA.   Very well! But I'll be revenged! And did not you tell your
master of this?

SHARP.   Tell him? No, Madam; had I told him, his love is so violent

---

117.   of this] *D*1, *D*2, *D*3, *O*1, *O*4, *O*6, *W*1, *W*2, *O*8; this *O*2, *O*3, *D*4, *O*5, *O*7,
     *D*5.

for you that he would certainly have murdered half the attorneys
in town by this time.

MELISSA. Very well! But I'm resolved not to go to your master's tonight.

SHARP (*aside*). Heavens and my impudence be praised!

KITTY. Why not, Madam? If you are not guilty, face your accusers.

SHARP (*aside*). Oh, the devil! ruined again!—To be sure, face 'em by
all means, Madam. They can but be abusive and break the windows a little. Besides, Madam, I have thought of a way to make
this affair quite diverting to you. I have a fine blunderbuss charged
with half a hundred slugs, and my master has a delicate large Swiss
broad sword; and between us, Madam, we shall so pepper and slice
'em, that you will die with laughing.

MELISSA. What, at murder?

KITTY. Don't fear, Madam, there will be no murder if Sharp's concerned.

SHARP. Murder, Madam! 'Tis self-defense; besides, in these sort of
skirmishes there are never more than two or three killed; for,
supposing they bring the whole body of militia upon us, down
but with a brace of them, and away fly the rest of the covey.

MELISSA. Persuade me never so much, I won't go. That's my resolution.

KITTY. Why then, I'll tell you what, Madam. Since you are resolved
not to go to the supper, suppose the supper was to come to you.
'Tis great pity such great preparations as Mr. Sharp has made
should be thrown away.

SHARP. So it is, as you say, Mistress Kitty. But I can immediately run
back and unbespeak what I have ordered. 'Tis soon done.

MELISSA. But then what excuse can I send to your master? He'll be
very uneasy at my not coming.

SHARP. Oh terribly so! But I have it—I'll tell him you are very much
out of order, that you were suddenly taken with the vapors or
qualms; or what you please, Madam.

MELISSA. I'll leave it to you, Sharp, to make my apology; and there's
half a guinea for you to help your invention.

SHARP (*aside*). Half a guinea! 'Tis so long since I had anything to do
with money that I scarcely know the current coin of my own
country. O Sharp, what talents hast thou! to secure thy master;
deceive his mistress; out-lie her chambermaid; and yet be paid

---

138. but with a brace] omit but *D*5.
141–44. Lines badly printed *D*1.
147–48. Lines badly printed *D*1.
157. her chambermaid] his chambermaid *W*1.

for thy honesty? But my joy will discover me.—Madam, you have eternally fixed Timothy Sharp your most obedient humble ser-
160   vant!—(*Aside.*) Oh, the delights of impudence and a good understanding!

Exit Sharp.

KITTY.   Ha, ha, ha! was there ever such a lying varlet? with his slugs and his broad swords; his attorneys and broken heads, and nonsense! Well, Madam, are you satisfied now? Do you want more proofs?

MELISSA.   Of your modesty I do; but I find, you are resolved to give me none.

KITTY.   Madam?

MELISSA.   I see through your little mean artifice; you are endeavoring
170   to lessen Mr. Gayless in my opinion, because he has not paid you for services he had no occasion for.

KITTY.   Pay me, Madam! I am sure I have very little occasion to be angry with Mr. Gayless for not paying me, when, I believe, 'tis his general practice.

MELISSA.   'Tis false! he's a gentleman and a man of honor, and you are —

KITTY (*curtsying*).   Not in love, I thank heaven.

MELISSA.   You are a fool.

KITTY.   I have been in love; but I am much wiser now.
180 MELISSA.   Hold your tongue, Impertinance!

KITTY (*aside*).   That's the severest thing she has said yet.

MELISSA.   Leave me.

KITTY.   Oh this love, this love is the devil!

Exit Kitty.

MELISSA.   We discover our weaknesses to our servants, make them our confidents, put 'em upon an equality with us, and so they become our advisers. Sharp's behavior, though I seemed to disregard it, makes me tremble with apprehensions; and though I have pretended to be angry with Kitty for her advice, I think it of too much consequence to be neglected.

Enter Kitty.

190 KITTY.   May I speak, Madam?

---

179. Line badly printed *D*1.
185. confidents] confidants *W*1, *W*2.
     upon an equality] upon equality *D*4; on an equality *W*1, *D*2, *D*3.
185. Line badly printed *D*3.

MELISSA.   Don't be a fool. What do you want?

KITTY.   There is a servant just come out of the country says he belongs
    to Sir William Gayless, and has got a letter for you from his mas-
    ter upon very urgent business.

MELISSA.   Sir William Gayless! What can this mean? Where is the
    man?

KITTY.   In the little parlor, Madam.

MELISSA.   I'll go to him—my heart flutters strangely.

Exit Melissa.

KITTY.   O woman, woman, foolish woman! She'll certainly have this
200   Gayless. Nay, were she as well convinced of his poverty as I am,
    she'd have him. A strong dose of love is worse than one of ratafia;
    when it once gets into our heads, it trips up our heels, and then
    goodnight to discretion. Here is she going to throw away fifteen
    thousand pounds; upon what? faith, little better than nothing—he's
    a man, and that's all—and heaven knows mere man is but small
    consolation.

    Be this advice pursued by each fond maid,
    Ne'er slight the substance for an empty shade.
    Rich, weighty sparks alone should please and charm ye:
210   For should spouse cool, his gold will always warm ye.

End of First Act.

ACT II.

[SCENE I. Gayless' lodgings.]
Enter Gayless *and* Sharp.

GAYLESS.   Prithee be serious, Sharp. Hast thou really succeeded?

SHARP.   To our wishes, Sir. In short, I have managed the business with
    such skill and dexterity, that neither your circumstances nor my
    veracity are suspected.

GAYLESS.   But how hast thou excused me from the ball and entertain-
    ment?

SHARP.   Beyond expectation, Sir. But in that particular I was obliged
    to have recourse to truth and declare the real situation of your
    affairs. I told her we had so long disused ourselves to dressing
10   either dinners or suppers, that I was afraid we should be but awk-

193.   a letter for you] for you omitted *W*1, *W*2.
201.   ratafia] ratifia *W*1, *W*2.

ward in our preparations. In short, Sir—at that instant a cursed gnawing seized my stomach, that I could not help telling her that both you and myself seldom make a good meal now-a-days once in a quarter of a year.

GAYLESS. Hell and confusion, have you betrayed me, villain? Did not you tell me this moment she did not in the least suspect my circumstances?

SHARP. No more she did, Sir, till I told her.

GAYLESS. Very well; and was this your skill and dexterity?

20 SHARP. I was going to tell you; but you won't hear reason. My melancholy face and piteous narration had such an effect upon her generous bowels, that she freely forgives all that's past.

GAYLESS. Does she, Sharp?

SHARP. Yes; and desires never to see your face again; and, as a farther consideration for so doing, she has sent you half a guinea. (*Shows the money.*)

GAYLESS. What do you mean?

SHARP. To spend it, spend it, Sir; and regale.

GAYLESS. Villain, you have undone me!

SHARP. What, by bringing you money, when you are not worth a
30 farthing in the whole world? Well, well, then to make you happy again, I'll keep it myself; and wish somebody would take it in their head to load me with such misfortunes. (*Puts up the money.*)

GAYLESS. Do you laugh at me, rascal?

SHARP. Who deserves more to be laughed at! ha, ha, ha! Never for the future, Sir, dispute the success of my negotiations, when even you, who know me so well, can't help swallowing my hook. Why, Sir, I could have played with you backwards and forwards at the end of my line, till I had put your senses into such a fermentation, that you should not have known in an hour's time, whether you
40 was a fish or a man.

GAYLESS. Why, what is all this you have been telling me?

SHARP. A downright lie from beginning to end.

GAYLESS. And have you really excused me to her?

SHARP. No Sir; but I have got this half guinea to make her excuses to you; and, instead of a confederacy between you and me to deceive her, she thinks she has brought me over to put the deceit upon you.

GAYLESS. Thou excellent fellow!

---

14. once in a quarter] once a quarter *W*1.
37. with you] with omitted *W*1.
44. to] letter "o" dropped *D*1.
45. you] you? And *O*6, *D*5.

SHARP. Don't lose time, but slip out of the house immediately; the
50   back way, I believe, will be the safest for you, and to her as fast
as you can. Pretend vast surprise and concern that her indisposition
has debarred you the pleasure of her company here tonight. You
need know no more. Away!

GAYLESS. But what shall we do, Sharp? here's her maid again.

SHARP. The devil she is—I wish I could poison her; for I'm sure, while
she lives I can never prosper.

Enter Kitty.

KITTY. Your door was open, so I did not stand upon ceremony.

GAYLESS. I am sorry to hear your mistress is taken so suddenly.

KITTY. Vapors, vapors only, Sir, a few matrimonial omens, that's all.
60   But I suppose Mr. Sharp has made her excuses.

GAYLESS. And tells me I can't have the pleasure of her company tonight. I had made a small preparation; but 'tis no matter. Sharp
shall go to the rest of the company and let 'em know 'tis put off.

KITTY. Not for the world, Sir. My mistress was sensible you must
have provided for her and the rest of the company; so she is resolved, though she can't, the other ladies and gentlemen shall partake of your entertainment. She's very good natured.

SHARP (*going*). I had better run and let 'em know 'tis deferred.
(*Going.*)

KITTY (*stopping him*). I have been with 'em already and told 'em my
70   mistress insists upon their coming, and they have all promised to
be here; so, pray, don't be under any apprehensions that your preparations will be thrown away.

GAYLESS. But as I can't have her company, Mrs. Kitty, 'twill be a
greater pleasure to me, and a greater compliment to her, to defer
our mirth; besides I can't enjoy anything at present, and she not
partake of it.

KITTY. Oh, no, to be sure; but what can I do? My mistress will have
it so, and Mrs. Gadabout and the rest of the company will be here
in a few minutes; there are two or three coachfuls of 'em.

80 SHARP (*aside*). Then my master must be ruined in spite of my parts.

GAYLESS (*aside to* Sharp). 'Tis all over, Sharp.

SHARP. I know it, Sir.

GAYLESS. I shall go distracted; what shall I do?

SHARP. Why, Sir, as our rooms are a little out of furniture at present,

---

63.   'em] them *O6, W*1.
      'tis put off] it is put off *W*1.
69.   (*Going.*)] *W*2.
80.   (aside)] omitted *W*2.

take 'em into the captain's that lodges here, and set 'em down to cards. If he should come in the meantime, I'll excuse you to him.

KITTY (*aside*). I have disconcerted their affairs I find; I'll have some sport with 'em.—Pray, Mr. Gayless, don't order too many things; they only make you a friendly visit; the more ceremony, you know, the less welcome. Pray, Sir, let me entreat you not to be profuse. If I can be of service, pray command me; my mistress has sent me on purpose. While Mr. Sharp is doing the business without doors, I may be employed within. (*To* Sharp.) If you'll lend me the keys of your sideboard I'll dispose of your plate to the best advantage. (*Knocking.*)

SHARP. Thank you, Mrs. Kitty; but it is disposed of already. (*Knocking at the door.*)

KITTY. Bless me, the company's come! I'll go to the door and conduct 'em into your presence.

Exit Kitty.

SHARP. If you'd conduct 'em into a horsepond and wait of 'em there yourself, we should be more obliged to you.

GAYLESS. I can never support this!

SHARP. Rouse your spirits and put on an air of gaiety, and I don't despair of bringing you off yet.

GAYLESS. Your words have done it effectually.

Enter Mrs. Gadabout, *her daughter and niece*, Mr. Guttle, Mr. Trippit *and* Mrs. Trippit.

MRS. GADABOUT. Ah, my dear Mr. Gayless! (*Kisses him.*)

GAYLESS. My dear Widow! (*Kisses her.*)

MRS. GADABOUT. We are come to give you joy, Mr. Gayless.

SHARP (*aside*). You never was more mistaken in your life.

MRS. GADABOUT. I have brought some company here, I believe, is not so well known to you, and I protest I have been all about the town to get the little I have.—Prissy, my Dear—Mr. Gayless, my daughter.

GAYLESS. And as handsome as her mother; you must have a husband shortly, my Dear.

PRISSY. I'll assure you I don't despair, Sir.

97–98. Lines badly printed *D*1.

99. 'em] them *D*1, *D*4.

101–3. Lines badly printed *D*1.

109. brought some] brought you some *D*5.

109–10. not so well] *D*1, *D*2, *D*3, *O*1, *O*2, *O*3, *D*4, *O*4, *O*5, *O*7, *D*5; not well *O*6, *W*1, *O*8, *W*2.

MRS. GADABOUT. My niece, too.

GAYLESS. I know by her eyes she belongs to you, Widow.

MRS. GADABOUT. Mr. Guttle, Sir, Mr. Gayless; Mr. Gayless, Justice
Guttle.

120 GAYLESS (*aside*). Oh, destruction! one of the quorum.

GUTTLE. Hem, though I had not the honor of any personal knowledge
of you, yet at the instigation of Mrs. Gadabout I have, without
any previous acquitance with you, throwed aside all ceremony to
let you know that I joy to hear the solemnization of your nuptials
is so near at hand.

GAYLESS. Sir, though I cannot answer you with the same elocution,
however, Sir, I thank you with the same sincerity.

MRS. GADABOUT. Mr. and Mrs. Trippit, Sir, the properest lady in the
world for your purpose, for she'll dance for four and twenty hours

130   together.

TRIPPIT. My dear Charles, I am very angry with you, faith; so near
marriage and not let me know, 'twas barbarous. You thought, I
suppose, I should rally you upon it; but dear Mrs. Trippit here has
long ago eradicated all my anti-matrimonial principles.

MRS. TRIPPIT. I eradicate! fie, Mr. Trippit, don't be so obscene.

KITTY. Pray, Ladies, walk into the next room. Mr. Sharp can't lay his
cloth till you are set down to cards.

MRS. GADABOUT. One thing I had quite forgot. Mr. Gayless, my nephew who you never saw will be in town from France presently, so I

140   left word to send him here immediately to make one.

GAYLESS. You do me honor, Madam.

SHARP. Do the ladies choose cards or the supper first?

GAYLESS (*aside*). Supper! what does the fellow mean?

GUTTLE. Oh, the supper by all means, for I have eat nothing to signify
since dinner.

SHARP (*aside*). Nor I, since last Monday was a fortnight.

GAYLESS. Pray, Ladies, walk into the next room. Sharp, get things
ready for supper, and call the music.

SHARP. Well said, Master.

150 MRS. GADABOUT. Without ceremony, Ladies.

Exeunt Ladies [*and* Gayless].

---

129.   world] word *O6*.
132–33.   I suppose] omitted *D5*.
142.   the supper] the omitted *D5*.
144.   GUTTLE.] GUT *D1*; GLUT. *O1*.
150.   MRS. GADABOUT.] *D1, D2, D3, O1, O3, O4, D5, O8, W1, W2*; GAY-
LESS. *O2, D4, O5, O6, O7*.
150.1.   *Exeunt Ladies] Ex. Ladies D1*.

KITTY (*aside*). I'll to my mistress and let her know everything is ready for her appearance.

Exit Kitty.

Guttle and Sharp.

GUTTLE. Pray Mr. What's-your-name, don't be long with supper; but hark'ee, what can I do in the meantime? Suppose you get me a pipe and some good wine. I'll try to divert myself that way till supper's ready.

SHARP. Or suppose, Sir, you was to take a nap till then; there's a very easy couch in that closet.

GUTTLE. The best thing in the world. I'll take your advice, but be sure to wake me when supper is ready.

Exit Guttle.

SHARP. Pray heaven you may not wake till then! What a fine situation my master is in at present! I have promised him my assistance, but his affairs are in so desperate a way, that I'm afraid 'tis out of all my skill to recover 'em. Well, fools have fortune, says an old proverb, and a very true one it is, for my master and I are two of the most unfortunate mortals in the creation.

Enter Gayless.

GAYLESS. Well, Sharp, I have set 'em down to cards, and now what have you to propose?

SHARP. I have one scheme left which in all probability may succeed. The good citizen, overloaded with his last meal, is taking a nap in that closet, in order to get him an appetite for yours. Suppose, Sir, we should make him treat us.

GAYLESS. I don't understand you.

SHARP. I'll pick his pocket, and provide us a supper with the booty.

GAYLESS. Monstrous! for without considering the villainy of it, the danger of waking him makes it impracticable.

SHARP. If he wakes, I'll smother him and lay his death to indigestion— a very common death among justices.

GAYLESS. Prithee be serious, we have no time to lose. Can you invent nothing to drive 'em out of the house?

SHARP. I can fire it.

GAYLESS. Shame and confusion so perplex me, I cannot give myself to a moment's thought.

---

159. be sure] besure *D*1.
163–64. 'tis out of all my skill] it is out of my skill *W*1.

SHARP. I have it. Did not Mrs. Gadabout say her nephew would be here?

GAYLESS. She did.

SHARP. Say no more, but [in to] your company. If I don't send 'em out of the house for the night, I'll at least frighten their stomachs away; and if this stratagem fails, I'll relinquish politics, and think
190   my understanding no better than my neighbors'.

GAYLESS. How shall I reward thee, Sharp?

SHARP. By your silence and obedience; away to your company, Sir.

Exit Gayless.

Now, dear Madam Fortune, for once, open your eyes and behold a poor unfortunate man of parts addressing you. Now is your time to convince your foes you are not that blind whimsical whore they take you for; but let 'em see by your assisting me, that men of sense, as well as fools, are sometimes entitled to your favor and protection.—So much for prayer; now for a great noise and a lie. (*Goes aside and cries out.*) Help, help, Master! Help, Gentlemen,
200   Ladies! Murder, fire, brimstone! Help, help, help!

Enter Mr. Gayless, [*Mr.* Trippit,] *and the ladies, with cards in their hands, and* Sharp *enters running, and meets 'em.*

GAYLESS. What's the matter?

SHARP. Matter, Sir! If you don't run this minute with that gentleman, this lady's nephew will be murdered. I am sure 'twas he; he was set upon the corner of the street, by four; he has killed two, and if you don't make haste, he'll be either murdered or took to prison.

MRS. GADABOUT. For heaven's sake, Gentlemen, run to his assistance. (*Aside.*) How I tremble for Melissa; this frolic of hers may be fatal.

GAYLESS. Draw, Sir, and follow me.

Exit Gayless *and* Gadabout.

210   TRIPPIT. Not I; I don't care to run myself into needless quarrels; I have suffered too much formerly by flying into passions; besides, I have pawned my honor to Mrs. Trippit, never to draw my sword again; and in her present condition, to break my word might have fatal consequences.

---

187. into] *O1, D1, D2, D3, O2, O3, D4, D5, O4, O5, O7;* in to *O6, O8, W1, W2.*
196. 'em] them *D5.*
198. and a lie] and lie *D5.*
209.1. *Exit.*] *D1, D2, D3, O1, O6, D5, O8, W1, W2; Exeunt O2, O3, D4, O4, O5, O7.*

SHARP.   Pray, Sir, don't excuse yourself. The young gentleman may
be murdered by this time.

TRIPPIT.   Then my assistance will be of no service to him. However,
I'll go to oblige you, and look on at a distance.

MRS. TRIPPIT.   I shall certainly faint, Mr. Trippit, if you draw.

Enter Guttle, *disordered, as from sleep.*

220 GUTTLE.   What noise and confusion is this?

SHARP.   Sir, there's a man murdered in the street.

GUTTLE.   Is that all? Zounds, I was afraid you had throwed the supper
down. A plague of your noise! I shan't recover my stomach this
half hour.

Enter Gayless *and* [*Mrs.*] Gadabout, *with* Melissa *in
boy's clothes, dressed in the French manner.*

MRS. GADABOUT.   Well, but my dear Jemmy, you are not hurt, sure?

MELISSA.   A little with riding post only.

MRS. GADABOUT.   Mr. Sharp alarmed us all with an account of your
being set upon by four men; that you had killed two, and was attacking the other when he came away, and when we met you at
230 the door, we were coming to your rescue.

MELISSA.   I had a small rencounter with half a dozen villains; but finding me resolute, they were wise enough to take to their heels. I believe I scrat some of 'em. (*Laying her hand to her sword.*)

SHARP (*aside*).   His vanity has saved my credit. I have a thought come
into my head may prove to our advantage, provided monsieur's
ignorance bears any proportion to his impudence.

MRS. GADABOUT.   Now my fright's over, let me introduce you, my
Dear, to Mr. Gayless. Sir, this is my nephew.

GAYLESS (*saluting her*).   Sir, I shall be proud of your friendship.

240 MELISSA.   I don't doubt but we shall be better acquainted in a little
time.

GUTTLE.   Pray, Sir, what news in France?

MELISSA.   Faith, Sir, very little that I know of in the political way; I
had no time to spend among the politicians. I was —

GAYLESS.   Among the ladies, I suppose.

MELISSA.   Too much, indeed. Faith, I have not philosophy enough to
resist their solicitations; (*To* Gayless *aside.*) you take me.

GAYLESS (*aside* to Sharp).   Yes, to be a most incorrigible fop; 'sdeath,

---

220.   What noise] what a noise *W*1.
227.   with an account] an accident of *W*1.
233.   scrat] *O*1, *O*2, *O*3, *D*4, *O*5, *O*7; scratcht *O*4, *O*6, *O*8, *W*1, *W*2; scratch'd
*D*1, *D*2, *D*3, *D*5.

this puppy's impertinence is an addition to my misery.

250 MELISSA (*aside to Mrs.* Gadabout). Poor Gayless, to what shifts is he reduced to? I cannot bear to see him much longer in this condition; I shall discover myself.

MRS. GADABOUT. Not before the end of the play; besides, the more his pain now, the greater his pleasure when relieved from it.

TRIPPIT. Shall we return to our cards? I have a *sans prendre* here, and must insist you play it out.

LADIES. With all my heart.

MELISSA. *Allons donc.*

As the company goes out, Sharp *pulls* Melissa *by the sleeve.*

SHARP. Sir, Sir, shall I beg leave to speak with you? Pray, did you find 260 a bank-note in your way hither?

MELISSA. What, between here and Dover do you mean?

SHARP. No, Sir, within twenty or thirty yards of this house.

MELISSA. You are drunk, Fellow.

SHARP. I am undone, Sir; but not drunk, I'll assure you.

MELISSA. What is all this?

SHARP. I'll tell you, Sir. A little while ago my master sent me out to change a note of twenty pounds; but I, unfortunately, hearing a noise in the street of, "Damme, Sir," and clashing of swords, and "rascal" and "murder," I runs up to the place, and saw four men 270 upon one; and having heard you was a mettlesome young gentleman, I immediately concluded it must be you; so ran back to call my master, and when I went to look for the note to change it, I found it gone, either stole or lost; and if I don't get the money immediately, I shall certainly be turned out of my place and lose my character.

MELISSA (*aside*). I shall laugh in his face.—Oh, I'll speak to your master about it, and he will forgive you at my intercession.

SHARP. Ah, Sir! you don't know my master.

MELISSA. I'm very little acquainted with him; but I have heard he's a 280 very good-natured man.

SHARP. I have heard so too, but I have felt it otherwise. He has so much good-nature, that, if I could compound for one broken head a day, I should think myself very well off.

---

251. reduced to] *D*1, *D*2, *D*3, *O*1, *W*1; reduced *O*2, *O*3, *O*4, *O*6, *D*4, *W*2, *D*5, *O*5, *O*7, *O*8.
258. (*goes out.*)] go out *D*5.
267. pounds] pound *W*2.
268. Damme] Damn me *W*1, *W*2, *D*4.
271. ran back] run back *D*1, *D*2, *D*3, *D*5.

MELISSA. Are you serious, Friend?

SHARP. Look'ee, Sir, I take you for a man of honor; there is something in your face that is generous, open, and masculine; you don't look like a foppish, effeminate telltale, so I'll venture to trust you. See here, Sir—(*shows his head.*) these are the effects of my master's good-nature.

290 MELISSA (*aside*). Matchless impudence!—Why do you live with him then after such usage?

SHARP. He's worth a great deal of money, and when he's drunk, which is commonly once a day, he's very free, and will give me anything; but I design to leave him when he's married, for all that.

MELISSA. Is he going to be married then?

SHARP. Tomorrow, Sir, and between you and I, he'll meet with his match both for humor and something else too.

MELISSA. What, she drinks too?

SHARP. Damnably, Sir; but mum.—You must know this entertainment
300 was designed for madam tonight; but she got so very gay after dinner, that she could not walk out of her own house; so her maid, who was half gone too, came here with an excuse, that Mrs. Melissa had got the vapors, and so she had indeed violently; here, here, Sir. (*Pointing to his head.*)

MELISSA (*aside*). This is scarcely to be borne.—Melissa! I have heard of her; they say she's very whimsical.

SHARP. A very woman, and please your honor, and between you and I, none of the mildest or wisest of her sex—but to return, Sir, to the twenty pounds.

310 MELISSA. I am surprised you who have got so much money in his ser- vice, should be at a loss for twenty pounds to save your bones at this juncture.

SHARP. I have put all my money out at interest; I never keep above five pounds by me; and if your honor would lend me the other fifteen, and take my note for it — (*Knocking.*)

MELISSA. Somebody's at the door.

SHARP. I can give very good security. (*Knocking.*)

MELISSA. Don't let the people wait, Mr. —

SHARP. Ten pounds will do. (*Knocking.*)

320 MELISSA. *Allez-vous-en!*

SHARP. Five, Sir. (*Knocking.*)

MELISSA. *Je ne puis pas.*

SHARP. (*aside*). "Je ne puis pas." I find we shan't understand one an- other, I do but lose time. And, if I had any thought, I might have

---

308. or wisest] omitted *W*2.

known these young fops return from their travels generally with
as little money as improvement.

Exit Sharp.

MELISSA. Ha, ha, ha, what lies doth this fellow invent, and what rogu-
eries does he commit for his master's service! There never sure
was a more faithful servant to his master, or a greater rogue to the
330   rest of mankind. But here he comes again; the plot thickens. I'll in
and observe Gayless.

Exit Melissa.

Enter Sharp *before several persons with dishes in their
hands, and a Cook, drunk.*

SHARP. (*aside*). Fortune, I thank thee. The most lucky accident!—
This way, Gentlemen, this way.
COOK. I am afraid I have mistook the house. Is this Mr. Treatwell's?
SHARP. The same, the same. What, don't you know me?
COOK. Know you? Are you sure there was a supper bespoke here?
SHARP. Yes. Upon my honor, Mr. Cook, the company is in the next
room and must have gone without had not you brought it. I'll draw
in a table. I see you have brought a cloth with you; but you need
340   not have done that, for we have a very good stock of linen—
(*Aside.*) at the pawnbroker's.

*Exit, and returns immediately,
drawing a table.*

Come, come, my boys, be quick, the company began to be very
uneasy; but I knew my old friend Lickspit here would not fail us.
COOK. Lickspit! I am no friend of yours; so I desire less familiarity.
Lickspit too!

Enter Gayless, *and stares.*

GAYLESS. What is all this?
SHARP (*aside to* Gayless). Sir, if the sight of the supper is offensive, I
can easily have it removed.
GAYLESS. Prithee explain thyself, Sharp.
350 SHARP. Some of our neighbors, I suppose, have bespoke this supper;

325. known these young fops] *D*1, *D*2, *D*3, *O*1, *O*4, *O*6, *D*5, *O*8, *W*2; known
young fops *O*2, *O*3, *D*4, *O*5, *O*7, *W*1.
334. Treatwell's] Treatwells *D*1, *D*2, *D*3.
338–39. draw in] in omitted *W*2.
340. very good] pretty good *W*2.
342. began] begin *D*1, *D*2, *D*3.

but the cook has drank away his memory, forgot the house, and brought it here; however, Sir, if you dislike it, I'll tell him of his mistake and send him about his business.

GAYLESS.   Hold, hold, necessity obliges me against my inclination to favor the cheat and feast at my neighbor's expense.

COOK.   Hark you, Friend, is that you[r] master?

SHARP.   Ay, and the best master in the world.

COOK.   I'll speak to him then.—Sir, I have, according to your commands, dressed as genteel a supper as my art and your price would admit of.

360

SHARP (*aside to* Gayless).   Good again, Sir, 'tis paid for.

GAYLESS.   I don't in the least question your abilities, Mr. Cook, and I am obliged to you for your care.

COOK.   Sir, you are a gentleman, and if you would but look over the bill and approve it, (*pulls out a bill*) you will ever and above return the obligation.

SHARP (*aside*).   Oh, the devil!

GAYLESS (*looking on a bill*).   Very well, I'll send my man to pay you tomorrow.

370 COOK.   I'll spare him that trouble and take it with me, Sir. I never work but for ready money.

GAYLESS.   Hah?

SHARP (*aside*).   Then you won't have our custom.—My master is busy now, Friend; do you think he won't pay you?

COOK.   No matter what I think; either my meat or my money.

SHARP.   'Twill be very ill-convenient for him to pay you tonight.

COOK.   Then I'm afraid it will be ill-convenient to pay me tomorrow, so d'ye hear —

Enter Melissa.

GAYLESS.   Prithee be advised! 'sdeath, I shall be discovered! (*Takes the Cook aside.*)

380 MELISSA (*to* Sharp).   What's the matter?

SHARP.   The cook has not quite answered my master's expectations about the supper, Sir, and he's a little angry at him, that's all.

MELISSA.   Come, come, Mr. Gayless, don't be uneasy; a bachelor cannot be supposed to have things in the utmost regularity; we don't expect it.

COOK.   But I do expect it and will have it.

MELISSA.   What does that drunken fool say?

---

356.   you[r] dropped letter *D*1, *D*2, *O*1, *D*3; your *O*2, *O*3, *D*4, *O*4, *W*1, *W*2, *O*5, *O*6, *O*7, *O*8, *D*5.
365.   ever] *D*1, *D*2, *D*3, *O*1, *O*4; over *O*2, *O*3, *O*5, *O*6, *O*7, *O*8, *D*4, *D*5, *W*1, *W*2.

COOK.   That I will have my money, and I won't stay till tomorrow, and, and —

390 SHARP (*runs and stops his mouth*).   Hold, hold, what are you doing? are you mad?

MELISSA.   What do you stop the man's breath for?

SHARP.   Sir, he was going to call you names.—Don't be abusive, Cook; the gentleman is a man of honor and said nothing to you. Pray be pacified; you are in liquor.

COOK.   I will have my —

SHARP (*holding, still*).   Why, I tell you, fool, you mistake the gentleman; he is a friend of my master's and has not said a word to you. Pray, good Sir, go into the next room; the fellow's drunk and takes
400 you for another.—You'll repent this when you are sober, Friend. —Pray, Sir, don't stay to hear his impertinence.

GAYLESS.   Pray Sir, walk in. He's below your anger.

MELISSA.   Damn the rascal! What does he mean by affronting me? Let the scoundrel go; I'll polish his brutality, I warrant you. Here's the best reformer of manners in the universe. (*Draws his sword.*) Let him go, I say.

SHARP.   So, so you have done finely now.—Get away as fast as you can. He's the most courageous mettlesome man in all England. Why, if his passion was up he could eat you. Make your escape, you fool!

410 COOK.   I won't. Eat me! he'll find me damned hard of digestion though.

SHARP.   Prithee come here; let me speak with you. (*They walk aside.*)

Enter Kitty.

KITTY.   Gad's me, is supper on the table already? Sir, pray defer it for a few moments; my mistress is much better and will be here immediately.

GAYLESS.   Will she indeed! Bless me—I did not expect—but however— Sharp?

KITTY (*aside to* Melissa).   What success, Madam?

MELISSA.   As we could wish, Girl. But he is in such pain and perplexity I can't hold it out much longer.

420 KITTY.   Ay, that not holding out is the ruin of half our sex.

SHARP.   I have pacified the cook, and if you can but borrow twenty pieces of that young prig, all may go well yet. You may succeed though I could not. Remember what I told you—about it straight, Sir.

GAYLESS (*to* Melissa).   Sir, Sir, I beg to speak a word with you. My

395.   pacified] pacify'd D_1, D_2, D_3.
408.   mettlesome man] mettlesome young man W_1, W_2.
420.   not holding out] not omitted $O8$.

servant, Sir, tells me he has had the misfortune, Sir, to lose a note
of mine of twenty pounds which I sent him to receive. And the
banker's shops being shut up, and having very little cash by me,
I should be much obliged to you if you would favor me with
430 twenty pieces till tomorrow.

MELISSA. Oh, Sir, with all my heart (*taking out her purse*), and so I
have a small favor to beg of you, Sir, the obligation will be mutual.

GAYLESS. How may I oblige you, Sir?

MELISSA. You are to be married, I hear, to Melissa.

GAYLESS. Tomorrow, Sir.

MELISSA. Then you'll oblige me, Sir, by never seeing her again.

GAYLESS. Do you call this a small favor, Sir!

MELISSA. A mere trifle, Sir. Breaking of contracts, suing for divorce,
committing adultery, and such like, are all reckoned trifles now-a-
440 days; and smart young fellows, like you and myself, Gayless, should
be never out of fashion.

GAYLESS. But pray, Sir, how are you concerned in this affair?

MELISSA. Oh, Sir, you must know that I have a very great regard for
Melissa, and, indeed, she for me; and, by the by, I have a most
despicable opinion of you; for *entre nous*, I take you, Charles,
to be a very great scoundrel.

GAYLESS. Sir!

MELISSA. Nay, don't look fierce, Sir, and give yourself airs. Damme,
Sir, I shall be through your body else in the snapping of a finger.

450 GAYLESS. I'll be as quick as you, Villain! (*Draws and makes at Melissa.*)

KITTY. Hold, hold, murder! You'll kill my mistress—the young gentleman, I mean.

GAYLESS. Ah, her mistress! (*Drops his sword.*)

SHARP. How! Melissa! Nay, then drive away cart. All's over now.

Enter all the company laughing.

MRS. GADABOUT. What, Mr. Gayless, engaging with Melissa before
your time. Ah, ah, ah!

KITTY (*to* Sharp). Your humble servant, good Mr. Politician. This is,
Gentlemen and Ladies, the most celebrated and ingenious Timothy Sharp, schemer general, and redoubted squire to the most re-
460 nowned and fortunate adventurer Charles Gayless, knight of the
woeful countenance. Ha, ha, ha! Oh, that dismal face and more
dismal head of yours. (*Strikes* Sharp *upon the head.*)

SHARP. 'Tis cruel in you to disturb a man in his last agonies.

438. Breaking of contracts] Breaking off contracts D5.
456. Ah, ah, ah!] Ha, ha, ha! O6, D5, O8, W1, W2.

MELISSA. Now, Mr. Gayless!—What, not a word? You are sensible
I can be no stranger to your misfortunes, and I might reasonably
expect an excuse for your ill treatment of me.

GAYLESS. No, Madam, silence is my only refuge; for to endeavor to
vindicate my crimes would show a greater want of virtue than
even the commission of 'em.

470 MELISSA. Oh, Gayless! 'Twas poor to impose upon a woman, and one
that loved you too.

GAYLESS. Oh, most unpardonable; but my necessities —

SHARP. And mine, Madam, were not to be matched, I'm sure, o' this
side starving.

MELISSA (*aside*). His tears have softened me at once.—Your necessities, Mr. Gayless, with such real contrition, are too powerful motives not to affect the breast already prejudiced in your favor. You
have suffered too much already for your extravagance; and as I
take part in your sufferings, 'tis easing myself to relieve you.

480 Know, therefore, all that's past I freely forgive.

GAYLESS. You cannot mean it, sure. I am lost in wonder.

MELISSA. Prepare yourself for more wonder. You have another friend
in masquerade here. Mr. Cook, pray throw aside your drunkenness
and make your sober appearance. Don't you know that face, Sir?

COOK. Ay, Master, what, have you forgot your friend Dick, as you
used to call me?

GAYLESS. More wonder indeed! Don't you live with my father?

MELISSA. Just after your hopeful servant there had left me, comes this
man from Sir William with a letter to me; upon which (being by
490 that wholly convinced of your necessitous condition) I invented,
by the help of Kitty and Mrs. Gadabout, this little plot, in which
your friend Dick there has acted miracles, resolving to tease you
a little, that you might have a greater relish for a happy turn in
your affairs. Now, Sir, read this letter and complete your joy.

GAYLESS (*reads*). "Madam, I am father to the unfortunate young
man, who, I hear by a friend of mine (that by my desire, has been
a continual spy upon him) is making his addresses to you. If he is
so happy as to make himself agreeable to you (whose character
I am charmed with) I shall own him with joy for my son and for-
500 get his former follies. I am,
Madam,
Your most humble servant,
William Gayless.

---

469. of 'em] of them *O6, O8, W2.*
499. I am] I'm *W2.*

P.S. I will be soon in town myself to congratulate his reformation and marriage."

O Melissa, this is too much. Thus let me show my thanks and
gratitude, (*kneeling; she raises him*) for here 'tis only due.

SHARP. A reprieve! A reprieve! A reprieve!

KITTY (*to* Gayless). I have been, Sir, a most bitter enemy to you. But
510   since you are likely to be a little more conversant with cash than
you have been, I am now, with the greatest sincerity, your most
obedient friend and humble servant. And I hope, Sir, all former
enmity will be forgotten.

GAYLESS. Oh, Mrs. Pry, I have been too much indulged with forgiveness myself not to forgive lesser offenses in other people.

SHARP. Well then, Madam, since my master has vouchsafed pardon to
your handmaid Kitty, I hope you'll not deny it to his footman
Timothy.

MELISSA. Pardon for what?

520 SHARP. Only for telling you about ten thousand lies, Madam, and,
among the rest, insinuating that your ladyship would —

MELISSA. I understand you; and can forgive anything, Sharp, that was
designed for the service of your master. And if Pry and you will
follow our example, I'll give her a small fortune as a reward for
both your fidelities.

SHARP. I fancy, Madam, 'twould be better to half the small fortune
between us, and keep us both single. For as we shall live in the
same house, in all probability we may taste the comforts of matrimony and not be troubled with its inconveniences. What say you,
530   Kitty?

KITTY. Do you hear, Sharp, before you talk of the comforts of matrimony, taste the comforts of a good dinner and recover your flesh a
little; do, Puppy.

SHARP. The devil backs her, that's certain; and I am no match for her
at any weapon.

MELISSA. And now, Mr. Gayless, to show I have not provided for you
by halves, let the music prepare themselves, and, with the approbation of the company, we'll have a dance.

ALL. By all means, a dance.

540 GUTTLE. By all means a dance—after supper though.

SHARP. Oh, pray, Sir, have supper first, or, I'm sure, I shan't live till
the dance is finished.

GAYLESS. Behold, Melissa, as sincere a convert as ever truth and beauty
made. The wild impetuous sallies of my youth are now blown
over, and a most pleasing calm of perfect happiness succeeds.

Thus Aetna's flames the verdant earth consume,
But milder heat makes drooping nature bloom.
So virtuous love affords us springing joy,
Whilst vicious passions, as they burn, destroy.

Finis

Epilogue

Spoken by Mr. Garrick.
[This Epilogue first appeared in the Second Edition, O₂, London:
Paul Vaillant, 1743.]

That I'm a lying rogue, you all agree:
And yet look round the world, and you will see
How many more, my betters, lie as fast as me.
Against this vice we all are ever railing,
And yet, so tempting is it, so prevailing,
You'll find but few without this useful failing.
Lady or Abigail, my lord or Will,
The lie goes round, and the ball's never still.
My lies were harmless, told to show my parts;
And not like those, when tongues belie their hearts.
In all professions you will find this flaw;
And in the gravest too, in physic and in law.
The gouty sergeant cries, with formal pause,
"Your plea is good, my friend, don't starve the cause."
But when my lord decrees for t'other side,
Your costs of suit convince you—that he lied.
A doctor comes with formal wig and face,
First feels your pulse, then thinks, and knows your case.
"Your fever's slight, not dangerous, I assure you,
Keep warm, and repetatur haustus, Sir, will cure you."
Around the bed, next day, his friends are crying:
The patient dies, the doctor's paid for lying.
The poet, willing to secure the pit,
Gives out his play has humor, taste and wit.
The cause comes on and, while the judges try,
Each groan and catcall gives the bard the lie.
Now let us ask, pray, what the ladies do:
They too will fib a little *entre nous*.
"Lord!" says the prude (her face behind her fan)

30   "How can our sex have any joy in man?
"As for my part, the best could ne'er deceive me,
"And were the race extinct 'twould never grieve me.
"Their sight is odious, but their touch—O Gad!
"The thought of that's enough to drive one mad."
Thus rails at man the squeamish Lady Dainty,
Yet weds, at fifty-five, a rake of twenty.
In short, a beau's intrigues, a lover's sighs,
The courtier's promise, the rich widow's cries,
And patriot's zeal, are seldom more than lies.
40   Sometimes you'll see a man belie his nation,
Nor to his country show the least relation.
For instance now —
A cleanly Dutchman, or a Frenchman grave,
A sober German, or a Spaniard brave,
An Englishman a coward or a slave.
Mine, though a fibbing, was an honest art:
I served my master, played a faithful part:
Rank me not therefore 'mong the lying crew,
For, though my tongue was false, my heart was true.

Miss in Her Teens:
or, The Medley
of Lovers
A Farce
1747

MISS *in her* TEENS:

OR, THE

MEDLEY of LOVERS.

A

FARCE.

IN TWO ACTS.

As it is Perform'd at the

THEATRE-ROYAL in *Covent-Garden.*

LONDON:

Printed for J. and R. TONSON and S. DRAPER
in the *Strand.* 1747.

[Price One Shilling.]

Advertisement

The Author takes this Opportunity to return the Publick his thanks for their so favorable Reception of the following Trifle; the Hint of which is taken from the *French*. Whether the Plot and Characters are alter'd for the better or worse, may be seen by comparing it with *La Parisienne* of *D'Ancourt*.

Prologue

Written by a Friend.

Too long has farce, neglecting nature's laws,
Debased the stage and wronged the comic cause.
To raise a laugh has been her sole pretense,
Though dearly purchased at the price of sense.
This child of folly gained increase with time,
Fit for the place, succeeded pantomime;
Revived her honors, joined her motley band,
And song and low conceit o'erran the land.
        More gen'rous views inform our author's breast,
From real life his characters are dressed;
He seeks to trace the passions of mankind,
And while he spares the person, paints the mind.
In pleasing contrast he attempts to show
The vap'ring bully and the frib'ling beau
Cowards alike—that full of martial airs,
And this as tender as the silk he wears.
        Proud to divert, not anxious for renown,
Oft has the bard essayed to please the town.
Your full applause out-paid his little art;
He boasts no merit but a grateful heart.
Pronounce your doom, he'll patiently submit,
Ye sovereign judges of all works of wit!
To you the ore is brought a lifeless mass;
You give the stamp and then the coin may pass.
        Now whether judgment prompt you to forgive,
Whether you bid this trifling offspring live,

10

20

---

8. o'erran] O_1, O_2, Q_1, D_1, O_3, D_2, O_4, D_3, O_5, D_4, W_1, O_6; o'er-run W_2.
14. frib'ling] O_1, O_2, Q_1, D_1, D_2, O_4, D_3, O_5, D_4, W_2, O_6; fribbling O_3, W_1.
20. grateful] O_1, O_2, Q_1, D_1, D_2, O_3, O_4, D_3, O_5, D_4, W_1, O_6; greatful W_2.

Or with a frown should send the sickly thing
To sleep whole ages under Dulness' wing;
To your known candor we will always trust.
30   You never were nor can you be unjust.

Dramatis Personae

Men.

Sir Simon Loveit.	Mr. *Hippisly*.
Captain Loveit.	Mr. *Havard*.
Fribble.	Mr. *Garrick*.
Flash.	Mr. *Woodward*.
Puff.	Mr. *Chapman*.
Jasper.	Mr. *Arthur*.

Women.

Miss Biddy.	Miss *Hippisly*.
Aunt.	Mrs. *Martin*.
Tag.	Mrs. *Pritchard*.

---

1. Mr. Hippisl[e]y] O_1, O_2, Q_1, D_1, D_2, O_4, D_3, O_6; Taswell] O_3, D_4, W_1, O_5, W_2.
5. Mr. Chapman] O_1, O_2, Q_1, D_1, D_2, O_4, D_3, O_6; Yates] O_3, D_4, W_1, W_2, O_5.
6. Mr. Arthur] O_1, O_2, Q_1, D_1, D_2, O_4, D_3, O_5; Blakes] O_3, D_4, W_1, W_2, O_6.
7. Miss Hippisl[e]y] O_1, O_2, Q_1, D_1, D_2, O_4, D_3, O_5; Mrs. Green] O_3, D_4, W_1, W_2, O_6.
8. Mrs. Martin] O_1, O_2, Q_1, D_1, O_3, D_2, O_4, D_3, O_5; Mrs. Cross] D_4, W_1, W_2, O_6.
9. Mrs. Pritchard] O_1, O_2, Q_1, D_1, O_3, D_2, O_4, D_3, O_5; Mrs. Clive] D_4, W_1, W_2, O_6.

Miss in Her Teens:
or, The Medley of Lovers

ACT I. SCENE I.

SCENE, *a street.*

Enter Captain Loveit *and* Puff.

CAPTAIN.   This was the place we were directed to; and now, Puff, if I can get no intelligence of her, what will become of me?

PUFF.   And me too, Sir. You must consider I am a married man and can't bear fatigue as I have done. But pray, Sir, why did you leave the army so abruptly and not give me time to fill my knapsack with common necessaries? Half a dozen shirts and your regimentals are my whole cargo.

CAPTAIN.   I was wild to get away, and, as soon as I obtained my leave of absence, I thought every moment an age till I returned to the place where I first saw this young, charming, innocent, bewitching creature —

PUFF.   With fifteen thousand pounds for her fortune. Strong motives, I must confess. And now, Sir, as you are pleased to say you must depend upon my care and abilities in this affair, I think I have a just right to be acquainted with the particulars of your passion, that I may be the better enabled to serve you.

CAPTAIN.   You shall have 'em. When I left the university, which is now seven months since, my father, who loves his money better than his son and would not settle a farthing upon me —

PUFF.   Mine did so by me, Sir.

CAPTAIN.   Purchased me a pair of colors at my own request. But before I joined the regiment, which was going abroad, I took a ramble into the country with a fellow collegian to see a relation of his who lived in Berkshire.

PUFF.   A party of pleasure, I suppose.

CAPTAIN.   During a short stay there I came acquainted with this young creature. She was just come from the boarding-school and, though she had all the simplicty of her age and the country, yet it was mixed with such sensible vivacity that I took fire at once.

30 PUFF. I was tinder myself at that age. But pray, Sir, did you take fire before you knew of her fortune?

CAPTAIN. Before, upon my honor.

PUFF. Folly and constitution. But on, Sir.

CAPTAIN. I was introduced to the family by the name of Rhodophil, for so my companion and I had settled it. At the end of three weeks I was obliged to attend the call of honor in Flanders.

PUFF. Your parting, to be sure, was heartbreaking.

CAPTAIN. I feel it at this instance. We vowed eternal constancy, and I promised to take the first opportunity of returning to her. I did

40 so, but we found the house shut up, and all the information, you know, that we could get from the neighboring cottage was that Miss and her aunt were removed to town and lived somewhere near this part of it.

PUFF. And now we are got to the place of action, propose your plan of operation.

CAPTAIN. My father lives but in the next street, so I must decamp immediately for fear of discoveries. You are not known to be my servant, so make what inquiries you can in the neighborhood, and I shall wait at the inn for your intelligence.

50 PUFF. I'll patrol hereabouts and examine all that pass. But I've forgot the word, Sir—Miss Biddy —

CAPTAIN. Bellair.

PUFF. A young lady of wit, beauty, and fifteen thousand pounds fortune. But, Sir —

CAPTAIN. What do you say, Puff?

PUFF. If your Honor pleases to consider that I had a wife in town whom I left somewhat abruptly half a year ago, you'll think it, I believe, but decent to make some inquiry after her first. To be sure, it would be some small consolation to me to know whether the

60 poor woman is living or has made away with herself, or —

CAPTAIN. Prithee don't distract me. A moment's delay is of the utmost consequence. I must insist upon an immediate compliance with my commands.

Exit Captain.

PUFF. The devil's in these fiery young fellows! They think of nobody's

---

30. that] *O*1, *O*2, *Q*1, *D*1, *O*3, *D*2, *O*4, *D*3, *O*5, *D*4, *W*1, *O*6; your *W*2.
34. Rhodophil] *O*1, *O*2, *Q*1, *D*1, *O*3, *O*4, *D*3, *O*5, *D*4, *W*1, *W*2, *O*6; Rodophil *D*2.
42. were] Omitted *W*2.

wants but their own. He does not consider that I am flesh and blood as well as himself. However, I may kill two birds at once; for I shan't be surprised if I meet my lady walking the streets. But who have we here? Sure, I should know that face.

Enter Jasper *from a house.*

Who's that? my old acquaintance Jasper?

70 JASPER. What, Puff! are you here?

PUFF. My dear friend! (*Kisses him.*) Well, and how Jasper! still easy and happy! *Toujours la méme!* What intrigues now? What girls have you ruined and what cuckolds made since you and I used to beat up together, eh?

JASPER. Faith, business has been very brisk during the war. Men are scarce, you know. Not as I can say I ever wanted amusement in the worst of times, but hark ye, Puff —

PUFF. Not a word aloud. I am *incognito.*

JASPER. Why, faith, I should not have known you if you had not spoke
80 first. You seem to be a little *dishabille* too, as well as *incognito.* Who do you honor with your service now? Are you from the wars?

PUFF. Piping hot, I assure you, Fire and smoke will tarnish, Jasper. A man that will go into such service as I have been in will find his clothes the worse for wear, take my word for it. But how is it with you? (*Salutes him.*) What, you still serve, I see? You live at that house, I suppose?

JASPER. I don't absolutely live, but I am most of my time there. I have within these two months entered into the service of an old gentleman, who hired a reputable servant and dressed him as you
90 see, because he has taken it into his head to fall in love.

PUFF. False appetite and second childhood! But, prithee, what's the object of his passion?

JASPER. No less than a virgin of sixteen, I assure you.

PUFF. Oh, the toothless old dotard!

JASPER. And he mumbles and plays with her till his mouth waters; then he chuckles till he cries, and calls it his Bid and his Biddy, and is so foolishly fond —

PUFF. Biddy! What's that?

---

71. how] now *W*2.
76. as] *O*1, *O*2, *D*2, *D*3, *O*5, *D*4, *O*6; that *Q*1, *D*1, *O*3, *O*4, *W*1, *W*2.
77. hark ye] harkee *W*2.
82. Jasper] Omitted, *Q*1, *O*3, *W*1, *W*2.
84–85. with you] *O*1, *O*2, *D*1, *D*2, *D*3, *O*5, *D*4; with you, friend Jasper *Q*1, *O*3, *O*4, *W*1, *W*2, *O*6.
    Salutes him.] Omitted *Q*1, *O*3, *D*2, *W*1, *W*2.
93. I assure you] Omitted *W*1, *W*2.

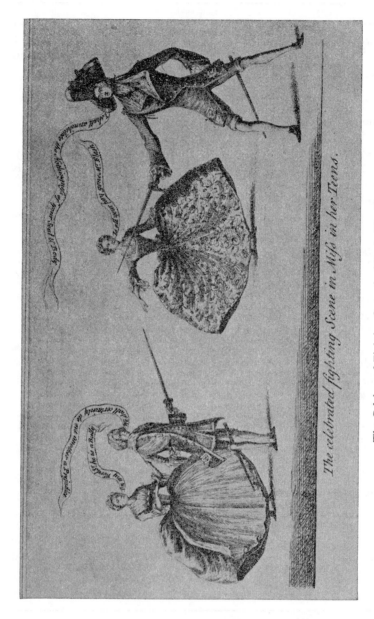

The Celebrated Fighting Scene in *Miss in Her Teens*.
Harvard Theatre Collection

JASPER. Her name is Biddy.

100   PUFF. Biddy! What, Miss Biddy Bellair?

JASPER. The same.

PUFF (*aside*). I have no luck, to be sure.—Oh! I have heard of her; she's of a pretty good family and has some fortune, I know. But are things settled? Is the marriage fixed?

JASPER. Not absolutely. The girl, I believe, detests him; but her aunt, a very good, prudent old lady, has given her consent if he can gain her niece's. How it will end I can't tell, but I am hot upon't myself.

PUFF. The devil! Not marriage, I hope?

JASPER. That is not yet determined.

110   PUFF. Who is the lady, pray?

JASPER. A maid in the same family, a woman of honor, I assure you. She has one husband already, a scoundrel sort of a fellow that has run away from her and listed for a soldier. So towards the end of the campaign she hopes to have a certificate he's knocked o' th' head. If not, I suppose we shall settle matters another way.

PUFF. Well, speed the plough. But, harkye! Consummate without the certificate if you can. Keep your neck out of the collar, do. I have wore it these two years, and damnably galled I am.

JASPER. I'll take your advice. But I must run away to my master, who
120   will be impatient for an answer to his message which I have just delivered to the young lady. So, dear Mr. Puff, I am your most obedient humble servant.

PUFF. And I must to our agent's for my arrears. If you have an hour to spare, you'll hear of me at George's or the Tiltyard. *Au revoir*, as we say abroad.

Exit Jasper.

Thus we are as civil and as false as our betters. Jasper and I were always the *Beau Monde* exactly. We ever hated one another heartily, yet always kiss and shake hands. But now to my master with a head full of news and a heart full of joy! (*Going, starts.*) *Angels and*
130   *ministers of grace defend me*! It can't be! By heavens, it is that fretful porcupine, my wife. I can't stand it. What shall I do? I'll try to avoid her.

Enter Tag.

TAG. It must be him! I'll swear to the rogue at a mile's distance; he either has not seen me or won't know me. If I can keep my temper I'll try him farther.

PUFF. I sweat, I tremble. She comes upon me!

TAG. Pray, good Sir, if I may be so bold —

PUFF. I have nothing for you, good woman. Don't trouble me.

TAG. If your Honor pleases to look this way —

140 PUFF. The kingdom is overrun with beggars. I suppose the last I gave
to has sent this, but I have no more loose silver about me. So, prithee,
woman, don't disturb me.

TAG. I can hold no longer. Oh, you villain, you! Where have you been,
scoundrel? Do you know me now, varlet? (*Seizes him.*)

PUFF. Here, Watch! Watch! Zounds, I shall have my pockets picked.

TAG. Own me this minute, hangdog, and confess everything, or by the
rage of an injured woman I'll raise the neighborhood, throttle you,
and send you to Newgate.

PUFF. Amazement! What, my own dear Tag? Come to my arms, and
150 let me press you to my heart that pants for thee and only thee, my
true and lawful wife. Now my stars have overpaid me for the
fatigue and dangers of the field. I have wandered about like Achilles
in search of faithful Penelope, and the gods have brought me to this
happy spot.

TAG. The fellow's cracked for certain. Leave your bombastic stuff
and tell me, rascal, why you left me and where you have been these
six months, heh?

PUFF. We'll reserve my adventures for our happy winter evenings.
And shall only tell you now that my heart beat so strong in my
160 country's cause and, being instigated either by honor or the devil,
I can't tell which, I set out for Flanders to gather laurels and lay
'em at thy feet.

TAG. You left me to starve, villain, and beg my bread, you did so.

PUFF. I left you too hastily, I must confess, and often has my conscience
stung me for it. I am got into an officer's service, have been in
several actions, gained some credit by my behavior, and am now
returned with my master to indulge the gentler passions.

TAG. Don't think to fob me off with this nonsensical talk. What have
you brought me home beside?

170 PUFF. Honor and immoderate love.

TAG. I could tear your eyes out.

PUFF. Temperance, or I walk off.

TAG. Temperance, traitor, temperance! What can you say for yourself?
Leave me to the wide world.

PUFF. Well, I have been in the wide world too, han't I? What would
the woman have?

TAG. Reduce me to the necessity of going to service. (*Cries.*)

PUFF. Why, I'm in service too; your lord and master, an't I, you saucy

159. And shall] *O*1, *O*2, *D*2, *D*3; I shall *Q*1, *O*3, *O*4, *D*4, *O*6, *W*1, *W*2.
167. gentler] *O*1, *O*2, *Q*1, *D*1, *D*2, *D*4, *O*5, *O*3, *O*4, *D*3; genteeler *W*1, *W*2, *O*6.
169. beside] *O*1, *O*2, *D*1, *D*2, *D*3, *O*5, *D*4, *O*6; besides *Q*1, *O*3, *O*4, *W*1, *W*2.

jade you? Come, where dost live hereabouts? Hast got good vails?
180   Dost go to market? Come, give me a kiss, darling, and tell me where
I shall pay my duty to thee.

TAG.   Why there I live, at that house. (*Pointing to the house* Jasper
came out of.)

PUFF.   What, there! that house?

TAG.   Yes, there, that house.

PUFF.   Huzza! We're made forever, you slut, you! Huzza! Everything
conspires this day to make me happy. Prepare for an inundation of
joy. My master is in love with your Miss Biddy over head and ears,
and she with him. I know she is courted by some old fumbler, and
her aunt is not against the match. But now we are come, the town
190   will be relieved and the Governor brought over. In plain English,
our fortune is made. My master must marry the lady, and the old
gentleman may go to the devil.

TAG.   Heyday, what is all this?

PUFF.   Say no more, the dice are thrown, doublets for us. Away to
your young mistress while I run to my master. Tell her Rhodophil will be with her immediately; then, if her blood does not
mount to her face like quicksilver in a weatherglass and point
to extreme hot, believe the whole a lie and your husband no
politician.

200 TAG.   This is news indeed! I have had the place but a little while, and
have not quite got into the secrets of the family. But part of your
story is true, and if you'll bring your master, and Miss is willing, I
warrant we'll be too hard for the old folks.

PUFF.   I'll about it straight. But hold, Tag, I had forgot. Pray how does
Mr. Jasper do?

TAG.   Mr. Jasper! What do you mean? I–I–I –

PUFF.   What, out of countenance, child? Oh fy! Speak plain, my dear.
And the certificate, when comes that, heh, love?

TAG (*aside*).   He has sold himself and turned conjurer, or he could never
210   have known it.

PUFF.   Are you not a jade? Are you not a Jezebel? Arn't you a —

TAG.   O ho, temperance! or I walk off.

PUFF.   I know I am not finished yet, and so I am easy; but more thanks
to my fortune than your virtue, Madam.

AUNT (*within*).   Tag, Tag; where are you, Tag?

TAG.   Coming, Madam. My old lady calls. Away to your master, and I'll
prepare his reception within.

195–96.   Rhodophil] *O*1, *O*2, *D*1, *D*2, *D*3, *D*4, *O*5; Rhodophil! Rhodophil! *Q*1, *O*3,
      *O*4, *O*6, *W*1, *W*2.
213.   I am easy] Omitted *W*2.

PUFF. Shall I bring the certificate with me?

Exit.

TAG. Go, you graceless rogue; you richly deserve it.

Exit.

SCENE [II.] *changes to a chamber.*

Enter Aunt *and* Tag.

AUNT. Who was that man you were talking to, Tag?

TAG. A cousin of mine, Madam, that brought me some news from my aunt in the country.

AUNT. Where's my niece? Why are not you with her?

TAG. She bid me leave her alone. She's so melancholy, Madam, I don't know what's come to her of late.

AUNT. The thoughtfulness that is natural upon the approach of matrimony generally occasions a decent concern.

TAG. And do you think, Madam, a husband of threescore and five —

10 AUNT. Hold, Tag. He protests to me he is but five and fifty.

TAG. He is a rogue, Madam, and an old rogue, and a fumbling old rogue, which is the worst of rogues.

AUNT. Alas! Youth or age, 'tis all one to her. She is all simplicity without experience. I would not force her inclinations, but she's so innocent she won't know the difference.

TAG. Innocent! Ne'er trust to that, Madam. I was innocent myself once, but "Live and learn" is an old saying and a true one. I believe, Madam, nobody is more innocent than yourself, and a good maid you are, to be sure. But though you really don't *know* the difference,
20 yet you can *fancy it*, I warrant you.

AUNT. I should prefer a large jointure to a small one, and that's all. But 'tis impossible that Biddy should have desires; she's but newly out of the country and just turned of sixteen.

TAG. That's a ticklish age, Madam. I have observed she does not eat nor she does not sleep; she sighs and she cries and she loves moonlight. These, I take it, are very strong symptoms.

AUNT. They are very unaccountable, I must confess. But you talk from a depraved mind, Tag; her's is simple and untainted.

---

2. some] Omitted *W2*.

10. five and fifty] fifty and five *W2*.

11–12. and a fumbling old rogue] *O1*, *D1*, *D2*, *D3*, *O5*, omitted *O2*, *Q1*, *O3*, *O4*, *D4*, *W1*, *W2*, *O6*.

14. I . . . inclinations] Omitted *W1*, *W2*.

25. and] Omitted *W2*.

TAG. She'll make him a cuckold though, for all that, if you force her
30   to marry him.
AUNT. You shock me, Tag, with your coarse expressions. I tell you her
        chastity will be her guard, let her husband be what he will.
TAG. Chastity! Never trust to that, Madam. Get her a husband that's
        fit for her, and I'll be bound for her virtue. But with such a one as
        Sir Simon, I'm a rogue if I'd answer for my own.
AUNT. Well, Tag, the child shall never have reason to repent of my
        severity. I was going before to my lawyer's to speak about the
        articles of marriage. I will now put a stop to 'em for some time, till
        we can make farther discoveries.
40   TAG. Heaven will bless you for your goodness. Look where the poor
        bird comes, quite moped and melancholy. I'll set my pump at work
        and draw something from her before your return, I warrant you.

                                                    Exit Aunt.

There goes a miracle. She has neither pride, envy, or ill-nature, and
yet is near sixty and a virgin.

                            Enter Biddy.

BIDDY. How unfortunate a poor girl am I. I dare not tell my secrets to
        anybody, an if I don't I'm undone. Heigho! (*Sighs.*) Pray, Tag, is
        my aunt gone to her lawyer about me? Heigho!
TAG. What's that sigh for, my dear young mistress?
BIDDY. I did not sigh, not I. (*Sighs.*)
50   TAG. Nay, never gulp 'em down. They are the worst things you can
        swallow. There's something in that little heart of yours that swells
        it and puffs it and will burst it at last, if you don't give it vent.
BIDDY. What would you have me tell you? (*Sighs.*)
TAG. Come, come, you are afraid I'll betray you, but you had as good
        speak. I may do you some service you little think of.
BIDDY. It is not in your power, Tag, to give me what I want. (*Sighs.*)
TAG. Not directly, perhaps; but I may be the means of helping you to
        it, as for example—If you should not like to marry the old man
        your aunt designs for you, one might find a way to break —
60   BIDDY. His neck, Tag?
TAG. Or the match. Either will do, Child.
BIDDY. I don't care which indeed, so I was clear of him. I don't think
        I'm fit to be married.
TAG. To him, you mean. You have no objection to marriage but the
        man, and I applaud you for it. But come; courage, Miss, never keep
        it in. Out with it all.

---

42. your] *O*1, *O*2, *Q*1, *D*1, *O*3, *D*2, *O*4, *D*3, *O*5, *D*4; you *W*1, *W*2, *O*6.

BIDDY. If you'll ask me any questions, I'll answer 'em; but I can't tell
you anything of myself. I shall blush if I do.

TAG. Well then—in the first place, pray tell me, Miss Biddy Bellair, if
70   you don't like somebody better than old Simon Loveit.

BIDDY. Heigho!

TAG. What's "Heigho!," Miss?

BIDDY. When I say "heigho," it means "yes."

TAG. Very well. And this somebody is a young, handsome fellow?

BIDDY. Heigho!

TAG. And if you were once his, you'd be as merry as the best of us?

BIDDY. Heigho!

TAG. So far so good; and since I have got you to wet your feet, souse
over head at once and the pain will be over.

80   BIDDY. There then. (*A long sigh.*) Now help me out, Tag, as fast as
you can.

TAG. When did you hear from your gallant?

BIDDY. Never since he went to the army.

TAG. How so?

BIDDY. I was afraid the letters would fall into my aunt's hands, so I
would not let him write to me. But I had a better reason then.

TAG. Pray let's hear that too.

BIDDY. Why, I thought if I should write to him and promise him to
love nobody else, and should afterwards change my mind, he might
90   think I was inconstant and call me a coquette.

TAG (*aside*). What a simple innocent it is!—And have you changed
your mind, Miss?

BIDDY. No indeed, Tag. I love him the best of any of 'em.

TAG. Of any of 'em! Why, have you any more?

BIDDY. Pray don't ask me.

TAG. Nay, Miss, if you only trust me by halves, you can't expect —

BIDDY. I will trust you with everything. When I parted with him, I
grew melancholy; so, in order to divert me, I have let two others
court me till he returns again.

100 TAG (*aside*). Is that all, my dear? Mighty simple, indeed.

BIDDY. One of 'em is a fine blustering man and is called Captain Flash.
He is always talking of fighting and wars; he thinks he's sure of me,
but I shall balk him. We shall see him this afternoon, for he pressed
strongly to come, and I have given him leave while my aunt's taking her afternoon's nap.

TAG. And who is the other, pray?

BIDDY. Quite another sort of man. He speaks like a lady for all the
world, and never swears as Mr. Flash does, but wears nice white
gloves and tells me what ribbons become my complexion, where

110   to stick my patches, who is the best milliner, where they sell the best tea, and which is the best wash for the face and the best paste for the hands. He's always playing with my fan and showing his teeth, and whenever I speak he pats me—so—and cries, "The devil take me, Miss Biddy, but you'll be my perdition!" ha, ha, ha!

TAG. Oh, the pretty creature! And what do you call him, pray?

BIDDY. His name's Fribble. You shall see him too, for by mistake I appointed 'em at the same time. But you must help me out with 'em.

TAG. And suppose your favorite should come too?

BIDDY. I should not care what became of the others.

120 TAG. What's his name?

BIDDY. It begins with an R—h—o—

TAG. I'll be hanged if it is not Rhodophil.

BIDDY. I'm frightened at you! You are a witch, Tag.

TAG. I am so, and I can tell your fortune too. Look me in the face. The gentleman you love most in the world will be at our house this afternoon. He arrived from the army this morning and dies till he sees you.

BIDDY. Is he come, Tag? Don't joke with me.

TAG. Not to keep you longer in suspense, you must know the servant

130   of your Strephon, by some unaccountable fate or other, is my lord and master. He has just been with me and told me of his master's arrival and impatience.

BIDDY. Oh my dear, dear Tag, you have put me out of my wits. I am all over in a flutter; I shall leap out of my skin. I don't know what to do with myself. Is he come, Tag? I am ready to faint. I'd give the world I had put on my pink and silver robings today.

TAG. I assure you, Miss, you look charmingly!

BIDDY. Do I indeed though? I'll put a little patch under my left eye and powder my hair immediately.

140 TAG. We'll go to dinner first, and then I'll assist you.

BIDDY. Dinner! I can't eat a morsel. I don't know what's the matter with me. My ears tingle, my heart beats, my face flushes, and I tremble every joint of me. I must run in and look myself in the glass this moment.

TAG. Yes, she has it, and deeply too. This is no hypocrisy.
       Not art but nature now performs her part,
       And every word's the language of the heart.

End of the First Act.

---

112. He's] *O*2, *Q*1, *O*3, *D*1, *O*4, *D*3, *O*5; He is *O*1, *D*2, *D*4, *W*1, *W*2, *O*6.

117. 'em] them *W*2.

147.1. *End . . . Act*] Omitted *W*2.

ACT II. SCENE I.

SCENE *continues.*
Enter Captain Loveit, Biddy, Tag, *and* Puff.

CAPTAIN. To find you still constant and to arrive at such a critical
juncture is the height of fortune and happiness.

BIDDY. Nothing shall force me from you. And if I am secure of your
affections —

PUFF. I'll be bound for him, Madam, and give you any security you
can ask.

TAG. Everything goes on to our wish, Sir. I just now had a second con-
ference with my old lady, and she was so convinced by my arguments that she returned instantly to the lawyer to forbid the draw-
10   ing out of any writings at all. And she is determined never to thwart
Miss's inclinations, and left it to us to give the old gentleman his
discharge at the next visit.

CAPTAIN. Shall I undertake the old dragon?

TAG. If we have occasion for help, we shall call for you.

BIDDY. I expect him every moment. Therefore I'll tell you what,
Rhodophil; you and your man shall be locked up in my bedchamber
till we have settled matters with the old gentleman.

CAPTAIN. Do what you please with me.

BIDDY. You must not be impatient though.

20   CAPTAIN. I can undergo anything with such a reward in view. One kiss
and I'll be quite resigned—and now, show me the way.

Exeunt.

TAG. Come, sirrah. When I have got you under lock and key, I shall
bring you to reason.

PUFF. Are your wedding clothes ready, my Dove? The certificate's
come.

TAG. Go follow your captain, sirrah, march! You may thank heaven
I had patience to stay so long.

Exeunt Tag *and* Puff.

Enter Biddy.

BIDDY. I was very much alarmed for fear my two gallants should come
in upon us unawares. We should have had sad work if they had.
30   I find I love Rhodophil vastly, for though my other sparks flatter
me more, I can't abide the thoughts of 'em now. I have business
upon my hands enough to turn my little head, but, egad, my heart's
good, and a fig for dangers. Let me see—what shall I do with my
two gallants? I must at least part with 'em decently. Suppose I set

'em together by the ears? The luckiest thought in the world! For if
they won't quarrel (as I believe they won't) I can break with 'em
for cowards and very justly dismiss 'em my service. And if they
will fight and one of 'em should be killed, the other will certainly
be hanged or run away, and so I shall very handsomely get rid of
both. I am glad I have settled it so purely.

Enter Tag.

Well, Tag, are they safe?

TAG. I think so. The door's double-locked and I have the key in my
    pocket.

BIDDY. That's pure; but have you given 'em anything to divert 'em?

TAG. I have given the Captain one of your old gloves to mumble, but
    my Strephon is diverting himself with the more substantial com-
    forts of a cold venison pasty.

BIDDY. What shall we do with the next that comes?

TAG. If Mr. Fribble comes first, I'll clap him up into my lady's store-
    room. I suppose he is a great maker of marmalade himself and will
    have an opportunity of making some critical remarks upon our
    pastry and sweetmeats.

BIDDY. When one of 'em comes, do you go and watch for the other;
    and as soon as you see him, run in to us and pretend it is my aunt;
    and so we shall have an excuse to lock him up till we want him.

TAG. You may depend upon me. Here is one of 'em.

Enter Fribble.

BIDDY. Mr. Fribble, your servant.

FRIBBLE. Miss Biddy, your slave. I hope I have not come upon you
    abruptly. I should have waited upon you sooner, but an accident
    happened that discomposed me so that I was obliged to go home
    again to take drops.

BIDDY. Indeed, you don't look well, Sir. Go, Tag, and do as I bid you.

TAG. I will, Madam.

Exit.

BIDDY. I have set my maid to watch my aunt, that we mayn't be sur-
    prised by her.

FRIBBLE. Your prudence is equal to your beauty, Miss, and I hope your
    permitting me to kiss your hands will be no impeachment of your
    understanding.

---

45. your] our *W*2.
47. pasty] pastry *W*2.
68. of] to *W*1, *W*2, O6.

70   BIDDY. (*aside*).   I hate the sight of him.—I was afraid I should not have
          had the pleasure of seeing you. Pray let me know what accident
          you met with and what's the matter with your hand? I shan't be
          easy till I know.

      FRIBBLE.   Well, I vow, Miss Biddy, you're a good creater. I'll endeavor
          to muster up what little spirits I have and tell you the whole affair.
          Hem! But first you must give me leave to make you a present of
          a small pot of my lip salve. My servant made it this morning. The
          ingredients are innocent, I assure you; nothing but the best Virgin's-
          wax, Conserve of Roses, and Lily of the Valley Water.

80   BIDDY.   I thank you, Sir, but my lips are generally red, and when they
          an't I bite 'em.

      FRIBBLE.   I bite my own sometimes to pout 'em a little, but this will
          give 'em a softness, color, and an agreeable moister. Thus let me
          make an humble offering at that shrine where I have already sacri-
          ficed my heart. (*Kneels and gives the pot.*)

      BIDDY.   Upon my word that's very prettily expressed. You are positively
          the best company in the world. (*Aside.*) I wish he was out of the
          house.

      FRIBBLE.   But to return to my accident and the reason why my hand is
90   in this condition—I beg you'll excuse the appearance of it, and be
          satisfied that nothing but mere necessity could have forced me to
          appear thus muffled before you.

      BIDDY.   I am very willing to excuse any misfortune that happens to
          you, Sir. (*Curtsies.*)

      FRIBBLE.   You are vastly good, indeed. Thus it was—hem!—You must
          know, Miss, there is not an animal in the creation I have so great an
          aversion to as those hackney-coach fellows. As I was coming out
          of my lodgings, says one of 'em to me, "Would your Honor have
          a coach?" "No, man," said I, "not now," (with all the civility
100   imaginable). "I'll carry you and your doll too," says he, "Miss
          Margery, for the same price." Upon which the masculine beasts
          about us fell a-laughing. Then I turned round in a great passion.
          "Curse me," says I, "fellow, but I'll trounce thee." And as I was hold-
          ing out my hand in a threatening poster, thus, he makes a cut at me
          with his whip, and striking me over the nail of my little finger it
          gave me such exquisite torter that I fainted away. And while I was
          in this condition, the mob picked my pocket of my purse, my scis-

---

72–73. I shan't . . . know] Omitted *W*1, *W*2.
   74.   creater] *O*1, *O*2, *Q*1, *D*1, *D*2, *D*4, *O*5, *W*2; creeter *O*3, *O*4, *W*1, *O*6;
          creature *D*3.
78–79. Virgin's-wax] *O*1, *O*2, *Q*1, *D*1, *D*2, *D*3, *O*5; Virgin-wax *O*3, *O*4, *D*4, *W*1,
          *W*2, *O*6.

sors, my Mocoa smellingbottle, and my huswife.

BIDDY (*aside*). I shall laugh in his face.—I am afraid you are in great
pain. Pray sit down. Mr. Fribble. But I hope your hand is in no
danger. (*They sit.*)

FRIBBLE. Not in the least, Maam; pray don't be apprehensive. A milk-
poultice and a gentle sweat tonight, with a little manna in the
morning, I am confident, will relieve me entirely.

BIDDY. But pray, Mr. Fribble, do you make use of a huswife?

FRIBBLE. I can't do without it, Maam. There is a club of us, all young
bachelors, the sweetest society in the world, and we meet three
times a week at each other's lodgings, where we drink tea, hear the
chat of the day, invent fashions for the ladies, make models of 'em
and cut out patterns in paper. We were the first inventors of knot-
ting, and this fringe is the original produce and joint labor of our
little community.

BIDDY. And who are your pretty set, pray?

FRIBBLE. There's Phil Whiffle, Jacky Wagtail, my Lord Trip, Billy
Dimple, Sir Dilbery Diddle, and your humble —

BIDDY. What a sweet collection of happy creatures!

FRIBBLE. Indeed and so we are, Miss. But a prodigious fracas disconcerted us a little on our visiting-day at Billy Dimple's. Three
drunken naughty women of the town burst into our clubroom,
cursed us all, threw down the china, broke six looking-glasses,
scalded us with the slop-basin, and scrat poor Phil Whiffle's cheek
in such a manner that he has kept his bed these three weeks.

BIDDY. Indeed, Mr. Fribble, I think all our sex have great reason to be
angry; for if you are so happy now you are bachelors, the ladies
may wish and sigh to very little purpose.

FRIBBLE. You are mistaken, I assure you. I am prodigiously rallied
about my passion for you, I can tell you that, and am looked upon
as lost to our society already. He, he, he!

BIDDY. Pray, Mr. Fribble, now you have gone so far, don't think me
impudent if I long to know how you intend to use the lady who
shall be honored with your affections.

108. Mocoa] Mocco *W*1, *W*2.
124. Jacky] Jackey *W*1, *W*2.
128. a little] Omitted *W*1.
      on our visiting day] *O*1, *O*2, *D*1, *O*3, *D*2, *O*4, *D*3, *O*5, *D*4, *O*6; some time
      ago *Q*1, *W*1, *W*2.
131. scrat] *O*1, *O*2, *Q*1, *D*1, *O*3, *O*4, *D*3, *O*5, *W*1, *D*2, *D*4; scratch'd *W*2, *O*6.
140. intend] *O*1, *O*2, *Q*1, *D*1, *O*3, *D*2, *O*4, *D*3, *O*5, *D*4; intended *W*1, *W*2,
      *O*6.
140-41. who shall be] *O*1, *O*2, *Q*1, *D*1, *O*3, *D*2, *O*4, *D*3, *O*5, *D*4, *W*1, *W*2; who
      have been *O*6.

FRIBBLE.   Not as most other wives are used, I assure you. All the domestic business will be taken off her hands. I shall make the tea, comb the dogs, and dress the children myself, if I should be blessed with any; so that, though I'm a commoner, Mrs. Fribble will lead the life of a woman of quality, for she will have nothing to do but lie in bed, play at cards, and scold the servants.

BIDDY.   What a happy creature she must be!

FRIBBLE.   Do you really think so? Then pray let me have a little serous
150   talk with you. Though my passion is not of a long standing, I hope the sincerity of my intentions —

BIDDY.   Ha, ha, ha!

FRIBBLE.   Go, you wild thing! (*Pats her.*) The devil take me but there is no talking to you. How can you use me in this barbarous manner? If I had the constitution of an alderman it would sink under my sufferings—*hooman nater* can't support it.

BIDDY.   Why, what would you do with me, Mr. Fribble?

FRIBBLE.   Well, I vow I'll beat you if you talk so. Don't look at me in that manner—flesh and blood can't bear it. I could—but I won't grow
160   indecent.

BIDDY.   But pray, Sir, where are the verses you were to write upon me? I find if a young lady depends too much upon such fine gentlemen as you, she'll certainly be disappointed.

FRIBBLE.   I vow, the flutter I was put into this afternoon has quite turned my senses. There they are, though, and I believe you'll like 'em.

BIDDY.   There can be no doubt of it.

FRIBBLE.   I protest, Miss, I don't like that curtsy. Look at me, and always rise in this manner. (*Shows her.*) But, my dear *Creater*, who
170   put on your cap today? They have made a fright of you, and it's as yellow as old Lady Crowfoot's neck. When we are settled, I'll dress your heads myself.

BIDDY.   Pray read your verses to me, Mr. Fribble.

FRIBBLE.   I obey—hem; William Fribble, Esq., to Miss Biddy Bellair— greeting.

> No ice so hard, so cold as I,
> Till warmed and softened by your eye;
> And now my heart dissolves away

144-45.   if I ... any] *O*1, *O*2, *D*1, *D*2, *D*3, *O*5; omitted *Q*1, *O*3, *O*4, *D*4, *W*1, *W*2, *O*6.

149.   serous] *O*1, *O*2, *Q*1, *D*1, *O*3, *D*2, *O*4, *O*5, *O*6, *W*1, *W*2; serious *D*3, *D*4.

165.   There] *O*1, *O*2, *Q*1, *D*1, *D*2, *D*3, *O*5, *D*4, *O*6; Here *O*3, *O*4, *W*1, *W*2.

169.   Creater] *O*1, *O*2, *Q*1, *D*1, *O*3, *D*2, *O*4, *D*3, *O*5; creeter *D*4, *W*1, *W*2, *O*6.

172.   heads] *O*1, *O*2, *Q*1, *D*1, *O*3, *D*2, *O*4, *D*3, *O*5, *D*4, *W*1, *W*2; head *O*6.

In dreams by night and sighs by day.
180   No brutal passion fires my breast,
Which loathes the object when possessed;
But one of harmless, gentle kind,
Whose joys are centered—in the mind.
Then take with me love's better part,
His downy wing, but not his dart.

How do you like 'em?

BIDDY.   Ha, ha, ha! I swear they are very pretty. But I don't quite understand 'em.

FRIBBLE.   These light pieces are never so well understood in reading as
190   singing. I have set 'em myself and will endeavor to give 'em you.—
La-la—, I have an abominable cold and can't sing a note. However,
the tune's nothing, the manner's all.

No ice so hard, &c. (*Sings.*)

Enter Tag, *running.*

TAG.   Your aunt! your aunt! your aunt, Madam!

FRIBBLE.   What's the matter?

BIDDY.   Hide, hide, Mr. Fribble, Tag, or we are ruined.

FRIBBLE.   Oh, for heaven's sake, put me anywhere so I don't dirty my
clothes.

BIDDY.   Put him into the storeroom, Tag, this moment.

200   FRIBBLE.   Is it a damp place, Mrs. Tag? The floor is boarded, I hope?

TAG.   Indeed it is not, Sir.

FRIBBLE.   What shall I do? I shall certainly catch my death! Where's
my cambric handkerchief and my salts? I shall certainly have my
hysterics!

Runs in.

BIDDY.   In, in, in! So now let the other come as soon as he will. I did
not care if I had twenty of 'em, so they would but come one after
another.

Enter Tag.

Was my aunt coming?

TAG.   No, 'twas Mr. Flash, I suppose, by the length of his stride and the
210   cock of his hat. He'll be here this minute. What shall we do with
him?

BIDDY.   I'll manage him, I warrant you, and try his courage. Be sure you
are ready to second me; we shall have pure sport.

TAG.   Hush! Here he comes.

---

179. and] *O1, O2, D1, D3, O5, D4;* in *Q1, D2, O3, O4, W1, W2, O6.*

Enter Flash, *singing.*

FLASH.   Well, my blossom, here am I! What hopes for a poor dog, eh? (*Aside.*) How! the maid here! then I've lost the town, dammee! Not a shilling to bribe the governor. She'll spring a mine and I shall be blown to the devil.

BIDDY.   Don't be ashamed, Mr. Flash, I have told Tag the whole affair,
220   and she's my friend, I can assure you.

FLASH (*aside*).   Is she? Then she won't be mine, I am certain.—Well, Mrs. Tag, you know, I suppose, what's to be done. This young lady and I have contracted ourselves, and so, if you please to stand bridemaid, why we'll fix the wedding-day directly.

TAG.   The wedding-day, Sir?

FLASH.   The wedding-day, Sir? Ay, Sir, the wedding-day, Sir. What have you to say to that, Sir?

BIDDY.   My dear Captain Flash, don't make such a noise. You'll wake my aunt.

230   FLASH.   And suppose I did, Child, what then?

BIDDY.   She'd be frightened out of her wits.

FLASH.   At me, Miss, frightened at me? *Tout au contraire*, I assure you. You mistake the thing, Child. I have some reason to believe I am not quite so shocking. (*Affectedly.*)

TAG.   Indeed, Sir, you flatter yourself. But pray, Sir, what are your pretensions?

FLASH.   The lady's promises, my own passion, and the best mounted blade in the three kingdoms. If any man can produce a better title, let him take her; if not, the D——l mince me if I give up an atom of
240   her.

BIDDY.   He's in a fine passion, if he would but hold it.

TAG.   Pray, Sir, hear reason a little.

FLASH.   I never do, Madam; it is not my method of proceeding. Here's my logic! (*Draws his sword.*) Sa, sa—my best argument is cart over arm, Madam, ha, ha! (*Lunges.*) And if he answers that, Madam, through my small guts, my breath, blood, and mistress are all at his service. Nothing more, Madam.

BIDDY.   This'll do, this'll do.

TAG.   But, Sir, Sir, Sir?

250   FLASH.   But Madam, Madam, Madam! I profess blood, Madam; I was bred up to it from a child. I study the book of fate, and the camp is my university. I have attended the lectures of Prince Charles

---

215.   eh?] he *D*3.
219.   ashamed] *O*1, *O*2, *Q*1, *D*1, *O*3, *D*2, *O*4, *O*5, *D*4, *O*6; alarmed *D*3, *W*1, *W*2.
252.   of] Dropped type *O*6.

upon the Rhine and Bathiani upon the Po, and have extracted knowledge from the mouth of a cannon. I'm not to be frightened with squibs, Madam. No, no.

BIDDY. Pray, dear Sir, don't mind her, but let me prevail wiih you to go away this time. Your passion is very fine, to be sure, and when my aunt and Tag are out of the way, I'll let you know when I'd have you come again.

260   FLASH. When you'd have me come again, Child? And suppose I never would come again, what do you think of that now, ha? You pretend to be afraid of your aunt. Your aunt knows what's what too well to refuse a good match when it's offered. Lookee, Miss, I'm a man of honor, glory's my aim. I have told you the road I am in, and do you see here, Child, (*Showing his aword.*) no tricks upon travelers.

BIDDY. But pray, Sir, hear me.

FLASH. No, no, no. I know the world, Madam. I am as well known at Covent-Garden as the Dial, Madam. I'll break a lamp, bully a con-
270   stable, bam a justice, or bilk a boxkeeper with any man in the liberties of Westminster. What do you think of me now, Madam?

BIDDY. Pray don't be so furious, Sir.

FLASH. Come, come, come, few words are best. Somebody's happier than somebody, and I'm a poor silly fellow, ha, ha! That's all. Look you, Child, to be short (for I'm a man of reflection) I have but a *baqatelle* to say to you. I am in love with you up to hell and desperation, may the sky crush me if I am not. But since there is another more fortunate than I, Adieu, Biddy! Prosperity to the happy rival, patience to poor Flash. But the first time we meet — gunpowder
280   be my perdition, but I'll have the honor to cut a throat with him. (*Going.*)

BIDDY (*stopping him.*)   You may meet with him now, if you please.

FLASH. Now, may I? Where is he? I'll sacrifice the villain! (*Aloud.*)

TAG. Hush, he's but in the next room.

FLASH. Is he? Ram me (*Low.*) into a mortarpiece but I'll have vengeance. My blood boils to be at him. Don't be frightened, Miss.

BIDDY. No, Sir, I never was better pleased, I assure you.

FLASH. I shall soon do his business.

BIDDY. As soon as you please. Take your own time.

290   TAG. I'll fetch the gentleman to you immediately. (*Going.*)

FLASH (*stopping her*). Stay, stay a little. What a passion I am in! Are

---

264. glory's] glory is my aim *W*2.
269. Dial] *O*1, *O*2, *Q*1, *D*1,*O*3, *D*2, *O*4, *D*3, *O*5, *D*4, *O*6; Dail *W*1, *W*2.
272. Pray . . . Sir] But pray, Sir, hear me. *W*2.
291. Stage direction *stopping her*] stoping her *W*2.

you sure he is in the next room? I shall certainly tear him to pieces;
I would fain murder him like a gentleman too. Besides, this family
shan't be brought into trouble upon my account. I have it—I'll
watch for him in the street and mix his blood with the puddle of
the next kennel. (*Going.*)

BIDDY (*stopping him*). No, pray Mr. Flash, let me see the battle. I
shall be glad to see you fight for me. You shan't go, indeed. (*Holding him.*)

TAG (*holding him*). Oh, pray let me see you fight. There were two
300   gentlemen fit yesterday, and my mistress was never so diverted in
her life. I'll fetch him out.

Exit.

BIDDY. Do stick him, stick him, Captain Flash. I shall love you the
better for it.

FLASH (*aside*). D——n your love! I wish I was out of the house.

BIDDY. Here he is. Now speak some of your hard words and run him
through.

FLASH (*aside to* Biddy). Don't be in fits now.

BIDDY. Never fear me.

Enter Tag *and* Fribble.

TAG (*to* Fribble). Take it on my word, Sir, he is a bully and nothing
310   else.

FRIBBLE (*frightened*). I know you are my good friend, but perhaps
you don't know his disposition.

TAG. I am confident he is a coward.

FRIBBLE. Is he? Nay, then I'm his man.

FLASH. I like his looks, but I'll not venture too far at first.

TAG. Speak to him, Sir.

FRIBBLE. I will. I understand, Sir—hem—that you—by Mrs. Tag here,
—Sir,—who has informed me—hem—that you have sent her to
inform me—Sir,—that you would be glad to speak with me—.

320   Demme! (*Turns off.*)

FLASH. I can speak to you, Sir, or to anybody, Sir—or I can let it alone
and hold my tongue, if I see occasion, Sir. Dammee — (*Turns off.*)

BIDDY. Well said, Mr. Flash. Be in a passion.

TAG (*to* Fribble). Don't mind his looks, he changes color already. To
him, to him! (*Pushes him.*)

FRIBBLE. Don't hurry me, Mrs. Tag, for heaven's sake! I shall be out
of breath before I begin if you do.—Sir, (*To* Flash.) if you can't

---

309. bully] bubble *D*3.
322. Dammee] Demme *W*1.

speak to a gentleman in another manner, Sir, why then I'll venture to say you had better hold your tongue. Oons!

330 FLASH. Sir, you and I are of different opinions.

FRIBBLE. You and your opinion may go to the devil. Take that. (*Turns off to* Tag.)

TAG. Well said, Sir, the day's your own.

BIDDY. What's the matter, Mr. Flash? Is all your fury gone? Do you give me up?

FRIBBLE. I have done his business.

FLASH. Give you up, Madam? No, Madam; when I am determined in my resolutions I am always calm. 'Tis our way, Madam. And now I shall proceed to business. Sir, I beg to say a word to you in private.

340 FRIBBLE. Keep your distance, fellow, and I'll answer you. That lady has confessed a passion for me, and as she has delivered up her heart into my keeping, nothing but my 'arts blood shall purchase it. Demnation!

TAG. Bravo! Bravo!

FLASH. If those are the conditions, I'll give you earnest for it directly. (*Draws.*) Now, villain, renounce all right and title this minute, or the torrent of my rage will overflow my reason and I shall annihilate the nothingness of your soul and body in an instant.

FRIBBLE. I wish there was a constable at hand to take us both up. We

350 shall certainly do one another a prejudice.

TAG. No you won't, indeed Sir. Pray bear up to him. If you would but draw your sword and be in a passion, he would run away directly.

FRIBBLE. Will he? (*Draws his sword.*) Then I can no longer contain myself. Hell and the Furies! Come on, thou savage brute!

TAG. Go on, Sir.

Here they stand in fighting postures, while Biddy
and Tag *push 'em forward.*

FLASH. Come on.

BIDDY. Go on.

FRIBBLE. Come on, rascal.

360 TAG. Go on, Sir.

Enter Captain Loveit *and* Puff.

CAPTAIN. What's the matter, my dear?

BIDDY. If you won't fight, here's one that will. Oh, Rhodophil, these two sparks are your rivals and have pestered me these two months

---

343. Demnation!] Damnation! *D*3, *W*1, *W*2.

with their addresses. They forced themselves into the house and have been quarreling about me and disturbing the family. If they won't fight, pray kick 'em out of the house.

CAPTAIN. What's the matter, gentlemen?

They both keep their fencing posture.

FLASH. Don't part us, Sir.

FRIBBLE No, pray Sir, don't part us. We shall do you a mischief.

370 CAPTAIN. Puff, look to the other gentleman and call a surgeon.

BIDDY and TAG. Ha, ha, ha!

PUFF. Bless me! How can you stand under your wounds, Sir?

FRIBBLE. Am I hurt, Sir?

PUFF. Hurt, Sir! Why you have, let me see—pray stand in the light—one, two, three through the heart and, let me see—hum—eight through the small guts. Come, Sir, make it up a round dozen and then we'll part you.

ALL. Ha, ha, ha!

CAPTAIN. Come here, Puff. (*Whispers and looks at* Flash.)

380 PUFF. 'Tis the very same, Sir.

CAPTAIN (*to* Flash). Pray, Sir, have I not had the pleasure of seeing your face abroad?

FLASH. I have served abroad.

CAPTAIN. Had not you the misfortune, Sir, to be missing at the last engagement in Flanders?

FLASH. I was found amongst the dead in the field of battle.

PUFF. He was the first that fell, Sir. The wind of a cannonball struck him flat upon his face. He had just strength enough to creep into a ditch, and there he was found after the battle in a most deplorable

390 condition.

CAPTAIN. Pray, Sir, what advancement did you get by the service of that day?

FLASH. My wounds rendered me unfit for service and I sold out.

PUFF. Stole out, you mean. We hunted him by scent to the waterside, thence he took shipping for England and, taking the advantage of my master's absence, has attacked his citadel, which we are luckily come to relieve and drive his Honor into the ditch again.

ALL. Ha, ha, ha!

FRIBBLE. He, he, he!

400 CAPTAIN. And now, Sir, how have you dared to show your face again in open day, or wear even the outside of a profession you have so

365. If] Omitted *W*2.
382. your face] Omitted *D*1, *D*2, *D*3, *D*4; you abroad *W*1, *W*2, *O*6.
396. his] *O*1, *O*2, *Q*1, *D*1, *D*2, *D*3, *D*4, *O*3, *O*4, *O*5; the *W*1, *W*2, *O*6.

much scandalized by your behavior? I honor the name of soldier and, as a party concerned, am bound not to see it disgraced. As you have forfeited your title to honor, deliver up your sword this instant.

FLASH. Nay, good Captain, —

CAPTAIN. No words, Sir. (*Takes his sword.*)

FRIBBLE. He's a sad scoundrel. I wish I had kicked him.

CAPTAIN. The next thing I command—leave this house, change the
410   color of your clothes and fierceness of your looks, appear from top to toe the wretch, the very wretch, thou art. If e'er I meet thee in the military dress again, or if you put on looks that belie the native baseness of thy heart, be it where it will, this shall be the reward of thy impudence and disobedience. (*Kicks him; he runs off.*)

[*Exit.*]

BIDDY. Oh, my dear Rhodophil!

FRIBBLE. What an infamous rascal it is! I thank you, Sir, for this favor; but I must after and cane him. (*Going, is stopped by the* Captain.)

CAPTAIN. One word with you too, Sir.

FRIBBLE. With me, Sir?

420 CAPTAIN. You need not tremble. I shan't use you roughly.

FRIBBLE. I am certain of that, Sir, but I am sadly troubled with weak nerves.

CAPTAIN. Thou art a species too despicable for correction. Therefore be gone. And if I see you here again, your insignificancy shan't protect you.

FRIBBLE. I am obliged to you for your kindness. (*Aside.*) But if ever I have anything to do with intrigues again —

[*Exit.*]

ALL. Ha, ha, ha!

PUFF. Shall I ease you of your trophy, Sir?

430 CAPTAIN. Take it, Puff, as some small recompense for thy fidelity. Thou can'st better use it than its owner.

PUFF. I wish your Honor had a patent to take such trifles from every pretty gentleman that could spare 'em. I would set up the largest cutler's shop in the kingdom.

CAPTAIN. Well said, Puff.

BIDDY. But pray, Mr. Fox, how did you get out of your hole? I thought you was locked in.

CAPTAIN. I shot the bolt back when I heard a noise, and thinking you

---

411. the very wretch] Omitted *W*1, *W*2.
427.1. [*Exit.*] Added stage direction *Q*1, *O*3, *O*4, *W*1, *W*2.

were in danger I broke my confinement without any other con-
440   sideration than your safety. (*Kisses her hand.*)

SIR SIMON (*without*).   Biddy, Biddy! Why, Tag!

BIDDY.   There's the old gentleman. Run in, run in.

Exeunt Captain *and* Puff. Tag *opens the door.*

Enter Sir Simon *and* Jasper.

SIR SIMON.   Where have you been, Biddy? Jasper and I have knocked
and called as loud and as long as we were able. What were you
doing, Child?

BIDDY.   I was reading part of a play to Tag, and we came as soon as we
heard you.

SIR SIMON.   What play, Moppet?

BIDDY.   *The Old Batchelor*—and we were just got to old Nykyn as you
450   knocked at the door.

SIR SIMON.   I must have you burn your plays and romances now that
you are mine. They corrupt your innocence; and what can you
learn from 'em?

BIDDY.   What you can't teach me, I'm sure.

SIR SIMON.   Fy, fy, Child. I never heard you talk at this rate before. I'm
afraid you, Tag, put these things into her head.

TAG.   I, Sir? I vow, Sir Simon, she knows more than you can conceive.
She surprises me, I assure you, though I have been married these
two years and lived with batchelors most part of my life.

460   SIR SIMON.   Do you hear, Jasper? I'm all over in a sweat. Pray, Miss, have
not you had company this afternoon? I saw a young fop go out
of the house as I was coming hither.

BIDDY.   You might have seen two, Sir Simon, if your eyes had been
good.

SIR SIMON.   Do you hear, Jasper? Sure the child is possessed. Pray, Miss,
what did they want here?

BIDDY.   Me, Sir; they wanted me.

SIR SIMON.   What did they want with you, I say?

BIDDY.   Why, what do you want with me?

470   SIR SIMON.   Do you hear, Jasper? I am thunderstruck! I can't believe my
own ears. Tell me the reason, I say, why —

TAG.   I'll tell you the reason why, if you please, Sir Simon. Miss, you
know, is a very silly young girl, and having found out, heaven
knows how, that there is some little difference between sixty-five

---

441.   Why, Tag!] Why, Tag, Tag! Q1, O3, O4, D4, W1, W2, O6.
455–56.   I'm . . . you, Tag] I'm afraid, Tag, you Q1, O3, O4, D4, W1, W2, O6.
468.   they] the D3.

and twenty-five, she's ridiculous enough to choose the latter; when if she'd taken my advice —

SIR SIMON. You are right, Tag. She would take me, eh?

TAG. Yes, Sir, as the only way to have both; for if she marries you the other will follow of course.

480 SIR SIMON. Do you hear, Jasper?

BIDDY. 'Tis very true, Sir Simon. From my knowing no better, I have set my heart upon a young man, and a young one I'll have. There have been three here this afternoon.

SIR SIMON. Three, Jasper!

BIDDY. And they have been quarreling about me, and one has beat the other two. Now, Sir Simon, if you'll take up the conqueror and kick him as he has kicked the others, you shall have me for your reward and my fifteen thousand pounds into the bargain. What says my hero, eh? (*Slaps him on the back.*)

490 SIR SIMON. The world's at an end! What's to be done, Jasper?

JASPER. Pack up and be gone. Don't fight the match, Sir.

SIR SIMON. Flesh and blood cannot bear it. I'm all over agitation, hugh, hugh! am I cheated by a baby, a doll? Where's your aunt, you young cockatrice? I'll let her know. She's a base woman, and you are —

BIDDY. You are in a fine humor to show your valor. Tag, fetch the Captain this minute, while Sir Simon is warm, and let him know he is waiting here to cut his throat.

Exit Tag.

I locked him up in my bedchamber till you came.

500 SIR SIMON. Here's an imp of darkness! What would I give that my son Bob was here to thrash her spark, while I ravished the rest of the family.

JASPER. I believe we had best retire, Sir.

SIR SIMON. No, no, I must see her bully first. And, do you hear, Jasper, if I put him in a passion do you knock him down.

JASPER. Pray keep your temper, Sir.

Enter Captain, Tag, *and* Puff.

CAPTAIN (*approaching angrily*). What is the meaning, Sir? Ounds! 'tis my father, Puff. What shall I do? (*Aside.*)

---

481. my] Omitted *W*2.
492. cannot] can't *W*1, *W*2, *O*6.
501. spark] sparks *D*3.
507. What is] What's *W*1, *W*2.
'tis] *O*1, *O*2, *Q*1, *O*3, *D*1, *D*2, *D*3, *O*5; it is *O*4, *D*4, *W*1, *W*2, *O*6.

PUFF (*drawing him by the coat*). Kennel again, Sir.

510 SIR SIMON (*staring*). I am enchanted.

CAPTAIN. There is no retreat. I must stand it.

BIDDY. What's all this?

SIR SIMON. Your humble servant, Captain Fireball. You are welcome from the wars, noble Captain. I did not think I should have the pleasure of being knocked o' th' head or cut up alive by so fine a gentleman.

CAPTAIN. I am under such confusion, Sir, I have not power to convince you of my innocence.

SIR SIMON. Innocence, pretty lamb! And so, Sir, you have left the
520 regiment and the honorable employment of fighting for your country to come home and cut your father's throat. Why, you'll be a great man in time, Bob.

BIDDY. His father, Tag!

SIR SIMON. Come, come. 'Tis soon done. One stroke does it; or, if you have any qualms, let your squire there perform the operation.

PUFF. Pray, Sir, don't throw such temptations in my way.

CAPTAIN. Hold your impudent tongue!

SIR SIMON. Why don't you speak, Mr. Modesty? What excuse have you for leaving the army, I say?

530 CAPTAIN. My affection to this lady.

SIR SIMON. Your affection, puppy!

CAPTAIN. Our love, Sir, has been long and mutual. What accidents have happened since my going abroad and her leaving the country, and how I have most unaccountably met you here, I am a stranger to. But whatever appearances may be, I still and ever was your dutiful son.

BIDDY. He talks like an angel, Tag!

SIR SIMON. Dutiful, Sirrah? Have you not rivalled your father?

CAPTAIN. No, Sir, you have rivalled me. My claim must be prior to yours.

540 BIDDY. Indeed, Sir Simon, he can show the best title to me.

JASPER. Sir, Sir, the young gentleman speaks well, and as the fortune will not go out of the family, I would advise you to drop your resentment, be reconciled to your son, and relinquish the lady.

SIR SIMON. Ay, ay, with all my heart. Lookye, Son, I give you up the girl. She's too much for me, I confess. And take my word, Bob, you'll catch a tartar.

BIDDY. I assure you, Sir Simon, I'm not the person you take me for. If

---

509. Kennel] Kneel *O6.*

510. Stage direction *staring*] *starting W*2.

544. give you up] *O*1, *O*2, *Q*1, *D*1, *O*3, *D*2, *O*4, *D*3, *O*5, *D*4; give you the girl *W*1, *W*2, *O*6.

I have used you any ways ill, 'twas for your son's sake, who had
my promise and inclinations before you. And though I believe I
550   should have made you a most uncomfortable wife, I'll be the best
daughter to you in the world. And if you stand in need of a lady,
my aunt is disengaged and is the best nurse —

SIR SIMON.   No, no, I thank you, Child. You have so turned my stomach
to marriage I have no appetite left. But where is this aunt? Won't
she stop your proceedings, think you?

TAG.   She's now at her lawyer's, Sir, and if you please to go with the
young couple and give your approbation, I'll answer for my old
lady's consent.

BIDDY.   The Captain and I, Sir —

560   SIR SIMON.   Come, come, Bob, you are but an ensign; don't impose on
the girl neither.

CAPTAIN.   I had the good fortune, Sir, to please my royal general by
my behavior in a small action with the enemy, and he gave me a
company.

SIR SIMON.   Bob, I wish you joy. This is news indeed. And when we
celebrate your wedding, Son, I'll drink a half pint bumper myself
to your benefactor.

CAPTAIN.   And he deserves it, Sir. Such a general by his example and
justice animates us to deeds of glory and insures us conquest.

570   SIR SIMON.   Right, my boy. Come along, then. (*Going.*)

PUFF.   Halt a little, gentlemen, and ladies, if you please. Everybody
here seems well satisfied but myself.

CAPTAIN.   What's the matter, Puff?

PUFF.   Sir, as I would make myself worthy of such a master, and the
name of soldier, I cannot put up the least injury to my honor.

SIR SIMON.   Heyday! What flourishes are these?

PUFF.   Here is the man. (*To* Jasper.) Come forth, caitiff! He hath confessed this day that, in my absence, he had taken freedoms with my
lawful wife and had dishonorable intentions against my bed; for
580   which I demand satisfaction.

SIR SIMON (*striking him*).   What stuff is here, the fellow's brain's
turned.

PUFF.   And cracked too, Sir. But you are my master's father and I
submit.

CAPTAIN.   Come, come, I'll settle your punctillios and will take care
of you and Tag hereafter, provided you drop all animosities and
shake hands this moment.

PUFF.   My revenge gives way to my interest, and I once again, Jasper,
take you to my bosom.

589.   you] *O1, O2, Q1, D1, O3, D2, O4, D3, O5, D4;* thee *W1, W2, O6.*

590 JASPER.   I'm your friend again, Puff. But harkee, I fear you not. And if
       you'll lay aside your steel there, as far as a broken head or a black
       eye, I'm at your service upon demand.

   TAG.   You are very good at crowing indeed, Mr. Jasper. But let me tell
       you, the fool that is rogue enough to brag of a woman's favors must
       be a dunghill every way. As for you, my dear Husband, show your
       manhood in a proper place and you need not fear these sheep-biters.

   SIR SIMON.   The Abigail is pleasant, I confess. He, he!

   BIDDY.   I'm afraid the town will be ill-natured enough to think I have
       been a little coquettish in my behavior; but I hope, as I have been
600   constant to the Captain, I shall be excused diverting myself with
       pretenders.

           Ladies, to fops and braggarts ne'er be kind.
           No charms can warm 'em and no virtues bind.
           Each lover's merit by his conduct prove,
           Who fails in honor will be false in love.

                                                            Exeunt.

Epilogue

By the same Hand as the Prologue.
Spoke by Mrs. PRITCHARD.

Good folks, I'm come at my young lady's bidding
To say, you all are welcome to her wedding.
Th' exchange she made, what mortal here can blame?
Show me the maid that would not do the same.
For sure the greatest monster ever seen
Is doting sixty coupled to sixteen!
When wintry age had almost caught the fair,
Youth clad in sunshine snatched her from despair.
Like a new Semele the virgin lay,
And clasped her lover in the blaze of day.
Thus may each maid, the toils almost entrapped-in,
Change old Sir Simon for the brisk young Captain.
    I love these men of arms, they know their trade;
Let dastards sue, these sons of fire invade.
They cannot bear around the bait to nibble,
Like pretty, powdered, patient Mr. Fribble.
To dangers bred, and skilful in command,
They storm the strongest fortress sword in hand.
Nights without sleep, and floods of tears when waking,
Showed poor Miss Biddy was in piteous taking.
She's now quite well; for maids in that condition
Find the young lover is the best physician;
And without helps of art or boast of knowledge,
They cure more women, faith, than all the college.
    But to the point. I come with low petition,
For, faith, poor Bayes is in a sad condition.
*The huge tall hangman stands to give the blow,
And only waits your pleasures—Ay or No.

---

* Alluding to *Bayes's* Prologue in the *Rehearsal*.

If you should—Pit, Box, and Gallery, egad!
Joy turns his senses and the man runs mad.
But if your ears are shut, your hearts are rock,
And you pronounce the sentence—block to block,
Down kneels the bard and leaves you when he's dead,
The empty tribute of an author's head.

30

Lilliput
A Dramatic Entertainment
1756

LILLIPUT.

A

Dramatic Entertainment.

As it is performed at the

THEATRE-ROYAL

IN

DRURY-LANE.

─────Eadem cupient, facientque MINORES.   JUVEN. Sat. 1.

LONDON:

Printed for PAUL VAILLANT, facing *Southampton-Street*, in the *Strand*.
MDCCLVII.

[Price One Shilling.]

Advertisement

Strand, Dec. 11, 1756

To the Reader.

The following letter came to my hands on Friday. I hope the author will excuse my printing it, as it will be impossible for me to read it to every person who has made, or shall make, objections to his performance.

> I am the Reader's
> Most obedient servant,
> PAUL VAILLANT.

R——, Dec. 8, 1756.

To Mr. VAILLANT.

Sir,

I thank you for your letter and the criticisms, which, by some mistake, I did not receive till this morning. I am surprised that you should seem uneasy at the objections which are made to Lilliput; for, be assured, if it is worth carping at, it will be worth buying; and then it will at least answer your end. However, since the critics, as you call 'em, will nibble at my dramatic morsel, I shall, like my Brother Bayes, throw a crust among 'em, that will rub their gums a little, I'll warrant ye. They are angry, you say, that I make Fripperel talk of firing a broadside, when it may be seen in Gulliver's Travels, that the people of Lilliput had not the use of gunpowder. In answer to which, I shall quote a passage from a Lilliputian manuscript, which was brought over by Gulliver, and shown to me by the gentleman to whom he left all his curiosities. The

passage is this: *Udel mis Aleph penden tipadel quif menef duren.* This, I think, will satisfy you, Mr. Vaillant, and stop the mouth of the most voracious critic of them all. They like-
30   wise complain with some warmth that in the magnificent en-
try of Gulliver into the capital there is but one lady of quality (Lady Flimnap) and her retinue in the procession. This objection, I must confess, has weight with it and is a great over-
sight, not of the author but of the manager; for in a letter to him, a copy of which I can produce, I gave him my full and free permission to make as many ladies of quality for the purpose, as he should think proper.

    Many, you tell me, think the performance too satirical upon the ladies—of Lilliput, I hope they mean; for I defy any of
40   the objectors to produce me a woman of fashion of their ac-
quaintance who has any follies in common with those in the following piece. The ingredients that compose the ladies of the two nations are as different (I speak it with great defer-
ence to Mr. Walter Baker) as those which are to be found in the powders of Dr. James and those of the late Baron Schwanberg. But their capital objection is that I have devi-
ated from Gulliver's true history, in order to defame a woman of the first quality, whose innocence has been so justly cel-
ebrated by Captain Lemuel himself.

50   Mr. Jacob Wilkinson, an old gentleman, who was former-
ly a haberdasher at Redriff and an intimate of Gulliver's, has frequently related to me many anecdotes of his friend, and particularly last summer at our Sunday Evening Club, when we had sat pretty late, and all the company had left us but Mr. R——, the attorney; the Reverend Mr. P——, Mr. Justice D——, and myself, he told us the following curious cir-
cumstance.

    My good friend the Captain (said he, with some emotion) protested to me upon his deathbed that, though he was a great
60   traveler and a writer of travels, he never published but one falsehood, and that was about the Lady Flimnap. He acknowledged that, notwithstanding his endeavors to justify her in-
nocence in his book, she had really confessed a passion for him and had proposed to elope with him and fly to England. And as he thought the knowledge of this fact, which lay heavy upon his conscience, could not, after so long a time,

---

27. tipadel] *O1, W2*; tapadel *W1*.
51. haberdasher] *O1, W1*; heberdasher *W2*.
53. Sunday] *O1, W1*; Suday *W2*.

sully the honor of the Flimnap family, he begged of me to publish it to the world. I have obeyed my friend's command in part. I have told it in conversation to a multitude of people;
70 but I think it also incumbent upon me to print it. Pray give me your opinion, gentlemen, in what manner shall I usher it into the world?

The clergyman said it was a pity the Captain had not left a sum of money for a funeral sermon, as the story might very aptly have been introduced in it among the rest of his virtues and given the sermon a great sale.

The Justice imagined that it might more properly be introduced in a charge to the Grand Jury, as it was a strong instance of the force of truth, in contra-distinction to the present loose
80 morals of the age.

My friend the attorney advised the printing a narrative and immediately prosecuting the publisher, that they then might proceed to trial, which being a rich one, would make a great noise, and the printing of it would quickly disperse the story throughout the three kingdoms. When my opinion was asked, I complimented my three neighbors upon their great sagacity and begged leave to give them a maxim of Horace:

Segnius irritant animos demissa per aurem,
Quam quae sunt oculis subjecta fidelibus,

90 And therefore I proposed throwing the story into a little drama, which might if properly spirited, have some success from its novelty. And, upon intimating that the playhouses are generally as much crowded as the courts of justice, the Quarter Sessions, or indeed the churches, they approved of my plan, laughed heartily at the conceit, and Mr. Wilkinson entreated me to undertake it.

Thus, sir, have I given you the history of my performance. What the merit of it is will be best known to the spectators. However, if it is the means of helping so many poor children
100 (as you tell me are employed in the piece) to some mince pies this Christmas, though your printed copies of it should be found at the bottom of 'em, I shall not think that I have spent some leisure hours unprofitably.

I am, Sir,
Your sincere Friend and Servant,
W. C.

68. command] *O*1, *W*1; commands *W*2.
82. that they then] *O*1, *W*1; that then they *W*2.

Prologue

By Mr. Garrick.
Spoken by Mr. Woodward.

Behold a conjurer—that's something new,
For, as times go, my brethren are but few.
I've come with magic ring and taper wand
To waft you far from this your native land.
Ladies, don't fear. My coach is large and easy,
I know your humors and will drive to please ye.
Gently you'll ride, as in a fairy dream,
Your hoops unsqueezed, and not a beau shall scream.
What, still disordered? Well, I know your fright;
You shall be back in times for cards tonight;
Swift as Queen Mab within her hazelnut,
I'll set you safely down at Lilliput.
Away we go—Ge'up!—Ladies, keep your places,
And gentlemen—for shame!—don't screw your faces.
Softly, my imps and fiends, you critics there,
Pray sit you still, or I can never steer,
My devils are not the devils you need to fear.
Hold fast, my friends above, for, faith, we spin it;
My usual rate's a thousand miles a minute.
A statesman, now, could tell how high we soar;
Statesmen have been these airy jaunts before.
I see the land, the folks. What limbs! What features!
There's lords and ladies, too, the pretty creatures.
  Now to your sight these puppets I'll produce
Which may, if rightly heeded, turn to use;

Puppets not made of wood and played with wires,
But flesh and blood, and full of strange desires.
So strange, you'll scarce believe me should I tell,
For giant vices may in pigmies dwell.
30   Beware you lay not to the conjurer's charge,
That these in miniature are you in large.
To you these little folks have no relation,
As different in their manners as their nation,
To show your pranks requires no conjuration.
Open your eyes and ears—your mouths be shut,
England is vanished. (*Waves his wand.*) Enter Lilliput.
(*Strikes the curtain and sinks.*)

32-34. To you . . . conjuration] *O1*, *W2*; lines bracketed *W2*.

Dramatis Personae

Lord Flimnap	*Master* CAUTHERLY.
Bolgolam	*Master* SIMPSON.
Fripperel	*Master* LARGEAU.
Lalcon	*Miss* POPE.
Gulliver	*Mr.* BRANSBY.

A number of Lilliputian *Citizens, etc.*
Messrs. POPE, HURST, MARTIN, *etc.*

Lady Flimnap	*Miss* SIMPSON.
Toadel	*Miss* MATHEWS.

Lilliput

SCENE I.

Lord Flimnap's *apartment.*
Enter Flimnap.

FLIMNAP. This marriage is the devil. I have sold my liberty, ease, and pleasure, and in exchange have got a wife, a very wife! Ambition began my misery and matrimony has completed it. But have not other men of quality wives, nay, fashionable wives, and yet are happy? Then why am not I? Because I am a fool, a singular fool, who am troubled with vulgar feelings and awkward delicacies, though I was born a nobleman, know the world, and keep the best company.

Enter Bolgolam

BOLGOLAM. What, in the dumps, Brother Flimnap?
10 FLIMNAP. Aye, brother, deeply so.
BOLGOLAM. Why, what's the matter?
FLIMNAP. I am married.
BOLGOLAM. And to my sister. If she wrongs you, I'll do you justice; and, if you wrong her, I shall cut your throat, that's all.
FLIMNAP. My dear Admiral, I know your friendship and your honor and can trust both. I have sent for you and your brother Fripperel, as my wife's nearest relations, to open my heart to you and to beg your advice and assistance.
BOLGOLAM. *He* advise you? What can he advise you about? He was
20 bred to nothing but to pick his teeth and dangle after a court. So, unless you have a coat to lace, a feather to choose, or a monkey to buy, Fripperel can't assist you.

---

19. advise] *O*1, *W*1; advice *W*2.

FLIMNAP. But he is the brother of my wife, Admiral.

BOLGOLAM. So much the worse for her and you too, perhaps. If she has listened to him, I shan't be surprised that you have a bad time of it. Such fellows as he, who call themselves fine gentlemen, forsooth, corrupt the morals of a whole nation.

FLIMNAP. Indeed, Admiral, you are too severe.

BOLGOLAM. Indeed, my Lord Flimnap, I speak the truth. Time was when we had as little vice here in Lilliput as anywhere; but since we imported politeness and fashions from Blefuscu, we have thought of nothing but being fine gentlemen. And a fine gentleman, in my dictionary, stands for nothing but impertinence and affectation, without any one virtue, sincerity or real civility.

FLIMNAP. But, dear brother, contain yourself.

BOLGOLAM. 'Zounds, I can't. We shall be undone by our politeness. Those cursed Blefuscudians have been polishing us to destroy us. While we kept our own rough manners, we were more than a match for 'em; but since they have made us fine gentlemen, we don't fight the better for't, I can assure you.

Enter Fripperel.

FRIPPEREL. What, is my dear brother and magnanimous Admiral firing a broadside against those wretches who wear clean shirts and wash their faces, eh?

BOLGOLAM. I would always fire upon those, good brother, who dare not show their faces when King and Country want 'em.

FLIMNAP. My dear brothers, let us not wander from the subject of our meeting. I have sent to you for your advice and assistance in an affair that nearly concerns me as a man, a nobleman, and the father of a family.

FRIPPEREL. What can possibly, my dear lord, disturb your tranquility, while you have the fortune to purchase pleasures and health to enjoy 'em?

BOLGOLAM. Well said, Fripperel. There spoke the genius of a fine gentleman. Give him but dainties to tickle his palate, women's to flatter his vanity, and money to keep the dice agoing, and you may purchase his soul and have his honor and virtue thrown into the bargain.

FRIPPEREL. Well said, Admiral. I would as soon undertake to steer thy ship as teach thee manners.

---

54. women's] *O*1; womens *W*1; women *W*2.
55. agoing] *O*1, *W*1; going *W*2.

60   BOLGOLAM.   And I would sooner sink my ship than suffer such fellows as thee to come on board of her.

FLIMNAP.   I find, gentlemen, you had rather indulge your own spleen than assist your friend.

BOLGOLAM.   I have done.

FRIPPEREL.   Come, come; let us hear your grievances.

FLIMNAP.   Your sister has dishonored me.

BOLGOLAM.   I'll cut her to pieces.

FRIPPEREL.   She is a fine woman, and a woman of quality, and therefore ought not to be cut to pieces for trifles.

70   BOLGOLAM.   Thou art a fine gentleman and ought to be hanged! But what has she done?

FLIMNAP.   Hurt me, injured me, beyond reparation.

BOLGOLAM.   The devil, what?

FLIMNAP.   I am ashamed to tell you.

BOLGOLAM.   Out with it.

FLIMNAP.   Fallen in love with a monster.

BOLGOLAM.   A monster? Land or sea monster?

FLIMNAP.   The new prodigy. This Quinbus Flestrin, the Man Mountain, Gulliver, the English giant.

80   FRIPPEREL.   Ha, ha! What, and are you afraid, Brother, he should swallow her? For you cannot possibly be afraid of anything else.

BOLGOLAM.   I don't know what to think of this, in love with a monster. My sister has a great soul, to be sure, but all the women in Lilliput are in love with him, I think. The devil is in 'em, and now they have seen the English giant, they'll turn up their noses at such a lusty fellow as I am. But how do you know this? Have you intercepted her love letters?

FRIPPEREL.   Or have you caught her in his sleeve or coat pocket? or has she been locked up in his snuff box? Ha, ha, ha!

90   FLIMNAP.   I cannot bear to jest when the honor of myself and family are at stake. I have witnesses that she visits him every day and allows and takes great familiarities.

FRIPPEREL.   She's a woman of quality, you know, and therefore I cannot possibly agree to abridge my sister of her natural rights and privileges.

BOLGOLAM.   What, is cuckolding her husband a natural right?

FRIPPEREL.   Lord, brother, how coarsely you talk. Besides, you know it can't be, it can't be; for did not Gulliver tell us, when we talked to him about the customs of his country, that it was a maxim with

100   the English never to lie with another man's wife.

BOLGOLAM.   No matter for that. Though he's a monster among us, he

Miss Clara Fisher as Lord Flimnap in *Lilliput*.
Folger Shakespeare Library

may be as fine a gentleman as you are in his own country; and then
I would not take his word for a farthing.

FRIPPEREL.   Brother, I have no time to quarrel with you now; for Gulliver, you know, is to make his entrance immediately; he is to be
created a Nardac of this kingdom, and we have all orders from the
king to assist at the ceremony. So, brother Flimnap, better spirits
to you; and better manners to you, my dear Bully Broadside. Ha,
ha, ha!

Exit.

110 BOLGOLAM.   A pretty counsellor, truly, to consult with in cases of
honor! What is the meaning of bringing this Man-Mountain into
the metropolis and setting him at liberty? Zounds, if the whim
should take him to be frolicsome, he'd make as much mischief in
the city as a monkey among china.

FLIMNAP.   He has signed the Treaty of Alliance with us and is brought
here to receive honors and to be ready to assist us.

BOLGOLAM.   I wish he was out of the kingdom; for should he prove an
ungrateful monster, like some other of our allies, and join our
enemies, we shall consume our meat and drain our drink to a fine
120   purpose.

FLIMNAP.   'Tis my interest in particular to get him hence, if I can;
and therefore I will join you most cordially in any scheme to send
him out of the kingdom.

BOLGOLAM.   We'll think of it. (*Trumpets sound.*) What's that noise
for?

FLIMNAP.   To call the guards together to attend the procession. I will
put on my robes and call upon you to attend the ceremony.

BOLGOLAM.   I'll wait for you. (*Going.*) But do you hear, Brother, talk
to your wife roundly. Don't fight her at a distance, but grapple
130   with her; but if she won't strike, sink her.

Exit Bolgolam.

FLIMNAP.   Grapple with her, and if she won't strike, sink her! 'Tis
easily said, but not so easily done. These bachelors are always great
heroes 'till they marry, and then they meet with their match. Let
me see, why should I disturb myself about my lady's conduct,
when I have not the least regard for my lady herself? However,
by discovering her indiscretions, I shall have an excuse for mine;
and people of quality should purchase their ease at any rate.

Let jealousy torment the lower life,
Where the fond husband loves the fonder wife:

140   Ladies and lords should their affections smother,
         Be always easy, and despise each other.
         With us no vulgar passions should abide;
         For none become a nobleman but pride.

                                                          Exit.

         Enter Lady Flimnap *and* Fripperel, *peeping and laughing.*

LADY FLIMNAP.   Come, brother, the owls are flown. Ha, ha, ha! This
    is the most lucky accident. But—how came the letter into your
    hands?
FRIPPEREL.   The moment I left your poor husband, and my wise broth-
    er, consulting how to punish you for your unnatural love of this
    Gulliver —
150 BOTH.   Ha, ha, ha!
FRIPPEREL.   And was hastening to the palace to prepare for the pro-
    cession, an elderly lady (who, though past love matters herself,
    seemed willing to forward 'em) pulls me gently by the sleeve, and
    with an insinuating curtsey and an eye that spoke as wantonly as
    it could, whispered me: "My Lord—My Lord Flimnap—I am com-
    missioned to deliver this into your own hands, and hope to have
    the honor of being better known to you." Then, curtseying again,
    mumbled something, looked roguishly, and left me.
LADY FLIMNAP.   Ha, ha, ha! I am glad that I have caught at last my
160   most virtuous lord and master. Oh, these modest men; they are
    very devils! However, I can balance accounts with him. But, pray,
    read the billet-doux to me. I am impatient to hear what his slut
    says.
FRIPPEREL.   'Tis a most exquisite composition, and a discharge in full
    to you for all kinds of inclinations that you may have now or con-
    ceive hereafter, either for man or monster. Ha, ha, ha!
LADY FLIMNAP.   Thou art the best of brothers, positively.
FRIPPEREL.   There's a bob for your ladyship too, I can tell you that.
LADY FLIMNAP.   Oh, pray let me have it.
170 FRIPPEREL (*reads*).   "Why did I not see my dearest Lord Flimnap last
    night? Did public affairs, or your lady, keep you from my wishes?"
LADY FLIMNAP.   Not his lady, I can assure her. Ha, ha!
FRIPPEREL (*reads on*).   "Time was when affairs of state could be post-
    poned for my company."
LADY FLIMNAP.   Could they so? Then the nation had a fine time of it.
FRIPPEREL (*reads on*).   "And if you sacrificed the last night to your

---

156. own] *O1, W1*; omitted *W2*.
170. (*reads*)] *O1*; reads on *W1, W2*.

lady, which by all the bonds of love should have been mine, you injured both of us; for I was panting for you, while she was wishing herself with her adorable Man-Mountain. Let me conjure you to leave her to her giants and fly this evening to the arms of your ever tender, languishing

Moretta."

LADY FLIMNAP.   Upon my word, the languishing Moretta makes very free with me. But this is a precious letter and will settle all our family quarrels for the future.

FRIPPEREL.   But come, let us to a little consultation of mischief. Shall we send for the Admiral and show it him? We shall have fine bouncing.

LADY FLIMNAP.   No, no, let us make the most of it. I'll fit him for calling in relations to assist him. If this hubbub is to be made every time I follow my inclinations, one might as well have married a tradesman as a man of quality.

FRIPPEREL.   I wonder that he does not insist upon your looking after his family and paying his bills.

LADY FLIMNAP.   And taking care of my children. Ha, ha, ha! Poor wretch!

FRIPPEREL.   Poor devil! But what shall we do with the letter?

LADY FLIMNAP.   Send it directly to my good lord. But first copy it, lest he should forswear it at the proper time.

FRIPPEREL.   Or suppose, when at our next consultation upon your indiscretions, that we send the letter to him before us all, to see how he will behave upon it. Let me alone for that.

LADY FLIMNAP.   Thou genius of mischief, and best of brothers! What can I do to thank you for your goodness to your poor sissy?

FRIPPEREL.   I'll tell you what you shall do. Confess to me sincerely whether you really like this Gulliver.

LADY FLIMNAP.   Why then, sincerely, I do think him a prodigious fine animal. And when he is dressed in his Nardac's robes, I am sure there will not be a female heart but will pit-a-pat as he passes by.

FRIPPEREL.   Egad, he ought to make a fine figure, I'm sure, for a hundred and fifty tailors have been working night and day these six weeks to adorn this pretty creature of yours. But, my dear sister, do you like him as a fine man or a fine monster?

LADY FLIMNAP.   Partly one, partly t'other.

FRIPPEREL.   Well, you have certainly a great soul, sister. I don't quite understand your taste, but so much the better; for I would have a woman of quality always a little incomprehensible.

LADY FLIMNAP.   For heaven's sake, let us make haste to join the cer-

emony. And be sure, brother, to prevent all conspiracies against
220   my dear Gulliver. Great men will always be envied. What an
honor will he be to Lilliput! Had we but a few more such lords,
how happy it would be for the nation as well as the ladies.
FRIPPEREL.   You are certainly mad.
LADY FLIMNAP.   Or I should not be thy sister.
FRIPPEREL.   Farewell, giddyhead.
LADY FLIMNAP.   Brother, I am yours.

Exeunt severally.

Enter a mob of Lilliputians *huzzaing.*

FIRST MOB.   What, is the Man-Mountain to be made a lord?
SECOND MOB.   To be sure, neighbor, he is.
FIRST MOB.   I suppose he is to be made a lord because he is of so much
230   service to the nation.
SECOND MOB.   We shall pay dear for it, though, for he eats more and
drinks more at a meal than would serve my wife and nine children
for a month. I wish his lordship was out of the kingdom, for he'll
certainly make free with us, should there be a scarcity of beef and
mutton.
THIRD MOB.   What countryman is this Gulliver, pray?
FIRST MOB.   Why, they say he comes from a strange country. The
women there are very near as tall as the men, aye, and as bold too,
and the children are as big as we are. All the people, they say, are
240   brave, free and happy; and for fear of being too happy, they are
always quarreling one among another.
SECOND MOB.   Quarrel? What do they quarrel for?
FIRST MOB.   Because they are brave and free; and if you are brave and
free, why you may quarrel whenever or with whom ever you
please.
SECOND MOB.   What, have they no laws to keep them quiet?
FIRST MOB.   Laws! Ay, laws enough; but they never mind laws if they
are brave and free.
SECOND MOB.   La, what a slaughter an army of such men-mountains
250   would make.
FIRST MOB.   And so they would, whilst they are brave and free, to be
sure, or else they may run away as well as lesser people. (*Trumpets
sound.*) Hark! Neighbors, they are coming. Now for a sight you
never saw before, nor mayhap will ever see again.

SCENE changes to MILDENDO, the Capital City of Lilliput;
then follows [*Scene II.*] THE PROCESSION.

SCENE [III.], Gulliver's *room.*
Lalcon, *the keeper, speaks without.*

LALCON (*without*).   Clear the way for the Nardac Gulliver.

Enter Lalcon *and* Gulliver.

LALCON.   Please your lordship to stoop a little. Most noble and tremen-
dous Nardac, behold the place allotted by his Majesty for thy residence. It has employed all the workmen belonging to the Public
Works these three months; and thy bed here is the joint labors of
all the upholsterers in this great metropolis.

GULLIVER.   I am bound to his Majesty for the honors he has done me;
and to you, Sir, for your friendship and attention to me.

LALCON.   When your lordship please to take the air, you will find a
10   large backdoor in your bedchamber, through which your lordship
may creep into the palace gardens. I shall now leave you to repose
after your fatigue. Should any company desire to see your lordship, may they be permitted to enter?

GULLIVER.   Without doubt, sir. But intreat 'em, if I should be asleep,
not to run over my face nor put their lances into my nose or shoot
their arrows into my eyes. For since the last time they did me that
honor I have been much afflicted with a violent sneezing and head-
ache.

LALCON.   It would be death to disturb you now. By our laws, nobody
20   can make free with a lord, but your lordship may make free with
anybody.

GULLIVER.   I shall not exert my privileges.

LALCON.   Will your lordship be pleased to lie down gently, and to
turn in your bed as easily as possible, lest the moving of your lordship's body should bring the palace about your ears.

GULLIVER.   I thank you, sir, for your caution. I am a little dry with my
fatigue today, shall beg something to moisten my mouth.

LALCON.   I shall order a hogshead of wine to quench your lordship's
thirst immediately.

Exit.

30   GULLIVER.   Notwithstanding the figure I make here, the honors I have
received, and the greater things intended me, I grow sick of my
situation. I shall either starve or be sacrificed to the envy and malice of my brother peers. They'll never forgive the service I have
done their country. I wish myself at home again, and plain Gul-

---

23.   down gently] *O*1, *W*1; down as gently *W*2.

liver. Everything is in miniature here but vice, and that is so disproportioned that I'll match our little rakes at Lilliput with any of our finest gentlemen in England.

Enter Lalcon.

LALCON.   A hundred and fifty tailors are without to pay their duty to your lordship, and have brought their bills —

40 GULLIVER.   Their bills! They are very pressing sure —

LALCON.   They have done nothing but work at your lordship's robes these six weeks, and therefore hope your indulgence for the sake of their wives and families.

GULLIVER.   I am so much fatigued that I must desire 'em to give me till tomorrow, and assure them, that notwithstanding my titles and privileges, I shall give 'em very little trouble.

Exit Lalcon.

My greatness begins to be troublesome to me.

Enter Lalcon.

LALCON.   Two ladies of the court to wait on your lordship.

Exit.

Enter Lady Flimnap *and* Toadel.

GULLIVER.   Lady Flimnap again! What can this mean?

50 TOADEL.   Would your ladyship have me retire?

LADY FLIMNAP.   Out of hearing only; should you leave us quite to ourselves, people might be censorious.

TOADEL.   I will walk into that gallery and amuse myself with the pictures.

LADY FLIMNAP.   Do so, Toadel, but be within call.

TOADEL.   Upon my word, the monster is a noble creature.

Exit.

LADY FLIMNAP.   I could not deter any longer wishing you joy of the honors which you so deservedly received this day. I take a particular interest in your welfare, I assure you.

60 GULLIVER.   And I a particular pride in your ladyship's good opinion.

LADY FLIMNAP.   I hope you don't think me imprudent in thus laying aside the formality of my sex to make you these frequent visits. Do the ladies of your country ever take these liberties?

---

49. What can this mean?] *O*1, *W*1; (*Aside.*) *W*2.

53. amuse] *O*1; muse *W*1, *W*2.

GULLIVER. Oh, yes, madam. Our English ladies are allowed some liberties, and take a great many more.

LADY FLIMNAP. What, the married ladies?

GULLIVER. Our married ladies, indeed, are so much employed with the care of their children and attention to their families, that they would take no liberties at all did not their husbands oblige 'em to
70   play at cards now and then, lest their great attachment to domestic affairs should throw 'em into fits of the vapors.

LADY FLIMNAP. Bless me! How different people are in different nations. I must confess to your Lordship, though I have some children, I have not seen one of them these six months; and though I am married to one of the greatest men in the kingdom, and, as they say, one of the handsomest, yet I don't imagine that I shall ever throw myself into a fit of sickness by too severe an attention to him or his family.

GULLIVER (*aside*). What a profligate morsel of nobility this is! [*To
80   Lady* Flimnap.] I must own your ladyship surprises me greatly; for in England I have been used to see the ladies employed in matters of affection and economy, that I cannot conceive, without these, how you can possibly pass your time or amuse yourself.

LADY FLIMNAP. What, are not tormenting one's husband and running him in debt tolerable amusements? It is below a woman of quality to have either affection or economy; the first is vulgar and the last is mechanic. And yet had I been an English lady, perhaps I might have seen an object that might have raised my affection and even persuaded me to live at home. (*Looking at him and sighing.*)

90   GULLIVER (*aside*). In the name of Queen Mab, what is coming now! Sure I have not made a conquest of this fairy?

LADY FLIMNAP. What a prodigious fine hand your Lordship has!

GULLIVER. Mine, madam! 'Tis brown sure, and somewhat of the largest.

LADY FLIMNAP. Oh, my lord, 'tis the nobler for that. I assure you that it was the first thing about your lordship that struck me. But, to return—I say, my lord, had I been happy enough to have been born, bred, and married in England, I might then have been as fond as I am now sick of matrimony. (*Approaching tenderly.*)

100 GULLIVER (*retreating*). Perhaps your ladyship has taken some just aversion to our sex.

LADY FLIMNAP. To one of it I have, my husband, but to the sex—Oh, no! I protest I have not. Far from it. I honor and adore your sex, when it is capable of creating tenderness and esteem. Have my visits to your lordship denoted any such aversion? My present

79-80. *To Lady* Flimnap] *O*1, *W*2; (*Aside to Lady* Flimnap.) *W*1.

visit, which I have imprudently made, rather indicates that, to one
of your sex at least, I have not taken so just an aversion as perhaps
I ought.

GULLIVER (*aside*). That is home, indeed. What can I possibly say to
110   her or do with her?

LADY FLIMNAP. A married woman, to be sure, ought not to visit a gentleman. She ought not to despise her husband. She ought to prefer
no company to him. And yet, such is my weakness, I have visited
a gentleman. I do despise my husband, heartily despise him. And
I am afraid I might be tempted even to quit Lilliput, were the proposal made to me by one whose honor, bravery, and affection
might make the loss of my own country less grievous to me.

GULLIVER (*aside*). I am in a fine situation. She certainly wants to elope
with me.

120 LADY FLIMNAP. Why won't your lordship converse with me upon
these topics?

GULLIVER. Upon my word, madam, I have been much at a loss to comprehend you. And now I do comprehend you, I am still at a loss
how to answer you. But, madam, look upon your delicate self
and me. Supposing there were no other objections, surely this dis-
porportion —

LADY FLIMNAP. I despise it, my lord. Love is a great leveller, and I
have ambition. And I think if I make no objections your lordship
need not.

130 GULLIVER. To pretend now not to understand you would be affectation, and not to speak my mind to you would be insincerity. I am
most particularly sorry, madam, that I cannot offer you my services; but, to speak the truth, I am unfortunately engaged.

LADY FLIMNAP. Engaged, my lord? To whom, pray?

GULLIVER. To a wife and six children.

LADY FLIMNAP. Is that all? Have not I, my lord, the same plea? And
does it weigh anything against my affection? Have I not a husband
and as many children?

GULLIVER. I allow that. But your ladyship is most luckily and politely
140   regardless of 'em. I, madam, not having the good fortune to be
born and bred in high life, am a slave to vulgar passions; and, to
expose at once my want of birth and education—with confusion
I speak it—I really love my wife and children.

LADY FLIMNAP. Is it possible?

---

115. quit] *O*₁, *W*₂; quite *W*₁.
117. loss] *O*₁, *W*₁; lose *W*₂.
118. I am in] *O*₁; I am certainly in *W*₁, *W*₂.
127. leveller] *O*₁, *W*₁; laveller *W*₂.

GULLIVER.   I am ashamed of my weakness, but it is too true, madam.

LADY FLIMNAP.   I am ashamed of mine, I must confess. What, have I really cast my affections upon a monster, a married monster, and who, still more monstrous, confesses a passion for his wife and children.

150 GULLIVER.   Guilty, madam.

LADY FLIMNAP.   Guilty indeed. Thou are tenfold guilty to me, but I am cured of one passion and shall now give way to another. As for your lordship's virtue, I leave and bequeath it, with all its purity, to your fair lady and her numerous offspring. Don't imagine that I'm quite unhappy at your coolness to me. I now as heartily despise you as before I loved you. And so, my dear Gully—Yours—yours—yours. Here, Toadel —

Enter Toadel.

Let us be gone. I am finely punished for my folly.

TOADEL.   For heaven's sake, madam, be composed, and don't exasper-
160 ate him; should he grow outrageous, he might commit violence upon us.

LADY FLIMNAP.   He commit violence! He is a poor, tame, spiritless creature. His great mountainous body promises wonders indeed; and where your expectations are raised, instead of the roaring dragon, out creeps the pusillanimous mouse.

TOADEL.   Dear my lady, be pacified. Here comes my lord and your ladyship's brothers. How will this end?

LADY FLIMNAP.   To my honor, assure yourself. Be sure do you second me, when I want you.

170 TOADEL.   Play what tune your ladyship pleases, I am always ready with the second part.

Enter Flimnap, Bolgolam, *and* Fripperel.

FLIMNAP.   Now, brother, am I unreasonably jealous or not? See and judge yourselves.

BOLGOLAM.   I have judged, and now I'll execute. (*Draws his sword.*)

FRIPPEREL.   What, without a trial? Fie, for shame, Admiral. That may be sea law but it is not land law.

GULLIVER.   What means this insult, Admiral, in my apartments? If you have no dread of a man who could puff you away with his breath, at least reverence him whom your king has honored.

180 BOLGOLAM.   No place shall protect a dishonorable sister.

FLIMNAP.   And no strength shall protect him who has dishonored Flimnap. (*Lays his hand upon his sword.*)

FRIPPEREL.   I say, hear the parties first. If then matters are not cleared, you shall draw your swords, and I'll—withdraw into the next room.

LADY FLIMNAP.   Hear me, my lord and brother, and then determine. I confess appearances are against me. An imprudent curiosity urged me to see this monster and hear him talk of his country and its customs.

FLIMNAP.   The infection, madam, that is taken in at the eyes and the
190   ears, will make a quick progress through the rest of the body.

LADY FLIMNAP.   Jealousy, my lord, will make a quicker. But I defy it. My friend, Toadel, here, can witness that curiosity was merely my motive.

TOADEL.   Oh yes, my lord, I'll swear that.

FRIPPEREL.   And so will I, too. Toadel is a woman of immense honor.

LADY FLIMNAP.   Having no harm myself, I suspected none. The monster has always behaved mild, tame, and gentle to me. But just now, his eyes flashing with desire, he owned a violent passion for me; nay, proposed even taking me away with him into his own
200   country.

FRIPPEREL.   In his greatcoat pocket, I suppose. And he would have made money of you, too, if his countrymen love rarities.

BOLGOLAM.   How can you jest at such a time as this?

FLIMNAP.   Fire and vengeance!

LADY FLIMNAP.   Pray, my dear, contain yourself. Then this wicked monster—aye, you may well turn up your eyes—upon my being shocked at his proposal, and declaring my unalterable love to you, began to grind his teeth and bite his knuckles. I trembled and begged for mercy. At last, gathering strength, from fear I fell into
210   rage. And, being strong in virtue and warm with my conjugal affections, I broke out into a bitterness against the villain who would have been my undoer. (*Bursts into tears.*)

TOADEL.   —which certainly hindered him from committing violence.

FRIPPEREL (*aside*).   Poor soul! By all that's mischievous, she's a genius.

FLIMNAP.   You have eased my heart, madam, of its suspicions; but my honor must have satisfaction here. (*Draws his sword.*)

GULLIVER.   Pray, my lord, sheath your anger. The odds are rather against you. I wave this private trial and insist upon a public one. And, till then, I beg to retire from the jealousy of a husband, the
220   partiality of brothers, and the irresistible eloquence of so fine a lady.

FLIMNAP.   Tomorrow the grand Court of Justice sits, and I summon thee, Nardac Gulliver, before the king and peers, to answer to the wrongs thou hast done me.

GULLIVER.   Clumglum Flimnap, I'll meet thee there. (*Goes into the inner room.*)

LADY FLIMNAP. For heaven's sake, my lord, let us leave this den of wickedness. (*Going.*)

Enter Keeper.

KEEPER. A letter to my Lord Flimnap.

FRIPPEREL (*aside*). Now for it, sister. Have at the other monster.

Flimnap *reads and seems disordered.*

230 LADY FLIMNAP. No bad news, I hope, my dear?

BOLGOLAM. Speak it out, brother. Your keeping it to yourself won't make it better.

FLIMNAP. Nothing at all—a private business.

FRIPPEREL. What, a petticoat business, brother?

LADY FLIMNAP. I shall grow uneasy, my lord. I must know. (*Soothing him.*)

FLIMNAP. You can't, my dear. It is a state affair.

LADY FLIMNAP. State affairs have been often postponed for a mistress. Why may they not for once be entrusted to a wife?

FRIPPEREL (*aside*). That's a choker.

240 BOLGOLAM. Zounds, what's all this mystery about?

LADY FLIMNAP. If you won't communicate, my dear Lord, I will.

FLIMNAP. What will you commuicate?

LADY FLIMNAP. Your state secret, the contents of that letter. What, confounded, my sweet husband? The paragon of chastity out of countenance? Ha, ha!

BOLGOLAM. Expound this riddle or I'll march off.

LADY FLIMNAP. There, brother, is a true copy of the negotiation that great statesman is carrying on for the good of the nation. (*Gives a paper.*)

FLIMNAP. Then I'm discovered.

250 BOLGOLAM. Hum—hum—hum—"the tender languishing Moretta!" Is this true, my lord?

FLIMNAP. I confess it.

BOLGOLAM. So, so; here are fine doings. What, do you keep a whore and are jealous of your wife too?

FRIPPEREL. That's damned unreasonable indeed.

BOLGOLAM. Look'ee, my lord, I promised you justice, if she had injured you; and, moreover, I promised to cut your throat if you should injure her. Therefore, if you'll walk with me into the burying ground, brother, I'll be as good as my word.

260 FLIMNAP. I should ill deserve the name of gentleman, if I was not as ready to defend my follies as commit them. I'll attend you.

Exit Flimnap *and* Bolgolam.

TOADEL. Won't you prevent mischief, my lady?

LADY FLIMNAP. No, no. The losing a little blood will do 'em both service. It will cool the wantonness of one and the choler of the other.

FRIPPEREL. Let the worst happen, I shall only be an elder brother, and you a husband, out of pocket.

LADY FLIMNAP. Oh, no, there will be no mischief. I'm confident the Admiral will bring him too. If my lord did not suffer himself to be bullied now and then, there would be no living with him. But what noise is that? Ho, here the heroes come.

Enter Bolgolam *and* Flimnap.

FRIPPEREL. Well, gentlemen, do either of you want a surgeon?

BOLGOLAM. Why here's the devil to do. The whole city's in an uproar. The man-mountain has made his escape out of his chamber. He has straddled over the walls of the palace garden, made the best of his way to the seaside, seized upon my ship, a firstrate, put his clothes on board her, weighed her anchor, and is now towing her over an arm of the sea towards Blefuscu.

FRIPPEREL. Then you have lost your commission, Admiral, and you your lover, sister.

LADY FLIMNAP. A good voyage to him. I was sure that he would run away. You see, my lord, that he durst not stand the trial. For all his mightiness, he could not bear the consciousness of his guilt nor the force of my virtue.

FLIMNAP. I see it, madam, and acknowledge my mistake.

LADY FLIMNAP. Is that a satisfaction, my lord, adequate to the injury? My innocence, my lord, is not to be thus wounded without having other remedies to heal it.

BOLGOLAM. If you don't apply one, my lord, instantly, I shall. (*Claps his hand to his sword.*)

FLIMNAP. I am ready, madam, this moment to make you easy and happy for the future.

LADY FLIMNAP. And how will your lordship bring it about?

FLIMNAP. By permitting you, madam, to follow your inclinations.

LADY FLIMNAP. Now your lordship really behaves like a nobleman. And to convince you that I am not unworthy of my rank and quality too, here I solemnly promise never to disturb your lordship in the pursuit of yours.

FRIPPEREL. Perfectly polite on both sides.

FLIMNAP. From this moment you have my full and free consent to spend what money you please, see what company you please, lie in bed and get up when you please, be abroad or at home when you please, be in and out of humor when you please; and, in short, to take every liberty of a woman of quality as you please; and, for the future, fall in love when you please with either man or monster.

LADY FLIMNAP.   To show your lordship that I will not be behind-hand with you in nobleness of sentiment, I most sincerely grant you a free access to the languishing Moretta whenever you please, and entreat you for the future that you will have as little regard for me as you have for the business of the nation.

FLIMNAP.   Let us seal and ratify the treaty in each other's arms, my dearest lady.

LADY FLIMNAP.   My beloved lord. (*They embrace.*)

BOLGOLAM.   I am astonished! From this moment I disown you all. I'll out to sea as fast as I can. Should these politenesses reach us, woe be to poor Lilliput! When they do, I'll let the sea into my great cabin and sink to the bottom with the honor, virtue, and liberty of my country.

Exit Bolgolam.

FRIPPEREL.   A queer dog my brother is, that's positive. But come, let me once again join your hands upon this your second happier union.

Let love be banished. We of rank and fashion,
Should ne'er in marriage mix one grain of passion.

LADY FLIMNAP.

To care and broils we now may bid defiance.
Give me my will and I am all compliance (*Curtsies.*)

LORD FLIMNAP.

Let low-bred minds be curbed by laws and rules,
Our higher spirit leaps the bounds of fools;
No law or custom shall to us say nay.
We scorn restriction—*vivè la Liberté.*

Finis

Epilogue

By a Friend.
Spoken by Lady Flimnap.

Well now! Could you who are of larger size
Bid to a bolder heighth your passions rise?
Was it not great? A lady of my span
To undertake this monstrous Mountain Man?

The prudes I know will censure and cry, "Fie on't!,
Preposterous, sure! A pigmy love a giant?"
Yet joy! No disproportion love can know;
It finds us equals, or it makes us so.
And to the sex, though power nor strength belong,
10   We yet have beauty to subdue the strong.

But what strange notions govern vulgar life!
The beau has qualms about an absent wife,
Were he at home, his dear might cut and carve,
But, if he can't partake, must others starve?
A theft like this he can't a robbery call;
"Let her not know it; she's not robbed at all."

Well, if so cold these English heroes prove,
Such squeamish creatures ne'er will gain my love.
Huge stupid things! not worth the pains to win 'em;
20   These great bodies have no spirit in 'em.
Mere dingbett fowl! unwieldy, dull, and tame;
The sprightly Bantams are the truest game.

0.2–0.3.] O_1, W_1; omitted W_2.
20.   great] O_1, W_1; giant W_2.
21.   dingbett] O_1; dunghill W_1, W_2.

In war, perhaps, these lubbers may have merit;
But to please us they must have fire and spirit:
For, let the giants say whate'er they can,
'Tis spirit! Spirit! ladies, makes the man.

Finis

The Male-Coquette;
or, Seventeen-Hundred
Fifty-Seven

1757

THE
MALE-COQUETTE:

OR,

Seventeen Hundred Fifty-Seven.

In TWO ACTS.

As it is Performed at the

THEATRE-ROYAL

In DRURY-LANE.

Jacentem lenis in Hostem. Virg.

LONDON:

Printed for P. Vaillant, facing *Southampton-Street,* in the *Strand.* MDCCLVII.

Facsimile title page of the First Edition.
Folger Shakespeare Library.

Advertisement

The following scenes were written with no other view than to serve Mr. Woodward last year at his benefit; and to expose a set of people (the Daffodils) whom the author thinks more prejudicial to the community, than the various characters of Bucks, Bloods, Flashes and Fribbles, which have by turns infested the town, and been justly ridiculed upon the stage. He expects no mercy from the critics: But the more indulgent public, perhaps, will excuse his endeavors to please them, when they shall know, that the performance was planned, written, and acted in less than a month.

0.1.   Advertisement] *W*1, *W*2; omitted *O*1.

Prologue

Written and spoken by Mr. GARRICK.

Why to this farce this title given,
Of Seventeen Hundred Fifty Seven?
Is it a register of fashions,
Of follies, frailties, fav'rite passions?
Or is't designed to make appear,
How happy, good, and wise you were
In this same memorable year?
Sure with our author wit was scarce,
To crowd so many virtues in a farce.
10 Perhaps 'tis meant to make you stare,
Like cloths hung out at country fair;
On which strange monsters glare and grin,
To draw the gaping bumpkins in.
Though 'tis the genius of the age,
To catch the eye with title-page;
Yet here we dare not so abuse ye.
We have some monsters to amuse ye.

Ye slaves to fashion, dupes of chance,
Whom fortune leads her fickle dance:
20 Who, as the dice, shall smile or frown,
Are rich and poor, and up and down;
Whose minds eternal vigils keep;
Who, like Macbeth, have murdered sleep.
Each modish vice this night shall rise,
Like Banquo's Ghost, before your eyes;

0.1. Written . . . Garrick] *O*1; omitted *W*1, *W*2.

While, conscious you, shall start and roar,
"Hence, horrid farce! we'll see no more!"
Ye ladies, too, maids, widows, wives,
Now tremble for your naughty lives.
30 How will your hearts go pit-a-pat?
Bless me! Lord, what's the fellow at?
Was poet e'er so rude before?
Why sure the brute will say no more.
Again? Oh, God, I cannot bear —
Here, you Boxkeeper, call my chair.
Peace, ladies, 'tis a false alarm.
To you our author means no harm.
His female failings all are fictions:
To which your lives are contradictions.
40 [Th' unnatural fool has drawn a plan,
Where women like a worthless man,
A fault ne'er heard of since the world began.]
This year he lets you steal away;
But if the next you trip or stray,
His muse, he vows, on you shall wait
In Seventeen Hundred Fifty-eight.

Dramatis Personae

Daffodil	Mr. Woodward.
Tukely	Mr. Palmer.
Lord Racket	Mr. Blakes.
Sir William Whister	Mr. Burton.
Sir Tan-Tivy	Mr. Jefferson.
Spinner	Mr. Walker.
Dizzy	Mr. Yates.
Ruffle	Mr. Usher.
First Waiter	Mr. Ackman.
Second Waiter	Mr. Atkins.
Harry	Mr. Clough.

WOMEN.

Sophia	Miss Macklin.
Arabella	Miss Minors.
Mrs. Dotterel	Miss Barton.
Widow Damply	Mrs. Cross.
Lady Fanny Pewit	Mrs. Bradshaw.

The Male-Coquette; or, Seventeen Hundred Fifty-Seven

ACT I. [SCENE I.]

[A hall in Sophia's *house.]*

Enter Arabella *and* Sophia *in men's clothes.*

ARABELLA.   Indeed, my dear, you'll repent this frolic.

SOPHIA.   Indeed, my dear, then it will be the first frolic I ever repented in all my life. Lookee, Bell, 'tis in vain to oppose me, for I am resolved the only way to find out his character is to see him thus and converse freely with him. If he is the wretch he is reported to be, I shall away with him at once; and if he is not, he will thank me for the trial, and our union will be the stronger.

ARABELLA.   I never knew a woman yet who had prudence enough to turn off a pretty fellow because he had a little more wickedness than the rest of his neighbors.

SOPHIA.   Then I will be the first to set a better example. If I did not think a man's character was of some consequence, I should not now run such risks and encounter such difficulties to be better acquainted with it.

ARABELLA.   Ha, Sophy! if you have love enough to be jealous, and jealousy enough to try these experiments, don't imagine, though you should make terrible discoveries, that you can immediately quit your inclinations with your breeches and return so very philosophically to your petticoats again, ha, ha!

SOPHIA.   You may be as merry with my weakness as you please, Madam; but I know my own heart and can rely upon it.

ARABELLA.   We are great bullies by nature, but courage and swaggering are two things, Cousin.

SOPHIA.   Since you are as little to be convinced as I am to be persuaded, your servant. (*Going.*)

ARABELLA.   Nay, Sophy, this is unfriendly. If you are resolved upon your scheme, open to me without reserve and I'll assist you.

SOPHIA.   *Imprimis*, then; I confess to you that I have a kind of whimsical attachment to Daffodil, not but I can see his vanities and laugh
30   at 'em.

ARABELLA.   And like him the better for 'em.

SOPHIA.   Pshaw! Don't plague me, Bell. My other lover, the jealous Mr. Tukely —

ARABELLA.   Who loves you too well to be successful —

SOPHIA.   And whom I really esteem —

ARABELLA.   As a good sort of man, ha, ha, ha.

SOPHIA.   Nay, should have loved him —

ARABELLA.   Had not a prettier fellow stept in between, who perhaps does not care a farthing for you.

40   SOPHIA.   That's the question, my dear. Tukely, I say, either stung by jealousy or unwilling to lose me without a struggle, has intreated me to know more of his rival before I engage too far with him. Many strange things he has told me which have piqued me, I must confess, and I am now prepared for the proof.

ARABELLA.   You'll certainly be discovered and put to shame.

SOPHIA.   I have secured my success already.

ARABELLA.   What do you mean?

SOPHIA.   I have seen him, conversed with him, and am to meet him again today by his own appointment.

50   ARABELLA.   Madness! It can't be.

SOPHIA.   But it has been, I tell you.

ARABELLA.   How? How? Quickly, quickly, dear Sophy.

SOPHIA.   When you went to Lady Fanny's last night, and left me, as you thought, little disposed for a frolic, I dressed me as you see, called a chair, and went to the King's Arms, asked for my gentleman and was shown into a room. He immediately left his company and came to me.

ARABELLA.   I tremble for you.

SOPHIA.   I introduced myself as an Italian nobleman, just arrived: *Il*
60   *Marchese di Macaroni.*

ARABELLA.   Ridiculous, ha, ha.

SOPHIA.   An intimate of Sir Charles Vainlove's, who is now at Rome, I told him my letters were with my baggage at the custom-house. He received me with all the openness imaginable, and would have introduced me to his friends. I begged to be excused, but promised

Portrait of Henry Woodward by Reynolds.
Folger Shakespeare Library

to attend him today, and am now ready, as you see, to keep my word.

ARABELLA. Astonishing! And what did you talk about?

SOPHIA. Of various things, women among the rest. And though I have
70   not absolutely any open acts of rebellion against him, yet I fear he is a traitor at heart. And then, such vanity! But I had not time to make great discoveries. It was merely the prologue; the play is to come.

ARABELLA. Act your part well, or we shall hiss you.

SOPHIA. Never fear me. You don't know what a mad, raking, wild young devil I can be, if I set my mind to it, Bell. (*Laying hold of her.*)

ARABELLA. You fright me. You shall positively be no bedfellow of mine any longer.

SOPHIA. I am resolved to ruin my woman and kill my man before I
80   get into petticoats again.

ARABELLA. Take care of a quarrel though. A rival may be too rough with you.

SOPHIA. No, no. Fighting is not the vice of these times. And as for a little swaggering, damn it, I can do it as well as the best of 'em.

ARABELLA. Hush, hush! Mr. Tukely is here.

SOPHIA. Now for a trial of skill. If I deceive him, you'll allow that half my business is done.

She walks aside, takes out a glass, and looks at the pictures.

Enter Tukely.

TUKELY. Your servant, Miss Bell. I need not ask if Miss Sophy be at home, for I believe I have seen her since you did.

90   ARABELLA. Have you, sir? You seem disconcerted, Mr. Tukely. Has anything happened?

TUKELY. A trifle, madam. But I was born to be trifled with, and to be made uneasy at trifles.

ARABELLA. Pray, what trifling affair has disturbed you thus?

SOPHIA (*aside*). What's the matter now?

TUKELY. I met Miss Sophy this moment in a hackney chair at the end of the street. I knew her by the pink negligée. But upon my crossing the way to speak to her, she turned her head away, laughed violently, and drew the curtain in my face.

100 SOPHIA (*aside*). So, so. Well said, jealousy.

ARABELLA. She was in haste, I suppose, to get to her engagement.

TUKELY. Yes, yes, madam. I amagine she had some engagement upon her hands. But sure, madam, her great desire to see her more agreeable friends need not be attended with contempt and disregard to the rest of her acquaintances.

ARABELLA. Indeed, Mr. Tukely, I have so many caprices and follies of my own that I can't possibly answer for my cousin's too.

SOPHIA (*aside*). Well said, Bell.

TUKELY. Answer, Miss! No—heaven forbid you should. For my part, I have given up all my hopes as a lover, and only now feel for her as a friend, and indeed as a friend, a sincere friend. I can't but say that going out in a hackney chair, without a servant, and endeavoring to conceal herself, is something incompatible with Miss Sophy's rank and reputation. This I speak as a friend, not as a lover, Miss Bell. Pray mind that.

ARABELLA. I see it very plainly, Mr. Tukely. And it gives me great pleasure that you can be so indifferent in your love and yet so jealous in your friendship.

TUKELY. You do me honor, Miss, by your good opinion. (*Walks about and sees* Sophy.) Who's that, pray?

ARABELLA. A gentleman who is waiting for Sophy.

TUKELY. I think she has gentlemen waiting for her everywhere.

SOPHIA (*coming up to him with her glass*). I am afraid, Sir, you'll excuse me, that notwithstanding your declaration and this lady's compliments, there is a little of the devil called jealousy at the bottom of all this uneasiness.

TUKELY. Sir!

SOPHIA. I say, Sir, wear your cloak as long as you please, the hoof will peep out, take my word for it.

TUKELY. Upon my word, Sir, you are pleased to honor me with a familiarity which I neither expected or indeed desired upon so slight an acquaintance.

SOPHIA. I dare swear you did not. (*Turns off and hums a tune.*)

TUKELY. I don't understand this.

ARABELLA (*aside*). This is beyond expectation.

SOPHIA (*picking her teeth*). I presume, Sir, you never was out of England.

TUKELY. I presume, Sir, that you are mistaken. I never was so foolishly fond of my own country to think nothing good was to be had out of it, nor so shamefully ungrateful to it, to prefer the vices and fopperies of every other nation to the peculiar advantages of my own.

SOPHIA. Ha, ha. Well said, old England, i'faith. Now, madam, if this gentleman would put this speech into a farce, and properly lard it with roast beef and liberty, I would engage the galleries would roar and halloo at it for half an hour together. Ha, ha, ha!

ARABELLA (*aside*).   Now the storm's coming.

TUKELY.   If you are not engaged, Sir, we'll adjourn to the next tavern and write this farce between us.

150 SOPHIA.   I fancy, Sir, by the information of your face, that you are more inclined to tragedy than comedy.

TUKELY.   I shall be inclined to treat you very ill, if you don't walk out with me.

SOPHIA.   I have been treated so very ill already, in the little conversation I have had with you, that you must excuse my walking out for more of it. But if you'll persuade the lady to leave the room, I'll put you to death. Damme! (*Going up to him.*)

ARABELLA.   For heaven's sake, what's the matter, gentlemen?

TUKELY.   What can I do with this fellow?

160 SOPHIA.   Madam, don't be alarmed. This affair will be very short. I am always expeditious, and will cut his throat without shocking you in the least. Come, Sir, (*draws*) if you won't defend yourself, I must kick you about the room. (*Advancing.*)

TUKELY.   Respect for this lady and this house has curbed my resentment hitherto. But as your insolence would take advantage of my forbearance, I must correct it at all events. (*Draws.*)

SOPHIA and ARABELLA.   Ha, ha, ha!

TUKELY.   What is all this?

SOPHIA.   What would you set your courage to a poor, weak woman?

170 You are a bold Briton, indeed. Ha, ha, ha!

TUKELY.   What, Sophia?

ARABELLA.   Sophia! No, no, she is in a hackney chair, you know, without a servant, in her pink negligée, ha, ha, ha.

TUKELY.   I am astonished and can scarce believe my own eyes. What means this metamorphosis?

SOPHIA.   'Tis in obedience to your commands. Thus equipped, I have got access to Daffodil and shall know whether your picture of him is drawn by your regard for me or resentment to him. *I will sound him from his lowest note to the top of his compass.*

180 TUKELY.   Your spirit transports me. This will be a busy and, I hope, a happy day for me. I have appointed no less than five ladies to meet me at the Widow Damply's; to each of whom, as well as yourself, the accomplished Mr. Daffodil has presented his heart;

---

146. halloo] *O1*, *W1*; haloo *W2*.

the value of which I am resolved to convince 'em of this night, for the sake of the whole sex.

SOPHIA. Pooh, pooh, that's the old story. You are so prejudiced.

TUKELY. I am afraid 'tis you who are prejudiced, Madam; for if you will believe your own eyes and ears —

SOPHIA. That I will, I assure you. I shall visit him immediately. He
190   thinks me in the country, and to confirm it, I'll write to him as from thence. But ask me no more questions about what I have done and what is to be done, for I have not a moment to lose. And so, my good friend Tukely, yours. My dear Bell, I kiss your hand. (*Kisses her hand.*) You are a fine woman, by heavens. Here, Joseppi, Brunello, Francesi—where are my fellows there? Call me a chair. Viva l'Amor and Liberté.

                                   Exit singing.

ARABELLA. Ha, ha, there's spirit for you. Well now, what do you stare at? You could not well desire more. Oh, fie, fie, don't sigh and bite your fingers. Rouse yourself, man. Set all your wits to
200   work. Bring this faithless Corydon to shame, and I'll be hanged if the prize is not yours. If she returns in time, I'll bring her to the Widow Damply's.

TUKELY. Dear Miss Arabella —

ARABELLA. Well, well. Make me a fine speech another time. About your business now.

TUKELY. I fly.

                                  Exit Tukely.

ARABELLA. What a couple of blind fools has love made of this poor fellow and my dear cousin Sophy. Little do they imagine, with all their wise discoveries, that Daffodil is as faithful a lover as he is an
210   accomplished gentleman. I pity these poor deceived women with all my heart. But how will they stare, when they find that he has artfully pretended a regard for them, the better to conceal his real passion for me. They will certainly tear my eyes out. And what will cousin Sophy say to me, when we are obliged to declare our passion? No matter what, 'tis the fortune of war. And I shall only serve her as she and every friend would serve me in the same situation.

         A little cheating never is a sin,
         At love or cards, provided that you win.

                                Exit Arabella.

[SCENE II.]

Daffodil's *lodgings.*
Enter Daffodil *and* Ruffle.

DAFFODIL. But are you sure, Ruffle, that you delivered the letter last
night in the manner I ordered you?

RUFFLE. Exactly, Sir.

DAFFODIL. And are you sure that Mr. Dotterel saw you slip the note
into his wife's hand?

RUFFLE. I have alarmed him, and you may be assured that he is as
uneasy as you would wish to have him. But I should be glad, with
your honor's leave, to have a little serious conversation with you;
for my mind forebodes much peril to the bones of your humble
10   servant, and very little satisfaction to your honor.

DAFFODIL. Thou art a most incomprehensible blockhead.

RUFFLE. No great scholar or wit, indeed; but I can feel an oak sapling
as well as another. Aye, and I should have felt one last night, if
I had not had the heels of all Mr. Dotterel's family. I had the whole
pack after me.

DAFFODIL. And did not they catch you?

RUFFLE. No, thank heaven.

DAFFODIL. You was not kicked, then?

RUFFLE. No, sir.

20 DAFFODIL. Nor caned?

RUFFLE. No, sir.

DAFFODIL. Nor dragged through a horse-pond?

RUFFLE. Oh lord, no, Sir!

DAFFODIL. That's unlucky.

RUFFLE. Sir!

DAFFODIL. You must go again, Ruffle; tonight perhaps you may be in
better luck.

RUFFLE. If I go again, sir, may I be caned, kicked, and horseponded
for my pains? I believe I have been lucky enough to bring an old
30   house over your head.

DAFFODIL. What d'ye mean?

RUFFLE. Mr. Dotterel only hobbled after me, to pay me the postage
of your letter; but being a little out of wind, he soon stopped to
curse and swear at me. I could hear him mutter something of
scoundrel and pimp, and my master, and villain, and blunderbuss
and sawpit. And then he shook his stick and looked like the devil.

---

12. sapling] *O*1, *W*1; suppling *W*2.

DAFFODIL. Blunderbuss and sawpit? This business grows a little serious, and so we will drop it. The husband is old and peevish, and
she so young and pressing, that I'll give it up, Ruffle. The town
40   talks of us, and I am satisfied.

RUFFLE. Pray, Sir, with submission, for what end do you write to so
many ladies and make such a rout about 'em? There are now upon
the list half a dozen maids, a leash of wives, and the Widow Damply. I know your honor don't intend mischief, but what pleasure
can you have in deceiving them and the world? For you are
thought a terrible young gentleman.

DAFFODIL. Why, that pleasure, Booby.

RUFFLE. I don't understand it. What do you intend to do with 'em
all? Ruin 'em?

50 DAFFODIL. Not I, faith.

RUFFLE. But you'll ruin their reputations.

DAFFODIL. That's their business, not mine.

RUFFLE. Will you marry any one of 'em?

DAFFODIL. Oh, no. That would be finishing the game at once. If I preferred one, the rest would take it ill; so, because I won't be particular, I give 'em all hopes without going a step further.

RUFFLE. Widows can't live upon such slender diet.

DAFFODIL. A true sportsman has no pleasure but in the chase. The game
is always given to those who have less taste and better stomachs.

60 RUFFLE. I love to pick a bit, I must confess. Really, sir, I should not
care what became of half the women you are pleased to be merry
with. But Miss Sophy, sure, is a heavenly creature and deserves
better treatment. And to make love to her cousin, too, in the same
house—that is very cruel.

DAFFODIL. But it amuses one; besides, they are both fine creatures.
And how do I know, if I loved only one, but the other might
poison herself?

RUFFLE. And when they know that you have loved 'em both, they
may poison one another. This affair will make a great noise.

70 DAFFODIL. Or I have taken a great deal of pains for nothing. But no
more prating, Sirrah; while I read my letters, go and ask Harry
what cards and messages he has taken in this morning.

RUFFLE. There is no mending him.

Exit Ruffle.

DAFFODIL *(opens letters).* This is from the Widow Damply. I know
her scrawl at a mile's distance. She pretends that the fright of her

---

64–72. Two speeches omitted *W*1, *W*2.

husband's death hurt her nerves so that her hand has shook ever
since, ha, ha, ha. It has hurt her spelling too, for here is joy with
a "G," ha, ha, poor creature. (*Reads.*) Hum—hum—hum. Well
said, Widow. She speaks plain, faith, and grows urgent. I must get
80   quit of her. She desires a tête à tête, which, with widows who have
suffered much for the loss of their husbands, is, as Captain Bobadil
says, a service of danger. So, I am off. (*Opens another.*) What the
devil have we here? A bill in Chancery. Oh, no; my tailor's bill,
sum total 374£ 11s. 5½d. Indeed, Monsieur Chicaneau, this is a
damned bill, and you will be damned for making it. Therefore,
for the good of your soul, Monsieur Chicaneau, you must make
another. (*Tears it.*) The French know their consequence and use us
accordingly. (*Opens another.*) This is from Newmarket. (*Reads.*)
        "May it please your Honor,
90   "I would not have you think of matching Cherry-
        "Derry with Gingerbread. He is a terrible horse,
        "and very covetous of his ground. I have chopped
        "Hurlotbrumbo for the Roan Mare, and fifty pounds.
        "Sir Roger has taken the match off your hands, which
        "is a good thing; for the mare has the distemper
        "and must have forfeited. I flung his Honor's
        "groom, though he was above an hour in the stable.
        "The nutmeg grey, Custard, is matched with Alderman.
        "Alderman has a long wind and will be too hard for
100   "Custard.
                    "I am, your Honor's
                        "Most obedient servant,
                            "Roger Whip."
Whip's a genius, and a good servant. I have not as yet lost above a
thousand pounds by my horses. But such luck can't always last.

                        Enter Ruffle *with cards.*

RUFFLE.   There's the morning's cargo, sir. (*Throws 'em down upon
    the table.*)
DAFFODIL.   Heighday! I can't read 'em in a month. Prithee, Ruffle, set
    down my invitations from the cards according to their date, and
    let me see 'em tomorrow morning. So much reading would dis-
110   tract me.
RUFFLE.   (*aside*).   And yet these are the only books that gentlemen
    read now-a-days.

                        Enter a Servant.

SERVANT.   And please your honor, I forgot to tell you that there was a gentleman here last night. I've forgot his name.

RUFFLE. Old Mr. Dotterel, perhaps.

SERVANT. Old? No, no, he looks younger than his honor. I believe he's
mad; he can't stand still a moment. He first capered out of the
chair, and when I told him your honor was not at home, he capered
into it again, said he would call again, jabbered something, and
120   away he went singing.

DAFFODIL. 'Tis the Marquis of Macaroni. I saw him at the King's Arms
yesterday. Admit him when he comes, Harry.

SERVANT. I shall, your honor. I can neither write or remember these
outlandish names.

Exit Servant.

DAFFODIL. Where is my list of women, Ruffle, and the places of their
abode, that we may strike off some and add the new acquisitions?

RUFFLE. What, alter again! I wrote it out fair but this morning. There
are quicker successions in your honor's list than the Court Calendar.

130 DAFFODIL. Strike off Mrs. Dotterel and the Widow Damply.

RUFFLE. They are undone. (*Strikes 'em out.*)

Enter Servant.

SERVANT. A lady, Mr. Ruffle, in a chair, must speak with you.

DAFFODIL. Did she ask for me? See, Ruffle, who it is.

Exit Ruffle.

SERVANT. No, your honor; but she looked quite flustrated.

DAFFODIL. Well, go below, and be careful not to let any old gentleman in this morning. And, d'ye hear, if any of the neighbors should
inquire who the lady is, you may say it is a relation; and be sure
to smile, do you hear? when you tell 'em so.

SERVANT. I shall, your honor. He, he, he, I am never melancholy.

Exit Servant.

140 DAFFODIL. That fellow's a character.

Enter Ruffle.

Sir, it is Mrs. Dotterel. She has had a terrible quarrel with her
husband about your letter, and has something to say of consequence to you both. She must see you, she says.

DAFFODIL. I won't see her. Why would you say that I was at home?
You know I hate to be alone with 'em, and she's so violent, too.
Well, well, show her up. This is so unlucky.

RUFFLE.   He hates to see duns he never intends to pay.

Exit Ruffle.

DAFFODIL.   What shall I do with her? This is worse than meeting her
husband with a blunderbuss in a sawpit.

Enter Mrs. Dotterel *and* Ruffle.

150   DAFFODIL.   Dear Mrs. Dotterel, this is so obliging. (*Aloud.*) Ruffle,
don't let a soul come near me. (*Aside.*) And harkee, don't leave
us long together; and let everybody up that comes.
RUFFLE.   What a deal of trouble here is about nothing.

Exit Ruffle.

MRS. DOTTEREL.   In the name of virtue, Mr. Daffodil, I hope you have
not given any private orders that may in the least derogate from
that absolute confidence which I place in your honor.
DAFFODIL.   You may be perfectly easy under this roof, madam. I hope
I am polite enough not to let my passions, of any kind, run too
great lengths in my own house.
160   MRS. DOTTEREL.   Nothing but absolute necessity could have made me
take this imprudent step. I am ready to faint with my apprehensions. Heighho!
DAFFODIL.   Heaven forbid! I'll call for some assistance. (*Going to ring.*)
MRS. DOTTEREL (*stopping him*).   Let your bell alone. You're always
calling for assistance, I think. You never give one time to come to
one's self. Mr. Dotterel has seen your letter and vows vengence
and destruction. Why would you be so violent and imprudent?
DAFFODIL.   The devil was in me, madam; but I repent it from my soul.
It has cured me of being violent.
170   MRS. DOTTEREL.   Come, come, don't take it too deeply neither. I thought
it proper at all hazards to let you know what had happened, and to
intreat you, by that affection you have sworn to me, to be careful
of my reputation.
DAFFODIL.   That I will indeed, madam. We can't be too careful.
MRS. DOTTEREL.   Well, Mr. Daffodil, I am an unhappy woman, married
to one I cannot love and loving one I ought to shun. It is a terrible
situation, Mr. Daffodil.
DAFFODIL.   It is indeed, madam. I am in a terrible one too. (*Aside.*)
Would I was well out of it.
180   MRS. DOTTEREL.   Do you know, Mr. Daffodil, that if I had not been
very religious my passions would have undone me. But you must
give me time; for nothing but that, and keeping the best company,
will ever conquer my prejudices.

DAFFODIL. I should be very ungenerous not to allow you time, madam. Three weeks or a month, I hope, will do the business, though, by my honor, I got the better of mine in half the time. (*Aside.*) What is Ruffle doing?

MRS. DOTTEREL [*aside*]. He's very cold, methinks; but I'll try him further. Lookee, Mr. Daffodil, you must curb your passions and keep
190   your distance. Fire is catching, and one does not know the consequences when once it begins to spread.

DAFFODIL. As you say, Madam, fire is catching; 'tis dangerous to play with it. And as I am of the tinder kind, as one may say, we had better—as you say, Madam,—change the subject. Pray did you ever hear of the pug-dog that you advertised? It was a very pretty creature. What was his name, Madam?

MRS. DOTTEREL (*stifling her passion*). Daffodil, sir!

DAFFODIL. Madam!

MRS. DOTTEREL. Could I love and esteem anything, and not call it Daf
200   fodil? (*Aside.*) What a wretch!

DAFFODIL. You do me honor, Madam. I don't like her looks; I must change the discourse (*aside*). Upon my soul, Mrs. Dotterel, this struggle is too much for man. My passions are now tearing me to pieces, and if you will stay, by heaven I will not answer for the consequences.

MRS. DOTTEREL. Consequences. What consequences? Thou wretched, base, false, worthless animal.

DAFFODIL (*bowing*). You do me honor.

MRS. DOTTEREL. Canst thou think that I am so blinded by my passion
210   not to see thy treacherous, mean, unmanly evasions? I have long suspected your infamy, and having this proof of it I could stab your treacherous heart and my own weak one. Don't offer to stir or ring your bell, for, by heavens, I'll — (*Catches hold of him.*)

DAFFODIL. I stir? I am never so happy as when I am in your company.

MRS. DOTTEREL. Thou liest. Thou art never so happy as when thou art deceiving and betraying our foolish sex. And all for what? Why, for the poor reputation of having that which thou hast neither power nor spirit to enjoy.

DAFFODIL (*aside*). Ha! I hear somebody coming. Now for a rapture.
220   [*To Mrs.* Dotterel.] Talk not of power or spirit. Heaven that has made you fair has made me strong. Oh, forgive the madness which your beauty has occasioned. (*Throws himself upon his knees.*)

Enter Servant.

---

223. Macaroons] *O1*; Macaroni *W1, W2.*

SERVANT. The Marquis of Macaroons.

Exit Servant.

Enter Sophia.

MRS. DOTTEREL. Ha! (*Screams.*) I am betrayed!

They all stare, and Daffodil *seemingly astonished.*

SOPHIA (*aside*). Mrs. Dotterel, by all that's virtuous. [*Aloud*] Signor
Daffodillo, *resto confuso*, tat I am com *si mal-a-proposito.*

DAFFODIL. Dear Marquis, no excuse, I beg.—Nothing at all, a relation
of mine, my sister only. Miss Daffodil, this is *il Merchese de Macaroni*, an intimate of Sir Charles Vainlove's. (*Aside.*) This was
230   lucky. [*Aloud*] Well then, my dear sister, I will wait upon you
tomorrow and settle the whole affair. (*Aside to Mrs.* Dotterel.)
I am the most miserable of mortals and have lost the most precious
moments of my life.

MRS. DOTTEREL. You are a villain. I despise you and detest you and
will never see you more.

Exit Mrs. Dotterel.

DAFFODIL. Ha, ha, ha! My sister has a noble spirit, my Lord.

SOPHIA. *Mi dispiace infinamente.* It tispils me, tat I haf *interrumpato,
gli affari* of you famili.

DAFFODIL. It is the old family-business, my Lord; and so old that, by
240   my honor, I am quite tired of it.

SOPHIA (*aside*). I hate him already. [*Aloud.*] Signor *Daffodillo*, she is
una belissima sorella in verità, a very prit' siss' intit.

DAFFODIL. I must confess to you, my Lord, that my sister is a young
distressed damsel, married to an old gentleman of the neighborhood. Ha, ha, ha!

SOPHIA. *O cara inghilterra!* vat a fortunate contreé is tis. Te olt men
marri de young fine girl and te young fine girl visite te young
Signors. O *preciosa libertà!*

DAFFODIL. Indeed, my Lord, men of fashion here have some small
250   privileges. We gather our roses without fear of thorns. Husbands
and brothers don't deal in poison and stilletos, as they do with you.

SOPHIA. *Il nostro amico*, Signor Carlo, has tol me a tousant *volte* dat
you vas de *Orlando Innamorato* himself.

DAFFODIL. But not *Furioso*, I can assure you, my Lord. Ha, ha, ha! I
am for variety and badinage without affection. Reputation is the
great ornament and ease the great happiness of life. To ruin women
would be troublesome; to trifle and make love to 'em amuses one.

I use my women as daintily as my tokay. I merely sip of both, but more than half a glass palls me.

260 SOPHIA. *Il mio proprio gusto.* (*Aside.*) Tukely is right; he's a villain. [*Aloud.*] Signor *Daffodillo*, vil you do me de favor to give me stranger *una introduzione* to some of your *signorine*, let *vostro amico* taste a littel, *un poco* of your *dulce* tokay.

DAFFODIL. Oh, *certmente!* I have half a hundred *signorines* at your service.

SOPHIA. *Multo obligato,* Signor *Daffodillo.*

Enter Servant.

SERVANT (*surlily*). Here's a letter for your honor.

DAFFODIL. What is the matter with the fellow?

SERVANT. Matter, your honor! The lady that went out just now gave
270 me such a souse on the ear as I made my bow to her that I could scarce tell for a minute whether I had a head or no.

DAFFODIL. Ha, ha! Poor fellow, there's smart money for you. (*Gives him money.*)

Exit Servant.

Will your lordship give me leave?

SOPHIA. *Senza ceremonie.* (*Aside.*) Now for it.

DAFFODIL (*reads*).

"Sir,

"I shall return from the country next week and shall

"hope to meet you at Lady Fanny Pewit's assembly next

"Wednesday.

280   "I am very much your humble servant,

           "Sophia Sprightly."

My lord Marquis, here is a letter has started game for you already, the most lucky thought imaginable.

SOPHIA. Cosa é questa—Cosa é—vat is?

DAFFODIL. There are two fine girls you must know, cousins who live together. This is a letter from one of 'em. Sophia is her name. I have addressed 'em both, but as matters become a little serious on their side, I must raise a jealousy between the friends, discover to one the treachery of the other, and so in the bustle steal off as
290 quietly as I can.

SOPHIA. Oh! *Spiritoso amico.* (*Aside.*) I can scarce contain myself.

DAFFODIL. Before the mine is sprung, I will introduce you into the town.

SOPHIA. You are great *generalissimo in verita mà.* I feel *in miò core* vat de poor *infelice* Sophia vil feel for de loss of Signor *Daffodillo*.

DAFFODIL.   Yes, poor creature; I believe she'll have a pang or two, tender indeed, and I believe will be unhappy for some time.

SOPHIA *(aside)*.   What a monster!

DAFFODIL.   You must dine with our club today, where I will introduce
300   you to more of Sir Charles's friends, all men of figure and fashion.

SOPHIA.   I must *primo* haf my *lettere*, dat your *amici* may be *assicurati*
dat I am no *impostore*.

DAFFODIL.   In the name of politeness, my lord Marquis, don't mention
your letters again. None but a justice of the peace or a constable
would ever ask for a certificate of a man's birth, parentage, and
education. Ha, ha, ha!

SOPHIA.   *Viva, viva il Signor Daffodillo!* You shall be *il mio conduttorè
in tutte le partite* of love and pleasure.

DAFFODIL.   With all my heart. You must give me leave now, my lord,
310   to put on my clothes. In the meantime, if your lordship will step
into my study there. If you choose music, there is a guitar and
some Venetian ballads; or, if you like reading, there's infidelity
and bawdy novels for you. Call Ruffle there.

Exit Daffodil.

SOPHIA *(looking after him)*.   I am shocked at him. He is really more
abandoned than Tukely's jealousy described him. I have got my
proofs and will not venture any further. I am vexed that I should
be angry at him, when I should only despise him. But I am so
angry that I could almost wish myself a man, that my breeches
might demand satisfaction for the injury he has done my petti-
320   coats.

Exit.

End of the First Act.

ACT II. [SCENE I.]

SCENE, *Mrs.* Damply's *Lodgings.*
Enter Arabella *and* Sophia.

SOPHIA.   In short, his own declarations, the unexpected meeting of Mrs.
Dotterel, his usage of my letter, and twenty things beside, determined me not to go among the set of 'em. So, making the best excuse I could, I got quit of him and his companions.

ARABELLA.   All this may be true, Sophy. Every young fellow has his
vanities. Fashion has made such irregularities accomplishments, and
the man may be worth having, for all your discoveries.

SOPHIA.   What! an abandoned, rash, profligate male-coquette, a wretch who can assume passions he never feels and sport with our sex's frailties. Fie, fie, Bell.

ARABELLA.   Well, well, you are too angry to be merciful. If he is such a monster, I am glad you are out of his clutches, and that you can so easily resign him to another.

SOPHIA.   To another? There is not that woman, be she ever so handsome, that I hate enough to wish her so much evil. And happy it is for you, Bell, that you have a heart to resist his allurements.

ARABELLA.   Yes, I thank my stars. I am not so susceptible of impressions of that kind. And yet I won't swear, if an agreeable man—I—I —

SOPHIA.   No, no, Bell, you are not absolute stone; you may be mollified. (*Aside.*) She is confounded.

ARABELLA (*aside*).   Surely he has not betrayed me. 'Tis impossible; I cannot be deceived.

SOPHIA.   Well, shall we go in to the ladies and Mr. Tukely? Were they not surprised when he opened the business to 'em?

ARABELLA.   'Twas the finest scene imaginable. You could see, though they all endeavored to hide their liking to Daffodil, all were uneasy at Tukely's discovery. At first they objected to his scheme, but they began to listen to his proposal the moment I was called out to you. What farther he intends is a secret to us all. But here he comes, and without the ladies.

Enter Tukely.

TUKELY.   Pray, Miss Bell—Bless me! Miss Sophy returned? I dare not ask, and yet if my eyes do not flatter my heart, your looks —

SOPHIA.   Don't rely too much upon looks, Mr. Tukely.

TUKELY.   Madam, why sure —

SOPHIA.   Don't imagine, I say, that you can always see the mind in the face.

TUKELY.   I can see, Madam, that your mind is not disposed to wish or make me happy.

SOPHIA.   Did not I bid you not to rely upon looks? For do you know now that my mind is at this time most absolutely disposed to do everything that you would have me. (*Curtsies.*)

TUKELY.   Then I have nothing more to wish or ask of fortune. (*Kneels and kisses her hand.*)

ARABELLA.   Come, come, this is no time to attend to one, when you have so many ladies to take care of.

TUKELY.   I will not yet inquire into your adventures 'till I have accomplished my own. The ladies within have at last agreed to attend me this evening, where, if you have a mind to finish the picture you have begun this morning, an opportunity may offer.

SOPHIA.   I am contented with my sketch. However, I'll make one; and
50   if you have an occasion for a second in anything, I am your man.
Command me.

TUKELY.   A match. From this moment I take you as my second, nay,
my first in every circumstance of our future lives.

ARABELLA.   Mighty pretty, truly. And so I am to stand cooling my
heels here, while you are making yourselves ridiculous.

SOPHIA.   Bell's in the right. To business, to business. Mr. Tukely, you
must introduce me to the ladies. I can at least make as good a figure
as Mr. Daffodil among 'em.

Exit Sophia *and* Tukely.

ARABELLA.   When Daffodil's real inclinations are known, how those
60   poor wretches will be disappointed.

Exit Arabella.

[SCENE II.]

SCENE, *The Club-Room.*
Lord Racket, Sir Tan-Tivy, Sir William Whister,
Spinner *writing, and* Daffodil. (*Waiter behind.*)

DAFFODIL.   What do you say, my lord, that I don't do it in an hour?

LORD RACKET.   Not in an hour and half, George.

DAFFODIL.   Done with you, my lord. I'll take your seven to five, seventy pound to fifty.

LORD RACKET.   Done. I'll lay odds again, with you, Sir William, and
with you, Sir Tivy.

SIR WILLIAM.   Not I, faith. Daffodil has too many fine women. He'll
never do it.

DAFFODIL.   I'll go into the country for a week, and not a petticoat shall
10   come near me. I'll take the odds again.

SIR TAN-TIVY.   Done, Daffodil.

LORD RACKET.   You are to hop upon one leg without changing, mind
that. Set it down, Spinner.

SPINNER.   I have. Shall I read it?

LORD RACKET.   Silence in the court.

SPINNER (*reads*).   "Lord Racket has betted 70 pounds to 50 with the
Honorable George Daffodil, that the latter does not walk from
Buckingham-Gate to the Bun-house at Chelsea, eat a bun there,

run back to the turnpike, and from thence hop upon one leg, with
the other tied to the cue of his wig, to Buckingham-Gate again,
in an hour and half."

DAFFODIL. I say, done.

LORD RACKET. And done.

SIR WILLIAM. Consider your women. You'll never do it, George.

DAFFODIL. Not do it? (*Hops.*) Why, I'll get a Chelsea pensioner shall
do it in an hour with his wooden leg. What day shall we fix for it?

SIR WILLIAM. The first of April, to be sure.

ALL. Ha, ha, ha!

LORD RACKET. Come, Daffodil, read the bets and matches of today;
then let us finish our champagne and go to the opera.

DAFFODIL (*reads*). "March 24, 1757, Sir Tan-Tivy has pitted Lady
Pettitoe against Dowager Lady Periwinkle, with Sir William
Whister, for 500 £." I'll pit my uncle, Lord Chalkstone, against
'em both.

SIR TAN-TIVY. Done.

LORD RACKET. The odds are against you, Daffodil. My lord has got to
plain Nantz now every morning.

DAFFODIL. And the ladies have been at it, to my knowledge, this half
year. Good, again, George.
"The Honorable George Daffodil has betted one hundred
"pound with Sir William Whister that he produces a
"gentleman, before the 5th of June next, that shall
"live for five days successively without eating, drinking,
"or sleeping."

SIR WILLIAM. He must have no books, George.

DAFFODIL. No, no; the gentleman I mean can't read.

SIR WILLIAM. 'Tis not yourself, George?

OMNES. Ha, ha, ha; 'tis impossible; it must kill him.

DAFFODIL. Why, then I lose my bet. (*Reads.*) "Lord Racket has
matched Sir Joslin Jolly against Major Calipash with Sir Tan-
Tivy, to run fifty yards upon the Mall after dinner. If either tumbles, the wages is lost for fifty pounds."

SPINNER. I'll lay fifty more neither of 'em run the ground in half an
hour.

DAFFODIL. Not in an hour.

SIR TAN-TIVY. Done, Daffodil. I'll bet you a hundred of that.

DAFFODIL. Done, Baronet. I'll double it, if you will.

SIR TAN-TIVY. With all my heart. Book it, Spinner (Spinner *writes*.)

LORD RACKET. You'll certainly lose, George.

DAFFODIL. Impossible, my lord. Sir Joslin is damnably out of wind.

LORD RACKET.   What, asthmatic?

DAFFODIL.   No, quite cured of his asthma—he died yesterday morning. Bite.

ALL.   Bravo, George.

LORD RACKET.   Now you talk of dying, how does your cousin Dizzy?

DAFFODIL.   Lingers on, better and worse. Lives upon asses' milk, panada, and Eringo root.

LORD RACKET.   You'll have a fine windfall there, George, a good two thousand a year.

70 DAFFODIL.   'Tis better, my lord. But I love Dick so well, and have had so many obligations to him—he saved my life once—that I could wish him better health.

SIR WILLIAM.   Or in a better place. There's devilish fine timber in Staunton Woods.

SIR TAN-TIVY.   Down with 'em, Daffodil.

LORD RACKET.   But let Dizzy drop first; a little blast will fell him.

Enter Dizzy.

DIZZY.   Not so little as you may imagine, my lord. Hugh, hugh. (*Coughs.*)

ALL.   Ha, ha, ha!

DAFFODIL.   Angels and ministers! What, Cousin? We were got among
80   your trees.

DIZZY.   You are heartily welcome to any one of 'em, gentlemen, for a proper purpose. Hugh, hugh.

LORD RACKET.   Well said, Dick. How quick his wit, and how youthful the rogue looks.

DAFFODIL.   Bloomy and plump; the country air is a fine thing, my Lord.

DIZZY.   Well, well, be as jocular as you please; I am not so ill as you may wish or imagine. I can walk to Knightsbridge in an hour for a hundred pound.

LORD RACKET.   I bet you a hundred of that, Dizzy.

90 DAFFODIL.   I'll lay you a hundred, Dick, that I can drive a sow and pigs to your lodgings before you can get there.

DIZZY.   Done, I say. (*Draws his purse.*) Done. Two hundred—done—three.

LORD RACKET.   I'll take Dizzy, against your sow and pigs.

SIR WILLIAM.   I take the field against Dizzy.

LORD RACKET.   Done.

SPINNER.   Done.

DIZZY.   Damn your sow and pigs. I am so sick with the thoughts of running with 'em that I shall certainly faint. (*Smells a bottle.*) Hugh,
100   hugh.

DAFFODIL (*aside to the rest*).   Cousin Dizzy can't bear the mention of pork. He hates it. I knew it would work.

DIZZY.   I wish you had not mentioned it. I can't stay. Damn your sow and pigs. Here, Waiter, call a chair. Damn your sow and pigs. Hugh, hugh.

Exit Dizzy.

DAFFODIL.   Poor Dizzy, what a passion he is in. Ha, ha, ha.

LORD RACKET.   The woods are yours, George; you may whet the ax. Dizzy won't live a month.

DAFFODIL.   Pooh, this is nothing. He was always weakly.

110 SIR WILLIAM.   'Tis a family misfortune, Daffodil.

Enter Waiter.

WAITER.   Mr. Dizzy, gentlemen, dropped down at the stair foot, and the cook has carried him behind the bar.

DAFFODIL.   Lay him upon a bed and he'll come to himself.

Exit Waiter.

LORD RACKET.   I'll bet fifty pound that he don't live till morning.

SIR WILLIAM.   I'll lay six to four he don't live a week.

DAFFODIL.   I'll take your fifty pound.

SPINNER.   I'll take your lordship again.

LORD RACKET.   Done, with you both.

SIR TAN-TIVY.   I'll take it again.

120 LORD RACKET.   Done, done, done. But I bar all assistance to him. Not a physician or surgeon sent for, or I am off.

DAFFODIL.   No, no; we are upon honor. There shall be none, else it would be a bubble bet. There shall be none.

SIR WILLIAM.   If I were my lord, now, the physicians should attend him.

Enter Waiter *with a letter.*

WAITER.   A letter for his honor. (*Gives it to* Daffodil. Daffodil *reads it to himself.*)

SIR WILLIAM.   Daffodil, remember the first of April, and let the women alone.

DAFFODIL.   Upon my soul you have hit it. 'Tis a woman, faith, some-

130 thing very particular, and if you are in spirits for a scheme —

LORD RACKET.   Aye, aye; come, come; a scheme, a scheme!

DAFFODIL.   There then, have among you. (*Throws the letter upon the table.*)

LORD RACKET (*reads, all looking on*).   Hum. "If the liking your person be a sin, what woman is not guilty?" Hum, hum—"at the end of the Bird-cage Walk about seven, where the darkness and privacy will befriend my blushes; I will convince you what trust I have in your secrecy and honor.—Yours, INCOGNITA."

DAFFODIL.   Will you go?

LORD RACKET.   What do you propose?

140 DAFFODIL.   To go—if after I have been with her half an hour you'll come upon us and have a blow up.

SIR WILLIAM.   There's a gallant for you!

DAFFODIL.   Prithee, Sir William, be quiet. Must a man be in love with every woman that invites him?

SIR WILLIAM.   No, but he should be honorable to 'em, George, and rather conceal a woman's weakness than expose it. I hate this work, so I'll go to the coffeehouse.

Exit Sir William.

LORD RACKET.   Let him go. Don't mind him, George; he's married and past fifty. This will be a fine frolic, devilish high.

150 DAFFODIL.   Very! Well, I'll go and prepare myself, put on my surtout and take my chair to Buckingham-Gate. I know the very spot.

LORD RACKET.   We'll come with flambeaux; you must be surprised, and —

DAFFODIL.   I know what to do. Here, Waiter, Waiter!

Enter Waiter.

How does cousin Dizzy?

WAITER.   Quite recovered, sir. He is in the Phoenix with two ladies and has ordered a boiled chicken and jellies.

LORD RACKET.   There's a blood for you, without a drop in his veins.

DAFFODIL.   Do you stay with him, then, till I have secured my lady.

160 And in half an hour from this time come away, and bring Dizzy with you.

LORD RACKET.   If he'll leave the ladies. Don't the Italian Marquis dine with us tomorrow?

DAFFODIL.   Certainly.

LORD RACKET.   Well, do you mind your business, and I'll speak to the cook to show his genius. Allons!

Exit Daffodil.

[*Enter* Second Waiter.]

Tom, bid the cook attend me tomorrow morning on special affairs.

Exit Lord Racket, *etc.*

SECOND WAITER.   I shall, my lord.

FIRST WAITER.   I'll lay you, Tom, five six-pences to three, that my lord
170   wins his bet with his Honor Daffodil.
SECOND WAITER.   Done with you, Harry. I'll take your half crown to
         eighteen pence. (*Bell rings within.*)
FIRST WAITER.   Coming, sir! I'll make it shillings, Tom.
SECOND WAITER.   No, Harry, you've the best on't. (*Bell rings.*) Com-
         ing, sir. I'll take five shillings to two. (*Bell rings.*) Coming, sir.
FIRST WAITER.   Coming, sir. No, five to three.
SECOND WAITER.   Shillings?—Coming, sir!
FIRST WAITER.   No, sixpences.
SECOND WAITER.   Done. Sixpences. (*Bell rings.*) Here, sir.
180 FIRST WAITER.   And done (*Bell rings.*) Coming, sir.

                                                        Exeunt.

                        [SCENE III.]

                      [SCENE, The Park.]
    Enter Arabella, Mrs. Damply, Lady Fanny Pewit, Mrs. Dotterel,
         Tukely *in women's clothes, and* Sophia *in men's.*

LADIES ALL.   Ha, ha, ha.
ARABELLA.   What a figure, and what a scheme!
TUKELY.   Dear ladies, be as merry with my figure as you please. Yet
         you shall see, this figure, awkward as it is, shall be preferred in
         its turn as well as you have been.
SOPHIA.   Why will you give yourself this unnecessary trouble, Mr.
         Tukely, to convince these ladies, who had rather still be deluded
         and will hate your friendship for breaking the charm?
ARABELLA.   My dear Cousin, though you are satisfied, these ladies are
10   not. And if they have their particular reasons for their infidelity,
         pray let 'em enjoy it 'til they have other proofs of your prejudices.
SOPHIA.   Aye, Bell, we have all our prejudices.
TUKELY.   What signifies reasoning when we are going upon the ex-
         periment? Dispose of yourselves behind those trees, and I will re-
         pair to the place of appointment and draw him hither. But you
         promise to contain yourselves, let what will happen. Hear and
         see, but be silent.

                                                  Exit Tukely.

SOPHIA.   A severe injunction indeed, ladies. But I must to my post.

                                                  Exit Sophia.

───

    0.1. Lady Fanny] *O1, W1*; Lady Fan *W2*.
    2. scheme] *O1, W1*; scene *W2*.

WIDOW DAMPLY. If he's a villain, I can never hold.

20 LADY PEWIT. I shall tear his eyes out.

MRS. DOTTEREL. For my part, if I was unmarried, I should not think him worth my anger.

ARABELLA. But as you are, Madam —

MRS. DOTTEREL. I understand your insinuations, Miss Bell; but my character and conduct need no justification.

ARABELLA. I beg pardon, madam. I intended no offence. But haste to your posts, ladies; the enemy's at hand.

> *They retire behind the trees.*

> *Enter* Tukely *and* Daffodil.

TUKELY (*in woman's voice*). For heaven's sake, let us be cautious. I am sure I heard a noise.

30 DAFFODIL. 'Twas nothing but your fear, my angel. Don't be alarmed; there can be no danger while we have love and darkness to befriend us.

TUKELY. Bless me, how my heart beats!

DAFFODIL. Poor soul, what a fright it is in. You must not give way to these alarms. Were you as well convinced of my honor as I am of your charms, you would have nothing to fear. (*Squeezes her hand.*)

ARABELLA (*aside*). Upon my word!

WIDOW DAMPLY (*aside*). So, so, so.

TUKELY. Hold, sir, you must take no liberties. But if you have the
40 least feeling for an unhappy woman, urged by her passion to this imprudent step, assist me—forgive me—let me go.

DAFFODIL. Can you doubt my honor? Can you doubt my love? What assurances can I give you to abate your fears?

MRS. DOTTEREL (*aside*). Very slender ones, I can assure her.

TUKELY. I deserve to suffer all I feel. For what, but the most blinded passion, could induce me to declare myself to one whose amours and infidelities are the common topic of conversation.

DAFFODIL (*aside*). Flattering creature!—May I never know your dear name, see your charming face, touch your soft hand, or hear your
50 sweet voice, if I am not more sincere in my affection for this little finger than for all the sex besides. (*The ladies seem astonished.*)

TUKELY. Except the Widow Damply.

DAFFODIL. She! Do you know her, Madam?

TUKELY. I have not that honor.

DAFFODIL. I thought so. Did you never see her, Madam, nodding and gogling in her old-fashioned heavy chariot, drawn by a pair of lean hackney horses, with a fat blackamoor footman behind in a scanty livery, red greasy stockings and a dirty turban? (*The Widow seems disordered.*)

TUKELY.   All which may be only a foil to her beauty. (*Sighs.*)

60 DAFFODIL.   Beauty! Don't sigh, Madam. She is past forty, wears a wig, and has lost two of her fore teeth. And then she has so long a beard upon her upper lip, and takes so much Spanish snuff, that she looks for all the world like the Great Mogul in petticoats. Ha, ha!

WIDOW DAMPLY (*aside*).   What falsehood and ingratitude!

TUKELY.   Could I descend to the slander of the town, there is a married lady —

DAFFODIL.   Poor Mrs. Dotterel, you mean.

MRS. DOTTEREL [*aside*].   Why am I to be mentioned? I have nothing to do —

70 WIDOW DAMPLY [*aside*].   Nay, nay; you must have your share of the panegyric.

TUKELY.   She is young and has wit.

DAFFODIL.   She's an idiot, Madam. And as fools are generally loving, she has forgot all her obligations to old Mr. Dotterel, who married her without a petticoat, and now seizes upon every young fellow she can lay her hands upon. She has spoiled me three suits of clothes with tearing the flaps and sleeves. Ha, ha, ha.

MRS. DOTTEREL [*aside*].   Monster of iniquity!

DAFFODIL.   She has even stormed me in my own house. But with all my
80   faults, Madam, you'll never find me overfond of age or ignorance.

WIDOW DAMPLY [*aside*].   I could tear him to pieces.

MRS. DOTTEREL [*aside*].   I will tear him to pieces.

ARABELLA [*aside*].   Be quiet, and we'll all tear him to pieces.

TUKELY (*aside*).   He has swallowed the hook and can't escape.

DAFFODIL.   What do you say, madam?

TUKELY.   I am only sighing, sir.

DAFFODIL (*aside*).   Fond creature. [*To* Tukely.] I know there are a thousand stories about me. You have heard, too, of Lady Fanny Pewit, I suppose? Don't be alarmed.

90 TUKELY.   I can't help it, sir. She is a fine woman, and a woman of quality.

DAFFODIL.   A fine woman, perhaps, for a woman of quality. But she is an absolute old maid, Madam, almost as thick as she is long, middle-aged, homely and wanton. That's her character.

LADY PEWIT (*going*).   Then there is no sincerity in man.

ARABELLA [*aside*].   Postively you shan't stir.

DAFFODIL.   Upon my soul, I pity the poor creature. She is now upon her last legs. If she does not run away with some foolish gentle-

100 man this winter, she'll run into the country and marry her footman. Ha, ha, ha.

LADY PEWIT [*aside*].   My footman shall break his bones, I can tell him
that.

DAFFODIL.   Hush, Madam. I protest I thought I heard a voice. (*Aside.*)
I wonder they don't come.

TUKELY.   'Twas only I, Mr. Daffodil. I was murmuring to you. (*Sighs.*)

DAFFODIL.   Pretty murmurer. (*Aside.*) Egad, if they don't come soon,
the lady will grow fond.

TUKELY.   But among your conquests, Mr. Daffodil, you forget Miss
Sophy Sprightly.

110 DAFFODIL.   And her cousin Arabella. I was coming to 'em; poor silly,
good-natured, loving fools. I made my addresses to one through
pique and the other for pity. That was all.

TUKELY.   Oh, that I could believe you.

DAFFODIL.   Don't be uneasy. I'll tell you how it was, Madam. You must
know, there is a silly, self-sufficient fellow, one Tukely —

TUKELY (*aside*).   So, so. [*To* Daffodil.] I know him a little.

DAFFODIL.   I am sorry for it. The less you know of him the better. The
fellow pretended to look fierce at me, for which I resolved to have
his mistress. So I threw in my line, and without much trouble
120 hooked her. Her poor cousin, too, nibbled at the bait and was
caught. So I have had my revenge upon Tukely, and now I shall
willingly resign poor Sophy, and throw him in her cousin for a
make-weight. Ha, ha, ha.

LADY PEWIT [*aside*].   This is some comfort at least.

ARABELLA [aside].   Your ladyship is better than you was. (*Noise without.*)

TUKELY.   I vow I hear a noise. What shall we do? It comes this way.

DAFFODIL.   They can't see us, my dear. (*Aside.*) I wish my friends
would come. [*To* Tukely.] Don't whisper or breathe.

Enter Sophia *in a surtout and slouched hat.*

SOPHIA.   If I could but catch her at her pranks. She certainly must be
130 this way, for the chair is waiting at the end of Rosamond's Pond.
I have thrown one of her chairmen into it, and if I could but catch
her —

TUKELY.   Oh, Sir, my passion has undone me. I am discovered. It is my
husband, Sir George, and he is looking for me.

DAFFODIL.   The devil it is! Why then, Madam, the best way will be for
you to go to him and let me sneak off the other way.

---

122.   throw him in] *O*1; throws in *W*1, *W*2.

TUKELY. Go to him, sir? What can I say to him?

DAFFODIL. Anthing, Madam; say you had the vapours and wanted air.

TUKELY. Lord, sir. He is the most passionate of mortals; and I am
140   afraid he is in liquor too; and then he is mad.

SOPHIA (*looking about*). If I could but catch her —

DAFFODIL. For your sake, Madam, I'll make the best of my way home.
(*Going.*)

TUKELY. What? Would you leave me to the fury of an enraged husband? Is that your affection? (*Holds him.*)

SOPHIA. If I could but catch her. Ha! What's that? I saw something
move in the dark. The point of my sword shall tickle it out, whatever it is. (*Draws and goes towards 'em.*)

TUKELY. For heaven's sake draw and fight him while I make my escape.

150 DAFFODIL. Fight him! 'Twould be cowardly to fight in the dark, and
with a drunken man. I'll call the sentry.

TUKELY. And expose us to the world?

DAFFODIL (*aside*). I would to heaven we were. (*He comes forward.*)
Let me go, Madam, you pinch me to the bone.

TUKELY. He won't know us. I have my mask on.

LADIES [*aside*]. Ha, ha, ha!

SOPHIA. What, is the devil and his imps playing at Blindman's Buff?
Aye, aye, here he is indeed, Satan himself, dressed like a fine gentleman. Come, Mr. Devil, out with your pitch-fork and let us take
160   a thrust or two.

DAFFODIL. You mistake me, Sir. I am not the person, indeed I am not.
I know nothing of your wife, Sir George. And if you knew how
little I care for the whole sex, you would not be so furious with
an innocent man.

SOPHIA. Who are you, then? And what are you doing with that blackamoor lady there, dancing a saraband with a pair of castanets?
Speak, Sir.

DAFFODIL. Pray forbear, Sir. Here's company coming that will satisfy you in everything. Hallo, hallo; here, here, here. (*Hallo's*
170   *faintly.*) My lord, my lord—Spinner, Dizzy—hallo!

         Enter Lord Racket, Sir Tan-Tivy, Spinner *and*
              Dizzy, *with torches.*

LORD RACKET. What's the matter here? Who calls for help?

DAFFODIL (*running to 'em with his sword drawn*). Oh, my friends, I
have been wishing for you this half hour. I have been set upon by
a dozen fellows. They have all made their escape, but this. My arm

is quite dead. I have been at Cart and Tierce with 'em all for near
a quarter of an hour.

SOPHIA.   In buckram, my Lord. He was got with my property here,
and I would have chastised him for it, if your coming had not prevented it.

180   DAFFODIL.   Let us throw the rascal into Rosamond's Pond.

LORD RACKET.   Come, Sir, can you swim?

> *All going up.* Tukely *snatches* Sophia's *sword*
> *and she runs behind him.*

TUKELY.   I'll defend you, my dear. What, would you murder a man
and lie with his wife, too? Oh, you are a wicked gentleman, Mr.
Daffodil. (*Attacks* Daffodil.)

DAFFODIL.   Why, the devil's in the woman, I think.

> *All the ladies advance from behind.*

LADIES.   Ha, ha, ha! Your humble servant, Mr. Daffodil. (*Curtseying.*)
Ha, ha, ha!

DAFFODIL.   This is all enchantment.

LADY PEWIT.   No, sir, the enchantment is broke. And the old maid,
190   Sir, homely and wanton, before she retires into the country, has
the satisfaction of knowing that the agreeable Mr. Daffodil is a
much more contemptible mortal than the footman which his goodness has been pleased to marry her to.

LADIES.   Ha, ha, ha.

WIDOW DAMPLY.   Would Mr. Daffodil please to have a pinch of Spanish snuff out of the Great Mogul's box? 'Tis the best thing in the
world for low spirits. (*Offers her box.*)

LADIES.   Ha, ha, ha.

MRS. DOTTEREL.   If a fool may not be permitted to speak, Mr. Daffodil,
200   let her at least be permitted to laugh at so fine a gentleman. Ha,
ha, ha.

ARABELLA.   Were you as sensible of shame as you are of fear, the sight
of me, whom you loved for pity, would be revenge sufficient. But
I can forgive your baseness to me much easier than I can myself,
for my behavior to this happy couple.

DAFFODIL.   Who the devil are they?

ARABELLA.   The Marquis and Marchioness of Macaroni, ladies. Ha, ha.

SOPHIA.   Ha! *Mio carrissimo amico, il Signior Daffodillo!*

DAFFODIL.   How! Tukely and Sophia! If I don't wake soon, I shall wish
210   never to wake again.

SOPHIA.   Who bids fairest now for Rosamond's Pond?

LORD RACKET. What, in the name of wonder, is all this business? I don't
understand it.

DIZZY. Nor I neither; but 'tis very droll, faith.

TUKELY. The mystery will clear in a moment.

DAFFODIL. Don't give yourself any trouble, Mr. Tukely. Things are
pretty clear as they are. The night's cool, and my cousin Dizzy
here is an invalid. If you please, another time when there is less
company. (*Ladies laugh.*) The ladies are pleased to be merry, and
220 you are pleased to be a little angry; and so, for the sake of tranquility, I'll go to the opera.

> Daffodil, *sneaking out by degrees.*

LORD RACKET. This is a fine blowup, indeed. Ladies, your humble servant. Hallo! Daffodil!

> *Exit Lord* Racket.

DIZZY. I'll lay you a hundred that my cousin never intrigues again.
George! George! Don't run—hugh, hugh —

> *Exit* Dizzy.

TUKELY. As my satisfaction is complete, I have none to ask of Mr.
Daffodil. I forgive his behavior to me, as it has hastened and confirmed my happiness here. (*To* Sophia.) But as a friend to you,
ladies, I shall insist upon his making you ample satisfaction. How-
230 ever, this benefit will arise, that you will hereafter equally detest
and shun these destroyers of your reputation.

In you coquettry is a loss of fame;
But in our sex 'tis that detested name
That marks the want of manhood, virtue, sense, and shame.

The Guardian

A Comedy

1759

THE
GUARDIAN.

A
COMEDY
OF
TWO ACTS.

As it is perform'd at the

THEATRE-ROYAL in *Drury-Lane.*

LONDON:

Printed for J. NEWBERY, at the *Bible* and *Sun*, in St. *Paul's*
Church-Yard ; and Sold by R. BAILYE, at *Litchfield* ;
J. LEAKE and W. FREDERICK, at *Bath*; B. COLLINS,
at *Salisbury* ; and S. STABLER at *York.*

MDCCLIX.

[Price One Shilling.]

Advertisement

The *Pupille* of Monsieur *Fagan* is mentioned by Voltaire, and other French writers, as the most complete *Petite-Piece* upon their stage.—It now appears in an English dress, with such alterations from the original as the difference of language and manners required.—It has more than answered the expectations of the author, who takes this opportunity to return thanks to the public for their kind indulgence, and to the performers for their great care.

Dramatis Personae

MEN

Mr. HEARTLY, *the Guardian.*   Mr. GARRICK.
Sir CHARLES CLACKIT.   Mr. YATES.
Mr. CLACKIT, *his Nephew.*   Mr. OBRIEN.
SERVANT.

WOMEN

Miss HARRIET, *an Heiress,*   Miss PRITCHARD.
LUCY, *the Maid.*   Mrs. CLIVE.

The Guardian

ACT I. SCENE I.

A hall in Mr. Heartly's house.

Enter Sir Charles Clackit, *his* Nephew, *and* servant.

SERVANT. Please to walk this way, Sir.

SIR CHARLES. Where is your master, Friend?

SERVANT. In his dressing room, Sir.

YOUNG CLACKIT. Let him know then —

SIR CHARLES. Prithee be quiet, Jack; when I am in company let me direct. 'Tis proper and decent.

YOUND CLACKIT. I am dumb, Sir.

SIR CHARLES. Tell Mr. Heartly his friend and neighbor, Sir Charles Clackit, would say three words to him.

10 SERVANT. I shall, Sir.

Exit.

SIR CHARLES. Now, Nephew, consider once again, before I open the matter to my neighbor Heartly, what I am going to undertake for you.—Why don't you speak?

YOUNG CLACKIT. Is it proper and decent, Uncle?

SIR CHARLES. Pshaw! Don't be a fool, but answer me. Don't you flatter yourself. What assurance have you that this young lady, my friend's ward, has a liking to you? The young fellows of this age are all coxcombs, and I am afraid you are no exception to the general rule.

YOUNG CLACKIT. Thank you, Uncle. But may I this instant be struck
20 old and peevish if I would put you upon a false scent to expose you for all the fine women in Christendom. I assure you again and again, and you may take my word, Uncle, that Miss Harriet has no kind of aversion to your nephew and most humble servant.

SIR CHARLES.   Aye, aye, vanity, vanity! But I never take a young fellow's word about women. They'll lie as fast, and with as little conscience, as the Brussels Gazette. Produce your proofs.

YOUNG CLACKIT.   Can't your eyes see 'em, Uncle, without urging me to the indelicacy of repeating 'em?

SIR CHARLES.   Why I see nothing but a fool's head and a fool's coat sup-
30   ported by a pair of most unpromising legs. Have you no better proofs?

YOUNG CLACKIT.   Yes I have, my good infidel Uncle, half a hundred.

SIR CHARLES.   Out with them then.

YOUNG CLACKIT.   First then—Whenever I see her, she never looks at me. That's a sign of love. Whenever I speak to her, she never answers me.—Another sign of love. And whenever I speak to anybody else, she seems to be perfectly easy.—That's a certain sign of love.

SIR CHARLES.   The devil it is!

YOUNG CLACKIT.   When I am with her, she's always grave. And the
40   moment I get up to leave her, then the poor thing begins, "Why will you leave me, Mr. Clackit? Can't you sacrifice a few moments to my bashfulness?—Stay, you agreeable runaway, stay; I shall soon overcome the fears your presence gives me." I could say more, but a man of honor, Uncle —

SIR CHARLES.   What, and has she said all these things to you?

YOUNG CLACKIT.   Oh yes, and ten times more—with her eyes.

SIR CHARLES.   With her eyes! Eyes are very equivocal, Jack. However, if the young lady has any liking to you, Mr. Heartly is too much a man of the world and too much my friend to oppose the match.
50   So do you walk into the garden, and I will open the matter to him.

YOUNG CLACKIT.   Is there any objection to my staying, Uncle? The business will be soon ended. You will propose the match, he will give his consent, I shall give mine, Miss is sent for, and *l'affair est fait.* (*Snapping his finger.*)

SIR CHARLES.   And so you think that a young beautiful heiress with forty thousand pounds is to be had with a scrap of French and a snap of your finger. Prithee, get away and don't provoke me.

YOUNG CLACKIT.   Nay, but, my dear Uncle —

SIR CHARLES.   Nay, but my impertinent Nephew, either retire or I'll
60   throw up the game. (*Putting him out.*)

YOUNG CLACKIT.   Well, well, I am gone, Uncle. When you come to the point, I shall be ready to make my appearance. *Bon voyage!*

Exit.

SIR CHARLES.   The devil's in these young fellows, I think. We send 'em abroad to cure their sheepishness, and they get above proof the other way.

Enter Mr. Heartly.

Good morrow to you, Neighbor.

HEARTLY. And to you, Sir Charles. I am glad to see you so strong and healthy.

SIR CHARLES. If I can return you the compliment, my Friend, without
70   flattery, you don't look more than thirty-five. And between ourselves, you are on the wrong side of forty. But mum for that.

HEARTLY. Ease and tranquility keep me as you see.

SIR CHARLES. Why don't you marry, Neighbor? A good wife would do well for you.

HEARTLY. For me? You are pleased to be merry, Sir Charles.

SIR CHARLES. No, faith, I am serious, and had I a daughter to recommend to you, you should say me nay more than once, I assure you,
Neighbor Heartly, before I would quit you.

HEARTLY. I am much obliged to you.
80 SIR CHARLES. But, indeed, you are a little too much of the philosopher
to think of being troubled with women and their concerns.

HEARTLY. I beg your pardon, Sir Charles. Though there are many who
call themselves philosophers that live single, and perhaps are in the
right of it, yet I cannot think that marriage is at all inconsistent
with true philosophy. A wise man will resolve to live like the rest
of the world, with this only difference, that he is neither a slave
to passions nor events. It is not because I have a little philosophy,
but because I am on the wrong side of forty, Sir Charles, that I
desire to be excused. (*Smiling.*)
90 SIR CHARLES. As you please, Sir. And now to my business. You have
no objection, I suppose, to tie up your ward, Miss Harriet, though
you have slipped the collar yourself? Ha, ha, ha!

HEARTLY. Quite the contrary, Sir. I have taken her some time from
the boarding school, and brought her home in order to dispose of
her worthily, with her own inclination.

SIR CHARLES. Her father, I have heard you say, recommended that particular care to you, when she had reached a certain age.

HEARTLY. He did so; and I am the more desirous to obey him scrupu-
lously in this circumstance, as she will be a most valuable acqui-
100   sition to the person who shall gain her—for, not to mention her
fortune, which is the least consideration, her sentiments are worthy
of her birth. She is gentle, modest, and obliging. In a word, my
Friend, I never saw youth more amiable or discreet. But perhaps I
am a little partial to her.

SIR CHARLES. No, no, she is a delicious creature. Everybody says so.

---

102. of her birth] *O*1, *O*2, *O*4; her birth *O*3, *W*1, *W*2.

Miss Pritchard as Harriet.

'Tis most sincerely and literally true.

Act 1.

Publish'd by Harrison & C°. May 1. 1779.

Miss Pritchard as Harriet in *The Guardian*.
Harvard Theatre Collection

But I believe, Neighbor, something has happened that you little think of.

HEARTLY.   What, pray, Sir Charles?

SIR CHARLES.   My nephew, Mr. Heartly —

Enter Young Clackit.

110   YOUNG CLACKIT.   Here I am, at your service, Sir. My Uncle is a little unhappy in his manner, but I'll clear the matter in a moment. Miss Harriet, Sir,—your ward —

SIR CHARLES.   Get away, you puppy!

YOUNG CLACKIT.   Miss Harriet, Sir, your ward—a most accomplished young lady, to be sure —

SIR CHARLES.   Thou art a most accomplished coxcomb, to be sure.

HEARTLY.   Pray, Sir Charles, let the young gentleman speak.

YOUNG CLACKIT.   You'll excuse me, Mr. Heartly. My Uncle does not set up for an orator,—a little confused, or so, Sir. You see me what I

120   am. But I ought to ask pardon for the young lady and myself. We are young, Sir. I must confess we were wrong to conceal it from you. But my Uncle, see, is pleased to be angry, and therefore I shall say no more at present.

SIR CHARLES.   If you don't leave the room this moment and stay in the garden till I call you —

YOUNG CLACKIT.   I am sorry I have displeased you. I did not think it was *mal-a-propos*. But you must have your way, Uncle. You command—I submit. Mr. Heartly, yours.

Exit Young Clackit.

SIR CHARLES (*aside*).   Puppy.—My nephew's a little unthinking, Mr.

130   Heartly, as you see, and therefore I have been a little cautious how I have proceeded in this affair. But, indeed, he has persuaded me in a manner that your ward and he are not ill together.

HEARTLY.   Indeed! This is the first notice I have had of it, and I cannot conceive why Miss Harriet should conceal it from me, for I have often assured her that I would never oppose her inclination, though I might endeavor to direct it.

SIR CHARLES.   'Tis human nature, Neighbor. We are so ashamed of our first passion that we would willingly hide it from ourselves. But will you mention my nephew to her?

140   HEARTLY.   I must beg your pardon, Sir Charles. The name of the gentleman whom she chooses must first come from herself. My ad-

---

120-21.   We are young] O_1, O_2, O_3, O_4; We are both young W_1, W_2.

128.   yours] O_1, O_2, O_4; your's O_3, W_1, W_2.

128.1.   *Exit* Young Clackit] O_1, O_2, O_4; Exit O_3, W_1, W_2.

vice or importunity shall never influence her. If guardians would
be less rigorous, young people would be more reasonable. And
I am so unfashionable to think that happiness in marriage can't
be bought too dear. I am still on the wrong side of forty, Sir
Charles.

SIR CHARLES. No, no, you are right, Neighbor. But here she is. Don't
alarm her young heart too much, I beg of you. Upon my word,
she is a sweet morsel.

Enter Miss Harriet *and* Lucy.

150 MISS HARRIET. He is with company. I'll speak to him another time.
(*Retiring.*)

LUCY. Young, handsome, and afraid of being seen. You are very particular, Miss.

HEARTLY. Miss Harriet, you must not go. (Harriet *returns.*) Sir Charles,
give me leave to introduce you to this young lady. (*Introduces
her.*) You know, I suppose, the reason of this gentleman's visit to
me? (*To Harriet.*)

MISS HARRIET. Sir! (*Confused.*)

HEARTLY. You may trust me, my dear (*smiling*). Don't be disturbed I
shall not reproach you with anything but keeping your wishes a
160   secret from me so long.

MISS HARRIET. Upon my word, Sir,—Lucy!

LUCY. Well, and Lucy! I'll lay my life 'tis a treaty of marriage. Is that
such a dreadful thing? Oh, for shame, Madam! Young ladies of
fashion are not frightened at such things nowadays.

HEARTLY (*to* Sir Charles). We have gone too far, Sir Charles. We must
excuse her delicacy and give her time to recover. I had better talk
with her alone. We will leave her now. Be persuaded that no endeavors shall be wanting on my part to bring this affair to a happy
and a speedy conclusion.

170 SIR CHARLES. I shall be obliged to you, Mr. Heartly. Young lady, your
servant. What grace and modesty! She is a most engaging creature,
and I shall be proud to make her one of my family.

HEARTLY. You do us honor, Sir Charles.

Exeunt Sir Charles *and* Heartly.

LUCY. Indeed, Miss Harriet, you are very particular. You was tired of
the boarding school, and yet seem to have no inclination to be married. What can be the meaning of all this? That smirking old

---

159. reproach you] *O*1, *O*2, *O*4; reproach not you *O*3, *W*1, *W*2.

gentleman is uncle to Mr. Clackit, and, my life for it, he has made some proposals to your guardian.

MISS HARRIET.   Prithee, don't plague me about Mr. Clackit.

180 LUCY.   But why not, Miss? Though he is a little fantastical, loves to hear himself talk, and is somewhat self-sufficient, you must consider he is young, has been abroad, and keeps good company. The trade will soon be at an end, if young ladies and gentlemen grow over nice and exceptious.

MISS HARRIET.   But if I can find one without these faults, I may surely please myself.

LUCY.   Without these faults? And is he young, Miss?

MISS HARRIET.   He is sensible, modest, polite, affable, and generous, and charms from the natural impulses of his own heart, as
190   much as others disgust by their senseless airs and insolent affectation.

LUCY.   Upon my word! But why have you kept this secret so long? Your guardian is kind to you beyond conception. What difficulties can you have to overcome?

MISS HARRIET.   Why, the difficulty of declaring my sentiments.

LUCY.   Leave that to me, Miss. But your spark, with all his accomplishments, must have very little penetration not to have discovered his good fortune in your eyes.

MISS HARRIET.   I take care that my eyes don't tell too much, and he has
200   too much delicacy to interpret looks to his advantage. Besides, he would certainly disapprove my passion; and if I should ever make the declaration and meet with a denial, I should absolutely die with shame.

LUCY.   I'll insure your life for a silver thimble. But what can possibly hinder your coming together?

MISS HARRIET.   His excess of merit.

LUCY.   His excess of a fiddlestick. But come, I'll put you in the way. You shall trust me with the secret; I'll entrust it again to half a dozen friends; they shall entrust it to half a dozen more, by which
210   means it will travel half the town over in a week's time. The gentleman will certainly hear of it, and then if he is not at your feet in the fetching of a sigh, I'll give up all my perquisites at your wedding. What is his name, Miss?

MISS HARRIET.   I cannot tell you his name. Indeed, I cannot. I am afraid of being thought too singular. But why should I be ashamed of my passion? Is the impression which a virtuous character makes upon our hearts such a weakness that it may not be excused?

---

192. this secret] *O*1, *O*2, *O*4, *W*1, *W*2; omit *this O*3.

LUCY.   By my faith, Miss, I can't understand you. You are afraid of being thought singular, and you really are so. I would sooner re-
220   nounce all the passions in the universe than have one in my bosom beating and fluttering itself to pieces. Come, come, Miss, open the window and let the poor devil out.

Enter Heartly.

HEARTLY.   Leave us, Lucy.
LUCY.   There's something going forward. 'Tis very hard I can't be of the party.

Exit.

HEARTLY (*aside*).   She certainly thinks, from the character of the young man, that I shall disapprove of her choice.
MISS HARRIET [*aside*].   What can I possibly say to him? I am as much ashamed to make the declaration as he would be to understand it.
230   HEARTLY.   Don't imagine, my dear, that I would know more of your thoughts than you desire I should. But the tender care which I have ever shown, and the sincere friendship which I shall always have for you, give me a sort of right to inquire into everything that concerns you. Some friends have spoken to me in particular. But that is not all. I have lately found you thoughtful, absent, and dis-turbed. Be plain with me. Has not somebody been happy enough to please you?
MISS HARRIET.   I cannot deny it, Sir. Yes, somebody indeed has pleased me. But I must entreat you not to give credit to any idle stories, or
240   inquire farther into the particulars of my inclination, for I cannot possibly have resolution enough to say more to you.
HEARTLY.   But have you made a choice, my dear?
MISS HARRIET.   I have, in my own mind, Sir, and 'tis impossible to make a better. Reason, honor, everything must approve it.
HEARTLY.   And how long have you conceived this passion?
MISS HARRIET (*sighs*).   Ever since I left the country—to live with you.
HEARTLY.   I see your confusion, my dear, and will relieve you from it immediately. I am informed of the whole —
MISS HARRIET.   Sir!
250   HEARTLY.   Don't be uneasy, for I can with pleasure assure you that your passion is returned with equal tenderness.
MISS HARRIET.   If you are not deceived, I cannot be more happy.
HEARTLY.   I think I am not deceived. But after the declaration you have made and the assurances which I have given you, why will you conceal it any longer? Have I not deserved a little more confidence from you?
MISS HARRIET.   You have indeed deserved it and should certainly have

it, were I not well assured that you would oppose my inclinations.

HEARTLY.   I oppose 'em? Am I then so unkind to you, my dear? Can

260   you in the least doubt of my affection for you? I promise you that I have no will but yours.

MISS HARRIET.   Since you desire it, then, I will endeavor to explain myself.

HEARTLY.   I am all attention. Speak, my dear.

MISS HARRIET.   And if I do, I feel I shall never be able to speak to you again.

HEARTLY.   How can that be, when I shall agree with you in everything?

MISS HARRIET.   Indeed you won't. Pray let me retire to my own chamber. I am not well, Sir.

270 HEARTLY.   I see your delicacy is hurt, my dear. But let me entreat you once more to confide in me. Tell me his name, and the next moment I will go to him and assure him that my consent shall confirm both your happiness.

MISS HARRIET.   You will easily find him. And when you have, pray tell him how improper it is for a young woman to speak first. Persuade him to spare my blushes and to release me from so terrible a situation. I shall leave him with you, and hope that this declaration will make it impossible for you to mistake me any longer.

Harriet is going, but, *upon seeing* Young Clackit,
remains upon the stage.

HEARTLY (*aside*).   Are we not alone? What can this mean?

[*Enter* Young Clackit.]

280 YOUNG CLACKIT [*aside*].   *Apropos*, faith! Here they are together.

HEARTLY (*aside*).   I did not see him, but now the riddle's explained.

MISS HARRIET (*aside*).   What can he want now? This is the most spiteful interruption.

YOUNG CLACKIT.   By your leave, Mr. Heartly. (*Crosses him to go to Harriet.*) Have I caught you at last, my divine Harriet? Well, Mr. Heartly, *sans façon*—but what's the matter, ho! Things look a little gloomy here. One mutters to himself and gives me no answer, and the other turns the head and winks at me. How the devil am I to interpret all this?

290 MISS HARRIET.   I wink at you, Sir? Did I, Sir?

YOUNG CLACKIT.   Yes, you, my angel. But mum. Mr. Heartly, for heaven's sake, what is all this? Speak, I conjure you; is it life or death with me?

---

261.   yours] *O*1, *O*2, *O*4; your's *O*3, *W*1, *W*2.

MISS HARRIET.   What a dreadful situation I am in!

YOUNG CLACKIT.   Hope for the best. I'll bring matters about, I warrant you.

HEARTLY.   You have both of you great reason to be satisfied. Nothing shall oppose your happiness.

YOUND CLACKIT.   Bravo, Mr. Heartly!

300 HEARTLY.   Miss Harriet's will is a law to me. And for you, Sir, the friendship which I have ever professed for your uncle is too sincere not to exert some of it upon this occasion.

MISS HARRIET (*aside*).   I shall die with confusion!

YOUNG CLACKIT.   I am alive again. Dear Mr. Heartly, thou art a most adorable creature. What a happiness it is to have to do with a man of sense, who has no foolish prejudices and can see when a young fellow has something tolerable about him.

HEARTLY.   Sir, not to flatter you, I must declare that it is from a knowl-edge of your friends and family that I have hopes of seeing you

310 and this young lady happy. I will go directly to your uncle and assure him that everything goes on to our wishes. (*Going.*)

MISS HARRIET.   Mr. Heartly! Pray, Sir, —

HEARTLY.   Poor Miss Harriet, I see your distress and am sorry for it; but it must be got over, and the sooner the better. Mr. Clackit, my dear, will be glad of an opportunity to entertain you for the little time that I shall be absent. (*Smiling.*) Poor Miss Harriet!

Exit.

YOUNG CLACKIT.   *Allez, allez, Monsieur!* I'll answer for that. Well, Madam, I think everything succeeds to our wishes. Be sincere, my Adorable. Don't you think yourself a very happy young lady?

320 MISS HARRIET.   I shall be most particularly obliged to you, Sir, if you would inform me what is the meaning of all this.

YOUNG CLACKIT.   Inform you, Miss? The matter, I believe, is pretty clear. Our friends have understanding; we have affections. And a marriage follows of course.

MISS HARRIET.   Marriage, Sir? Pray what relation or particular con-nection is there between you and me, Sir?

YOUNG CLACKIT.   I may be deceived, faith. But upon my honor I always supposed that there was a little smattering of inclination between us.

MISS HARRIET.   And have you spoke to my guardian upon this sup-

330 position, Sir?

YOUNG CLACKIT.   And are you angry at it? I believe not. (*Smiling.*) Come, come, I believe not. 'Tis indelicate in you to be upon the reserve.

MISS HARRIET.   Indeed, Sir, this behavior of yours is most extraordinary.

YOUNG CLACKIT.   Come, come, my dear, don't carry this jest too far,
   è troppo, è troppo, mia carissima. What the devil, when everything
   is agreed upon, and uncles and guardians and such folks have given
   their consent, why continue the hypocrisy?

MISS HARRIET.   They may have consented for you; but I am mistress of
340   my affections and will never dispose of 'em by proxy.

YOUNG CLACKIT.   Upon my soul, this is very droll. What, has not your
   guardian been here this moment and expressed all imaginable pleasure at our intended union?

MISS HARRIET.   He is in an error, Sir. And had I not been too much
   astonished at your behavior, I had undeceived him long before now.

YOUNG CLACKIT (*humming a tune*).   But pray, Miss, to return to business, what can be your intention in raising all this confusion in the
   family and opposing your own inclinations?

MISS HARRIET.   Opposing my own inclinations, Sir?

350   YOUNG CLACKIT.   Aye, opposing your own inclinations, Madam. Do
   you know, Child, if you carry on this farce any longer, I shall begin to be a little angry.

MISS HARRIET.   I would wish it, Sir, for be assured that I never in my
   life had the least thought about you.

YOUNG CLACKIT.   Words, words, words.

MISS HARRIET.   'Tis most sincerely and literally true.

YOUNG CLACKIT.   Come, come, I know what I know.

MISS HARRIET.   Don't make yourself ridiculous, Mr. Clackit.

YOUNG CLACKIT.   Don't you make yourself miserable, Miss Harriet.

360   MISS HARRIET.   I am only so when you persist to torment me.

YOUNG CLACKIT (*smiling*).   And you really believe that you don't love
   me?

MISS HARRIET.   Positively not.

YOUNG CLACKIT (*conceitedly*).   And you are very sure now that you
   hate me?

MISS HARRIET.   Oh, most cordially.

YOUNG CLACKIT.   Poor young lady! I do pity you from my soul.

MISS HARRIET.   Then why won't you leave me?

YOUNG CLACKIT.   "She never told her love,
370   But let concealment like a worm i'th' bud,
   Feed on her damask cheek."
   Take warning, Miss, when you once begin to pine in
   thought, it's all over with you, and be assured, since
   you are obstinately bent to give yourself airs, that,
   if you once suffer me to leave this house in a pet—

---

336.   *è troppo, è troppo*] O1, O2, O3, O4, W1; omit one *è troppo* W2.

Do you mind me?—not all your sighing, whining, fits,
vapors, and hysterics, shall ever move me to take the
least compassion on you, *coute qui coute*.

Enter Heartly *and* Sir Charles.

SIR CHARLES. I am overjoyed to hear it. There they are, the pretty
380   doves! That is the age, Neighbor Heartly, for happiness and
pleasure.
HEARTLY. I am willing, you see, to lose no time, which may convince
you, Sir Charles, how proud I am of this alliance in our families.
SIR CHARLES. The thoughts of it rejoices me. Gad, I will send for the
fiddles and take a dance myself, and a fig for the gout and rheumatism. But, hold, hold! The lovers, methinks, are a little out of
humor with each other. What is the matter, Jack? Not pouting,
sure, before your time.
YOUNG CLACKIT (*hums a tune*). A trifle, Sir. The lady will tell you.
390   HEARTLEY. You seem to be troubled, Harriet. What can this mean?
MISS HARRIET. You have been in an error, Sir, about me. I did not
undeceive you, because I could not imagine that the consequences
could have been so serious and so sudden. But I am now forced to
tell you that you have misunderstood me, that you have distressed
me.
HEARTLY. How, my dear?
SIR CHARLES. What do you say, Miss?
YOUNG CLACKIT. Mademoiselle is pleased to be out of humor, but I
can't blame her, for, upon my honor, I think a little coquetry be-
400   comes her.
SIR CHARLES. Aye, aye, aye. Oh, ho! Is that all? These little squalls
seldom overset the lovers' boat, but drive it the faster to port. Aye,
aye, aye.
HEARTLY. Don't be uneasy, my dear, that you have declared your passion. Be consistent now, lest you should be thought capricious.
YOUNG CLACKIT. Talk to her a little, Mr. Heartly. She is a fine lady and
has many virtues, but she does not know the world.
SIR CHARLES. Come, come, you must be friends again, my children.
MISS HARRIET. I beg you will let me alone, Sir.
410   HEARTLEY. For heaven's sake, Miss Harriet, explain this riddle to me.
MISS HARRIET. I cannot, Sir. I have discovered the weakness of my
heart. I have discovered it to you, Sir. But your unkind interpreta-
tions and reproachful looks convince me that I have already said
too much.

Exit.

SIR CHARLES (*as* Heartly *muses*). Well, but hark 'ye, Nephew. This is going a little too far. What have you done to her?

HEARTLY. I never saw her so much moved before!

YOUNG CLACKIT. Upon my soul, gentlemen, I am as much surprised at it as you can be. The little *brouillerie* between us arose upon her
420 persisting that there was no passion, no *penchant*, between us.

SIR CHARLES. I'll tell you what, Jack. There is a certain kind of impudence about you that I don't approve of; and were I a young girl those coxcomical airs of yours would surfeit me.

YOUNG CLACKIT. But as the young ladies are not quite so squeamish as you, Uncle, I fancy they will choose me as I am. Ha, ha! But what can the lady object to? I have offered to marry her; is not that a proof sufficient that I like her? A young fellow must have some affection that will go such lengths to indulge it. Ha, ha!

SIR CHARLES. Why really, Friend Heartly, I don't see how a young
430 man can well do more, or a lady desire more. What say you, Neighbor?

HEARTLY. Upon my word, I am puzzled about it. My thoughts upon the matter are so various and so confused. Everything I see and hear is so contradictory, is so—. She certainly cannot like anybody else?

YOUNG CLACKIT. No, no; I'll answer for that.

HEARTLY. Or she may be fearful then that your passion for her is not sincere, or like other young men of the times you may grow careless upon marriage and neglect her.

440 YOUNG CLACKIT. Ha! Egad, you have hit it. Nothing but a little natural delicate sensibility. (*Hums a tune.*)

HEARTLY. If so, perhaps the violence of her reproaches may proceed from the lukewarmness of your professions.

YOUNG CLACKIT. *Je vous demande pardon!* I have sworn to her a hundred and a hundred times that she should be the happiest of her sex. But there is nothing surprising in all this; it is the misery of an over-fond heart to be always doubtful of its happiness.

HEARTLY (*half-aside*). And if she marries thee I fear that she'll be kept in a state of doubt as long as she lives.

Enter Lucy.

450 LUCY. Pray, gentlemen, what is the matter among you? And which of you has affronted my mistress? She is in a most prodigious taking yonder, and she vows to return into the country again. I can get nothing but sighs from her.

---

416. *as* Heartly *muses*] omit *as* O3, *W*1, *W*2.
418. her so much] O1, O2, O3, O4, *W*1; her much *W*2.
443. professions] O1, O2, O4, *W*1, *W*2; reproaches O3.

YOUNG CLACKIT. Poor thing!

LUCY. Poor thing! The devil take this love, I say. There's more rout about it than 'tis worth.

YOUNG CLACKIT. I beg your pardon for that, Mrs. Abigail.

HEARTLY. I must inquire further in this. Her behavior is too particular for me not to be disturbed at it.

460 LUCY (*to* Heartly). She desires, with the leave of these gentlemen, that when she has recovered herself she may talk with you alone, Sir.

HEARTLY. I shall with pleasure attend her.

Exit Lucy.

YOUNG CLACKIT (*sings*). Divine Bacchus! la, la, la!

SIR CHARLES. I would give, old as I am, a leg or an arm to be beloved by that sweet creature as you are, Jack.

YOUNG CLACKIT. And throw your gout and rheumatism into the bargain, Uncle? Ha, ha! Divine Bacchus, la, la, la, etc. (*Sings*.)

SIR CHARLES. What the plague are you quavering at? Thou hast no more feeling for thy happiness than my stick here.

470 YOUNG CLACKIT. I beg your pardon for that, my dear Uncle. (*Takes out a pocket looking-glass*.)

SIR CHARLES. I wonder what the devil is come to the young fellows of this age, Neighbor Heartly? Why, a fine woman has no effect upon 'em. Is there no method to make 'em less fond of themselves and more mindful of the ladies?

HEARTLY. I know but of one, Sir Charles.

SIR CHARLES. Aye, what's that?

HEARTLY. Why, to break all the looking-glasses in the kingdom. (*Pointing to* Young Clackit.)

SIR CHARLES. Aye, aye, they are such fops, so taken up with themselves! Zounds, when I was young and in love —

480 YOUNG CLACKIT. You were a prodigious fine sight, to be sure.

HEARTLY. Look'ye, Mr. Clackit, if Miss Harriet's affections declare for you, she must not be treated with neglect or disdain. Nor could I bear it, Sir. Any man must be proud of her partiality to him, and he must be fashionably insensible indeed, who would not make it his darling care to defend from every inquietude the most delicate and tender of her sex.

SIR CHARLES. Most nobly and warmly said, Mr. Heartly. Go to her,

---

456. 'tis] *O*1, *O*2, *O*4, *W*1, *W*2; its *O*3.
458. in] *O*1, *O*2, *O*4, *W*1, *W*2; into *O*3.
463. Divine Bacchus] *O*1, *O*2, *O*4, *W*1; Divin Bacchus *O*3, *W*2.
467. Divine Bacchus] *O*1, *O*2, *O*4, *W*1; Divin Bacchus *O*3, *W*2.
468. hast] *O*1, *O*2, *O*4, *W*1, *W*2; has *O*3.

Nephew, directly. Throw yourself at her feet and swear how much her beauty and virtue have captivated you, and don't let her go till you have set her dear little heart at rest.

YOUNG CLACKIT. I must desire to be excused. Would you have me say the same thing over and over again? I can't do it, positively. It is my turn to be piqued now.

SIR CHARLES. Damn your conceit, Jack, I can bear it no longer.

HEARTLY. I am very sorry to find that any young lady so near and dear to me should bestow her heart where there is so little prospect of its being valued as it ought. However, I shall not oppose my authority to her inclinations, and so — Who waits there?

Enter Servant.

Let the young lady know that I shall attend her commands in the library.

Exit Servant.

Will you excuse me, gentlemen?

SIR CHARLES. Aye, aye. We'll leave you to yourselves, and pray convince her that I and my nephew are most sincerely her very humble servants.

YOUNG CLACKIT. On yes, you may depend upon me.

HEARTLY (*aside*). A very slender dependence, truly.

Exit.

YOUNG CLACKIT. We'll be with you again to know what your *tete-a-tete* produces and, in the mean time, I am her's,—and your's—Adieu. Come, Uncle,—Fal, lal, la, la!

SIR CHARLES (*aside*). I could knock him down with pleasure.

Exeunt Sir Charles and Young Clackit.

[*End of* ACT I.]

ACT II.

SCENE, a library.

HEARTLY (*speaking to a servant*). Tell Miss Harriet that I am here. If she is indisposed, I will wait upon her in her own room.

Exit Servant.

However mysterious her conduct appears to me, yet still it is to be decyphered. This young gentleman has certainly touched her. There are some objections to him, and, among so many young men of fashion that fall in her way, she certainly might have made a better choice. She has an understanding to be sensible of this; and, if I am not mistaken, it is a struggle between her reason and her passion that occasions all this confusion. But here she is.

Enter Miss Harriet.

10 MISS HARRIET.   I hope you are not angry, Sir, that I left you so abruptly, without making any apology?

HEARTLY.   I am angry that you think any apology necessary. The matter we were upon was of such a delicate nature that I was more pleased with your confusion than I should have been with your excuses. You'll pardon me, my dear.

MISS HARRIET.   I have reflected that the person for whom I have conceived a most tender regard may, from the wisest motives, doubt of my passion. And therefore I would endeavor to answer all his objections and convince him how deserving he is of my highest esteem.

20 HEARTLY.   I have not yet apprehended what kind of dispute could arise between you and Mr. Clackit. I would advise you both to come to a reconciliation as soon as possible. The law of nature is an imperious one and cannot, like those of our country, be easily evaded; and though reason may suggest some disagreeable reflections, yet when the stroke is to be given we must submit to it.

MISS HARRIET (*aside*).   He still continues in his error, and I cannot undeceive him.

HEARTLY.   Shall I take the liberty of telling you, my dear—(*Taking her hand.*) You tremble, Harriet; what is the matter with you?

30 MISS HARRIET.   Nothing, Sir, Pray go on.

HEARTLY.   I guess whence proceeds all your uneasiness. You fear that the world will not be so readily convinced of this young gentleman's merit as you are. And, indeed, I could wish him more deserving of you. But your regard for him gives him a merit he otherwise would have wanted and almost makes me blind to his failings.

MISS HARRIET.   And would you advise me, Sir, to make choice of this gentleman?

HEARTLY.   I would advise you, as I always have done, to consult your
40 own heart upon such an occasion.

MISS HARRIET.   If that is your advice, I will most religiously follow it. And for the laste time I am resolved to discover my real sentiments.

---

12. any] *O*1, *O*2, *O*3, *O*4, *W*1; an *W*2.
23. evaded] *O*1, *O*2, *O*3, *O*4, *W*1; envaded *W*2.

But as a confession of this kind will not become me, I have been thinking of some innocent stratagem to spare my blushes and in part to relive me from the shame of a declaration. Might I be permitted to write to him?

HEARTLY.   I think you may, my dear, without the least offence to your delicacy. And indeed you ought to explain yourself; your late misunderstanding makes it absolutely necessary.

50 MISS HARRIET.   Will you be kind enough to assist me? Will you write it for me. Sir?

HEARTLY.   Oh, most willingly! And as I am made a party, it will remove all objections.

MISS HARRIET.   I will dictate to you in the best manner I am able. (*Sighing.*)

HEARTLY.   And here is pen, ink, and paper, to obey your commands. (*Draws the table.*)

MISS HARRIET (*aside*).   Lord, how my heart beats! I fear I cannot go through it.

HEARTLY.   Now, my dear, I am ready. Don't be disturbed. He is certainly a man of family, and though he has some little faults, time

60 and your virtues will correct them. Come, what shall I write? (*Preparing to write.*)

MISS HARRIET.   Pray give me a moment's thought; 'tis a terrible task, Mr. Heartly.

HEARTLY.   I know it is. Don't hurry yourself. I shall wait with patience. Come, Miss Harriet.

MISS HARRIET (*dictating*).   "It is in vain for me to conceal, from one of your understanding, the secrets of my heart."

HEARTLY (*writing*).   "—the secrets of my heart —"

MISS HARRIET.   "Though your humility and modesty will not suffer you to perceive it."

70 HEARTLY.   Do you think, my dear, that he is much troubled with those qualities?

MISS HARRIET.   Pray indulge me, Sir.

HEARTLY.   I beg your pardon. "—your humility and modesty will not suffer you to perceive it." (*Writes.*) So.

MISS HARRIET.   "Everything tells you that it is you that I love."

HEARTLY.   Very well. (*Writes.*)

MISS HARRIET.   Yes—you "that I love," do you understand me?

HEARTLY.   Oh, yes, yes. I understand you — "—that it is *you* that I love." This is very plain, my dear.

80 MISS HARRIET.   I would have it so. "And though I am already bound in gratitude to you —"

HEARTLY.   In gratitude to Mr. Clackit?

MISS HARRIET.   Pray write, Sir.

HEARTLY. Well "—in gratitude to you. (*Writes.*) (*Aside.*) I must write what she would have me.

MISS HARRIET. "Yet my passion is a most disinterested one."

HEARTLY (*writes*). "—most disinterested one."

MISS HARRIET. "And to convince you that you owe much more to my affections —"

90   HARRIET. And then?

MISS HARRIET. "I could wish that I had not experienced —"

HEARTLY. Stay, stay. (*Writes.*) "—had not experienced —"

MISS HARRIET. "Your tender care of me in my infancy."

HEARTLY (*disturbed*). What did you say? (*Aside.*) Did I hear right, or am I in a dream?

MISS HARRIET (*aside*). Why have I declared myself? He'll hate me for my folly.

HEARTLY. Harriet!

MISS HARRIET. Sir!

100   HEARTLY. To whom do you write this letter?

MISS HARRIET. To—to—Mr. Clackit, is it not?

HEARTLY. You must not mention then the care of your infancy. It would be ridiculous.

MISS HARRIET. It would indeed. I own it; it is improper.

HEARTLY. What, did it escape you in your confusion?

MISS HARRIET. It did indeed.

HEARTLY. What must I put in its place?

MISS HARRIET. Indeed I don't know. I have said more than enough to make myself understood.

110   HEARTLY. Then I'll only finish your letter with the usual compliment, and send it away.

MISS HARRIET. Yes, send it away, if you think I ought to send it.

HEARTLY (*troubled*). Ought to send it! Who's there?

Enter a Servant.

Carry this letter.

An action escapes from Harriet, *as if to hinder the sending the letter.*

Is it not for Mr. Clackit?

MISS HARRIET (*peevishly*). Who can it be for?

HEARTLY (*to the Servant*). Here, take this letter to Mr. Clackit. (*Gives the letter.*)

Exit Servant.

MISS HARRIET (*aside*). What a terrible situation!

HEARTLY (*aside*). I am thunderstruck!

120 MISS HARRIET (*aside*). I cannot speak another word.
HEARTLY (*aside*). My prudence fails me.
MISS HARRIET (*aside*). He disapproves my passion, and I shall die with confusion.

Enter Lucy.

LUCY (*aside*). The conversation is over and I may appear. Sir Charles is without, Sir, and is impatient to know your determination. May he be permitted to see you?
HEARTLY (*aside*). I must retire to conceal my weakness.

Exit.

LUCY. Upon my word, this is very whimsical. What is the reason, Miss, that your guardian is gone away without giving me an answer?
130 MISS HARRIET (*aside*). What a contempt he must have for me, to behave in this manner!

Exit.

LUCY. Extremely well, this, and equally foolish on both sides. But what can be the meaning of it? Ho, ho! I think I have a glimmering at last. Suppose she should not like young Shatter-brains after all; and indeed she has never absolutely said she did. Who knows but she has at last opened her mind to my good master, and he, finding her taste (like that of other girls of her age) most particularly ridiculous, has not been so complaisant as he used to be. What a shame it is that I don't know more of this matter, a wench of spirit
140 as I am, a favorite of my mistress, and as inquisitive as I ought to be. It is an affront to my character, and I must have satisfaction immediately. (*Going.*) I will go directly to my young mistress, tease her to death till I am at the bottom of this. And if threatening, soothing, scolding, whispering, crying, and lying will not prevail, I will e'en give her warning,—and go upon the stage.

Exit.

Enter Heartly.

HEARTLY. The more I reflect upon what has passed, the more I am convinced that she did not intend writing to this young fellow. What am I to think of it, then? Let a man be ever so much upon his guard against the approaches of vanity, yet he will find himself weak in
150 that quarter. Had not my reason made a little stand against my presumption, I might have interpreted some of Harriet's words in my own favor. But I may well blush, though alone, at my extravagant folly. Can it be possible that so young a creature should even

cast a thought of that kind upon me? Upon me! Presumptious
vanity! No, no; I will do her and myself the justice to acknowledge
that, for a very few slight appearances, there are a thousand reasons
that destroy so ridiculous a supposition.

Enter Sir Charles.

SIR CHARLES.   Well, Mr. Heartly, what are we to hope for?

HEARTLY.   Upon my word, Sir, I am still in the dark. We puzzle about,
160   indeed, but we don't get forward.

SIR CHARLES.   What the devil is the meaning of all this? There never
sure were lovers so difficult to bring together. But have you not
been a little too rough with the lady? For as I passed by her but
now, she seemed a little out of humor, and, upon my faith, not the
less beautiful for a little pouting.

HEARTLY.   Upon my word, Sir Charles, what I can collect from her
behavior is, that your Nephew is not so much in her good graces as
he made you believe.

SIR CHARLES.   Egad, like enough. But hold, hold; this must be looked a
170   little into. If it is so, I would be glad to know why and wherefore
I have been made so ridiculous. Eh, Master Heartly, does he take
me for his fool, his beast, his Merry Andrew? By the Lord Harry —

HEARTLY.   In him a little vanity is excusable.

SIR CHARLES.   I am his Vanity's humble servant for that, though.

HEARTLY.   He is of an age, Sir Charles —

SIR CHARLES.   Aye, of an age to be very impertinent; but I shall desire
him to be less free with his Uncle for the future, I assure him.

Enter Lucy.

LUCY.   I have it, I have it, gentlemen! You need not puzzle anymore
about the matter. I have got the secret. I know the knight-errant
180   that has wounded our distressed lady.

SIR CHARLES.   Well, and who, and what, Child?

LUCY (*to* Heartly).   What, has not she told you, Sir?

HEARTLY.   Not directly.

LUCY.   So much the better. What pleasure it is to discover a secret and
then tell it to all the world! I pressed her so much that she at last
confessed.

SIR CHARLES.   Well, what?

LUCY.   That, in the first place, she did not like your Nephew.

SIR CHARLES.   And I told the puppy so.

190   LUCY.   That she had a mortal antipathy for the young men of this age;
and that she had settled her affections upon one of riper years and
riper understanding.

SIR CHARLES. Indeed?

LUCY. And that she expected from a lover in his autumn more affection, more complaisance, more constancy, and more discretion, of course.

HEARTLY. That is very particular.

SIR CHARLES. Aye, but it is very prudent for all that.

LUCY. In short, as she had openly declared against the Nephew, I took upon me to speak of his Uncle.

200 SIR CHARLES. Of me, Child?

LUCY. Yes, of you, Sir. And she did not say me nay, but cast such a look and fetched such a sigh, that if ever I looked and sighed in my life, I know how it is with her.

SIR CHARLES. What the devil? Why surely,—eh, Lucy, you joke for certain. Mr. Heartly, eh —?

LUCY. Indeed, I do not, Sir. 'Twas in vain for me to say that nothing could be so ridiculous as such a choice. Nay, Sir, I went a little further (you'll excuse me) and told her—"Good God, Madam," said I, "why he is old and gouty, asthmatic, rheumatic, sciatic,

210 spleenatic—" It signified nothing; she had determined.

SIR CHARLES. But you need not have told her all that.

HEARTLY. I am persuaded, Sir Charles, that a good heart and a good mind will prevail more with that young lady than the more fashionable accomplishments.

SIR CHARLES. I'll tell you what, Neighbor, I have had my days and have been well received among the ladies, I have. But, in truth, I am rather in my winter than my autumn; she must mean somebody else. Now I think again, it can't be me. No, no, it can't be me.

LUCY. But I tell you it is, Sir. You are the man; her stars have decreed

220 it. And what they decree, though ever so ridiculous, must come to pass.

SIR CHARLES. Say you so, Why then, Monsieur Nephew, I shall have a little laugh with you. Ha, ha, ha! The titbit is not for you, my nice Sir. Your betters must be served before you. But here he comes. Not a word, for your life! We'll laugh at him most triumphantly. Ha, ha! But mum, mum.

Enter Young Clackit. *Music plays without.*

YOUNG CLACKIT (*to the Musicians*). That will do most divinely well. Bravo, bravo, Messieurs Vocal and Instrumental! Stay in that chamber and I will let you know the time for your appearance. (*To*

230 Heartly.) Meeting by accident with some artists of the string, and my particular friends, I have brought 'em to celebrate Miss Harriet's and my approaching happiness.

SIR CHARLES (*to* Lucy). Do you hear the puppy?

HEARTLY. It is time to clear up all mistakes.

SIR CHARLES. Now for it.

HEARTLY. Miss Harriet, Sir, was not destined for you.

YOUNG CLACKIT. What do you say, Sir?

HEARTLY. That the young lady has fixed her affections upon another.

YOUNG CLACKIT. Upon another?

240 SIR CHARLES. Yes, Sir, *another*. That is *English*, Sir, and you may translate it into *French*, if you like it better.

YOUNG CLACKIT. *Vous êtes bien drole, mon Oncle.* Ha, ha!

SIR CHARLES. Aye, aye, show your teeth, you have nothing else for it. But she has fixed her heart upon *another*, I tell you.

YOUNG CLACKIT. Very well, Sir, extremely well.

SIR CHARLES. And that other, Sir, is one to whom you owe great respect.

YOUNG CLACKIT. I am his most respectful, humble servant.

SIR CHARLES. You are a fine youth, my sweet Nephew, to tell me a story of a cock and a bull, of you and the young lady, when you have no

250 more interest in her than the Czar of Muscovy.

YOUNG CLACKIT (*smiling*). But, my dear Uncle, don't carry this jest too far. I shall begin to be uneasy.

SIR CHARLES. Aye, aye, I know your vanity. You think now that the women are all for you young fellows.

YOUNG CLACKIT. Nine hundred and ninety-nine in a thousand, I believe, Uncle. Ha, ha, ha!

SIR CHARLES. You'll make a damned foolish figure by and by, Jack.

YOUNG CLACKIT. Whoever my precious rival is, he must prepare himself for a little humility. For be he ever so mighty, my dear Uncle,

260 I have that in my pocket will lower his topsails for him. (*Searching his pocket.*)

SIR CHARLES. Well, what's that?

YOUNG CLACKIT. A fourteen-pounder only, my good Uncle, a letter from the lady. (*Takes it out of his pocket.*)

SIR CHARLES. What, to you?

YOUNG CLACKIT. To me, Sir. This moment received, and overflowing with the tenderest sentiments.

SIR CHARLES. To you?

YOUNG CLACKIT. Most undoubtedly. She reproaches me with my excessive modesty. There can be no mistake.

270 SIR CHARLES (*to* Heartly). What letter is this he chatters about?

HEARTLY. One written by me and dictated by the young lady.

SIR CHARLES. What, sent by her to him?

HEARTLY. I believe so.

SIR CHARLES. Well, but then—how the devil?—Mrs. Lucy, eh? What becomes of your fine story?

LUCY. I don't understand it.

SIR CHARLES. Nor I.

HEARTLY (*hesitating*). Nor—I—

YOUNG CLACKIT. But I do, and so you will all, presently. Well, my dear
280   Uncle, what, are you astonished, petrified, annihilated?

SIR CHARLES. With your impudence, Jack! But I'll see it out.

Enter Miss Harriet.

MISS HARRIET. Bless me, Mr. Heartly, what is all this music for in the
next room?

YOUNG CLACKIT. I brought the gentlemen of the string, Mademoiselle,
to convince you that I feel, as I ought, the honor you have done me.
(*Showing the letter.*) But for heaven's sake be sincere a little with
these good folks. They tell me here that I am nobody and there is
another happier than myself, and for the soul of me I don't know
how to believe 'em. Ha, ha, ha!

290   SIR CHARLES. Let us hear Miss speak.

MISS HARRIET. It is a most terrible task, but I am compelled to it, and to
hesitate any longer would be injurious to my guardian, his friend,
this young gentleman, and my own character.

YOUNG CLACKIT. Most judicious, upon my soul.

SIR CHARLES. Hold your tongue, Jack.

YOUNG CLACKIT. I am dumb.

MISS HARRIET. You have all been in an error. My bashfulness may have
deceived you. My heart never did.

YOUNG CLACKIT. *C'est vrai.*

300   MISS HARRIET. Therefore, before I declare my sentiments, it is proper
that I disavow any engagement, but at the same time must confess —

YOUNG CLACKIT. Ho, ho!

MISS HARRIET. —with fear and shame confess —

YOUNG CLACKIT. *Courage, Mademoiselle!*

MISS HARRIET (*to* Young Clackit). —that another, not you, Sir, has
gained a power over my heart.

SIR CHARLES. *Another*, not you. Mind that, Jack. Ha, ha!

MISS HARRIET. It is a power, indeed, which he despises. I cannot be
deceived in his conduct. Modesty may tie the tongue of our sex,
310   but silence in him could proceed only from contempt.

SIR CHARLES. How prettily she reproaches me! But I'll soon make it up
with her.

MISSS HARRIET (*to* Young Clackit). As to that letter, Sir, your error
there is excusable; and I own myself in that particular a little blame-
able. But it was not my fault that it was sent to you; and the contents
must have told you that it could not possibly be meant for you.

SIR CHARLES. Proof positive, Jack. Say no more. Now is my time to begin. Hem!—Hem! Sweet young lady! Hem! whose charms are so mighty, so far transcending everything that we read of in history or fable, how could you possibly think that my silence proceeded from contempt? Was it natural or prudent, think you, for a man of sixty-five, nay, just entering into his sixty-sixth year —

YOUNG CLACKIT. O *misericorde!* What, is my Uncle my rival? Nay, then, I shall burst, by Jupiter. Ha, ha, ha!

MISS HARRIET. Don't imagine, Sir, that to me your age is any fault.

SIR CHARLES (*bowing*). You are very obliging, Madam.

MISS HARRIET. Neither is it, Sir, a merit of that extraordinary nature that I should sacrifice to it an inclination which I have conceived for another.

SIR CHARLES. How is this?

YOUNG CLACKIT. Another! not you,—mind that, Uncle.

LUCY. What is the meaning of all this?

YOUNG CLACKIT. Proof positive, Uncle, and very positive.

SIR CHARLES. I have been led into a mistake, Madam, which I hope you will excuse; and I have made myself very ridiculous, which I hope I shall forget. And so, Madam, I am your humble servant. This young lady has something very extraordinary about her.

HEARTLY. What I now see and the remembrance of what is past force me to break silence.

YOUNG CLACKIT. Aye, now for it. Hear him, hear him.

HEARTLY. Oh, my Harriet! I too must be disgraced in my turn. Can you think that I have seen and conversed with you unmoved? Indeed I have not. The more I was sensible of your merit, the stronger were my motives to stifle the ambition of my heart. But now I can no longer resist the violence of my passion, which casts me at your feet, the most unworthy indeed of all your admirers, but of all the most affectionate.

YOUNG CLACKIT. So, so, the moon has changed and the grown gentlemen begin to be frisky.

LUCY (*aside*). What, my master in love too? I'll never trust these tie-wigs again.

MISS HARRIET. I have refused my hand to Sir Charles and this young gentleman. The one accuses me of caprice, the other of singularity. Should I refuse my hand a third time, (*smiling*) I might draw upon myself a more severe reproach, and therefore I accept your favor, Sir, and will endeavor to deserve it.

HEARTLY. And thus I seal my acknowledgments, and from henceforth

---

319-20. in history] *O*1, *O*2, *O*4, *W*1, *W*2; omit *in O*3.

devote my every thought and all my services to the author of my
happiness. (*Kisses her hand.*)

360 LUCY. Since matters are so well settled, give me leave, Sir, to congratulate you on your success and my young lady on her judgment. You have my taste exactly, Miss. Ripe fruit for my money!
When it is too green it sets one's teeth on edge, and when too mel-
low it has no flavor at all.

SIR CHARLES (*to* Lucy). Hold your tongue, you baggage. Well, my
dear discreet Nephew, are you satisfied with the fool's part you
have given me and played yourself in the farce?

YOUNG CLACKIT. What would you have me say, Sir? I am too much a
philosopher to fret myself because the wind, which was East this
370 morning, is now West. The poor girl in pique has killed herself to
be revenged on me; but, hark'ye, Sir, I believe Heartly will be
cursed mad to have me live in his neighborhood. A word to the
wise —

SIR CHARLES. Thou hast a most incorrigible vanity, Jack, and nothing
can cure thee. Mr. Heartly, I have sense enough and friendship
enough not to be uneasy at your happiness.

HEARTLY. I hope, Sir Charles, that we shall still continue to live as
neighbors and friends. For you, my Harriet, words cannot express
my wonder or my joy. My future conduct must tell you what a
380 sense I have of my happiness, and how much I shall endeavor to
deserve it.

> My friendly care shall change to grateful love,
> And the fond husband still the Guardian prove.

Finis

382–83. My friendly ... prove] *O*1, *O*2, *O*3, *O*4; two lines added *W*1, *W*2: "For
every charm that ever yet blessed youth,/Accept compliance, tenderness
and truth;/My friendly care shall change to grateful love,/And the fond
husband still the Guardian prove."

Harlequin's Invasion;
or, A Christmas Gambol
1759

HARLEQUINS Invasion

with

Transparency's &c.

Facsimile cover page of the manuscript
in the Boston Public Library.

Dramatis Personae

Bog.	
Taffy.	
Forge,	Mr. Burton.
Barnably Bounce,	Mr. Bransby.
Gasconade, *a Frenchman*,	Mr. Blakes.
Joe Snip, *a Tailor*,	Mr. Yates.
Mrs. Snip,	Mrs. Bennet.
Mercury,	Mr. Dodd.
Harlequin,	Mr. King.
Simon, *a Clown*,	Mr. Moody.

10

	Mr. Hartry.
Justices,	Mr. Clough.
	Mr. Castle.
	Mr. Strange.

Clerk.	
Constable,	Mr. Ackman.
Four old Women.	
Dolly Snip,	Miss Pope.
Abram,	Mr. Weston.
Sukey Chitterlin,	Mrs. Millidge.
Jailor.	

20

Other parts by: Packer, Scrase, Vaughan, Fox.
Vocals by: Champness, Reinhold, Mrs. Vernon,
Miss Young, Miss Spencer.
Dances by: Grimaldi, Giorgi, Sga. Giorgi, Miss Baker.

Harlequin's Invasion;
or, A Christmas Gambol

Act I

SCENE I. *Charing Cross* (2nd *Grove*)
Enter Bog, Taffy, Forge, *with a paper*, Crib, *etc., huzzaing.*

FORGE. Here! Here it is. Huzza, Boys! Here it is, my Jolly Hearts.
This will be the making of us all. Huzza!

[(2) Bounce *a stick*]

TAFFY. Vat you got, Neipor Forge?
FORGE. Damn me if I know what it is. But it will be the making of us
all. Here, read it. Read it, Taffy. It will be the making of us all.

[(3) Gasconade]

TAFFY. I will put on my best eyes, Neipor Forge, and do your likings.
BOG. Hold your hand, my dear, for though you read it very well, I
don't understand a word you say.

[(4) Mercury, *followers and* Chorus.]

TAFFY. Read it yourself.
BOG. Faith, I can't, Honey. I write very well, but I forgot my reading
long ago.

[*Enter* Bounce *Pd.*]

BOUNCE. Where is it? Where is it? Zounds! Let me see it.
TAFFY. Here it is, Neibor Pounce, the Corporal.
BOUNCE. What do you give it me for? You know I can't read. I can
swear, I can fight, I can drink, I can wench. I can —
TAFFY. You can teeve and steal, too.
BOUNCE. Zounds, I can do anything but read. And as for that, why,
I am a soldier and above it.

TAFFY.　'Tis apove you, you mean, foolish man.

[*Enter* Gasconade *O.P.*]

20　GASCONADE.　*Pourquoy faites vous tant de bruit?* Vat is all dis noise?

BOUNCE.　For my pleasure. I love noise and hate the French, and my name is Barnaby Bounce.

GASCONADE.　Your name is Barnaby Villaine, poltroon. And, begar, if you are not a little more poli, *je vous donnerai le coup de pied!* I vil kicka you behind.

BOUNCE.　Well, well. I believe you dare fight. So I won't quarrel with you. Here's my hand. I'm your friend.

GASCONADE.　*De tout mon coeur!* Look you, Sir, I dare fight de Devil, but I had much rather be friend with the Devil. So, Sir, I am your

30　*tres* humble *serviteur. Mais allons.* Vat *papier* is dat?

BOUNCE.　Give it me, give it me! Here you, Dismal! (*To* Crib.) You can read, I know. He's a special scholar. He was formerly a parish clerk and was turned out of his office for robbing the Poor's Box.

CRIB.　And so I was, indeed. (*Sound and shout.*)

BOUNCE.　Stand clear, stand clear! Here comes the Herald himself. Huzza!

[(5) Snip, Mrs. Snip, *measures and shears.*]

ALL.　Huzza! Huzza! (*Flourish.*)

Enter 2 Heralds, Staves [*P.S.*], 2 trumpets, drum *and*
fife, Mercury, 2 Heralds, Staves, *all the* Chorus.

Roar trumpet, squeak fife, blow horn and beat drum! [*Flourish.*]
To Dramatica's realm from Apollo I come.

40　Whereas it is feared French trick may be played ye,
Be it known Monsieur Harlequin means to invade ye.
And hither transporting his legions, he floats
On an ocean of canvas in flat bottom boats.
With fairies, hags, genii, hobgoblins all shocking,
And many a devil in flame-colored stocking,
Let the light troops of Comedy march to attack him,
And Tragedy whet all her daggers to hack him.
Let all hands and hearts do their utmost endeavor.
Sound trumpet, beat drum, King Shakespear forever.

[*Flourish and shout.*]

AIR

50　To arms, you brave mortals, to arms,
The road to renown is before you.

The name of King Shakespear has charms,
To rouse you to actions of glory.

2

Away, ye brave mortals, away,
'Tis nature calls on you to save her.
What man but would nature obey
And fight for her Shakespear forever.

[*Shout, flourish and exeunt* O P]

SCENE II. Plain Chamber

(*Border bell and Wings bell*)
Enter Joe Snip *and* Wife *pushing him on* P.S.

WIFE. Get along with you, cowardly rascal, and make your fortune at once. Follow 'em, follow 'em. Don't you hear the trumpet?

SNIP. Yes, and you too, Wife. You are both loud enough, I am sure.

WIFE. Sirrah, Sirrah, and I'll be louder still. What, have you no manhood left? Have not you spirit enough to take fire at the proclamation?

SNIP. You have spirit enough, Wife, to take fire at anything. You make a proclamation in my ears every day of my life. The trumpets are a fool to you.

10 WIFE. You poor, mean, low minded fellow! Can nothing rouse you? Is all my greatness of soul thrown away upon you? Upon a tailor?

[(6) Simon, Harlequin, *all the* Children.]

SNIP. I wish it had been thrown into the sea, with all my soul, before I had been honored with it.

WIFE. How, villain! Do you wish *me* in the sea?

SNIP. Yes, from my soul do I, if wishing would do me any good.

WIFE. Here's a wicked wretch for you. Don't provoke me, I say, with your disobedience. Away with your thread lists and your measures. Put on a sword and bring me this Frenchman's head on the point of it, and at once make me a lady and yourself a lord.

20 SNIP. Make you a widow and myself a fool you mean. I bring you his head upon the point of a sword. Bring you a flea's head upon the point of a needle.

WIFE. Sirrah! Sirrah, don't provoke me, I say.

SNIP. You shall never provoke me to fight, Wife. When can I find a heart to cut off heads? Your tongue must be a little quieter than it is, I can assure you that.

John Moody as Simon in *Harlequin's Invasion.*
Harvard Theatre Collection

WIFE.   Did you ever hear such a wicked wretch? Such an ungrateful
wretch? Have I not refused the best men and the best matches for
your sake. Had I not been bewitched by your person and deluded
30   by your tongue, I might have held up my head with the proudest
she in the parish.
SNIP.   I have not held up mine, I'm sure, since you did me the favor.
Heigh-ho!
WIFE.   Don't stand sighing and sniv'ling here, but rouze your manhood. Clap a sword by your side and march.
SNIP.   Yes, I'll march to my shop-board and finish the work I'm about.
(*Crosses to* P.S.) Here's my two edged sword (*Takes out his
shears*). No tailor in Christendom can fight a piece of broadcloth
better than I can. I'll say that for myself.
40   WIFE.   You say for yourself, you poor, mean, beggarly, cowardly
fellow, you! Don't put me in a passion. I hate to be quarrelsome.
But you will force me to break through the meekness of my spirit
and do something. I'll tell you what, Joe. If you won't exert yourself for my sake, I'll no longer be virtuous for yours. I have my
revenge in my own hands. And so, fetch me this outlandish man's
head or take care of your own, I say. A word to the wise; take
care of your own.

Exit O.P.

SNIP.   Aye, there she has me. She knows how delicate I am about my
honor. And she always attacks me in that tender point. I must do
50   my best to please her. I must either make a fool of myself or she'll
make something worse of me.
Devils, we say, and justly too, are wives.

> And all do know
> As well as Joe,
> He needs must go
> The devil drives.

Exit P.S.

SCENE III. *Barn to change to trees. And a cave behind*
stump of a tree to change to armor. [2. En[trance] O.P.]
Harlequin *discovered asleep before the barn.*
[*Enter* Simon O.P. *First Entrance.*]

SIMON.   Ha, ha, ha! What a plague is the matter with all my neighbors? The murrain has seized 'em, I believe. They will have it that

there is some strange creature got into the parish. The women are
agog to see it. The children are frighted out of their wits. Our
parson shakes his head, and the squire and his dogs are all in high
hunt after it. His Worship, our Justice, and Master Cramp the
lawyer called to me at the end of the lane. "Simon, Simon," said
they, "what strange creature is that in our parish?" "And please,
your Worship," says me, "I, I don't think we want strange crea-
10   tures in our parish." And so I whistled away and left it with them.
But I can't see nothing, not I. If I do chance to light on 'em, I shall
make bold to tickle 'em a little with the prongs of my fork. Ha,
ha, ha! (*Going, he sees* Harlequin.) So, so! So talk of the devil and
here's one of his imps. Why sure this can't be a living creature.
'Ecod, but it is. 'Tis either drunk or asleep or both. Shall I take it
dead or alive? Has it nothing about it to do mischief? I'll e'en put
a fork into it and make all sure at once. (*Touches* Harlequin, *who
tumbles.*) Ha, ha, ha! I have set 'en a-dancing already; Hollo!
HARLEQUIN.   Hollo! (*Sits up and rubs his eyes.*)
20   SIMON.   Who are you? Whence came you?
HARLEQUIN.   I am nobody and came from nowhere. (*Rising.*)
SIMON.   Where are you going then?
HARLEQUIN.   To my own parish. Your Ta. (*Going.*)
SIMON.   Hold, hold, Mr. Nobody. Hold, hold a bit. As you came from
     nowhere and are going to the same place, it can be no great dam-
     age to stop you a little. (*Holds his fork at him.*)
HARLEQUIN.   Pray don't hurt me, merciful Sir! I am a very harmless
     creature. I have been taking a nap here and am not quite awake.
SIMON.   Whence came you?
30   HARLEQUIN (*looking up*).   There.
SIMON.   There? What, as far as I can see?
HARLEQUIN.   Farther . . . there!
SIMON.   Where?
HARLEQUIN.   There. (*Strikes his hand and catches the fork.*)
SIMON.   Give me my fork.
HARLEQUIN.   Take it, then. (*Pointing it at him.*)
SIMON.   Pray don't hurt me, merciful Sir! I am but a poor, harmless
     creature.
HARLEQUIN.   Ha, ha, ha! Shall we be friends?
40   SIMON.   Why, shall we, eh?
HARLEQUIN.   Ouy.
SIMON.   Ouy? What's that?
HARLEQUIN.   Yes.
SIMON.   Well, then, We, with all my heart.
HARLEQUIN.   Done. (*Holds out his hand.*)

SIMON. Done. (*Holds out his.*)

HARLEQUIN. And done. (*Strikes him with his sword.*)

SIMON. Is that the way you show your friendship?

HARLEQUIN. Friend Simon, take your fork.

[(7)Snip *in armor.*]

50 SIMON. Will you give it me?

HARLEQUIN. Here, take it. (*Sinks it.*)

SIMON. Pray, Friend, what's your name?

HARLEQUIN. Whirligig.

SIMON. Whirligig. And pray, Friend Whirligig, what profession are you of?

HARLEQUIN. A flycatcher. I was formerly altogether among the stars. I plied as a ticket porter in the Milky Way and carried the Howdyes from one planet to another. But, finding that too fatiguing, I got into the service of the rainbow. And now I wear his livery. Don't

60   you think I fib now, Friend Simon?

SIMON. Yea, in troth, do I, Friend Whirligig. He, he, he!

HARLEQUIN. I'll settle your faith in a moment and show you some of my little family. (*Strikes the barn.*)

[*Tr. Bell*]

It turns into a cut wood, backed by a cave (4 G). *Several children in pantomime characters come down and dance, at which* Simon *appears delighted.*

HARLEQUIN (*End of dance*). Away, away! Vanish!

[*Children exeunt severally.*]

I'm pursued! They are at my heels! O, Friend Simon, I'm undone. They'll roast me alive if they take me. (*Runs about.*)

SIMON. And boil me, perhaps, for keeping you company. What shall we do?

HARLEQUIN. Courage, Simon, I'll protect thee. (*They get up into the*

70   *tree.*) Friend Simon, I'll show you some sport. Keep in your head, the enemy's at hand.

[(8) Mr. Bounce, Gasconade.]
[*P S Enter* Snip *loaded with armor.*]

SNIP. What a dismal thing it is to live in fear of one's wife. Here am I sent, a poor harmless tailor, shaking and trembling to kill something who would make no more of killing me than I would of stealing a piece of cloth. Every bush and every blast of wind is an ague to me. As I came along a sheep did but clap his nose through a hedge and cry "Baa," and I have been in sweat ever since. I borrowed this armor of a friend of mine formerly of the Train Bands. But he couldn't tell me how to put it on. I wish I could see any of my neighbors to show me home again, for I have almost frighted myself blind.

HARLEQUIN. Neighbor Snip. Neighbor Snip!

SNIP. Eh? What's that? I am a dead man.

HARLEQUIN. Be not in panics, I am your friend and neighbor, Taffy.

SNIP. Where are you, Neighbor Taffy?

HARLEQUIN. I am got into this tree to hide myself from Harlequin. He is just gone by with a sword in his hand as long and as broad as a scythe and looks as crabbed as if he had eaten sour pippins.

SNIP. Pray, Neighbor, make room for me.

HARLEQUIN. Here's but just room for Neighbor Pog and I.

SNIP. What, is he there too?

HARLEQUIN. I don't know whether I am here or no, faith, for the gentleman with his long sword has frightened me out of my senses and remembrances too joy.

SNIP. What must I do, then? Pray tell me, for I am most sadly frighted.

HARLEQUIN. Yes, faith, are you. I hear it very visibly. Go into that cave there and you'll be very safe and may have very good time to sleep yourself into your senses again.

SNIP. Thank you, I'll take your advice. Pray, Neighbor Taffy, tell me when you go home, that I mayn't go alone.

HARLEQUIN. Dat I will, Neighbor Snip.

SNIP. Thank you, good Neighbor. (*Going.*) Bless me. Oh! 'Tis nothing.

Exit into the cave.

SIMON. What, is he gone? Hark ye, Friend Whirligig. You aren't afraid of a tailor?

HARLEQUIN. Silence! Here are some more of 'em.

[*Enter* Bounce *and* Gasconade *P.S.*]

BOUNCE. Look about. He must be here about.

GASCONADE. *Ne faites pas tant de bruit.* Don't you make a noise. And if we canna trap him asleep, we will cut his troat and save ourselves de trouble of an engagement.

BOUNCE (*softly*). 'Sblood, you are not afraid, are you?

[(9) Forge *drunk*]

GASCONADE. *Non, non,* I am only prudent.

BOUNCE. You don't like to kill your countryman, then?

GASCONADE. I beg your pardon. I would kill anything for my interest.

BOUNCE. You remember the bargain? We go snacks in the murder.

GASCONADE. *Ouy, ouy!* Begar, he shall cut off de head himself and I will snacka de money. Eh! Monsieur Bounce, what is de *raison* your one-two knees knicky-knocky together, *come sa?*

BOUNCE. Oh, that proceeds from my eagerness for fighting. My flesh
120   quivers to be at him. Trembling is a sure sign of resolution.

GASCONADE. Upon my word, den, *vous et moy*, you and I have so much resolution as any two in all de varld.

BOUNCE (*aside*). What can be the matter with me? If I should continue sweating for a day as I do now, I should be melted down to the lathy consistency of Joe Snip the tailor.

HARLEQUIN. Who call's me?

BOUNCE. Eh! What the devil's that?

GASCONADE. If you no like it, I vil go home *avec a vous vid* all mine heart.

130 HARLEQUIN. 'Tis only I, Joseph Snip, in the tree here.

GASCONADE. Vat you do dere, eh?

HARLEQUIN. Hush, hush! Harlequin is hard by.

BOTH. Where! Where?

HARLEQUIN. In that cave there. I believe he is asleep.

BOUNCE. Will you go and wake him and tell him I'm come to murder him?

GASCONADE. *Non, non.* You had much better kill him first, and there will be no occasion to wake him at all.

BOUNCE. We'll nap him sleeping.

140 GASCONADE. *De tout mon coeur. Allons!*

BOUNCE. Lead the way.

GASCONADE. *Non*, indeed, sir.

BOUNCE. Go first, I say!

GASCONADE. I am *une Francoise* and understand civility. I vil not go first, upon my vard.

BOUNCE. We'll go together. Give me your hand.

Exit into cave.

SIMON. Well, but, Friend Whirligig, you won't let 'em kill the poor tailor?

HARLEQUIN. They'll cut off his head only. But I'll give him a better.

150 BOUNCE *and* GASCONADE (*Huzza within*).

Enter Forge *drunk P S.*

[FORGE] What the devil do you make such a noise for?

Enter Bounce *and* Gasconade (*from Top*).

BOUNCE. 'Tis done, 'tis done! This is the arm that gave the blow. (*Gives the head to* Forge.)

GASCONADE. Vat is you say? *Parblieu*! I say and I swear dis vas de *bon* sword dat did cut off de head.

BOUNCE. Right, Frenchman, but this was the sword that laid him low first.

GASCONADE. *Vous mentez*, you lie, you villain. How could you knock him down ven I did cut his throat when he vas fast asleep?

160 FORGE. Upon my word you are two very pretty fellows. You have killed a sleeping tailor and are quarreling about the glory of the victory.

BOUNCE. A tailor?

GASCONADE. Eh? *Un tailleur!*

FORGE. Really you are two very great champions. You set out a couple of lion hunters and return a couple of sheep stealers.

BOUNCE. Confusion chokes me. (*Crosses to O P.*)

GASCONADE. Begar, I am very much afraid un rope vil choke a me. (*Takes the head.*)

HARLEQUIN. Now, Simon, observe the virtue of this shrub. Where's my head? Where's my head?

Gets from the tree and is changed to the tailor without a head.

170 BOUNCE. Fire and brimstone! The Devil! The Devil!

Exit running O P.

HARLEQUIN. Frenchman, give me my head. Frenchman, give me my head.

GASCONADE. Here, begar, take your head vile I take a to my heel.

Exit running P S.

FORGE. What a parcel of cowardly dogs are my neighbors. As if they had never seen a tailor without a head before. Pray, my good friend, Joseph Snip, what are your commands?

HARLEQUIN. Take my head home to my wife and bid her prosecute my murderers.

[Act]

FORGE. If she won't, I will. But Neighbor, if they have really murdered
180 you, you had better appear yourself as an evidence and you'll certainly hang 'em.

HARLEQUIN. They shall hear farther from me.

FORGE. Well, I'll be your porter for once (*takes the head*). Upon my word, 'tis wondrous light. Damn me if I don't think he looks better

without a head than with. We see by this of what consequence a
head is to a tailor. (*Going.*)

HARLEQUIN.   Bless you, good Neighbor.

FORGE.   Very well, Joe, I am satisfied. No more words. Pray stay where
you are. You know I hate ceremony. You have lost your head and
190   may lose your way too. Pray stay where you are.

Exit Forge *P.S.*

Harlequin *goes to the side scene, slips his dress,
and returns immediately.*

HARLEQUIN.   So they are disposed of.

SIMON.   What, are you there, Friend Whirligig? Egad, I thought I had
lost you.

HARLEQUIN.   Friend Simon, I'll step into the cave, stitch the tailor a
new head on, and then you shall go to town with me and see my
pranks there. Eh, Simon?

Exit into the cave.

SIMON.   Indeed I will not, Master Whirligig. Egad, I have had enough
of your pranks here. No more devil's dances for Simon. He must
be Old Nick himself for sartain, and I am dealing with him. Heav-
200   ens, bless me! The thoughts of it puts me into a grievous taking.
He talks of heads as if they were so many buttons, and cuts 'em
off and sews 'em on as fast. I'll e'en steal home while I have legs to
walk upon and my head upon my shoulders. But is it there? Yes,
it is. But I had best hold it for fear of the worst.

Exit O.P.

Drop: Bar bell.

Act ends.

ACT II

SCENE [I] *Justices' Room* (2nd *Groove.*)
Table 5 Chairs
The Bench of Justices all discovered.
[(2) Constables]

FIRST JUSTICE.   And now we have got him, this Harlequin, what must
we do with him? What think you, Brother Cramp?

SECOND JUSTICE.   Why, for my part, Mr. Chairman, I think this Harlequin comes within the statute description of incorrigible rogue.

He's an old offender, and I think we have a power to transport him.

FIRST JUSTICE. I don't know that. We must have a care of informations above, Mr. Cramp. We can't be too wary. A burnt child, you know. Call in the Head Borough. Call in Joseph Harrow.

CLERK. Joseph Harrow! Come into court.

10 THIRD JUSTICE. What think you, Brothers, of setting our hands to his pass and having him whipped from constable to constable?

FIRST JUSTICE. But where must we pass him to, Mr. Justice Spindle? This fellow is a vagabond, 'tis true. But he is son to nobody, servant to nobody, belongs to nobody, comes from nowhere and is going to nowhere. And we none of us, no, none of us, know nothing at all about him.

> [(3) Harlequin *and* Constables]
> *Enter* Constable P.S.

FIRST JUSTICE. Well, Mr. Constable, where is your prisoner?

CONSTABLE. He's without. And, please your Worships, I wish we were well rid of him. For, under favor, I don't think he's of this world.

20 He is certainly something, as I may say, of the magical order about him.

FIRST JUSTICE. Ay, how so?

CONSTABLE. Why there's Simon Clodby of Gander Green says as how this blackamoor man has cut off a tailor's head and sewed it on again.

SECOND JUSTICE. Did you ever hear the like. Why, he has cut off all your heads, I think.

CONSTABLE. I think we are all in some danger, aye, and your Worships, too. For I heard him say myself that he could cut off all your Worships' heads and no harm done neither.

30 FIRST JUSTICE. He'll cut off our heads, will he? We'll lay him by the heels first. Bring him before us. He'll cut off our heads, quotha? And now we have got him.

> *Enter* Harlequin *and* Constable P.S.

FIRST JUSTICE. Let us first examine the prisoner. I hear, Sir, that you have been doing a great deal of mischief about this country.

HARLEQUIN. Yes. A great deal.

FIRST JUSTICE. Very well. He confesses it. Set that down, Clerk. And I hear that you cut off people's heads.

HARLEQUIN. Yes, to cure the toothache. Is your Worship troubled with it?

40 THIRD JUSTICE. You impudent vagabond! How dare you talk to the court so? Did you tell this honest constable here that you would cut off our heads?

HARLEQUIN.   Yes, and mend 'em for nothing.

THIRD JUSTICE.   Did you ever hear the like? Let us send him to prison
   directly. A little whipping will mend his manners.

ALL JUSTICES.   Commit him! Commit him!

HARLEQUIN.   Mercy, mercy, dear, good, wise, reverend, worshipful
   Old Gentlewomen.

ALL JUSTICES.   No mercy. Away with him, away with him!

[(4) Dolly, Mrs. Snip]

50   HARLEQUIN.   Nay then, have at your heads.

[*Loud whistle and Wing Bell*]
Strikes the table with his sword. The wigs all fly off.
Harlequin *runs off. And in their places where the Justices
was seated comes 4* Old women. *Soon an old woman
comes forward.*
[*Curtain Bell*]

SONG.

Old women we are
And as wise in the chair
As fit for the quorum as men.
We can scold on the bench
Or examine a wench
And like them can be wrong now and then.

Chorus.

For search the world through
And you'll find nine in ten
Old women can do as much as old men.

Second.

60   We can hear a sad case
With a no-meaning face
And though shallow yet seem to be dark.
Leave all to the clerk
For when matters grow dark
Their worships had better go sleep.

Chorus, etc.

Third.

When our wisdom is tasked

And hard questions are asked
We'll answer them best with a snore.
We can mump a tidbit
70   And can joke without wit,
And what can their worships do more?

Chorus, etc., exit O.P.

Curtain Bell.

[Scene II] *Wainscot Chamber* (First *Groove*).
Enter Dame Snip *and* Dolly, *crying P. S.*

MRS. SNIP. What do you cry for Dolly, my daughter, and want a
proper spirit? I am ashamed of your principles, Dolly. What do
you cry for, Child?

DOLLY. I can't help it, Mama. I am ashamed to see my Papa so blood
thirsty and look so like a madman as he did, with his breastpan
and headpan and a long sword to kill that dear, sweet, charmingest
of all creatures—Harlequin.

MRS. SNIP. How dare you be so wicked to say this of a creature that
your Papa is gone to murder? Have you no delicacy, you dis-
10   obedient slut, you. My dear Joe is coming home in triumph to us.
He has done the business before this.

DOLLY. But he han't nor won't, nor shan't nor can't. That I am sure
of, and I hope he never will.

MRS. SNIP. What's that you mutter, Madam? Won't your Papa comprehend Harlequin?

[(5) Abraham]

DOLLY. How can he, Mama? Nobody can comprehend him, he's too
nimble for 'em. That's my comfort. They hunted him last week
all about the town, and he turn himself into ten thousand shapes.
First he shrunk himself into a dwarf, then he stretched himself into
20   a giant. Then he was a beau, then a monkey, then a peacock, then
a wheelbarrow. And then he made himself an ostelige, and he
walked about so stately and looked so grand, and when I went up
to him he clapped his wings so (*mimics the ostrich*) that my very
heart leaped within me.

MRS. SNIP. More shame for you, Dolly. So hold your tongue.

DOLLY. Can't hold my tongue. Wiser folks than you and I, Mama,
prize him more than your tragedies or your comedies, aye, or your
singing, either. Cousin Chitterlin and I doat on him. Where do you

30 think he was, Mama, when he was lost for three days? You'd never
guess. I hid him in my bedchamber.

MRS. SNIP. In your bedchamber?

DOLLY. Yes, I did. And I'd hide him there again, and again and again.
Sure I'm old enough to know what's best for me. Lord, what a
creature! He was here and there and everywhere. Now he was
out of the window, then atop of the house, then down in the street,
then he run up the leaden spout. Then he jumped behind the glass,
then over the table and chairs. Then he run under the bed and over
the bed and in the bed. And there was such a bustle, and I was in
such a flutter. And at last, when he had played all his tricks over
40 and over again, he whipped across Jenny's broom, gave me a hearty
kiss, whisks up the chimney and flew into the country, where he
has been ever since.

MRS. SNIP. I am shocked at your impudence. You'll break my heart,
Dolly. You're a Jack-bite hussy.

DOLLY. A Jack-bite, am I? Oh, law!

MRS. SNIP. You are a rebel, Madam. You hide rebels, and whoever
hides rebels is a Jackbite all the world over. Read the newspapers.

DOLLY. Bless me, I tremble every joint of me.

MRS. SNIP. And well you may, Dolly. For if your Papa can kill Harle-
50 quin, we shall not only be rich, Child, but qualitified.

DOLLY. Ay, indeed, qualitified. Show me that and I'll send him packing, I'll warrant you.

MRS. SNIP. Your Papa will be a Barrow-Knight, a lord at least, and
they'll call me my ladyship. And you'll be Lady Doll Snip all the
world over.

DOLLY. Shall I? I'd cut off his head myself if I had him here.

MRS. SNIP. My dear sweet child! Now you are your mother's own
daughter. How I love your spirit. You have it all from my family.
You have nothing sneaking about you, like your Father.

60 DOLLY. Pray, should I let our Abraham court me and slop me about
any more till I hear farther from my Papa?

MRS. SNIP. You may easily pick a quarrel with him.

DOLLY. I'll frump him the next time he speaks to me. (*Crosses to P.S.*)
I can't bear to think of a tailor now. If I were to choose for myself
I should like a captain.

MRS. SNIP. A captain?

DOLLY. Yes, a captain. They look so bold, and are so bold, and are so
grand. And when they march up to one so, they look as if they
could eat a body. It frightens one a little. But it does one's heart
70 good to see 'em. I will have a captain, Mama!

MRS. SNIP. So thou shalt. I love a soldier, too. Everybody loves 'em.

They have done so much and deserve so much that they may do
what they will with us.

DOLLY.   Let 'em do their worst. I defy 'em. But here comes Abram.
I can't bear the sight of him.

Enter Abram, *P.D.*

[ABRAM].   Mistress, Master Forge below wants to speak with you. He
has news of my master but won't tell it to nobody but yourself.

MRS. SNIP.   Where is he, Abram? 'Tis all over, Daughter. We are made
forever. I'll go to him.

Exit Mrs. Snip *P.S.*

80 ABRAM.   Miss Dolly. Miss Dolly! Shall we fetch a walk together this
fine evening?

DOLLY.   Fetch a walk, no, I won't fetch a walk. I beg, Abraham, that
you'll keep to your shop and not talk so familiarly to me. Fetch a
walk. I don't think ever to walk again.

ABRAM.   Heigh to pass, what's the matter now, Miss Dolly? You ben't
false hearted like the great ladies, be ye?

DOLLY.   But I be, though, don't talk to me. Go and mind your business.

ABRAM.   Here's for you, indeed. You told me another story last Saturday night, when I was kissing and toying with you in my Mas-
90 ter's hall above stairs. But those happy hours are past, they are
gone to be sure. And so, if you are changed why I am changed.
Your servant. Your servant. Your servant, Miss Dolly.

Exit P.S.

DOLLY.   I have begun pretty well with him. I'll quite turn him off the
next time. Not but I'll do him some kindness. Perhaps I may make
him one of my footmen. He's genteel, and I shall like to have him
about me. O Law, if I should be Lady Doll Snip, the first thing
I do, I'll be half lame and half blind like Lady Totteridge. And
I'll have a long train draggling after me, which when I want to be
smart I shall tuck under my arm, thus, and jig it away. My teeth
100 shall be white as ivory and my cheeks as red as a cherry. I'm not
an ugly girl, I know that. I won't be stuffed up twice or thrice a
year at holiday time at the top of the playhouse among folks that
laugh and cry, just as they feel. Then I'll carry my head as high
and have as high a head as the best of 'em, and it shall be all set out
with curls. It shall be too high to go in at any door without stoop-
ing, and so broad that I must always go in sideways. Then I shall
keep a chair with a cupola o'top to hold my featherhead in, and I
shall be carried in it by day and by night, dingle-dangle, bobbing

110 and nodding, all the way I go. Then I shall sit in the side boxes among my equals, laugh, talk loud, mind nothing, stare at the low people in the galleries without ever looking at them. Thus! Then they'll hate me as much as I shall my old acquaintance. What a life shall I lead when I'm a fine lady. I'll be as fine as any of 'em and will be turned quite topsy turvey as well as the best of 'em.

Exit.

Act Ends.
Drop. Abram *dresses*

ACT III
[Scene I] Drop Chamber

Enter Dolly Snip O P

[DOLLY].   Was there ever anything so unlucky. I was this morning out of my senses and thought my Father a great man and myself a fine lady. And now my dream's out. My Father has lost his head, my Mother is breaking her heart, and, what is worse than all, I must work for my living. It is a sad thing, a terrible thing, to be obliged to work when one has set one's mind upon lying abed and think-ing of nothing. Then there's Abram, too. I wish I had not turned him off. I must not let him go. I know he can't help loving me, and he knows his interest. So I will e'en marry him, make my mother
10 give up the shop to him, allow her a trifle to maintain her, and take the business into my own hands. I can't think of anything better at present.

[(3) Abram]

Enter Sukey Chitterlin. *P. S.*

SUKEY.   Cousin Dolly! Cousin Dolly. Cousin Dolly.
DOLLY.   Lord, what a noise you make, always roaring and romping.
SUKEY.   Why, would not you have me merry and in spirits?
DOLLY.   I would not have you so boisterous, Ma'am.
SUKEY.   I am sorry to see you so frumpish, Miss Dolly. I came for a little advice. Your Abram, since you turned him off, has made pro-posals to me. Now as we have always opened our hearts to each
20 other, Cousin, and you are my most intimate friend, I want to know if you think it a good match for me. He's a handsome man, to be sure, though he's a little of the rakish cast. I don't like him the worse for it. I have a turn for high fun myself. Eh, Cousin?

DOLLY. Then you'll both be ruined. You are too young. A little waiting will do you no harm.

SUKEY. Egad, I don't know that, Cousin. I'm sure it will do me no
good. If he don't think me too young I'm sure I won't. I may wait
longer and fare worse, mayn't I, Cousin?

DOLLY. But such things should not be done in a hurry, Cousin.

30 SUKEY. One may do worse things in a hurry, Cousin. And so, if you
have no better advice to give, I'll e'en follow my own.

DOLLY. You are grown very glib of your tongue, Miss.

SUKEY. You left it off, Miss, and I took it up. I make a shift with your
leavings—Abram. Among the rest, I'm not proud and fantastical,
Miss.

DOLLY. You are very impertinent, Miss, and deserve to have your ears
boxed.

SUKEY. The sooner the better, for my fingers hate to be idle.

DOLLY. Get out of the room, you saucy flirt, you.

40 SUKEY. You fancy yourself a lady in good earnest. But pride will have
a fall. I know you hate me, and I know the reason of it. I happen
to be handsomer than Somebody, and have as much money as
Somebody, and I was toasted last Friday night at the Spouting
Club before Somebody. All this gives pain to Somebody, who
from thinking herself a lady, forsooth, is become Nobody. And
so, my Lady Doll Somebody-Nobody, your humble servant. But
here comes your Abram. My Abram, I mean. Lord, he's a fine man
and looks so rakish and so amorous. Oh, 'tis a charming, bewitching fellow.

Enter Abram, *dressed. P.S.*

50 ABRAM. Come, Miss Sukey, will you fetch a walk with me? I did not
know your Ladyship was here, or I should not have intruded.
Come, Miss Sukey. (*Going.*)

SUKEY. There's wit and a fleer for you. Oh, he's a charming fellow
and a perfect satyr.

DOLLY. Mr. Abram, may I have the favor of speaking a word to you?

ABRAM. With *me*, my Lady? No, my Lady. I know my distance
which you have taught me, my Lady. "Keep to your shop, Abraham, and don't talk so familiarly to me. Fetch a walk! I don't think
ever to walk again." I'll keep my distance, my Lady. Come, Miss

60 Chitterlin! I know my distance, my Lady.

[(4) Bounce, Gasconade *in chains*]

SUKEY. What a satyr he is. I'm glad I've got him.

DOLLY. Pray let me speak with you, Cousin.

SUKEY.   Oh, not for the world, my Lady.

[(5) Goaler, *bunch of keys*]

BOTH [SUKEY *and* ABRAM].   Ha, ha, ha!

DOLLY.   Why then I must tell you, Sukey Chitterlin, that you are a treacherous, base girl to take my sweetheart from me.

ABRAM.   That's me. I knew she'd repent it. (*Struts.*)

SUKEY.   And I must tell you, Miss Madam, My Lady Doll Snip, that you falsify yourself to say so. You bid me take him, so you did.
70   And I have taken him. And I'll keep him, too. Shan't I, Abram?

[(6) Harlequin, *wine, etc. ready*]

ABRAM.   That you shall, body and soul of me, Miss Sukey. And no bad bargain neither.

DOLLY.   Go, you poor, pitiful, low-minded . . .

ABRAM (*crosses to center and back*).   As good a man as your Father, Miss. Aye, and better too, for I've got my head upon my shoulders. (*Struts.*)

DOLLY.   Yes. Yes, you have a head. And it will be finely furnished shortly.

SUKEY.   And so it shall, Madam. He shall want for nothing that I can help him to.

80 ABRAM.   I shall want for nothing that she can help me to. (*Struts.*) Come, wife that is to be. Don't let us lose time with a mad lady. Your servant, my Lady Doll. Ha, ha, ha!

SUKEY.   Your Ladyship's most obedient.

BOTH.   Ha, ha, ha!

ABRAM.   I knew she's repent at last.

Struts out with Sukey. P.S.

DOLLY.   I am mad indeed. I could tear both their eyes out. A low-bred foolish girl in my situation would run distracted. But I don't mind it no more than a pin's point, not I. I despise and laugh at it, he, he, he. I can't bear it neither. I must go and cry a little to recover
90   myself.

Exit O.P.

[Scene II] B.B.W. SCENE *a Prison. Table to change & sink.*

Bounce *and* Gasconade *discovered.*

BOUNCE.   Is not this a most lamentable situation for a man of my soul and ambition, I who have thinned nations, mowed down armies, to be hanged at last for killing a tailor? It is not death, 'tis the disgrace, the dishonor is all my concern.

GASCONADE. *En verite* inteed that no concerns me at all. If they will give me my life, I will put my disgrace in my pocket.

BOUNCE. Is there no way to get out of this damned hole? I had always a good hand at getting into prisons, I wish I knew as well how to get out of one. Egad, I have it! My dear friend, you shall help me up to that window there, and then I can easily make my escape over the top of the next house.

[(7) Mrs. Snip]

GASCONADE. *Eh bien*, my dear friend, and vat must I do den, eh?

BOUNCE. Faith, that's true. Why you shall stay here and let 'em know that I am gone, but that I will certainly come again when they want me.

[(8) Mr. Snip, Turnkey]

GASCONADE. I very much tank you for dat, Monsieur Bounce. *Non, non*, if I must be hanged, *mon amie*, I love that my dear friend should keep a me *compagnie*.

[Enter Jailor P.S. *(Bunch of Keys)]*

[JAILOR]. Well, Gentlemen, I bring you good news, good news.

BOUNCE. What, a reprieve?

GASCONADE. Vat, a reprieve?

JAILOR. A reprieve, no, no. You'll certainly be hanged and tomorrow too. But the good news I have brought you is that your friends have got permission for a friar to attend you. And here behold your Father and Comforter.

[P S Enter Harlequin *(like a friar)]*

HARLEQUIN. Peace be with the afflicted. Jailor, a chair and a bottle of sack. The body requires rest and refreshment.

[Exit Jailor P.S.*]*

As you are under misfortunes, what I am going to say shall be uttered with the utmost gentleness and humanity. You are without doubt gentlemen. I speak it from my soul, a couple of horrid rascals.

GASCONADE. Dat is very gentile indeed.

BOUNCE *(aside)*. And very true.

[Enter Jailor *with wine P.S.]*

HARLEQUIN.   Gentlemen, to your speedy execution!

GASCONADE.   *Je vous remercie.* He's very complaisant indeed.

HARLEQUIN.   Another to your repentence, and then to business.

GASCONADE.   Begar, you vas sent here to give us consolation, and you take all de consolation yourself.

HARLEQUIN.   Son, I shall give you spiritual consolation. But in the first
40   place, I must examine the sullen sinner. Of what religion are you?

BOUNCE.   None.

HARLEQUIN.   Of what religion are you?

GASCONADE.   Whatever you please.

HARLEQUIN.   'Tis really a pity you should suffer, for you have been both exceedingly well educated. Will you confess anything?

BOUNCE.   No.

HARLEQUIN.   Will you confess, sir?

GASCONADE.   I do confess and profess too, sir, that I have no great desire to be hanged.

[Enter Mrs. Snip *P.S.D.]*

50   MRS. SNIP.   Let me come, let me come! And let me indulge myself with the sight of poor Joe's murderers. Oh, you base, base villains, to deprive so civil and peaceable a woman as I am of as good a husband and as good a workman. I can't bear the thoughts of it. Let me come at 'em, let me come at 'em! If I were in a passion now, I could tear their execratious eyes out. Well, poor Joe, thou wert a little too domineering and robustious sometimes, but my quiet temper soon appeased thee. Thy passion was soon over. I shall never get such another for my purpose.

[Enter Snip *PS]*

A ghost! A ghost! I shall die. I shall die.

60   BOUNCE.   No ghost, no ghost! I shall live, I shall live! 'Tis he himself.

GASCONADE.   Ah, *je vive aussi.* I am alive too.

BOUNCE.   Off with my chains. I'll swear to his face.

GASCONADE.   Ouy, I'll swear to his face, for I did cut off his head.

JAILOR.   Where have you been, Joe?

SNIP.   I have been murdered, neighbor Padlock.

MRS. SNIP.   And are you really flesh and blood? Let me feel you. Come nearer. Don't touch me, if you are not a man. He's warm. Kiss me. Kiss me again. 'Tis my Joe, I know 'tis he. I am glad to see you again, but I am sorry you came back so soon too. Had you but
70   stayed a day longer, these two would have been hanged for murdering of you.

JAILOR.   But since things have happened otherwise, I'll e'en release

my prisoners. [*Takes off their chains and throws 'em off P.S.*]
GASCONADE.   *De tout mon coeur.*
BOUNCE.   Huzza!
TURNKEY [*within (Prompter)*].   Lock up all the doors. Bar up all the windows. Keep a good look out the back way.
JAILOR.   What's the matter, Turnkey?
TURNKEY [*Prompter*].   Look about ye; Harlequin's in the prison.
80 JAILOR.   The devil he is, that would be a prize indeed.
BOUNCE.   Now Monsieur, now's our time.
GASCONADE.   *Pardonnez moi.* I vil burn my finger no more.
HARLEQUIN.   Give me some sack. Oh, I shall faint, I shall faint. Harlequin's in the prison.
MRS. SNIP.   Poor soul! Pour soul!
SNIP.   May I never handle needle again, if this is not the blackamoor gentleman that sowed my head on.
ALL.   'Tis Harlequin! 'Tis Harlequin himself.
JAILOR.   Now for it boys, the prize is our own.

[*They advance to seize him*]
Tr. bell to change table—to the Devil.
Trap bell to sink table.

90 GASCONADE.   Vat is all dis? I am fright out of my wits.
MRS. SNIP.   Mercy on us, they are raising the Devil here.
BOUNCE.   Oh! Oh! Oh!

[*Music in the orchestra*]
Trap bell—border bell—Wing bell.
Prison returns. 1st Transparency

SNIP.   We are all bewitched. I shall certainly lose my head again.
JAILOR.   Why, I am in my own jail again.
BOUNCE.   And I'll get out of it as fast as I can.
TURNKEY [*without*].   Bring him along. Bring him along.
BOUNCE.   What have we got here? My father and confessor.

[Harlequin *brought on by* Mercury Pd.]

GASCONADE.   Eh! Monsieur Consolation, are you caught with all your tricks, you dam black dog?
100 MERCURY.   Come, come, strip hypocrisy lined with folly. [*Draws off the friar's gown—Harlequin tries to escape.*] Not so fast, Monsieur Harlequin. I have heels shall match yours. Run, fly, swim, leap! I am after you, and if you are for fighting, I have a weapon here. *Ecce signum.* [*Showing his caduceus*].
GASCONADE.   There is consolation for you, *mon bon pere.*

MERCURY.   In a true glass I'll set to view
Your fate and that of all your crew.
Hence, you profane, without delay.
This scene is not for you. Away.

Exeunt Snip, Mrs. Snip, Gasconade, Bounce *and* Jailor *OP.*

Mercury *waves his caduceus (Music in orchestra)*
Tr. bell. Border bell. Wing bell. Prison sinks.

The second transparency appears representing the powers
of pantomime going to attack Mount Parnassus. A storm
comes on, destroys the fleet. (When the ship splits —
whistle) Rock flat. Shuts up transparency.

110 MERCURY.   Hear Earthly Proteus, hear great Jove's decree.
His thunder sleeps, and thus he speaks by me.
Descend to earth, be sportive as before,
Wait on the muses' train like fools of yore,
Beware encroachment and invade no more.

Harlequin *stands on front trap OP*
Mercury *waves his caduceus.*
Tr. bell. Wing bell. Border bell.
Temple of the Gods.

MERCURY.   Now let immortal Shakespear rise
Ye sons of Taste adore him.
As from the sun each vapor flies,
Let folly sink before him. [*Wave caduceus*]

Trap bell
Shakespear rises: Harlequin sinks.

SONG.

Thrice happy th' nation that Shakespear has charmed,
120   More happy the bosom his genius has warmed.
Ye children of Nature, of Fashion, and Whim,
He painted you all, all join to praise him.
Come away, come away, come away.
His genius calls and you must obey.

At the Chorus many of Shakespear's characters enter P.S.
and O.P., also the three Graces, who dance to the repeat.

II.

To praise him ye fairies and genii repair,
He knew where you haunted in earth or in air.

No phantom so subtle could glide from his view,
The wings of his fancy were swifter than you.
    Come away, come away.
130   His genius calls and you must obey.

    At the Chorus several fairies and genii enter.
    The fairies dance to the repeat.

III.

Ye Britons may fancy ne'er lead you astray,
Nor e'er through your senses your reason betray.
By your love to the Bard may your wisdom be known,
Nor injure his fame to the loss of your own.
    Come away, come away.
    His genius calls and we must away.

    During the 3rd verse the figure dancers enter. When over,
the Grand Dance is executed while the Chorus is sung and repeated.
    Ring. Curtain.
    Finis

The Enchanter;
or, Love and Magic
A Musical Drama
1760

THE
ENCHANTER;

O R,

LOVE and MAGIC.

A MUSICAL DRAMA.

As it is performed at the

Theatre-Royal in Drury-Lane.

The MUSIC composed

By Mr. SMITH.

LONDON:

Printed for J. and R. TONSON, in the Strand.
MDCCLX.

Advertisement

As the recitative commonly appears the most tedious part of the musical entertainment, the writer of the following little piece has avoided it as much as possible; and has endeavored to carry on what fable there is, chiefly by the songs.—The reader is desired to take notice that the passages distinguished by inverted commas are omitted in the representation.

Persons

Moroc, the Enchanter, by Mr. CHAMPNESS.
Kaliel, Attendant Spirit, by Master LIONI
Zoreb, contracted to Zaida, by Mr. LOWE.

Zaida, by Mrs. VINCENT.
Lyssa, by Miss YOUNG.

Chorus, Attendants, Dancers, *etc.*

The Enchanter;
or, Love and Magic

ACT I. SCENE I.

A Room in the Enchanter's Castle.

RECITATIVE.

MOROC. Oh Love, destroyer Love, this ravage cease,
Or give me conquest, or restore my peace.

AIR.

I burn! I burn!
Where e'er I turn
Each object feeds my flame;
The hinds that whistle care away,
The birds that sing, the beasts that play,
    Show what a wretch I am!
'A wretch of reason and of power,
'Who in this trying hour
'Cannot conquer or retreat,
'Passion all my pow'r disarms,
'Moroc yields to woman's charms,
'And trembles at her feet.'

SCENE II.

Moroc, Kaliel.

RECITATIVE.

MOROC. Oh, Kaliel! Kaliel! Speak, thou faithful slave,
What hope? Will Zaida yield? Alas, I rave.

RECITATIVE.

KALIEL. Torn from her lover's arms, the mournful fair

Rejects your vows and cherishes despair;
Like a transplanted flower, the blooming spoil
20 Droops in a foreign, though a richer soil.

AIR.

In vain I tried
Each soothing art,
To swell her pride
Or melt her heart.

In vain your love
Your power displayed,
Nor power could move,
Nor love persuade.

With lifted eyes
30 She Zoreb calls,
Then strikes her breast!
The sighs that rise,
The tear that falls,
Declare the rest.

MOROC. Obdurate fair one! What uncommon mold
Impressed thy mind, that pleasure, power, nor gold
Can soften or allure it. Take this wand. (*Gives a wand to* Kaliel.)
Again persuade, implore, at thy command
Joys shall attend, while I with other arms
40 My rival seek, and hell shall aid my charms.

AIR.

My slaves below,
Prepare, prepare!
Enchant the foe,
Deceive the fair.
Magic now with magic vies,
Moroc's art with Zaida's eyes. (*Sinks.*)

SCENE III.

AIR.

KALIEL. Fly, airy sprites,
Around her fly.
Sooth her with delights,
50 Charm her ear and eye.

20. though] *O*1, *W*1; tho' *W*2.

Fly swifter than the wind,
Let your spells her fancy bind,
Through her senses reach her mind.)

Exit.

SCENE IV.

A garden belonging to the Enchanter.

AIR.

ZAIDA.   Intruder sleep! In vain you try
To hush my breast and close my eye;
The morning dews refresh the flower,
     That unmolested blows;
But ineffectual falls the shower
     Upon the cankered rose.

SCENE V.

Zaida, Kaliel.
RECITATIVE.

60   KALIEL.   Oh let not grief your bloom destroy,
Youth's fairest blossoms spring from joy,
And beauty's cheek with tints supply,
Which nipt by sorrow fade and die.

AIR.

Sigh not your hours away,
Youth should be ever gay;
Ever should dance around
Pleasure's enchanted ground:
     Reason invites you,
     Passion excites you,
70   Raptures abound.

Spring shall her sweets display,
     Nature shall view with art;
No clouds shall shade the day,
     No grief the heart.

Love shall his treasures bring,)
Beauty shall sport and sing, }
Free as the zephyr's wing,)

72. view] *O*1, *W*1; vie *W*2.

Soft as his kiss,
'Changing
80   'and
'Ranging
'From bliss to bliss.'
Free as the zephy'rs wing, *etc.*

Come then sweet liberty,
Let us be ever free.
What's life without love, what love without thee?

RECITATIVE, ACCOMPANIED.

ZAIDA.   To Zaida's ears thy strains might sweetly flow,
Had Zoreb's air or face her bosom fired;
No transient passion caught her heart, oh no!
90   Can passion die, that virtue has inspired?

AIR.

Whate'er you say, whate'er you do,
My heart shall still be fixed and true;
The vicious bosom love deforms,
And rages there in gusts and storms;
But love with us a constant gale
Just swells the sea and fills the sail;
Neither of winds or waves the sport,
We rule the helm and gain the port.

RECITATIVE.

KALIEL.   Ye votaries of mirth and love,
100   In all your various mazes move,
Be frolic, changeable, and free,
Charm her with sweet variety:
The happiest union known on earth,
Is mirth and love, and love with mirth.
(Kaliel *waves his wand.*)

SCENE VI.

*Lyssa enters with her followers, as the votaries of
Mirth and Love.*

AIR.

LYSSA.   When youthful charms
Fly pleasure's arms,
Kind nature's gifts are vain;

We should not save
What nature gave,

110   But kindly give again.

Though scorn and pride
Our wishes hide,
And though the tongue says, Nay!
The honest heart
Takes pleasure's part,
Denying all we say.

The birds in spring
Will sport and sing,

And revel through the grove;
120   And shall not we,
As blithe and free,
With them rejoice and love?

Let love and joy
Our spring employ,
Kind nature's law fulfill;
Then sport and play
Now whilst we may,
We cannot when we will.

(*A dance by the followers of Lyssa.*)

RECITATIVE.

LYSSA.   'Tis thus we revel, dance and play,
130   Life with us is holiday:
Constancy would pall our joys,
Varied passion never cloys.

DUET.

LYSSA.   Would you taste the sweets of love,
Ever change and ever rove,
Fly at pleasure and away.
Love's the cup of bliss and woe,
Nectar if you taste and go,
Poison if you stay.

ZAIDA.   Would you taste the sweets of love,
140   Never change and never rove,

---

111. Though] *O*1, *W*1; Tho' *W*2.
132.1. Duet] *O*1, *W*1, Duett *W*2.

Fly from pleasures that betray.
Love's the cup of bliss and woe,
Poison if you taste and go,
Nectar if you stay.

Exeunt severally.

End of the First Act.

ACT II. SCENE I.

A Garden.
Zaida, Lyssa, *and other female spirits following.*

RECITATIVE.

ZAIDA.   Shame of thy sex, begone, nor haunt me more.

RECITATIVE.

LYSSA.   Will Zaida's bosom from a woman hide,
What to conceal from man is art and pride?
Behold power's sovereign charm to soften hate,
What melts us most—variety and state!

(*Waves her wand, and the whole scene
and decorations change.*)

AIR.

Turn and see what pleasures woo you,
Let not love in vain pursue you.
Seize his blessings while you may,
Love has wings and will not stay.
10   CHORUS.   Seize his blessings whilst you may,
Love has wings and will not stay.

RECITATIVE. ACCOMPANIED.

ZAIDA.   Deluders hence! Your spells are weak,
My Zoreb's stronger spells to break;
For him alone I draw my breath,
With him I could rejoice in death.

*It thunders, grows dark, and the garden shakes. All the
women run off but* Zaida *and* Lyssa.

RECITATIVE.

LYSSA.   'Tis past; the softer passions take their flight.
Moroc comes armed in terrors and in night,
Destruction in his eye, and in his hand
The scepter of his wrath, his ebon wand.

144.2.   End of ... Act] *O*1, *W*1; omitted *W*2.

SCENE II.

Moroc, Zaida, Lyssa.

RECITATIVE. ACCOMPANIED.

20 MOROC.   No more I come with sighs and prayers,
                          A proud ungrateful fair to sue:
                   Revenge a festival prepares,
                          A festival for love and you.

TRIO.

LYSSA (*to* Moroc).   Oh hear her sighs, believe her tears,
                   The heart may change that pants with fears.

ZAIDA.   Hear not my sighs, nor trust my tears,
                   My heart may pant, but not with fears:
                   His treasure lost, the miser mourns.

LYSSA.   More treasure found, his joy returns.

30 MOROC.   Hence jealousy and lovesick cares!
                   Vengeance now my bosom tears.

LYSSA.   'The joys of power will here attend thee.

ZAIDA.   'The joys of love will Zoreb send me.

LYSSA.   'With him your heart new woes would prove.

ZAIDA.   'I fear no woes with him I love.

MOROC.   'Away with love and fond desires.
                   'Vengeance rage with all thy fires.'

RECITATIVE.

Lyssa, depart. This is no hour for joy.
I come not now to pity but destroy.

Exit Lyssa, *etc.*

40   To Zaida's arms her lover I resign;
            He's dead, and dying thought you mine.
            For him alone you drew your breath,
            With him you shall rejoice in death.

(*Dead march.*)

SCENE III.

A tomb rises from the ground, in which Zoreb *lies,* Kaliel *standing by him with his wand on his breast.*

---

28. treasure] *O*1, *W*1; treasure's *W*2.
39. but destroy] *O*1, *W*1; but to destroy *W*2.

Scene from *The Enchanter* (Watercolor by Tannai).
Folger Shakespeare Library

RECITATIVE. ACCOMPANIED.

ZAIDA.   My Zoreb dead! Then sorrow is no more.
                 Now let the lightning flash, the thunder roar.

AIR.

                 Back to your source weak, foolish tears,
                 Away, fond love, and woman's fears;
                     A nobler passion warms.
                 The dove shall soar with eagle's wings,
50   From earth I spring
                 And fly to heav'n and Zoreb's arms.

Offers to stab herself. Moroc *runs to prevent her, and in
his fright drops his ebon wand, which* Kaliel *takes up.*

MOROC.   Hold, deperate fair. (*Takes away the dagger.*)
                     No more will I employ
                 Love's softer arts, but seize and force my joy.

                     (*Takes hold of her.*)

ZAIDA.   Help, heav'nly Powers!
MOROC.   What power can Moroc fear?
KALIEL.   The power of virtue, which I now revere.
                 With thy own arms thy guilty reign I end,
                 No longer Moroc's slave but Zaida's friend.
60   Thus do I blast thee, as the thunder's stroke
                 Blasts the proud cedar. All thy charms are broke.

Kaliel *strikes* Moroc *with the wand and he sinks.*

SCENE IV.

ZAIDA. How shall I thank the guardian of my fame?
        (*Kneels to* Kaliel.)
KALIEL. Rise, Zaida. Peace! More thanks shall Kaliel claim.
        Behold thy Zoreb, dead to mortal view,
        The spells dissolved, shall wake to life and you.

RECITATIVE, ACCOMPANIED.
                 This magic wand in Moroc's hand
                     Did wound, oppress:
                 In Kaliel's hand this magic wand
                     Shall heal and bless.

_____

        49. wings] *O*1, *W*1; wing *W*2.

AIR.

70
<blockquote>
Oh faithful youth,
To shake thy truth
   No more shall fiends combine.
Now gently move
To meet that love,
   That truth which equals thine.
</blockquote>

While the symphony is playing, Zoreb *rises gradually from the tomb.*

AIR.

ZOREB.   'What angel's voice, what sweet enchanting breath
   'Calls hapless Zoreb from the bed of death?
   'In terror's gloom,
   'Night's awful womb,

80
   'My soul imprisoned lay,
   'But now I wake to day,
'Too weak my power's to bear this flood of light,
'For all Elysium opens to my sight.'

(*Looks rapturously on* Zaida.)

ZAIDA. Oh, Zoreb! Oh, my lord, my bosom guest!
  Transport is mute; my eyes must speak the rest.
ZOREB.   And do I wake to bliss as well as life?
  'Tis more than bliss, 'tis Zaida, 'tis my wife.
KALIEL. In fate's mysterious web this knot was wove;
  Thus heaven rewards your constancy and love. (*Joins their hands.*)

DUET.

90 ZOREB, ZAIDA. No power could divide us, no terror dismay,
     No treasures could bribe us, no falsehood betray.
     No demons could tempt us, no pleasure could move,
     No magic could bind us, but the magic of love.
ZOREB.   The spell round my heart was the image of you;
    Then how could I fail to be constant and true.

RECITATIVE.

KALIEL. Hence ye wicked spirits away.
    Passion yields to reason's sway.
    Purer beings of the air

75.1. *symphony*] O1; sympathy W1, W2.
83. opens] O1, W1; open's W2.
94–95. Zaida repeats these lines W1, W2.
96. spirits] O1, W1; sprites W2.

Hover round and guard this pair.
100   Love and innocence appear!
Love and virtue triumph here. (*Waves his wand.*)

SCENE V.

Enter Shepherds, Shepherdesses, *etc.*

AIR.

KALIEL.
    Ye sons of simplicity,
    Love and felicity,
Ye shepherds who pipe on the plain;
    Leave your lambs and your sheep,
    Our revels to keep,
Which Zoreb and Zaida ordain.

    Your smiles of tranquility,
    Hearts of humility,
110   Each fiend of the bosom destroy.
    For virtue and mirth
    To blessings give birth,
Which Zoreb and Zaida enjoy.

CHORUS:
    How happy the hour,
    When passion and power
No longer united, no longer oppress.
    When beauty and youth
    With love and with truth,
Forever united, forever shall bless.

A dance of Shepherds, Shepherdesses, etc., etc.

Finis

The Farmer's
Return from London

An Interlude

1762

THE

FARMER's RETURN

FROM

LONDON.

AN

INTERLUDE.

As it is PERFORMED at the

THEATRE ROYAL in DRURY-LANE.

LONDON:

Printed by DRYDEN LEACH,

For J. and R. TONSON, in the Strand.

MDCCLXII.

Facsimile title page of the First Edition.
Folger Shakespeare Library.

Advertisement

The following Interlude was prepared for the stage, merely with a view of assisting Mrs. Pritchard at her benefit; and the desire of serving so good an actress is a better excuse for its defects than the few days in which it was written and represented. Notwithstanding the favorable reception it has met with, the author would not have printed it, had not his friend, Mr. Hogarth, flattered him most agreeably by thinking *The Farmer and his Family* not unworthy of a sketch of his pencil. To him, therefore, this trifle, which he has so much honored, is inscribed, as a faint testimony of the sincere esteem which the writer bears him, both as a man and an artist.

10

Persons of the Interlude

Farmer,		Mr. GARRICK.
Wife,		Mrs. BRADSHAW.
Sally, ⎫		⎛ Miss HEATH.
Dick, ⎬	Children,	⎨ Master POPE.
Ralph, ⎭		⎝ Master CAPE.

SCENE, The Farmer's Kitchen.

1.   Garrick] *O*1, *Q*1, *W*1; Garric *W*2.
5.   Master Cape] *O*1, *Q*1, *W*1; Master Capf *W*2.

The Farmer's Return from London

Enter Wife *busily.*

[WIFE.]   Where are you, my children? Why Sally, Dick, Ralph!

Enter Children *running.*

Your father is come, heaven bless him, and safe.

Enter Farmer.

Oh, John! My heart dances with joy thou art come.
FARMER.   And troth so does mine, for I love thee and whoam. (*Kisses.*)
WIFE.   Now kiss all your children—and now me agen. (*Kisses.*)
Oh bless thy sweet feace! For one kiss gi' me ten!
FARMER.   Keep some for anon, Dame. You quoite stop my breath.
You kill me wi' koindness, you buss me to death.
Enough, Love! Enough is as good as a feast.
10   Let's ha' some refreshment for me and my beeast.
Dick, get me a poipe.

Exit Dick.

Ralph, go to the mare;
Gi' poor wench some oaats.

Exit Ralph.

Dame, reach me a chair.
Sal, draw me some aal to wash the dirt down,

Exit Sally.

0.1. busily] *O*1; hastily *Q*1, *W*1, *W*2.
1. Ralph] *O*1, *W*2; Raaph *Q*1, *W*1.
12. Ralph] *O*1, *W*1, *W*2; Raaph *Q*1.

And then I will tell you of London fine town. (*Sits down.*)
WIFE. Oh, John, you've been from me the Lord knows how long!
    Yo've been with the false ones and done me some wrong.
FARMER. By the zooks but I ha'nt, so hold thy fool's tongue.
20   Some tittups I saw, and they maade me to stare,
    Tricked noice out for saale, like our cattle at fair:
    So tempting, so fine! and i'cod, very cheap.
    But, Bridget, I know, as we sow we must reeap,
    And a cunning old ram will avoid rotten sheep.

Enter Dick *with a pipe and a candle, and* Sally *with some ale.*

WIFE. But London, dear John!
FARMER.   Is a fine hugeous city,
    Where the geese are all swans and the fools are all witty.
WIFE. Did you see ony wits?
FARMER.   I looked up and down,
30   But 'twas labor in vain. They were all out of town.
    I asked for the maakers o' news and such things,
    Who know all the secrets of kingdoms and kings.
    So busy were they, and such matters about,
    That six days in the seven they never stir out.
    Koind souls, with our freedom they make such a fuss,
    That they lose it themselves to bestow it on us.
WIFE. But was't thou at court, John? What there hast thou seen?
FARMER. I saw 'em, heaven bless 'em! You know whom I mean.
    I heard their healths prayed for agen and agen,
40   With provoiso that one may be sick now and ten.
    Some looks speak their hearts, as it were with a tongue.
    Oh, Dame! I'll be damned if they e'er do us wrong:
    Here's to 'em, bless 'em boath. Do you take the jug.
    Woud't do their hearts good, I'd swallow the mug. (*Drinks.*)
    (*To* Dick.) Come, pledge me, my boy.
    Hold, lad; hast nothing to say?
DICK. Here, Daddy, here's to 'em! (*Drinks.*)
FARMER.   Well said, Dick, boy!
DICK.   Huzza!
50 WIFE. What more did'st thou see to beget admiration?

---

18. Yo've] *O1, Q1, W1*; You've *W2.*
20. made me stare] *O1, Q1, W1*; made me to stare *W2.*
28. ony] *O1*; only *Q1, W1, W2.*
32. know] *O1, Q1, W1*; knew *W2.*
34. never] *O1, W1, W2*; neer *Q1.*
49. Huzza!] *O1, Q1, W2*; Hazza *W1.*

Wm Hogarth delin.   James Basire. Sculp.

The Farmer's Return.

Garrick and Mary Bradshaw, with Edward Cape Everard and Ann Heath
in *The Farmer's Return from London* by Hogarth.
Harvard Theatre Collection

FARMER. The city's fine show,—but first the crownation!
'Twas thof all the world had been there with their spouses;
There was street within street, and houses on houses!
I thought from above (when the folk filled the pleaces)
The streets paved with heads and the walls made of feaces.
Such justling and bustling! 'twas worth all the pother.
I hope, from my soul, I shall ne'er see another.
SALLY. Dad, what did you see at the pleays and the shows?
FARMER. What did I see at the pleays and the shows?
60   Why bouncing and grinning, and a power of fine cloaths:
From top to the bottom 'twas all 'chanted ground,
Gold, painting, and music, and blaazing all round!
Above 'twas like Bedlam, all roaring and rattling!
Below, the fine folk were all curts'ying and prattling:
Strange jumble together—*Turks, Christians,* and *Jews!*
At the temple of folly all crowd to the pews.
Here, too, doizened out, were those seame freakish leadies,
Who keep open market, though smuggling their treade is.
I saw a new pleay, too. They called it *The School* —
70   I thought it pure stuff, but I thought like a fool.
'Twas *The School of*—? Pize on it! my mem'ry is naught.
The great ones disliked it; they heate to be taught.
The cratticks too grumbled. I'll tell you for whoy.
They wanted to laugh, and were ready to croy.
WIFE. Pray what are your cratticks?
FARMER.   Like watchmen in town,
Lame, feeble, half-blind, yet they knock poets down.
Like old Justice Wormwood, a crattick's a man
That can't sin himself, and he heates those that can.
80   I ne'er went to operas. I thought it too grand
For poor folk to like what they don't understand.
The top joke of all, and what pleased me the moast,
Some wise ones and I sat up with a ghoast.
WIFE *and* CHILDREN (*starting*). A ghoast!
FARMER.   Yes, a ghoast.
WIFE.   I shall swoond away, Love!
FARMER. Odzooks! thou'rt as bad as thy betters above.
With her nails and her knuckles she answered so noice.
For *Yes* she knocked once, and for *No* she knocked twoice.

---

61. top to bottom] *O*1, *Q*1, *W*1; to the bottom *W*2.
66. crowd] *O*1, *Q*1; croud *W*1, *W*2.
80. operas] *O*1, *Q*1, *W*1; opras *W*2.
87. Odzooks] *O*1; Odrooks *Q*1, *W*1, *W*2.

90   I asked her one thing —

WIFE.   What thing?

FARMER.   If yo', Dame, was true.

WIFE.   And the poor soul knocked *one*.

FARMER.   By the zounds, it was *two*!

WIFE (*cries*). I'll not be abused, John.

FARMER.   Come, prithee, no croying,

The ghoast, among friends, was much given to loying.

WIFE. I'll tear out her eyes —

FARMER.   I thought, Dame, of matching

100   Your nails against hers, for you're both good at scratching.

They may talk of the country, but, I say, in town

Their throats are much woider to swallow things down.

I'll uphold, in a week—by my troth I don't joke —

That our little Sal shall fright all the town folk.

Come, get me some supper. But first let me peep

At the rest of my children—my calves and my sheep. (*Going.*)

WIFE. Ah, John!

FARMER.   Nay, cheer up. Let not ghoats trouble thee. ⎞

Bridget, look in thy glass, and *there* thou may'st see, ⎬

110   I defy mortal man to maake cuckold o' me. ⎠

Exeunt.

The End

---

110. a cuckold] *O*1, *Q*1, *W*1; cuckold *W*2.

110.2. The End] *O*1, *Q*1; End of The Farmer's Return *W*1, *W*2.

The Clandestine Marriage

A Comedy

1766

THE

Clandeſtine Marriage,

A

COMEDY.

As it is ACTED at the

Theatre-Royal in *Drury-Lane.*

BY

GEORGE COLMAN
AND
DAVID GARRICK.

---

*Hac adhibe vultus, et in unâ parce duobus :
Vivat, et ejuſdem ſimus uterque parens !* OVID.

LONDON,

Printed for T. BECKET and P. A. DE HONDT, in the Strand;
R. BALDWIN, in Pater-noſter-Row; R. DAVIS, in Pic-
cadilly; and T. DAVIES, in Ruſſel-Street, Covent-
Garden.

M.DCC.LXVI.

Facsimile title page of the First Edition.
Folger Shakespeare Library.

Advertisement

Hogarth's Marriage-a-la-Mode has before furnished materials to the author of a novel, published some years ago, under the title of *The Marriage-Act*. But as that writer pursued a very different story, and as his work was chiefly designed for a political satire, very little use could be made of it for the service of this comedy.

In justice to the person who has been considered as the sole author, the party who has hitherto lain concealed thinks it incumbent on him to declare that the disclosure of his name was, by his own desire, reserved till the publication of the piece.

Both the authors, however, who have before been separately honored with the indulgence of the public, now beg leave to make their joint acknowledgements for the very favorable reception of *The Clandestine Marriage*.

10

---

7. *C* omits the last two paragraphs and substitutes the following: "Some friends, and some enemies, have endeavored to allot distinct portions of this play to each of the authors. Each, however, considers himself as responsible for the whole; and though they have, on other occasions, been separately honored with the indulgence of the public, it is with peculiar pleasure that they now make their joint acknowledgements for the very favorable reception of *The Clandestine Marriage*."

Prologue

Written by Mr. Garrick.
Spoken by Mr. Holland.

Poets and painters, who from nature draw
Their best and richest stores, have made this law:
That each should neighborly assist his brother,
And steal with decency from one another.
Tonight, your matchless Hogarth gives the thought,
Which from his canvas to the stage is brought.
And who so fit to warm the poet's mind,
As he who pictured morals and mankind?
But not the same their characters and scenes;
10 Both labor for one end, by different means:
Each, as it suits him, takes a separate road,
Their one great object, marriage-a-la-mode!
Where titles deign with cits to have and hold,
And change rich blood for more substantial gold!
And honored trade from interest turns aside,
To hazard happiness for titled pride.
The painter dead, yet still he charms the eye;
While England lives, his fame can never die.
But he who struts his hour upon the stage
20 Can scarce extend his fame for half an age;
Nor pen nor pencil can the actor save,
The art and artist share one common grave.
Oh, let me drop one tributary tear,
On poor Jack Falstaff's grave, and Juliet's bier!
You to their worth must testimony give;
'Tis in your hearts alone their fame can live.
Still as the scenes of life will shift away,
The strong impressions of their art decay.
Your children cannot feel what you have known;

30   They'll boast of QUINS and CIBBERS of their own.
      The greatest glory of our happy few
      Is to be felt and be approved by you.

Dramatis Personae

MEN

LORD OGLEBY	Mr. *King*
SIR JOHN MELVIL	Mr. *Holland*
STERLING	Mr. *Yates*
LOVEWELL	Mr. *Powell*
CANTON	Mr. *Baddeley*
BRUSH	Mr. *Palmer*
SERJEANT FLOWER	Mr. *Love*
TRAVERSE	Mr. *Lee*
TRUEMAN	Mr. *Aickin*

WOMEN

MRS. HEIDELBERG	Mrs. *Clive*
MISS STERLING	Miss *Pope*
FANNY	Mrs. *Palmer*
BETTY	Mrs. [*Abington*]
CHAMBERMAID	Miss *Plym*
TRUSTY	Miss *Mills*

10

---

13. Mrs. ——] in all editions until *C*, 1777; Mrs. Abington *C*. Mrs. Abington, who also played Miss Crotchet in the epilogue, refused to have her name appear in the printed plays, apparently because both are minor parts. Her name appeared on the bills.

The Clandestine Marriage

ACT I. [Scene I.]

SCENE, *A room in* Sterling's *house.*

Miss Fanny *and* Betty *meeting.*

BETTY (*running in*). Ma'am! Miss Fanny, ma'am!

FANNY. What's the matter, Betty?

BETTY. Oh la, ma'am, as sure as I'm alive, here is your husband —

FANNY. Hush, my dear Betty! If any body in the house should hear
you, I am ruined.

BETTY. Mercy on me, it has frighted me to such a degree that my heart
is come up to my mouth. But as I was saying, ma'am, here's that
dear, sweet —

FANNY. Have a care, Betty.

10 BETTY. Lord, I'm bewitched, I think. But as I was a saying, ma'am,
here's Mr. Lovewell, just come from London.

FANNY. Indeed!

BETTY. Yes indeed; and indeed, ma'am, he is. I saw him crossing the
courtyard in his boots.

FANNY. I am glad to hear it. But pray now, my dear Betty, be cautious.
Don't mention that word again on any account. You know, we
have agreed never to drop any expressions of that sort for fear of
an accident.

BETTY. Dear ma'am, you may depend upon me. There is not a more
20 trustier creature on the face of the earth than I am. Though I say
it, I am as secret as the grave—and if it's never told till I tell it, it
may remain untold till doomsday for Betty.

FANNY. I know you are faithful—but in our circumstances we cannot
be too careful.

BETTY. Very true, ma'am!—and yet I vow and protest, there's more plague than pleasure with a secret, especially if a body mayn't mention it to four or five of one's particular acquaintance.

FANNY. Do but keep this secret a little while longer, and then I hope you may mention it to anybody. Mr. Lovewell will acquaint the
30   family with the nature of our situation as soon as possible.

BETTY. The sooner the better, I believe; for if he does not tell it, there's a little tell-tale I know of will come and tell it for him.

FANNY (*blushing*). Fie, Betty!

BETTY. Ah, you may well blush, but you're not so sick and so pale and so wan, and so many qualms —

FANNY. Have done! I shall be quite angry with you.

BETTY. Angry? Bless the dear puppet, I am sure I shall love it as much as if it was my own. I meant no harm, heaven knows.

FANNY. Well, say no more of this. It makes me uneasy. All I have to
40   ask of you is to be faithful and secret, and not to reveal this matter till we disclose it to the family ourselves.

BETTY. Me reveal it? If I say a word, I wish I may be burned. I would not do you any harm for the world. And as for Mr. Lovewell, I am sure I have loved the dear gentleman ever since he got a tide-waiter's place for my brother. But let me tell you both, you must leave off your soft looks to each other, and your whispers, and your glances, and your always sitting next to one another at dinner, and your long walks together in the evening. For my part, if I had not been in the secret I should have known you were a pair
50   of loviers at least, if not man and wife, as —

FANNY. See there now! Again! Pray be careful.

BETTY. Well—well—nobody hears me. Man and wife—I'll say so no more. What I tell you is very true for all that —

MR. LOVEWELL (*calling within*). William!

BETTY. Hark! I hear your husband —

FANNY. What!

BETTY. I say, here comes Mr. Lovewell. Mind the caution I give you. I'll be whipped now if you are not the first person he sees or speaks to in the family. However, if you choose it, it's nothing at all to
60   me. As you sow, you must reap; as you brew, so you must bake. I'll e'en slip down the back stairs and leave you together.

Exit.

FANNY. I see, I see I shall never have a moment's ease till our marriage is made public. New distresses crowd in upon me every day. The

---

50. loviers] O1, O2, O3, O4, O5, O6, O7, O8, O9, D1, D2; *loviers* C; lovers W1, W2.

52. say so] O1, O2, O3, O4, O5, O6, D1, D2; say O7, O8, O9, W1, W2, C.

Thomas King as Lord Ogleby and Mrs. Baddeley
as Fanny Sterling in *The Clandestine Marriage*.
Harvard Theatre Collection

solicitude of my mind sinks my spirits, preys upon my health, and destroys every comfort of my life. It shall be relieved, let what will be the consequence.

Enter Lovewell.

LOVEWELL.   My love! How's this? In tears? Indeed this is too much. You promised me to support your spirits and to wait the determination of our fortune with patience. For my sake, for your
70   own, be comforted! Why will you study to add to our uneasiness and perplexity?

FANNY.   Oh, Mr. Lovewell! The indelicacy of a secret marriage grows every day more and more shocking to me. I walk about the house like a guilty wretch. I imagine myself the object of the suspicion of the whole family and am under the perpetual terrors of a shameful detection.

LOVEWELL.   Indeed, indeed, you are to blame. The amiable delicacy of your temper and your quick sensibility only serves to make you unhappy. To clear up this affair properly to Mr. Sterling is
80   the continual employment of my thoughts. Every thing now is in a fair train. It begins now to grow ripe for a discovery, and I have no doubt of its concluding to the satisfaction of ourselves, of your father, and the whole family.

FANNY.   End how it will, I'm resolved it shall end soon—very soon. I would not live another week in this agony of my mind to be mistress of the universe.

LOVEWELL.   Do not be too violent neither. Do not let us disturb the joy of your sister's marriage with the tumult this matter may occasion. I have brought letters from Lord Ogleby and Sir John
90   Melvil to Mr. Sterling. They will be here this evening—and, I dare say, within this hour.

FANNY.   I am sorry for it.

LOVEWELL.   Why so?

FANNY.   No matter. Only let us disclose our marriage immediately!

LOVEWELL.   As soon as possible.

FANNY.   But directly.

LOVEWELL.   In a few days, you may depend on it.

FANNY.   Tonight—or tomorrow morning.

LOVEWELL.   That, I fear, will be impracticable.

100   FANNY.   Nay, but you must.

LOVEWELL.   Must? Why?

FANNY.   Indeed you must. I have the most alarming reasons for it.

LOVEWELL.   Alarming, indeed, for they alarm me even before I am acquainted with them. What are they?

FANNY.   I cannot tell you.

LOVEWELL.   Not tell me?

FANNY.   Not at present. When all is settled, you shall be acquainted with everything.

LOVEWELL.   Sorry, they are coming! Must be discovered! What can
110 this mean? Is it possible you can have any reasons that need be concealed from me?

FANNY.   Do not disturb yourself with conjectures, but rest assured that, though you are unable to divine the cause, the consequence of a discovery, be it what it will, cannot be attended with half the miseries of the present interval.

LOVEWELL.   You put me upon the rack. I would do anything to make you easy. But you know your father's temper. Money—you will excuse my frankness—is the spring of all his actions, which nothing but the idea of acquiring nobility or magnificence can ever
120 make him forego—and these he thinks his money will purchase. You know too your aunt's, Mrs. Heidelberg's, notions of the splendor of high life, her contempt for everything that does not relish of what she calls Quality, and that from the vast fortune in her hands, by her late husband, she absolutely governs Mr. Sterling and the whole family. Now, if they should come to the knowledge of this affair too abruptly they might perhaps be incensed beyond all hopes of reconciliation.

FANNY.   But if they are made acquainted with it otherwise than by ourselves, it will be ten times worse; and a discovery grows every
130 day more probable. The whole family have long suspected our affection. We are also in the power of a foolish maidservant, and if we may even depend on her fidelity, we cannot answer for her discretion. Discover it therefore immediately, lest some accident should bring it to light and involve us in additional disgrace.

LOVEWELL.   Well—well—I meant to discover it soon but would not do it too precipitately. I have more than once sounded Mr. Sterling about it, and will attempt him more seriously the next opportunity. But my principal hopes are these. My relationship to Lord Ogleby, and his having placed me with your father, have been,
140 you know, the first links in the chain of this connection between the two families, in consequence of which I am at present in high favor with all parties. While they all remain thus well effected to me, I propose to lay our case before the old Lord; and if I can prevail on him to meditate in this affair, I make no doubt but he will be able to appease your father; and, being a lord and a man

___

123.   Quality] *O*1, *O*2, *O*3, *O*4, *O*5, *O*6, *O*7, *O*8, *O*9, *D*1, *D*2; quality *W*1, *W*2, *C*.

of quality, I am sure he may bring Mrs. Heidelberg into good humor at any time. Let me beg you, therefore, to have but a little patience, as you see we are upon the very eve of a discovery that must probably be to our advantage.

150 FANNY. Manage it your own way. I am persuaded.

LOVEWELL. But in the meantime make yourself easy.

FANNY. As easy as I can, I will. We had better not remain together any longer at present. Think of this business, and let me know how you proceed.

LOVEWELL. Depend on my care. But pray be cheerful.

FANNY. I will.

As she is going out, enter Sterling.

STERLING. Hey day! Who have we got here?

FANNY (*confused*). Mr. Lovewell, sir.

STERLING. And where are you going, hussey?

160 FANNY. To my sister's chamber, sir.

Exit.

STERLING. Ah, Lovewell! What, always getting my foolish girl yonder into a corner? Well, well, let us but once see her elder sister fast married to Sir John Melvil, we'll soon provide a good husband for Fanny, I warrant you.

LOVEWELL. Wou'd to heaven, sir, you would provide her one of my recommendation!

STERLING. Yourself, eh, Lovewell?

LOVEWELL. With your pleasure, sir!

STERLING. Mighty well!

170 LOVEWELL. And I flatter myself that such a proposal would not be very disagreeable to Miss Fanny.

STERLING. Better and better!

LOVEWELL. And if I could but obtain your consent, sir.

STERLING. What? You marry Fanny? No, no, that will never do, Lovewell. You're a good boy, to be sure—I have a great value for you—but can't think of you for a son-in-law. There's no *stuff* in the case, no money, Lovewell!

LOVEWELL. My pretensions to fortune, indeed, are but moderate, but tho' not equal to splendor, sufficient to keep us above distress.

180 Add to which, that I hope by diligence to increase it and have love, honor —

STERLING. But not the *stuff*, Lovewell! Add one little round o to the sum total of your fortune, and that will be the finest thing you can say to me. You know I've a regard for you—would do any thing to serve you—any thing on the footing of friendship—but—

LOVEWELL.   If you think me worthy of your friendship, sir, be assured that there is no instance in which I should rate your friendship so highly.

STERLING.   Psha, psha, that's another thing, you know. Where money or interest is concerned, friendship is quite out of the question.

LOVEWELL.   But where the happiness of a daughter is at stake, you would not scruple, sure, to sacrifice a little to her inclinations.

STERLING.   Inclinations? Why, you wou'd not persuade me that the girl is in love with you, eh, Lovewell?

LOVEWELL.   I cannot absolutely answer for Miss Fanny, sir, but am sure that the chief happiness or misery of my life depends entirely upon her.

STERLING.   Why, indeed, now, if your kinsman, Lord Ogleby, would come down handsomely for you—but that's impossible. No, no, 'twill never do. I must hear no more of this. Come, Lovewell, promise me that I shall hear no more of this.

LOVEWELL (*hesitating*).   I am afraid, sir, I shou'd not be able to keep my word with you if I did promise you.

STERLING.   Why, you would not offer to marry her without my consent, would you, Lovewell?

LOVEWELL (*confused*).   Marry her, sir?

STERLING.   Ay, marry her, sir! I know very well that a warm speech or two from such a dangerous young spark as you are will go much farther towards persuading a silly girl to do what she has more than a month's mind to do than twenty grave lectures from fathers or mothers or uncles or aunts to prevent her—But you wou'd not, sure, be such a base fellow, such a treacherous young rogue, as to seduce my daughter's affections and destroy the peace of my family in that manner. I must insist on it that you give me your word not to marry her without my consent.

LOVEWELL.   Sir—I—I—as to that—I—I—I beg, sir—Pray, sir, excuse me on this subject at present.

STERLING.   Promise, then, that you will carry this matter no further without my approbation.

LOVEWELL.   You may depend on it, sir, that it shall go no further.

STERLING.   Well, well, that's enough. I'll take care of the rest, I warrant you. Come, come, let's have done with this nonsense. What's doing in town? Any news upon 'Change?

LOVEWELL.   Nothing material.

STERLING.   Have you seen the currants, the soap, and Madeira safe in the warehouses? Have you compared the goods with the invoice and bills of lading, and are they all right?

LOVEWELL. They are, sir.

STERLING. And how are stocks?

230 LOVEWELL. Fell one and an half this morning.

STERLING. Well, well, some good news from America and they'll be up again. But how are Lord Ogleby and Sir John Melvil? When are we to expect them?

LOVEWELL. Very soon, sir. I came on purpose to bring you their commands. Here are letters from both of them. (*Giving letters.*)

STERLING. Let me see—let me see—'slife, how his Lordship's letter is perfumed! It takes my breath away. (*Opening it.*) And French paper, too, with a fine border of flowers and flourishes—and a slippery gloss on it that dazzles one's eyes. (*Reading.*) *My dear*
240 *Mr. Sterling.* Mercy on me, his lordship writes a worse hand than a boy at his exercise. But how's this? Eh? (*Reading.*)—*with you tonight—lawyers tomorrow morning.* Tonight! That's sudden indeed. Where's my sister Heidelberg? She should know of this immediately. (*Calling the servants.*) Here John! Harry! Thomas! Hark ye, Lovewell!

LOVEWELL. Sir!

STERLING. Mind now how I'll entertain his Lordship and Sir John. We'll show your fellows at the other end of the town how we live in the city. They shall eat gold and drink gold, and lie in gold.
250 (*Calling.*) Here cook, butler! What signifies your birth and education and titles? Money, money, that's the stuff that makes the great man in this country.

LOVEWELL. Very true, sir!

STERLING. True, sir? Why then, have done with your nonesense of love and matrimony. You're not rich enough to think of a wife yet. A man of business should mind nothing but his business. Where are these fellows? (*Calling.*) John! Thomas! Get an estate, and a wife will follow of course. Ah, Lovewell, an English merchant is the most respectable character in the universe. 'Slife, man,
260 a rich English merchant may make himself a match for the daughter of a nabob. Where are all my rascals? Here, William!

Exit, calling.

LOVEWELL. So! As I suspected. Quite averse to the match, and likely to receive the news of it with great displeasure. What's best to be done? Let me see. Suppose I get Sir John Melvil to interest himself in this affair. He may mention it to Lord Ogleby with a better grace than I can, and more probably prevail on him to interfere in it. I can open my mind also more freely to Sir John. He told me, when I left him in town, that he had something of consequence to communicate, and that I could be of use to him. I am glad of

270   it, for the confidence he reposes in me and the service I may do
     him will insure me his good offices. Poor Fanny! It hurts me to
     see her so uneasy, and her making a mystery of the cause adds to
     my anxiety. Something must be done upon her account, for at all
     events her solicitude shall be removed.

                                                              Exit.

                          [Scene II.]

             SCENE *changes to another chamber.*

          Enter Miss Sterling *and* Miss Fanny.

MISS STERLING. Oh, my dear sister, say no more. This is downright
     hypocrisy. You shall never convince me that you don't envy me
     beyond measure. Well, after all, it is extremely natural. It is im-
     possible to be angry with you.
FANNY. Indeed, sister, you have no cause.
MISS STERLING. And you really pretend not to envy me?
FANNY. Not in the least.
MISS STERLING. And you don't in the least wish that you was just in
     my situation?
10 FANNY. No, indeed, I don't. Why should I?
MISS STERLING. Why should you? What, on the brink of marriage,
     fortune, title—But I had forgot. There's that dear sweet creature
     Mr. Lovewell in the case. You would not break your faith with
     your true love now for the world, I warrant you.
FANNY. Mr. Lovewell, always Mr. Lovewell! Lord, what signifies Mr.
     Lovewell, sister?
MISS STERLING. Pretty peevish soul! Oh, my dear, grave, romantic
     sister! A perfect philosopher in petticoats! Love and a cottage,
     eh, Fanny! Ah, give me indifference and a coach and six!
20 FANNY. And why not the coach and six without the indifference?
     But, pray, when is this happy marriage of yours to be celebrated?
     I long to give you joy.
MISS STERLING. In a day or two—I can't tell exactly. Oh, my dear sis-
     ter—(*aside*) I must mortify her a little.—I know you have a pretty
     taste. Pray give me your opinion of my jewels. How d'ye like the
     style of this esclavage? (*Showing jewels.*)
FANNY. Extremely handsome indeed, and well fancied.
MISS STERLING. What d'ye think of these bracelets? I shall have a
     miniature of my father, set round with diamonds, to one, and Sir
30   John's to the other. And this pair of earrings set transparent. Here,

the tops, you see, will take off to wear in a morning, or in an undress. How d'ye like them? (*Shows jewels.*)

FANNY. Very much, I assure you. Bless me, sister, you have a prodigious quantity of jewels. You'll be the very queen of diamonds.

MISS STERLING. Ha, ha, ha! Very well, my dear, I shall be as fine as a little queen indeed. I have a bouquet to come home tomorrow made up of diamonds and rubies and emeralds and topazes and amethysts, jewels of all colors—green, red, blue, yellow, intermixt —the prettiest thing you ever saw in your life! The jeweler says
40   I shall set out with as many diamonds as anybody in town except Lady Brilliant and Polly What-d'ye-call-it, Lord Squander's kept mistress.

FANNY. But what are your wedding clothes, sister?

MISS STERLING. Oh, white and silver, to be sure, you know. I bought them at Sir Joseph Lutestring's, and sat above an hour in the parlor behind the shop consulting Lady Lutestring about gold and silver stuffs on purpose to mortify her.

FANNY. Fie, sister, how could you be so abominably provoking?

MISS STERLING. Oh, I have no patience with the pride of your city-
50   knights' ladies. Did you never observe the airs of Lady Lutestring drest in the richest brocade out of her husband's shop, playing crown whist at Haberdasher's Hall? While the civil smirking Sir Joseph, with a snug wig trimmed round his broad face as close as a new-cut yew hedge, and his shoes so black that they shine again, stands all day in his shop, fastened to his counter like a bad shilling?

FANNY. Indeed, indeed, sister, this is too much. If you talk at this rate, you will be absolutely a bye-word in the city. You must never venture on the inside of Temple Bar again.

60 MISS STERLING. Never do I desire it—never, my dear Fanny, I promise you. Oh, how I long to be transported to the dear regions of Grosvenor Square, far, far from the dull districts of Aldersgate, Cheap, Candlewick, and Farringdon Without and Within! My heart goes pit-a-pat at the very idea of being introduced at court— gilt chariot!—pyebald horses!—laced liveries!—and then the whispers buzzing round the circle, "Who is that young lady? Who is she?"—"Lady Melvil, ma'am." Lady Melvil! My ears tingle at the sound. And then at dinner, instead of my father perpetually asking, "Any news upon 'Change?" to cry, "Well, Sir John, any
70   thing new from Arthur's?"—or to say to some other woman of quality, "Was your Ladyship at the Dutchess of Rubber's last

---

58. bye-word] *O1, O2, O3, O4, O5, O6, O7, O8, O9, W1, W2, C*; By-word *D1, D2*.

night? Did you call in at Lady Thunder's? In the immensity of the
crowd I swear I did not see you. Scarce a soul at the opera last
Saturday. Shall I see you at Carlisle House next Thursday?" Oh,
the dear beau-monde! I was born to move in the sphere of the
great world.

FANNY.   And so, in the midst of all this happiness, you have no compassion for me, no pity for us poor mortals in common life?

MISS STERLING (*affectedly*). You? You're above pity. You would not
80   change conditions with me—you're over head and ears in love, you
know. Nay, for that matter, if Mr. Lovewell and you come together, as I doubt not you will, you will live very comfortably, I
dare say. He will mind his business, you'll employ yourself in the
delightful care of your family, and once in a season perhaps you'll
sit together in a front box at a benefit play, as we used to do
at our dancing master's, you know; and perhaps I may meet you
in the summer with some other citizens at Tunbridge. For my part,
I shall always entertain a proper regard for my relations. You
shan't want my countenance, I assure you.

90 FANNY.   Oh, you're too kind, sister.

Enter Mrs. Heidelberg.

MRS. HEIDELBERG (*at entering*). Here this evening! I vow and pertest
we shall scarce have time to provide for them. (*To* Miss Sterling.)
Oh, my dear, I'm glad to see you're not quite in dish-abille. Lord
Ogleby and Sir John Melvil will be here tonight.

MISS STERLING.   Tonight, ma'am?

MRS. HEIDELBERG.   Yes, my dear, tonight. Do put on a smarter cap, and
change those ordinary ruffles. Lord, I have such a deal to do, I
shall scarce have time to slip on my Italian lutestring. Where is
this dawdle of a house-keeper?

Enter Mrs. Trusty.

100   Oh, here, Trusty! Do you know that people of qualaty are expected here this evening?

TRUSTY.   Yes, ma'am.

MRS. HEIDELBERG.   Well, do you be sure now that everything is done
in the most genteelest manner—and to the honor of the famaly.

TRUSTY.   Yes, ma'am.

MRS. HEIDELBERG.   Well, but mind what I say to you.

TRUSTY.   Yes, ma'am.

---

100. qualaty] *O*1, *O*2, *O*3, *O*4, *O*5, *O*6, *O*7, *D*1, *D*2, *C*; quality *O*8, *O*9, *W*1, *W*2.
104. famaly] *O*1, *O*3, *O*4, *O*6, *O*7, *O*8, *O*9, *D*1, *D*2, *W*1, *W*2, *C*; fammaly *O*2,
      *O*5.

MRS. HEIDELBERG. His Lordship is to lie in the chintz bedchamber,
d'ye hear? And Sir John in the blue damask room. His Lordship's
110   valet-de-shamb in the opposite —
TRUSTY. But Mr. Lovewell is come down, and you know that's his
room, ma'am.
MRS. HEIDELBERG. Well—well—Mr. Lovewell may make shift—or get
a bed at the George. But hark ye, Trusty —
TRUSTY. Ma'am?
MRS. HEIDELBERG. Get the great dining room in order as soon as pos-
sible. Unpaper the curtains, take the civers off the couch and the
chairs, and put the china figures on the mantlepiece immediately.
TRUSTY. Yes, ma'am.
120   MRS. HEIDELBERG. Be gone then. Fly this instant. Where's my brother
Sterling?
TRUSTY. Talking to the butler, ma'am.
MRS. HEIDELBERG. Very well.

Exit Trusty.

Miss Fanny, I pertest I did not see you before. Lord, child, what
is the matter with you?
FANNY. With me? Nothing, ma'am.
MRS. HEIDELBERG. Bless me, why, your face is as pale and black and
yellow—of fifty colors, I pertest. And then you have drest yourself as loose and as big—I declare there is not such a thing to be
130   seen now as a young woman with a fine waist. You all make yourselves as round as Mrs. Deputy Barter. Go, child! You know the
qualaty will be here by and by. Go and make yourself a little more
fit to be seen.

Exit Fanny.

She is gone away in tears—absolutely crying, I vow and pertest.
This ridiculous love; we must put a stop to it. It makes a perfect
nataral of the girl.
MISS STERLING (*affectedly*). Pour soul, she can't help it.
MRS. HEIDELBERG. Well, my dear, now I shall have an opportunity of
convincing you of the absurdity of what you was telling me con-
140   cerning Sir John Melvil's behavior to you.
MISS STERLING. Oh, it gives me no manner of uneasiness. But indeed,

---

118. immediately] O_1, O_2, O_3, O_4, O_5, O_6, O_7, O_8, O_9, D_1, D_2, W_1, W_2;
immediately. And set them o'nodding as soon as his lordship comes in,
d'ye hear, Trusty? C.
138. opportunity] O_1, O_2, O_3, O_4, O_5, O_6, D_1, D_2, W_1, W_2; opportoonity
O_7, O_8, O_9, C.

ma'am, I cannot be persuaded but that Sir John is an extremely cold lover. Such distant civility, grave looks and lukewarm professions of esteem for me and the whole family! I have heard of flames and darts, but Sir John's is a passion of mere ice and snow.

MRS. HEIDELBERG. Oh, fie, my dear! I am perfectly ashamed of you. That's so like the notions of your poor sister. What you complain of as coldness and indiffarence is nothing but the extreme gentilaty of his address, an exact picture of the manners of qualaty.

150 MISS STERLING. Oh, he is the very mirror of complaisance—full of formal bows and set speeches! I declare, if there was any violent passion on my side, I should be quite jealous of him.

MRS. HEIDELBERG. I say, jealus indeed. Jealus of who, pray?

MISS STERLING. My sister Fanny. She seems a much greater favorite than I am, and he pays her infinitely more attention, I assure you.

MRS. HEIDELBERG. Lord, d'ye think a man of fashion, as he is, can't distinguish between the genteel and the wulgar part of the famaly? Between you and your sister, for instance—or me and my brother? Be advised by me, child; it is all politeness and good breeding. No-

160 body knows the qualaty better than I do.

MISS STERLING. In my mind the old Lord, his uncle, has ten times more gallantry about him than Sir John. He is full of attentions to the ladies, and smiles and grins and leers and ogles and fills every wrinkle in his old wizen face with comical expressions of tenderness. I think he would make an admirable sweetheart.

Enter Sterling.

STERLING (*at entering*). No fish? Why, the pond was dragged but yesterday morning. There's carp and tench in the boat. Pox on't, if that dog Lovewell had any thought, he would have brought down a turbot, or some of the land-carriage mackarel.

170 MRS. HEIDELBERG. Lord, brother, I am afraid his Lordship and Sir John will not arrive while it's light.

STERLING. I warrant you. But pray, sister Heidelberg, let the turtle be drest tonight, and some venison, and let the gardener cut some pineapples. And get out some ice—I'll answer for wine, I warrant you. I'll give them such a glass of champagne as they never drank in their lives—no, not at a Duke's table.

---

157. wulgar] O1, O2, O3, O4, O5, O6, O7, O8, O9, D1, D2, C; vulgar W1, W2.
famaly] O1, O2, O3, O4, O5, O6, O7, O8, O9, D1, D2, W1, W2; family C.

159. politeness] O1, O2, O3, O4, O5, O6, D1, D2, W1, W2; puliteness O7, O8, O9, C.

167. boat] O1, O2, O3, O4, O5, O6, O7, O8, O9, W1, W2, C; boot D1, D2.

MRS. HEIDELBERG.   Pray now, brother, mind how you behave. I am always in a fright about you with people of qualaty. Take care that you don't fall asleep directly after supper, as you commonly
180   do. Take a good deal of snuff, and that will keep you awake. And don't burst out with your horrible loud horse-laughs. It is monstrous wulgar.

STERLING.   Never fear, sister. Who have we here?

MRS. HEIDELBERG.   It is Mons. Cantoon the Swish gentleman, that lives with his Lordship, I vow and pertest.

Enter Canton.

STERLING.   Ah, Mounseer! your servant. I am very glad to see you, Mounseer.

CANTON.   Mosh oblige to Mons. Sterling. Ma'am, I am yours. Matemoiselle, I am yours.

(*Bowing round.*)

190   MRS. HEIDELBERG.   Your humble servant, Mr. Cantoon!

CANTON.   I kiss your hands, matam!

STERLING.   Well, Mounseer, and what news of your good family? When are we to see his Lordship and Sir John?

CANTON.   Mons. Sterling, Milor Ogleby and Sir Jean Melvile will be here in one quarter-hour.

STERLING.   I am glad to hear it.

MRS. HEIDELBERG.   Oh, I am perdigious glad to hear it. Being so late I was afeard of some accident. Will you please to have any thing, Mr. Cantoon, after your journey?

200   CANTON.   No, I tank you, ma'am.

MRS. HEIDELBERG.   Shall I go and show you the apartments, sir?

CANTON.   You do me great honeur, ma'am.

MRS. HEIDELBERG.   Come then. (*To* Miss Sterling.) Come, my dear.

Exeunt.

STERLING.   Pox on't, it's almost dark. It will be too late to go round the garden this evening. However, I will carry them to take a peep at my fine canal at least, I am determined.

Exit.

---

184.   Mons. Cantoon] *O*1, *O*2, *O*3, *O*4, *O*5, *O*6, *O*7, *O*8, *O*9, *D*1, *D*2; mons. Cantoon *W*1, *W*2; mounseer Cantoon *C*.

206.   at least, I am] *O*1, *O*2, *O*3, *O*4, *O*5, *O*6, *O*7, *O*8, *O*9, *D*1, *D*2, *W*1, *W*2; at least; that I am *C*.

ACT II. [Scene I.]

SCENE, *an antichamber to* Lord Ogleby's *bedchamber.*
Table with chocolate, and small case for medicines.

Enter Brush, *my lord's valet-de-chambre, and* Sterling's
chambermaid.

BRUSH. You shall stay, my dear. I insist upon it.

CHAMBERMAID. Nay, pray, sir, don't be so positive; I can't stay indeed.

BRUSH. You shall take one cup to our better acquaintance.

CHAMBERMAID. I seldom drinks chocolate; and if I did, one has no
satisfaction, with such apprehensions about one. If my Lord should
wake, or the Swiss gentleman should see one, or Madam Heidelberg should know of it, I should be frighted to death. Besides, I
have had my tea already this morning. (*In a fright.*) I'm sure I
hear my Lord.

10 BRUSH. No, no, madam, don't flutter yourself. The moment my Lord
wakes, he rings his bell, which I answer sooner or later, as it suits
my convenience.

CHAMBERMAID. But should he come upon us without ringing —

BRUSH. I'll forgive him if he does. This key (*takes a phial out of the
case*) locks him up till I please to let him out.

CHAMBERMAID. Law, sir, that's potecary's-stuff!

BRUSH. It is so; but without this he can no more get out of bed than he
can read without spectacles. (*Sips.*) What with qualms, age, rheumatism, and a few surfeits in his youth, he must have a great deal

20 of brushing, oiling, screwing, and winding up to set him a-going
for the day.

CHAMBERMAID. (*Sips.*) That's prodigious indeed. (*Sips.*) My Lord
seems quite in a decay.

BRUSH. Yes, he's quite a spectacle (*sips*), a mere corpse, till he is revived and refreshed from our little magazine here. When the re-
storative pills and cordial waters warm his stomach and get into
his head, vanity frisks in his heart, and then he sets up for the lover,
the rake, and the fine gentleman.

CHAMBERMAID. (*Sips.*) Poor gentleman! (*Frightened.*) But should the

30 Swiss gentleman come upon us —

BRUSH. Why then the English gentleman would be very angry. No
foreigner must break in upon my privacy. (*Sips.*) But I can assure
you Monsieur Canton is otherwise employed. He is obliged to

---

8. had my tea] *O*1, *O*2, *O*3, *O*4, *O*5, *O*6, *O*7, *O*8, *O*9, *W*1, *W*2, *C*; made my
tea *D*1, *D*2.

skim the cream of half a score newspapers for my Lord's breakfast
—ha, ha, ha. Pray, madam, drink your cup peaceably. My Lord's
chocolate is remarkably good; he won't touch a drop but what
comes from Italy.

CHAMBERMAID. (*Sipping.*) 'Tis very fine indeed, (*sips*) and charmingly perfumed. It smells for all the world like our young ladies'
40   dressing boxes.

BRUSH. You have an excellent taste, madam, and I must beg of you
to accept of a few cakes for your own drinking (*takes 'em out of
a drawer in the table*), and in return I desire nothing but to taste
the perfume of your lips. (*Kisses her.*) A small return of favors,
madam, will make, I hope, this country and retirement agreeable
to both. (*He bows; she curtsies.*) Your young ladies are fine girls,
faith (*sips*), tho' upon my soul I am quite of my old Lord's mind
about them; and were I inclined to matrimony, I should take the
youngest. (*Sips.*)

50 CHAMBERMAID. Miss Fanny's the most affablest and the most best-
natered creter!

BRUSH. And the eldest a little haughty or so —

CHAMBERMAID. More haughtier and prouder than Saturn himself—but
this I say quite confidential to you, for one would not hurt a young
lady's marriage, you know. (*Sips.*)

BRUSH. By no means, but you can't hurt it with us. We don't consider
tempers—we want money, Mrs. Nancy. Give us enough of that,
we'll abate you a great deal in other particulars—ha, ha, ha.

CHAMBERMAID. (*Bell rings.*) Bless me, here's somebody. Oh, 'tis my
60   Lord. Well, your servant, Mr. Brush. I'll clean the cups in the
next room.

BRUSH. Do so; but never mind the bell. I shan't go this half hour. Will
you drink tea with me in the afternoon?

CHAMBERMAID. Not for the world, Mr. Brush. I'll be here to set all
things to rights, but I must not drink tea indeed. And so your
servant.

Exit maid with tea board.

Bell rings again.

BRUSH. It is impossible to stupify one's self in the country for a week
without some little flirting with the abigails. This is much the
handsomest wench in the house, except the old citizen's youngest
70   daughter, and I have not time enough to lay a plan for her. (*Bell
rings.*) And now I'll go to my Lord, for I have nothing else to do.

Going.

Enter Canton *with newspapers in his hand.*

CANTON. Monsieur Brush—Maistre Brush, my Lor stirra yet?

BRUSH. He has just rung his bell. I am going to him.

Exit Brush.

CANTON. Depechez vous donc. (*Puts on spectacles.*) I wish de Deviel
had all dese papiers. I forget as fast as I read. De Advertise put out
of my head de Gazette, de Gazette de Chronique, and so dey all
go l'un apres l'autre. I must get some nouvelle for my Lor, or he'll
be enragée contre moi. (*Reads in the papers.*) Voyons! Here is
nothing but Anti-Sejanus and advertise —

Enter maid with chocolate things.

80   Vat you vant, child?

CHAMBERMAID. Only the chocolate things, sir.

CANTON. O, ver well, dat is good girl—and ver prit too!

Exit Maid.

LORD OGLEBY (*within*). Canton, he, he—(*coughs*) Canton!

CANTON. I come, my Lor. Vat shall I do? I have no news. He vill make
great tintamarre!

LORD OGLEBY (*within*). Canton, I say, Canton! Where are you?

Enter Lord Ogleby *leaning on* Brush.

CANTON. Here, my Lor. I ask pardon, my Lor, I have not finish de
papiers —

LORD OGLEBY. Dem your pardon, and your papers. I want you here,
90   Canton.

CANTON. Den I run, dat is all.

Shuffles along. Lord Ogleby *leans upon* Canton
too, and comes forward.

LORD OGLEBY. You Swiss are the most unaccountable mixture: you
have the language and the impertinence of the French, with the
laziness of Dutchmen.

CANTON. 'Tis very true, my Lor. I can't help —

LORD OGLEBY (*cries out*). O diavolo!

CANTON. You are not in pain, I hope, my Lor.

LORD OGLEBY. Indeed but I am, my Lor. That vulgar fellow Sterling,
with his city politeness, would force me down his slope last night
100   to see a clay colored ditch which he calls a canal; and with the

---

88. papers] O₁, O₂, O₃, O₄, O₅, O₆, O₇, D₁, D₂, W₁, W₂; papiers O₈, O₉,
C.

dew and the east wind, my hips and shoulders are absolutely screwed to my body.

CANTON. A littel veritable eau d'arquibusade vil set all to right again.

My Lord *sits down*, Brush *gives chocolate.*

LORD OGLEBY. Where are the palsy drops, Brush?

BRUSH. Here, my Lord. (*Pouring out.*)

LORD OGLEBY. Quelle nouvelle avez vous, Canton?

CANTON. A great deal of papier, but no news at all.

LORD OGLEBY. What, nothing at all, you stupid fellow?

CANTON. Yes, my Lor, I have littel advertise here vil give you more
110   plaisir den all de lies about nothing at all. La voila!

(*Puts on his spectacles.*)

LORD OGLEBY. Come, read it, Canton, with good emphasis and good discretion.

CANTON. I vil, my Lor. (Canton *reads.*) Dere is no question but dat de Cosmetique Royale vil utterlie take away all heats, pimps, frecks and oder eruptions of de skin, and likewise de wrinque of old age, etc., etc.—A great deal more, my Lor—be sure to ask for de Cosmetique Royale, signed by de docteur own hand. Dere is more raison for dis caution dan good men vil tink. En bein, my Lor!

LORD OGLEBY. En bien, Canton! Will you purchase any?

120   CANTON. For you, my Lor?

LORD OGLEBY. For me, you old puppy! For what?

CANTON. My Lor?

LORD OGLEBY. Do I want cosmetics?

CANTON. My Lor!

LORD OGLEBY. Look in my face. Come, be sincere. Does it want the assistance of art?

CANTON (*with his spectacles*). En verite, non. 'Tis very smoose and brillian—but I tote dat you might take a little by way of prevention.

130   LORD OGLEBY. You thought like an old fool, monsieur, as you generally do. The surfeit-water, Brush! (Brush *pours out.*) What do you think, Brush, of this family we are going to be connected with, eh?

BRUSH. Very well to marry in, my Lord; but it would not do to live with.

---

127. smoose] *O*1, *O*2, *O*3, *O*4, *O*5, *O*6, *O*7, *O*8, *O*9, *D*1, *D*2, *C*; smooth *W*1, *W*2.

128. little] *O*1, *O*2, *O*3, *O*4, *O*5, *O*6, *D*1, *D*2, *W*1, *W*2; like *O*7, *O*8, *O*9; litt *C*.

LORD OGLEBY. You are right, Brush. There is no washing the blackamoor white. Mr. Sterling will never get rid of Blackfriars, always taste of the borachio—and the poor woman his sister is so
busy and so notable to make one welcome that I have not yet
140   got over her first reception; it almost amounted to suffocation!
I think the daughters are tolerable. Where's my cephalic snuff?
(Brush *gives him a box.*)

CANTON. Dey tink so of you, my Lor, for dey look at nothing else,
ma foi.

LORD OGLEBY. Did they? Why, I think they did a little. Where's my
glass? (Brush *puts one on the table.*) The youngest is delectable.

(Takes snuff.)

CANTON. O, ouy, my Lor—very delect, inteed; she made doux yeux
at you, my Lor.

LORD OGLEBY. She was particular. The eldest, my nephew's lady, will
be a most valuable wife; she has all the vulgar spirits of her father
150   and aunt, happily blended with the termagant qualities of her
deceased mother. Some peppermint water, Brush! How happy is
it, Cant, for young ladies in general that people of quality over-
look everything in a marriage contract but their fortune.

CANTON. C'est bien heureaux, et commode aussi.

LORD OGLEBY. Brush, give me that pamphlet by my bedside. (Brush
goes for it.) Canton, do you wait in the antichamber, and let nobody interrupt me till I call you.

CANTON. Mush goot may do your Lordship!

LORD OGLEBY (*to* Brush, *who brings the pamphlet*). And now, Brush,
160   leave me a little to my studies.

Exit Brush.

LORD OGLEBY. What can I possibly do among these women here with
this confounded rheumatism! It is a most grievous enemy to gallantry and address. (*Gets off his chair.*) He! Courage, my Lor! By
heavens, I'm another creature. (*Hums and dances a little.*) It will
do, faith. Bravo, my Lor! These girls have absolutely inspired me.
If they are for a game of romps—Me voila pret! (*Sings and dances.*)
Oh—that's an ugly twinge—but it's gone. I have rather too much
of the lily this morning in my complexion; a faint tincture of the
rose will give a delicate spirit to my eyes for the day.

*Unlocks a drawer at the bottom of the glass
and takes out rouge; while he's painting
himself, a knocking at the door.*

170   Who's there? I won't be disturbed.

CANTON (*without*).   My Lor, my Lor, here is Monsieur Sterling to pay his devoir to you this morn in your chambre.

LORD OGLEBY.   (*Softly.*) What a fellow! (*Aloud.*) I am extremely honored by Mr. Sterling. Why don't you see him in, monsieur? (*Aside.*) I wish he was at the bottom of his stinking canal. (*Door opens.*) Oh, my dear Mr. Sterling, you do me a great deal of honor.

Enter Sterling *and* Lovewell.

STERLING.   I hope, my Lord, that your Lordship slept well in the night. I believe there are no better beds in Europe than I have. I spare no pains to get 'em, nor money to buy 'em. His Majesty, God bless
180   him, don't sleep upon a better out of his palace; and if I said *in* too, I hope no treason, my Lord.

LORD OGLEBY.   Your beds are like every thing else about you, incomparable! They not only make one rest well, but give one spirits, Mr. Sterling.

STERLING.   What say you then, my Lord, to another walk in the garden? You must see my water by daylight, and my walks, and my slopes, and my clumps, and my bridge, and my flowering trees, and my bed of Dutch tulips. Matters looked but dim last night, my Lord. I feel the dew in my great toe, but I would put on a cut
190   shoe that I might be able to walk you about. I may be laid up tomorrow.

LORD OGLEBY (*aside*).   I pray heav'n you may!

STERLING.   What say you, my Lord?

LORD OGLEBY.   I was saying, sir, that I was in hopes of seeing the young ladies at breakfast. Mr. Sterling, they are, in my mind, the finest tulips in this part of the world—he, he.

CANTON.   Bravissimo, my Lor! Ha, ha, he.

STERLING.   They shall meet your Lordship in the garden—we won't lose our walk for them. I'll take you a little round before break-
200   fast, and larger before dinner, and in the evening you shall go the Grand Tower, as I call it, ha, ha, ha.

LORD OGLEBY.   Not a foot, I hope, Mr. Sterling. Consider your gout, my good friend. You'll be laid by the heels for your politeness—he, he, he.

CANTON.   Ha, ha, ha—'Tis admirable, en veritè! (*Laughing very heartily.*)

STERLING.   If my young man (*to* Lovewell) here would but laugh at my jokes, which he ought to do, as monsieur does at yours, my Lord, we should be all life and mirth.

LORD OGLEBY.   What say you, Cant, will you take my kinsman under

210   your tuition? You have certainly the most companionable laugh
       I ever met with, and never out of tune.
       CANTON. But when your Lordship is out of spirits.
       LORD OGLEBY. Well said, Cant. But here comes my nephew to play
       his part.

                      Enter Sir John Melvil.

       Well, Sir John, what news from the island of love? Have you been
       sighing and serenading this morning?
       SIR JOHN. I am glad to see your Lordship in such spirits this morning.
       LORD OGLEBY. I'm sorry to see you so dull, sir.—What poor things, Mr.
       Sterling, these very young fellows are! They make love with faces
220   as if they were burying the dead—though, indeed, a marriage
       sometimes may be properly called a burying of the living, eh, Mr.
       Sterling?
       STERLING. Not if they have enough to live upon, my Lord—ha, ha, ha.
       CANTON. Dat is all Monsieur Sterling tink of.
       SIR JOHN (*apart to* Lovewell). Prithee, Lovewell, come with me into
       the garden. I have something of consequence for you and I must
       communicate it directly.
       LOVEWELL (*apart*). We'll go together. (*Aloud.*) If your Lordship
       and Mr. Sterling please, we'll prepare the ladies to attend you in
230   the garden.

                      Exeunt Sir John *and* Lovewell.

       STERLING. My girls are always ready. I make 'em rise soon and to bed
       early; their husbands shall have 'em with good constitutions and
       good fortunes if they have nothing else, my Lord.
       LORD OGLEBY. Fine things, Mr. Sterling!
       STERLING. Fine things, indeed, my Lord! Ah, my Lord, had not you
       run off your speed in your youth, you had not been so crippled
       in your age, my Lord.
       LORD OGLEBY. Very pleasant, I protest (*half laughing*), he, he, he.
       STERLING. Here's Monseer now, I suppose, is pretty near your Lord-
240   ship's standing; but having little to eat and little to spend in his
       own country, he'll wear three of your Lordship out. Eating and
       drinking kills us all.
       LORD OGLEBY. Very pleasant, I protest. (*Aside.*) What a vulgar dog!
       CANTON. My Lor so old as me? He is shicken to me, and look like a
       boy to pauvre me.

---

212. spirits] *O*1, *O*2, *O*3, *O*4, *O*5, *O*6, *O*7, *O*8, *O*9, *D*1, *D*2, *W*1, *W*2; spirit *C*.
224. Sterling] *O*1, *O*2, *O*3, *O*4, *O*5, *O*6, *O*7, *O*8, *O*9, *D*1, *D*2, *W*1, *W*2; Steerling
       C.

STERLING. Ha, ha, ha. Well said, Mounseer—keep to that and you'll
live in any country of the world—ha, ha, ha. But, my Lord, I will
wait upon you into the garden; we have but a little time to breakfast. I'll go for my hat and cane, fetch a little walk with you, my
250   Lord, and then for the hot rolls and butter!

Exit Sterling.

LORD OGLEBY. I shall attend you with pleasure.—Hot rolls and butter
in July! I sweat with the thoughts of it.—What a strange beast it is!
CANTON. C'est un barbare.
LORD OGLEBY. He is a vulgar dog, and if there was not so much money
in the family, which I can't do without, I would leave him and his
hot rolls and butter directly. Come along, Monsieur!

Exeunt Lord Ogleby *and* Canton.

[Scene II.]

SCENE *changes to the garden.*
Enter Sir John Melvil *and* Lovewell.

LOVEWELL. In my room this morning? Impossible.
SIR JOHN. Before five this morning, I promise you.
LOVEWELL. On what occasion?
SIR JOHN. I was so anxious to disclose my mind to you that I could
not sleep in my bed. But I found that you could not sleep neither.
The bird was flown, and the nest long since cold. Where was you,
Lovewell?
LOVEWELL. Pooh! prithee! ridiculous!
SIR JOHN. Come now, which was it? Miss Sterling's maid? A pretty
10   little rogue! Or Miss Fanny's abigail? A sweet soul too! Or —
LOVEWELL. Nay, nay, leave trifling and tell me your business.
SIR JOHN. Well, but where was you, Lovewell?
LOVEWELL. Walking—writing—what signifies where I was?
SIR JOHN. Walking! Yes, I dare say. It rained as hard as it could pour.
Sweet refreshing showers to walk in. No, no Lovewell. Now
would I give twenty pounds to know which of the maids —
LOVEWELL. But your business, your business, Sir John!
SIR JOHN. Let me a little into the secrets of the family.
LOVEWELL. Psha!

---

6. Where was] O1, O2, O3, O4, O5, O6, O7, O8, O9, W1, W2; Where were]
D1, D2, C.
12. where was] O1, O2, O3, O4, O5, O6, O7, O8, O9, W1, W2; where were
D1, D2, C.

20 SIR JOHN. Poor Lovewell, he can't bear it, I see. She charged you
not to kiss and tell, eh, Lovewell? However, though you will not
honor me with your confidence, I'll venture to trust you with
mine. What dy'e think of Miss Sterling?
LOVEWELL. What do I think of Miss Sterling?
SIR JOHN. Ay, what dy'e think of her?
LOVEWELL. An odd question! But I think her a smart, lively girl, full
of mirth and sprightliness.
SIR JOHN. All mischief and malice, I doubt.
LOVEWELL. How?
30 SIR JOHN. But her person—what dy'e think of that?
LOVEWELL. Pretty and agreeable.
SIR JOHN. A little grisette thing.
LOVEWELL. What is the meaning of all this?
SIR JOHN. I'll tell you. You must know, Lovewell, that notwithstand-
ing all appearances—(*Seeing* Lord Ogleby, *etc.*) We are inter-
rupted. When they are gone I'll explain.

                Enter Lord Ogleby, Sterling, Mrs. Heidelberg,
                        Miss Sterling, *and* Fanny.

LORD OGLEBY. Great improvements indeed, Mr. Sterling! Wonderful
improvements! The four seasons in lead, the flying Mercury, and
the basin with Neptune in the middle are all in the very extreme of
40   fine taste. You have as many rich figures as the man at Hyde Park
Corner.
STERLING. The chief pleasure of a country house is to make improvements, you know, my Lord. I spare no expense, not I. This is quite
another-guess sort of a place than it was when I first took it, my
Lord. We were surrounded with trees. I cut down above fifty to
make the lawn before the house and let in the wind and the sun—
smack-smooth, as you see. Then I made a greenhouse out of the
old laundry, and turned the brew-house into a pinery. The high
octagon summer house you see yonder is raised on the mast of a
50   ship given me by an East India captain who has turned many a
thousand of my money. It commands the whole road. All the
coaches and chariots and chaises pass and repass under your eye.
I'll mount you up there in the afternoon, my Lord. 'Tis the pleas-
antest place in the world to take a pipe and a bottle, and so you
shall say, my Lord.
LORD OGLEBY. Ay—or a bowl of punch, or a can of flip, Mr. Sterling,
for it looks like a cabin in the air. If flying chairs were in use, the

---

32. little grisette thing] *O*1, *O*2, *O*3, *O*4, *O*5, *O*6, *O*7, *O*8, *O*9, *D*1, *W*1, *W*2;
little grisetta thing *D*2; little thing *C*.

captain might make a voyage to the Indies in it still, if he had but
a fair wind.

60 CANTON. Ha! ha! ha! ha!

MRS. HEIDELBERG. My brother's a little comical in his ideas, my Lord!
But you'll excuse him. I have a little gothic dairy, fitted up entirely in my own taste. In the evening I shall hope for the honor of
your Lordship's company to take a dish of tea there, or a sullabub
warm from the cow.

LORD OGLEBY. I have every moment a fresh opportunity of admiring
the elegance of Mrs. Heidelberg—the very flower of delicacy, and
cream of politeness.

MRS. HEIDELBERG. Oh, my Lord! ⎫
70 LORD OGLEBY. Oh, madam!   ⎬ (*leering at each other.*)
                             ⎭

STERLING. How dy'e like these close walks, my Lord?

LORD OGLEBY. A most excellent serpentine! It forms a perfect maze
and winds like a true-lover's knot.

STERLING. Ay, here's none of your strait lines here, but all taste—zig-
zag—crinkum crankum—in and out—right and left—to and again—
twisting and turning like a worm, my Lord!

LORD OGLEBY. Admirably laid out indeed, Mr. Sterling! One can hardly see an inch beyond one's nose any where in these walks. You
are a most excellent economist of your land, and make a little go
80 a great way. It lies together in as small parcels as if it was placed
in pots out at your window in Gracechurch Street.

CANTON. Ha! ha! ha! ha!

LORD OGLEBY. What d'ye laugh at, Canton?

CANTON. Ay, que cette similitude est drole! So clever what you say,
mi Lor!

LORD OGLEBY (*to* Fanny). You seem mightily engaged, madam. What
are those pretty hands so busily employed about?

FANNY. Only making up a nosegay, my Lord. Will your Lordship do
me the honor of accepting it? (*Presenting it.*)

90 LORD OGLEBY. I'll wear it next my heart, madam! (*Apart.*) I see the
young creature doats on me.

MISS STERLING. Lord, sister, you've loaded his Lordship with a bunch
of flowers as big as the cook or the nurse carry to town on Monday morning for a beaupot. Will your Lordship give leave to present you with this rose and a sprig of sweet briar?

62–63. gothic] O1, O3, O4, O6, D2, W1, W2; gothick O2, O5, O7, O8, O9, D1,
C.
entirely] O1, O2, O3, O4, O5, O6, O7. O8, O9, D2, W1, C; intirely D1,
W2.
91. doats] O1, O2, O3, O4, O5, O6, O7, O8, O9, D1, D2, W1, W2; dotes C.

LORD OGLEBY.   The truest emblems of yourself, Madam! All sweetness and poignancy. (*Apart.*) A little jealous, poor soul!

STERLING.   Now, my Lord, if you please, I'll carry you to see my ruins.

MRS. HEIDELBERG.   You'll absolutely fatigue his Lordship with over-
100   walking, brother!

LORD OGLEBY.   Not at all, madam. We're in the garden of Eden, you know, in the region of perpetual spring, youth, and beauty.

(*Leering at the women.*)

MRS. HEIDELBERG (*apart*).   Quite the man of qualaty, I pertest.

CANTON.   Take a my arm, mi Lor! (Lord Ogleby *leans on him.*)

STERLING.   I'll only show his Lordship my ruins, and the cascade, and the Chinese bridge, and then we'll go to breakfast.

LORD OGLEBY.   Ruins, did you say, Mr. Sterling?

STERLING.   Ay, ruins, my Lord! And they are reckoned very fine ones too. You would think them ready to tumble on your head. It has
110   just cost me a hundred and fifty pounds to put my ruins in thor-ough repair. This way, if your Lordship pleases.

LORD OGLEBY (*going, stops*).   What steeple's that we see yonder? The parish church, I suppose.

STERLING.   Ha! ha! ha! that's admirable. It is no church at all, my Lord. It is a spire that I have built against a tree, a field or two off, to terminate the prospect. One must always have a church, or an obelisk, or a something, to terminate the prospect, you know. That's a rule of taste, my Lord.

LORD OGLEBY.   Very ingenious indeed! For my part, I desire no finer
120   prospect than this I see before me. (*Leering at the women.*) Sim-ple, yet varied; bounded, yet extensive.—Get away, Canton! (*Push-ing away* Canton.) I want no assistance. I'll walk with the ladies.

STERLING.   This way, my Lord.

LORD OGLEBY.   Lead on, sir! We young folks here will follow you.—Madam! Miss Sterling! Miss Fanny! I attend you.

Exit after Sterling, *gallanting the ladies.*

CANTON (*following*).   He is cock o' de game, ma foy!

Exit.

SIR JOHN.   At length, thank heaven, I have an opportunity to unbosom. I know you are faithful, Lovewell, and flatter myself you would rejoice to serve me.

---

103.   qualaty] *O*1, *O*2, *O*3, *O*4, *O*5, *O*6, *O*7, *O*8, *O*9, *C*; quality *D*1, *W*1, *W*2; Qualaty *D*2.

126.   foy] *O*1, *O*2, *O*4, *O*5, *O*7, *O*8, *O*9, *D*1, *D*2, *C*; foi *O*3, *O*6, *W*1, *W*2.

130 LOVEWELL.   Be assured, you may depend on me.

SIR JOHN.   You must know then, notwithstanding all appearances, that this treaty of marriage between Miss Sterling and me will come to nothing.

LOVEWELL.   How!

SIR JOHN.   It will be no match, Lovewell.

LOVEWELL.   No match?

SIR JOHN.   No.

LOVEWELL.   You amaze me. What should prevent it?

SIR JOHN.   I.

140 LOVEWELL.   You! Wherefore?

SIR JOHN.   I don't like her.

LOVEWELL.   Very plain indeed! I never supposed that you was extremely devoted to her from inclination, but thought you always considered it as a matter of convenience rather than affection.

SIR JOHN.   Very true. I came into the family without any impressions on my mind—with an unimpassioned indifference ready to receive one woman as soon as another. I looked upon love, serious, sober love, as a chimaera and marriage as a thing of course, as you know most people do. But I, who was lately so great an infidel in love,

150 am now one of its sincerest votaries. In short, my defection from Miss Sterling proceeds from the violence of my attachment to another.

LOVEWELL.   Another! So! so! Here will be fine work. And pray who is she?

SIR JOHN.   Who is she? Who can she be but Fanny, the tender, amiable, engaging Fanny.

LOVEWELL.   Fanny! What Fanny?

SIR JOHN.   Fanny Sterling. Her sister. Is not she an angel, Lovewell?

LOVEWELL.   Her sister? Confusion! You must not think of it, Sir John.

160 SIR JOHN.   Not think of it? I can think of nothing else. Nay, tell me, Lovewell, was it possible for me to be indulged in a perpetual intercourse with two such objects as Fanny and her sister and not find my heart led by insensible attraction toward Her? You seem confounded. Why don't you answer me?

LOVEWELL.   Indeed, Sir John, this event gives me infinite concern.

SIR JOHN.   Why so? Is not she an angel, Lovewell?

LOVEWELL.   I foresee that it must produce the worst consequences. Consider the confusion it must unavoidably create. Let me persuade you to drop these thoughts in time.

---

142.   you was] *O*1, *O*2, *O*3, *O*4, *O*5, *O*6, *O*7, *O*8, *O*9, *W*1, *W*2; you were *D*1, *D*2, *C*.

163.   Her] *O*1, *O*2, *O*3, *O*4, *O*5, *O*6, *D*1; her *O*7, *O*8, *O*9, *D*2, *W*1, *W*2, *C*.

170 SIR JOHN. Never, never, Lovewell!

LOVEWELL. You have gone too far to recede. A negotiation so nearly concluded cannot be broken off with any grace. The lawyers, you know, are hourly expected, the preliminaries almost finally settled between Lord Ogleby and Mr. Sterling, and Miss Sterling herself ready to receive you as a husband.

SIR JOHN. Why, the bans have been published, and nobody has forbidden them, 'tis true; but you know either of the parties may change their minds even after they enter the church.

LOVEWELL. You think too lightly of this matter. To carry your ad-
180   dresses so far, and then to desert her—and for her sister too!—it will be such an affront to the family that they can never put up with it.

SIR JOHN. I don't think so. For as to my transferring my passion from her to her sister, so much the better, for then, you know, I don't carry my affections out of the family.

LOVEWELL. Nay, but prithee be serious and think better of it.

SIR JOHN. I have thought better of it already, you see. Tell me honestly, Lovewell, can you blame me? Is there any comparison between them?

190 LOVEWELL. As to that now—why that—that is just—just as it may strike different people. There are many admirers of Miss Sterling's vivacity.

SIR JOHN. Vivacity! A medley of Cheapside pertness and Whitechapel pride. No, no, if I do go so far into the city for the wedding dinner, it shall be upon turtle at least.

LOVEWELL. But I see no probability of success; for, granting that Mr. Sterling would have consented to it at first, he cannot listen to it now. Why did not you break this affair to the family before?

SIR JOHN. Under such embarrassed circumstances as I have been, can
200   you wonder at my irresolution or perplexity? Nothing but despair, the fear of losing my dear Fanny, could bring me to a declaration even now. And yet I think I know Mr. Sterling so well that, as strange as my proposal may appear, if I can make it advantageous to him as a money transaction, as I am sure I can, he will certainly come into it.

LOVEWELL. But even suppose he should, which I very much doubt, I don't think Fanny herself would listen to your addresses.

SIR JOHN. You are deceived a little in that particular.

LOVEWELL. You'll find I am in the right.

210 SIR JOHN. I have some little reason to think otherwise.

LOVEWELL. You have not declared your passion to her already?

SIR JOHN. Yes, I have.

LOVEWELL.   Indeed! And—and—and how did she receive it?

SIR JOHN.   I think it is not very easy for me to make my addresses to any woman without receiving some little encouragement.

LOVEWELL.   Encouragement! Did she give you any encouragement?

SIR JOHN.   I don't know what you call encouragement, but she blushed, and cried, and desired me not to think of it any more; upon which I prest her hand, kissed it, swore she was an angel—and I could see it tickled her to the soul.

LOVEWELL.   And did she express no surprise at your declaration?

SIR JOHN.   Why faith, to say the truth, she was a little surprised—and she got away from me, too, before I could thoroughly explain myself. If I should not meet with an opportunity of speaking to her, I must get you to deliver a letter from me.

LOVEWELL.   I? A letter! I had rather have nothing —

SIR JOHN.   Nay, you promised me your assistance, and I am sure you cannot scruple to make yourself useful on such an occasion. You may, without suspicion, acquaint her verbally of my determined affection for her, and that I am resolved to ask her father's consent.

LOVEWELL.   As to that, I—your commands, you know—that is, if she— Indeed, Sir John, I think you are in the wrong.

SIR JOHN.   Well, well, that's my concern. Ha! There she goes, by heaven, along that walk yonder, d'ye see? I'll go to her immediately.

LOVEWELL.   You are too precipitate. Consider what you are doing.

SIR JOHN.   I would not lose this opportunity for the universe.

LOVEWELL.   Nay, pray don't go! Your violence and eagerness may overcome her spirits. The shock will be too much for her. (*Detaining him.*)

SIR JOHN.   Nothing shall prevent me. Ha! Now she turns into another walk. Let me go! (*Breaks from him.*) I shall lose her. (*Going, turns back.*) Be sure now to keep out of the way. If you interrupt us, I shall never forgive you.

Exit hastily.

LOVEWELL.   'Sdeath! I can't bear this. In love with my wife! Acquaint me with his passion for her! Make his addresses before my face!

217. encouragement] O1, O2, O3, O4, O5, O6, O7, O8, O9, D1, D2, W1, W2; *encouragement* C.

221. surprise] O1, O2, O3, O4, O5, O6, D1, D2, W1, W2; surprize O7, O8, O9, C.

222. surprised] O1, O2, O3, O4, O5, O6, D1, D2, W1, W2; surprized O7, O8, O9, C.

250

I shall break out before my time. This was the meaning of Fanny's uneasiness. She could not encourage him—I am sure she could not. Ha! They are turning into the walk and coming this way. Shall I leave the place, leave him to solicit my wife? I can't submit to it.—They come nearer and nearer. If I stay, it will look suspicious. It may betray us and incense him.—They are here—I must go. I am the most unfortunate fellow in the world.

Exit.

Enter Fanny *and* Sir John.

FANNY. Leave me, Sir John, I beseech you leave me! Nay, why will you persist to follow me with idle solicitations which are an affront to my character and an injury to your own honor?

SIR JOHN. I know your delicacy and tremble to offend it; but let the urgency of the occasion be my excuse. Consider, madam, that the future happiness of my life depends on my present application

260

to you. Consider that this day must determine my fate; and these are perhaps the only moments left me to incline you to warrant my passion and to intreat you not to oppose the proposals I mean to open to your father.

FANNY. For shame, for shame, Sir John! Think of your previous engagements! Think of your own situation, and think of mine! What have you discovered in my conduct that might encourage you to so bold a declaration? I am shocked that you should venture to say so much, and blush that I should even dare to give it a hearing. Let me be gone!

270

SIR JOHN. Nay, stay, madam, but one moment! Your sensibility is too great. Engagements! What engagements have even been pretended on either side than those of family convenience? I went on in the trammels of matrimonial negotiation with a blind submission to your father and Lord Ogleby, but my heart soon claimed a right to be consulted. It has devoted itself to you, and obliges me to plead earnestly for the same tender interest in your's.

FANNY. Have a care, Sir John! Do not mistake a depraved will for a virtuous inclination. By these common pretences of the heart, half of our sex are made fools, and a greater part of yours despise them

280

for it.

SIR JOHN. Affection, you will allow, is involuntary. We cannot always direct it to the object on which it should fix. But when it is once inviolably attached, inviolably as mine is to you, it often creates reciprocal affection. When I last urged you on this sub-

---

276. your's] *O1, O2, O3, O4, O5, O6, O7, O9, D1, D2, W1, W2*; yours *O8, C.*

ject, you heard me with more temper, and I hoped with some compassion.

FANNY. You deceived yourself. If I forebore to exert a proper spirit —nay, if I did not even express the quickest resentment of your behavior—it was only in consideration of that respect I wish to pay you, in honor to my sister. And be assured, sir, woman as I am, that my vanity could reap no pleasure from a triumph that must result from the blackest treachery to her. (*Going.*)

SIR JOHN. One word, and I have done. (*Stopping her.*) Your impatience and anxiety, and the urgency of the occasion, oblige me to be brief and explicit with you. I appeal therefore from your delicacy to your justice. Your sister, I verily believe, neither entertains any real affection for me or tenderness for you. Your father, I am inclined to think, is not much concerned by means of which of his daughters the families are united. Now, as they cannot, shall not be connected otherwise than by my union with you, why will you, from a false delicacy, oppose a measure so conducive to my happiness and, I hope, your own? I love you, most passionately and sincerely love you, and hope to propose terms agreeably to Mr. Sterling. If then you don't absolutely loath, abhor, and scorn me—if there is no other happier man —

FANNY. Hear me, sir! Hear my final determination. Were my father and sister as insensible as you are pleased to represent them, were my heart forever to remain disengaged to any other, I could not listen to your proposals. What? You on the very eve of a marriage with my sister; I living under the same roof with her, bound not only by the laws of friendship and hospitality, but even the ties of blood, to contribute to her happiness and not to conspire against her peace—the peace of a whole family, and that my own too! Away! away, Sir John! At such a time, and in such circumstances, your addresses only inspire me with horror. Nay, you must detain me no longer. I will go.

SIR JOHN. Do not leave me in absolute despair! Give me a glimpse of hope! (*Falling on his knees.*)

FANNY. I cannot. Pray, Sir John! (*Struggling to go.*)

SIR JOHN. Shall this hand be given to another? (*Kissing her hand.*) No, I cannot endure it. My whole soul is yours, and the whole happiness of my life is in your power.

Enter Miss Sterling.

FANNY. Ha! My sister is here. Rise for shame, Sir John.

SIR JOHN. Miss Sterling!

MISS STERLING. I beg pardon, sir! You'll excuse me, madam! I have broke in upon you a little unopportunely, I believe. But I did not mean to interrupt you. I only came, sir, to let you know that breakfast waits, if you have finished your morning's devotions.

SIR JOHN. I am very sensible, Miss Sterling, that this may appear par-
330 ticular, but —

MISS STERLING. Oh dear, Sir John, don't put yourself to the trouble of an apology. The thing explains itself.

SIR JOHN. It will soon, madam! In the meantime I can only assure you of my profound respect and esteem for you, and make no doubt of convincing Mr. Sterling of the honor and integrity of my intentions. And—and—your humble servant, madam!

Exit in confusion.

MISS STERLING. Respect? Insolence! Esteem? Very fine, truly! And you, madam, my sweet, delicate, innocent, sentimental sister, will you convince my papa too of the integrity of your intentions?

340 FANNY. Do not upbraid me, my dear sister! Indeed, I don't deserve it. Believe me, you can't be more offended at his behavior than I am, and I am sure it cannot make you half so miserable.

MISS STERLING. Make me miserable? You are mightily deceived, madam! It gives me no sort of uneasiness, I assure you. A base fellow! As for you, miss, the pretended softness of your disposition, your artful good nature, never imposed upon me. I always knew you to be sly and envious and deceitful.

FANNY. Indeed you wrong me.

MISS STERLING. Oh, you are all goodness, to be sure! Did not I find
350 him on his knees before you? Did not I see him kiss your sweet hand? Did not I hear his protestations? Was not I witness of your dissembled modesty? No, no, my dear, don't imagine that you can make a fool of your elder sister so easily.

FANNY. Sir John, I own, is to blame; but I am above the thoughts of doing you the least injury.

MISS STERLING. We shall try that, madam! I hope, miss, you'll be able to give a better account to my papa and my aunt, for they shall both know of this matter, I promise you.

Exit.

FANNY. How unhappy I am! My distresses multiply upon me. Mr.
360 Lovewell must now become acquainted with Sir John's behavior to me—and in a manner that may add to his uneasiness. My father, instead of being disposed by fortunate circumstances to forgive any transgression, will be previously incensed against me. My sister and my aunt will become irreconcilably my enemies and re-

joice in my disgrace. Yet, at all events, I am determined on a discovery. I dread it, and am resolved to hasten it. It is surrounded with more horrors every instant, as it appears every instant more necessary.

Exit.

ACT III. SCENE I.

A hall.

Enter a servant leading in Serjeant Flower *and*
Counsellors Travers *and* Trueman, *all booted.*

SERVANT.   This way, if you please, gentlemen. My master is at break-fast with the family at present, but I'll let him know, and he will wait on you immediately.

FLOWER.   Mighty well, young man, mighty well.

SERVANT.   Please to favor me with your names, gentlemen.

FLOWER.   Let Mr. Sterling know that Mr. Serjeant Flower and three other gentlemen of the bar are come to wait on him according to his appointment.

SERVANT.   I will, sir. (*Going.*)

10   FLOWER.   And harkee, young man! (Servant *returns*.) Desire my ser-vant—Mr. Serjeant Flower's servant—to bring in my green and gold saddle cloth and pistols, and lay them down here in the hall with my portmanteau.

SERVANT.   I will, sir.

Exit.

FLOWER.   Well, gentlemen, the settling these marriage-articles falls conveniently enough almost just on the eve of the circuits. Let me see—the Home, the Midland, Oxford, and Western, ay, we can all cross the country well enough to our several destinations. Trav-erse, when do you begin at Abingdon?

20   TRAVERSE.   The day after tomorrow.

FLOWER.   That is commission day with us at Warwick too. But my clerk has retainers for every cause in the paper, so it will be time enough if I am there the next morning. Besides, I have about half a dozen cases that have lain by me ever since the spring assizes,

---

6.   three] *O1, O3, O4, O6, D1, D2, W1, W2*; two *O2, O5, O7, O8, O9, C.*

17.   Midland, Oxford, and Western] *O1, O3, O4, O6, D1, D2, W1, W2*; Mid-land, and Western *O2, O5, O7, O8, O9, C.*

19.   Abingdon] *O1, O3, O4, O6, D1, D2, W1, W2*; Hertford *O2, O5, O7, O8, O9, C.*

and I must tack opinions to them before I see my country clients
again. So I will take the evening before me—and then *currente*
calamo, as I say—eh, Traverse!

TRAVERSE.   True, Mr. Serjeant.

FLOWER.   Do you expect to have much to do on the home circuit these
30   assizes?

TRAVERSE.   Not much *nisi prius* business, but a good deal on the crown
side, I believe. The gaols are brimfull—and some of the felons in
good circumstances and likely to be tolerable clients. Let me see.
I am engaged for three highway robberies, two murders, one for-
gery, and half a dozen larcenies at Kingston.

FLOWER.   A pretty decent gaol delivery! Do you expect to bring off
Darkin for the robbery on Putney Common? Can you make out
your *alibi?*

TRAVERSE.   Oh, no! The crown witnesses are sure to prove our iden-
40   tity. We shall certainly be hanged; but that don't signify. But, Mr.
Serjeant, have you much to do? Any remarkable cause on the
Midland this circuit?

FLOWER.   Nothing very remarkable except two rapes, and Rider and
Western at Nottingham, for *crim. con.*—but on the whole, I believe, a good deal of business. Our associate tells me there are above
thirty *venires* for Warwick.

TRAVERSE.   Pray, Mr. Serjeant, are you concerned in Jones and Thomas
at Lincoln?

FLOWER.   I am—for the plantiff.

50   TRAVERSE.   And what do you think on't?

FLOWER.   A nonsuit.

TRAVERSE.   I thought so.

FLOWER.   Oh, no manner of doubt on't—*luce clarius*. We have no right
in us; we have but one chance.

TRAVERSE.   What's that?

FLOWER.   Why, my Lord Chief does not go the circuit this time, and
my brother Puzzle being in the commission, the cause will come
on before him.

TRUEMAN.   Ay, that may do, indeed, if you can but throw dust in the
60   eyes of the defendant's counsel.

FLOWER.   True. (*To* Trueman.) Mr. Trueman, I think you are con-

---

25. must tack opinions] *D*1 omits tack.
28. True, Mr. Serjeant] *O*1, *O*3, *O*4, *O*5, *O*6, *D*1, *D*2, *W*1, *W*2; True, Mr.
Serjeant—and the easiest thing in the world too, for those country at-
tornies are such ignorant dogs that in case of the devise of an estate to A.
and his heirs for ever, they'll make a query, whether he takes in fee or
in tail. *O*2, *O*7, *O*8, *O*9, *C*.

cerned for Lord Ogleby in this affair?

TRUEMAN.   I am, sir. I have the honor to be related to his Lordship and hold some courts for him in Somersetshire, go to the Western circuit, and attend the sessions at Exeter, merely becauuse his Lordship's interest and property lie in that part of the kingdom.

FLOWER.   Ha! And pray, Mr. Trueman, how long have you been called to the bar?

TRUEMAN.   About nine years and three quarters.

70 FLOWER.   Ha! I don't know that I ever had the pleasure of seeing you before. I wish you success, young gentleman!

Enter Sterling.

STERLING.   Oh, Mr. Serjeant Flower, I am glad to see you. Your servant, Mr. Serjeant! Gentlemen, your servant. Well, are all matters concluded? Has the snail-paced conveyancer, old Ferret of Gray's Inn, settled the articles at last? Do you approve of what he has done? Will his tackle hold? Tight and strong? Eh, master Serjeant?

FLOWER.   My friend Ferret's slow and sure, sir, but then *serius aut citius*, as we say—sooner or later, Mr. Sterling, he is sure to put

80 his business out of hand as he should do. My clerk has brought the writings and all other instruments along with him, and the settlement is, I believe, as good a settlement as any settlement on the face of the earth.

STERLING.   But that damned mortgage of 60,000 l. There don't appear to be any other incumbrances, I hope.

TRAVERSE.   I can answer for that, sir—and that will be cleared off immediately on the payment of the first part of Miss Sterling's portion. You agree, on your part, to come down with 80,000 l.

STERLING.   Down on the nail. Ay, ay, my money is ready tomorrow

90 if he pleases. He shall have it in India bonds, or notes, or how he chooses. Your lords and your dukes and your people at the court-end of the town stick at payments sometimes—debts unpaid, no credit lost with them—but no fear of us substantial fellows, eh, Mr. Serjeant?

FLOWER.   Sir John, having last term, according to agreement, levied a fine and suffered a recovery, has thereby cut off the entail of the Ogleby estate for the better effecting the purposes of the present intended marriage, on which above-mentioned Ogleby estate

84.   60,000 l.] *O*1, *O*2, *O*3, *O*4, *O*5, *O*6, *O*7, *O*8, *O*9, *D*1, *D*2; £60,000 *W*1, *W*2; sixty thousand pounds *C*.

88.   80,000 l.] *O*1, *O*2, *O*3, *O*4, *O*5, *O*6, *O*7, *O*8, *O*9, *D*1, *D*2; £80,000 *W*1, *W*2; eighty thousand pounds *C*.

a jointure of 2000 l per ann. is secured to your eldest daughter,
now Elizabeth Sterling, spinster, and the whole estate, after the
death of the aforesaid Earl, descends to the heirs male of Sir John
Melvil on the body of the aforesaid Elizabeth Sterling lawfully
to be begotten.

TRAVERSE. Very true—and Sir John is to be put in immediate possession of as much of his Lordship's Somersetshire estate as lies in
the manors of Hogmore and Cranford, amounting to between
two and three thousands per ann., and at the death of Mr. Sterling,
a further sum of seventy thousand —

Enter Sir John Melvil.

STERLING. Ah, Sir John! Here we are, hard at it, paving the road to
matrimony. We'll have no jolts; all upon the nail, as easy as the
new pavement. First the lawyers, then comes the doctor. Let us
but dispatch the long-robe, we shall soon set Pudding-sleeves to
work, I warrant you.

SIR JOHN. I am sorry to interrupt you, sir, but I hope that both you
and these gentlemen will excuse me. Having something very particular for your private ear, I took the liberty of following you,
and beg you will oblige me with an audience immediately.

STERLING. Ay, with all my heart. Gentlemen, Mr. Serjeant, you'll excuse it. Business must be done, you know. The writings will keep
cold till tomorrow morning.

FLOWER. I must be at Warwick, Mr. Sterling, the day after.

STERLING. Nay, nay, I shan't part with you tonight, gentlemen, I
promise you. My house is very full, but I have beds for you all,
beds for your servants, and stabling for all your horses. Will you
take a turn in the garden and view some of my improvements before dinner? Or will you amuse yourself in the green with a game
of bowls and a cool tankard? My servants shall attend you. Do you
choose any other refreshment? Call for what you please, do as
you please, make yourselves quite at home, I beg of you. Here,
Thomas, Harry, William, wait on these gentlemen!

Follows the lawyers out, bawling, and talking,
and then returns to Sir John.

And now, sir, I am entirely at your service.—What are your commands with me, Sir John?

SIR JOHN. After having carried the negotiation between our families

---

99. 2000 l.] O1, O2, O3, O4, O5, O6, O7, O8, O9, D1, D2, £2000 W1, W2;
     two thousand pounds C.
107. thousands] O1, O2, O3, O4, O5, O6, O8, D1, D2, W1, W2, C; thousand
     O7, O9.

to so great a length, after having assented so readily to all your proposals as well as received so many instances of your cheerful compliance with the demands made on our part, I am extremely concerned, Mr. Sterling, to be the unvoluntary cause of an uneasiness.

STERLING.   Uneasiness? What uneasiness? Where business is transacted
140   as it ought to be and the parties understand one another, there can be no uneasiness. You agree, on such and such conditions, to receive my daughter for a wife; on the same conditions I agree to receive you as a son-in-law; and as to all the rest, it follows of course, you know, as regularly as the payment of a bill after acceptance.

SIR JOHN.   Pardon me, sir; more uneasiness has arisen than you are aware of. I am myself at this instant in a state of inexpressible embarrassment. Miss Sterling, I know, is extremely disconcerted too; and unless you will oblige me with the assistance of your friend-
150   ship, I foresee the speedy progress of discontent and animosity through the whole family.

STERLING.   What the deuce is all this? I don't understand a single syllable.

SIR JOHN.   In one word, then—it will be absolutely impossible for me to fulfill my engagements in regard to Miss Sterling.

STERLING.   How, Sir John? Do you mean to put an affront upon my family? What? Refuse to —

SIR JOHN.   Be assured, sir, that I neither mean to affront nor forsake your family. My only fear is that you should desert me; for the
160   whole happiness of my life depends on my being connected with your family by the nearest and tenderest ties in the world.

STERLING.   Why, did not you tell me but a moment ago that it was absolutely impossible for you to marry my daughter?

SIR JOHN.   True. But you have another daughter, sir —

STERLING.   Well?

SIR JOHN.   Who has obtained the most absolute dominion over my heart. I have already declared my passion to her; nay, Miss Sterling herself is also apprized of it, and if you will but give a sanction to my present addresses, the uncommon merit of Miss Sterling
170   will no doubt recommend her to a person of equal, if not superior, rank to myself, and our families may still be allied by my union with Miss Fanny.

STERLING.   Mighty fine, truly! Why, what the plague do you make of us, Sir John? Do you come to market for my daughters, like ser-

---

174.   daughters] *O*1, *O*2, *O*3, *O*4, *O*5, *O*6, *D*1, *D*2, *W*1, *W*2; daughter *O*7, *O*8, *O*9, *C*.

vants at a statute fair? Do you think that I will suffer you, or any man in the world, to come into my house like the Grand Signior and throw the handkerchief first to one and then t'other, just as he pleases? Do you think I drive a kind of African slave-trade with them? And —

180 SIR JOHN. A moment's patience, sir! Nothing but the excess of my passion for Miss Fanny should have induced me to take any step that had the least appearance of disrespect to any part of your family; and even now I am desirous to atone for my transgression by making the most adequate compensation that lies in my power.

STERLING. Compensation? What compensation can you possibly make in such a case as this, Sir John?

SIR JOHN. Come, come, Mr. Sterling; I know you to be a man of sense, a man of business, a man of the world. I'll deal frankly with you, and you shall see that I do not desire a change of measures for 190 my own gratification without endeavoring to make it advantageous to you.

STERLING. What advantage can your inconstancy be to me, Sir John?

SIR JOHN. I'll tell you, sir. You know that by the articles at present subsisting between us, on the day of my marriage with Miss Sterling you agree to pay down the gross sum of eighty thousand pounds.

STERLING. Well?

SIR JOHN. Now, if you will but consent to my waving that marriage —

STERLING. I agree to your waving that marriage? Impossible, Sir John!

200 SIR JOHN. I hope not, sir, as on my part I will agree to wave my right to thirty thousand pounds of the fortune I was to receive with her.

STERLING. Thirty thousand, d'ye say?

SIR JOHN. Yes, sir, and accept of Miss Fanny with fifty thousand instead of fourscore.

STERLING. Fifty thousand — (*Pausing.*)

SIR JOHN. Instead of fourscore.

STERLING. Why—why—there may be something in that. Let me see; Fanny with fifty thousand instead of Betsey with fourscore—But how can this be, Sir John? For you know I am to pay this money 210 into the hands of my Lord Ogleby, who, I believe—between you and me, Sir John,—is not overstocked with ready money at present; and threescore thousand of it, you know, is to go to pay off the present incumbrances on the estate, Sir John.

SIR JOHN. That objection is easily obviated. Ten of the twenty thousand which would remain as a surplus of the fourscore after paying off the mortgage was intended by his Lordship for my use, that we might set off with some little *eclat* on our marriage, and

the other ten for his own. Ten thousand pounds therefore I shall
be able to pay you immediately, and for the remaining twenty
220   thousand you shall have a mortgage on that part of the estate
which is to be made over to me, with whatever security you shall
require for the regular payment of the interest, 'till the principal
is duly discharged.

STERLING. Why, to do you justice, Sir John, there is something fair
and open in your proposal; and since I find you do not mean to
put an affront upon my family —

SIR JOHN. Nothing was ever farther from my thoughts, Mr. Sterling.
And, after all, the whole affair is nothing extraordinary—such
things happen every day; and as the world has only heard gen-
230   erally of a treaty between the families, when this marriage takes
place nobody will be the wiser, if we have but discretion enough
to keep our own counsel.

STERLING. True, true; and since you only transfer from one girl to
the other, it is no more than transferring so much stock, you know.

SIR JOHN. The very thing.

STERLING. Odso! I had quite forgot. We are reckoning without our
host here. There is another difficulty —

SIR JOHN. You alarm me. What can that be?

STERLING. I can't stir a step in this business without consulting my
240   sister Heidelberg. The family has very great expectations from
her, and we must not give her any offence.

SIR JOHN. But if you come into this measure, surely she will be so
kind as to consent.

STERLING. I don't know that. Betsey is her darling, and I can't tell
how far she may resent any slight that seems to be offered to her
favorite niece. However, I'll do the best I can for you. You shall
go and break the matter to her first, and by that time that I may
suppose that your rhetoric has prevailed on her to listen to reason,
I will step in to reinforce your arguments.

250 SIR JOHN. I'll fly to her immediately. You promise me your assistance?

STERLING. I do.

SIR JOHN. Ten thousand thanks for it! And now success attend me!
(*Going.*)

STERLING. Harkee, Sir John!

Sir John returns.

STERLING. Not a word of the thirty thousand to my sister, Sir John.

SIR JOHN. Oh, I am dumb, I am dumb, sir. (*Going.*)

STERLING. You remember it is thirty thousand.

SIR JOHN. To be sure I do. (*Going.*)

STERLING. But, Sir John, one thing more. (Sir John *returns.*) My Lord must know nothing of this stroke of friendship between us.

260 SIR JOHN. Not for the world. Let me alone! Let me alone! (*Offering to go.*)

STERLING (*holding him*). And when everything is agreed, we must give each other a bond to be held fast to the bargain.

SIR JOHN. To be sure. A bond by all means! A bond, or whatever you please.

Exit hastily.

STERLING (*alone*). I should have thought of more conditions; he's in a humor to give me everything. Why, what mere children are your fellows of quality, that cry for a plaything one minute and throw it by the next, as changeable as the weather and as uncertain as the stocks. Special fellows to drive a bargain, and yet they are 270 to take care of the interest of the nation truly! Here does this whirligig man of fashion offer to give up thirty thousand pounds in hard money with as much indifference as if it was a china orange. By this mortgage I shall have a hold on his *terra firma*; and if he wants more money, as he certainly will—let him have children by my daughter or no—I shall have his whole estate in a net for the benefit of my family. Well, thus it is that the children of citizens who have acquired fortunes prove persons of fashion; and thus it is that persons of fashion who have ruined their fortunes reduce the next generation to cits.

Exit.

[Scene II.]

SCENE *changes to another apartment.*
Enter Mrs. Heidelberg *and* Miss Sterling.

MISS STERLING. This is your gentle-looking, soft-speaking, sweet-smiling, affable Miss Fanny for you!

MRS. HEIDELBERG. My Miss Fanny! I disclaim her. With all her arts she never could insinuat herself into my good graces—and yet she has a way with her that deceives man, woman, and child, except you and me, niece.

---

4. insinuat] *O1, O2, O4, O5, O7,* C; insinuate *O3, O6, O8, O9, D1, D2, W1, W2.*

MISS STERLING. Oh ay; she wants nothing but a crook in her hand and a lamb under her arm to be a perfect picture of innocence and simplicity.

10 MRS. HEIDELBERG. Just as I was drawn at Amsterdam when I went over to visit my husband's relations.

MISS STERLING. And then she's so mighty good to servants—*pray, John, do this—pray, Tom, do that—thank you, Jenny,*—and then so humble to her relations—*to be sure, Papa!—as my aunt pleases— my sister knows best.* But with all her demureness and humility she has no objection to be Lady Melvil, it seems, nor to any wickedness that can make her so.

MRS. HEIDELBERG. She Lady Melvil? Compose yourself, niece! I'll ladyship her indeed—a little creepin, cantin, she shan't be the bet-
20 ter for a farden of my money. But tell me, child, how does this intriguing with Sir John correspond with her partially to Lovewell? I don't see a concatunation here.

MISS STERLING. There I was deceived, madam. I took all their whisperings and stealing into corners to be the mere attraction of vulgar minds; but behold, their private meetings were not to contrive their own insipid happiness but to conspire against mine. But I know whence proceeds Mr. Lovewell's resentment to me. I could not stoop to be familiar with my father's clerk, and so I have lost his interest.

30 MRS. HEIDELBERG. My spurrit to a T, my dear child! (*Kissing her.*) —Mr. Heidelberg lost his election for member of parliament because I would not demean myself to be slobbered about by drunken shoemakers, beastly cheesemongers, and greasy butchers and tallow-chandlers. However, niece, I can't help diffuring a little in opinion from you in this matter. My experience and sagucity makes me still suspect that there is something more between her and that Lovewell, notwithstanding this affair of Sir John. I had my eye upon them the whole time of breakfast. Sir John, I observed, looked a little confounded, indeed, though I knew nothing
40 of what had passed in the garden. You seemed to sit upon thorns too; but Fanny and Mr. Lovewell made quite another-guess sort of a figur, and were as perfet a pictur of two distrest lovers as

34. diffuring] O1, O2, O3, O4, O5, O6, D1, D2, W1, W2; diffurring O7, O8, O9, C.
42. figur] O1, O2, O3, O4, O5, O6, O7, O8, O9, D2, W1, W2, C; figure D1. perfet] O1, O2, O3, O4, O5, O6, D1, D2, W1, W2; perfect O7, O8, O9, C. pictur] O1, O2, O3, O4, O5, O6, O7, O8, O9, D2, W1, W2, C; picture D1. distrest] O1, O2, O3, O4, O5, O6, O7, O8, O9, D1, D2, W1, W2; distress'd C.

if it had been drawn by Raphael Angelo. As to Sir John and Fanny, I want a matter of fact.

MISS STERLING.   Matter of fact, madam! Did not I come unexpectedly upon them? Was not Sir John kneeling at her feet and kissing her hand? Did not he look all love, and she all confusion? Is not that matter of fact? And did not Sir John, the moment that Papa was called out of the room to the lawyer-men, get up from breakfast and follow him immediately? And I warrant you that by this time he has made proposals to him to marry my sister. Oh, that some other person, an earl or a duke, would make his addresses to me, that I might be revenged on this monster!

MRS. HEIDELBERG.   Be cool, child! You *shall* be Lady Melvil in spite of all their caballins, if it costs me ten thousand pounds to turn the scale. Sir John may apply to my brother, indeed; but I'll make them all know who governs in this famaly.

MISS STERLING.   As I live, madam, yonder comes Sir John. A base man! I can't endure the sight of him. I'll leave the room this instant. (*Disordered.*)

MRS. HEIDELBERG.   Poor thing! Well, retire to your own chamber. I'll give it him, I warrant you; and by and by I'll come and let you know all that has past between us.

MISS STERLING.   Pray do, madam. (*Looking back.*)—A vile wretch!

Exit in a rage.

Enter Sir John Melvil.

SIR JOHN.   Your most obedient humble servant, madam! (*Bowing very respectfully.*)

MRS. HEIDELBERG.   Your servant, Sir John! (*Dropping a half courtsey and pouting.*)

SIR JOHN.   Miss Sterling's manner of quitting the room on my approach and the visible coolness of your behavior to me, madam, convince me that she has acquainted you with what past this morning.

MRS. HEIDELBERG.   I am very sorry, Sir John, to be made acquainted with any thing that should induce me to change the opinion which I could always wish to entertain of a person of quallaty. (*Pouting.*)

SIR JOHN.   It has always been my ambition to merit the best opinion from Mrs. Heidelberg; and when she comes to weigh all circumstances, I flatter myself —

47.   hand] *O*1, *O*2, *O*3, *O*4, *O*5, *O*6, *O*7, *D*1, *D*2, *W*1, *W*2; hands *O*8, *O*9, *C.*
62.   past] *O*1, *O*2, *O*3, *O*4, *O*5, *O*6, *O*7, *O*8, *O*9, *D*1, *D*2, *W*1, *W*2; pass'd *C.*
68.   past] *O*1, *O*2, *O*3, *O*4, *O*5, *O*6, *O*7, *O*8, *O*9, *D*1, *D*2, *W*1, *W*2; pass'd *C.*
71.   quallaty] *O*1, *O*2, *O*3, *O*4, *O*5, *O*6, *D*1, *D*2; qualaty *O*7, *O*8, *O*9, *W*1, *W*2, *C.*

MRS. HEIDELBERG (*warmly*).   You *do* flatter yourself if you imagine
that I can approve of your behavior to my niece, Sir John. And
give me leave to tell you, Sir John, that you have been drawn into
an action much beneath you, Sir John; and that I look upon every
injury offered to Miss Betty Sterling as an affront to myself, Sir
80   John.

SIR JOHN.   I would not offend you for the world, madam! But when
I am influenced by a partiality for another, however ill-founded,
I hope your discernment and good sense will think it rather a
point of honor to renounce engagements which I could not fulfil
so strictly as I ought; and that you will excuse the change in my
inclinations, since the new object, as well as the first, has the honor
of being your niece, madam.

MRS. HEIDELBERG.   I disclaim her as a niece, Sir John; Miss Sterling
disclaims her as a sister, and the whole family must disclaim her
90   for her monstrous baseness and treachery.

SIR JOHN.   Indeed she has been guilty of none, madam. Her hand and
heart are, I am sure, entirely at the disposal of yourself and Mr.
Sterling.

Enter Sterling *behind.*

And if you should not oppose my inclinations, I am sure of Mr.
Sterling's consent, madam.

MRS. HEIDELBERG.   Indeed!

SIR JOHN.   Quite certain, madam.

STERLING (*behind*).   So they seem to be coming to terms already! I
may venture to make my appearance.

100   MRS. HEIDELBERG.   To marry Fanny? (*Sterling advances by degrees.*)

SIR JOHN.   Yes, madam.

MRS. HEIDELBERG.   My brother has given his consent, you say?

SIR JOHN.   In the most ample manner, with no other restriction than
the failure of your concurrence, madam. (*Sees* Sterling.)—Oh,
here's Mr. Sterling, who will confirm what I have told you.

MRS. HEIDELBERG.   What? Have you consented to give up your own
daughter in this manner, brother?

STERLING.   Give her up? No, not give her up, sister; only in case that
you—(*Apart to* Sir John.) Zounds, I am afraid you have said too
110   much, Sir John.

MRS. HEIDELBERG.   Yes, yes. I see now that it is true enough what my
niece told me. You are all plottin and caballin against her. Pray,
does Lord Ogleby know of this affair?

SIR JOHN.   I have not yet made him acquainted with it, madam.

MRS. HEIDELBERG.   No, I warrant you. I thought so, and so his Lordship and myself, truly, are not to be consulted 'till the last.

STERLING. What? Did not you consult my Lord? Oh, fie for shame, Sir John.

SIR JOHN. Nay, but Mr. Sterling —

120 MRS. HEIDELBERG. We who are the persons of most consequence and experunce in the two fammalies are to know nothing of the matter 'till the whole is as good as concluded upon. But his Lordship, I am sure, will have more generosaty than to countenance such a perceeding. And I could not have expected such behavior from a person of your quallaty, Sir John. And as for you, brother —

STERLING. Nay, nay but hear me, sister!

MRS. HEIDELBERG. I am perfectly ashamed of you. Have you no spurrit, no more concern for the honor of our fammaly than to consent —

130 STERLING. Consent? I consent? As I hope for mercy, I never gave my consent. Did I consent, Sir John?

SIR JOHN. Not absolutely, without Mrs. Heidelberg's concurrence. But in case of her approbation —

STERLING. Ay, I grant you, if my sister approved. (*To* Mrs. Heidelberg.) But that's quite another thing, you know.

MRS. HEIDELBERG. Your sister approve, indeed! I thought you knew her better, brother Sterling! What, approve of having your eldest daughter returned upon your hands and exchanged for the younger? I am surprized how you could listen to such a scandalus pro-

140 posal.

STERLING. I tell you, I never did listen to it. Did not I say that I would be governed entirely by my sister, Sir John? And unless she agreed to your marrying Fanny —

MRS. HEIDELBERG. I agree to his marrying Fanny? Abominable! The man is absolutely out of his senses. Can't that wise head of yours foresee the consequence of all this, brother Sterling? Will Sir John take Fanny without a fortune? No. After you have settled the largest part of your property on your youngest daughter, can there be an equal portion left for the eldest? No. Does not this overturn

150 the whole systum of the fammaly? Yes, yes, yes. You know I was always for my niece Betsey's marrying a person of the very first quallaty. That was my maxum. And therefore much the largest settlement was of course to be made upon her. As for Fanny, if she could, with a fortune of twenty or thirty thousand pounds, get a knight, or a member of parliament, or a rich common-councilman for a husband, I thought it might do very well.

---

117. fie] *O1, O2, O3, O4, O5, O6, O7, O8, O9, D1, D2, W1, W2;* fy *C.*

SIR JOHN.   But if a better match should offer itself, why should not it
be accepted, madam?

MRS. HEILDELBERG.   What, at the expence of her elder sister? Oh fie,
160   Sir John! How could you bear to hear of such an indignaty, brother Sterling?

STERLING.   I? Nay, I shan't hear of it. I promise you. I can't hear of it
indeed, Sir John.

MRS. HEIDELBERG.   But you *have* heard of it, brother Sterling. You
know you have, and sent Sir John to propose it to me. But if you
can give up your daughter, I shan't forsake my niece, I assure you.
Ah, if my poor dear Mr. Heidelberg and our sweet babes had been
alive, he would not have behaved so.

STERLING.   Did I, Sir John? Nay, speak! Bring me off, or we are
170   ruined.

SIR JOHN.   Why, to be sure, to speak the truth.

MRS. HEIDELBERG.   To speak the truth, I'm ashamed of you both. But
have a care what you are about, brother! Have a care, I say. The
lawyers are in the house, I hear; and if everything is not settled
to my liking, I'll have nothing more to say to you, if I live these
hundred years. I'll go over to Holland and settle with Mr. Vander-
spracken, my poor husband's first cousin; and my own fammaly
shall never be the better for a farden of my money, I promise you.

Exit.

STERLING.   I thought so. I knew she never would agree to it.
180 SIR JOHN.   'Sdeath, how unfortunate! What can we do, Mr. Sterling?

STERLING.   Nothing.

SIR JOHN.   What? Must our agreement break off the moment it is made,
then?

STERLING.   It can't be helped, Sir John. The family, as I told you before, have great expectations from my sister; and if this matter
proceeds, you hear yourself that she threatens to leave us. My
brother Heidelberg was a warm man, a very warm man, and died
worth a Plumb at least, a Plumb! Ay, I warrant you, he died worth
a Plumb and a half.

---

159.   fie] O1, O2, O3, O4, O5, O6, O7, O8, O9, D1, D2, W1, W2; fy C.

160.   indignaty] O1, O2, O3, O4, O5, O6, O7, O8, O9, D1, D2, W1, W2; in-
dignety C.

174.   lawyers] O1, O2, O3, O4, O5, O6, D1, D2, W1, W2; counsellors O7, O8,
O9, C.

187.   warm man, a very warm man, and died] O1, O2, O3, O4, O5, O6, O7, O8,
O9, D1, D2, C; warm man, and died W1, W2.

190   SIR JOHN.   Well, but if I —

STERLING.   And then, my sister has three or four very good mortgages, a deal of money in the three per cents. and old South-Sea annuities, besides large concerns in the Dutch and French funds. The greatest part of all this she means to leave to our family.

SIR JOHN.   I can only say, sir —

STERLING.   Why, your offer of the difference of thirty thousand was very fair and handsome to be sure, Sir John.

SIR JOHN.   Nay, but I am even willing to —

STERLING.   Ay, but if I was to accept it against her will, I might lose
200   above a hundred thousand; so you see the ballance is against you, Sir John.

SIR JOHN.   But is there no way, do you think, of prevailing on Mrs. Heidelberg to grant her consent?

STERLING.   I am afraid not. However, when her passion is a little abated —for she's very passionate—you may try what can be done. But you must not use my name any more, Sir John.

SIR JOHN.   Suppose I was to prevail on Lord Ogleby to apply to her, do you think that would have any influence over her?

STERLING.   I think he would be more likely to persuade her to it than
210   any other person in the family. She has a great respect for Lord Ogleby. She loves a lord.

SIR JOHN.   I'll apply to him this very day. And if he should prevail on Mrs. Heidelberg, I may depend on your friendship, Mr. Sterling?

STERLING.   Ay, ay, I shall be glad to oblige you when it is in my power; but as the account stands now, you see it is not upon the figures. And so your servant, Sir John.

Exit.

SIR JOHN.   What a situation am I in! Breaking off with her whom I was bound by treaty to marry, rejected by the object of my af-
220   fections, and embroiled with this turbulent woman who governs the whole family. And yet opposition, instead of smothering, increases my inclination. I must have her. I'll apply immediately to Lord Ogleby; and if he can but bring over the aunt to our party, her influence will overcome the scruples and delicacy of my dear Fanny, and I shall be the happiest of mankind.

Exit.

---

200.   ballance] *O*1, *O*2, *O*4, *O*5, *D*2; balance *O*3, *O*6, *O*7, *O*8, *O*9, *D*1, *W*1, *W*2, *C*.

ACT IV. SCENE I.

A room.
Enter Sterling, Mrs. Heidelberg, *and* Miss Sterling.

STERLING. What! Will you send Fanny to town, sister?

MRS. HEIDELBERG. Tomorrow morning. I've given orders about it already.

STERLING. Indeed?

MRS. HEIDELBERG. Positively.

STERLING. But consider, sister, at such a time as this, what an odd appearance it will have.

MRS. HEIDELBERG. Not half so odd as her behavior, brother. This time was intended for happiness, and I'll keep no incendaries here to destroy it. I insist on her going off tomorrow morning.

STERLING. I'm afraid this is all your doing, Betsey!

MISS STERLING. No indeed, Papa. My aunt knows that it is not. For all Fanny's baseness to me, I am sure I would not do or say anything to hurt her with you or my aunt for the world.

MRS. HEIDELBERG. Hold your tongue, Betsey! I will have my way. When she is packed off, everything will go on as it should do. Since they are at their intrigues, I'll let them see that we can act with vigur on our part; and the sending her out of the way shall be the purlimunary step to all the rest of my perceedings.

STERLING. Well, but sister —

MRS. HEIDELBERG. It does not signify talking, brother Sterling, for I am resolved to be rid of her, and I will. (*To* Miss Sterling.) Come along, child! The post-shay shall be at the door by six o'clock in the morning; and if Miss Fanny does not get into it, why, *I* will, and so there's an end of the matter. (*Bounces out with* Miss Sterling.)

Mrs. Heidelberg *returns.*

One word more, brother Sterling! I expect that you will take your eldest daughter in your hand and make a formal complaint to Lord Ogleby of Sir John Melvil's behavior. Do this, brother; show a proper regard for the honor of your fammaly yourself, and I shall

---

5. positively] O1, O2, O3, O4, O5, O6, D1, D2, W1, W2; posatively O7, O8, O9, C.

18. vigur] O1, O2, O3, O4, O5, O6, O7, O8, O9, D2; vigour D1, W1, W2, C.

19. perceedings] O1, O2, O3, O4, O5, O6, O7, O8, O9, D2, W1, W2, C; proceedings D1.

30   throw in my mite to the raising of it. If not—but now you know
        my mind. So act as you please, and take the consequences.

                                                            Exit.

STERLING.   The devil's in the woman for tyranny—mothers, wives, mis-
        tresses, or sisters, they always will govern us. As to my sister
        Heidelberg, she knows the strength of her purse and domineers
        upon the credit of it. (*Mimicking.*) "I will do this" and "you shall
        do that" and "you must do t'other, or else the fammaly shan't have
        a farden of"—So absolute with her money! But to say the truth,
        nothing but money can make us absolute, and so we must e'en
        make the best of her.

                            [SCENE II.]

                    SCENE *changes to the garden.*
                    Enter Lord Ogleby *and* Canton.

LORD OGLEBY.   What? Mademoiselle Fanny to be sent away? Why?
        Wherefore? What's the meaning of all this?
CANTON.   Je ne sais pas. I know noting of it.
LORD OGLEBY.   It can't be; it shan't be. I protest against the measure.
        She's a fine girl, and I had much rather that the rest of the family
        were annihilated than that she should leave us. Her vulgar father,
        that's the very abstract of 'Change Alley—the aunt, that's always
        endeavoring to be a fine lady—and the pert sister, forever show-
        ing that she is one, are horrid company indeed, and without her
10   would be intolerable. Ah, la petit Fanchon! She's the thing. Isn't
        she, Cant?
CANTON.   Dere is very good sympatie entre vous and dat young lady,
        mi Lor.
LORD OGLEBY.   I'll not be left among these Goths and Vandals, your
        Sterlings, your Heidelbergs, and Devilbergs. If she goes, I'll pos-
        itively go too.
CANTON.   In de same post-chay, mi Lor? You have no object to dat, I
        believe, nor mademoiselle neider too—ha, ha, ha.
LORD OGLEBY.   Prithee hold thy foolish tongue, Cant. Does thy Swiss
20   stupidity imagine that I can see and talk with a fine girl without
        desires? My eyes are involuntarily attracted by beautiful objects.
        I fly as naturally to a fine girl —
CANTON.   As de fine girl to you, my Lor, ha, ha, ha. You alway fly
        togedre like un pair de pigeons.
LORD OGLEBY (*Mocks him.*) Like un pair de pigeons—Vous êtes un sot,

Mons. Canton. Thou art always dreaming of my intrigues, and
never seest me *badiner* but you suspect mischief, you old fool, you.

CANTON. I am fool, I confess; but not always fool in dat, my Lor,
he, he, he.

30 LORD OGLEBY. He, he, he. Thou art incorrigible, but thy absurdities
amuse one. Thou art like my rappee here (*takes out his box*), a
most ridiculous superfluity, but a pinch of thee now and then is
a most delicious treat.

CANTON. You do me great honeur, my Lor.

LORD OGLEBY. 'Tis fact, upon my soul. Thou art properly my ceph-
alick snuff, and art no bad medicine against megrims, vertigoes and
profound thinking—ha, ha, ha.

CANTON. Your flatterie, my Lor, vil make me too prode.

LORD OGLEBY. The girl has some little partiality for me, to be sure.
40 But prithee, Cant, is not that Miss Fanny yonder?

CANTON (*looking with a glass*). En verite, 'tis she, my Lor, 'tis one of
de pigeons—de pigeons d'amour.

LORD OGLEBY. Don't be ridiculous, you old monkey. (*Smiling.*)

CANTON. I am monkee, I am ole, but I have eye, I have ear, and a little
understand, now and den.

LORD OGLEBY. Taisez vous, bête!

CANTON. Elle vous attend, my Lor. She vill make a love to you.

LORD OGLEBY. Will she? Have at her then! A fine girl can't oblige me
more. Egad, I find myself a little enjouée. Come along, Cant! She
50 is but in the next walk—but there is such a deal of this damned
crinkum-crankum, as Sterling calls it, that one sees people for half
an hour before one can get to them. Allons, Mons. Canton, allons
donc!

Exit singing in French.

Another part of the garden.
Lovewell *and* Fanny

LOVEWELL. My dear Fanny, I cannot bear your distress; it overcomes
all my resolutions, and I am prepared for the discovery.

FANNY. But how can it be effected before my departure?

LOVEWELL. I'll tell you. Lord Ogleby seems to entertain a visible partiality for you; and notwithstanding the peculiarities of his behavior, I am sure that he is humane at the bottom. He is vain to an

---

33. most] *O1, O2, O3, O4, O5, O6, D1, D2, W1, W2, C;* more *O7, O8, O9.*

35–36. cephalick] *O1, O2, O4, O5, D1, D2, C;* cephalic *O3, O6, O7, O8, O9, W1,
W2.*

49. enjouée] *O1, O2, O4, O5, D2;* enjouee *O3, O6, D1, W1, W2;* enjoué *O7,
O8, O9; enjouè C.*

60   excess, but withal extremely goodnatured, and would do anything
      to recommend himself to a lady. Do you open the whole affair
      of our marriage to him immediately. It will come with more ir-
      resistible persuasion from you than from myself, and I doubt not
      but you'll gain his friendship and protection at once. His influence
      and authority will put an end to Sir John's solicitations, remove
      your aunt's and sister's unkindness and suspicions, and, I hope, rec-
      oncile your father and the whole family to our marriage.

FANNY.   Heaven grant it! Where is my Lord?

LOVEWELL.   I have heard him and Canton since dinner singing French
70   songs under the great walnut tree by the parlor door. If you meet
      with him in the garden, you may disclose the whole immediately.

FANNY.   Dreadful as the task is, I'll do it. Anything is better than this
      continual anxiety.

LOVEWELL.   By that time the discovery is made, I will appear to second
      you.—Ha! here comes my Lord. Now, my dear Fanny, summon
      up all your spirits, plead our cause powerfully, and be sure of
      success. (*Going.*)

FANNY.   Ah, don't leave me!

LOVEWELL.   Nay, you must let me.

80 FANNY.   Well, since it must be so, I'll obey you, if I have the power.
      Oh, Lovewell!

LOVEWELL.   Consider, our situation is very critical. Tomorrow morn-
      ing is fixt for your departure, and if we lose this opportunity we
      may wish in vain for another. He approaches—I must retire. Speak,
      my dear Fanny, speak, and make us happy.

Exit.

FANNY.   Good heaven, what a situation I am in! What shall I do? What
      shall I say to him? I am all confusion.

Enter Lord Ogleby *and* Canton.

LORD OGLEBY.   To see much beauty so solitary, madam, is a satire upon
      mankind, and 'tis fortunate that one man has broke in upon your
90   reverie for the credit of our sex. I say *one*, madam, for poor Can-
      ton here, from age and infirmities, stands for nothing.

CANTON.   Noting at all, inteed.

FANNY.   Your Lordship does me great honor. I had a favor to request,
      my Lord.

LORD OGLEBY.   A favor, madam! To be honored with your commands
      is an inexpressible favor done to me, madam.

---

83.   fixt] *O*1, *O*2, *O*3, *O*4, *O*5, *O*6, *O*7, *O*8, *O*9, *D*1, *D*2, *W*1, *W*2; fix'd *C*.

FANNY.   If your Lordship could indulge me with the honor of a moment's—(*Aside.*) What is the matter with me?

LORD OGLEBY (*to* Canton).   The girl's confused—he!—here's something in the wind, faith. I'll have a tête-à-tête with her—allez vous en!

CANTON.   I go—Ah, pauvre, mademoiselle! My Lor, have pitié upon de poor *pigeone!*

LORD OGLEBY (*smiling*).   I'll knock you down, Cant, if you're impertinent.

CANTON.   Den I mus avay—(*Shuffles along.*) (*Aside.*) You are mosh please, for all dat.

Exit.

FANNY (*aside*).   I shall sink with apprehension.

LORD OGLEBY.   What a sweet girl! She's a civilized being and atones for the barbarism of the rest of the family.

FANNY.   My Lord, I — (*She courtsies and blushes.*)

LORD OGLEBY (*addressing her*).   I look upon it, madam, to be one of the luckiest circumstances of my life that I have this moment the honor of receiving your commands and the satisfaction of confirming with my tongue what my eyes perhaps have but too weakly expressed—that I am literally—the humblest of your servants.

FANNY.   I think myself greatly honored by your Lordship's partiality to me; but it distresses me that I am obliged in my present situation to apply to it for protection.

LORD OGLEBY.   I am happy in your distress, madam, because it gives me an opportunity to show my zeal. Beauty to me is a religion in which I was born and bred a bigot and would die a martyr. (*Aside.*) I'm in tolerable spirits, faith!

FANNY.   There is not perhaps at this moment a more distressed creature than myself. Affection, duty, hope, despair, and a thousand and different sentiments are struggling in my bosom; and even the presence of your Lordship, to whom I have flown for protection, adds to my perplexity.

LORD OGLEBY.   Does it, madam? (*Aside and smiling.*) Venus forbid! My old fault; the devil's in me, I think, for perplexing young women.—Take courage, madam! Dear Miss Fanny, explain. You have a powerful advocate in my breast, I assure you—my heart, madam. I am attached to you by all the laws of sympathy and delicacy. By my honor, I am.

FANNY.   Then I will venture to unburden my mind. Sir John Melvil, my Lord, by the most misplaced and mistimed declaration of affection for me, has made me the unhappiest of women.

LORD OGLEBY.   How, madam? Has Sir John made his addresses to you?

FANNY.   He has, my Lord, in the strongest terms. But I hope it is needless to say that my duty to my father, love to my sister, and regard
140   to the whole family, as well as the great respect I entertain for your
Lordship (*curtseying*), made me shudder at his addresses.

LORD OGLEBY.   Charming girl! Proceed, my dear Miss Fanny, proceed!

FANNY.   In a moment—give me leave, my Lord!—But if what I have to disclose should be received with anger or displeasure —

LORD OGLEBY.   Impossible, by all the tender powers! Speak, I beseech you, or I shall divine the cause before you utter it.

FANNY.   Then, my Lord, Sir John's addresses are not only shocking to me in themselves, but are more particularly disagreeable to me at this time, as—as —(*hesitating.*)

150   LORD OGLEBY.   As what, madam?

FANNY.   As—pardon my confusion—I am entirely devoted to another.

LORD OGLEBY.   (*Aside.*) If this is not plain, the devil's in it.—But tell me, my dear Miss Fanny, for I must know; tell me the how, the when, and the where. Tell me —

Enter Canton *hastily.*

CANTON.   My Lor, my Lor, my Lor!

LORD OGLEBY.   Damn your Swiss impertinence! How durst you interrupt me in the most critical melting moment that ever love and beauty honored me with?

CANTON.   I demande pardonne, my Lor! Sir John Melvil, my Lor, sent
160   me to beg you to do him the honor to speak a little to your Lordship.

LORD OGLEBY.   I'm not at leisure—I am busy. Get away, you stupid old dog, you Swiss rascal, or I'll —

CANTON.   Fort bien, my Lor.   Canton *goes out tiptoe.*

LORD OGLEBY.   By the laws of gallantry, madam, this interruption should be death; but as no punishment ought to disturb the triumph of the softer passions, the criminal is pardoned and dismissed. Let us return, madam, to the highest luxury of exalted minds—a declaration of love from the lips of beauty.

170   FANNY.   The entrance of a third person has a little relieved me, but I cannot go thro' with it. And yet I must open my heart with a discovery, or it will break with its burden.

LORD OGLEBY.   (*Aside.*) What passion in her eyes! I am alarmed to agitation.—I presume, madam—and as you have flattered me by mak-

160.   you to do] *O*1, *O*2, *O*3, *O*4, *O*5, *O*6, *D*1, *D*2, *W*1, *W*2; you do *O*7, *O*8, *O*9, *C.*

171.   thro'] *O*1, *O*2, *O*3, *O*4, *O*5, *O*6, *D*1, *D*2, *W*1, *W*2; through *O*7, *O*8, *O*9, *C.*

ing me a party concerned, I hope you'll excuse the presumption
—that —

FANNY.   Do you excuse my making you a party concerned, my Lord,
and let me interest your heart in my behalf, as my future happiness
or misery in a great measure depend —

180   LORD OGLEBY.   Upon me, Madam?

FANNY.   Upon you, my Lord. (*Sighs.*)

LORD OGLEBY.   There's no standing this. I have caught the infection—
her tenderness dissolves me. (*Sighs.*)

FANNY.   And should you too severely judge of a rash action which
passion prompted and modesty has long concealed —

LORD OGLEBY (*taking her hand*).   Thou amiable creature, command my
heart, for it is vanquished. Speak but thy virtuous wishes, and enjoy them.

FANNY.   I cannot, my Lord—indeed, I cannot. Mr. Lovewell must tell
190   you my distresses; and when you know them, pity and protect me!

Exit in tears.

LORD OGLEBY.   How the devil could I bring her to this? It is too much—
too much. I can't bear it. I must give way to this amiable weakness
—(*Wipes his eyes.*) My heart overflows with sympathy, and I feel
every tenderness I have inspired—(*Stifles the tear.*) How blind have
I been to the desolation I have made! How could I possibly imagine that a little partial attention and tender civilities to this young
creature should have gathered to this burst of passion? Can I be
a man and withstand it? No, I'll sacrifice the whole sex to her.—
But here comes the father, quite *apropos.* I'll open the matter im-
200   mediately, settle the business with him, and take the sweet girl
down to Ogleby House tomorrow morning. But what the devil!
Miss Sterling too! What mischief's in the wind now?

Enter Sterling *and* Miss Sterling.

STERLING.   My Lord, your servant! I am attending my daughter here
upon rather a disagreeable affair. Speak to his Lordship, Betsy!

LORD OGLEBY.   Your eyes, Miss Sterling—for I always read the eyes of
a young lady—betray some little emotion. What are your commands, madam?

MISS STERLING.   I have but too much cause for my emotion, my Lord!

LORD OGLEBY.   I cannot commend my kinsman's behavior, madam. He
210   has behaved like a false knight, I must confess. I have heard of his
apostacy. Miss Fanny has informed me of it.

MISS STERLING.   Miss Fanny's baseness has been the cause of Sir John's
inconstancy.

LORD OGLEBY.   Nay, now, my dear Miss Sterling, your passion trans-
ports you too far. Sir John may have entertained a passion for Miss
Fanny; but believe me, Miss Fanny has no passion for Sir John.
(*Conceitedly.*) She has a passion, indeed a most tender passion.
She has opened her whole soul to me and I know where her affec-
tions are placed.

220 MISS STERLING.   Not upon Mr. Lovewell, my Lord, for I have great
reason to think that her seeming attachment to him is, by his consent, made use of as a blind to cover her designs upon Sir John.

LORD OGLEBY.   Lovewell! No, poor lad, she does not think of him.
(*Smiling.*)

MISS STERLING.   Have a care, my Lord, that both the families are not
made the dupes of Sir John's artifice and my sister's dissimulation.
You don't know her—indeed, my Lord, you don't know her—a
base, insinuating, perfidious—It is too much. She has been beforehand with me, I perceive. Such unnatural behavior to me! But
since I see I can have no redress, I am resolved that some way or
230 other I will have revenge.

Exit.

STERLING.   This is foolish work, my Lord!

LORD OGLEBY.   I have too much sensibility to bear the tears of beauty.

STERLING.   It is touching indeed, my Lord—and very moving for a
father.

LORD OGLEBY.   To be sure, sir. You must be distrest beyond measure!
Wherefore, to divert your too exquisite feelings, suppose we
change the subject and proceed to business.

STERLING.   With all my heart, my Lord!

LORD OGLEBY.   You see, Mr. Sterling, we can make no union in our fam-
240 ilies by the proposed marriage.

STERLING.   And very sorry I am to see it, my Lord.

LORD OGLEBY.   Have you set your heart upon being allied to our house,
Mr. Sterling?

STERLING.   'Tis my only wish at present, my omnium, as I may call it.

LORD OGLEBY.   Your wishes shall be fulfilled.

STERLING.   Shall they, my Lord? But how—how?

LORD OGLEBY.   I'll marry in your family.

STERLING.   What! My sister Heidelberg?

LORD OGLEBY.   You throw me into a cold sweat, Mr. Sterling. No, not
250 your sister, but your daughter.

STERLING.   My daughter?

230.1.   stage direction: (*manet* LORD *Ogleby and* Sterling.) C.

LORD OGLEBY. Fanny!—Now the murder's out!

STERLING. What, *you*, my Lord?

LORD OGLEBY. Yes—I, I, Mr. Sterling!

STERLING. No, no, my Lord—that's too much. (*Smiling.*)

LORD OGLEBY. Too much? I don't comprehend you.

STERLING. What, you, my Lord, marry my Fanny! Bless me, what will the folks say?

LORD OGLEBY. Why, what will they say?

260 STERLING. That you're a bold man, my Lord—that's all.

LORD OGLEBY. Mr. Sterling, this may be city wit for ought I know. Do you court my alliance?

STERLING. To be sure, my Lord.

LORD OGLEBY. Then I'll explain. My nephew won't marry your eldest daughter—nor I neither. Your youngest daughter won't marry him. I will marry your youngest daughter.

STERLING. What? With a younger daughter's fortune, my Lord?

LORD OGLEBY. With any fortune, or no fortune at all, sir. Love is the idol of my heart, and the demon Interest sinks before him. So, sir,

270 as I said before, I will marry your youngest daughter; your youngest daughter will marry me.

STERLING. Who told you so, my Lord?

LORD OGLEBY. Her own sweet self, sir.

STERLING. Indeed?

LORD OGLEBY. Yes, sir. Our affection is mutual; your advantage double and treble. Your daughter will be a countess directly; I shall be the happiest of beings, and you'll be father to an earl instead of a baronet.

STERLING. But what will my sister say—and my daughter?

280 LORD OGLEBY. I'll manage that matter. Nay, if they won't consent I'll run away with your daughter in spite of you.

STERLING. Well said, my Lord! Your spirit's good. I wish you had my constitution! But if you'll venture, I have no objection, if my sister has none.

LORD OGLEBY. I'll answer for your sister, sir. Apropos, the lawyers are in the house. I'll have articles drawn, and the whole affair concluded tomorrow morning.

STERLING. Very well; and I'll dispatch Lovewell to London immediately for some fresh papers I shall want, and I shall leave you

290 to manage matters with my sister. You must excuse me, my Lord, but I can't help laughing at the match—he! he! he! What will the folks say? *Exit.*

---

267. younger] *O1, O2, O3, O4, O5, O6, O8, D1, D2, W1, W2*; youngest *O7, O9, C.*

LORD OGLEBY. What a fellow am I going to make a father of? He has no more feeling than the post in his warehouse. But Fanny's virtues tune me to rapture again, and I won't think of the rest of the family.

Enter Lovewell *hastily.*

LOVEWELL. I beg your Lordship's pardon, my Lord; are you alone, my Lord?

LORD OGLEBY. No, my Lord, I am not alone! I am in company, the best
300   company.

LOVEWELL. My Lord!

LORD OGLEBY. I never was in such exquisite enchanting company since my heart first conceived or my senses tasted pleasure.

LOVEWELL. Where are they, my Lord? (*Looking about.*)

LORD OGLEBY. In my mind, sir.

LOVEWELL. What company have you there, my Lord? (*Smiling.*)

LORD OGLEBY. My own ideas, sir, which so crowd upon my imagination and kindle it to such a delirium of extasy that wit, wine, music, poetry, all combined and each perfection, are but mere mortal
310   shadows of my felicity.

LOVEWELL. I see that your Lordship is happy, and I rejoice at it.

LORD OGLEBY. You *shall* rejoice at it, sir; my felicity shall not selfishly be confined, but shall spread its influence to the whole circle of my friends. I need not say, Lovewell, that you shall have your share of it.

LOVEWELL. Shall I, my Lord? Then I understand—you have heard— Miss Fanny has informed you —

LORD OGLEBY. She has. I have heard, and she shall be happy—'tis determined.

320 LOVEWELL. Then I have reached the summit of my wishes. And will your Lordship pardon the folly?

LORD OGLEBY. Oh yes, poor creature, how could she help it? 'Twas unavoidable—fate and necessity.

LOVEWELL. It was indeed, my Lord. Your kindness distracts me.

LORD OGLEBY. And so it did the poor girl, faith.

LOVEWELL. She trembled to disclose the secret and declare her affections?

LORD OGLEBY. The world, I believe, will not think her affections ill placed.

330 LOVEWELL (*bowing*). You are too good, my Lord. And do you really excuse the rashness of the action?

LORD OGLEBY. From my very soul, Lovewell.

LOVEWELL. Your generosity overpowers me—(*Bowing.*) I was afraid of her meeting with a cold reception.

LORD OGLEBY. More fool you then.
> Who pleads her cause with never-failing beauty,
> Here finds a full redress. (*Strikes his breast.*)
She's a fine girl, Lovewell.

LOVEWELL. Her beauty, my Lord, is her least merit. She has an understanding.

LORD OGLEBY. Her choice convinces me of that.

LOVEWELL (*bowing*). That's your Lordship's goodness. Her choice
was a disinterested one.

LORD OGLEBY. No—no—not altogether. It began with interest and ended
in passion.

LOVEWELL. Indeed, my Lord, if you were acquainted with her goodness of heart and generosity of mind as well as you are with the
inferior beauties of her face and person —

LORD OGLEBY. I am so perfectly convinced of their existence, and so
totally of your mind touching every amiable particular of that
sweet girl, that were it not for the cold unfeeling impediments of
the law, I would marry her tomorrow morning.

LOVEWELL. My Lord!

LORD OGLEBY. I would by all that's honorable in man and amiable in
woman.

LOVEWELL. Marry her! Who do you mean, my Lord?

LORD OGLEBY. Miss Fanny Sterling, that is—the Countess of Ogleby
that shall be.

LOVEWELL. I am astonished.

LORD OGLEBY. Why could you expect less from me?

LOVEWELL. I did not expect this, my Lord.

LORD OGLEBY. Trade and accounts have destroyed your feeling.

LOVEWELL. No, indeed, my Lord. (*Sighs.*)

LORD OGLEBY. The moment that love and pity entered my breast, I
was resolved to plunge into matrimony and shorten the girl's tortures. I never do any thing by halves, do I, Lovewell?

LOVEWELL. No, indeed, my Lord—(*Sighs.*) What an accident!

LORD OGLEBY. What's the matter, Lovewell? Thou seem'st to have lost
thy faculties. Why don't you wish me joy, man?

LOVEWELL. Oh, I do, my Lord.

LORD OGLEBY. She said that you would explain what she had not power
to utter, but I wanted no interpreter for the language of love.

LOVEWELL. But has your Lordship considered the consequences of
your resolution?

LORD OGLEBY. No, sir; I am above consideration when my desires are
kindled.

LOVEWELL. But consider the consequences, my Lord, to your nephew, Sir John.

LORD OGLEBY. Sir John has considered no consequences himself, Mr. Lovewell.

380

LOVEWELL. Mr. Sterling, my Lord, will certainly refuse his daughter to Sir John.

LORD OGLEBY. Sir John has already refused Mr. Sterling's daughter.

LOVEWELL. But what will become of Miss Sterling, my Lord?

LORD OGLEBY. What's that to you? You may have her if you will. I depend upon Mr. Sterling's city philosophy to be reconciled to Lord Ogleby's being his son-in-law instead of Sir John Melvil, Baronet. Don't you think that your master may be brought to that without having recourse to his calculations? Eh, Lovewell?

390

LOVEWELL. But, my Lord, that is not the question.

LORD OGLEBY. Whatever is the question, I'll tell you my answer. I am in love with a fine girl, whom I resolve to marry.

Enter Sir John Melvil.

What news with you, Sir John? You look all hurry and impatience —like a messenger after a battle.

SIR JOHN. After a battle, indeed, my Lord. I have this day had a severe engagement, and wanting your Lordship as an auxiliary, I have at last mustered up resolution to declare what my duty to you and to myself have demanded from me some time.

LORD OGLEBY. To the business then, and be as concise as possible; for

400

I am upon the wing—eh, Lovewell? (*He smiles, and Lovewell bows.*)

SIR JOHN. I find 'tis in vain, my Lord, to struggle against the force of inclination.

LORD OGLEBY. Very true, nephew. I am your witness and will second the motion—shan't I, Lovewell? (*Smiling and* Lovewell *bows.*)

SIR JOHN. Your Lordship's generosity encourages me to tell you— that I cannot marry Miss Sterling.

LORD OGLEBY. I am not at all surprised at it. She's a bitter potion, that's the truth of it; but as you were to swallow it and not I, it was your business and not mine. Anything more?

410

SIR JOHN. But this, my Lord—that I may be permitted to make my addresses to the other sister.

LORD OGLEBY. Oh, yes, by all means. Have you any hopes there, nephew? Do you think he'll succeed, Lovewell? (*Smiles and winks at* Lovewell *gravely.*)

LOVEWELL. I think not, my Lord.

LORD OGLEBY. I think so too, but let the fool try.

SIR JOHN. Will your Lordship favor me with your good offices to remove the chief obstacle to the match, the repugnance of Mrs. Heidelberg.

LORD OGLEBY. Mrs. Heidelberg! Had not you better begin with the young lady first? (*Conceitedly.*) It will save you a great deal of trouble, won't it, Lovewell?—Why don't you laugh at him?

LOVEWELL. I do, my Lord. (*Forces a smile.*)

SIR JOHN. And your Lordship will endeavor to prevail on Mrs. Heidelberg to consent to my marriage with Miss Fanny?

LORD OGLEBY. I'll go and speak to Mrs. Heidelberg about the adorable Fanny as soon as possible.

SIR JOHN. Your generosity transports me.

LORD OGLEBY (*aside*). Poor fellow, what a dupe! He little thinks who's in possession of the town.

SIR JOHN. And your Lordship is not offended at this seeming inconstancy?

LORD OGLEBY. Not in the least. Miss Fanny's charms will even excuse infidelity. I look upon women as the *ferae naturae*—lawful game—and every man who is qualified has a natural right to pursue them —Lovewell as well as you, and I as well as either of you. Every man shall do his best, without offence to any. What say you, kinsman?

SIR JOHN. You have made me happy, my Lord.

LOVEWELL. And me, I assure you, my Lord.

LORD OGLEBY. And I am superlatively so. Allons donc—to horse and away, boys! You to your affairs and I to mine. (*Sings.*) Suivons l'amour!

Exeunt severally.

ACT V. SCENE I.

Fanny's *apartment.*
Enter Lovewell *and* Fanny, *followed by* Betty.

FANNY. Why did you come so soon, Mr. Lovewell? The family is not yet in bed, and Betty certainly heard somebody listening near the chamber door.

BETTY. My mistress is right, sir! Evil spirits are abroad, and I am sure you are both too good not to expect mischief from them.

LOVEWELL. But who can be so curious, or so wicked?

BETTY. I think we have wickedness and curiosity enough in this family, sir, to expect the worst.

FANNY. I do expect the worst. Prithee, Betty, return to the outward
10   door and listen if you hear anybody in the gallery; and let us
        know directly.

BETTY. I warrant you, madam. The Lord bless you both.

Exit.

FANNY. What did my father want with you this evening?

LOVEWELL. He gave me the key of his closet, with orders to bring
        from London some papers relating to Lord Ogleby.

FANNY. And why did not you obey him?

LOVEWELL. Because I am certain that his Lordship has opened his
        heart to him about you, and those papers are wanted merely on
        that account. But as we shall discover all tomorrow, there will be
20   no occasion for them, and it would be idle in me to go.

FANNY. Hark!—hark! Bless me, how I tremble! I feel the terrors of
        guilt—indeed, Mr. Lovewell, this is too much for me.

LOVEWELL. And for me too, my sweet Fanny. Your apprehensions
        make a coward of me. But what can alarm you? Your aunt and
        sister are in their chambers, and you have nothing to fear from
        the rest of the family.

FANNY. I fear everybody, and every thing, and every moment. My
        mind is in continual agitation and dread; indeed, Mr. Lovewell,
        this situation may have very unhappy consequences. (*Weeps.*)

30 LOVEWELL. But it shan't—I would rather tell our story this moment
        to all the house and run the risk of maintaining you by the hardest
        labor, than suffer you to remain in this dangerous perplexity.
        What, shall I sacrifice all my best hopes and affections in your dear
        health and safety for the mean, and in such a case the meanest,
        consideration of our fortune? Were we to be abandoned by all
        our relations, we have that in our hearts and minds will weigh
        against the most affluent circumstances. I should not have proposed
        the secrecy of our marriage but for your sake, and with hopes
        that the most generous sacrifice you have made to love and me
40   might be less injurious to you by waiting a lucky moment of rec-
        onciliation.

FANNY. Hush! Hush! For heaven sake, my dear Lovewell, don't be
        so warm. Your generosity gets the better of your prudence; you
        will be heard, and we shall be discovered. I am satisfied, indeed I
        am. Excuse this weakness, this delicacy—this what you will. My
        mind's at peace—indeed it is; think no more of it, if you love me!

LOVEWELL. That one word has charmed me, as it always does, to the most implicit obedience; it would be the worst of ingratitude in me to distress you a moment. (*Kisses her.*)

Re-enter Betty.

50 BETTY (*in a low voice*). I'm sorry to disturb you.
FANNY. Ha, what's the matter?
LOVEWELL. Have you heard anybody?
BETTY. Yes, yes, I have, and they have heard *you* too, or I am mistaken. If they had *seen* you too, we should have been in a fine quandary.
FANNY. Prithee don't prate now, Betty!
LOVEWELL. What did you hear?
BETTY. I was preparing myself, as usual, to take me a little nap.
LOVEWELL. A nap!
60 BETTY. Yes, sir, a nap; for I watch much better so than wide awake. And when I had wrapped this handkerchief round my head, for fear of the earache, from the keyhole I thought I heard a kind of a sort of a buzzing, which I first took for a gnat, and shook my head two or three times and went so with my hand —
FANNY. Well, well, and so —
BETTY. And so, madam, then I heard Mr. Lovewell a little loud, I heard the buzzing louder to; and pulling off my handkerchief softly, I could hear this sort of noise — (*Makes an indistinct noise like speaking.*)
FANNY. Well, and what did they say?
70 BETTY. Oh, I could not understand a word of what was said.
LOVEWELL. The outward door is locked?
BETTY. Yes; and I bolted it too, for fear of the worst.
FANNY. Why did you? They must have heard you if they were near.
BETTY. And I did it on purpose, madam, and coughed a little, too, that they might not hear Mr. Lovewell's voice. When I was silent, they were silent, and so I came to tell you.
FANNY. What shall we do?
LOVEWELL. Fear nothing; we know the worst. It will only bring on our catastrophe a little too soon. But Betty might fancy this noise.
80 She's in the conspiracy and can make a man of a mouse at any time.
BETTY. I can distinguish a man from a mouse as well as my betters. I am sorry you think so ill of me, sir.
FANNY. He compliments you, don't be a fool! (*To* Lovewell.) Now you have set her tongue a-running, she'll mutter for an hour. I'll go and hearken myself.

Exit.

BETTY (*half aside, and muttering*).   I'll turn my back upon no girl for sincerity and service.

LOVEWELL.   Thou art the first in the world for both, and I will reward
90   you soon, Betty, for one and the other.

BETTY.   I'm not marcenary neither. I can live on a little with a good *carreter*.

Re-enter Fanny.

FANNY.   All seems quiet. Suppose, my dear, you go to your own room —I shall be much easier then—and tomorrow we will be prepared for the discovery.

BETTY (*half aside and muttering*).   You may discover, if you please, but for my part I shall still be secret.

LOVEWELL.   Should I leave you now, if they still are upon the watch we shall lose the advantage of our delay. Besides, we should con-
100   sult upon tomorrow's business. Let Betty go to her own room and lock the outward door after her. We can fasten this, and when she thinks all safe, she may return and let me out, as usual.

BETTY.   Shall I, madam?

FANNY.   Do! Let me have my way tonight, and you shall command me ever after. I would not have you surprized here for the world. Pray leave me! I shall be quite myself again if you will oblige me.

LOVEWELL.   I live only to oblige you, my sweet Fanny! I'll be gone this moment. (*Going.*)

FANNY.   Let us listen first at the door, that you may not be inter-
110   cepted. Betty shall go first, and if they lay hold of her —

BETTY.   They'll have the wrong sow by the ear, I can tell them that. (*Going hastily.*)

FANNY.   Softly, Betty! Don't venture out if you hear a noise. Softly, I beg of you! See, Mr. Lovewell, the effects of indiscretion!

LOVEWELL.   But love, Fanny, makes amends for all.

Exeunt all softly.

[SCENE II.]

SCENE *changes to a gallery which leads to several bedchambers.*
Enter Miss Sterling *leading* Mrs. Heidelberg *in a nightcap.*

MISS STERLING.   This way, dear madam, and then I'll tell you all.

---

91.   marcenary] *O*1, *O*2, *O*3, *O*4, *O*5, *O*6, *O*7, *O*8, *O*9, *D*2, *C*; mercenary *D*1, *W*1, *W*2.

MRS. HEIDELBERG. Nay, but niece, consider a little. Don't drag me out
in this figur. Let me put on my fly-cap! If any of my Lord's
fammaly or the councellors at law should be stirring, I should be
perdigus disconcarted.

MISS STERLING. But, my dear madam, a moment is an age in my situation. I am sure my sister has been plotting my disgrace and ruin
in that chamber. Oh, she's all craft and wickedness!

MRS. HEIDELBERG. Well, but softly, Betsey! You are all in emotion.
Your mind is too much flustrated; you can neither eat nor drink,
nor take your natural rest. Compose yourself, child; for if we are
not as warysome as they are wicked, we shall disgrace ourselves
and the whole fammaly.

MISS STERLING. We are disgraced already, madam. Sir John Melvil
has forsaken me; my Lord cares for nobody but himself—or, if
for anybody, it is my sister; my father, for the sake of a better
bargain, would marry me to a 'Change broker; so that if you,
madam, don't continue my friend—if you forsake me—if I am to
lose my best hopes and consolation—in your tenderness—and affect—ions—I had better—at once—give up the matter—and let my
sister enjoy—the fruits of her treachery—trample with scorn upon
the rights of her eldest sister, the will of the best of aunts, and the
weakness of a too interested father. (*She pretends to be bursting
into tears all this speech.*)

MRS. HEIDELBERG. Don't, Betsey—keep up your spurrit. I hate whim-
pering. I am your friend; depend upon me in every partickler, but
be composed and tell me what new mischief you have discovered.

MISS STERLING. I had no desire to sleep and would not undress myself,
knowing that my Machiavel sister would not rest till she had broke
my heart. I was so uneasy that I could not stay in my room, but
when I thought that all the house was quiet I sent my maid to discover what was going forward. She immediately came back and
told me that they were in high consultation; that she had heard only,
for it was in the dark, my sister's maid conduct Sir John Melvil to
her mistress and then lock the door.

MRS. HEIDELBERG. And how did you conduct yourself in this dalimma?

MISS STERLING. I returned with her and could hear a man's voice,
though nothing that they said distinctly; and you may depend
upon it that Sir John is now in that room, that they have settled
the matter and will run away together before morning if we don't
prevent them.

MRS. HEIDELBERG. Why, the brazen slut! Has she got her sister's hus-

---

3. figur] *O*1, *O*2, *O*3, *O*4, *O*5, *O*6, *O*7, *O*8, *O*9, *D*2, *W*1, *W*2, *C*; figure *D*1.

band that is to be locked up in her chamber? At night too! I tremble at the thoughts!

MISS STERLING.   Hush, madam. I hear something.

MRS. HEIDELBERG.   You frighten me! Let me put on my fly-cap; I
would not be seen in this figur for the world.

MISS STERLING.   'Tis dark, madam. You can't be seen.

MRS. HEIDELBERG.   I protest there's a candle coming, and a man too.

50   MISS STERLING.   Nothing but servants; let us retire a moment.

They retire.

Enter Brush *half drunk, laying hold of the*
Chambermaid, *who has a candle in her hand.*

CHAMBERMAID.   Be quiet, Mr. Brush; I shall drop down with terror!

BRUSH.   But my sweet and most amiable chambermaid, if you have no
love, you may hearken to a little reason; that cannot possibly do
your virtue any harm.

CHAMBERMAID.   But you will do me harm, Mr. Brush, and a great deal
of harm too. Pray let me go. I am ruined if they hear you. I tremble like an asp.

BRUSH.   But they shan't hear us. And if you have a mind to be ruined,
it shall be the making of your fortune, you little slut, you! There-

60   fore I say it again, if you have no love, hear a little reason!

CHAMBERMAID.   I wonder at your impudence, Mr. Brush, to use me in
this manner; this is not the way to keep me company, I assure you.
You are a town rake, I see, and now you are a little in liquor, you
fear nothing.

BRUSH.   Nothing, by heavens, but your frowns, most amiable chambermaid; I am a little electrified, that's the truth on't. I am not used
to drink port, and your master's is so heady that a pint of it over-
sets a claret-drinker.

CHAMBERMAID.   Don't be rude! Bless me, I shall be ruined! What will

70   become of me?

BRUSH.   I'll take care of you, by all that's honorable.

CHAMBERMAID.   You are a base man to use me so. I'll cry out if you
don't let me go. (*Pointing.*) That is Miss Sterling's chamber, that
Miss Fanny's, and that Madam Heidelberg's.

BRUSH.   And that my Lord Ogleby's, and that my Lady what d'ye
call 'em. I don't mind such folks when I'm sober, much less when
I am whimsical—rather above that, too.

CHAMBERMAID.   More shame for you, Mr. Brush! You terrify me. You
have no modesty.

---

49.   protest] *O*1, *O*2, *O*4, *O*5, *O*7, *O*8, *O*9, *D*1, *D*2; pertest *O*3, *O*6, *W*1, *W*2, *C.*

80 BRUSH.   Oh, but I have, my sweet spider-brusher! For instance, I reverence Miss Fanny; she's a most delicious morsel and fit for a prince. With all my horrors of matrimony, I could marry her myself; but for her sister —

MISS STERLING.   There, there, madam, all in a story!

CHAMBERMAID.   Bless me, Mr. Brush, I heard something!

BRUSH.   Rats, I suppose, that are gnawing the old timbers of this execrable old dungeon. If it was mine I would pull it down and fill your fine canal with the rubbish, and then I should get rid of two damned things at once.

90 CHAMBERMAID.   Law, law, how you blaspheme! We shall have the house upon our heads for it.

BRUSH.   No, no it will last our time. But as I was saying, the eldest sister, Miss Jezabel —

CHAMBERMAID.   Is a fine young lady, for all your evil tongue.

BRUSH.   No, we have smoked her already; and unless she marries our old Swiss, she can have none of us. No, no, she won't do; we are a little too nice.

CHAMBERMAID.   You're a monstrous rake, Mr. Brush, and don't care what you say.

100 BRUSH.   Why, for that matter, my dear, I am a little inclined to mischief; and if you won't have pity upon me, I will break open that door and ravish Mrs. Heidelberg.

MRS. HEIDELBERG (*coming forward*).   There's no bearing this, you profligate monster!

CHAMBERMAID.   Ha! I am undone!

BRUSH.   Zounds! Here she is, by all that's monstrous.

Runs off.

MISS STERLING.   A fine discourse you have had with that fellow!

MRS. HEIDELBERG.   And a fine time of night it is to be here with that drunken monster.

110 MISS STERLING.   What have you to say for yourself?

CHAMBERMAID.   I can say nothing. I am so frightened, and so ashamed— but indeed I am vartuous; I am vartuous indeed.

MRS. HEIDELBERG.   Well, well, don't tremble so, but tell us what you know of this horrable plot here.

MISS STERLING.   We'll forgive you if you'll discover all.

CHAMBERMAID.   Why, madam, don't let me betray my fellow servants. I shan't sleep in my bed if I do.

---

86. Rats, I suppose] O1, O2, O3, O4, O5, O6, O7, O8, O9, D1, D2, W1, W2; Rats! Rats, I suppose C.

MRS. HEIDELBERG. Then you shall sleep somewhere else tomorrow night.

120 CHAMBERMAID. Oh, dear! What shall I do?

MRS. HEIDELBERG. Tell us this moment, or I'll turn you out of door directly.

CHAMBERMAID. Why, our butler has been treating us below in his pantry—Mr. Brush forced us to make a kind of a holiday night of it.

MISS STERLING. Holiday? For what?

CHAMBERMAID. Nay, I only made one.

MISS STERLING. Well, well, but upon what account?

CHAMBERMAID. Because as how, madam, there was a change in the
130 family, they said—that his honor, Sir John, was to marry Miss Fanny instead of your Ladyship.

MISS STERLING. And so you made a holiday for that. Very fine!

CHAMBERMAID. I did not make it, ma'am.

MRS. HEIDELBERG. But do you know nothing of Sir John's being to run away with Miss Fanny tonight?

CHAMBERMAID. No indeed, ma'am.

MISS STERLING. Not of his being now locked up in my sister's chamber?

CHAMBERMAID. No, as I hope for marcy, ma'am.

MRS. HEIDELBERG. Well, I'll put an end to all this directly. Do you run
140 to my brother Sterling —

CHAMBERMAID. Now, ma'am? 'Tis so very late, ma'am —

MRS. HEIDELBERG. I don't care how late it is. Tell him there are thieves in the house—that the house is o'fire. Tell him to come here immediately. Go, I say!

CHAMBERMAID. I will, I will, though I am frightened out of my wits.

MRS. HEIDELBERG. Do you watch here, my dear, and I'll put myself in order, to face them. We'll plot 'em, and counter-plot 'em too.

Exit into her chamber.

MISS STERLING. I have as much pleasure in this revenge as in being made a countess! Ha, they are unlocking the door. Now for it.

Retires.

Fanny's *door is unlocked and* Betty *comes
out with a candle.* Miss Sterling *approaches her.*

150 BETTY (*calling within*). Sir, sir, now's your time—all's clear. (*Seeing* Miss Sterling.) Stay, stay—not yet. We are watched.

MISS STERLING. And so you are, Madam Betty!

---

134. MRS. HEIDELBERG] Miss *O6.*

Miss Sterling *lays hold of her while* Betty
locks the door and puts the key into her pocket.

BETTY (*turning round*). What's the matter, madam?

MISS STERLING. Nay, that you shall tell my father and aunt, madam.

BETTY. I am no tell-tale, madam, and no thief; they'll get nothing
from me.

MISS STERLING. You have a great deal of courage, Betty; and considering the secrets you have to keep, you have occasion for it.

BETTY. My mistress shall never repent her good opinion of me, ma'am.

Enter Sterling.

160 STERLING. What is all this? What's the matter? Why am I disturbed
in this manner?

MISS STERLING. This creature, and my distresses, sir, will explain the
matter.

Re-enter Mrs. Heidelberg, *with another headdress.*

MRS. HEIDELBERG. Now I am prepared for the rancounter. Well,
brother, have you heard of this scene of wickedness?

STERLING. Not I—but what is it? Speak! I was got into my little closet
—all the lawyers were in bed—and I had almost lost my senses in
the confusion of Lord Ogleby's mortgages when I was alarmed
with a foolish girl who could hardly speak; and whether it's fire,
170 or thieves, or murder, or a rape I am quite in the dark.

MRS. HEIDELBERG. No, no, there's no rape, brother! All parties are
willing, I believe.

MISS STERLING. (*Detaining* Betty, *who seemed to be stealing away.*)
Who's in that chamber?

BETTY. My mistress.

MISS STERLING. And who's with your mistress?

BETTY. Why, who should there be?

MISS STERLING. Open the door, then, and let us see.

BETTY. The door is open, madam. (Miss Sterling *goes to the door.*)
I'll sooner die than peach!

Exit hastily.

180 MISS STERLING. The door's locked, and she has got the key in her
pocket.

MRS. HEIDELBERG. There's impudence, brother, piping hot from your
daughter Fanny's school!

---

164. rancounter] *O*1, *O*2, *O*3, *O*4, *O*5, *O*6, *O*7, *O*8, *O*9, *D*2, *W*1, *W*2, *C*; rencounter *D*1.

STERLING. But, zounds! what is all this about? You tell me of a sum total, and you don't produce the particulars.

MBS. HEIDELBERG. Sir John Melvil is locked up in your daughter's bed-chamber. There is the particular!

STERLING. The devil he is? That's bad!

MISS STERLING. And he has been there some time too.

190 STERLING. Ditto!

MRS. HEIDELBERG. Ditto! Worse and worse, I say, I'll raise the house and expose him to my Lord and the whole family.

STERLING. By no means! We shall expose ourselves, sister! The best way is to insure privately—let me alone! I'll make him marry her tomorrow morning.

MISS STERLING. Make him marry her? This is beyond all patience! You have thrown away all your affection, and I shall do as much by my obedience. Unnatural fathers make unnatural children. My revenge is in my own power, and I'll indulge it. Had they made

200 their escape, I should have been exposed to the derision of the world—but the deriders shall be derided; and so—help! help, there! thieves! thieves!

MRS. HEIDELBERG. Tit-for-tat, Betsey! You are right, my girl.

STERLING. Zounds! You'll spoil all; you'll raise the whole family. The devil's in the girl.

MRS. HEIDELBERG. No, no, the devil's in *you*, brother. I am ashamed of your principles. What, would you connive at your daughter's being locked up with her sister's husband? (*Cries out.*) Help! thieves, thieves, I say!

210 STERLING. Sister, I beg you!—daughter, I command you. If you have no regard for me, consider yourselves! We shall lose this opportunity of ennobling our blood and getting above twenty percent for our money.

MISS STERLING. What, by my disgrace and my sister's triumph? I have a spirit above such mean considerations; and to show you that it is not a low-bred, vulgar 'Change Alley spirit—help! help! thieves! thieves! thieves, I say!

STERLING. Ay, ay, you may save your lungs—the house is in an up-roar. Women at best have no discretion, but in a passion they'll

220 fire a house, or burn themselves in it, rather than not be revenged.

Enter Canton *in a nightgown and slippers.*

CANTON. Eh, diable! Vat is de raison of dis great noise, this tintamarre?

STERLING. Ask those ladies, sir; 'tis of their making.

---

192.   family] *O*1, *O*2, *O*4, *O*5, *O*7, *D*1, *D*2; fammaly *O*3, *O*6, *O*8, *O*9, *W*1, *W*2, C.

LORD OGLEBY (*calls within*). Brush! Brush! Canton, where are you? What's the matter? (*Rings a bell.*) Where are you?
STERLING. 'Tis my Lord calls, Mr. Canton.
CANTON. I com, mi Lor!

Exit Canton.

Lord Ogleby *still rings.*

FLOWER (*calls within*). A light! A light here! Where are the servants? Bring a light for me and my brothers.
STERLING. Lights here! Lights for the gentlemen!

Exit Sterling.

230 MRS. HEIDELBERG. My brother feels, I see—your sister's turn will come next.
MISS STERLING. Ay, ay, let it go round, madam; it is the only comfort I have left.

Re-enter Sterling *with lights, before* Serjeant
Flower (*with one boot and a slipper*) *and* Traverse.

STERLING. This way, sir; this way, gentlemen.
FLOWER. Well, but Mr. Sterling, no danger, I hope. Have they made a burglarious entry? Are you prepared to repulse them? I am very much alarmed about thieves at circuit-time. They would be particularly severe with us gentlemen of the bar.
TRAVERSE. No danger, Mr. Sterling? No trespass, I hope?
240 STERLING. None, gentlemen, but of those ladies making.
MRS. HEIDELBERG. You'll be ashamed to know, gentlemen, that all your labors and studies about this young lady are thrown away. Sir John Melvil is at this moment locked up with this lady's younger sister.
FLOWER. The thing is a little extraordinary, to be sure, but why were we to be frightened out of our beds for this? Could not we have tried this cause tomorrow morning?
MISS STERLING. But, sir, by tomorrow morning perhaps even your assistance would not have been of any service. The birds now in
250 that cage would have flown away.

Enter Lord Ogleby *in his robe de chambre, nightcap,*
etc., leaning on Canton.

LORD OGLEBY. I had rather lose a limb than my night's rest. What's the matter with you all?

---

240. ladies] O1, O2, O3, O4, O5, O6, O7, O8, O9, D1, D2, W1, W2; ladies' C.

STERLING. Ay, ay, 'tis all over! Here's my Lord too.

LORD OGLEBY. What's all this shrieking and screaming? Where's my angelick Fanny? She's safe, I hope.

MRS. HEIDELBERG. Your angelick Fanny, my Lord, is locked up with your angelick nephew in that chamber.

LORD OGLEBY. My nephew! Then will I be excommunicated.

MRS. HEIDELBERG. Your nephew, my Lord, has been plotting to run
260   away with the younger sister; and the younger sister has been plotting to run away with your nephew; and if we had not watched them and called up the fammaly, they had been upon the scamper to Scotland by this time.

LORD OGLEBY. Look'ee, ladies, I know that Sir John had conceived a violent passion for Miss Fanny; and I know too that Miss Fanny has conceived a violent passion for another person; and I'm so well convinced of the rectitude of her affections that I will support them with my fortune, my honor, and my life. Eh, shan't I, Mr. Sterling? (*Smiling.*) What say you?

270   STERLING (*sulkily*). To be sure, my Lord. (*Aside.*) The bawling women have been the ruin of everything.

LORD OGLEBY. But come, I'll end this business in a trice. If you ladies will compose yourselves and Mr. Sterling will insure Miss Fanny from violence, I will engage to draw her from her pillow with a whisper through the keyhole.

MRS. HEIDELBERG. The horrid creatures! I say, my Lord, break the door open.

LORD OGLEBY. Let me beg of your delicacy not to be too precipitate! Now to our experiment! (*Advancing towards the door.*)

280   MISS STERLING. Now what will they do? My heart will beat thro' my bosom.

Enter Betty *with the key.*

BETTY. There's no occasion for breaking open doors, my Lord; we have done nothing that we ought to be ashamed of, and my mistress shall face her enemies. (*Going to unlock the door.*)

MRS. HEIDELBERG. There's impudence.

LORD OGLEBY. The mystery thickens. (*To* Betty.) Lady of the bed chamber, open the door and intreat Sir John Melvil—for these ladies will have it that he is there—to appear and answer to high crimes and misdemeanors. Call Sir John Melvil into the court!

Enter Sir John Melvil *on the other side.*

255-57. angelick] *O*1, *O*2, *O*4, *O*5, *O*7, *O*8, *O*9, *D*1, *D*2, *C*; angelic *O*3, *O*6, *W*1, *W*2.

290   SIR JOHN.   I am here, my Lord.

MRS. HEIDELBERG.   Heyday!

MISS STERLING.   Astonishment!

SIR JOHN.   What is all this alarm and confusion? There is nothing but hurry in the house. What is the reason of it?

LORD OGLEBY.   Because you have been in that chamber—*have* been? Nay, you *are* there at this moment, as these ladies have protested, so don't deny it.

TRAVERSE.   This is the clearest *alibi* I ever knew, Mr. Serjeant.

FLOWER.   *Luce clarius.*

300   LORD OGLEBY.   Upon my word, ladies, if you have often these frolics it would be really entertaining to pass a whole summer with you. But come (*to* Betty), open the door and intreat your amiable mistress to come forth and dispel all our doubts with her smiles.

BETTY (*opening the door pertly*).   Madam, you are wanted in this room.

Enter Fanny *in great confusion.*

MISS STERLING.   You see she's ready dressed—and what confusion she's in.

MRS. HEIDELBERG.   Ready to pack off, bag and baggage! Her guilt confounds her!

310   FLOWER.   Silence in the court, ladies!

FANNY.   I *am* confounded, indeed, madam.

LORD OGLEBY.   Don't droop, my beauteous lilly, but with your own peculiar modesty declare your state of mind. Pour conviction into their ears and raptures into mine. (*Smiling.*)

FANNY.   I am at this moment the most unhappy—most distrest—the tumult is too much for my heart—and I want the power to reveal a secret, which to conceal has been the misfortune and misery of my—my — (*Faints away.*)

LORD OGLEBY.   She faints! Help, help, for the

320   fairest, and best of women!

BETTY (*running to her*).   Oh, my dear mistress! Help, help, there!

SIR JOHN.   Ha! let me fly to her assistance.

(*Speaking all at once.*)

Lovewell *rushes out from the chamber.*

LOVEWELL.   My Fanny in danger! I can contain no longer. Prudence were now a crime; all other cares are lost in this! Speak, speak to me, my dearest Fanny! Let me but hear thy voice; open your eyes and bless me with the smallest sign of life. (*During this speech they are all in amazement.*)

MISS STERLING. Lovewell!—I am easy.

MRS. HEIDELBERG. I am thunderstruck!

330 LORD OGLEBY. I am petrified!

SIR JOHN. And I undone!

FANNY (*recovering*). O Lovewell!—even supported by thee I dare not look my father nor his Lordship in the face.

STERLING. What now! did not I send you to London, sir?

LORD OGLEBY. Eh!—What?—How's this? By what right and title have you been half the night in that lady's bedchamber?

LOVEWELL. By that right that makes me the happiest of men, and by a title which I would not forego for any the best of kings could give me.

340 BETTY. I could cry my eyes out to hear his magnimity.

LORD OGLEBY. I am annihilated!

STERLING. I have been choked with rage and wonder; but now I can speak. Zounds! what have you to say to me? Lovewell, you are a villain. You have broke your word with me.

FANNY. Indeed, sir, he has not. You forbade him to think of me when it was out of his power to obey you; we have been married these four months.

STERLING. And he shan't stay in the house four hours. What baseness and treachery! As for you, you shall repent this step as long as
350 you live, madam.

FANNY. Indeed, sir, it is impossible to conceive the tortures I have already endured in consequence of my disobedience. My heart has continually upbraided me for it; and tho' I was too weak to struggle with affection, I feel that I must be miserable forever without your forgiveness.

STERLING. Lovewell, you shall leave my house directly; (*to* Fanny.) and you shall follow him, madam.

LORD OGLEBY. And if they do, I will receive them into mine. Look ye, Mr. Sterling, there have been some mistakes which we had all bet-
360 ter forget for our own sakes; and the best way to forget them is to forgive the cause of them, which I do from my soul. Poor girl! I swore to support her affection with my life and fortune; 'tis a debt of honor and must be paid. You swore as much too, Mr. Sterling; but your laws in the city will excuse *you*, I suppose, for you never strike a ballance without errors excepted.

STERLING. I am a father, my Lord; but for the sake of all other fathers I think I ought not to forgive her, for fear of encouraging other

---

365. ballance] O1, O2, O4, O5, D1, D2; balance O3, O6, O7, O8, O9, W1, W2, C.

silly girls like herself to throw themselves away without the consent of their parents.

370 LOVEWELL. I hope there will be no danger of that, sir. Young ladies with minds like my Fanny's would startle at the very shadow of vice; and when they know to what uneasiness only an indiscretion has exposed her, her example, instead of encouraging, will rather serve to deter them.

MRS. HEIDELBERG. Indiscretion, quoth a! A mighty pretty delicat word to express disobedience!

LORD OGLEBY. For my part, I indulge my own passions too much to tyrannize over those of other people. Poor souls, I pity them. And you must forgive them too. Come, come, melt a little of your flint,
380 Mr. Sterling.

STERLING. Why, why—as to that, my Lord—to be sure he is a relation of yours, my Lord—what say *you*, sister Heidelberg?

MRS. HEIDELBERG. The girl's ruined, and I forgive her.

STERLING. Well—so do I then. (*To* Lovewell *and* Fanny, *who seem preparing to speak.*) Nay, no thanks. There's an end of the matter.

LORD OGLEBY. But, Lovewell, what makes you dumb all this while?

LOVEWELL. Your kindness, my Lord. I can scarce believe my own senses; they are all in a tumult of fear, joy, love, expectation, and gratitude. I ever was and am now more bound in duty to your
390 Lordship. For you, Mr. Sterling, if every moment of my life spent gratefully in your service will in some measure compensate the want of fortune, you perhaps will not repent your goodness to me. And you, ladies, I flatter myself, will not for the future suspect me of artifice and intrigue. I shall be happy to oblige and serve you. As for you, Sir John —

SIR JOHN. No apologies to me, Lovewell; I do not deserve any. All I have to offer in excuse for what has happened is my total ignorance of your situation. Had you dealt a little more openly with me, you would have saved me and yourself and that lady—who
400 I hope will pardon my behavior—a great deal of uneasiness. Give me leave, however, to assure you that, light and capricious as I may have appeared, now my infatuation is over, I have sensibility enough to be ashamed of the part I have acted and honor enough to rejoice at your happiness.

LOVEWELL. And now, my dearest Fanny, though we are seemingly the happiest of beings, yet our joys will be dampt if his Lordship's

---

375. delicat] *O*1, *O*2, *O*4, *O*5, *O*7, *O*8, *O*9, *D*1, *D*2, *C*; delicate *O*3, *O*6, *W*1, *W*2.

generosity and Mr. Sterling's forgiveness should not be succeeded (*to the audience*) by the indulgence, approbation, and consent of these our best benefactors.

Finis

Epilogue

Written by Mr. Garrick.

CHARACTERS of the EPILOGUE.

LORD MINUM	Mr. *Dodd*
COLONEL TRILL	Mr. *Vernon*
SIR PATRICK MAHONY	Mr. *Moody*
MISS CROTCHET	Mrs. [*Abington*]
MRS. QUAVER	Mrs. *Lee*
FIRST LADY	Miss *Bradshaw*
SECOND LADY	Miss *Mills*
THIRD LADY	Miss *Dorman*

SCENE, *an assembly.*

*Several persons at cards, at different tables; among
the rest* Colonel Trill, Lord Minum, Mrs. Quaver, Sir
Patrick Mahony.
At the Quadrille table.

COL. TRILL. Ladies, with leave —
SECOND LADY.   Pass!
THIRD LADY.   Pass!
MRS. QUAVER.   You must do more.
COL. TRILL. Indeed I can't.
MRS. QUAVER.   I play in hearts.
COL. TRILL.   Encore!
SECOND LADY. What luck!
COL. TRILL.   Tonight at Drury Lane is played

---

4. Mrs. ——] All editions except *C*; Mrs. Abington *C*.

10   A comedy, and *toute nouvelle*–a spade!
      Is not Miss Crotchet at the play?
MRS. QUILL.   My niece
      Has made a party, sir, to damn the piece.

                  At the Whist table.

LORD MINUM.   I hate a playhouse–Trump! It makes me sick.
FIRST LADY.   We're two by honors, ma'am.
LORD MINUM.   And we the odd trick.
      Pray do you know the author, Colonel Trill?
COL. TRILL.   I know no poets, Heav'n be praised!–spadille!
FIRST LADY.   I'll tell you who, my Lord! (*Whispers my Lord.*)
20 LORD MINUM.   What, he again?
      "And dwell such daring souls in little men?"
      Be whose it will, they down our throats will cram it!
COL. TRILL.   Oh, no–I have a club–the best. We'll damn it.
MRS. QUAVER.   O bravo, Colonel! Music is my flame.
LORD MINUM.   And mine, by Jupiter! We've won the game.
COLONEL TRILL.   What, do you love all music?
MRS. QUAVER.   No, not Handel's
      And nasty plays –
LORD MINUM.   Are fit for Goths and Vandals.
                        (*Rise from the table, and pay.*)

            From the Picquette table.

30 SIR PATRICK.   Well, faith and troth! that Shakespeare was no fool!
COL. TRILL.   I'm glad you like him, sir! So ends the pool!
                        (*Pay and rise from the table.*)

            SONG *by the* Colonel.

            I hate all their nonsense.
            Their Shakespeares and Johnsons,
      Their plays and their playhouse and bards!
            'Tis singing, not saying;
            A fig for all playing
      But playing, as we do, at cards!
            I love to see Jonas,
            Am pleased too with Comus;
40   Each well the spectator rewards.
            So clever, so neat in
            Their tricks and their cheating!
      Like them we would fain deal our cards.

---

33. Johnsons] All editions except *C*; Jonsons *C*.

SIR PATRICK.

    King Lare is touching!—And how fine to see
    Ould Hamlet's Ghost! "To be, or not to be."
    What are your op'ras to Othello's roar?
    Oh, he's an angel of a Blackamoor!

LORD MINUM. What, when he chokes his wife?

COL. TRILL.   And calls her whore?

SIR PATRICK.

50   King Richard calls his horse—and then Macbeth,
    Whene'er he murders, takes away the breath.
    My blood runs cold at every syllable
    To see the dagger—that's invisible. (*All laugh.*)

SIR PATRICK. Laugh if you please, a pretty play —

LORD MINUM.   Is pretty,

SIR PATRICK. And when there's wit in't —

COL. TRILL.   To be sure, 'tis witty.

SIR PATRICK.

    I love the playhouse now, so light and gay,
    With all those candles they have ta'en away! (*All laugh.*)

60   For all your game, what makes it so much brighter?

COL. TRILL. Put out the light, and then —

LORD MINUM.   'Tis so much lighter.

SIR PATRICK. Pray do you mane, sirs, more than you express?

COL. TRILL. Just as it happens —

LORD MINUM.   Either more, or less.

MRS. QUAVER (*to* Sir Patrick). An't you ashamed, sir?

SIR PATRICK.   Me? I seldom blush.

    For little Shakespear, faith! I'd take a push!

LORD MINUM. News! news! Here comes Miss Crotchet from the play.

Enter Miss Crotchet.

70 MRS. QUAVER. Well, Crotchet, what's the news?

MISS CROTCHET.   We've lost the day.

COL. TRILL. Tell us, dear Miss, all you have heard and seen.

MISS CROTCHET. I'm tired—a chair—here, take my capuchin!

LORD MINUM. And isn't it damned, Miss?

MISS CROTCHET.   No, my lord, not quite.

    But we shall damn it.

COL. TRILL.   When?

MISS CROTCHET.   Tomorrow night.

    There is a party of us, all of fashion,

80   Resolved to exterminate this vulgar passion.
    A playhouse, what a place! I must forswear it.

A little mischief only makes one bear it.
Such crowds of city folks! So rude and pressing!
And their horse-laughs, so hideously distressing!
When e'er we hissed, they frowned and fell a swearing
Like their own Guildhall giants—fierce and staring!
COL. TRILL. What said the folks of fashion? Were they cross?
LORD MINUM. The rest have no more judgment than my horse.
MISS CROTCHET.
Lord Grimly swore 'twas execrable stuff.
90   Says one. Why so, my Lord?—My Lord took snuff.
In the first act Lord George began to doze
And criticized the author through his nose;
So loud indeed that as his Lordship snored
The pit turned round, and all the brutes encored.
Some Lords, indeed, approved the author's jokes.
LORD MINUM. We have among us, miss, *some* foolish folks.
MISS CROTCHET.
Says poor Lord Simper, well, now, to my mind
The piece is good—but he's both deaf and blind.
SIR PATRICK.
Upon my soul a very pretty story!
100   And Quality appears in all its glory!
There was some merit in the piece, no doubt.
MISS CROTCHET. Oh, to be sure! if one could find it out.
COL. TRILL. But tell us, miss, the subject of the play.
MISS CROTCHET.
Why, 'twas a marriage—yes, a marriage—stay!
A Lord, an aunt, two sisters, and a merchant.
A baronet—ten lawyers—a fat serjeant
Are all produced to talk with one another
And about something make a mighty pother.
They all go in, and out, and to, and fro,
110   And talk, and quarrel—as they come and go —
Then go to bed, and then get up—and then —
Scream, faint, scold, kiss—and go to bed again. (*All laugh.*)
Such is the play. Your judgment? Never sham it.
COL. TRILL. O damn it!
MRS. QUAVER.   Damn it!
FIRST LADY.   Damn it!
MISS CROTCHET.   Damn it!
LORD MINUM.   Damn it!
SIR PATRICK.
Well, faith, you speak your minds, and I'll be free —

120   Goodnight; this company's too good for me. (*Going.*)

COL. TRILL.   Your judgment, dear Sir Patrick, makes us proud.
(*All laugh.*)

SIR PATRICK.   Laugh if you please, but pray don't laugh too loud.

Exit.

RECITATIVE.

COL. TRILL.

Now the barbarian's gone, miss, tune your tongue,
And let us raise our spirits high with song.

RECITATIVE.

MISS CROTCHET.

Colonel, *de tout mon coer*—I've one *in petto*
Which you shall join, and make it a *duetto.*

RECITATIVE.

LORD MINUM.

Bella signora, et amico mio!
I too will join, and then we'll make a *trio.*

COL. TRILL.

Come all and join the full mouthed chorus,
130   And drive all tragedy and comedy before us!

*All the company rise, and advance to the front of
the stage.*

AIR.

COL. TRILL.   Would you ever go to see a tragedy?

MISS CROTCHET.   Never, never.

COL. TRILL.   A comedy?

LORD MINUM.

Never, never.
Live forever!
Tweedle-dum and Tweedle-dee!

COL. TRILL, LORD MINUM, *and* MISS CROTCHET.

Live for ever
Tweedle-dum and Tweedle-dee!

CHORUS

Would you ever go to see, &c.

FINIS.

Neck or Nothing
A Farce
1766

NECK or NOTHING,

A FARCE.

IN TWO ACTS.

AS IT IS PERFORMED AT THE

THEATRE ROYAL

IN DRURY-LANE.

LONDON:

Printed for T. Becket and Co. near Surry-Street, in the Strand. MDCCLXVI.

[Price One Shilling.]

Advertisement

The author of the following piece will claim no merit that
does not belong to him.—He therefore takes this opportunity
of acknowledging his obligation to the celebrated author of
Gil Blas.—Trifling as it is, the following farce is an imitation of
the *Crispin Rival de Son Maitre* of Le Sage.

Dramatis Personae

Neck or Nothing

ACT I. [Scene I.]

SCENE, *a street.*

Enter Martin.

MARTIN. I am sick as a dog of being a valet, running after other people's business and neglecting my own. This low life is the devil! I've had a taste of the gentleman and shall never lose it. 'Tis thy own fault, my little Martin. Thou would'st always play small games, when, had you but had the face to put yourself forward a little, some well jointured widow had taken you into her post-chariot and made your fortune at once. A fellow of my wit and spirit should have broke twice and set up again by this time.

Enter Slip.

SLIP. Hey, is not that that rascal, Martin, yonder?

10 MARTIN (*aside*). Can that be my modest friend, Slip?

SLIP. The same, i'faith!

MARTIN. 'Tis he, as I live!

SLIP. My friend, happily met.

MARTIN. My dear, I embrace you! Not seeing you among the beau-monde, I was afraid there had been some fresh misunderstanding between you and the law.

SLIP. Faith, my dear, I have had a narrow escape since I saw you. I had like to have been preferred in some of our settlements abroad, but I found there was no doing the business by deputy—so —

20 MARTIN. Did not accept of the place, ha! Why, what little mischief had'st thou been at?

SLIP. Why, I don't know. Meeting one night with a certain Portuguese Jew-merchant in one of the back streets here by the Exchange (I

14–15. beau-monde] *O1, O2, O3, D2*; beau-mode *D1*.

was a little in liquor, I believe—piping hot from a turtle-feast), it came into my giddy head to stop him out of mere curiosity to ask what news from Germany—nothing more—and the fellow, not understanding good English, would needs have it that I asked him for something else. He bawled out, up came the watch, down was I laid in the kennel and then carried before a magistrate. He clapped
30 me on a stone-doublet that I cou'd not get off my back for two months.

MARTIN.   Two months, say you?

SLIP.   And there I might have rotted, if I had not had great friends. A certain lady of quality's woman's cousin, that was kept by Mr. Quirk, of Thavies-Inn, you must know, was in love with me, and she —

MARTIN.   Brought you in not guilty, I warrant. Oh, great friends is a great matter.

SLIP.   This affair really gave me some serious reflections.

40 MARTIN.   No doubt it spoiled you for a news-monger. No more intelligence from foreign countries, ha!

SLIP.   Well but, Martin, what's thy history since I saw thee?

MARTIN.   Um—a novel only, sir. Why, I am ashamed to say it; I am but an honorary rascal, as well as yourself. I did try my luck indeed at Epsom and Newmarket; but the knowing ones were taken in, and I was obliged to return to service again. But a master without money implies a servant without wages; I am not in love with my condition, I promise you.

SLIP.   I am with mine, I assure you. I am retired from the great world—
50 that's my taste now—and live in the country with one Mr. Harlowe, piping hot from his travels. 'Tis a charming young fellow. Drinking, hunting, and wenching, my boy—a man of universal knowledge. Then I am his privy counsellor, and we always play the devil together. That amuses one, you know, and keeps one out of mischief.

MARTIN.   Yes, pretty lambs! But what makes you at London now? Whither are you bound?

SLIP.   To yonder great house.

MARTIN.   What, Mr. Stockwell's?

60 SLIP.   The same. You must know his daughter is engaged to my master.

MARTIN.   Miss Stockwell to your master?

SLIP.   'Tis not above six weeks ago that my master's father, Sir Henry Harlowe, was here upon a visit to his old friend, and then the matter was settled between 'em—quite a-la-mode, I assure you.

MARTIN.   How do you mean?

51. 'Tis] *O*1, *O*2, *O*3, *D*2; He's *D*1.

Mr. Palmer.

ighton Pinx   *R.Laurie S.*

blishd as the Act Directs, July 10. 1779   *by W. Richardson Nº 68 High Holbo*

John Palmer in *Neck or Nothing*.
Engraving by R. Lawrie, after Dighton.
Harvard Theatre Collection

SLIP. The old folk struck the bargain without the consent of the young ones, or even their seeing one another.

MARTIN. Tip top, I assure you; and everything's agreed?

SLIP. Signed and sealed by the two fathers; the lady and her fortune
70 both ready to be delivered. Twenty thousand, you rogue, ready rhino down, and only wait for young master to write a receipt.

MARTIN. Whew! Then my young master may e'en make a leg to his fortune and set up his staff somewhere else.

SLIP. Thy master!

MARTIN. Ay, he's dying for the twenty thousand, that's all; but since your master — *Going.*

SLIP. Oh, there you're safe enough. My master will never marry Miss Stockwell; there happens to be a small rub in the way.

MARTIN. What rub?

80 SLIP. Only married already.

MARTIN. How!

SLIP. Why, his father would marry him here in town, it seems, and he chose to be married in the country, that's all. The truth is, our young gentleman managed matters with the young lady so ill—or so well—that upon his father's return there was hot consulting among the relations; and the lady being of a good family, and having a smart, fighting fellow of a brother in the army—why, my master, who hates quarrelling, spoke to the old gentleman, and the affair's hushed up by a marriage, that's all.

90 MARTIN. Um, an entire new face of affairs!

SLIP. My master's wedding-clothes, and mine, are all ordered for the country, and I am to follow them as soon as I have seen the family here and redeemed my old master's promise, that lies in pawn.

MARTIN. Old master's promise? Let me think —

SLIP. 'Twas what brought me to town, or I had not shook my honest friend by the fist. Martin, good morrow! What, in the dumps? We shall meet again, man.

MARTIN. Let me alone. I have a thought—hark you, my dear, is thy master known to old Stockwell?

100 SLIP. Never saw him in his life.

MARTIN. That's brave, my boy! (*Hits him a slap on the back.*) Art thou still a cock of the game, Slip? And shall we—no, I doubt—I doubt that damned Jew-merchant sticks in thy stomach and you are turned dunghill, you dog!

SLIP. Try me. A good sailor won't die a dry death at land for one hurricane. Speak out. You would pass your master upon the family for mine and marry him to the lady? Is not that the trick?

MARTIN. That! I have a trick worth two on't; I know Miss Nancy is a girl of taste, and I have a prettier fellow in my eye for her.

110 SLIP.   Ay, who's he?

MARTIN.   Myself, you puppy.

SLIP.   That's brave, my boy! (*Slaps him on the back.*)

MARTIN.   I'm in love with her to —

SLIP.   To the value of twenty thousand pounds. I approve your flame.

MARTIN.   I will take the name and shape of your master.

SLIP.   Very well!

MARTIN.   Marry Miss Stockwell —

SLIP.   Agreed.

MARTIN.   Touch the twenty thousand —

120 SLIP.   Um! Well, well!

MARTIN.   And disappear before matters come to an ecclaircissement.

SLIP.   Um! That article wants a little explanation, my honest friend.

MARTIN.   How so?

SLIP.   You talk of disappearing with the lady's fortune and never mention Slip in the treaty.

MARTIN.   Oh! we shall disappear together, to be sure. I have more honor
than to go without you.

SLIP.   Well, on that condition, I am content to play your back hand.
But hold, hold! How will you pass yourself for my master in a
130   family where you are so well known?

MARTIN.   Hold your fool's tongue; this is my first visit to 'em. I returned but yesterday to my master. You must know, I asked his
leave to be absent a week, and I made free with a month; 'twas a
party of pleasure, so I made bold. During my absence he saw this
lady, liked her person, adored her fortune, and now, by my help,
hopes to be in possession of both in a few days.

SLIP.   And you'll do the lady the honor to help her to a better match.

MARTIN.   She'll think so, I believe.

SLIP.   Well said, Conceit! But what sort of people are your father and
140   mother-in-law?

MARTIN.   I am told he is a mere citizen who, thinking himself very
wise, is often outwitted; and his lady has as much vanity in her
way; will never be old, though turned of sixty, and as irresolute
and capricious as a girl of fifteen.

SLIP.   And Miss, I suppose, is like all other misses; wants to be her own
mistress and her husband's, and in the meantime is governed by her
chambermaid, who will be too hard for us both if we don't look
about us.

MARTIN.   A fig for dangers! I am prepared for 'em.

---

145. And Miss] O1, O2, O3 omit cue for Slip; D1, D2 correct the error.

150 SLIP.   But hearkee, what shall we do with the old gentleman's letter
that I'm to deliver? This will knock us all up.

MARTIN.   Write another.

SLIP.   That's easier said than done; but I'll do my best, as you can't
write.

MARTIN.   Do you see after my wedding clothes, that they do not set
out for the country. We have no time to lose.

SLIP.   My master's will fit you to a hair.

MARTIN.   But stay, stay, I must see my master first. If he should appear
and surprise us, we're in a fine pickle. I must make him keep house

160 for a few days—I'll think of a lie as I go. 'Egad, I have it already.
I'll tell him and meet you afterwards at the tavern, there take a
glass, cast this coarse skin, whip on the gentleman, and shame the
first men of fashion in the kingdom.   *Exit* Martin.

SLIP.   If impudence will do our business, 'tis done, and the twenty
thousand are our own.   *Exit* Slip.

SCENE II.

An apartment in Mr. Stockwell's *house.*
Enter Miss Nancy *and* Jenny.

NANCY.   You know, Jenny, that Belford has got into my heart, and if
I consent to marry this man, 'twill be the death of me. Advise me
then, and don't be so teasing.

JENNY.   Lud, what advice can I give you? I have but two in the world;
one is to forget your lover, and t'other to disobey your father. You
have too much love to take the one, and I too much conscience to
give t'other; so we are just where we were, madam.

NANCY.   Don't torment me, Jenny.

JENNY.   Why, I fancy we might find a way to reconcile your love and
10   my conscience.

NANCY.   How, how, my dear girl?

JENNY.   Suppose we were to open the affair to your mama?

NANCY.   Nay, now your jesting is cruel.

JENNY.   I never was more in earnest, madam. She loves flattery dearly;
and she loves her daughter dearly. I'll warrant, with a sigh and a
tear and a handkerchief, she makes her husband break his word
with young Harlowe in a quarter of an hour after his arrival.

NANCY.   Not unlikely, but if —

JENNY.   What at your ifs? No doubts, I beg, where I am concerned.

20 NANCY.   But you know my poor mother is so unsettled a creature.

JENNY.   Why, that's true enough. The last speaker is her oracle; so let

us lose no time to bring her over to—Hark! Here she comes. Do
you retire till I have prepared her for you.   *Exit* Miss Nancy.

Enter Mrs. Stockwell.

JENNY.   Well, of all the women in London, sure there never was such
a temper as my lady's.
MRS. STOCKWELL (*aside*).   What can have set this girl against me?
JENNY.   Such good humor and good sense together seldom meet—then
such a perpetual smile upon her features. Well, her's is a sort of
face that can never grow old. What would I give for such a lasting
30   face as she has.
MRS. STOCKWELL.   Hussey, hussey, you're a flatterer. (*Taps her on the
shoulder.*)
JENNY.   Ah! Madam, is it you? I vow you made me start. Miss Nancy
and I had just been talking of you, and we agreed you were one of
the best of women, the most reasonable friend, the tenderest mother,
and the—the—the —
MRS. STOCKWELL.   Nay, that's too much. I have my failings, and my
virtues too, Jenny. In one thing indeed I am very unlike other
women; I always hearken to reason.
JENNY.   That's what I said, madam.
40 MRS. STOCKWELL.   I am neither headstrong nor fantastical, neither —
JENNY.   No, sweet lady, the smallest twine may lead you. Miss, says I,
hear reason, like your mama; will so good a mother, do you think,
force her daughter to marry against her inclinations?
MRS. STOCKWELL.   I force my child's inclinations! No, I make the case
my own. But tell me—there's a good girl—has my daughter an aversion to young Harlowe?
JENNY.   I don't say that, madam. That is, aversion, to be sure, but I believe she hates him like the devil.
MRS. STOCKWELL.   Poor thing, poor thing! And perhaps her little heart
50   is beating for another?
JENNY.   Oh, that's a certain rule! When a young woman hates her husband, 'tis taken for granted she loves another man. For example, you
yourself, as you have often told me, hated the sight of Mr. Stockwell when first he was proposed for your husband. Why? Only
because you were in love, poor lady, with captain—you know who
that was killed at the siege—you know where.
MRS. STOCKWELL.   Why will you name him, Jenny? (*Wipes her eyes.*) —
JENNY.   Tender lady!
MRS. STOCKWELL.   Why, indeed, had that fine young creature survived
60   his wounds, I should never have married Mr. Stockwell—that I will
say.

JENNY.   Then you know how to pity your daughter. Her heart suffers now what yours did before that siege, madam.

MRS. STOCKWELL.   Say you so? Poor girl! And who is it has found the way to her heart?

JENNY.   No other than the young gentleman that has been so constant at cards with you lately.

MRS. STOCKWELL.   Who, Belford?

JENNY.   The same, and a fine spirited young fellow it is.

Enter Miss Nancy.

70 MISS NANCY.   Pardon my folly, my misfortunes, dear madam, if I cannot conform in all my sentiments with yours and my father's —

MRS. STOCKWELL.   It will happen, child, sometimes that a daughter's heart may not be disposed to comply exactly with the views and schemes of a parent—but then, a parent should act with tenderness. My dear, I pity your distress. Belford has my approbation, I assure you.

NANCY.   You are too good, madam!

JENNY.   Your approbation is not enough, madam; will you answer for master's too? He's a stubborn bit of stuff, you know; he will not always hearken to reason.

80 MRS. STOCKWELL.   But he shall, Jenny; stubborn as he is, I'll soften him. I'll take Belford under my protection. Here comes my husband, I have taken my resolutions, and you shall see how I'll bring him about presently.

Enter Mr. Stockwell.

My dear, you're come in the very nick of time. I have just changed my mind.

MR. STOCKWELL.   You are always changing it, I think.

MRS. STOCKWELL.   I always hearken to reason, Mr. Stockwell.

MR. STOCKWELL.   Well, and which way does the wind set now?

MRS. STOCKWELL.   Why, I have taken a resolution not to marry my
90 daughter to young Harlowe.

MR. STOCKWELL.   Hey, that's chopping about, indeed!

MRS. STOCKWELL.   Nay, but my dear, hear me, and let us reason a little. Here's a better offer for Nancy: Belford has asked her of me.

MR. STOCKWELL.   Belford a better?

MRS. STOCKWELL.   Nay, but don't be obstinate, child! He is not indeed so rich as the other; but what are riches to content, Mr. Stockwell?

MR. STOCKWELL.   And what is content without riches, Mrs. Stockwell?

MRS. STOCKWELL.   But he's a gentleman, my dear, and out of regard to his family we may very well excuse his fortune.

100 JENNY.   Well said, madam. (*Aside.*) This will do.

MR. STOCKWELL.   Ha, ha, ha! That's because you were a gentlewoman. But I, being a downright cit, think just the reverse and, out of regard to his fortune, if he had one, might excuse his family. I have no great objection to the man; but is not our word and honor engaged to another?

MRS. STOCKWELL.   Eh? That's true, indeed, but —

MR. STOCKWELL.   Has my old friend, Sir Harry Harlowe, done anything to —

MRS. STOCKWELL.   I don't accuse him, my dear.

110   MR. STOCKWELL.   Or has his son refused to comply?

MRS. STOCKWELL.   Not in the least, that I know of.

JENNY (*aside*).   Never flinch, madam.

MRS. STOCKWELL (*aside*).   Never fear, Jenny.

NANCY.   But I have never seen him, papa.

MRS. STOCKWELL.   No, Mr. Stockwell, she has never seen him —

MR. STOCKWELL.   So much the better, Mrs. Stockwell. He'll be a greater novelty and please her the better and the longer for it.

MRS. STOCKWELL.   There is some reason in that, Jenny.

JENNY.   Is there, madam? Then I have not a bit about me.

120   NANCY.   But to marry without inclination, sir, think of that.

MRS. STOCKWELL.   Ay, think of that, Mr. Stockwell.

MR. STOCKWELL.   I never thought of it for myself, nor you neither, my dear; and why should our daughter think herself wiser than her parents?

MRS. STOCKWELL.   Ay, why indeed? There's no answering that, Jenny.

JENNY.   I see there is not. (*Aside.*) What a woman!

MR. STOCKWELL.   It would be such an affront as never could be forgiven. Consider, dame, the instruments are signed, preparations made, and the bridegroom expected every minute; 'tis too far gone to be re-
130   called with any honor.

MRS. STOCKWELL.   Good lack a day, very true, very true!

JENNY (*aside*).   Well said, weather-cock. About and about we go. This woman betrays the whole sex: she won't contradict her own husband.

MRS. STOCKWELL.   You are witness, Jenny, I did all I could for poor Belford.

JENNY.   To be sure, you took him under your protection—a noble patroness, truly!

MR. STOCKWELL.   Hey, whom have we got here? I'll be hanged if this
140   is not my son-in-law's servant. Now, girl, we shall hear.

Enter Slip, *in a hurry.*

SLIP.   Ladies and gentlemen, I am come—let me recover my breath—I come—Oh! I come with mine and my master's compliments to your honor and my lady, our best love and services to pretty Miss, and (*to* Jenny) madam, I'm your obedient Blackamoor.

MR. STOCKWELL.   Um, the fellow has humor, I promise you. Well, sirrah, where's your master?

SLIP.   My master, and your son, is on his way to throw himself at the feet of this angelic creature. His impatience, madam, can equal nothing but your beauty.

150   MR. STOCKWELL.   Well, but where is he, where is he?

SLIP.   He's but just arrived from the country; he treads upon my heels, and I had only the start of him to tell you that he will but whip on clean linen and wait on you in the snapping of a finger.

MR. STOCKWELL.   Oh, fie upon him, what need all this ceremony between us? Why did not he come hither directly? He knows he may make my house his own.

SLIP.   Oh, sir, he designs it; but the first time—Pardon me, sir—he knows the world better than to treat you so cavalierly as that. No, no, he's not that man, I can assure you; though I'm his valet, yet I'd give

160   the devil his due.

MRS. STOCKWELL.   Is he so extremely well bred? Daughter, you'll be infinitely happy.

MR. STOCKWELL.   Does not my old friend, Harlowe, his father, come with him?

SLIP.   Sir, I grieve to tell it you, such was his design, but an unforeseen accident has prevented him, which I assure you gives him great pain.

MR. STOCKWELL.   Ay, what's the matter?

SLIP.   The gout, sir, the gout!

170   MRS. STOCKWELL.   Poor gentleman!

SLIP.   He was seized in his right foot the evening before we set out, but—I have a letter from him. (*Gives a letter.*)

MR. STOCKWELL (*Puts on his spectacles and reads.*)   "To Doctor, Doctor Clackit, physician, near St. Sepulchre's church."

SLIP.   Lud! lud! that's not it. (*Takes out letters.*) Let me see.

MR. STOCKWELL.   St. Sepulchre's church! I find the doctor chooses to live among his patients.

SLIP.   Eh! eh! that's so good! You're a very wag, sir! He, he, he! Let me see. Oh, here's one like it. To Mr. Stockwell, the same. I am

180   afraid you'll hardly be able to make it out. Shall I read it to you? Oh, this unlucky gout!

MR. STOCKWELL.   I see it has affected his hands too. Why, 'tis scarce legible, and ill spelt too.

---

182. Why] Wyh in O_1, O_2, O_3; Why D_1, D_2.

SLIP. The gout, sir. May it never affect you, sir, nor Madam Stockwell, Miss Nancy, that young woman there, nor any of the good
company.

MR. STOCKWELL. (*Reads.*) "My much honored friend, few words are
best in my condition; this damned gout has laid hold upon me and
won't let me attend my son for to be present at his matrimony." For
190   to be present at his matrimony! I think his hand and style too much
altered.

SLIP. The gout, sir.

MR. STOCKWELL. (*Reading.*) "I look upon this conjuncture of our
families." Conjuncture! A very odd phrase!

SLIP. The gout, dear sir, the gout! He's quite another man in it.

MR. STOCKWELL. "I look upon this conjuncture of our families as the
comfort of my age. The sooner it is done the more comfort I shall
have. I don't doubt but you'll like my son, whom I have sent with
a most trusty and faithful servant, who deserves your friendship
200   and favor."

SLIP. Oh, law, sir, I am quite ashamed.

MR. STOCKWELL. "I am, my dear brother, yours, &c., till death, Henry
Harlowe." I am very sorry we can't have the old gentleman's company. But who is this gay young fellow coming towards us? Can
this be my son-in-law?

SLIP (*aside*). What the devil should ail him?—Look at him, miss; observe him, madam. Is not he a pretty fellow?

MR. STOCKWELL. What is he doing?

SLIP. Only paying his chairman. (*To* Jenny.) Generous as a prince.

210 MRS. STOCKWELL. Not ill made, indeed! You'll only be too happy, child.

NANCY. I wish I could think so, madam.

SLIP (*aside*). Dress us but as well, and we'll cut out our masters ten to
one.—All my fancy, I assure you, ladies.

Enter Martin *as young* Harlowe.

MARTIN. Slip!

SLIP. Your honor!

MARTIN. Mr. Stockwell, I presume, my illustrious father —

SLIP. The same, sir, in *proprium personum.*

MR. STOCKWELL. My dear son, welcome! Let me embrace you.

MARTIN. You do me too much honor. My superabundant joy is too in-
220   expressible to express the—This, I flatter myself (*to* Mrs. Stockwell),
is the brilliant beauty destined to the arms of happy Mart—Harlowe.
(*Aside*) Gad! I'd like to have forgot my own name.

NANCY (*aside*). An impertinent, absurd coxcomb!

MR. STOCKWELL. Nay, nay, son-in-law, not so fast; that's my wife. Here's my daughter Nancy!

MARTIN. A fine creature! (*Salutes her.*) Madam, I have seen the world, and from all the world here would I choose a wife and a mistress— a family of beauties. Let me die.

MRS. STOCKWELL. Excessively gallant! He has wit, I assure you, daughter.

230

JENNY. And taste too, madam.

NANCY. And impudence, I'm sure!

MARTIN (*singing to* Mrs. Stockwell). "With a shape, and a face, and an air, and a grace!" Ha, ha! Just, just as our old gentleman told me. There you'll see Madam Stockwell, says he, the agreeable still —take care of your heart, boy; she's a dangerous beauty, though her daughter may be by.

MRS. STOCKWELL. Oh, fie, fie, fie!

MARTIN. I but repeat my father's words, madam, confirmed by my own observation. Ah, boy, says he, I wish with all my heart that my dear friend Mr. Stockwell was dead; I'd marry her tomorrow.

240

MR. STOCKWELL. I'm much obliged to him, faith!

MRS. STOCKWELL. And so am I, I am sure, sir.

MARTIN. I but repeat my father's words, sir.

MRS. STOCKWELL. My esteem for your father, sir, is mutual, and I am heartily sorry we could not have the pleasure of his company.

MARTIN. Oh, madam, he was damned mad that he could not be at the wedding. He had flattered himself these two months with the hopes of dancing a minuet with Mrs. Stockwell.

250

SLIP (*aside*). Two months? Whew!—and 'tis but six weeks he has known her. He'll knock us all up if I don't interfere.—Sir, Sir Harry begs you'll hasten the ceremonials, that he may have the pleasure of his daughter's company as soon as possible.

MR. STOCKWELL. Well, well, everything is signed and sealed; nothing remains that I know of but to finish the affair at once and pay you my daughter's portion.

MARTIN (*aside*). "Pay you my daughter's portion"—(*aloud*) that's all, sir. Come along, sir; I wait on you to your closet. Slip, go with my civilities to the marquis of—(*Softly.*) Go this moment, you dog, and secure us horses, and let 'em be bridled and saddled and ready at a minute's warning—(*aloud*) and don't forget my compliments to the marchioness.

260

SLIP. I fly, sir. Ladies, your most obedient.   *Exit* Slip.

MARTIN. Come along, sir, to your closet.

MR. STOCKWELL. Stay, son, stay! To return to the old gentleman —

MARTIN. Oh, sir, we'll return to him when the portion's paid.

MR. STOCKWELL.   No, no; first satisfy my curiosity about this unlucky lawsuit of his.

MARTIN (*aside*).   Oh, lud! Slip not here now!

270 MR. STOCKWELL.   You seem disturbed, son-in-law. Has anything —

MARTIN (*aside*).   Eh! pox o' this question—I have such a memory! (*Puts his hand to his forehead.*) As much forgot to send Slip to the duke of—as if I had no manner of acquaintance with him. I'll call him back. Slip!

MR. STOCKWELL.   He'll be back again presently. But, sir—

MARTIN (*aside*).   He should have told me of this damned lawsuit.

MR. STOCKWELL.   Has it been brought to a hearing?

MARTIN.   Oh, yes, sir, and the affair is quite over.

MR. STOCKWELL.   Ay, already?

280 MARTIN (*aside*).   The wrong box, I'm afraid!

MR. STOCKWELL.   And I hope you have got your cause?

MARTIN.   With costs of suit, I assure you, sir.

MR. STOCKWELL.   I am extremely glad of it.

MRS. STOCKWELL.   Thank heaven 'tis so well over.

MARTIN.   Oh, the family had the lawsuit so much at heart, the lawyers should have had every farthing we were worth in the world before we'd have been cast.

MR. STOCKWELL.   Um, that would have been carrying it a little too far. But as it was, it cost him a pretty penny, ha?

290 MARTIN.   That it did, sir. But justice—Oh, justice, sir, is so fine a thing, we cannot pay too dear for it.

MR. STOCKWELL.   Very true; but exclusive of the expense, this has been a troublesome affair to my friend.

MARTIN.   You can have no idea of it, sir—especially with such a tricking son of a whore as he had to do with.

MR. STOCKWELL.   Son of a whore? He told me his antagonist was a lady.

MARTIN (*aside*).   I thought I was in the wrong box.—A lady call you her? Yes, yes, a fine lady! But she had got an old pettifogging rascal for her attorney, and he—it was he that was such a plague to our

300 old gentleman. But damn this cause; let us call another. I'm for nothing now but flames, darts, daggers, Cupids and Venuses, and Madam Stockwell and Miss Nancy. (*Bowing to them.*)

MRS. STOCKWELL.   The pink of complaisance!

NANCY (*aside*).   The fellow's a fool, and I'll die before I'll have him.

MR. STOCKWELL.   Well said, son-in-law. A spirited fellow, faith! Come, we'll in and see things ready.

MARTIN.   Shan't I wait upon you to your closet first, sir?

MR. STOCKWELL.   As soon as the ceremony's over, son. Come, I'll show you the way.

310 MARTIN (*aside*). Eh! If I could but have touched beforehand, I'd have
waved the ceremony.—Madam (*to* Mrs. Stockwell), may I hope for
the honor. (*Offering to lead her out.*)

MRS. STOCKWELL. Oh, sweet sir—(*Aside to* Nancy.) Daughter, you'll
have a pretty fellow for your husband.   *Exeunt.*

NANCY. There's a lover for you, Jenny!

JENNY. Not for me, madam, I assure you. What, snap at the old kite
when such a tender chick is before him?

NANCY. Not a civil word to his mistress, but quite gallant to her mother.

JENNY. As much as to say, a fig for you—I'm in love with your fortune.

320 NANCY. A fig for him, a conceited puppy; I'm in love with Belford.
But how to get at him, Jenny?

JENNY. Ah, poor bird, you're limed by the wing, and struggling will
but make it worse.

NANCY. Not struggle! Ruin is better than this coxcomb! Prithee, advise me.

JENNY. Don't tempt me. I pity you so that I could give you a sprightly
piece of advice; and you are in so desperate a way that I know you'd
follow it.

NANCY. Follow it! I'll follow any advice, Jenny.

330 JENNY. Oh, yes, to follow your own inclinations, that's a good young
lady. Well, I am at present much given to mischief. So if you'll go
into your chamber, lock the door, and let us lay our little heads together for half an hour, if we don't counterplot your wise papa and
his intended son-in-law, we deserve never to be married, or if we
are, to be governed by our husbands.   *Exeunt.*

ACT II. [Scene I.]

SCENE, *a hall in* Stockwell's *house.*
Enter Belford.

BELFORD. I am surprised that Martin has not returned to tell me his
success with Jenny. He advised me not to stir from home, and said
I might be assured every thing goes well and I should hear from
him. But still, the impatience of my heart cannot bear this delay.
I must be near the field of battle, let what will be the consequence.
I hope I shall get sight of Martin and not unluckily light on the
old gentleman. 'Sdeath! he's here! Oh, no, 'tis Jenny. My heart was
in my mouth.

Enter Jenny.

Dear Jenny, where's your mistress?

10 JENNY.   Winding herself up for your sake, and by my advice, to a
       proper pitch of disobedience, that's all. But —
   BELFORD.   But what? You hesitate, Jenny, and seem concerned.
   JENNY.   Concerned! Why, we're undone, that's all. Your rival is come
       to town.
   BELFORD.   How!
   JENNY.   And is this morning to marry madam.
   BELFORD.   Not while I'm alive, I can tell him that. But prithee, who is
       this happy rival of mine?
   JENNY.   'Tis one Mr. Harlowe.
20 BELFORD.   Harlowe!
   JENNY.   A gentleman of Dorsetshire.
   BELFORD.   I know all of that country and can recollect no Harlowe but
       the son of Sir Harry Harlowe, and he —
   JENNY.   Ay, and he is your rival.
   BELFORD.   If I had no more to fear from your mistress than from my
       rival, as you call him —
   JENNY.   Oh, you are very clever now, an't you? What would you be
       at now?
   BELFORD.   The truth only, the real certain truth.
30 JENNY.   Ay, what's that?
   BELFORD.   Why, that this Harlowe is the son of Sir Harry Harlowe of
       Dorsetshire and my friend, my particular friend.
   JENNY.   Yes, and so particular that he will take your mistress from you.
   BELFORD.   He shall take my life first.
   JENNY.   You said that before. Have you nothing else to say?
   BELFORD.   I say that this Harlowe, my friend, was married last week in
       the country, that's all.
   JENNY.   And that's enough, if it is true; but I have a small addition to
       your news.
40 BELFORD.   What's that?
   JENNY.   That the aforesaid John Harlowe, Esq., your particular friend
       and son to Sir Harry Harlowe of Dorsetshire, is now within, wait-
       ing for my young lady's hand, that's all.
   BELFORD.   Jenny, no jesting; you distract me!
   JENNY.   'Tis but too true. He's this minute gone in with my master and
       mistress to settle preliminaries.
   BELFORD.   Impossible! He's my intimate acquaintance and writ to me
       not a week ago, as I tell you. I have his letter at my lodgings.
   JENNY.   And what says he there?
50 BELFORD.   That he's privately married to a lady of condition.
   JENNY.   How can this be reconciled? Go fetch that letter. We have no
       time to lose.

BELFORD. But what is Martin doing?

JENNY. Martin? Who's he?

BELFORD. Martin, my servant, whom I sent to assist you.

JENNY. Why, sure love has turned your brain, sir; I have seen no Martin, not I.

BELFORD. The rascal then is run away from me again. I have spoiled him by my indulgence. He left me for a month and returned but yes-
60 terday; then I sent him hither to assist you, and now the scoundrel has left me again.

JENNY. 'Tis the luxury of the times, sir; though we are poor, we have good tastes and can be out of the way now and then as well as our betters.

BELFORD. How this villain has used me! But we must lose no time. I'll fetch the letter and be back in an instant.

Exit.

JENNY. Let me see; can't I strike some mischief out of this intelligence? I warrant me, I can delay the marriage at least. Here's my master. I'll try my skill upon him. If I don't quite bring him about, I'll set
70 his brains in such a ferment they shan't settle in haste again.

Enter Mr. Stockwell.

MR. STOCKWELL. I think I saw a glimpse of young Belford. But now, what business has he here?

JENNY. Business enough, sir; the best friend you have, that's all. He has been telling me a piece of news that will surprise you.

MR. STOCKWELL. Let's hear this piece of news.

JENNY. O' my word, a bold man, this Mr. Harlowe, to take two wives at once, when most folk we see have enough of one.

MR. STOCKWELL. Two wives! Bless us, what do you mean?

JENNY. Why, the poor man's married already, sir, that's all.

80 MR. STOCKWELL. Married!

JENNY. Married, I say, to a young lady in the country, and very near marrying another in town; a new fashion, I suppose.

MR. STOCKWELL. Pooh, pooh, the thing's impossible, I tell you.

JENNY. That may be, but so it is. He has writ to Belford, who is his friend.

MR. STOCKWELL. All romance and invention!

JENNY. All truth, I say. Belford is gone to fetch the letter, and he'll convince you.

MR. STOCKWELL. I will never be convinced that —

90 JENNY. Why not, sir? The young fellows of this age are capable of anything.

MR. STOCKWELL. Very true, Jenny, they are abominable!

JENNY.   And for aught we know this Mr. Harlowe here may be one of
those gentlemen that make no scruple of a plurality of wives, provided they bring a plurality of portions. But by your leave, good
sir, as this young lady—she in the country, I mean—has the first and
best title, we must look a little about us for the sake of our young
lady in town.

MR. STOCKWELL. Very true—'tis worth attending to.

100 JENNY.   Attending to! If I were you, sir, before I delivered up my
daughter I should insist upon the affair's being cleared up to my
satisfaction.

MR. STOCKWELL. You're in the right, Jenny. Here's his man. I'll sound
him about his master's marriage, and then—Leave us together—go.
I'll make him speak, I warrant you.

JENNY.   If this marriage is but confirmed, I shall leap out of my skin.

Exit.

Enter Slip.

MR. STOCKWELL. Mr. Slip, come hither. My old friend Sir Harry has
recommended you to me, and I like your physiognomy. You have
an honest face; it pleases me much.

110 SLIP.   Your humble servant, sir. That's your goodness. But if I was no
honester than my face, gad a mercy poor me!

MR. STOCKWELL. Well, well, hark you me. This master of yours is a
lad of spirit—a favorite of the ladies, I warrant him, ha?

SLIP.   That he is, I can tell you, sir; a pretty fellow, no woman can resist him. I'll warrant, this marriage in your family will set you the
hearts of thirty families at ease all round the country.

MR. STOCKWELL. Odd! A terrible man, I profess. I don't wonder now
that one wife can't serve him.

SLIP.   Wife, sir? What wife, sir?

120 MR. STOCKWELL. You see, I know all, my friend; so you may as well
confess.

SLIP.   Confess? What, sir?

MR. STOCKWELL. I know all the conspiracy, and will take care that you,
rascal, shall have your desert as an accomplice.

SLIP.   Accomplice? Rascal? And a conspiracy? Let me die if I comprehend a word you say.

MR. STOCKWELL. But I'll make you, villain.

SLIP.   O very well, sir—ha! ha! ha! I protest you half frightened me.
Very well, indeed! Ha! ha! ha!

130 MR. STOCKWELL. Do you laugh at me, sirrah?

SLIP.   If I had not remembered to have heard my old master say what a dry joker you were, I protest I should have been taken in. Very good, indeed! Ha! ha! ha!

MR. STOCKWELL.   None of your buffoonery, sirrah, but confess the whole affair this minute or be sent to Newgate the next.

SLIP.   Newgate! Sure, sir, that would be carrying the joke too far.

MR. STOCKWELL.   You won't confess, then? Who waits there? Send for a constable this moment.

SLIP.   Nay, good sir, no noise, I beseech you. Though I am innocent as
140   the child unborn, yet that severe tone of voice is apt to disconcert one. What was it your honor was pleased to hint about my master's being married? Who could possibly invent such a fib as that?

MR. STOCKWELL.   No fib, sirrah. He wrote it himself to a friend of his at London—to Belford.

SLIP.   Oh, oh! Your humble servant, Mr. Belford! A fine fetch, i'faith! Nay, I can't blame the man neither, ha, ha. Pray, sir, is not this same Mr. Belford in love with your daughter?

MR. STOCKWELL.   Suppose he is, puppy, and what then?

SLIP.   Why then Jenny is his friend and at the bottom of all his fetches.
150   I'll lay a wager that she is author of this whopper.

MR. STOCKWELL.   Um!

SLIP.   Our arrival put 'em to their trumps, and then, slap, my poor master must be married; and Belford must show a forged letter, forsooth, under his own hand to prove it—and, and, and, you understand me, sir —

MR. STOCKWELL.   Why, this has a face.

SLIP.   A face? Ay, like a full moon. And while you're upon a false scent after this story, Jenny will gain time to work upon your daughter. I heard her say myself that she could lead you by the nose.

160   MR. STOCKWELL.   Oh, she could, could she? Well, well, we'll see [*to*] that.

SLIP.   By the bye, sir, where did you meet with this Mrs. Jenny?

MR. STOCKWELL.   How should I know? I believe my wife hired her half a year ago out of the country. She had a good character and is very notable, but pert, very pert.

SLIP.   Yes, yes, she is notable. (*Half aside.*) Out of the country! And a good character! Well said, Mrs. Jenny!

MR. STOCKWELL.   What's the matter, Slip? You have something in your head, I'm sure.

SLIP.   No, nothing at all—but the luck of some people! Out of the
170   country!

MR. STOCKWELL.   You must tell me. I shan't think you mean me well if you conceal anything from me.

SLIP.   Why, among ourselves sir, I knew Mrs. Jenny the last year very well. Born and bred in Convent Garden. Some time ago barmaid to a Jelly-house, and two children (very fine ones indeed) by little Tom the waiter. I knew when I saw her here that we should have some sport.

MR. STOCKWELL. Ay, ay! I know enough. Well said, Mrs. Jenny, in-deed! But mind the cunning of this fellow, this Belford; he says he's

180   the most intimate friend your master has.

SLIP. Ay, sir! Ha! ha! ha! And I dare say my master would not know him if he met him. However, that's well observed, sir. Um! Noth-ing escapes you.

MR. STOCKWELL. Why, I am seldom out, seldom —

SLIP. Never.

MR. STOCKWELL. I don't say never. But here is your master. I must have a laugh with him about this marriage. Ha! ha! ha!

SLIP. 'Twill be rare sport for him, He, he, he!

Enter Martin

MR. STOCKWELL. So, son-in-law, do you hear what the world says of

190   you? I have had intelligence here—ay, and certain intelligence too—that you are married, it seems—privately married to a young lady of Dorsetshire. What say you, sir? Is not this fine! Ha, ha, ha!

SLIP. Very merry, faith! (*Laughing, and making signs to* Martin.)

MARTIN. Ha, ha, ha! 'Tis such a joke! What, you have heard so? This Mr. World is a facetious gentleman.

MR. STOCKWELL. Another man now would have given plumb into this foolish story, but I—no, no, your humble servant for that.

SLIP. No, plague! Mr. Stockwell has a long head. He — (*Pointing still.*)

MARTIN. I would fain know who could be the author of such a ridicu-

200   lous story.

SLIP. Mr. Stockwell tells me 'tis one Belford, I think he calls him. Is not that his name, sir?

MARTIN. Belford? Belford? I never heard of his name in my life.

SLIP. As I said, sir. You see, master knows nothing of the fellow. Stay, stay, is it not the youngster that—you know whom I mean—that, that —

MARTIN. Rot me, if I do!

SLIP. He that—you must know him—that is your rival here, as the re-port goes.

210 MARTIN. Oh, ay! Now I recollect. By the same token, they said he had but little and owed much. That this match was to wipe off old scores, and that his creditors had stopped proceedings till he's married.

---

196. plumb] O_1, O_2, O_3; plump D_1, D_2.

MR. STOCKWELL.   Ay! ay! there let 'em stop. Ha, ha, ha! They'll be tired
of stopping, I believe, if they are to stop till he has married my
daughter. Ha, ha, ha.

SLIP.   He's no fool, let me tell you, this Mr. Belford.

MR. STOCKWELL.   No, nor Mr. Stockwell neither. And to convince them
of that, I will go this instant to my banker's and —

220 MARTIN.   Sir, I'll wait on you.

MR. STOCKWELL.   Stay, son-in-law, I have a proposal to make—I own,
I agreed with my old friend to give you £10,000 down.

MARTIN.   Ay, *down* was the word, sir—it was so—*down.*

MR. STOCKWELL.   Now, could you conveniently take some houses that
I have in the Borough instead of half that sum? They are worth a
great deal more than that, I assure you.

MARTIN.   Oh, dear sir, your word is not to be disputed. I'll take anything. But between friends, ready money is the truth. *Down,* you
know, sir; that was the word, *down.*

230 SLIP.   Specious, your honor knows, is of easier conveyance.

MR. STOCKWELL.   Yes, sure, that's true; but —

MARTIN.   Ay, ay, one can't put houses in one's portmanteau, you know.
He! he! he! Besides, there is a pretty estate to be sold in Dorsetshire, near my father's, and I have my eye upon that.

SLIP.   As pretty a conditioned thing as any in the country, and then so
contagious that a hedge only parts 'em.

MARTIN.   I may have it for £9,000, and I'm told 'tis worth ten at least.

SLIP.   The least penny, sir; the timber's worth half the money.

MR. STOCKWELL.   Well, well—Look you, son; I have a round £10,000

240 now in my banker's hands which I thought to have made immediate advantage of. You shall have a moiety of it.

MARTIN.   Sir, I am infinitely obliged to you. Are you agoing to your
banker's now, sir?

MR. STOCKWELL.   I will but step and let my wife know of it, fetch the
cash directly, and you shall marry my daughter in an hour.

MARTIN.   Sir, suppose we invite Mr. Belford to the wedding? Ha, ha,
ha!

SLIP.   Ha, ha, ha! What a droll devil my master is!

MR. STOCKWELL.   Ha, ha, ha!   *Exit* Stockwell.

250 MARTIN.   Wind and tide, my boy! My master has certainly had an
interview with Miss Nancy Stockwell.

SLIP.   And as certainly knows Harlowe too.

MARTIN.   They correspond, you see.

SLIP.   But, thanks to my wit, I have so set the old man against Belford
that I am in hopes we shall pack up Madam's fortune in the portmanteau before he's set to rights again; and — (Martin *going, stops.*)

MARTIN. Zounds! My master!

SLIP. Where?

MARTIN. Don't you see him reading a letter?

260 SLIP. This is my unlucky star! What will become of us?

Enter Belford.

BELFORD. This letter gets me admittance to Miss Stockwell at least; and if I can but save her from ruin, I shall be happy. But I hope this may have better consequences. Ha! what's this? 'Tis he! 'tis Martin, as I live.

MARTIN. Ay, 'tis I—and well for you it is. What do you here?

BELFORD. Nay, what are *you* doing here, and what have you done here? What clothes are these? What's your scheme? And why have I not known it?

MARTIN. Not so fast and so loud, good master of mine. Walls have
270   ears. These are your rival's clothes, who is to follow them in a few days; but his servant there is an old friend of mine, and so, as they fit me so well—he's—I pass upon the family for the young fellow himself.

BELFORD. Well, and where's the joke of that?

MARTIN. A very good joke, I think. I'll undertake to put these two old fools—your papa and mama that shall be—so out of conceit with their son-in-law that—why, already I have heard the old folks agreeing that you were much the properer match for their daughter, so that I expect every moment they'll send for you to deliver them
280   from me. And nothing can prevent our success but your being —

BELFORD. Ha, ha, ha! A very good stratagem. But there is no need of it now; for this rival, as you call him, is my particular friend, and married to another woman. So I tell you we have nothing to fear.

MARTIN. But I tell you, you will knock us all to pieces. The finest plot that ever was laid, and you'll spoil it in the hatching.

BELFORD. But what occassion is there? He can't marry 'em both.

MARTIN. Speak lower! You think yourself mighty wise now; but here's Harlowe's servant, whom I have tickled in the palm, will tell you another story.

290 BELFORD. Why, here's a letter under his own hand—read it.

MARTIN. (*Reading.*) Um—um—"Some days privately married." (*Apart to* Slip.) Slip.

SLIP. This is easily cleared up, sir! There was such a thing proposed by my young master; but you must understand, sir, that Mr. Harlowe, not approving of the terms, has tipped the young woman's father a good round sum, and so the affair is made up.

BELFORD. Can it be possible that he is not married?

SLIP.   I'll take my oath of it before any magistrate in England.

MARTIN.   Pooh—married! What, his old boots?

300 BELFORD.   Well, I'll decamp then. But why is not Jenny in your plot?

MARTIN.   She? No, no, she is not to be trusted. I soon found out that. Tooth and nail against us.

BELFORD.   Good heavens, how have I been deceived!

MARTIN.   You have indeed, master; but we have no time for reflections. If Jenny should see you we are undone.

BELFORD.   Well, well, I go. I'll make both your fortunes if you succeed.

MARTIN.   Succeed? Nothing can prevent us but your being seen.

BELFORD.   I'll away then.

MARTIN.   And come not near this house today. If you do I must decamp.

310 BELFORD.   Well. But my dear lads, take care; I depend on you.

SLIP.   That's all you have to do—put your fortune into our hands —

MARTIN.   And I'll warrant we give a good account of it.

BELFORD.   Think how my happiness —

MARTIN.   Prithee, no more.

BELFORD.   Depends on you.

MARTIN.   Begone, I say; or I'll throw up the cards.   *Exit* Belford.

SLIP.   At last he's gone!

MARTIN.   And we have time to take a little breath; for this was a hot alarm, faith!

320 SLIP.   I was only afraid the old gentleman or Jenny would have surprised us together.

MARTIN.   That would have been a clincher; but now I must after the old gentleman for the money.   *Exit.*

SLIP.   And I'll be upon the watch for fear of mischief.   *Exit.*

[Scene II.]

SCENE, *an apartment in* Mr. Stockwell's *house.*
Enter Mr. Stockwell *and* Jenny.

JENNY.   Still I say, sir —

MR. STOCKWELL.   And still I say, madam —

JENNY.   That Mr. Belford's a very honest gentleman, and you ought to search it.

MR. STOCKWELL.   I tell you, I have searched and probed it to the quick— and that he shall feel. I know well enough you are in his interest and have your interest in so doing; and I'm sorry you could find no prettier plot than this to defer the wedding.

JENNY.   Lud, sir, do you believe —

---

8. prettier] *O*1, *O*2, *O*3, *D*2; prittier *D*1.

10   MR. STOCKWELL.   No—but I'm sure on't. That's better.

JENNY.   Lud! You'd make one mad.

MR. STOCKWELL.   And you'd make me a fool if you could. No, no, I'm an ass, a poor simpleton that may be led by the nose. But you may tell my daughter that she shall marry Harlowe this night. And you may tell your friend Belford to let his creditors know that they need not stop proceedings. And you, madam, may return to your Jelly-shop and give my compliments to little Tom and all the little family. Ha, ha, ha!   *Exit.*

JENNY.   What does he mean by his Jelly-house—little Tom and all the
20   little family? There's something at the bottom of this I cannot yet fathom. But I will fathom it. I never was out of a secret yet that I had a mind to find out—and that's all that have come across me— and my pride won't let me be long out of this. I will go directly to Mr. Belford's, where we'll lay our heads together and beget such a piece of mischief that shall be hard for the devil himself, if he has the impudence to try confusions with me.   *Exit.*

[Scene III.]

SCENE, *the street before* Stockwell's *house.*
Mr. Stockwell, Martin, *and* Slip.

MR. STOCKWELL.   Come, son-in-law, we'll go to my banker's and see how our cash stands, and settle matters as well as we can.

MARTIN.   I'll attend you, sir, with pleasure. Cash or notes—all the same to me.

MR. STOCKWELL.   I wish you'd take the houses, son-in-law; 'twould be more convenient for me and a greater advantage to you.

MARTIN.   Advantage, sir? I scorn to take any advantage of you. I hate mean views. I desire nothing better than my bargain. The money and your daughter's charms are sufficient for your poor Mart—
10   humble servant.

MR. STOCKWELL.   Well, well, come along; we don't quite understand one another.   *Exit.*

MARTIN.   But we do. (*To* Slip.) The day's our own. Get everything ready to make our retreat good.

SLIP.   Ay, ay, get you the money, and I'll be ready with the equipage.

Exit Martin.

"Thus far our arms have with success been crowned." I have only one doubt remaining, and that's about this same portion. I don't relish this dividing a booty. How shall I cheat Martin? I should deserve to be canonized could I but cheat that rogue of

20   rogues. I must e'en throw the young lady in his way and persuade him, for our better security, to pass the night with her; so leave him with the shell while I slip off with the kernel. A tempting bait! But no—stand off, Satan! 'Tis against our fundamental laws. We adventurers have ten times the honor of your fair traders. (*Going and stops.*) Why, what? Sure it can't be! Zounds, if it should! It is the very man! Our little old withered fiery gentleman, by all that's terrible! From what a fine dream will this gouty spitfire awake us? He's certainly going to Mr. Stockwell's, and his gunpowder will blow up all at once. If Martin and Mr. Stockwell don't return too

30   soon from the banker's, I may send him away; 'tis our last stake, and I must play it like a gamester.

Enter Sir Harry Harlowe.

SIR HARRY.   I don't know how my old friend Stockwell may receive me after this disappointment.

SLIP (*aside*).   Stay till you see Mr. Stockwell, my old friend.—Bless me, what do I see! Sir Harry, is it you? Indeed your honor? Your very humble servant.

SIR HARRY.   I don't know you, friend. Keep your distance. (*Claps his hands on his pockets.*)

SLIP.   Don't you know me, sir?

SIR HARRY.   It cannot be Slip, sure! Is this the fool's coat my son ordered

40   you for his wedding?

SLIP.   Yes, sir, and a genteel thing it is upon me. What, you had a mind to surprise your friends who thought of you at London, sir?

SIR HARRY.   I set out soon after you, lame as I was. I bethought me, it looked better to settle matters of such consequence with Mr. Stockwell viva voce than to trust it to a servant.

SLIP.   You were always a nice observer of decorums. You are going now to Mr. Stockwell's?

SIR HARRY.   Directly. (*Going to knock.*)

SLIP.   Hold your desperate hand, and thank fortune that brought me

50   hither for your rescue.

SIR HARRY.   Why, what's the matter? Rescue me, quoth-a! Have you seen 'em, Slip?

SLIP.   Seen 'em? Ay, and felt 'em too. I am just escaped. The old lady is in a damned passion with you, I can tell you.

SIR HARRY.   With me?

SLIP.   Ay, that she is. How, says she, does the old fool think to fob us off with a flam and a sham of a dirty trollop? Must my daughter's reputation—and then she bridled and stalked up to me thus, sir.

SIR HARRY. How? But there's no answering a silly woman. How can
60   this affect her daughter's character?

SLIP.   That's what I said. Madam, says I—but you can't expect a woman
in a fury to hear reason. 'Tis almost as much as they can do when
they are cool. No, no; as for her argument, it was sad stuff! Will the
world, says she, believe such a—No, no, they'll think the old hunks
has found some flaw in our circumstances, and so won't stand to his
bargain.

SIR HARRY. Poh! Nothing disguises a woman like passion. Though it
may become a man sometimes.

SLIP.   Lud, sir, you would not know her again—her eyes stare in her
70   head, and she can't see a creature. On a sudden—for I pushed the
argument pretty home—she caught hold of my throat, thus, sir,
and knocked me down with the butt end of her fan.

SIR HARRY. Did she? But what did her husband say to this? Let us hear
that.

SLIP.   Oh, sir, I found him pretty reasonable. He only showed me the
door and kicked me down stairs.

SIR HARRY. If he's for that work, we can kick too.

SLIP.   Dear sir, consider your gout.

SIR HARRY. No, sir; when my blood is up I never feel the gout. But
80   could they possibly take it amiss that I consented to my son's marriage? I doubt you did not explain circumstances.

SLIP.   I told 'em plain enough, I thought, that my young master, having begun the ceremony at the wrong end, the family were going
ding-dong to law; and that you had behaved like a man of honor
and—very wisely compounded matters.

SIR HARRY. And did not this convince 'em?

SLIP.   I say, convince! They're in a pretty temper to be convinced. If
you'd take a fool's counsel, you should return to your inn and never
think of convincing them.

90 SIR HARRY.   They are for kicking, are they? I could have kicked pretty
well myself once. We shall see what they would be at — (*Going, is
stopped by* Slip.)

SLIP.   Indeed, sir, you shall not. What, have your face scratched by an
old woman, or be run thro' the body with a rusty sword? Indeed
you shall not.

SIR HARRY (*endeavoring to draw his sword*).   We have swords that run
thro' bodies as well as they; ay, and pistols too. If he will quarrel, I'm his man. Steel or lead, 'tis all one to me. A passionate fool!
I'll cool him. Kick me down stairs!

SLIP.   Lord, sir, you are so hot! You forget it was me he kicked down
100   stairs, not you.

SIR HARRY. 'Tis the same thing, sir. Whoever kicks you kicks me by
    proxy—nay, worse; you have only the kicks, but I have the affront.
SLIP.   If the kicks are the best, I shall be content with the worst another
    time. (*Aside.*) Undone, undone!—This way, this way, sir. Let us go
    this way—there will certainly be bloodshed.
SIR HARRY.   What is the matter, you fool? What art afraid of?
SLIP.   Don't you see Mr. Stockwell coming this way? Bless me, how he
    stares! He's mad with passion. Don't meet him, Sir Harry. You are
    out of wind and have not pushed a great while, and he'll certainly
110   be too much for you.
SIR HARRY.   I won't avoid him. My blood's up as well as his. If the fool
    will be for fighting, let him take what follows. Hold my cane, Slip.
    (*Cocks his hat.*)

SLIP (*aside*).   Ay, 'tis all over. If Martin has but got the money we may
    retire while the champions are at it.

> *Enter old* Stockwell *and* Martin, Stockwell
> *with a bag, and notes in his hand.*

MR. STOCKWELL.   We will count our money and bills over again, sign
    the writings, and then, son, for singing and dancing and —
MARTIN.   Don't give yourself that trouble, Mr. Stockwell—among
    friends, you know. Pray let me ease you of that weight. (*Offers to
    take the money.*)
MR. STOCKWELL.   No, no, son; you shan't have a farthing more or less
120   than your bargain. We citizens are exact and must have our way, in
    form.
SLIP.   Zounds! He has not got the money! We must have a scramble for
    it at last, then.
SIR HARRY.   Now he eyes me! I'll be as fierce as he. Now for it—hem,
    hem! (*Bustles up.*)

> *During this* Martin *and* Slip *make signs, and approach
> each other by degrees.*

MR. STOCKWELL.   Eh! Sure, if my eyes don't deceive me, there is some-
    body very like my old friend and your father, Sir Harlowe!
SLIP.   Damnably like indeed, sir.
SIR HARRY.   He looks like the devil at me, but I'll be even with him.
130 MR. STOCKWELL.   What, my dear friend, is it you?
SIR HARRY.   None of your hypocritical palavers with me. Keep your

---

106. what art] *O1, O2, O3, D2*; what are you *D1*.
112.1. *Cocks his hat*] *D1* omits the direction.

distance, you dissembling old fool you, or I'll teach you better manners than to kick my servant down stairs.

MR. STOCKWELL.   What do you mean, Sir Harry? (*Aside.*) He's mad sure!

> *They stand and stare at each other, and* Sir Harry
> *shakes his sword.*

MARTIN.   Nothing can save us now, Slip!

SLIP.   Trip up his heels and fly with the money to the post-chaise, while I tread upon my old master's toes that he mayn't follow us.

MARTIN.   We have nothing else for it. Have at 'em.

140 MR. STOCKWELL.   Nay, but Sir Harry!

> *As they approach the old gentlemen,* Belford *comes in
> behind with constables and seizes them.*

BELFORD.   Have I caught you, rascals? In the very nick, too! Secure 'em, constables.

MR. STOCKWELL.   What in the name of wonder are you about?

BELFORD.   I have a double pleasure in this, for I have not only discovered two villains, but at the very time, sir, their villainy was taking effect to make you miserable.

SIR HARRY.   Two villains! Mr. Stockwell, do you hear this? Explain yourself, sir, or blood and brimstone —

MR. STOCKWELL.   Explain, Mr. Belford. Sir Harry Harlowe, what is all
150 this? I am all stupefaction!

BELFORD.   Is this Sir Harry? I am your humble servant, sir. I have not the honor to be known to you, but am a particular acquaintance of your son's, who has been misrepresented here by that pretty gentleman, once a rascal of mine.

SIR HARRY.   I'm in a wood and don't know how to get out of it.

MR. STOCKWELL.   Is not this your son, Sir Harry?

SIR HARRY.   No, you passionate old fool; but this is my servant, and my son's pimp, whom I understand you have been kicking down stairs.

MR. STOCKWELL.   Here's a fine heap of roguery!

160 BELFORD.   It was my good fortune, by the intelligence and instigation of Mrs. Jenny, to discover the whole before these wretches had accomplished their designs.

MR. STOCKWELL.   What a hair-breadth 'scape have I had! As the poet says, the very brink of destruction, for I should have given him the cash in five minutes. I'm in a cold sweat at the thoughts of it. Dear Mr. Belford! (*Shakes him by the hand.*)

> *Enter* Mrs. Stockwell, Miss [Nancy], *and* Jenny.

MRS. STOCKWELL.   Oh, Mr. Stockwell, here are fine doings going forward. Did not I tell you that I was for Mr. Belford from the
beginning?

170   MR. STOCKWELL.   Don't trouble us now, wife; you have been for and
against him twenty times in four and twenty hours.

JENNY (*to* Martin *and* Slip).   Your humble servant, gentlemen! What,
dumb and ashamed too? The next scheme you go about, take care
that there is not such a girl as I within twenty miles of you.

MARTIN.   I wish we were twenty miles from you, with all my soul.

SLIP.   As you don't like our company, madam, we'll retire. (*Going
away.*)

BELFORD.   Hold 'em fast, constables. They must give some account of
themselves at the Old Bailey, and then perhaps they may retire to
our plantations.

180   SIR HARRY.   But what have they done? Or what will you do? Or what
am I to do? I'm all in the dark—pitch-dark.

MR. STOCKWELL.   Is your son married, Sir Harry?

SIR HARRY.   Yes, a fortnight ago. And this fellow you kicked down stairs
was sent with my excuses.

MR. STOCKWELL.   I kicked him down stairs? You villain you.

BELFORD.   Don't disturb yourself with what is past, but rejoice at your
deliverance. If you and Sir Harry will permit me to attend you
within, I will acquaint you with the whole business.

SIR HARRY.   I see the whole business now, sir. We have been their fools.

190   MR. STOCKWELL.   And they are our knaves and shall suffer as such.
Thanks to Mr. Belford here, my good angel that has saved my
£10,000.

SIR HARRY.   He has saved your family, Mr. Stockwell.

BELFORD.   Could you but think, sir, my good services to your family
might entitle me to be one of it.

---

182.   Is your son married, Sir Harry?] *O*1, *D*1, *D*2; *O*2, *O*3 add two speeches:

> MARTIN.   I'll bring you a light immediately.
>
> (*Going, and* Slip *following.*)
>
> MR. STOCKWELL.   Don't let them stir a step 'till I lay them by the heels. But
> is your son married, Sir Harry?

185.   I kicked him down] *O*1, *O*2, *O*3, *D*1; I kick'd down *D*2.
You villain you] *O*1, *D*1, *D*2; *O*2, *O*3 add the following:

> MR. STOCKWELL (*to* Slip).   You villain, you, did I kick you down the
> stairs?
> SLIP.   If you did, sir, you were heartily welcome. And if you would kick
> me out of the house now I should be much obliged to you.
> MR. STOCKWELL.   Matchless impudence.

MISS NANCY.   You'd make your daughter happy by giving her to your
best friend.

MRS. STOCKWELL.   My dear, for once hear me and reason and make 'em
both happy.

200 MR. STOCKWELL.   You shall be happy, Belford. Take my daughter's
hand. You have her heart. You have deserved her fortune and shall
have that too. Come, let us go in and examine these culprits.

SIR HARRY.   Right, Mr. Stockwell. 'Tis a good thing to punish villainy,
but 'tis a better to make virtue happy. And so let us about it.

Finis

---

201. hand] *O1, D1, D2*; and *O2, O3*.
202. examine these culprits.] *O1, D1, D2*; *O2, O3* add this exchange:

MARTIN.   Won't it give you too much trouble, sir, and break [in] upon
better business?

SLIP.   An Act of Grace would become your present happiness.

MR. STOCKWELL.   An Act of Grace for such villains as you would be an
act of cruelty to the rest of the world.

SIR HARRY.   Right, friend Stockwell. Let everyone be rewarded according
to their deserts. We are both of the quorum and ought to see justice
done. Well done, and quickly done. About it, brother. *Those (indicating* Martin *and* Slip) should be ty'd up one way, *these (indicating*
Belford *and* Miss Nancy) another.

Finis

You'd make your daughter happy by giving her to your heart...

The End.

List of References
Commentary and Notes
Index to Commentary

List of References

In this edition references to works are given by short title only. This list of references does not include the newspapers and other periodicals of the time.

Anon. *Lethe Rehearsed; or, A Critical Discussion of the Beauties and Blemishes of that Performance, etc.* London, 1749.

Addison, Joseph. *The Drummer; or, The Haunted House.* London, 1716.

Allen, Ralph G. "A Christmas Tale, or Harlequin Scene Painter." *Tennessee Studies in Literature* (1974), 149–61.

Angelo, Henry. *Reminiscences of Henry Angelo.* 2 vols. London, 1828–30.

Ashmole, Elias. *The History of the Order of the Garter.* London, 1672.

Baker, David Erskine. *A Companion to the Playhouse.* 2 vols. London, 1764.

Baker, David Erskine, Isaac Reed, and Stephen Jones. *Biographia Dramatica.* London, 1812.

Baker, Thomas. *Tunbridge Walks.* London, 1703.

Barton-Ticknor Collection. Boston Public Library, Boston, Massachusetts.

Beatty, Joseph M. "Garrick, Colman, and *The Clandestine Marriage.*" *Modern Language Notes*, 36 (1921), 129–41.

Bergmann, Fredrick L. "David Garrick and *The Clandestine Marriage.*" *PMLA*, 67 (1952), 148–62.

Boaden, James, ed. *The Private Correspondence of David Garrick.* 2 vols. London, 1831–32.

Boswell, James. *Life of Samuel Johnson.* Edited by George Birbeck Hill; rev. L. F. Powell. 6 vols. London, 1934–50.

Burnim, Kalman A. *David Garrick, Director.* Pittsburgh, Pa., 1961.

Bushwell, John. *An Historical Account of the Knights of the Most Noble Order of the Garter.* London, 1757.

Cibber, Colley. *The Careless Husband.* London, 1705.

Colman, George (the Elder). *The English Merchant.* London, 1767.

Colman, George (the Younger). *Posthumous Letters from Various Celebrated Men.* London, 1820.

Cooke, J. *Lethe.* London, 1745.

Cozens-Hardy, Basil, ed. *The Diary of Sylas Neville, 1767–1788.* Oxford, 1950.

———. Typescript of the Neville MS. Microfilm in Folger Shakespeare Library, Washington, D.C.

Cradock, Joseph. *Literary and Miscellaneous Memoirs.* 4 vols. London, 1828.

Cross, Richard. MS Diary, 1747–60, 1760–68. Folger Shakespeare Library, Washington, D.C.

Dancourt, Florent Carton Sieur. *La Parisienne*. La Haye, 1694.

Davies, Thomas. *Memoirs of the Life of David Garrick*. 2 vols. London, 1808.

Deelman, Christian. *The Great Shakespeare Jubilee*. New York, 1964.

Dodsley, Robert. *A Collection of Poems*. London, 1748.

Doran, John. *Annals of the English Stage*. 3 vols. London, 1888.

England, Martha Winburn. *Garrick and Stratford*. New York, 1962.

Etherege, Sir George. *The Man of Mode*. London, 1676.

Fagan, Barthélemi-Christophe. *La Pupille*. Paris, 1758.

Fawcett, John. Commonplace Book of Clippings. Folger Shakespeare Library, Washington, D.C.

Fiske, Roger. *English Theatre Music in the Eighteenth Century*. Oxford, 1973.

Fitzgerald, Percy. *The Life of David Garrick*. 2 vols. London, 1868.

———. *A New History of the English Stage*. 2 vols. London, 1882.

Forster, John. *Life of Oliver Goldsmith*. London, 1848.

———. *Life and Times of Oliver Goldsmith*. 2nd ed. 2 vols. London, 1854.

Garrick, David. *The Poetical Works of David Garrick*. London, 1785.

Genest, John. *Some Acount of the English Stage*. Bath, 1832.

Hedgcock, Frank A. *A Cosmopolitan Actor: David Garrick and His French Friends*. London, 1912.

Highfill, Philip H., Jr., Kalman A. Burnim, and Edward A. Langhans. *A Biographical Dictionary of Actors, Actresses, Musicians, Dancers, Managers, and Other Stage Personnel in London, 1660–1800*. Carbondale, Ill., 1973–.

Hopkins, William. MS Diary, 1769–76. Folger Shakespeare Library, Washington, D.C.

Hughes, Leo. *A Century of English Farce*. Princeton, 1956.

Iacuzzi, Alfred. *The European Vogue of Favart*. New York, 1932.

Kelly, John A. *German Visitors to English Theaters in the Eighteenth Century*. Princeton, 1936.

Kinne, Willard Austin. *Revivals and Importations of French Comedies in England 1749–1800*. New York, 1939.

Knapp, Mary E. *A Checklist of Verse by David Garrick*. Charlottesville, Va., 1955 (revised 1974).

Knight, Joseph. *David Garrick*. London, 1894.

Lamb, Charles. *Dramatic Essays of Charles Lamb*. Edited by Brander Matthews. New York, 1892.

Lee, Sir Sidney. *A Life of William Shakespeare*. London, 1925.

Le Sage, Alain René. *Crispin, rival de son maître*. Paris, 1707.

Little, David Mason, George M. Kahrl, and Phoebe de K. Wilson, eds. *The Letters of David Garrick*. 3 vols. Cambridge, Mass., 1963.

Macmillan, Dougald. *Catalogue of the Larpent Plays in the Huntington Library*. San Marino, Calif., 1939.

———. *Drury Lane Calendar, 1747–1776*. Oxford, 1938.

Miller, James. *An Hospital for Fools*. London, 1739.

Molière, Jean-Baptiste. *The Dramatic Works of J. B. Poquelin-Molière*. Translated by Henri Van Laun. 6 vols. Edinburgh, 1878.

Motteux, Peter Antony. *The Novelty; or, Every Act a Play*. London, 1697.

Murphy, Arthur. *The Life of David Garrick.* 2 vols. London, 1801.

Nicoll, Allardyce. *British Drama.* New York, 1925.

———. *A History of Restoration Drama, 1660–1700.* Cambridge, 1923.

———. *A History of Early Eighteenth-Century Drama, 1700–1750.* Cambridge, 1929.

———. *A History of Late Eighteenth-Century Drama, 1750–1800.* Cambridge, 1937.

Otway, Thomas. *The Orphan.* London, 1680.

Oulton, W. C. *The History of the London Theatres.* 2 vols. London, 1796.

Page, E. R. *George Colman, The Elder.* New York, 1935.

Pedicord, Harry William. *The Theatrical Public in the Time of David Garrick.* New York, 1954.

Perrin, Michel. *David Garrick Homme de Theatre.* 2 vols. Dissertation., Universite de Lille, 1978.

Scouten, Arthur H. *The London Stage. Part 3: 1729–1747.* 2 vols. Carbondale, Ill., 1961.

Seldon, John. *Titles of Honor.* London, 1614.

Stein, Elizabeth P. *Three Plays by David Garrick.* New York, 1926.

———. *David Garrick, Dramatist.* New York, 1938.

Stone, George Winchester, Jr. *The London Stage. Part 4: 1747–1776.* 3 vols. Carbondale, Ill., 1962.

Swift, Jonathan. *Works.* Vol. III. Dublin, 1735.

Vanbrugh, Sir John. *The Provok'd Wife.* London, 1697.

Victor, Benjamin. *The History of the Theatres of London.* 3 vols. London, 1761–71.

West, Gilbert. *The Institution of the Garter.* London, 1742.

Wilkinson, Tate. *Memoirs of His Own Life.* York, 1790.

———. *The Wandering Patentee.* London, 1795.

Wycherley, William. *The Country Wife.* London, 1675.

Commentary and Notes

Lethe; or, Esop in the Shades

Two seasons before his extraordinary debut as an actor, David Garrick had his first play produced. Henry Giffard and his wife were members of the Drury Lane company in the 1739–40 season and for Giffard's benefit night, 15 April 1740, the couple appeared as Sir Charles and Lady Betty in Colley Cibber's *The Careless Husband*. Their afterpiece that evening was "a new Dramatic Satire," Garrick's *Lethe; or, Esop in the Shades*. For its second performance, however, the new play had to wait an entire season, while the Giffard family took advantage of a relaxation in the enforcing of the Licensing Act to reopen "the Late Theatre" in Goodman's Fields (15 October 1740) and establish an efficient repertoire. Once Garrick had become an acting sensation on 19 October 1741, *Lethe* was revived at Goodman's Fields on 7 April 1741 for seven (benefit) performances that season and twenty-six in 1741–42. After an inauspicious beginning, *Lethe* became an established property and, with many changes in its scenes, one of the standard afterpieces during Garrick's lifetime.

Lethe has no formal plot, rather a framework within which Garrick could add or subtract scenes throughout his stage career. Using a formula of trial by derision the author is able to satirize any group of characters appropriate to his whim and the changing taste of his audiences. In what would seem a daring gesture, Garrick seized upon James Miller's *An Hospital for Fools*, a comedy performed quite recently at Drury Lane (15 November 1739) and hissed off the stage two nights later. Miller's play had in turn been based partially on Vadé's *L'Hopital des Foux* and damned by Miller's enemies because he had introduced scenes in a previous play, *The Coffee-House* (Drury Lane, 26 January 1738), which the Templars thought disparaged their pet haunt.

From Miller Garrick took his basic structure. Aesculapius, at Jupiter's order, is assigned the task of assisting mortals to rid themselves of folly. But when the mortals fail to respond to Mercury's invitation because they won't admit their follies, the call goes out to have them bring friends and neighbors so afflicted. This summons they do heed, and the stage is soon filled with fools of every persuasion. At this point Mercury calls for wise men to present themselves, and with one exception the entire company answers. The lone holdout, the only true wise man, advises Aesculapius to test his suppliants by their own opinion of themselves. The result is a dance of fools, and the company is dismissed no wiser than its members when they came.

Instead of Miller's Aesculapius, Garrick borrowed his Esop from Sir John Vanbrugh's *Aesop* (1697), especially the situation in which the foolish visitors to Learcus's home react to the sage's advice. Garrick's characters come at the invitation of Pluto and the suggestion of Proserpine, the anniversary of whose abduction is being celebrated. Qualified mortals are to be allowed to drink water from the river Lethe and to forget their problems. They are brought to the River Styx, ferried by Charon, the boatman, across to Elysium, where Esop is the judge of their worthiness to drink from Lethe. As they are about to enter, the mortals are greeted by Mercury and Esop in a song:

> Ye mortals whom fancies and troubles perplex,
> Whom folly misguides and infirmities vex;
> Whose lives hardly know what it is to be blest,
> Who rise without joy and lie down without rest;
>   Obey the glad summons, to Lethe repair,
>   Drink deep of the stream and forget all your care.[1]

There follows a series of comic portraits satirizing the misfits of London society: the Poet whose play has been damned; an Old Man afraid to die because he cannot take his money with him; a Fine Gentleman or Beau who wishes to forget his two qualities, modesty and good nature; Mr. and Mrs. Tatoo, a young couple three months married and already wanting a divorce; a Frenchman who wishes to forget his English creditors and wed a lady of fortune; Mrs. Riot, who considers herself a fashionable lady and is embarrassed by her loutish husband; a Drunken Man, who turns out to be Mr. Riot, accompanied by his tailor, who desires to forget an unfaithful wife. Finally, Charon enters to describe the confusion among the other mortals still waiting on the other side of the Styx. They are ladies who "have been disputing so long and so loud about taking place and precedency that they have set their relations a tilting at one another, to support their vanity."[2] Charon has left these creatures "to settle their prerogatives by themselves and be friends at their leisure." The comedy ends when Esop decides to discharge those now in the grove; and, while the characters already interviewed return to the stage, Mercury invites the company to drink from Lethe as Esop reminds the audience that " 'Tis vice alone disturbs the human breast; / Care dies with guilt; be virtuous and be blest."[3]

Any discussion of *Lethe* depends upon the version in hand. The reader may refer to the following tabulation of the character variations in the *dramatis personae* from 1740 through 1772.

---

1. Lines 60–65.
2. Lines 775–77.
3. Lines 824–25.

GARRICK'S ALTERATIONS IN *Lethe* EPISODES

[Names italicized represent their first appearance in a revival.]

L 4/15/'40	GF 4/7/'41	GF 1745[4]	DL 1749[5]	DL 1757	DL 1/11/'72[6]
sop	Esop	Esop	Aesop	Aesop	Aesop
lercury	Mercury	Mercury	Mercury	Mercury	Mercury
haron	Charon	Charon	Charon	Charon	Charon
Drunken Man	Drunken Man	Drunken Man	Drunken Man	Drunken Man	Drunken Man
eau	Beau	Beau	*Fine Gentleman*	Fine Gentleman	*Fribble*
Attorney	Attorney				
Thomas	Thomas	Thomas			
	Irishman	Irishman			*Irishman*
	Frenchman	Frenchman	Frenchman	Frenchman	Frenchman
			Poet		
			Mr. Tatoo	Mr. Tatoo	*Mr. Carbine* (Tatoo)
			Old Man	Old Man	Old Man
			Tailor		Tailor
				[Bowman]	Bowman
				Ld. Chalkstone	Ld. Chalkstone
					Snap
ady	1st Lady	1st Lady			
ady	2nd Lady	2nd Lady			
		Miss Lucy	*Mrs. Riot*	Mrs. Riot	
			Mrs. Tatoo	*Fine Lady*	Fine Lady
				Mrs. Tatoo	*Mrs. Carbine* (Tatoo)

The script used on the first night at Drury Lane is presumably that which the manager, Charles Fleetwood, dispatched to the Lord Chamberlain's office for licensing, signed 1 April 1740. This manuscript is now part of the Larpent Collection in the Huntington Library and differs considerably from the first authorized edition published in 1749. Miss Lucy, Vanbrugh's Hortensia, who is later to become Mrs. Tatoo, is also the basis for the later Mrs. Riot and the Fine Lady. In this Larpent manuscript Lucy describes the tastes of a fine lady in a song of eight stanzas later to be billed as "Life of a Belle," which begins

> What lives are so happy as those of the Fair,
> Who scarcely a moment from pleasure can spare,
> But leave their husband's reflection and care,
> Such, such is the Life of a Belle.[7]

The substance of this song was developed in prose in all the later versions.

When Garrick revived the play for Goodman's Fields in the next two seasons, he lengthened it by the addition of two more characters, an Irishman and a Frenchman, while continuing the character of the Attorney. But by

4. Surreptitious edition published by J. Cooke.
5. First authorized edition.
6. *The London Stage*, Part 4, III, 1599.
7. Quoted with the permission of the Huntington Library.

1745 he had dropped the Attorney and added another Lady, if we are to credit an unauthorized version of the play published by J. Cooke (London, 1745) and advertising it "As Acted in the Theatres in London, With Universal Applause. Written by Mr. Garrick." This version amounts to only twenty-two pages, the curtailment of over three hundred lines in what appears to be an auditor's or an actor's memorial account or sketch of the characters and dialogue. Issued during Garrick's second season in Dublin, this version is of little value except that it prints for the first time the Epilogue to *Lethe*, 1740, as spoken by Mrs. Clive and James Raftor.

The play was then put aside until Garrick had established himself as manager at Drury Lane. On 2 January 1749 *Lethe* was again revived, and Richard Cross noted in his *Diary*, "This farce of Lethe was wrote some years ago and play'd with Success, & was reviv'd this Night with great Alterations, & was but indifferently receiv'd by the Audience." On the following night Cross comments, "Great Applause to ye Farce, some little Hiss."[8] Nevertheless, *Lethe* was performed sixteen times before the end of the season. In this alteration Garrick introduced three additional characters, the Poet, the Old Man, and the Old Man's tailor. The Beau has now become the Fine Gentleman; Thomas is now Mr. Tatoo; the two Ladies have become Mrs. Riot and Mrs. Tatoo. The Irishman has been dropped and will not appear again until the 1771–72 season, when Garrick rewrote the role to fit John Moody.

In the same season (1 February 1749) there appeared what Professor Stone calls "a fifty-two page puff of *Lethe*," a piece entitled *Lethe Rehearsed; or, A Critical Discussion of the Beauties & Blemishes of that Performance, etc.*[9] Written in the usual conversational manner, the piece has several comments which, while purporting to be derogative, show what Garrick was about in this alteration. Dr. Heartfree thinks "His piece seems to be a Copy of one of Lucian's Dialogues; and as from the Action it moves us more, methinks it ought not to charm us less. Instruction, is the Business of the Stage, and therefore in minding that he minds his own Business, and at the same Time puts us on minding ours." Mr. Snipsnap, however, thinks otherwise: "Ha! ha! ha! The first Time that ever I knew Business and the Play-House brought together; why now I thought we went there to forget Business, and to Church to hear Sermons? Then, for Lucian, I'll be hanged if he knows any more of him than I do. Walsh's *Hospital for Fools*, and Sir John Vanbrugh's *Aesop*, furnished the Materials. Dodsley's *Toy-Shop* was the Original, and this but a Copy."[10]

As for the new characters introduced in this alteration, Mr. Snipsnap declares, "Lord, Sir! you are in love with the Fellow to Madness. Now to me his *Poet* is his own Character, and I think every new Farce he writes, is a Proof that the last is not the *worst* that could be written! His *Lying Valet* was poor, his *Miss in her Teens* Trash, his *Lethe* fetched from *Hell*, and I wish it and *him* both at the Devil. Why, Sir, you talk of Society; this Fellow's an

8. *The London Stage*, Part 4, I, 86.
9. London: J. Roberts, 1749.
10. *Lethe Rehearsed*, pp. 2–3.

Enemy to Society, he makes us all a Jest to one another."[11] Dr. Heartfree has
some things to say about the two featured ladies in the farce: "Mrs. *Tatoo* is,
in my Judgment Madam, a *fine Lady* in her leading-strings; whereas Mrs.
Riot is a fine Lady full-grown; the former *would* be she cannot tell *what*, the
latter is the very thing she *would* be and could not *tell*. Mrs. *Tatoo* is just
running wild. Mrs. *Riot* is come to Maturity in Madness. The one fills us with
fear of what she may come *to*, and the other is the Picture of *that* of which
we are afraid—A Woman of Fashion equally *distracted* in her *Notions* and
corrupted in her *Manners*."[12] Mr. Snipsnap concludes by saying, "for a Man
to play *three* top Parts in the same *Farce*, and that *Farce* his own,—is, in my
shallow Judgment, a little *extraordinary*, and not a little *fantastical*."[13]

On 27 March 1756 Garrick added his most famous characterization in
farce, the part of Lord Chalkstone, the only one who does not desire to drink
the waters of Lethe. This Lord has come out of curiosity to meet and converse with the immortal Aesop and to take a good look at the Elysian Fields.
He is the uncle of the Fine Gentleman whom he expects to meet in the grove;
but before he leaves he has pertinent remarks for Aesop concerning such
matters as pain and pleasure, wagering, landscape gardening, and his ideas on
the marriage-contract. "I married for a fortune; she for a title. When we both
had got what we wanted, the sooner we parted the better—We did so; and
are now waiting for the happy moment, that will give to one of us the liberty
of playing the same farce over again."[14] A little over a month later the re-
viewer in *The Old Maid* was happy with Mrs. Clive's Italian Song as Mrs. Riot,
but not so charmed with Lord Chalkstone: "What is there now in a Lord's
having Gout, loving a bottle, pretending to taste, or being follow'd by a flatterer?"[15] Nevertheless, Lord Chalkstone became the feature of the new *Lethe*
and so remains to this day. His scene, taken from the fifth edition (London,
1757), immediately follows the text of the first edition of the play in this
volume.

In the 1772 alteration the Fine Gentleman has been replaced by a Fribble,
and the Tatoo characters have become the Carbines, a horse-grenadier and his
new wife. The scene with Fribble was submitted for licensing on 26 December
1771 and is now a part of the Larpent Collection.[16] Since the part of the Fine
Gentleman had become obsolete because of his remarks on the behavior of
gentlemen behind Garrick's scenes, no problem at this late date, he was replaced by a Fribble. This gentleman is bothered by an extreme case of nerves:
"(*Taking off his coat.*) I wish I was got back again with all my Soul—what
with the damp of the River, the nastiness of the Boat, the Vulgarity of the
boat fellow—my Nerves are in a terrible flutter—& I have nothing to smell to,

---

11. Ibid., pp. 4–5.
12. Ibid., p. 21.
13. Ibid., p. 35.
14. The Lord Chalkstone scene is added from the Fifth Edition. Lines 130–34.
15. *The London Stage*, Part 4, II, 534.
16. Stone has a curious note in *The London Stage*, Part 4, III, 1599, in which he
     states "Macmillan notes lack of Fribble parts in Larpent MS." (But see *Cata-
     logue of the Larpent Plays*, p. 13.)

but my Essence of Roses! (*Seeing Aesop.*) what in the name of Delicacy in-duc'd me to visit this lower World! when from a babe I could not bear the thoughts of being in the dark, or meeting hobgobblins."[17] He wishes to drink of Lethe and forget his nerves long enough to cuckold the horse-grenadier who stole his beloved. The grenadier may just be the same Mr. Carbine now strolling with his young wife in the grove. Aesop dismisses the fop with these words: "Go thy ways for the most unaccountable Animal I ever beheld or heard of—'tis beyond the power of fable to describe thee."[18]

Five years later Garrick was in retirement when he made one further al-teration of *Lethe*. When invited to Windsor to read before the royal family he added the character of a Jew. W. C. Oulton has described the incident: "In the year 1777 Mr. Garrick was desired to read a play before the king and queen at Buckingham house in the manner of Mons. Le Texier, who had obtained great reputation by reading them, sitting at a table, and acting them as he went on. Mr. Garrick fixed upon his own farce of *Lethe*, in which he introduced for the occasion the character of an ungrateful Jew; there were present the king, queen, princes royal, duchess of Argyle, and one or two more of the ladies-in-waiting; but the coldness with which this select party heard him, so opposite to the applause he had always been used to on the stage, had such an effect upon him, as to prevent his exertions; or, to use Mr. Garrick's own words in relating the circumstance, 'it was,' said he, 'as if they had thrown a wet blanket over me.' "[19]

In this his first play Garrick discovered stage personalities, stage business and situations that in his later work would evolve into great and lasting char-acterizations. Mrs. Riot's mispronunciation of words will become the distinc-tive feature of Mrs. Heidelberg in *The Clandestine Marriage* (later to appear again in Sheridan's Mrs. Malaprop in *The Rivals*). Lord Chalkstone and his companion, Bowman, will become Lord Ogleby and his valet Canton. If, as Leo Hughes reminds us, "the chief, even the exclusive, business of farce is to stimulate the risibilities of the audience,"[20] in *Lethe* Garrick proved himself at once a master of farce and social satire. His eight other farces only confirm this auspicious beginning.

Yet there have been critical voices that would deny Garrick's very real art in this form. Frank A. Hedgcock, with his usual severity, takes a scornful look at *Lethe* in *David Garrick and His French Friends* (London, 1912) and tries to describe Garrick's idea of comedy: "This little sketch is light, but sparkling; the dialogue is good and the characters vigorously drawn. From it one may judge of the meaning of the word *comedy* for Garrick—a series of situations in which amusing and ridiculous types of humanity can be brought together to expose their peculiarities before the eyes of the audience. As for the plot, that was always as slight as might be, and he preferred to take it ready-made from the works of some predecessor. Here, as in the poems,

---

17. Quoted with the permission of the Huntington Library.
18. Quoted with the permission of the Huntington Library.
19. *History of the London Theatres*, I, 44.
20. *A Century of English Farce*, p. 19.

composing power is lacking, and it is worthy of note, that, in the only one of his pieces which is important from its structure, he had the assistance of his friend George Colman."[21] But we can no longer confuse "comedy" with "farce" as Garrick understood the term. A busy manager with entertainment on his mind, Garrick would have been delighted with Hedgcock's account of his writing method (except in the matter of *The Clandestine Marriage*, which is discussed thoroughly in Garrick's favor in this edition). The writer of the farce afterpiece aimed no higher than to construct or adapt pieces which would prop up mainpieces and delight the galleries as well as pit and boxes and bring money to the box-office. The longevity of Garrick's *Lethe* attests the measure of Garrick's art and predicts his lifelong success as a writer of afterpieces for his theatre—263 performances in 26 seasons.

TEXTS

O1   London: Printed by J. Cooke, 1745 (Surreptitious)
O2   1st edition. London: Paul Vaillant, 1749.
D1   Dublin: G. and A. Ewing, 1749.
O3   3rd edition. London: Paul Vaillant, 1752.
O4   London: Printed for H. D. Symonds [1755?].
O5   5th edition. London: Paul Vaillant, 1757. "With the Additional Character of Lord Chalkstone."
O6   Dublin: Printed for G. and A. Ewing, G. Faulkner, etc., 1759.
O7   Edinburgh: Printed for A. Donaldson, 1760.
O8   6th edition. London: Paul Vaillant, 1762.
D2   Glasgow: N.p., 1766. "The Sixth Edition."
O9   6th edition. London: Paul Vaillant, 1767.
W1   *Dramatic Works of David Garrick.* [London.] N.p., 1768, I, 105-52.
O10   7th edition. Dublin: Printed for W. Spotswood, 1774.
W2   *Dramatic Works of David Garrick.* London: Printed for R. Bald, T. Blaw, and J. Kurt, 1774. I, 81-112.

[THE PLAY]

0.2. Lethe] one of the rivers of Hades. Souls of the dead must taste of its waters and forget all said and done when they were alive.

0.3. Charon] the ferryman at the River Styx. Aesop] the deformed Phrygian slave of the sixth century B.C., author of *Aesop's Fables.*

3. Styx] the river of Hades, which flows nine times round the Infernal Regions.

6. Proserpine] wife of Pluto and Queen of the Infernal Regions. Pluto] king of the Infernal Regions.

18. Elysium] the happy land, the abode of the blessed.

29.1 Mercury] the god of science and commerce, patron of travelers, rogues, thieves and vagabonds.

102-3. Stone of Sysiphus] Sisyphus (Sisyphos) was punished in the underworld by being forced to roll a huge stone up a hill. Having reached the top, the stone would roll down again. Thirst of Tantalus] for his crimes Tantalus was placed in water which he longed for but could never drink.

---

21. P. 90.

108. *Tempora mutantur*] How times have changed!

129. catcall] a squeaking whistle used in theatres to express derision.

170. Helicon] mountain home of the Greek Muses.

261. drawer] a bartender.

444. front] affront.

459. polir] polish.

525. Serbeerus] Cerberus, three-headed dog guarding entrance to the Infernal Regions.

540. Pump Room] place at a spa where medicinal waters are distributed.

552. Johnson] Ben Jonson.

605. vapors] depressed spirits, hypochondria.

652. arrack] Oriental alcoholic drink made from rice or molasses.

662. bum-bailiffs] officers of the law always close to one's rear.

691. hump] Aesop was supposed to be hunchbacked.

709. cabbaged] stolen, appropriated by a tailor in cutting out clothes.

The Lying Valet

David Garrick's acting debut was made under the management of Henry Giffard at Goodman's Fields Theatre on Monday evening 19 October 1741. The next day he was writing to his brother Peter about his triumph and adding a postscript: "I have a farce (yᵉ Lying Valet) coming out at Drury Lane."[1] For some reason Drury Lane, which had produced his first play, *Lethe* (15 April 1740), rejected his second (or, what is more probable, Giffard made a better offer), and a little more than a month after his debut, while excitement mounted over the young unknown's *Richard III*, the farce was produced at Goodman's Fields. *The Lying Valet* followed Garrick's appearance as Chamont in Otway's *The Orphan* on Monday evening, 30 November, with Garrick playing the valet Sharp in the afterpiece.

The enthusiastic reception accorded this farce is reflected in another letter to brother Peter which began: "On Monday last I sent by yᵉ Carrier . . . The Lying Valet; the Valet takes Prodigiously, & is approv'd of by Men of Genius & thought yᵉ Most diverting Farce that ever was perform'd; I believe You'll find it read pretty well, & in performance tis a general Roar from beginning to End; & I have got as much Reputation in yᵉ Character of Sharp & is in any Other Character I have perform'd tho far different from yᵉ Others."[2] The approval of "Men of Genius" is the subject of a reproof Garrick received from the Reverend Thomas Newton in a letter on 18 January 1742: "I am sorry it happened so that you could not oblige us with the "Orphan" and the "Lying Valet" last week; and it appears the more unlucky, as you was able to act the Lying Valet and something else almost every night. It would certainly have been a very great honour to you, if of no other advantage, for such a person as Mr. Pultney to come so far to be one of your audience; and, if I had been in your capacity, I should have thought it worth while to have strained a point, or done almost any thing, rather than have disappointed him.

1. *Letters*, I, 28.
2. Ibid., I, 33–34.

I would have acted that night, if I had spared myself all the rest for it."[3] Garrick did act the Otway play and the farce on 19 January 1742, and *The Lying Valet* was given thirty-five performances that first season, to become one of the favorite afterpieces of the century. We may assume that the Reverend Mr. Newton and the minister, William Pulteney, who became Earl of Bath that year, eventually witnessed a performance.

The Lying Valet opened on Monday 30 November 1741, and before the year's end one J. Rhames, of The Bee-Hive in Dame-Street, Dublin, was offering a printed text with a title-page reading: "*The Lying Valet*; / As it is now performing with Great Applause, / at the THEATRE in *Goodman's Fields* / By D. Garrick." This volume is a badly printed duodecimo but with surprisingly few differences from the first edition published in 1742 by Paul Vaillant and J. Roberts. Whether the Irish edition actually was published within a month of the first night of Garrick's farce (which appears most unlikely), whether J. Rhames dated his edition to supercede the legitimate publishers, or whether the Irish edition was completely unauthorized, we have no way of knowing. As a newly discovered dramatist, Garrick experienced an embarrassment which was to be repeated later in the instance of J. Cooke's unauthorized publication of the truncated version of *Lethe*, London 1745: "As acted in the Theatres in London, With Universal Applause. Written by Mr. Garrick." We have treated the Rhames edition of *The Lying Valet* simply as a first "Dublin," taking the 1742 octavo to be the "first" for the purposes of copy-text. Two more Rhames editions were published in 1742.

Garrick's farce is based on *All Without Money*, the second act of the curious entertainment called *The Novelty*; *or, Every Act a Play*, which Peter Antony Motteux, a Norman merchant in London, had written for Lincoln's Inn Fields in 1697. Motteux, the translator of Rabelais and Cervantes, in making his "novelty" had produced with minor changes an almost literal prose translation of the French verse comedy *Le Souper mal-apprêté* by Noël Le Breton sieur de Hauteroche (1616–1707).

Needmore, a spendthrift youth in Motteux's play, aims to marry in order to redeem himself from bankruptcy and his creditors. Having invited his love, Theodosia, to supper, he finds himself unable to finance the evening's entertainment. Two other friends, Freeman and Clara, also wish to attend. It is up to the valet, Speedwell, to save the occasion. He goes to Theodosia, suggests that her calling at Needmore's house is a matter of consequence to her reputation, and persuades the lady to refuse Needmore's invitation. However, jealousy prevails, and Theodosia joins Freeman and Clara for the supper. Even Speedwell's trumped-up story that Theodosia's brother has been gravely wounded in a duel fails to daunt the heroine, especially when the brother appears to prove the valet's lie. Speedwell wants to get rid of their guests by setting fire to the house. When his master is reluctant to join in such a plan, Speedwell puts a final suggestion into action. When he informs Theodosia and the others that the landlady's daughter has just been taken with the smallpox, the visitors flee and Needmore announces his own reform.

In act 1 Garrick follows his originals faithfully. Gayless is told by Me-

3. *Private Correspondence*, I, 5.

lissa, his bride-to-be, that she wishes him to give her an elegant supper and entertainment at his house. But Gayless is bankrupt and pursued by creditors who have learned that he has been disinherited by his father. The valet, Sharp, offers to relieve his master of his obligation by visiting Melissa and, without his master's knowledge, warns the young lady not to attend the dinner party. He suggests that her previous visits to Gayless are a matter of gossip among the neighbors and cast unsavory implications on her reputation. Melissa decides not to attend the party. But her maid, Kitty, suspects subterfuge in Sharp's behavior and tries to inform Melissa of Gayless's true financial plight. While pretending to disregard her maid's information, Melissa now has second thoughts about refusing her lover's invitation, especially after she receives a letter from Gayless's father, Sir William Gayless.

Thus far Garrick has followed his originals, but improved upon them with superior humor and brilliant dialogue. It is in act 2 that the important changes in characterization and action take place. Motteux's heroine is a jealous woman. Melissa is not jealous but extremely sympathetic. She decides to attend the Gayless party to determine for herself just how critical her lover's financial situation may be. And she invents a plot of her own, comes to the supper in disguise, and persuades Dick, an old friend of Sir William, to pretend he is a drunken cook. Garrick also amplifies the comedy by having four guests appear, and by having Gayless and Sharp try to borrow money from the disguised Melissa. When the furor dies down Sharp has been unable to send the guests packing, and the company laughs at both Sharp and Gayless for having been taken in by Melissa's stratagem. With the father's forgiveness and blessing, Gayless finally obtains consent to marry Melissa, and in an amusing scene of repentance and gratitude he declares his reformation.

Of greater moment are the changes Garrick made in the latter part of the second act. The episode of the cook is greatly expanded from Motteux's treatment. Garrick's cook is a benevolent prankster at Melissa's bidding. He is a long-time friend of Sir William, and instead of demanding payment for past meals, as in the originals, he supplies the company with the supper so sorely needed. His actions lead to the amusing scene in which Gayless and Sharp try to borrow money from the guests to pay this unusual cook. Omitting the scene in Motteux in which the law makes its appearance, Garrick concentrates on the defeat and outfacing of Sharp and his lies. The valets in Hauteroche and Motteux are able to get rid of the invited company, but poor Sharp is defeated. The company laughs at his failure at the close of the comedy.

The reformation of Gayless, making this the sole Garrick comedy to be purely sentimental, is carefully plotted. In the French original the hero, finding himself alone and again in command of his situation, reverts to his old extravagant self. Motteux's hero is brought to what amounts to an instant reformation. Garrick is more deliberate with Gayless. He has his hero repent his extravagance at the beginning of the play.

SHARP. ... Now, Sir, if you marry this young lady, who as yet, thank heaven, knows nothing of your misfortunes, and by that means procure a better fortune than that you squandered away, make a good husband and turn

economist, you still may be happy, may still be Sir William's heir, and the lady too no loser by the bargain. There's reason and argument, Sir.
GAYLESS. 'Twas with that prospect I first made love to her; and though my fortune has been ill spent, I have at least purchased discretion with it.[4]

Despite Sharp's plans and argument, Gayless declares he will not deceive Melissa. Only Sharp's threat to leave forces Gayless to acquiesce in the deception.

GAYLESS. Well then, I am resolved to favor the cheat, and as I shall quite change my former course of life, happy may be the consequences. At least of this I am sure —
SHARP. That you can't be worse than you are at present.[5]

The sentimental is apparent in both hero and heroine throughout the farce. Gayless, after the disclosure that his dueling partner has been the disguised Melissa, pleads his "necessities." Melissa in an aside cries,

His tears have softened me at once.—Your necessities, Mr. Gayless, with such real contrition, are too powerful motives not to affect the breast already prejudiced in your favor. You have suffered too much already for your extravagance; and as I take part in your sufferings, 'tis easing myself to relieve you. Know, therefore, all that's past I freely forgive.
GAYLESS. You cannot mean it, sure. I am lost in wonder.[6]

When Gayless is allowed to read his father's letter to Melissa, in which he is forgiven and restored to parental favor, he exclaims: "O Melissa, this is too much. Thus let me show my thanks and gratitude, (*kneeling: she raises him*) for here 'tis only due."[7]
Only the two servants, Sharp and Kitty, redeem the farce from its sentimentality. When Melissa proposes to reward Kitty with "a small fortune" for the couple's fidelity, Sharp's reaction is:

I fancy, Madam, 'twould be better to half the small fortune between us, and keep us both single. For as we shall live in the same house, in all probability we may taste the comforts of matrimony and not be troubled with its inconveniences. What say you, Kitty?
KITTY. Do you hear, Sharp, before you talk of the comforts of matrimony, taste the comforts of a good dinner and recover your flesh a little; do, Puppy.[8]

Sharp is a direct descendant of the valets of the French stage, while Kitty is the soubrette who advises her mistress in the ways of the world. In his later plays Garrick will sometimes have the pair working together, but in *The Lying Valet* they are at odds until the play's end.
From this early farce and its sentimentality Garrick will depart to in-

4. Act I, lines 39–47.
5. Act I, lines 60–63.
6. Act II, lines 475–81.
7. Act II, lines 506–7.
8. Act II, lines 526–33.

dulge his own preference for the spirit of Restoration comedy. His leading characters in the future will transgress, acknowledge their follies, but they will not stage a reformation. Garrick accomplished this by creating in most of his comedies a character who acts as a commentator or mouthpiece for the author. This person hints at such reformation, points out the errant follies for the audience, then asks the spectators to join him in a hope for reformation. Only Sharp, in this comedy, is unrepentant to the end.

Every actor aspiring to become a playwright dreams of writing himself a great part. Garrick achieved this many times; but no part in his comedies fits him as well as the valet Sharp. When he was through acting it, the role became one of Richard Yates's popular vehicles. *The Lying Valet* is fast-paced and filled with fashionable and amusing dialogue, a farce that served not only at Goodman's Fields but became the functional support of main-pieces in the Drury Lane repertoire during the thirty-five years of Garrick's management. In all these years the farce had 374 performances (at all theatres), 3 "By Command," 23 "By Desire," and 114 benefit performances. Thirty-five additional performances occurred from Garrick's retirement in 1776 to 1800, according to the figures of George Winchester Stone, Jr., and Charles Beecher Hogan.[9]

Confirmation of the farce's continuing popularity is found in David Erskine Baker's *Companion to the Playhouse*,[10] where it is noted that . . . the little dramatic work . . . whether original, translation, or copy, has undoubtedly great merit, if character, plot, incident, and a rank of diction well adapted to those characters, can give it a just title to the praise I have bestowed on it.— Nor can there be stronger evidence borne to its deserts, than that approbation which constantly attends on it through the numerous repetitions of it in every season at both Theatres.

TEXTS

D1   Dublin: J. Rhames, 1741.
D2   Dublin: J. Rhames, 1742.
D3   Dublin: J. Rhames, 1742.
O1   1st edition. London: Paul Vaillant and J. Roberts, 1742.
O2   2nd edition. London: Paul Vaillant, 1743.
O3   3rd edition. London: Paul Vaillant, 1743.
D4   Dublin: Peter Wilson, 1746.
O4   4th edition. London: Paul Vaillant, 1749.
O5   5th edition. London: Paul Vaillant, 1751.
O6   6th edition. London: Paul Vaillant, 1756.
O7   Glasgow: J. Newbury, 1759, "eighth edition."
D5   Dublin: Peter Wilson, 1767.
W1   *Dramatic Works of David Garrick.* [London.] N.p., 1768, I, 1–52.
O8   7th edition. London: Paul Vaillant, 1769.
W2   *Dramatic Works of David Garrick.* London: Printed for R. Bald, T. Blaw, and J. Kurt, 1774, I, 13–46.

9.   *The London Stage*, Parts 4 and 5.
10.   London, 1764, Vol. I. *The Lying Valet*, p. 3.

[ACT I, i]

6–7. movables] small furniture and bric-a-brac.
51. keep house] remain inside the house.
149. pure] excellent.

[ACT I, ii]

103. fine taper crab] a crab-tree club.
150. vapors] depressed spirits, hypochondria.
151. qualms] a sudden fit of nausea.
201. ratafia] cordial or liqueur, brandy.

[ACT II, i]

22. bowels] interior of the body, seat of tender emotions.
120. the quorum] designating the body of justices of the peace.
226. riding post] from one set of fresh horses to another.
233. scrat] scratched.
255. a *sans prendre*] a card hand which could win without help from a partner.
258. *Allons donc*] Go, then.
307. A very woman] a true woman. and] if it.
320. *Allez-vous-en*] Go.
322. *Je ne puis pas*] I cannot.
445. *entre nous*] betwween ourselves.
454. drive away cart] let me hang.
460–61. knight of the woeful countenance] Sancho Panza called Don Quixote the "Knight of the Rueful Countenance."

Miss in Her Teens; or, The Medley of Lovers

Garrick's third play for the professional theatre was an adaptation of Florent Carton sieur Dancourt's *La Parisienne* (1691), to which he gave the title *Miss in Her Teens*. It was produced while he was engaged at Covent Garden in the 1746–47 season on Saturday 17 January 1747 as the afterpiece following a performance of Joseph Addison's *The Drummer; or, The Haunted House*. The resounding success of this little comedy could easily have been predicted by the artfully scheduled puffs beforehand—a note placed discreetly in the *General Advertiser* (December 1746) which hinted at something very special: "We hear there is now in rehearsal a Farce of two acts call'd *Miss in Her Teens*; and will be acted soon after the holidays." There followed a warning in the same newspaper that nothing under full prices would be taken during the time of the first performance on 17 January. Finally, the same warning was continued in every bill for *Miss in Her Teens* that season.[1]

There was the usual author's benefit on the third night (20 January 1747), and then the piece continued the remarkable run of eighteen nights, 17 January to 7 February. Ultimately, the company at Goodman's Fields was allowed

---

1. *The London Stage*, Part 3, II, 1275 and 1280.

to play it for thirteen performances, the Haymarket for two, Covent Garden for another eleven, Bartholomew and Southwark Fairs one each, for a total of forty-six performances to end the first season. When Garrick subsequently became the new manager of Drury Lane Theatre in September 1747, he and his partner established the piece in its new home for nineteen additional performances that season beginning on 24 October 1747.

The cast of the first production was a distinguished one, with Garrick as William Fribble; Henry Woodward as Captain Flash; John Hippisley as Sir Simon; Hippisley's daughter Jane as Miss Biddy; and Hannah Pritchard in the comic servant role of Tag. But after the initial run at Covent Garden Garrick transferred the comedy to Drury Lane, and only four members of the original cast were retained—Garrick, William Havard (the original Captain Loveit), John Arthur (Jasper), and Jane Hippisley (known from this date on as Mrs. Green). Charles Macklin replaced Woodward as Flash; Richard Yates assumed George Chapman's role as Puff; Arthur replaced Hippisley as Sir Simon, relinquishing the Jasper part to Charles Blakes. Mrs. Richard Cross, wife of Garrick's long-time prompter, played the Aunt, while Kitty Clive took over Mrs. Pritchard's part as Tag.

In all there were thirteen separate printings of *Miss in Her Teens* published during Garrick's lifetime. Three editions by J. and R. Tonson and S. Draper, and another printing for W. Webb, appeared in the first year. Alterations and variants in the succeeding texts are negligible, consisting for the most part in small changes the actors made to modify their stage speech. Other differences and a few cuts in later editions are clearly the result of changing public taste as the century wore on.

While contemporary criticism of this early piece is scarce, there is one which appeared in *The Anatomist and News Regulator* for 31 January 1747 and was reprinted in the *Gentleman's Magazine* for February as "The Farce of *Miss in Her Teens Anatomiz'd*."[2]

I have given uncommon attention to the success of a dramatic performance which whether in respect for the author, or the merit of the production, has been indulged a very long run, having all along equally filled *Covent Garden* Theatre with *company* and *laughter*.

Having been one of the numerous spectators twice myself, and having also read the piece with attention, so I venture to make a *dissection* of *Miss in Her Teens; or, The Medley of Lovers*.

This farce has little of *novelty* to recommend it, the subject having often been handled with equal *mastership* and *delicacy*. Some characters are *unnatural*, and others *faulty*; there is very little *plot*, and no *moral*: But these are blemishes which it shares in common with many celebrated comedies: It is merit enough, to entitle it to be made a *skeleton*, that

Mr. G–rr–k is the author of it,
The best actors have performed in it.
And the Town have been hugely diverted
with it.

---

2. Pp. 71–72.

This was also the opinion of Mary Granville, Mrs. Delaney, who wrote, "Last Saturday [29 January] I went to . . . the new farce . . . composed by Garrick; *nothing can be lower*, but the part he acts in it himself (Mr. Fribble) he makes so very ridiculous that it is really entertaining. It is said he mimics eleven men of fashion."[3] At the turn of the century, however, Arthur Murphy described *Miss in Her Teens* as

a piece at that time greatly admired, and to this day worthy of more notice than it meets with from those, whose province it is to cater for the public taste. The severest critic must allow that the fable is well imagined; the incidents spring out of one another in a well connected series, with frequent turns of surprise, but never violating the rules of probability. *Captain Flash* and *Fribble* are not the mere offspring of the poet's imagination, they were copied from life. The coffee-houses were infested by a set of young officers, who entered with a martial air, fierce *Kavenhuller* hats, and long swords. They paraded the room with ferocity, ready to draw without provocation. In direct contrast to this race of braggarts, stood the pretty gentlemen, who chose to unsex themselves, and make a display of delicacy that exceeded female softness. To expose these two opposite characters to contempt and ridicule was the design of *Miss in Her Teens*, and this was effectually done by *Woodward*, in *Captain Flash*, and Garrick in the mincing character of *Fribble*. The ferocious, swaggering *Bravo* did not choose to be called Captain Flash, and the delicate beau was frightened out of his little wits by the name of *Fribble*. They were both laughted out of society.[4]

In his adaptation of *La Parisienne* Garrick claimed only that the source of his comedy was French. The advertisement in the printed text concludes with the statement: "Whether the Plot and Characters are alter'd for the better or worse, may be seen by comparing it with *La Parisienne* of D'Ancourt." And such a comparison makes abundantly clear what Garrick was about in his alteration. By following Dancourt's text literally in most instances, by paraphrasing occasionally, transposing scenes, and cutting bits of the French original, he arrived at a more sparkling and vigorous English comedy filled with his own humor and interesting turns of stage business.

Both dramatists have their heroes fall in love at first sight with young ladies, Angélique and Miss Biddy, and then promptly send them off to foreign climes while their respective fathers become amorous and plan to marry their sons' loves. Each hero returns to find this complication and to discover the fact that his young lady has been flirting with other suitors. Garrick's principal departure from the Dancourt play lies in his treatment of the situation in which the heroine has arranged visits from her two admirers at the very moment the hero returns to claim her. In Dancourt's comedy Lisimon and Dorante are casual young men, Lisimon the more virile of the two, Dorante a weak and timid second. But in Garrick's adaptation these characters become Captain Flash, a swaggering bully, and Fribble, the effeminate fop Garrick always enjoys ridiculing as a plague upon society.

3.   *Letters*, I, 88.
4.   *Life*, I, 117–18.

Elizabeth Stein has drawn attention to the fact that John Genest, the nineteenth-century stage historian, saw in Flash and Fribble borrowings from Thomas Baker's *Tunbridge Walks* (Drury Lane, January 1702–3) and calls this "not unlikely." She points out, however, that while Baker's character Maiden is averse to women, except for the demands of the fashionable world, Garrick's Fribble shows "no aversion to women" and expects his wooing of Miss Biddy to end in marriage. She also subscribes to Genest's thought that Captain Squib in the Baker comedy is the suggestion to Garrick for the blustering Captain Flash, but credits Garrick with giving the character irascibility and cowardice.[5]

In any event, the comic duel scene between Flash and Fribble is the highlight of the Garrick play. With Captain Loveit shut up in Biddy's chamber, Fribble is the first suitor upon the scene. After an hilarious account of an accident to the nail of his little finger, Fribble continues his wooing of Miss Biddy by a fulsome description of her future life as Mrs. William Fribble: "All the domestic business will be taken off her hands. I shall make the tea, comb the dogs, and dress the children myself, if I should be blessed with any; so that, though I'm a commoner, Mrs. Fribble will lead the life of a woman of quality, for she will have nothing to do but lie in bed, play at cards, and scold the servants."[6] Fribble's visit is interrupted by the noisy arrival of Captain Flash. The little fellow is secreted in the Aunt's storehouse by the time the bully enters. Suspecting a rival, Flash threatens to cut the gentleman's throat. Whereupon Miss Biddy invites Fribble to come forth and engage with the Captain, only to find that both her suitors are cowards. Forced into a duelling position, and actually being prodded by Biddy and Tag, the ludicrous pair is frozen in fencing stance at the entrance of Captain Loveit and Puff. The so-called "Captain" Flash is unmasked as an army deserter and the Fribble dismissed with derision.

The comedy ends with the reconciling of father and son and the Aunt's consent to the marriage of Captain Loveit and Miss Biddy. After Tag has advised her husband Puff to show his manhood in a "proper place," Miss Biddy ends the piece by asking the Town to forgive her coquettish behavior since she has proved constant to her captain.

Taking into account his almost literal borrowings from the French comedy, Garrick proves himself adept at elaborating characters in order to move the stage action and convulse his audience. In *Miss in Her Teens* he produced what was to become a standard afterpiece in the repertoire of most English theatres, achieving under his own management a grand total of 324 performances, 9 "By Command," 20 "By Desire," and 121 benefit nights.

TEXTS

O1   1st edition. London: J. and R. Tonson and S. Draper, 1747.
O2   2nd edition. London: J. and R. Tonson and S. Draper, 1747.
Q1   3rd edition. London: J. and R. Tonson and S. Draper, 1747.
D1   London: Printed for W. Webb [1747].

5.   *David Garrick, Dramatist*, p. 84.
6.   II, i, lines 142–47.

O3   4th edition. London: J. and R. Tonson and S. Draper, 1748.
D2   5th edition. Dublin: Printed for G. and A. Ewing . . . and G. Faulkner, 1752.
O4   5th edition. London: J. and R. Tonson, 1758.
D3   6th edition. Belfast: James Magee, 1767.
O5   6th edition. London: T. Becket and Co., 1771.
D4   7th edition. Belfast: James Magee, 1759.
W1   *Dramatic Works of David Garrick.* [London.] N.p. 1768, I, 53–104.
W2   *Dramatic Works of David Garrick.* London: Printed for R. Bald, T. Blaw, and J. Kurt, 1774, I, 47–80.
O6   "A new edition." London: T. Becket, 1777.

[ADVERTISEMENT]

5. D'Ancourt] Florent Carton sieur Dancourt (1661–1725), French actor and dramatist with over fifty comedies to his credit.

[ACT I, i]

2. a pair of colors] two silken flags carried by the senior Ensigns in each regiment.

80. *dishabille*] dressed negligently.

124. George's] a tavern. the Tiltyard] military officers' quarters in Whitehall.

152–53. Achilles . . . Penelope] Puff affects a knowledge of classical mythology and his obvious error is intended to raise laughter.

161. Flanders] modern Belgium.

179. vails] tips and gratuities.

194. doublets] the same number turning up on both the dice at a throw.

[ACT I, ii]

110. patches] small bits of black silk or court plaster worn on the face to hide a blemish or to show off complexion.

116. Fribble] a trifler, one not in serious employment.

130. Strephon] popular term for a lover, derived from the Shepherd in Sir Philip Sidney's *Arcadia*.

[ACT II, i]

45. mumble] to chew or bite softly.

62. drops] lozenges or sugar-plums for medicinal purposes.

78–79. Virgin's-wax] a preparation of fresh, new, or unused white bee's wax.

79. Conserve] medicinal or confectionary preparation of some part of a plant or flower preserved with sugar.

108. Mocoa smelling-bottle] a clouded bottle for smelling-salts. Huswife] a pocket-case for needles, pins, thread, scissors.

120–21. knotting] fancy work of knitting threads into knots.

172. heads] coiffures.

244. cart] *carte*, a position in fencing with the smallsword.

252. Prince Charles] Karl Alexander (1712–80), prince of Lorraine, youngest son of Leopold, duke of Lorraine. His elder brother, Francis, married Maria Theresa, who made Charles an Austrian officer. Charles advanced from field marshal to governor-general of the Austrian Netherlands.

253. Bathiani] Marshal Bathiany, commander of Austrian forces at Lauffeld, 2 July 1747, prior to the Treaty of Aix-la-Chapelle in April 1748.

269. the Dial] Seven Dials. Traffic from Charing Cross, Soho, St. Giles, Drury Lane, and Covent Garden converged here around a seven-faced sundial.

449. *The Old Batchelor*] William Congreve's first comedy (Drury Lane, March 1693).

504. bully] the "gallant" or protector of a prostitute, a pimp.

509. Kennel] contemptuous slang for "Return home, you dog!"

577. caitiff] wretch, villain.

585. punctillios] trifles, niceties.

Lilliput

On 3 December 1756 Garrick presented his audience with an afterpiece in the form of a one-act comedy of manners called *Lilliput*. The piece had great advance drawing power in that it was derived almost literally from the fifth, sixth, and seventh chapters of the first book of Jonathan Swift's *Gulliver's Travels*, and, with the exception of the role of Gulliver, was acted by "not less than a hundred" children. But despite excellent preparations and well-disciplined child actors, the afterpiece was indifferently received. *The London Chronicle* for 6–8 January 1757 could only remark, "This dramatic piece contains a Mixture of Satire, and of that kind of Ridicule which [arises?] from the Disproportion between the Importance of the Speech and the Insignificance of the Speaker. It was, agreeably to the Place where the Scene was supposed to be, acted by Children, and introduced by the following Prologue, writ by Mr. Garrick, and Spoke by Mr. Woodward." After quoting the Prologue in its entirety, the critic continues, "We shall present our Readers with Part of one Scene." The scene noted is that in which Lady Flimnap tries to seduce Gulliver after he has been made a Nardac in Lilliput, and the critic uses it to point up the suggestive dialogue put into the mouth of a child actress.

The Theatrical Examiner went to greater lengths to excoriate all who had a hand in the production.

Lilliput is, I think, the most petit, trifling, indecent, immoral, stupid parcel of rubbish I ever yet met with; and I can't help judging it a scandal to the public, to suffer such a *thing* to pass a second night, which at best was alone calculated to please boys and girls, and fools of fashion; it may gratify them: the manager to debauch the minds of infants, by putting sentiments and glances in their breasts and eyes, that should never be taught at any years, which are sufficiently bad when naturally imbibed. The question of Gulliver, in answer to the infant lady's gross addresses, is horrid, if we allow an audience a common share of delicacy, *what should he do with her?* and what the devil does it mean? Finally, where is the instruction, or even tolerable language, to gild the dirt over. O tempora! O mores![1]

Lilliput was played for seventeen performances that season, and then

---

1.   London, 1757, p. 89.

was shelved during the remainder of Garrick's management. But on 15 May 1777 George Colman opened his management of the Haymarket Theatre with *The English Merchant*, to which was added *Lilliput*, as altered by David Garrick, and a "burlesque pageant in the characters of cards, Gulliver appearing as the knave of Clubs."[2]

In order to provide motivation for his manners comedy, Garrick supposes a violent love passion on the part of Lady Flimnap toward the "man-mountain" Gulliver. This and Lord Flimnap's desire to satisfy his honor in turn become the reasons for Gulliver's hasty escape from Lilliput to the country of the Blefuscudians. Through the tiny lady and her family Garrick coldly satirizes the contemporary Englishman's lack of morality, especially in the conventions of the marriage contract. Lord Flimnap's situation is commented upon by the lady's brothers, Fripperel, the fine gentleman of the court, and Bolgolam, chief of Lilliput's navy and a stern advocate of personal honor and virtue. Fripperel's defense of his sister's impulsive actions toward Gulliver stems from his wish to "have a Woman of Quality always a little incomprehensible." His brother Bolgolam, the spokesman for Garrick, holds Fripperel in contempt. "Such fellows," he declares, "who call themselves fine gentlemen, forsooth, corrupt the morals of a whole nation." He continues: "I speak the truth. Time was when we had as little vice here in Lilliput as anywhere; but since we imported politeness and fashions from Blefuscu, we have thought of nothing but being fine gentlemen. And a fine gentleman, in my dictionary, stands for nothing but impertinence and affection, without any one virtue, sincerity or real civility."[3] Lord Flimnap himself decides to remain true to the ideals of a Restoration rake.

Let me see, why should I disturb myself about my lady's conduct, when I have not the least regard for my lady myself? However, by discovering her indiscretions, I shall have an excuse for mine; and people of quality should purchase their ease at any rate.

. . . .

Ladies and lords should their affections smother,
Be always easy, and despise each other.[4]

After Gulliver's escape, Flimnap and his wife reconcile on condition that each maintain his inclinations. And once again Bolgolam pronounces his abhorrence of their morality, while Fripperel declares: "Let love be banished. We of rank and fashion, / Should ne'er in marriage mix one grain of passion."[5] The afterpiece ends with Lord Flimnap's salute to sexual liberty.

We may shrink even today from the idea of tiny child actors being charged with speaking the dialogue of this comedy and being directed in the stage business required by the dramatic situation. Even in the Epilogue little Miss Simpson was given suggestive lines such as

2.   W. E. Oulton, *History of the London Theatres*. London, 1796, I, 61.
3.   Scene I, lines 29–34.
4.   Scene I, lines 133–37, 140–41.
5.   Scene III, lines 322–23.

Was it not great? A lady of my span
To undertake this monstrous Mountain Man?

.   .   .   .

The beau has qualms about an absent wife,
Were he at home, his dear might cut and carve,
But, if he can't partake, must others starve? [6]

Granting the moral issues, we still have to admit, however, that in *Lilliput*
Garrick achieved a degree of sophistication not to be matched until nineteen
years later with his production of *Bon Ton* on 18 March 1775.

TEXTS

*O*1   1st edition. London: Paul Vaillant, 1757.
*W*1   *Dramatic Works of David Garrick*. [London.] N.p., 1768, I, 255–92.
*W*2   *Dramatic Works of David Garrick*. London: Printed for R. Bald, T. Blaw,
and J. Kurt, 1774, I, 179–204.

[TITLE PAGE]

Eadem . . . MINORES] "our descendants will desire and do the same things."

[ADVERTISEMENT]

9. Paul Vaillant] printer and bookseller patronized by Garrick between 1750
and 1761, after which T. Becket became Garrick's regular publisher.

10. R——] Redriff. Gulliver's house was in the parish of Rotherhithe or Redriff,
a seafaring population in the Borough of Bermondsey, London.

19. Brother Bayes] character satirizing John Dryden in *The Rehearsal*, by
George Villiers, second Duke of Buckingham.

27–28. *Udel . . . duren*] nonsensical quotation imitating Swift's artificial language
for the Lilliputians.

44. Mr. Walter Baker] attorney, administrator to Baron Schwanberg, Baker
represented the deceased "Baron" in legal efforts "to vacate the Patent obtained by
Dr. Robert James for Schwanberg's Powder."

45. Dr. James] Dr. Robert James (1703–76), inventor of "James's Powder," a
fabrifuge popular in the eighteenth and early nineteenth centuries to drive away or
reduce a fever.

45–46. Baron Schwanberg] supposed inventor of "Schwanberg's Powder and
the Aurum Horizontal Pill," whose products were allegedly plagiarized by Dr.
Robert James.

50. Jacob Wilkinson] fictitious character invented by Garrick.

55–56. Mr. R——, Reverend Mr.——, Mr. Justice D——] fictitious characters.

88–89. *Segnius . . . fidelibus*] From *Ars Poetica*, lines 180–81: "The things that
are impressed by ear stimulate the mind more slowly than the things which are
exposed to the dependable eyes."

106. W. C.] fictitious signature used by Garrick to avoid the critics.

---

6.   *Epilogue*, lines 3–4; 12–14.

[PROLOGUE]

0.3. Mr. Woodward] Henry Woodward (1717–77, pantomimist, first appeared at Covent Garden under John Rich in 1730 as "Lun. Junior." He joined the Drury Lane Company in 1738 and acted there for the next twenty years.

[SCENE i]

31. Blefuscu] island situated north-northeast of Lilliput, a rival kingdom.
106. a Nardac] the highest title of honor Lilliput can bestow.
189. fit him] cuckold him.

[SCENE iii]

71. vapors] depressed spirits, hypochondria.
225. Clumglum] expression invented by Swift.

The Male-Coquette; or, Seventeen Hundred Fifty-Seven

When Henry Woodward took his benefit on 24 March 1757 the evening's entertainment included Garrick as Leontes in Shakespeare's *The Winter's Tale* as mainpiece, followed by a new Garrick farce called *The Modern Fine Gentleman*. The following season, when the second performance of the farce was given, it was billed under a new title, *The Male-Coquette; or, Seventeen Hundred Fifty-Seven*. We do not know how this miniature comedy of manners was received at the Woodward benefit, but the change in title suggests that the piece did not make much of an impression on its first appearance. With the new title, however, the farce caught the public fancy and was performed fifteen more nights in the 1757–58 season. The two following seasons saw eight performances, and revivals in 1763–64, 1772–73, and 1774–75 brought the total of performances to thirty-four at Garrick's retirement.

The actor-manager's position in regard to the manners of his age is apparent from the beginning of his career. In *Lethe*, his first produced play (1740), Garrick explores the whole range of manners with cameo portraits of his targets—the Poet, the miserly Old Man, the Fine Gentleman, newly-weds, a Frenchman, Mrs. Riot, and, of course, Bowman and Lord Chalkstone (later additions to the cast). In *Lilliput* (1756) he first makes public his abhorrence of persons of quality who hold the marriage contract in derision, a social evil he was to explore in considerable depth in *Bon Ton* (1775), which was probably written in the same period as *Lilliput* and *The Male-Coquette*.

In *The Male-Coquette* he is satirizing the men of London society, their affected inconstancy toward the opposite sex and their strong addiction to wagering. Garrick is quite explicit in declaring his purpose in the advertisement: "The following Scenes were written with no other view than to serve Mr. *Woodward* last year at his Benefit; and to expose a Set of People, (the Daffodils) whom the Author thinks more prejudicial to the Community, than the various Characters of Bucks, Bloods, Flashes, and Fribbles, which have by Turns infested the Town, and have been justly ridicul'd upon the Stage."[1] He "expects no mercy from the critics" but seeks to be excused by his public for preparing the entire production "in less than a month."

Such a declaration, if true, only shows again that Garrick was a master of manners comedy in the Restoration mode. His dialogue is filled with vivacious wit as he moves swiftly from one telling scene to another. The basic situation involves a spirited young lady, Sophia, who must keep her faithful suitor Tukely waiting while she makes up her mind about the fascinating but fickle Daffodil. This dandy has built himself a reputation as a great lover and is inordinately proud of his many conquests. Needless to say, he has not the slightest intention of becoming serious about any of these ladies. "I give 'em all hopes without going a step further. . . . A true sportsman has no pleasure but in the chase. The game is always given to those who have less taste and better stomachs."[2]

Sophia and her cousin Arabella are both intended conquests on Daffodil's list, but poor Arabella stubbornly believes she is his own true love. But when Sophia assumes male attire and impersonates an Italian nobleman, the Marchese di Macaroni, she soon discovers how treacherous her dandy can be. When she describes Daffodil as "de *Orlando Innamerato* himself," the dandy quickly adds: "But not *Furioso* . . . I am for variety and bandinage without affection. Reputation is the greatest ornament and ease the great happiness of life. To ruin women would be troublesome; to trifle and make love to 'em amuses one. . . . I merely sip of both, but more than half a glass palls me."[3] Daffodil, the perfect host, even offers the "Marchese" two ladies from his own list— none other than Sophia and her cousin. "I have addressed 'em both, but as matters become a little serious on their side, I must raise a jealousy between the friends, discover to one the treachery of the other, and so in the bustle steal off as quietly as I can."[4] Sophia declines an invitation to visit Daffodil's club and departs instead for the Widow Damply's house, where Tukely has assembled five of the women duped by Daffodil. There the disillusioned Sophia agrees not only to marry Tukely but also to further his plans to expose Daffodil.

Meanwhile at the club a very comic scene ridicules the current vogue for wagering. Garrick excels in portraying such scenes of bustle, and in this one he attacks the ignorance and childish nature of the fine gentleman. And there Daffodil receives a letter from an unknown lady asking him to meet her in the park. He decides to accept the invitation only if his wagering friends agree to accompany him and break up the rendezvous.

The closing scene in the park is hilarious, with Tukely in drag and Sophia again disguised as the woman's husband. There the five women join in exposing Daffodil before his fine friends. Tukely speaks the closing lines and advises the ladies on stage and those in the audience to

---

1. Lines 1–6.
2. I, ii, lines 56; 58–59.
3. I, ii, lines 254–59.
4. I, ii, lines 286–90.

hereafter equally detest and shun these
destroyers of your reputation.
      In your coquettry is a loss of fame:
      But in our sex 'tis that detested name
      That marks the want of manhood, virtue,
            sense and shame.[5]

Garrick was to use the characters and situations of *The Male-Coquette* many times in later plays, but never would he so completely borrow all his characters from Restoration comic tradition. Daffodil, as a character for Henry Woodward, is almost an exact copy of the rake Horner in Wycherley's *The Country Wife* or the Dorimant of Etherege's *The Man of Mode*, lacking only the viciousness and sublety of both characters. When finally trapped, he resembles one of Garrick's favorite comic roles, Sir John Brute in Vanburgh's *The Provok'd Wife*. Sophia is typical of the eighteenth century's idea of a breeches role, the heroine being very moral and assuming male dress for practical reasons. Tukely is the typical honest member of the bourgeois class in London, and later will mature into such a Garrick spokesman as Sir John Trotley in *Bon Ton*. The neglected ladies at the Widow Damply's are the Lady Cockwoods, Lady Wishforts, and the Margery Pinchwifes of the earlier comedies. From curtain to curtain *The Male-Coquette* is one of the finest illustrations of Garrick's devotion to the Restoration mode. Never again was he to appear so successfully unoriginal!

We can agree with the contemporary critic who, in a lengthy review in 1757, wrote: "On the whole the beauties of this little comedy exceed the faults in number and importance."[6] While this critic was at a loss to identify the author of the play, hazarding a guess that it might have come from Arthur Murphy's hand, he knew a successful piece when he saw it. Thirty-four performances proved his judgment.

TEXTS

O1   1st edition. London: P. Vaillant, 1757.
W1   *Dramatic Works of David Garrick.* [London.] N.p. 1768, I, 199–254.
W2   *Dramatic Works of David Garrick.* London: Printed for R. Bald, T. Blaw, and J. Kurt, 1774, I, 143–77.

[PROLOGUE]

23. Macbeth] Act II, i, line 36.
25. Banquo's Ghost] *Macbeth*, Act III, iv.

[ACT I, i]

28. *Imprimis*] In the first place.
97. negligée] a loose-fitting gown.
200. Corydon] a rustic.

---

5.   II, iii, lines 230–34.
6.   *The Theatrical Review, 1757, and Beginning of 1758.* Quoted in *The London Stage*, Part 4, II, 631.

[ACT I, ii]

81. Captain Bobadil] the blustering braggart in Ben Jonson's *Every Man in His Humour*.

83. Chancery] Court of the Lord Chancellor of England, the highest judicatory next to the House of Lords.

96–97. flung . . . groom] threw the rider off his back.

226. *resto confuso*] I' ashamed. *si mal-a-proposito*] so inopportunely.

237–38. *Mi dispiace infinamente*] my utmost chagrin. *interrumpato, gli affari*] intruded on the affairs.

242. *una belissima sorella in verità*] a very pretty sister indeed.

246. *O cara inghilterra!*] O dear England!

252–53. *volte . . . Orlando Innamorato*] times that you was the Orlando the Lover.

260. *Il mio proprio gusto*] exactly my taste.

274. *Senza ceremonie*] without ceremony.

284. *Cosa é questa*] Such as what?

291. *Spiritoso amico*] lively friend.

294. *generalissimo in verita mà*] but you are truly a commanding officer.

307–8. *il mio conduttorè in tutte le partite*] my guide in all the ways.

[ACT II, ii]

37. plain Nantz] a liquor of France.

66–67. panada] a dish of boiled bread. Eringo root] candied root of the Sea Holly, regarded as an aphrodisiac.

74. Staunton Woods] situated in Gloucestershire.

[ACT II, iii]

175. Cart and Tierce] positions in fencing.

177. In buckram] starched, stuck up, a false appearance of strength.

180. Rosamond's Pond] in southwest corner of St. James's Park, a favorite spot for skaters and suicides.

The Guardian

On Saturday, 3 February 1759, friends of Christopher Smart supported a benefit performance for that unfortunate poet, who was currently indulging his wildly convivial genius in the confines of a madhouse. The benefit bill that evening consisted of Aaron Hill's *Meropé* as mainpiece, followed by a new two-act comedy by Garrick, *The Guardian*. Richard Cross, the prompter, noted that the afterpiece was greeted with "universal applause."[1] Its popularity can be estimated by a record of fourteen performances in its first season, after which it became a standard afterpiece in the Drury Lane repertoire as long as Garrick acted. In all, *The Guardian* was performed forty-eight nights in fifteen seasons, being acted at least once every season through

---

1.   *MS. Diaries of the Drury Lane Theatre*, 3 February 1759.

Garrick's final season of 1775–76. It was published six times before Garrick's retirement from the stage, and continued as a viable property well into the nineteenth century.

The popularity of *The Guardian* was assured perhaps from its inception, as Garrick proudly indicates in his brief advertisement to the first edition. He reminds the public that its source, *La Pupille* by Barthélemi-Christophe Fagan (1702–55), is considered to be "the most complete *Petite-Piece*" on the contemporary French stage. He modestly states that his translation faithfully represents the French original, with only such "alterations from the original as the difference of language and manners" require. Textually, Garrick's changes prove to be little more than to place the scene in London, to give the characters English names, some minor cuts in the French text, and to change the characterizations and quicken the stage business.

The dominant feature of this adaptation is its difference in characterization. Garrick increases the sentimental tone of the Fagan play in order to ridicule the vogue for sentimental comedy in England. Both Harriet and her guardian Heartly display their delicacy of feeling to such an extent that the audience must laugh at their hypersensitivity. From the beginning we are aware of Harriet's love for her guardian, a man past forty; but Heartly cannot allow himself the thought of responding to such a situation, and it is not until the final scene of the comedy that all barriers have been swept away. Harriet confides to her maid Lucy: "I take care that my eyes don't tell too much, and he has too much delicacy to interpret looks to his advantage. Besides, he would certainly disapprove my passion; and if I should ever make the declaration and meet with a denial, I should absolutely die with shame."[2] When Lucy asks her what can "hinder your coming together," the quick reply is, "His excess of merit."

Heartly is blinded by his own excessive delicacy. When the thought of Harriet's love for him first presents itself he soliloquizes: "Let a man be ever so much upon his guard against the approaches of vanity, yet he will find himself weak in that quarter. Had not my reason made a little stand against my presumption, I might have interpreted some of Harriet's words in my own favor. But I may well blush, though alone, at my extravagant folly. Can it be possible that so young a creature should even cast a thought of that kind upon me? . . . No, no; I will do her and myself the justice to acknowledge that, for a very few slight appearances, there are a thousand reasons that destroy so ridiculous a supposition."[3]

Julie and Ariste, the French counterparts of Harriet and Heartly, are sentimental, but so drawn that the audience is persuaded to sympathize with them. Garrick, however, has so overloaded the pair with sensitivity as to ridicule the very substance of sentimental comedy. In a scene strongly reminiscent of the letter scene in Wycherley's *The Country Wife* Harriet dictates a message to be sent to Young Clackit but actually meant for her guardian. When Heartly sends off the letter the action elicits no less than six passionate asides.

2. Act I, lines 199–203.
3. Act II, lines 148–57.

MISS HARRIET (*aside*). What a terrible situation!

HEARTLY (*aside*). I am thunderstruck!

MISS HARRIET (*aside*). I cannot speak another word.

HEARTLY (*aside*). My prudence fails me.

MISS HARRIET (*aside*). He disapproves my passion, and I shall die with confusion.

Enter Lucy.

LUCY (*aside*). The conversation is over and I may appear . . .[4]

The foil for this burlesquing of the two lovers is the excellent comic interpretation of the rest of the small cast. Sir Charles Clackit is the opposite of Heartly, an outgoing type of country gentleman. He is older than his neighbor Heartly, but he is quick to respond to the idea that Harriet may be in love with him despite his age. His nephew, Young Clackit, is Garrick's familiar portrait of the fop addicted to the affected dress and manners of the Englishman returned from travels on the Continent.

Garrick's principal instrument in ridiculing the rest of the characters is Lucy, Harriet's maid and confidante. She speaks for the author, and many of her sallies represent Garrick's additions to the French original. When Harriet confides that she dare not reveal her infatuation toward her guardian, Lucy finds a practical answer which nearly ends the comedy before it has properly begun: "I'll put you in the way. You shall trust me with the secret; I'll entrust it again to half a dozen friends; they shall entrust it to half a dozen more, by which means it will travel half the town over in a week's time. The gentleman will certainly hear of it, and then if he is not at your feet in the fetching of a sigh, I'll give up all my perquisites at your wedding."[5] When Harriet muses about "the impression which a virtuous character makes upon our hearts," and wants to know if "such a weakness" may not be excused, Lucy's reply is: "You are afraid of being thought singular, and you really are so. I would sooner renounce all the passions in the universe than have one in my bosom beating and fluttering itself to pieces. Come, come, Miss, open the window and let the poor devil out."[6]

Having exploited the hypersensibility of Harriet and the astounding lack of perception on the part of Heartly, Garrick has prepared his audience for a final scene of hilarious comedy. Young Clackit accepts his rejection with foolish élan. "The poor girl in pique has killed herself to be revenged on me; but, hark'ye, Sir, I believe Heartly will be cursed mad to have me live in his neighbourhood. A word to the wise—"[7] Sir Charles at sixty-five, "nay, just entering into his sixty-sixth year," knows he has made a fool of himself and hopes Heartly will understand that he has "sense enough and friendship enough not to be uneasy" at his neighbor's happiness. And the Guardian himself capitulates with reckless ardor to the demands of a new-found love. "The more I was sensible of your merit, the stronger were my motives to

---

4.   Act II, lines 118–24.

5.   Act I, lines 207–12.

6.   I, lines 218–22.

7.   II, lines 370–73.

stifle the ambition of my heart. But now I can no longer resist the violence of my passion, which casts me at your feet, the most unworthy indeed of all your admirers, but of all the most affectionate."[8]

However close Garrick kept to the Fagan original, his is the more lively and vivacious, and the attack on sentimental comedy gives the piece an identity of its own. With Garrick playing Heartly, Miss Pritchard as Harriet, the incomparable Kitty Clive as the maid, with Yates and O'Brien to broaden the humor, this little comedy must have been welcomed by an audience surfeited with the *comedie larmoyante* and now afforded an opportunity to laugh it off the stage.

TEXTS

O1   1st edition. London: J. Newberry, 1759.
O2   2nd edition. Dublin: George Faulkner, 1760.
W1   *Dramatic Works of David Garrick*. [London.] N.p., 1768, I, 153–98.
O3   Dublin: George Faulkner, 1771.
O4   4th edition. London: T. Carman and F. Newberry, Jr., 1773.
W2   *Dramatic Works of David Garrick*. London: Printed for R. Bald, T. Blaw, and J. Kurt, 1774, I, 113–41.

[ADVERTISEMENT]

1. Monsieur *Fagan*] Barthélemi-Christophe Fagan (1702–55).
2. *Petite-Piece*] afterpiece.

[ACT I, i]

53–54. *l'affair est fait*] the matter is done.
286. *sans façon*] without ceremony.
336. *è troppo, mia carissima*] too much, my darling.
370–72. "She . . . cheek"] Shakespeare, *Twelfth Night*, II, iv, lines 113–15.
378. vapors] depressed spirits, hypochondria.
379. *coute qui coute*] whatever the cost.
420. *brouillerie*] falling-out, quarrel.
421. *penchant*] inclination.

[ACT II, i]

323. O misericorde!] Have mercy upon me!
350–51. tie-wigs] in which the hair is gathered into a knot behind and tied with a ribbon.

Harlequin's Invasion; or, A Christmas Gambol

Nowhere was the rivalry between Drury Lane and Covent Garden theatres so evident as in the production of the traditional Christmas entertainment or pantomime. In Dr. Johnson's famous Prologue for the opening of Drury Lane

---

8.   II, lines 343–47.

under Garrick's management in 1747, the new regime was emphatic in its idealism.

> But forc'd at length, her ancient reign to quit,
> She saw great Faustus lay the ghost of wit;
> Exulting Folly hail'd the joyous day,
> And Pantomime and Song confirm'd her sway.
>   But who the coming changes can presage,
> And mark the future periods of the stage?
> Perhaps if skill could distant times explore,
> New Behns, new Durfeys, yet remain in store;
> Perhaps where Lear has raved, and Hamlet died,
> On flying cars new sorcerers may ride;
> Perhaps (for who can guess the effects of chance?)
> Here Hunt may box, or Mahomet may dance.
> . . . .
> Then prompt no more the follies you decry,
> As tyrants doom their tools of guilt to die;
> 'Tis yours, this night, to bid the reign commence
> Of rescued Nature, and reviving Sense.

Unfortunately for Garrick, the "new reign" did not commence, the new day didn't dawn. And Drury Lane played to very thin houses every time John Rich dusted off one of his old, familiar pantomimes. In 1750, at the opening of a new season at Drury Lane, Garrick spoke another prologue:

> Sacred to Shakespeare was this spot design'd,
> To pierce the heart, and humanize the mind.
> But if an empty House, the Actor's curse,
> Show us our Lears and Hamlets lose their force;
> Unwilling we must change the nobler scene,
> And in our turn present you Harlequin;
> Quit Poets, and set Carpenters to work,
> Shew gaudy scenes, or mount the vaulting Turk:
> For tho' we Actors, one and all, agree
> Boldly to struggle for our—vanity,
> If want comes on, importance must retreat;
> Our first great ruling passion is—to eat.
> To keep the field, all methods we'll pursue;
> The conflict glorious! for we fight for you:
> And should we fail to gain the wish'd applause,
> At least we're vanquished in a noble cause.[1]

At Christmastime that season Garrick gave the public his Harlequin, challenging the supremacy of "Lun" with Henry Woodward's spectacular *Queen Mab* pantomime. And the success of this piece called for five other

---

1. *Poetical Works*, I, 102.

Woodward pantomimes for Drury Lane before the comedian departed with Spranger Barry for Dublin in 1756.[2]

With "Lun jun" off to Dublin, Garrick had to provide his own Christmas entertainments. *Harlequin's Invasion*, his only pantomime, was the first of four Christmas productions. It opened at Drury Lane on 31 December 1759 and achieved 25 performances that season. With additions and alterations it had 18 performances the next season and 13 in 1761–62. In a life-span of 11 seasons through 1773–74 *Harlequin's Invasion* was given 167 times.

To the casual observer it would appear that with the six Woodward productions, and now *Harlequin's Invasion*, Garrick had finally accepted the rage for pantomime. Not so—for with his own pantomime he was decidedly revolutionary. He gave his astonished audience a *speaking* Harlequin and dialogue for all the major characters. In a moving prologue written at the time of John Rich's death, Garrick took the trouble to explain why he had given such characters speech.

> But why a speaking Harlequin?—'tis wrong,
> The wits will say, to give the fool a tongue:
> When Lun appear'd, with matchless art and whim,
> He gave pow'r of speech to ev'ry limb;
> Tho' mask'd and mute, convey'd his quick intent,
> And told in frolic gestures all he meant.
> But now the motly coat, and sword of wood,
> Requires a tongue to make them understood.[3]

The manager knew his company and its abilities; nowhere did he perceive a true pantomimic artist. His company indeed required "a tongue to make them understood." But, even as he complimented his rival at Covent Garden, Garrick was deprecating pantomime. Once again he was prepared to fight for Shakespeare. And it is significant that his other three Christmas entertainments were not to be pantomimes.

In his apprentice days under Henry Giffard at Goodman's Fields and Ipswich, Garrick was rumored to have been a hasty substitute for an ailing Richard Yates in two or three scenes of *Harlequin Student; or, The Fall of Pantomime*. In a letter to his brother Peter, Garrick admitted as much. The matter is of little significance for us, except for the fact that this production saluted the completion and unveiling of William Kent's statue of Shakespeare in Westminster Abbey, a project to which actors at Drury Lane had contributed a performance of *Julius Caesar* and those at Covent Garden a performance of *Hamlet*. Lord Burlington, Garrick's future wife's benefactor, had been one of the chief promoters of the Shakespeare project. All this com-

---

2.   The five other pantomimes by Woodward were: *Harlequin Ranger* (26 December 1751); *The Genii, an Arabian Nights Entertainment* (26 December 1752); *Fortunatus* (later *Harlequin Fortunatus*) (26 December 1753); *Proteus; or, Harlequin in China* (4 January 1755); and *Harlequin Mercury* (27 December 1756).

3.   *Poetical Works*, I, 158. It is titled "Part of a Prologue to *Harlequin's Invasion*."

bined to influence Garrick as he prepared his own pantomime eighteen years later, and it was perhaps only natural for him to turn to this old piece which was ready-made for his intentions toward pantomime.

With scenery by John Devoto and music by Peter Prelleur,[4] the libretto for *Harlequin Student* had its comic action interrupted by the gods themselves. Mercury brought a warning word from Jupiter: "Genius and Taste to Britain he'll restore, / And Farce and Harlequin shall be no more."[5] When Jupiter himself appeared, it was to inveigh against the patent theatres for indulging pantomime, and to charge Goodman's Fields with the obligation to avoid foreign mimes and "Eunuchs to Sloth." The final scene was a representation of the new monument to Shakespeare, with Jupiter's parting demand that this minor theatre "Doat on Shakespeare's manly Sense, / Send th'invading Triflers Home, / To lull the Fools of France and Rome!"[6] Garrick too was happy to end his pantomime with the Harlequin discarded in favor of the god of his idolatry.

Harlequin's Invasion employs Garrick's usual roster of comic characters. The country folk are in commotion over a printed document which none of them can read. They are spared the trouble when Mercury and a full chorus with trumpets, drum and fife warns of Harlequin's invasion of Shakespeare's right to the public stage. In the sung Chorus it is commanded:

> Let the light troops of Comedy march to attack him,
> And Tragedy whet all her daggers to hack him.
> Let all hands and hearts do their utmost endeavour,
> Sound trumpet, beat drum, King Shakespeare forever.[7]

After this brief scene we meet the tailor, Joe Snip, and his wife. That worthy lady orders Joe to arm for the battle and to bring her back the head of Harlequin. The tailor's efforts to obey his wife bring about his adventures with Harlequin, who, with the clownish Simon as companion, conspires to have Bounce and Gasconade cut off the tailor's head. Then Harlequin, assuming Snip's shape, arranges for Forge to take the head to Mrs. Snip and have her bring Joe's murderers into court.

Harlequin himself is captured and brought before three Justices and, when they hear him declare that he can decapitate them and sew their heads on again, they sentence him to a whipping. Harlequin's retaliation is to turn the Justices into old women and to escape from the court.

Back at Snip's home, a subplot further entangles the family. Daughter Dolly has fallen in love with Harlequin and is enraged to learn that her father is bent on killing him. Her mind is soon set at rest, however, when Mrs. Snip describes how Harlequin's head can lead the family to money and a title. Dolly then makes short shrift of Abram, her father's apprentice, and plans to aspire to a more attractive suitor. Just then the family learns that Snip himself has lost his head, and Dolly tries to recapture Abram—but the young swain

4. Roger Fiske, *English Theatre Music*, pp. 169–70.
5. Ibid.
6. Ibid.
7. I, i, lines 46–49.

has found her cousin Sukey more attractive. Now Dolly is left without either Harlequin or Abram.

The scene shifts to the prison, where Bounce and Gasconade have been doomed to execution. Their release comes when Tailor Snip appears once more with his own head. And when Harlequin's person is discovered in the prison, they all try to capture him, but are foiled when Harlequin causes the prison to disappear.

Only then does Mercury reappear and announce Harlequin's final fate. With a wave of his caduceus, Mercury shows a vision (transparency) in which pantomimic powers prepare an attack on Parnassus. Pantomime's fleet is destroyed in a storm, and Mercury pronounces Jupiter's final word: "Descend to Earth, be Sportive as before, / Wait on the Muses' Train, like Fools of Yore, / Beware encroachment and invade no more."[8] As Harlequin disappears, Garrick causes Shakespeare to rise and Shakespearean characters to appear for a song and a grand dance. The final song includes Garrick's advice to his audience: "By your Love to the Bard may your Wisdom be known, / Nor injure his Fame to the loss of your own."[9]

Highlighting Garrick's production of this pantomime were three scene transparencies devised by Domenico Angelo and executed by the scene designer Samuel French. With all other scenery painted in opaque colors, the transparency was usually depicted on the backcloth. This scenery was of linen or calico, painted with transparent dyes, and when lighted from behind it revealed yet another scene. Henry Angelo describes how his father assisted Garrick with scenes for *Harlequin's Invasion*.

One evening, after dining with my father, and sitting over the wine, Garrick, conversing upon a speaking pantomime which he had long projected, asked him to contrive a scene, such as would be likely to attract by its novelty.

The projected piece was *"Harlequin's Invasion,"* and Garrick, describing the various situations in which the character of the "tailor in armour," was to be placed, it was suggested to lead him through an enchanted wood, in the pursuit of Harlequin . . .

Angelo's ideas were conveyed to French, who

produced a very fine composition, which was painted with masterly execution; the slips or screens in the usual opaque manner, but the back scene was a transparency, behind which, visionary figures were seen flitting across, upon the plan of the *Tableau mouvant*.

That which rendered this scene apparently the work of enchantment, however, was a contrivance, which originated in the inventive faculties of my father.

He caused screens to be placed diagonally, which were covered with scarlet, crimson, and bright blue moreen, which, having a powerful light before them, by turning them towards the scenes, reflected these various colours alternately, with a success that astonished and delighted the audience. Indeed, the whole stage appeared on fire.

---

8.   III, ii, lines 112–14.
9.   III, ii, lines 133–34.

The success of this novel experiment gave rise to other scenes, in which transparent paintings were adopted.[10]

Two other transparencies were used in *Harlequin's Invasion*, the return of the Prison Scene after Harlequin had made it disappear, and the view of Harlequin's forces going to attack Mount Parnassus, the storm's destruction of his fleet, both in act 3, scene 2. These innovations, combined with the harlequinade tricks developed long since by John Rich and Henry Woodward, must have made *Harlequin's Invasion* a thing to behold.

Another reputed highlight was the musical score. Although William Boyce is credited with the music, according to Roger Fiske this score was a hodge-podge of composition: "By now the Seven Years War was at its height, and the big hit of the pantomime was Boyce's patriotic sea song, "Heart of Oak," the tune differing a good deal from the Victorianized version known today. [Theodore] Aylward and Michael Arne also contributed songs and probably Comic Tunes, but the latter were never published."[11]

Harlequin's Invasion remained unpublished until Elizabeth P. Stein discovered the manuscript in the Boston Public Library's Department of Rare Books and Manuscripts and published it in *Three Plays by David Garrick*, New York, 1926, with an interpretation of the stage directions by William Seymour. This edition is based once again on the manuscript by courtesy of the Trustees of the Boston Public Library and acknowledgment of Stein's original contributions.

[ACT I, i]

0.4. 2nd Grove] 2nd Groove. Groove sets, in which flats or wings were run, were numbered from the front of the stage at six-feet intervals, excepting the first entrance from the proscenium—from wing to curtain line was about four feet. Thus Scene I, Charing Cross, 2nd Groove, was set at a depth of ten feet.

2.1. Bounce *a stick*] This is the prompter's indicated warning to prepare for entrance of Bounce some speeches later. See entrance and stagehands' warnings *passim*.

6. my best eyes] eyeglasses.

11.1 *Enter* Bounce *Pd.*] Enters by the prompt door, *stage left*.

19.1. O.P.] Opposite prompter's side, *stage right*.

23. poltroon] a thorough coward.

36.1. *measures*] tape measures.

37.1. Staves] official staffs.

39. Apollo] god of music, poetry, prophecy.

40. French trick] a reference to rivalry between England and France, especially in terms of theatrical criticism. Contemporary reference would also include a hit at the defeat of the French in this year.

[ACT I, ii]

0.2. *Border bell and Wings bell*] Warning signals to stagehands for the coming change from the Charing Cross scene to the Plain Chamber scene.

---

10. *Reminiscences*, I, 10–15.
11. *English Theatre Music*, p. 236. Fiske states, "In fact, Garrick, who devised the plot and the song words (there must also have been recitatives), had rewritten *Harlequin Student, or The Fall of Pantomime*."

[ACT I, iii]

0.2. 2. *Entrance* O.P.] 2nd entrance opposite prompter, *stage right.*

0.4. OP. *First Entrance*] First entrance opposite prompter's side, *stage right.*

2. murrain] pestilence or plague.

23. Your Ta.] Your thanks.

57. Howdyes] greetings.

63.1. *Tr. bell*] Transformation bell.

63.2. cut wood] cloth scene on battens with cut foliage openings. 4 G.] Fourth groove; the stage is now about twenty-two feet deep.

76. ague] fever.

78. Train Bands] citizens trained as soldiers to supplement the regular army.

115. snacks] shares.

125. lathy] tall and thin.

151.1. *from Top*] from the "top" or rear of a raked stage.

178.1. ACT] warning for the end of act 1.

204.2. *Drop: Bar Bell.*] act curtain dropped and a bell rung for opening the refreshment bar to the audience.

[ACT II, i]

11. pass] permission to go and come.

31. quotha] indeed.

49.1. *Curtain Bell*] warning bell to lower curtain after song.

69. mump] mumble.

[ACT II, ii]

14–15. comprehend] catch hold of.

44. Jack-bite] Jacobite, supporters of James II after his abdication and later.

53. Barrow-Knight] Baron-Knight.

63. frump him] jeer him.

85. Heigh to pass] exclamation of surprise.

104. as high a head] reference to the ridiculously high coiffures of the time.

107. cupola o' top] trapdoor in roof of sedan chair for headdresses.

109. side boxes] seating for the fashionable.

114.3. *Drop. Abram dresses*] Stagehands' alert to change to a drop curtain for act 3, secene 1, and warning to Abram to change costume for act 3.

[ACT III, i]

0.2. Drop Chamber] scenic drop depicting a room.

17. frumpish] ill-tempered.

43–44. Spouting Club] organization for declamation practice.

53. fleer] sneer.

[ACT III, ii]

49.1. P.S.D.] Prompt side down.

55. execratious] cursed.

89.2. *Tr. bell*] transformation bell.

89.3. *Trap bell*] warning for trapdoor to sink table.

104. *Ecce Signum*] Behold the sign. caduceus] Mercury's staff, a winged staff with two serpents entwined.

The Enchanter; or, Love and Magic

Encouraged by the success of his Christmas offering, *Harlequin's Invasion* (1759), Garrick grew venturesome and determined to vary his formula for spectacle. For the following Christmas show he wrote *The Enchanter; or, Love and Magic* and engaged John Christopher Smith, Handel's pupil, to set the piece to music. The miniature opera was successful as an afterpiece. Prompter William Hopkins noted that this new entertainment "wrote by Mr. Garrick, and set by Mr. Smith, very well received. Master Leoni, a Jew, made his first appearance in this piece [as Kaliel] and was received with great applause."[1]

The Enchanter is in two acts and was first produced at Drury Lane on 13 December 1760. The libretto tells a "Turkish" story of an evil magician named Moroc who is in love with the beautiful maiden Zaida. Determined to put an end to the contracted love of Zaida and her Zoreb, Moroc spirits her away to his castle to woo and win the maiden for his own evil purposes. But the beautiful maiden is determined to remain faithful to her lover. The frustrated Moroc then uses his magic powers to convince Zaida that her Zoreb is dead. He conjures Zoreb's tomb from the ground to fulfill his promise to deliver the body to Zaida. After a dead march Zaida attempts to stab herself. In the confusion of trying to prevent the suicide Moroc accidentally drops his magic wand. At this point, Kaliel, Moroc's slave attendant, snatches up the wand, strikes Moroc, and, as Moroc sinks into the earth, restores Zoreb to life and love. When Zaida and Zoreb are reunited Kaliel declares "Love and Virtue triumph here." The opera closes with a dance of shepherds and their lasses who have been conjured to the happy scene.

Elizabeth Stein pointed out that this miniature opera "has all the features of Italian opera; its pageantry and its scenic effects. Most important of all, and what makes this play most like the Italian musical drama, is the fact that its plot is carried on entirely through airs and recitatives."[2] But Miss Stein neglected to add that Garrick, if not particularly gifted musically, was sufficiently influenced by his composer to make it very plain in the advertisement to the printed text what revolutionary aims, what new departures, were intended in this collaboration. "As the recitative commonly appears the most tedious part of the musical entertainment, the writer of the following little piece has avoided it as much as possible; and has endeavoured to carry on what fable there is, chiefly by the songs." Roger Fiske, in his sensitive treatment of Smith's compositions, notes that the Smith score "omits recitatives, dances and choruses, though it does include the Dead March." He points out that the composer of music for *The Tempest* (1756) and *The Fairies* (1755) "has gone even further towards lightening his style. Only one of the songs is in *Da Capo* form, and in general they are short, simple, and reasonably tuneful; but they are not very interesting. There is less than half the quantity of music to be found in *The Fairies* and *The Tempest*."[3]

---

1. *The London Stage*, Part 4, II, 830.
2. *David Garrick, Dramatist*, p. 119.
3. *English Theatre Music*, p. 246.

We infer from the above quotations that *The Enchanter* represents an adventure toward something more than another dull, sententious or mindless piece of buffoonery dressed out in the latest elaborate stage machinery. Underneath Garrick's "gingerbread" production one can observe an innovation daring for its time and pointing toward what was eventually to materialize as modern musical staging, especially now that the modern musical has elected to become serious and polemic. While Fiske maintains that "the success of the piece lay mainly in its Eastern story, so much more fascinating than that of any previous all-sung English opera," it was the musical form which carried this piece of undeserving libretto to a successful run of seventeen nights in its initial season, and six more nights the following season.

TEXTS

O1 1st edition. London: J. and R. Tonson, 1760.
W1 *Dramatic Works of David Garrick*. [London.] N.p., 1768, III, 155–74.
W2 *Dramatic Works of David Garrick*. London: R. Bald. T. Blaw, and J. Kurt, 1774, II, 271–86.

The Farmer's Return From London

The success of this very popular interlude served to link the names of Hannah Pritchard, William Hogarth, and David Garrick. In the advertisement to the printed text Garrick stated that the piece was written to support a benefit for Mrs. Pritchard, and that it owed a great measure of its life to Hogarth's sketch of Garrick as the Farmer. When the interlude was staged, however, it was not with Mrs. Pritchard as the Farmer's wife but Mrs. Mary Bradshaw, a veteran actress at Drury Lane for thirty-seven years, whose specialty was older women. Mrs. Pritchard was the recipient of the benefit, when part of the pit was laid into boxes. *The Farmer's Return from London* was first staged at Drury Lane on 20 March 1762, programmed for the benefit between Vanbrugh's *The Mistake* and Arthur Murphy's *The Old Maid*. It was played for twelve nights in its first season and three nights in the following year.

This *petite piece*, despite its brevity, allowed Garrick as a countryman to relate to his family the sights and experiences he had met with while attending the coronation celebrations in honor of King George III and Queen Charlotte. While the whole family listens avidly, the Farmer describes the citizens of London as they viewed the "crownation," from those seated on the scaffoldings erected for the occasion to those crowding the streets or peering from upper-story windows and rooftops: "I thought from above, (when the Folk fill'd the Places) / The streets pav'd with Heads, and the walls made of Feaces!"[1] He readily admits to his wife that he has seen "the false ones" and found them "Tricked noice out for saale, like our cattle at fair:" but he dismisses them with: "But, Bridget, I know, as we sow we must reap, / And a cunning old ram will avoid rotten sheep."[2] All of this provided Gar-

1. Lines 54–55.
2. Lines 21; 23–24.

rick with opportunity to satirize current idiocies of city folks, from their taste and behavior at the theatre and opera to their fascination with the Cock Lane Ghost.

The Farmer had attended a performance of Paul Whitehead's *The School for Lovers* (Drury Lane, 10 February 1762) and thought it "pure stuff" because "The Great Ones disliked it," and the "Cratticks" grumbled because the piece given out as a comedy had made them tearful. Thus Garrick hits at sentimental comedy as he had in his own comedy, *The Guardian*, exaggerating the hypersensitivity of his characters in the vain hope of turning public taste back to true comedy.

Having had his laugh at the critics as "Lame, feeble, half-blind" creatures who rail at poets because they can't write plays themselves, Garrick had a turn at the Cock Lane Ghost. Benjamin Victor describes the furor over this phenomenon:

The *Drummer* was revived at this Period at both Theatres, and confessedly allowed by a Prologue spoken at *Covent Garden* House (well suited to the silly Occasion) to take Advantage of the reigning Weakness of the People, who went in Crowds many Days and Nights to an *Haunted House*, by what was called the *Cock-Lane Ghost*—a Delusion set on foot, and very ingeniously carried on, by a Girl of twelve Years of age, the Daughter of the Clerk of *St. Sepulchre's* Church, who resided in *Cock-Lane* near *Smithfield*.

The Story of this Ghost was founded on the sudden Death of a young Woman, whose Name was *Fanny* . . . the supposed Mistress of a Gentleman . . . Her Ghost (which was reported to haunt this Girl by strange knockings and scratchings) was to insinuate that some foul Practices had been used to deprive her of Life; and to bring the Gentleman (as it did) into Trouble.

It would be incredible to relate the Numbers of Persons of Distinction that attended this Delusion! many of whom treated it as a serious and most important Affair . . . at last—the Girl's Father and three or four others were tried in the King's Bench—found guilty—pilloried and imprisoned. This most effectively laid the Ghost; and is the best and properest Cure for every Ghost that may arise hereafter.[3]

When the Farmer's family is terrified to learn that he has "sat up with a Ghoast," the Farmer exclaims: "'Ozooks!—thou'rt as bad as thy Betters above!" And again "The Ghoast, among Friends, was much giv'n to Loying."[4]

Despite the brevity of this interlude, its popularity was deserved. In it Garrick proved once again his delight in good humor, in ridiculing the follies of the day, and in the presentation of "older comedy," the robust comic characters of the "lower" order.

TEXTS

O1   1st edition. London: Printed by Dryden Leach for J. and R. Tonson, 1762.
Q   2nd edition. London: Printed by Dryden Leach for J. and R. Tonson, 1762.

---

3.   *History of the Theatres*, III, 22–24.
4.   Lines 87; 97.

W   *Dramatic Works of David Garrick*. [London.] N.p. 1768, III, 175–82.
W 2   *Dramatic Works of David Garrick*. London: Printed for R. Bald, T. Blaw, and J. Kurt, 1774, II, 287–94.

[ADVERTISEMENT]

2. Mrs. Pritchard] Hannah Pritchard (1711–68), first known as Miss Vaughan, began her career at fair booths. After a brief engagement at the Haymarket, she joined the Drury Lane company as Mrs. Pritchard. Her farewell performance was as Lady Macbeth on 24 April 1768.
7. Mr. Hogarth] William Hogarth (1697–1764), painter and engraver; known for his satirical pictures of eighteenth-century English life.

[THE INTERLUDE]

20. tittups] frolicsome, capering ladies.
51. crownation] coronation.
69. The School——] *The School for Lovers*, by William Whitehead, produced by Garrick 10 February 1762. *The Farmer's Return from London* was first performed on 20 March 1762.
83. ghoast] topical allusion to the current excitement in London over the Cock Lane Ghost, created by a twelve-year-old girl and her father, a Mr. Parsons.

The Clandestine Marriage

One of the most celebrated of eighteenth-century debates may well be that of the authorship of *The Clandestine Marriage*, that "unhappy comedy," as Garrick called it when the trials of joint authorship threatened his long friendship with George Colman. Until recently the question of how much of the play belongs to Garrick, how much to Colman has been clouded by lack of evidence and by faction. For the quarrel has existed since December 1765, a few months before the comedy was first performed at Drury Lane, as indicated in the celebrated correspondence of that month between the two playwrights. The authors themselves could not agree upon their respective shares before three acts had been written.[1] With the first publication of the play they nevertheless acknowledged joint authorship, Garrick's early biographers and commentators either accepting this fact without question (e.g. Thomas Davies) or giving the major share to Garrick (e.g. Arthur Murphy, Benjamin Victor, Tate Wilkinson, Joseph Cradock, and the actor Cautherly).[2] After that the issue became less clearcut, and it is only recently that manuscript evidence has revealed Garrick to have had the major hand in the writing of the play. It will be of value to trace briefly here the progress of the quarrel.

It is Mrs. Inchbald in the nineteenth century who first "suspects" that

---

1. See Colman to Garrick, 4 December 1765, Boaden I, 209–11; Garrick's reply, 5 December, Boaden I, 213, and Little et al., *Letters*, No. 378, II, 481–83; and Colman's response, 6 December, Boaden I, 215.
2. Davies, *Life*, II, 102; Murphy, II, 27; Victor, III, 73; Wilkinson, III, 254; Cradock, I, 201; Fitzgerald, *Life*, II, 171–73.

Garrick merely "cast a directing hand and eye" on the composition,[3] an opinion backed up by Colman's son, George the Younger, with his publication of some Colman manuscript drafts.[4] John Doran gives Colman the lion's share, Percy Fitzgerald neatly divides the honors, and Joseph Knight swings the pendulum again in Colman's favor by maintaining that the play is too good for Garrick to have had much of a share in it.[5] Twentieth-century biographers in effect throw in the sponge by barely alluding to the problem; and indeed Carola Oman, the latest, omits all references to it.

Critical comment in our time begins with Joseph M. Beatty, who revived speculation in 1921 by maintaining that the chief characters are "simply amplifications of Colman's notes" and that "Colman was responsible for the basic characterization . . . including Lord Ogleby, and also for the details of the first four acts."[6] Six years later Allardyce Nicoll suggested the possibility that Garrick was merely the reviser, that his "facile genius" had not the strength to create the play.[7] Indeed, in his *British Drama* Nicoll omits mention of Garrick's name, giving Colman "a place among the true masters of comic portraiture" for Lord Ogleby.[8] In 1935, E. R. Page, in his book *George Colman the Elder*, concludes that Garrick merely polished the dialogue and resolved the plot.[9] A telling rebuttal came two years later from Elizabeth P. Stein, who in *David Garrick, Dramatist* set out to prove a long line of Colmanites wrong. Largely through internal evidence she gives Garrick almost the entire play and suggests that the role of reviser is really Colman's.[10] New manuscript evidence presented in 1952 establishes that Garrick wrote no less than half the play, including the most important scenes.[11] Now additional evidence from Garrick's pen confirms the fact that the major portion of the play is indeed his.

In determining the authorship of the play it is possible today to examine more primary sources than ever before. The chief sources are these:

1. The Garrick-Colman correspondence of 1764–65, particularly that of December, 1765.

2. John Forster's abstracts from a part of a Garrick synopsis which Forster took from an article in the *Observer* newspaper. On these and on the Garrick-Colman correspondence has rested much of the conjecture regarding Garrick's share of the play.

3. The *Observer* article itself, which quotes Garrick's preliminary syn-

3. *The British Theatre*, Vol. XVI, "The Clandestine Marriage," p. 5.
4. *Posthumous Letters*, pp. 328, 345.
5. *Annals*, II, 45; Fitzgerald, *Life*, II, 172; Knight, p. 227.
6. "Garrick, Colman, and *The Clandestine Marriage*," *Modern Language Notes*, 36 (March), 129–41.
7. *A History of Late Eighteenth Century Drama, 1750–1800* (Cambridge, 1927), p. 168.
8. 1925, pp. 290–91.
9. Pp. 122–24.
10. Pp. 272–73.
11. Fredrick L. Bergmann, "David Garrick and *The Clandestine Marriage*," *PMLA*, 67 (1952), 148–62.

nopsis. It appeared on 26 October 1845 but was not thereafter consulted, primarily because Forster, typically, failed to be precise as to his source.

4. Colman's rough drafts and hints for the play published by Colman the Younger in 1820. Young Colman considered these the original of the comedy.

5. The working copy of the play in the Folger Shakespeare Library.

6. Garrick's manuscript outline of the play entitled *The Sisters*, referred to in the Colman correspondence of 1765 but since lost sight of except for the excerpts given by the anonymous writer for the *Observer*. The manuscript has been found among the holdings of the Garrick Club in London.[12]

Those claiming the major share of authorship for Colman have had the better of the argument almost to the present day. First, in the exchange of letters in 1765 Garrick refused to tilt against Colman, thus leaving the known facts in Colman's favor. Second, the rough drafts published by Colman the Younger in 1820, when considered without reference to other materials, naturally suggest that Colman did the greater part of the planning and even the writing. It is upon this transcript that several commentators have relied entirely. Third, Forster's abstracts of the Garrick synopsis were presented in a way that would cast some doubt upon their value. In the first edition of his *Life of Oliver Goldsmith* (1848) he states that "Garrick's synopsis . . . did not see the light till the other day."[13] In the second edition of the work (1854) he gives, in a footnote, his source as "the *Observer* newspaper" and quotes part of it.[14] All later editions of the work drop the footnote with its abstracts. This curious fact, together with the fact that Forster's source was not fully documented and that no one took the trouble to find the original, tended to demote Garrick's position as joint author. Moreover, with the discovery of this article it is now known that Forster ignored a major point made in it: that Garrick's sketch was made prior to Colman's.

The most important evidence of authorship lies in the Folger Shakespeare Library manuscript working copy and the more recently discovered Garrick manuscript sketch for *The Sisters*. The latter proves Garrick's inspiration— not Colman's—for the comedy, lays out the main action, and gives the outline upon which Colman based his own rough drafts. Of the eight characters which Garrick develops in *The Sisters*, seven remain in the completed play. The *dramatis personae* names, however, actors and actresses intended for the various roles rather than giving names to the characters, and then outlines the first three acts. Garrick opens his sketch with the Fanny and Lovewell scene, adds the scene of altercation between the sisters, and follows this with Lord Ogleby's famous toilet scene. In act 2 Garrick develops a theme of the aunt's being in love with the clandestine husband and sketches the scenes in which the young couple decide to appeal to Ogleby, Ogleby's misunderstanding Fanny's intentions, and Lovewell's attempt to reveal to Ogleby his secret

---

12. Fredrick L. Bergmann, "The Authorship of *The Clandestine Marriage*," a paper presented to the English 14 section of the Modern Language Association of America in Philadelphia, Pa., on 28 December 1960.

13. P. 374.

14. II, 26 ff.

marriage to Fanny. Act 3 develops Ogleby's infatuation with Fanny and further develops the aunt's love affair. Except for the idea of a lovesick Mrs. Heidelberg, then, Garrick's sketch gives the basic materials of the finished play. That this is the earliest version of the comedy Colman accedes in his letter to Garrick of 4 December 1765.[15] Colman drew out of it his "rough draught," in which he gives names to most of the characters: Garrick becomes the Earl of Oldsap, the nephew becomes Lord Sapplin, O'Brien becomes Lovewell. He adds to it the city or merchant characters he found in the first plate of Hogarth's "Marriage à la Mode": Traffick, his sister, and his two daughters, keeping, however, Garrick's comic Ogleby rather than substituting Hogarth's proud lord—but "this notion," Colman writes to Garrick in his draft, "you are more fully possest of than I."[16] Colman has the younger rather than the older sister be the secretly married one, introduces the satire on contemporary gardening, and alludes to the young lord's declaration to Fanny and to the lawyer scene of act 3. He adds further suggestions not found in the finished play, such as a foolish character intended as a match for Fanny.

Chronologically, the last manuscript evidence of the joint writing effort is the group of papers in the Folger Shakespeare Library. They include a synopsis of almost the entire play, with the cast and an outline of the first two acts in Colman's hand—this material extensively revised by Garrick, who eliminates Colman's act 2 entirely. The remainder of this synopsis is in Garrick's hand. Here Colman's Earl of Oldsap becomes the Earl of Kexy, Traffick becomes Sterling, Canton is named, and Mrs. Heidelberg is called Miss Sterling. Colman's outline for act 1 as revised by Garrick (who, for example, changes Sterling's sister from a spinster to a widow) follows the finished play rather closely, the only significant change being the shifting of the lawyer scene to act 3. The remainder of the Folger manuscript material, made up of fully written acts and scenes, is in three hands: that of Garrick predominately; that of William Hopkins, the prompter, as amanuensis; and that of a second amanuensis, the material in the latter two hands being extensively revised by Garrick. All this reveals that Garrick wrote at least half of the play. He must have credit for the opening scene of act 2 and the levee scene; for the scene between Mrs. Heidelberg and Miss Sterling in act 3; for the garden scene of act 4, including the repartee of Ogleby and Canton, the Lovewell-Fanny episode, Fanny's interview with Ogleby, and Sir John's scene with his uncle; and all of act 5.

This would leave for Colman—or undecided—all of act 1, the Sir John Melvil scenes of act 2; the lawyer scene of act 3 and Sir John's interview with Sterling and Mrs. Heidelberg; and two episodes of act 4, Mrs. Heidelberg's threat to cut the family out of her will and Miss Sterling's appeal to Lord Ogleby. Thus, other than act 1, the major parts of the play not in the Folger manuscript are most of the Sir John Melvil scenes and the satire on lawyers. Regarding act 1, we know that Garrick had sketched its opening scene in his synopsis. Colman, after reading Garrick's sketch, had added the scene of the

---

15. Boaden I, 209-11.
16. *Posthumous Letters*, p. 333.

City family awaiting the arrival of the nobility, the episode which completes the act. Moreover, to Colman's brief sketch of the act in the manuscript Garrick added the point of the elder sister's contempt for the younger, of Mrs. Heidelberg's partiality for the elder, and of making the younger a girl of "great Spirit & Sweetness." Clearly, act 1 was a cooperative venture. Only one important question remains—the authorship of the excellent satiric portrait of Ogleby in act 4, the scene in which the old fop mistakenly assumes that Fanny is in love with him. Whereas there has been general agreement (as Colman himself agreed in his letter of 4 December 1765) that Garrick wrote the Ogleby material in act 2 and all of act 5, the authorship of the act 4 material has been vague. The manuscript material suggests that it is Garrick's. It is in his hand in the Folger manuscript, and it is no mere copy of a previously written scene but original writing, replete with reworking and polishing. There is also the manuscript sheet headed "G—— takes——" in Garrick's hand which indicates that Garrick was to write, in addition to the levee of act 2 and certain other scenes, this very garden episode, described as "Fanny's discovering Scene to my Lord / his mistake in his own Favor & Consequences. / previous to this a Short Scene with Canton." Here is strong evidence that Garrick had taken the scene as his own. Colman's case depends mainly on his letter of 4 December, in which he says that "in the conduct as dialogue of the fourth act, I think your favourite, Lord Ogleby, has some obligations to me," a claim which Garrick surely refutes in his reply of 5 December in which he refers to Ogleby as "my portion of the play."[17] The manuscript factors involved—Garrick's taking on the writing of the scene, and the original nature of his manuscript version—indicate that Garrick wrote this satiric portrait.

In summary, we can give Garrick credit for the inspiration of the plot and for the chief characters, including Ogleby. And we can give Colman credit for contributing the idea of the city or merchant family. Traffick (later Sterling) is Colman's inspiration, although the aunt and the two sisters had already appeared in Garrick's draft. As for act 1, Garrick first sketched the opening scene and detailed the characterization of the older sister. Colman added the scene of the city family awaiting the arrival of the nobility. In act 2 Garrick gets credit for the opening scene, the scene between Brush and the chambermaid, and Lord Ogleby's levee, whereas it seems just to credit Colman with the Sir John Melvil scenes. In act 3 the scene between Mrs. Heidelberg and Miss Sterling comes from Garrick; the lawyer scene and Sir John's interview with Sterling and Mrs. Heidelberg would be Colman's. In act 4 most of the happenings in the garden come from the pen of Garrick, including the episode between Ogleby and Canton, the scene in which Lovewell and Fanny determine to enlist the aid of Ogleby, the matter of Ogleby's misunderstanding Fanny's intentions, and Sir John's interview with Ogleby. To act 4 Colman contributes Mrs. Heidelberg's threat to cut the family out of her will and Miss Sterling's appeal to Ogleby. Act 5 is without question Garrick's.

The two authors shared ideas and exchanged manuscripts until the late

---

17. *Letters*, No. 378, II, 482.

summer of 1763, when Garrick went to the Continent. His letters to Colman during the period contained frequent references to the venture: from Rome—"Speed y^r Plow my d^r friend. have you thought of the *Clandestine M*.? I am at it—"; from Paris—"I have consider'd our 3 acts, & with some little alterations they will do—I'll ensure them"; and again—"why didn't you finish ye first Act as you would have it? & if you had hinted at Ld Ogleby's vanity & amorous disposition, by way of preparation to ye 4th Act (as we talk'd it over) would it not have made ye strong scene there more natural?"[18] That each collaborator was, after an exchange of ideas, to deal with certain scenes is suggested by the manuscript sheet in the Folger Shakespeare Library headed "G—— takes ——" which lists scenes to be written by Garrick. It points up a method used by the collaborators. Again Colman writes to Garrick regarding the denouement: "when you have thrown y^r thoughts on paper, as I have done mine, we will lay our heads together, Brother Bayes."[19]

But act 5 gave endless trouble. Colman tried some "Loose Hints" but failed to please Garrick.[20] After the two had consulted he tried again, with better success. Finally the two exchanged their last acts, Colman writing to Garrick: "I have sent you the fifth act as you desired, but have had neither leisure nor inclination to compare it with that left by your brother yesterday. You know it was my opinion, that it wanted retrenching; but for near two months past I have been totally incapable of that task, as I could never without pain turn my eyes or thoughts on 'The Clandestine Marriage,'—this unhappy comedy, as you very properly call it."[21] This seems to have been the end of Colman's effective help with the play. And even after Garrick wrote the last act and put the play into production he continued to rewrite. Percy Fitzgerald says that "so many alterations had been made, up to the very last moment, that the players did not know what they were to say, or what to leave out; . . . There was a deal of rushing in and out, from bedrooms, &c.; but the energetic 'Pivy' Clive, who to the last was full of spirits and animal motion, came bustling on, and threw such life and vigour into the scene, that she restored the day, and brought the piece triumphantly through."[22]

So the play was at length completed, and was presented with success. *The Critical Review* said that "with very few improvements [it] would excel any which has been exhibited on the English stage for many years past."[23] Yet old wounds remained, wounds deepened by Garrick's refusal to play Lord Ogleby. Garrick tried to heal them with an addition to the advertisement of the printed play to the effect that "Each [author] considers himself responsible for the whole." The final attitude of the collaborators may perhaps be seen in the fact that Colman, when in Paris in July 1766, presented a copy to Diderot as "*donum ex authoribus*" without mentioning Garrick, whereas the

---

18.   Letters of 11 April 1764 (*Letters*, No. 329, I, 410–12); to November 1764 (*Letters*, No. 341, II, 429–31); and Xmas Day [1765] (*Letters*, No. 381, II, 485–86).
19.   *Posthumous Letters*, pp. 341–42.
20.   Ibid., pp. 343–44.
21.   Boaden, I, 215.
22.   Fitzgerald, *Life*, II, 178.
23.   21 March 1766.

latter, during the same week, told Madame Riccoboni that his own share had been merely a "touch of the fingers."[24]

The result of the collaboration of Garrick and Colman was popular and profitable. During its first season (1765–66) it ran for thirteen nights without a break and continued to be acted once a week for six additional weeks, without the usual requisite of an afterpiece, singing, and dancing. The play continued for fifteen performances the following season and for more than fifty more during the next nine years. Although box office receipts for the first year's run are not available, the Drury Lane *Treasurer's Account Book* for the second season indicates that the play led all others in number of performances and box receipts except for the new play *Cymon*, Garrick's own dramatic romance. *The Clandestine Marriage* brought in £2476/12/– in its fifteen nights as opposed to £5093/1/6 for the twenty-eight nights of *Cymon*. Its closest rival was still another Garrick venture, his alteration of Wycherley's *The Country Wife*, which brought in £1733/18/– in fourteen performances.[25] *The Clandestine Marriage* was published shortly after its initial presentation—on 4 March 1766—and went through three editions in six weeks, besides being published twice in Dublin and once in Edinburgh.

A noteworthy characteristic of the play lies in the fact that Garrick conceived it in terms of actual contemporary stage personalities rather than in terms of stock characters of literary tradition. The earliest draft, called *The Sisters*, indicates that Garrick is to play "an Old Beau, vain, &c," that Yates is to be his brother, O'Brien their nephew, King "an old flattering Serv.ᵗ of G's" (later Canton), Clive the aunt (Mrs. Heidelberg), Bride the elder sister, and Pope the younger sister. The entire sketch continues in this vein; for example: "Enter *Bride* and *O'Brien* (who are secretly married) She complaining how unhappy she is, and how disagreeably she is situated on acctᵗ of their concealing the marriage . . . the audience must learn that *Mrs. Clive* yᵉ aunt has two nieces Coheiresses & one of them is to be married to *O'Brien* the Son of *Garrick* & Nephew to Yates."[26]

Colman's later synopsis, published by his son as addenda to his edition of the Colman letters in 1820, gives the names of the characters (all but one of which were later changed) but also adds the names of the chief players. The Folger manuscript, apparently the last in chronological order, again begins with a cast of characters and players. All this indicates that the first consideration of the dramatists was to write the play for the best comedians available at Drury Lane. It is obvious in all three synopses that the part of Lord Ogleby was written for Garrick, that Mrs. Clive was to be Mrs. Heidelberg, Miss Pope was to act Miss Sterling, and Miss Bride was to be Fanny. Lord Ogleby is a kind of summary of Garrick's comic talents—of the simple-minded Abel Drugger, the coxcomb Bayes, Lord Chalkstone the dandy, even drunken Sir John Brute. The cross and passionate Mrs. Clive is the perfect Mrs. Heidelberg; had there been no Clive there would have been no Mrs. Heidelberg as we know her. The genius of Miss Pope for expressing the humor of whims,

24. Fitzgerald, *Life*, II, 308.
25. Folger Shakespeare Library.
26. The Garrick Club, London.

pretentiousness, anger, even rant, was exploited as her role was written. The style of John Palmer (Charles Lamb remarks that he was "a *gentleman* with a slight infusion of the *footman*"[27]) was written into the part of Brush; and Garrick had Richard Yates in mind for Sterling before a line of the play was written. The "star" system had developed considerably since Marlowe wrote parts to display the genius of Edward Alleyn and Shakespeare to capitalize on the comic talents of Robert Armin. Here was a play designed to exploit the abilities of virtually a company of actors.

Some changes in the original conception occurred before the play was first presented on 20 February 1766. As Garrick had decided, after his return from France in 1765, to take on no new roles (thus causing a rift between Colman and himself for the actor's refusal to play Ogleby), the part of Ogleby fell to Thomas King, who made the most of his talent for dry, epigrammatic humor in creating the part. Likewise the Lovewell role, intended from the start for "Gentleman" O'Brien, known for his ease and naturalness in playing, was given to William Powell because the former had left the stage before the play was ready. Powell, known as an actor of "tragic passion" who whined and blubbered well, easily fit the role of the sensitive Lovewell. The final cast, then, consisted of King as Ogleby, Yates as Sterling, Powell as Lovewell, Holland as Sir John Melvil, Baddeley as Canton, Palmer as Brush, Love as Serjeant Flower, Lee as Traverse, Aickin as Trueman, Mrs. Clive as Mrs. Heidelberg, Miss Pope as Miss Sterling, Mrs. Palmer as Fanny, Miss Plym as the chambermaid, Mrs. Abington as Betty, and Miss Mills as Trusty. King and Mrs. Clive had Lord Ogleby and Mrs. Heidelberg as their best parts for the remainder of their stage careers. The play was chosen by five actors as the piece that would bring them the best returns for their benefit nights (Mrs. Clive, Mrs. Palmer, Miss Rogers, King, and Ackman), and it was commanded several times by King George III and Queen Charlotte. Mrs. Baddeley, who succeeded Mrs. Palmer in the role of Fanny, made a great reputation in the play. A note in John Fawcett's *Commonplace Book* of clippings and scraps of eighteenth-century theatrical information contains this interesting note: "In the softer characters of both comedy and tragedy, she [Mrs. Baddeley] had few if any superiors. In the part of Fanny in *Clandestine Marriage*, the beauty of her person, and the elegant simplicity of her performance were extremely conspicuous, and so much attracted his Majesty's notice, that he commanded a picture to be taken of Fanny's principal scene with Lord Ogleby in the fourth act; for which purpose Mrs. Baddeley and that excellent comedian, Mr. King, sat to Zoffany the painter."[28]

The Clandestine Marriage was translated into French and German and was made into an Italian opera, *Il Matrimonio Segreto*. It had a long run on the American stage and was seen on 5 June 1789 by George Washington in New York. It continued well into the nineteenth century and is, indeed, sometimes performed today.

27. *Dramatic Essays of Charles Lamb*, p. 60.
28. Folger Shakespeare Library.

TEXTS

O_1 1st edition. London: T. Becket and P. A. DeHondt, R. Baldwin, R. Davis, and T. Davies., 1766.

O_2 2nd edition. London: T. Becket et al., 1766. A new setting of type.

O_3 3rd (?) edition. London: T. Becket et al., 1766. Another new setting of type.

O_4 London: T. Becket et al., 1766.

O_5 London: T. Becket et al., 1766.

O_6 Edinburgh: Printed (by Permission of the Authors) for R. Fleming, 1766.

D_1 Dublin: G. Faulkner, J. Hoey, Sen., W. and W. Smith, P. Wilson, W. Whitestone, J. Potts, and J. Williams, 1766.

D_2 Colman, George. *The Clandestine Marriage*. Dublin: A. Leathley, J. Hoey, Sen., P. Wilson, J. Exshaw, E. Watts, H. Sanders, J. Hoey, Jun., W. Sleater, and S. Watson, 1766.

W_1 *Dramatic Works of David Garrick*. [London.] N.p., 1768, III, 183-286.

O_7 "A New Edition." London: T. Becket and P. A. DeHondt, 1768.

O_8 "A New Edition." London: T. Becket and P. A. DeHondt, 1770.

W_2 *Dramatic Works of David Garrick*. London: R. Bald, T. Blaw, and J. Kurt, 1774, II, 295-376.

C *Dramatic Works of George Colman*. London: T. Becket, 1777, I, [151]-[292].

O_9 "A New Edition." London: T. Becket, 1778.

[TITLE PAGE]

Hac adhibe . . . parens] Turn your face this way, and by sparing one spare both; / Let her live, and let us both be parent to the same one! (Ovid, *Amores* 2.13.15-16). Apparently this is a somewhat altered version, for Burmann's variorum edition of 1727 and following editions through Kenney's Oxford text of 1961 give the second line as *"nam vitam dominae tu dabis, illa mihi"* (for you will be giving life to my mistress, she to me). The latter reading makes better sense in terms of Garrick and Colman's plot. The context in Ovid is that the speaker's girl has tried (successfully?) to produce an abortion and has injured herself to the point of endangering her life. The speaker here calls on Isis (as he later does on Ilithyia, the goddess of childbirth) to save her. Disregarding the reference to childbirth, the first line as given on the title page together with the second line as given in the Ovid texts make a suitable plea for Lovewell to have uttered.

[ADVERTISEMENT]

1. Hogarth's Marriage-a-la-Mode] the English painter Hogarth (1697-1764) produced his popular satire on married life in the fashionable world in 1745.

3. *The Marriage Act*] by John Shebbeare, M.D. (1709-88) and published anonymously in two volumes in 1745.

8. sole author] George Colman the Elder (1732-94), Garrick's collaborator in this play.

[PROLOGUE]

13. cits] citizens, the middle class, especially the merchant class.

19. struts his hour upon the stage] *Macbeth*, V, v.

24. Falstaff's] Sir John Falstaff of Shakespeare's *Henry IV* and *The Merry Wives of Windsor*. Juliet's] heroine of Shakespeare's *Romeo and Juliet*.

30. Quins and Cibbers] James Quin (1693–1766), actor who was supplanted in popularity by young David Garrick. Colley Cibber (1671–1757), dramatist and poet laureate (1730–57).

[ACT I, i]

44–45. tide waiter] an officer of the customs who awaits incoming ships and boards them to insure payment of duties.

210. more than a month's mind] i.e. something strongly desired.

223. 'Change] The Royal Exchange, generally referred to at this time as the 'Change and its location as Change Alley, was the center of commercial activity of the nation. It was the stock market and, until 1766, housed more than two hundred shops at which the fashionable purchased their finery.

227. bills of lading] documents listing the contents of shipments of goods and providing for acknowledgment of receipt of the goods.

231. good news from America] Relations with the Colonies were strained because of the Stamp Act, passed the year before this play was first performed. Good news would be news that the colonists had accepted the burden imposed by the act. The Stamp Act was repealed two days after the first performance of the play (22 Ferbuary 1766).

248. other end of the town] the West End or fashionable part of London.

261. nabob] in the eighteenth century, an Englishman who had returned from India with a fortune.

[ACT I, ii]

26. esclavage] a necklace of several gold chains or strings of beads or jewels, worn by women in the eighteenth century.

31–32. undress] informal attire.

41. Polly What-d'ye-call-it] Lavinia Fenton, who first played Polly Peachum in Gay's *The Beggar's Opera* (1728), left the stage after the sixty-second performance (19 June 1728) to become mistress to the Duke of Bolton. The duke married her after his wife's death in 1751. She died in 1760. The reference is to the fact that actresses frequently became intimate acquaintances of the nobility.

49–50. city-knights] wealthy merchants rewarded with titles.

52. crown whist] a version of whist, a forerunner of bridge.

59. Temple Bar] Temple Bar divided the City, where the merchant class was dominant, from the West End, or Westminster, where the fashionable lived.

62. Grosvenor Square . . . dull districts] Grosvenor Square was in the heart of the West End, whereas the dull districts are in the mercantile areas.

65. chariot] a four-wheeled pleasure carriage with a coach box and only a back seat.

70. Arthur's] Robert Arthur was proprietor of White's Chocolate House, fundamentally a gambling house which burned in 1733. Arthur restored it as a club in 1755; it was supposed to be political, was conservative and extremely aristocratic.

74. Carlisle House] After the mid-'60s this former residence of the Earls of Carlisle in Soho was the scene of fashionable assemblies, balls, and concerts.

87. Tunbridge] Tunbridge Wells, a watering-place.

98. lutestring] a dress of glossy silk fabric.

114. the George] an inn.

136. nataral] a natural, one naturally deficient in intellect.

[ACT II, i]

53. Saturn] i.e. Satan.

68. abigails] maidservants.

79. Anti-Sejanus] The Rev. James Scott, a political writer employed by Lord Sandwich to write in the newspapers against Pitt, signed his pieces *Anti-Sejanus*.

85. tintamarre] racket.

103. eau d'arquibusade] Harquebusade water, a lotion.

123. want] i.e. need.

137. Blackfriars] a part of the City of London, hence meaning here the merchant class. So named because it was formerly property held by the order of Black Friars.

138. borachio] Spanish for wine bag. Hence the reference is very likely to a dealer in wines; thus a merchant.

145. glass] mirror.

146. doux yeux] to ogle.

186. see my water] Satire on current fashions in gardening is found frequently on the eighteenth-century stage.

201. Grand Tower] i.e. Grand Tour.

[ACT II, ii]

40–41. man at Hyde Park Corner] a seller of plaster of Paris statues.

48. pinery] a place for growing pineapples.

56. flip] a seaman's drink of beer mixed with spirits and sugar and heated with a hot iron. Cf. Congreve's *Love for Love*, III, iv: "Thus we live at sea, eat biscuit, and drink flip."

64. sullabub] syllabub, milk or cream mixed with wine.

71. close walks] enclosed walks, as in a maze.

94. beaupot] a large ornamental vase for cut flowers.

98. ruins] continued satire on gardening, here on the building of ruins and (as with the steeple, line 112) follies.

193. Cheapside] a principal street of business, inhabited by goldsmiths, linen drapers, haberdashers, etc. Whitechapel] a district in London inhabited by persons of low character. As an adjective it signified low or vulgar.

329–30. particular] i.e. peculiar, odd (obs.).

[ACT III, i]

21. commission day] the opening of assizes, when the commission authorizing the judge to hold them is read.

22. cause] i.e. case.

26–27. *currente calamo*] with running pen.

31. *nisi prius*] civil as opposed to criminal action. The satire on lawyers which follows is a typical part of eighteenth-century comedy.

44. *crim. con.*] criminal conversation, i.e. adultery.

46. *venires*] summoning of a jury. The meaning is that more than thirty groups of people have been summoned from which to choose juries.

53. *luce clarius*] clear as day.

57. commission] those justices authorized to hold court on a particular circuit.

91–92. court-end] Westminster.

112. long-robe] i.e. lawyer.

Pudding-sleeves] large bulging sleeves drawn in at the wrist, resembling bags in which puddings are cooked. They are part of a doctor's gown; hence, as here, a clergyman.

175. statute fair] a fair held annually in certain towns and villages for the hiring of servants.

272. china orange] *Citrus aurantium*, the sweet table orange, originally brought from China.

[ACT III, ii]

10. drawn at Amsterdam] i.e. as a shepherdess, a favorite pose for a lady's portrait.

188. Plumb] slang for £100,000.

[ACT IV, ii]

31. rappee] snuff.

433. *ferae naturae*] wild animals.

[ACT V, i]

14. closet] office or study.

[ACT V, ii]

3. fly-cap] a fashionable headdress, the fly-cap was fixed upon the forehead to form the figure of an enormous butterfly resting upon its head, its outstretched wings edged with precious stones.

57. asp] aspen tree.

[EPILOGUE]

0.5 Quadrille] a popular card game played by four persons with forty cards (a regular deck with the tens, nines, and eights removed). The poet Gay told Swift in 1726 that the game was the universal employment in fashionable circles.

13.1 Whist] Ancestor of bridge, whist is played by four persons with a deck of fifty-two cards. Originally played chiefly by the clergy, after 1726 it became the rage and was much used in gambling. Horace Walpole wrote in 1742, "Whist has spread an universal opium over the whole nation."

15. honors] the ace, king, queen, and jack of trumps.

18. spadille] the ace of spades.

21. "And ... men"] The quotation has not been identified. Hermann J. Real of the Westfälische Wilhelms-Universität conjectures that it is not a quotation but an allusion to Pope's *Rape of the Lock*, I, 11–12: "In Tasks so bold, can Little Men engage, / And in soft Bosoms dwell such mighty Rage?" which in turn are based upon *AEneid* I, 11 and Boileau's *Lutrin*, I, 12 (G. Tillotson, Twickenham ed. of *Rape*, p. 145).

27. Handel's] George Frederick Handel (1685–1759) had been court composer and was highly feted in England in his time.

29. Goths and Vandals] the tribes which conquered Rome, here suggesting those of no taste in the arts.

29.2. *Picquette*] piquet, a card game for two. The cards from two to six are removed from the deck.

44. Lare] Lear.

73. capuchin] a woman's cloak and hood, having some resemblance to the apparel of Capuchin monks.

86. Guildhall giants] Gog and Magog, two colossal wooden statues in London's Guildhall. They were constructed in 1708 to replace older effigies burned in the 1666 fire.

125. *in petto*] in one's own breast, privately.

Neck or Nothing

Garrick's farce, *Neck or Nothing*, one of five plays he adapted from French originals,[1] is a lively and humorous afterpiece which did not, however, prove to be popular with Drury Lane audiences. Garrick staged it during only two seasons, for a total of eighteen performances. It was popular enough, however, to be printed in three editions between 1766 and 1774 and to find its way into some of the anthologies of the time.

The farce was first presented at Drury Lane on 18 November 1766 as the afterpiece with *The Siege of Damascus*, a long-lived John Hughes play which had been resurrected that season after having lain dormant for seven years. Garrick first called the farce *The Narrow Escape*, as indicated in the Larpent MS. copy. Originally he intended having King play Martin,[2] one of the two tricky servants, but eventually assigned the part to Palmer, Yates playing his companion, Slip. He also originally assigned the role of Stockwell to Parsons and that of Harlowe to Castle, later giving them to Hartry and Parsons respectively. When the farce was revived for the 1773–74 season, however, King did play Martin to Palmer's Slip. Hartry as Stockwell, Miss Pope as Jenny, and Mrs. Bradshaw as Mrs. Stockwell were retained from the original casting of seven years earlier, with Waldron playing Harlowe, Brereton playing Belford, and Miss Hopkins in Miss Plym's role of Miss Nancy.

Neck or Nothing made its stage debut without benefit of the author's name attached to it, a practice Garrick often employed in order to spare his work the attacks of disappointed playwrights whose efforts had been turned down by the manager. Garrick presented it eleven times in the 1766–67 season, then dropped it from the repertoire for seven seasons. It was revived on 19 January 1774 as the afterpiece with *A Christmas Tale* and played six times more that season; the last performance under Garrick's managership, on 17 May with *King Lear*, was a benefit "for relief of those, who from their infirmities, shall be oblig'd to retire from the stage." The Treasurer's Book shows receipts of £300/3/6, with profit to the Fund of £282/11/-. The farce was attempted once more at Drury Lane—after Garrick's death and seven years following its last previous performance—on 10 February 1784 as the

---

1. The others include *The Lying Valet*, based on *The Novelty; or, Every Act a Play* (1697) by Peter Antony Motteux; *Miss in Her Teens*, based on *La Parisienne* (1691) of Florent Carton sieur Dancourt; *The Guardian*, from Barthelemi-Christophe Fagan's *La Pupille* (1734); and *The Irish Widow*, which owes a debt to Molière's *Le Mariage forcé*.

2. Larpent MS. 260.

afterpiece with John Home's *Douglas*. Presumably it has not been acted since.

In his advertisement to the printed play Garrick acknowledges his indebtedness to "the celebrated Author of *Gil Blas*," Alain René Le Sage, whose *Crispin, rival de son maître* (1707) is the source of Garrick's farce. At a time when, as Allardyce Nicoll says, "French playwrights, from Molière to the authors of contemporary Paris, were eagerly ransacked and provided many a theme and suggestion"[3] to English playwrights, Garrick would have considered himself to be on safe ground in producing a free translation of Le Sage's successful playlet.

In adapting *Crispin* to the English stage Garrick anglicized the whole. The scene is shifted from Paris to London, and the characters (Valere, Crispin, La Branche, Angélique, etc.) take English names (Belford, Martin, Slip, Miss Nancy, etc.). He omitted some few scenes of Le Sage's original, amplified others, and improved the ending. The result is an English farce, a "fair specimen," as Nicoll calls it, "of the humours-intrigue type. The devices of the servant Martin are full of good fun, and the dialogue teems with sentences which, if, like Cibber's, are not wit, sound very much like it."[4]

Garrick's departures from Le Sage include omission of the original first scene, Valere (Belford) telling Crispin (Martin) of his attraction to Angélique (Nancy). Le Sage repeats this information in his second scene, Garrick's I, i, when Crispin meets La Branche (Slip) and plans the attempt to defraud Oronte (Stockwell) of his daughter's dowry. Thus Garrick's version opens with the lively action which characterizes the whole. Garrick also enlarged upon the scene in which Orgon (Sir Harry Harlowe) visits Oronte (Stockwell) to withdraw in person his consent to the marriage of his son to the other's daughter. Garrick's change makes the valet, Slip, a greater—and a funnier—rogue. The conversation between Slip and Sir Harry on the supposed harsh treatment of the former as a result of the break in the marriage negotiations—the supposed kicking of Slip down the stairs by Stockwell and Sir Harry's determination to kick back:

SLIP.   Lord, sir, you are so hot! You forget it was me he kicked down stairs, not you.

SIR HARRY.   'Tis the same thing, sir. Whoever kicks you kicks me by proxy—nay, worse; you have only the kicks, but I have the affront—[5]

is pure Garrick and gives his play, as Elizabeth P. Stein has said, "an even greater vivacity and briskness of movement than are encountered in the French play.[6]

Garrick intensifies Slip's roguery by having him defame the character of the maid, Jenny. And he brings the two intriguing servants to book for their trickery. Whereas Le Sage's Crispin and La Branche are, following the disclosure of their attempted extortion of Angélique's dowry, pardoned for no adequate reason by Oronte with a promise to establish each in business and

3.   *A History of Late Eighteenth-Century Drama, 1750–1800*, p. 118.
4.   Nicoll, p. 185.
5.   II, iii, 99–102.
6.   *David Garrick, Dramatist*, p. 94.

even to supply one with a wife, Garrick's Martin and Slip are taken into custody with the obvious notion that their villainy will be punished.

Doggerel verse in the *Gentleman's Magazine* attacking the offerings at the two patent theatres during the 1766–67 season complained that the farce was "too low,"[7] and Garrick himself, in reference to his play, pointed out a weakness when he told a friend and would-be playwright that "an audience will not Suffer the Dupe to be cheated too extravagantly even in a Farcical piece."[8] Wrote Garrick: "To convince you how over delicate the Publick may be at times—I will relate to you a passage in a Farce call'd *Neck or Nothing*—Two Servants agree to impose upon on old Citizen Stockwell—one of 'em is to pass for his Master & to receive a portion with the Daughter, whom he is to marry—they agree to divide the Booty & run away—the business is comically enough manag'd & had great applause 'till upon the old Citizens asking the Sham Gentlemen to take a Mortgage upon Some Houses for part of the Fortune—the other Answers he is Sorry that he could not—but that he had bargain'd for an Estate that was *Contagious* to his own, & must be oblig'd to pay the Money in two days or forfeit—Is the Estate good, says the old Man? in fine Condition answers the cheat, & the Wood upon it will very near pay the Purchas[e]—indeed!—O Yes, says the Confederate, & then the fine ponds upon the Estate!—ponds (cries Stockwell) what signify Ponds—O Sir they make a great deal of the Ponds, many Pounds a year!—indeed! what are they good for?—Slip replies—to Catch Gudgeons Sir—great Proffit & pleasure. —I thought it dangerous and, so it prov'd, tho' but in a Farce, & which 'till the Gudgeons came had met with great applause."

And so the farce lasted for only two seasons, and those widely separated. The lively action and mild humor of the play were not sufficient to keep it on the boards. Frank Hedgcock's complaint that the actor-manager's comedies, including this one, "betray little talent on Garrick's part beyond that of knowing how to choose in his predecessors' works incidents or characters capable of development in different surroundings, and of giving them new life by the addition of smart, up-to-date dialogue"[9] does not offer sufficient reason for the lack of success of *Neck or Nothing*. But Madame Riccoboni's admission that Garrick's "charming pieces" lacked the charm of novelty[10] may suggest the public had had a surfeit of tricky servants and romantic farces.

TEXTS

O1   1st edition. London: T. Becket, 1766.
D1   Dublin: P. Wilson, J. Exshaw, H. Saunders, W. Sleater, D. Chamberlain, J. Potts, J. Hoey, Jun., J. Mitchell, J. Williams, L. Flin, S. Watson, W. Colles, O. Adams, and T. Ryder, 1767.
O2   "A New Edition." London: T. Becket, 1774.
O3   In *A Collection of Plays*. London: F. Longe, 1774 (?).

7.   January 1767.
8.   To Herbet Lawrence, in *Letters*, III, No. 817 (p. 917).
9.   *A Cosmopolitan Actor*, p. 92.
10. Letter to Garrick, October, 1768, in Boaden II, 544.

D2 In *Supplement to Bell's British Theatre*. London: John Bell, 1784, II, [259]–91.

[ADVERTISEMENT]

5. Le Sage] Alain René Le Sage (1668–1747), French novelist and playwright. His picaresque novel *L'Histoire de Gil Blas de Santillane* was published in four volumes between 1715 and 1735. The play *Crispin, rival de son maître* appeared in 1707.

[ACT I, i]

5–6. well jointured] well provided for by a late husband.

6. post-chariot] a light four-wheeled carriage differing from a post-chaise in having a driver's seat in front.

14–15. beau-monde] fashionable society.

18. settlements abroad] i.e. penal colonies.

23. Exchange] the Royal Exchange, the center of commercial activity for the nation.

24. turtle-feast] a turtle is a young prostitute; thus, consorting with a prostitute.

28. the watch] a picked body of men charged with maintaining order in the streets, especially during the night.

29. kennel] gutter.

30. stone-doublet] prison or prison sentence.

40. news-monger] news vendor.

45. Epsom . . . Newmarket] English race tracks.

70–71. ready rhino] ready money. Rhino is a slang term for money, perhaps carrying an allusion to the size of the rhinoceros.

104. dunghill] coward (a cockpit term; all but game cocks are dunghill).

121. ecclaircissement] *eclaircissement*, clearing up.

151. knock us all up] alarm or confuse, "floor us."

162. coarse skin] i.e. servant's livery.

[ACT I, ii]

4. Lud] the ejaculation Lord, as to a judge (my Lud) or a titled person (m'Lud).

91. chopping about] A chopper is a blow struck on the face with the back of the hand; thus a blow.

102. cit] short for citizen, but with a measure of scorn; it means a townsman or tradesman as opposed to a gentleman.

128. instruments] marriage contracts.

132. weather-cock] weather vane, thus changeable, inconsistent.

144. Blackamoor] used as a playful endearment; also a servant.

177. among his patients] i.e. in the graveyard.

209. chairman] one of the porters of the sedan chair.

217. *proprium personum*] in [my] own person.

233–34. "With a shape . . . a grace"] from Altisidora's song in Part 3 of Tom D'Urfey's *Don Quixote*, reprinted as the first song ("A Mad Song") in volume I of *Wit and Mirth: or, Pills to Purge Melancholy*, 1719. It was set to music by Henry Purcell.

266. portion] marriage share.

297. wrong box] from *balk*, a piece of ground carelessly plowed; hence a disap-

pointment, a waste, a missed opportunity.

303. pink] exceedingly fashionable, elegant.

307. closet] office, study.

316. kite] a bird of the hawk family.

322. limed] caught. Lime (birdlime) was used in snares.

[ACT II, i]

135. Newgate] a noted London prison.

174. Covent Garden] the Covent Garden district teemed, in the eighteenth century, with brothels.

175. Jelly-house] a jelly was a buxom and pretty girl. It also referred to the male semen (a jelly bag was the scrotum). Thus a house of prostitution.

198. Long head] a shrewd head.

230. specious] i.e. specie, hard money.

236. contagious] i.e. contiguous.

238. timber] trees to be sold for lumber.

276. out of conceit with] dissatisfied with.

288. tickled in the palm] tipped.

316. throw up the cards] give up the plan.

[ACT II, iii]

16. Opening line of Dryden's *Tyrannick Love*, but "my arms." Horace Walpole quotes it as Garrick does ("our arms") in a letter to George Montagu, 23 July 1763 (*Horace Walpole's Correspondence with George Montagu*, ed. W. S. Lewis and Ralph S. Brown, Jr. [New Haven: Yale University Press, 1941], II, 88).

45. viva voce] by word of mouth.

51. quoth-a] said he; indeed.

57. flam] a trick, a sham story.

64. hunks] miser.

84. ding-dong] in a hasty and disorderly manner; quickly.

85. compounded] settled amicably, adjusted by agreement.

178. Old Bailey] London criminal court.

Index to Commentary